SACRED HUNGER

BY BARRY UNSWORTH

Mooncranker's Gift

Pascali's Island (published in the United States
under the title *The Idol Hunter*)

The Rage of the Vulture

Stone Virgin

Sacred Hunger

SACRED
HUNGER

BARRY UNSWORTH

NAN A. TALESE

DOUBLEDAY

New York   London   Toronto   Sydney   Auckland

PUBLISHED BY NAN A. TALESE
an imprint of Doubleday,
a division of
Bantam Doubleday Dell Publishing Group, Inc.
666 Fifth Avenue, New York, New York 10103

DOUBLEDAY and the portrayal of an anchor
with a dolphin are trademarks of
Doubleday, a division of Bantam Doubleday Dell
Publishing Group, Inc.

Published by arrangement with Hamish Hamilton Ltd., London.

Library of Congress Cataloging-in-Publication Data

Unsworth, Barry, 1930–
  Sacred hunger / Barry Unsworth.—1st ed.
    p.   cm.
  I. Title.
PR6071.N8S3   1992
823'.914—dc20   91-33237
                                            CIP

ISBN 0-385-26530-1

Printed in the United States of America
June 1992

1   3   5   7   9   10   8   6   4   2

First Edition in the United States of America

TO JOHN, MADELEINE AND FELIX REISS.
WITH LOVE.

I should like to thank the British Council for the grant of a six-month Visiting Scholarship to Sweden and the staffs of the English Department and Library of Lund University, where the background reading for this novel was done, for their unfailing help and kindness.

Some safer world in depths of woods embrac'd,
Some happier island in the watry waste . . .

Alexander Pope

PROLOGUE

According to Charles Townsend Mather, the mulatto was dark amber in colour and grey-haired and nearly blind. He was small-boned and delicately made and he had a way of tilting his head up when he spoke, as if seeking to admit more light to the curdled crystals of his eyes. He was an old plantation slave from Carolina, freed when he was past work and turned off the land. In the spring and summer of 1832 he was begging every day in the streets of New Orleans and down on the waterfront. He would wait on the quayside for paid-off sailors, to whom some clouded impulse of pity or contempt might come. He was a talker; whether there was anyone to hear or not, he went on muttering or shouting the details of his life.

His slave name was Luther, then Sawdust was added, because an overseer made him eat sawdust once to discourage him from answering back – it seemed he had always been a talker. So Luther Sawdust. But in the bars along the waterfront he was known as the Paradise Nigger. He lived on scraps and spent what he had in the bars, where he was suffered for his gifts as an entertainer, until he got too drunk. People bought rum for him; he became something of an institution. He would sometimes play a tune on an old harmonica that he wore slung round his neck, or sing a song of the plantations. But mainly he talked – of a Liverpool ship, of a white father who had been doctor aboard her and had never died, a childhood of wonders in a place of eternal sunshine, jungle hummocks, great flocks of white birds rising from flooded savannahs, a settlement where white and black lived together in perfect accord. He claimed he could read. Also – and Mather vouches for this – he quoted snatches

I

from the poetry of Alexander Pope. In one of his occasional pieces for the *Mississippi Recorder* Mather declares that he actually heard him do it. These pieces were afterwards collected and published privately under the title *Sketches of Old Louisiana*. The only record of the Paradise Nigger that we have is contained in this little-known work, in the chapter entitled 'Colourful Characters of the Waterfront'. Mather says that when he returned to New Orleans after an absence of a year or so he found the mulatto gone and no one able to say what had become of him.

Continued observation of colourful characters took Mather frequently down cellar steps and he became in the course of time a colourful and visionary character himself, dying at last in a state of delirium in a Jacksonville sanatorium in 1841. His widow, preparing his papers for a collected edition, conceived it her duty to suppress the low-life material, and so the mulatto beggar was discarded, along with Big Suzanne and a transvestite guitarist named Angelo and a number of others.

Not exactly scrapped, but he was cast into the margin, into that limbo of doubtful existence where he lurks still, begging, boasting, talking about paradise, somewhere between Mather's two trips to New Orleans, the two editions of his book. Can Mather have invented him? But this author grew lurid and disordered only in his latter days; the mulatto belongs to a cooler time. Besides, there are the quotations. I don't believe Mather would have invented a thing like that. The mulatto invented himself – it was why he was tolerated in the bars. Some aura of my own invention lies about him too. The kneading of memory makes the dough of fiction, which, as we know, can go on yeasting for ever; and I have had to rely on memory, since the newspaper itself has been long defunct and its files have been destroyed or simply mouldered away. My own copy of the *Sketches* was lost years ago and I have never been able to unearth another or even to trace any reference to the work.

But the mulatto haunts my imagination still, with his talk of a lost paradise, raising his blind face to solicit something from me. Nothing can restore him now to Mather's text, but he sits at the entrance to the labyrinth of mine . . .

BOOK ONE
1752–1753

PART ONE

ONE

The ship he meant was the *Liverpool Merchant*, Captain Saul Thurso, and he had never seen her, though she carried the seeds of all his dreams in her hold.

She carried death for the cotton broker who owned her, or so at least his son believed. For Erasmus Kemp it was always to seem that the ship had killed his father, and the thought poisoned his memories. Grief works its own perversions and betrayals: the shape of what we have lost is as subject to corruption as the mortal body, and Erasmus could never afterwards escape the idea that his father had been scenting his own death that drab afternoon in the timber yard on the banks of the Mersey when, amid colours of mud and saffron, he had lowered himself rather awkwardly down to sniff at the newly cut sections of mast for his ship. Not odours of embalmment, nothing sacramental; the reek of his own death.

It was an ugly thought, confirmed somehow by other remembered details, thought naturally only Erasmus himself, as host to it, could have found these admissible as evidence: smell of wet sawdust and trodden mud – the mud was flecked with sawdust; cold swamp smell of the river only some hundred yards off; another odour too, stink of neglect, not really belonging here, transferred from another day by the same ugly workings of grief.

The sections of the mast were pale yellow; they lay in trestles under the rough plank roof – the shed was open at the sides. It had been raining heavily and the men had made a causeway of wood blocks down the churned slope of the bank. Erasmus had felt embarrassed at the theatrical way his father had brought his face so close up to snuffle at the raw wood. At twenty-one he was reticent, not given to gestures, moreover just then in a state of inflamed sensitivity, being in the early phase of his undeclared love for Sarah Wolpert.

'Prime quality.' Kemp straightened himself for the pronouncement. 'When this tree was cut it was drinking sweetly. You can smell it in the sap. If you want to test the soundness of the timber, smell the sapwood. Isn't that right, lads?' He had made himself an expert on timber too.

It was imported fir from the Baltic. 'Fir for a mast,' Kemp said. 'Fir is one thing breeds better out of England. By God, there are not many.'

Those round him laughed. They all knew him. They had seen him about the yards, with his quick movements, darkly flushed face, something careless in his dress without being slovenly, the short unpowdered wig, the long, square-cut outer coat usually hanging open.

'See, my boy,' he said to the aloof Erasmus. 'Come over here and see. The pieces are all cut and ready. Here are the two parts of the spindle. D'you mark the taper on them? They'll be coaked together in the middle here, and bolted after. Look at these woundy great fellows, d'you know what they are? See the thickness of them.'

His accent was still that of the rural Lancashire he had left as a child but warmer and more precipitate than is common there. He explained to his son how the spindle would be assembled and the massive side-trees jointed round it, how the mast would be thickened athwartships and fore and aft with heels of plank, then further secured by great iron hoops driven on the outside. And the mast was braced stronger in his mind with every word he spoke, every mark of assent from those around him, and his ship made proof against the violence of men and weather, ensuring a speedy passage and a good return on his outlay – and only Kemp could know how desperately this was needed.

Not knowing, Erasmus was bored and ill at ease – he had no natural friendliness towards inferiors as his father had. Remorse for the boredom would come too, in its season, and even for the ignorance, his failure to understand this striving to make the ship indestructible.

8

The signs were there for anyone to see. Kemp was a busy man but he would find occasion several times a week to ride down from his house in the town or his place of business near the Old Pool Dock to spend some time in Dickson's Yard on the river bank, where his ship was being built, poking about, chatting to the shipwrights. Wealth had not dimmed his need to be liked, his desire to appear knowledgeable; and for a man who had come from nothing it was a gratifying thing to command this labour, to see the flanks of his ship swell on the stocks from day to day as by the patient breath of a god.

Not that there was much unusual about her. Ships had not changed significantly for a long time now. They were still built of wood, still powered by the action of the wind on sails of flax canvas attached to masts and yards supported by hemp rigging. Columbus, set down on any vessel of the time, would not have found much to puzzle him. All the same, these Liverpool ships had some special features: they were built high in the stern so that the swivel guns mounted on their quarterdecks could be the more easily, the more *commodiously* as might have been said then – a word curiously typical of the age – trained down on their waists to quell slave revolt; they had a good width of beam and a good depth of hold and they were thickened at the rails to make death leaps more difficult.

Nothing very special then about the *Liverpool Merchant*. Her purpose was visible from the beginning, almost, of her construction, in the shape of her keel, the gaunt ribs of her hull: a Liverpool snow, two-masted, brig-rigged, destined for the Atlantic trade. But Kemp's natural optimism had been inflamed to superstition by the mounting pressure of his debts, and his hope in the ship was more than commercial.

He was a sanguine, handsome man, dark-complexioned, with straight brows and bright, wide-open black eyes and a habit of eager gesture that was something of a joke among his generally more stolid acquaintance – a limited joke, because Kemp, at least so far as anyone then knew, was successful in his enterprises and rich, with a wealth he was not reluctant to display: fine stone house in Red Cross Street among the principal merchants of the town; his own carriage with a liveried groom; a wife

9

expensively turned out, though languid-looking – the positive, quick-mannered father and the glowering son together seemed to have drained her.

Father and son looked at each other now, standing beside the still-bleeding mast-pieces in the great draughty shed, divided in their sense of the occasion but with the same handsome brows and dark eyes, wide-open, bright, somehow dazed-looking, show-ing the same capacity for excess. 'A thousand oaks to make this ship of mine,' Kemp said, with satisfaction. 'D'you know how to tell if the heart of an oak is sound? Veins of dried pith in it, that's the danger sign, means the wood is rotten. That's what you look for. Ask these fellows, they know. Pity you can't do the same with people, eh, lads?'

He was attractive, even in his condescension; there was some-thing magnetic about him. But not all filings will fly the same way, and the visit to the sailmaker's loft was less successful. Erasmus could never remember how long afterwards this was, or indeed whether it was afterwards at all – his memories of those days had no ordered sequence. But he remembered feeling over-exposed here, in the large square loft brimming with light from its long windows, water-light thrown up from the grey river, austere and abundant, falling without distinction on faces and hands, on the dusty planks of the floor, the low benches, the tarred post in the centre with its rope and tackle for hanging the sails. A horizontal bar came out from this, with a square of thin sail-cloth draped over it.

There were three men on stools, with canvas spread over their knees, two journeymen and the sailmaker, a pale sparse-haired man. It was to him that Kemp spoke, with that warmth of manner that came naturally to him.

'Well, my friend, and how is the work proceeding?'

The two others had risen at the merchant's entrance, clutching the work in their laps; but he gave only a single glance upwards, then resumed his stitching. 'Well enough, as the times are,' he said.

Erasmus had noted the failure to rise, the absence of respectful title, the implicit complaint. This was some radical, atheist fellow – the yards were full of them. 'See to your sails, you were best,' he said. 'Let those that are fitted for office see to the times.'

The man made no reply. He was stitching the edge of the sail with an extra layer of canvas, using a small iron hook with a cord spliced in it to confine the sail while he worked.

'Let us leave this fellow to his stitching,' Erasmus said to his father.

Kemp, however, was not yet deterred. 'I trust you are making stout sails for my ship?'

'It is the best hemp flax,' the sailmaker said, barely pausing in his work.

After a moment or two, as if baffled slightly, Kemp turned to his son. 'These sails, now,' he said, with a conscious energy of tone, 'they cut them out cloth by cloth, the width and depth down to a fraction, depending on the mast or yard they hang from. You need a devilish good eye for it, I can tell you. Ill-made sails will bring a ship to grief, however stout she is else. This fellow now is lining round the edges of the sail to –'

'Not all the way round.' The man still kept his head obstinately lowered. 'Only at the leeches we have the lining.'

' 'Twas that I meant to say.' Kemp spoke sharply – he had not liked being interrupted.

Nothing changed in the sailmaker's expression but he paused in his stitching. 'Was it so?' he said. 'Aye, the leeches, and some would say the bunts also. There are those as will line you all the middle parts of the foot of square sails and the foremost leech of staysails. I don't know if you hold with that, sir?'

'No.' Kemp's face had darkened, but he could never admit ignorance – it was like a defeat. 'I take my stand on common practice,' he said.

'Practice is various, sir. What do you think should be done in the matter of the goring cloths, if I might be so bold?'

Erasmus felt himself flush with rage at this sly pedant who was contriving to discomfit his father. His loved father too he blamed, for persisting. This fellow should not be talked to, but quitted instantly – or kicked off his stool. He moved away to a window and stood with his back to the room, looking out across the faintly glimmering, slate-grey water of the Mersey at the masts of ships at anchor in the Pool. Gulls were wheeling overhead. Their plumage looked leaden against the dull sky and they seemed to hurtle like lead through the air. This coincidence, the justness of his observation, impressed Erasmus and took away his rage. He resolved to write it down later. His love had inclined him, not to poetry exactly, but to a sort of doom-laden note-taking. She is there now, he thought. Less than five miles from where I am standing.

Since falling in love with Sarah Wolpert, his being had become tidal, he could brim with her at any time, the channels were there already, the tracks his obsession had so quickly made. A twitch of recollection, a pang of sense, and the tide of her perfections would come flooding in, the clear pallor of her skin, the slight motions of her hands, the look of her eyelids when she glanced down, the imagined life of her body inside the hooped dress . . .

He had known her most of his life; their fathers were old acquaintances who had sometimes done business together; but real knowledge dated only from ten days before, from the occasion of her elder brother's coming of age – Charles was a few months younger than himself. He had gone rather unwillingly, being always ill at ease in a crowd, disliking broken talk, shared place. He was farouche, intractable. But some grace descended on his eyes that night. He had thought her childish and affected until this descent of knowledge – knowledge she must surely have shared: she had given him some looks. But she had looked at others too . . .

Turning his mind from this he began with a sort of stricken patience to piece that evening together again, the lamplight, bare arms, inflections of voice, whispers of silk. Filigree of a miracle. Again his being flooded with her.

He kept his back to the room a while longer, hearing the voices continuing still. A daub of sunlight from some invisible rift in the cloud lay far out on the water. Below him the tide lapped, muddy and sullen. Here along the open bank were the yards where Liverpool's ships were built, theirs among the others, not framed yet, not much more than the spine of her keel, yet to his eager father already freighted and on her way south. Erasmus felt a rush of surprised affection. He had none of this transfiguring enthusiasm. His need to possess the present was too urgent. Lately the sense of this difference between them had complicated his feelings with a kind of sorrow, though whether for himself or for his father he could not have said.

He turned back into the room, where silence had now fallen. Some accommodation had been reached – his father's face was florid and calm. The sailmaker he did not look at. He saw the sheet of canvas over the bar stir and creep a little in some current of air. It is always through arbitrary combinations that experience enslaves the memory. New shackles were being forged here, in the light-filled loft, amid smells of oiled canvas and raw hemp and tar, the creeping fringes of the sail-cloth, his feelings for Sarah Wolpert and for his father.

TWO

Then there was the supper party, his father's visionary gleam in the firelight, candle-light, face darkly flushed below the ash-grey line of his wig, heated with talking and wine. Not the same man at all as that sniffer of timbers, the bluffer in the sailmaker's loft. One of those in receipt of his father's eloquence that evening was his cousin, Matthew Paris. It was his cousin's arrival, the looming quality of his presence there, a man newly released from prison – though of course the other guests knew nothing of this – that fixed the evening so clearly in Erasmus's mind. He had hated his cousin from the age of ten, because of an incident on a beach in Norfolk. Paris was to be the ship's surgeon.

The ladies had left the table, headed by his mother, who was always prompt to rise, as far as her habitual languidness could show it, to escape from the oppression of loud male voices and spirituous breath.

The voices grew louder with the ladies gone. Light played over the long, beast-footed sideboard, flickered on the heavy brass clasps that held its doors, on glasses and decanter, on the triple-headed silver candlesticks that had belonged to his mother's mother. These, and the gilded mahogany clock above the fireplace and the ebony book-ends carved as ravens holding the big Bible with its purple silk marker, were things he had grown up with, as was his father's voice, which had never to his recollection sounded the faintest note of doubt or misgiving.

It was confident as ever now, while the two different sorts of flame, ruddy and pale in concert, danced assent to his views of the profits to be made in the Africa trade, the voice warm, insistent, with sudden rising inflections, telling his guests assembled there that this very time, this year of grace 1752, was the best, the most auspicious possible: 'Now that the wars are over, now that the Royal African Company has lost its charter and the monopoly that went with it, now that we can trade to Africa without paying dues to those damned rogues in London . . .'

Paris there among the others, silent – he hardly spoke at all; but more physically present than anyone else, solid among shadows, with his big-knuckled hands and awkward bulk and long pale face and the aura of shame and disgrace he brought with him.

'The trade is wide open. Wide open, I tell you, gentlemen. The colonies grow more populous by the year, by the month. The more land that is planted, the more they will want negroes. It is a case of first come, first served. And who is best placed to take it on? London is away there on the wrong side, with the Thames up her arse. Bristol's costs are twice ours here. I tell you, if God picked this town up in the palm of his hand and studied where best in England to set her down for the Africa trade, he would put her exactly back where she is, exactly where she stands at present.'

He thumped his fist on the table so that the glasses rattled and sat looking round the faces, challenging contradiction.

'Why should God want to do Liverpool a kindness?'

The source of this levity Erasmus could not afterwards remember, but he remembered the frown of displeasure that came to his father's face.

'It was a manner of speaking,' Kemp said. 'I am not the man to take God's name in vain.' Though profane by thoughtless habit, he was a church-going man and devout, especially now, with his ship on the stocks and his thoughts on the hazardous business of capturing and selling negroes. God is polycephalous, as the diversity of our prayers attests; his aspect varies with men's particular hopes, and Kemp's were pinned on fair winds and good prices. 'I tell you,' he said, 'sure as I sit here, the future of Liverpool lies with the Africa trade. It is patent and obvious to the meanest understanding. The trade goods are all in our own backyard, the cottons, the trinkets, the muskets, everything we –'

'For my part, I'll stick to what I know.' An old man's voice, drink-thickened and truculent. Old Rolfson, who died of a stroke not long after, on the steps of the Exchange, leaving more than one hundred thousand pounds, most of it made provisioning the army during the recent wars.

'And what may that be?' somebody asked him. Jocular, not very friendly. 'We have peace now, Isaac, your contracts are finished. Fortunately for our brave army. I make no doubt your victuals killed more of them than the French did.'

There was laughter at this, which the old man heard through with a sort of malevolent composure. He was making to speak again, but someone on his right got in first.

'He means the Spanish trade, don't you, Rolfson?'

'A contraband trade?' Kemp waxed scornful. 'So you'd found this city's fortune on smuggled tobacco? I am talking about a commerce that will be worth millions. A lawful commerce – it is sanctioned by the law of the land. Merchants trading to Africa can hold up their heads with the best.'

In later times, when commercial enterprise came to be a virtue in itself, and a good return on capital was blessing enough, the need to invoke legitimacy was not so much felt, but the men seated around this table still felt it strongly. Kemp had made his assertion with triumphant authority and it was greeted without demur. He waited a moment, then continued more quietly: 'Those that get in now will be the ones best situated. I'd be surprised if there are more than twenty Liverpool ships in the trade at present. In the next ten years you'll see that go up to a hundred. Why, my tailor is in it. He was telling me just the other day. He has bought a tenth part in a thirty-ton sloop that will carry you seventy-five negroes to the West Indies.'

'That's no more than a fishing-smack.' Paris this, his one remembered contribution to the talk. The voice rather deep, vibrant, softened by the growling inflections of Norfolk. 'Hardly longer than a pitch for quoits,' he added after a moment. Incredulity in the tone, though what he was questioning – the size of the vessel, the number of negroes – Erasmus couldn't determine.

His father, it seemed, had heard quite a different question.

16

'Aye,' he said, 'that is the beauty of it. Ten men can sail her. One prime slave will make you a profit of twenty-five pounds in Kingston market – enough to pay ten men's wages for two months at sea.'

Kemp looked smiling round the table. 'And look what is happening to sugar,' he said. 'I don't need to tell you gentlemen what raw sugar is worth on the home market nowadays.' He raised a hand and made a rapid sketch of a triangle in the air before him. 'Three separate profits,' he said. 'One in Africa, one in Jamaica, one back here. And each one better than the last.'

With the exception of Paris, these were all Liverpool men. There could scarcely have been one of them who had not a full understanding of the Triangular Trade, as it was called – cheap trade goods to Africa for the purchase of negroes, these then carried to America or the West Indies and sold there; rum and tobacco and sugar bought with the proceeds and resold in England. Most of them were involved in the trade to some degree, as manufacturers, brokers or wholesalers.

Kemp was telling them what they already knew. He was aware himself that he was doing so. But he was in fear, and needed these days the temporary sedative of approval to take the edge off it, as one might need a drug, and he was ready to spend his best efforts to obtain this. There were those who afterwards recalled the garrulity that descended on Kemp towards the end of his life, and gave it out that they had always seen the weakness, known he was not sound by the way he sought to involve you in his purposes, get you on his side, working for it, casting round his energetic glances, gesturing with his hands like a confounded Frenchman. Kemp could not keep his own counsel, they said, and that will bring a man to ruin sooner or later.

These were people who added to their satisfaction at another's downfall the gloss of worldly wisdom. In the period after his father's death, Erasmus was sometimes aware of it hanging in the air of conversations, in silences, in shifts of subject, too elusive for a cause of quarrel – he would have fought any man of whatever degree who spoke in disrespect of his father's memory.

17

This evening he had not seen anything amiss. Drink had made his father eloquent, but there was nothing wrong in that. He had been proud of the way his father had stared that old ruffian Rolfson down, and dominated the table. He had thought him right in everything he said. It was true that the presence of Matthew Paris had been disturbing; it was hateful to have a jail-bird for a cousin and to be obliged to sit at table with him. But Erasmus had drunk quite a lot too; and something had happened earlier that day which occupied his thoughts and possibly blunted his observation. In the afternoon he had taken his courage in both hands and ridden over to the Wolpert house, ostensibly to see Charles. And there, without quite knowing how or why, he, who had always hated acting, had allowed himself to be enrolled in the cast of a play.

THREE

It had been on the morning of that day – the day of his involvement in these theatricals – that his cousin from Norfolk had arrived, about whom there hung the shadow of failure and disgrace; terrible blemishes to Erasmus, like deformities. If people stayed in their places, he felt, they would not incur such misfortunes. Even Paris's sufferings, of which he had heard his parents speak, his broken career, the loss of his wife, these seemed shameful too. He had felt, from the first moment, oppressed by his cousin's presence, as if literally in shadow, as if this meeting existed in shadow time, along with certain other incidents of darkness occurring then, while the ship was being built, which he afterwards remembered.

'This is your cousin Matthew. Do you remember him?'

Erasmus saw a tall, ungainly-looking man with a face deeply marked below the short, bobbed wig. He was dressed in a suit of black cloth and his necktie came down in two straight folds like a parson's.

'No, I don't remember him at all.' He spoke with his eyes turned towards his father, as if talking of some person not there in the room.

'You were too young when we last met,' Paris said. 'There are ten years between us, I think.' His voice was deep and soft, with a husky vibrance in it, strangely distinctive.

Erasmus felt a slight prickling sensation at the nape of his neck. He was amazed at this nonchalance. On their last meeting Paris had lifted him, helpless and raging, away from a dam he had been trying to build against the sea, lifted him clear and swung him and set him down yards away. The mortal offence of

19

it, the violation of his body and his will, were as vivid now to his mind as they had been thirteen years ago. 'I am glad to see you, cousin,' he said. 'You are very welcome here.' Glancing aside again, he saw that his father was smiling and nodding in a way he had when highly pleased.

'I am glad of this opportunity to renew my cousin's acquaintance,' Paris said, with a slight inclination of the head. After this he stood silent for some moments looking from one to the other, from chuckling father to stiff son. 'After so many years,' he added heavily. He had felt his cousin's hostility. Suddenly, again, he wondered if he could go through with this visit, had to suppress an impulse to quit the room. Father and son aimed the same level brows at him, had the same staring regard.

'What I haven't yet told you,' William Kemp said to his son, 'because it has only now been finally agreed between us, is that Matthew here will be sailing with the *Liverpool Merchant* as surgeon.'

'Will he so?' Erasmus had not imagined anyone related to him going with the ship. And that it should be this person, whom he had always hated, who had now compounded his offence by being convicted of sedition – he had brought disgrace on them all – this was a thought intensely disagreeable to him. 'You did not tell me you had this in mind,' he said to his father.

'In case it came to naught when we were building upon it. Matthew is more than qualified. He studied three years in Surgeons' Hall in the City of London. Then he was assistant something or other at the Westminster Hospital, what was it . . .?'

'Assistant lithotomist,' Paris said gravely. 'That was before entering into private practice in Norwich.'

'And he is, er was, a member of the Royal Company of Surgeon Apothecaries. And he has writ a treatise, entitled *Syllabus of Anatomy*, which has been published by Blackie and Son of Paternoster Row in London. I trust I have these details right?'

Early in this recital Kemp's face had commenced to glow. There was nothing like a qualified man. Each item was a rivet, a strong bolt for the ship's timbers. 'Ah, yes, I almost forgot, he obtained the Bishop of Norwich's licence as a physician and ran his own practice, with his own premises for retail transactions. Is that not so, Matthew?'

20

'H'm, yes.' Those who knew Paris would have recognized the quality of his hesitation now, and the sudden prominence of his cheekbones. He had enjoined humility upon himself, or, failing that, caution; but he had felt both receding during this catalogue of his virtues. That he was taking his uncle's charity did not oblige him to take his commendations too, though he was amused in a way to see these enlisted as commercial assets. But it was the unexpected reference to this cleric who had so damaged his life that caused him to break his promises to himself. 'Aye,' he said, 'you must have your piece of paper with the bishop's scrawl upon it, there is no doing without that. Though why it should be so I cannot see, as the man knows even less of medicine than of theology. His scrawl was on the paper that sent me to prison too – he knows something about prisons, at least. He owns Norwich Jail at present; not the building, of course – that belongs to good King George. No, the revenue from it, which is quite considerable, you know: people will pay for their comforts inside prison just as they will outside, if they have money.'

Some moments of silence followed this. Erasmus could not fully credit what he had heard. That Paris should so gratuitously refer to his experience of prison struck him as in such execrable taste that it almost deserved pity. It was as if his cousin had made some terrible blunder which he needed to be saved from. And it was with some sense of coming to the rescue, some urge to cover the offence, that he cast around now for a new topic. 'What is a lithotomist exactly?' he said at last.

'Lithotomy is the operation of cutting for stone in the bladder,' Paris said, in his deep, unhurried voice. His face relaxed in a rueful, slightly lop-sided smile that narrowed one eye more than the other. 'As for the premises your father speaks of,' he said, 'it was a shop.' He raised a large hand in a gesture of repudiation. 'My wife and I kept an apothecary's shop and had rooms above it.'

The words were merely modest in intention; but they gave Erasmus what he needed, a reason for legitimizing his dislike, giving it official status, so to speak. Antipathy for a fellow-being, like love, is a story that we relate to ourselves, varying in the elements that feed it but always the same in its need for a formal opening, so that it can become properly conscious of itself and not remain for ever inchoate, mere vague repugnance or resentment or prejudice. This opening Erasmus found in the twisted smile, in what seemed a sardonic belittling of his father's enthusiasm; and with the opening once found things proceeded apace, as always: what right had this pauper, this recipient of charity, to correct his benefactor, to choose the way he was to be regarded?

A little later, in the drawing-room, where his mother joined them for tea, he found himself adding his cousin's strangely unfashionable shoes to the count against him. They were large, black, square-toed, with big square buckles – this at a time when buckles of any sort were quite out – and they creaked slightly. They somehow completed the suggestion of the necktie, with its two straight folds, and the black, low-crowned hat he had seen hanging in the hall, of some country preacher, a hedge parson dressed up for a visit. This seemed like hypocrisy – it was for denying Holy Writ that his cousin had been imprisoned . . .

In the smaller space of this room it was impossible not to feel a kind of force emanating from Paris. This lay not so much in any distinction of bearing as in the potential for damage that seemed to invest him, conveyed by something awkward in his movements, something constrained or perhaps not fully coordinated. Sitting there in his thick black suit, impassive now that grimace of a smile had faded, with his pale eyes and long, furrowed face turned attentively to his hostess, the stranger looked somehow as if the space wasn't enough, as if he might break into disastrous action.

It was the chief fear of Mrs Kemp, as she afterwards confessed, that her nephew might break something. 'I was on the edge of my seat the *whole* time Matthew was in the room,' she said. 'So unsettling.' Her voice, as always, threatening to expire before the final syllables were reached.

She had joined them for tea, in this room she loved best in the house, with its pale green brocaded chairs and little oval tables, its lawn curtains admitting a discreet view of the street and the opposite house fronts, its cabinets of things she had had from

22

her mother, things precious to her, tea-sets, Dresden figurines, the prized collection of china pomanders and pill-boxes – all well within reach of her nephew's arm.

She was fond of Matthew, who was her sister's son, and had always followed his career with interest, in spite of seeing him only rarely. She often spoke of him, a fact galling to Erasmus, though his pride would not allow him to show it. Her pity and distress at her nephew's misfortune she disguised in accustomed weariness and these exaggerated fears that he might break something. With a husband and a son always ready to correct her errors of feeling, she had learned disguise long ago.

'Yes,' she said in her expiring tones, 'I was prepared for the very worst.'

And yet the movements of his hands were precise enough, his management of shallow saucer and small-handled cup and diminutive spoon beyond reproach. It was an uneasy constraint of body, not any evident clumsiness, that gave others a sense of possible disaster. And it was obvious that he was strong.

'He quite wearied me out,' Mrs Kemp said. 'And then, of course, knowing that he had not been long out of prison . . .'

'You think his capacity for wreckage was thereby increased?' Kemp asked. Though not given to regarding himself with any degree of irony – and perhaps because of this – he had stores of it for his wife.

'Well, it restricts them, doesn't it?' she said in a reasonable tone. 'My nephew has been kept within close bounds. Now that he is restored to society, it would not be surprising if he felt a need to move himself about.'

It astonished Erasmus – who had never understood his mother – that she seemed so little sensible of the disgrace her sister's son had brought on the family. From her manner of speaking about it Paris might as well have just emerged from some illness.

'You can say what you like,' she said. 'I thought him charming. And his manners, for the occasion, a good deal better than those of some' – this last a rebuke, more direct than she usually had energy for, to her son for his brusqueness, which she had not failed to see.

The manners were a source of amazement to Paris himself. A

23

man whose heart feels dead within him, whose desire it is to disappear from the face of the earth, who is about to take employment on a slaveship as a first step to this, still balancing his cup, passing the sugar, writhing politely on a hard chair.

However, such is our nature, what begins as social pretence quite often becomes a reality of feeling. He saw his aunt's face near his own, marks of sympathy in it as well as petulance and hypochondria, and he found himself drawn to her. The lines of strain on his face softened as he observed her fussing to settle her skirts, watched the play of her scented handkerchief as she leaned forward to converse with him. Nor was it wholly fear for her pretty things that kept Mrs Kemp's attention on her nephew. It soon became obvious, both to the husband and to the son, that Matthew Paris, in his wincing shoes and subfusc suit and bob wig, was making a distinctly favourable impression.

'So you are going with the ship?'

'As surgeon, yes.'

'It will be very comforting for us to know that.'

'I am glad you take that view, aunt.' Paris spoke with a sort of solemn courtesy. 'However, I am not entirely clear how you mean it.'

'Why, sir,' she said, with a little air of wonder at his failure to see, 'naturally we shall all feel much better with a member of the family on board.'

It now appeared that Paris possessed a different smile from the wry one they had seen: it came to his face slowly, lighting it with an expression of great sweetness. 'Ah, yes, of course.'

He was touched by the sentiment as well as amused by what seemed a lapse of logic. Of late he had become very sensitive to kindness, and it was this that the pale, languid woman, who hardly knew him, who seemed half extinguished between husband and son, was seeking to show. 'You may rest assured,' he said, traces of the smile still remaining, 'that I shall be mindful of my responsibilities.'

'Good heavens, woman,' Kemp said with a certain testiness, 'he is not going as a member of the family, or at any rate not primarily, but as a qualified medical man to ensure the best possible condition of health for the negroes.'

24

'And crew,' Paris said mildly.

'Eh? Oh, aye, the crew too, naturally. Matthew has studied at Surgeons' Hall,' he told his wife. 'He was resident surgeon at one of our great hospitals, he has writ books . . .'

'Yes, my dear, you have told us all that. And besides, I knew it before.' Mrs Kemp turned again to Paris. 'I have sometimes a kind of fluttering here, below the heart,' she said. She laid a white hand among the lace trimmings that rose above her stomacher. 'When I get at all agitated or beyond myself. Do you know of anything for it?'

'For palpitations,' Paris said with restored gravity, 'I have always found tincture of hellebore to answer very well. I can make one up for you if you wish. And a draught of warm cinnamon water, taken night and morning, is generally soothing to the nerves.'

Erasmus saw his mother, thus encouraged, preparing to launch on a more detailed account of her symptoms. 'Have you been to sea before?' he said to Paris.

'Not what one would call going to sea. I went out with the fishing boats sometimes when I was a boy. At Brancaster on the Norfolk coast.' Paris paused as if in some doubt. His eyes, Erasmus now noticed, were pale green in colour, not blue as he had thought at first; they were set at a slight downward slant, giving his face in repose an expression of mingled obstinacy and melancholy. After some further moments of hesitation, he said, 'It was there we last met, all of us – both the families, I mean. You had come on a visit. We went down to the sea one day. There was quite a party of us, I remember – some other people too, who lived nearby. I was eighteen that summer, so you must have been eight or perhaps nine. Quite small.'

'I have no recollection of it.'

The words came too coldly and emphatically to be altogether trusted; but there was no mistaking the intention to rebuff, the rejection of a shared past his cousin had thus diffidently held out to him.

'I remember it clearly.' Paris sought refuge once again in his aunt – it was to her that he kept coming back. 'I think because of a dam we tried to build that day. My cousin showed great

25

determination of character. He did his very best to stay the tide.'

He went on to tell her in his gentle baritone about a channel and a reservoir they had built that distant day at the edge of the tide, using stones and driftwood and the thick black mud of the salt flats to line the banks and make a barrier, and how the sea constantly frustrated their efforts, scooping below the foundations so that the walls kept crumbling and the water leaking away, until the others got tired of it and went to divert themselves elsewhere – all but Erasmus.

'He would not give it up. We went to ask him to come away, but he would not. He would not speak to anyone. He had mud all over him. He went on plastering over the stones and bits of plank and the sea went on wrecking his efforts. I thought to myself then that what my cousin sets his mind on it will come hard but he gets it.'

Paris paused, swallowing at a feeling of a self-contempt. Was it to ingratiate himself with the mother that he was telling this story of heroic persistence? He had found shelter in her invalidism – was he now trying to creep further into her good graces, trying to cement an alliance of the weak? The truth of his memory was quite different . . .

'It was as if you were possessed,' he said, looking steadily and rather sternly at Erasmus. 'You were white in the face and staring. I remember that your hands were black with the mud but blood from your fingers showed through it where you had lacerated them scrabbling with the stones. It was . . . quite a spectacle.' And no joy in it, he thought, looking with a kind of curiosity at his cousin, no prospect of joy – there would have been no joy in success; that lonely passion had needed defeat as a condition of its being.

'I do not recollect anything of it.' Erasmus had quivered internally at the touch of his cousin's impertinent curiosity, though meeting it with an appearance of indifference and the same obstinate lie. This stranger, with his lined face and pale eyes, the mounds of his knees showing under the cloth of his breeches, was claiming rights which by his disgrace he had forfeited. Worse, he was vindicating his claims: he had brought

26

the episode vividly, irresistibly, back; Erasmus could deny remembering, but he could not defend himself against the memory; he felt it again now, the loneliness of it, the indifferent sky, the gleaming, elusive water, the exquisite rage. He saw himself as the others must have seen him, dogged and ridiculous. And all this he had to endure now again, and at Paris's bidding. Worst of all, his cousin showed no awareness of the wrong he had done, he made no slightest mention of it . . .

FOUR

Soon after the midday meal, at which she ate little, Mrs Kemp retired for her afternoon rest. Before she did so she made Paris a present of a very handsome lacquered box, lined with baize and decorated on the outside with a design of gold peacocks on a blue background. ''Tis Chinese lacquer,' she said. 'I have been used to keep recipes in it, but it will serve just as well for your log books and such like.'

'It is the captain who keeps a log, not the doctor,' Kemp said.

'I was speaking of a medical log, not a nautical one,' his wife said with dignity. 'Matthew will want to keep notes of the ailments he encounters on the ship. I should much enjoy to read them when he returns.' She had an abiding interest in illness of every kind.

'I am sure to find a use for it,' Paris said, holding the box rather awkwardly between his large hands. 'It is indeed kind of you, aunt.'

Erasmus too excused himself early. It was a Sunday and he had made up his mind to ride over to the Wolpert house on the pretext of a visit to Charles Wolpert, with whom he had never been on very close terms. The decision had involved a struggle with himself, with his pride, his fear of ridicule, shame at the element of declaration he felt in it – though this was less obvious than it seemed to his exasperated self-consciousness. This travail once over, his intention was cast firm and unalterable. The only element of choice remaining lay in what clothes to wear for the occasion; and in order to give his best attention to this Erasmus repaired to his room at the earliest opportunity.

This left the two men alone, Paris without refuge in a third party, Kemp possessed by a kind of impatience: he would have liked, in the span of this single afternoon, to take this studious, clumsy-seeming nephew of his through all the stages of his own enthusiasm for the slaving venture – an ambition inflamed, if anything, by the Malaga wine he had taken with his meal. But speech lets us down very often, and the merchant found he had nowhere to begin except in a reiteration of his good intentions. 'You are welcome to stay here, Matthew, in the days before you join the ship,' he said, not for the first time.

They were in the room on the first floor of the house which Kemp regarded as his sanctum and sometimes called his study, though nothing much but ledgers were studied there. Pipe in mouth, he looked through curls of smoke at the young man sitting opposite, hunched forward in the easy-chair as if set on maintaining a notion of sufferance, his large hands loosely clasped between his knees. 'You must regard my house as your own for as long as you choose,' he said.

'It is indeed kind of you. But I have things to see to at home, as I told you, and must take the stage for Norwich the day after tomorrow at latest.'

'It is as you choose. All I am intending to say is that the past is the past and you must set it behind you. Nothing that has happened places a term to your welcome here.'

The sound of his own words animated Kemp with a renewed sense of the excellence of his motives. His spirits rose. He was behaving generously towards his nephew and at the same time gaining the services of a qualified medical man. A less qualified medical man would have done, he knew that: most of the slavers that sailed out of Liverpool would have some sawbones apprentice or drunken quack aboard, or no one; but that was not good enough for the *Liverpool Merchant*. Moreover, he was killing other pigeons with the same shot: by this kindness to a bankrupt he was dressing his ship in the colours of charity and compassion.

Kemp held a moral view of the universe. God balanced the ledgers. Nothing went unrecognized. A good deed was an entry on the credit side, a bill drawn on destiny which could not fail to be met one day. He saw his ship home in port again, riding at anchor in the Pool, laden with goods high in demand, saw his creditors satisfied, temporarily at least, with the interest on their loans, till the cotton trade took a turn for the better, as it soon must. The vision glowed in his cheeks and eyes as he leaned forward. 'Africa,' he said, 'you will be going to Africa, Matthew. Think of it.'

'I have thought much of it.' Paris sat up a little, straightening his shoulders in polite response. He did not know what to say to his uncle, whom he thought looked rather hectic and high-coloured this afternoon, feverish almost; he would have liked to take his pulse.

Not feeling able to suggest this, he looked away towards the window. Sunshine had come to the day after a misty start and there was a breeze outside, stirring the new leaves on the elms round the little square. Some pigeons flew up as he watched. The movement of the trees and the flight of the pigeons sent quick shoals of shadows across the room, over the ceiling and walls. For some moments he watched this without speaking. Despite the inertness of his body, he felt light, without substance. Misty mornings bring fine weather when the season is turning, he thought vaguely, almost sleepily. First songs of warblers through the mist, the sycamores in first leaf. By the river. Ruth and I hand in hand, light raining down on leaf and bud, shadows moving on the water. Light of love in her face. We sat together on the bank. By then she was carrying the child. A day to be remembered, because we knew – and told each other – that we need do nothing but wait. We only had to be as we were. Everything was calm and satisfactory. The house not very grand but with room enough, and the income from shop and practice sufficient. We only had to wait, with our love, for the child to come. Now Ruth is nowhere in the world any more and I am going to Africa. 'Yes,' he said, 'well, it is very far away. It is a place I had never thought to visit. But it might as well be there as anywhere.' Lest this should sound ungrateful, he added quickly, 'I thank you once again for your letter, uncle, and for wishing to do me a service.'

'Blood is thicker than water.' Kemp's tone held an increased alertness. He had sensed some reservation in the other's words. 'You did yourself express an interest in what I had to propose,' he added after a short pause. After all, it is why you are here, he was on the point of adding, but refrained, as it might seem to suggest there could be no other reason.

All the same, the question hung in the air for some moments. Paris did not reply immediately. He was a man who, Kemp suspected, might gnaw at his own purposes indefinitely if left alone to do so.

'You have taken into account the advantages, of course,' he said. 'As I outlined them in my letter. You will be calling at places with many marvels to offer.'

'Indeed yes.' Paris nodded gravely. 'It was said by Pliny that out of Africa there comes always something new.'

'Oh, aye, was it? Well, he was in the right of it. And then, being a man of science you will find a quantity of things to notice.'

'I have no doubt of it.'

'I don't mention money,' the merchant said. 'You have incurred expenses and these have been met. We need say no more about that. But there is something else which I think will interest you.' Kemp leaned forward again, marking a pause. 'I had been keeping it till the ship's articles were signed, but there is no harm in telling you now. I am purposing to allow you three negroes privilege to be paid out of the cargo at cost, your choice of the blacks to be marked at the time of purchase. There now, what do you think of that?'

He was disappointed to discern no change of expression on his nephew's face. 'That is in addition to salary,' he added in a tone of reproach.

After a long moment Paris smiled slightly and said, 'That is an unlooked-for generosity on your part.'

'And then, just now, a break, a period away from home, new fields of endeavour. To dispel those unfortunate associations which must . . . to an extent at least . . . I had hoped to have your final answer.'

'Oh, I am going,' the other replied quickly and, it seemed, almost carelessly, certainly not as though capitulating to argument.

In fact he had known from the first, from first receiving his

31

uncle's letter, that he would go. This exile of a long voyage, a commerce he had every reason to believe degraded, and suitable therefore for such as himself – it was a combination, in his wretchedness, impossible to resist. He had not doubted since then, was so far from doubting now that he was surprised to see relief show on his uncle's face. 'Certainly, I am going,' he repeated.

'That's the spirit, we'll drink to that,' Kemp said. Next to signatures, he had found brandy the best way of sealing a bargain. Getting out the bottle and glasses, however, he felt suddenly exhausted, as if he had been through an ordeal of some kind. These moments of doubt, just when everything had seemed settled, had brought home to the merchant why this awkward nephew of his exercised such a spell, why he was so set on having him for surgeon. It had little to do with charity, except perhaps to himself. What had befallen Paris was the worst possible thing, the thing most to be feared. He stalked through the rooms of the house in Red Cross Street, a spectre of bankruptcy and ruin, his own, Kemp's, everyone's; he was a wincing ghost that had to be, not laid to rest, but rehabilitated, undemonized, brought back into the world of collective enterprise. Then the fear that haunted most of Kemp's dawns might also pass away.

'Well, nephew,' he said, holding up his glass, 'here's to success!'

FIVE

It took Erasmus an hour to choose his clothes for the visit. He tried on various suits, but all of them were lacking in one way or another. Finally he decided on the claret-coloured satin suit with the white, corded-silk waistcoat to go with it, a sumptuous garment this, embroidered all over with small flowers in a darker shade. His hair was dark and naturally lustrous; he had taken recently to wearing it in a bang across his forehead and tied behind with ribbon. Worn thus, it softened his looks, reduced the impression of fanaticism. In the smoothness of his face the eyes were extraordinary: long, narrow, very dark, with a gaze of singular intensity. This narrowness of regard, and the high cheek-bones, gave him an appearance of aiming his eyes at people, which his father had too.

The day was bright, the air still slightly engrained with the mist of earlier. Going was slow at first: the lanes above the river were miry and fetid and his mare was soon splashed to her knees. There were no pavements anywhere in the town, he had trouble keeping clear of pedestrians and had frequently to rein in for street-vendors with handcarts and for the little broad-backed ponies labouring up from the waterfront, laden below the belly with goods for next day's market.

His main concern was to prevent any besmirching of his person above the riding boots; for larger thoughts there was no space in his mind. The visit lay on him now like a heavy sentence, one which there was no evading – he was serving it already as he made his way through the bemusing sunlight amidst sewage smells from the open drains, impatient snortings from his horse, the ring of clogs on the plank walks, quarrelling shouts over right of way.

33

Coming out of Castle Street he heard the hoarse, glottal whoops of a water-seller and the clatter of his pails, and found his way blocked by the huge barrel mounted on its cart, the skinny horse standing listless while the man slopped out the water into waiting buckets. Edging by between cart and wall, Erasmus cursed the man and his parents and his buckets and barrel. The man grinned and waved his hat in an attempt to make the mare shy up, and one of the waiting women screeched at him, whether joke or abuse he could not tell.

Once north of Pool Lane and on the outskirts of the town, both he and the horse felt easier. The Wolpert house was in open country, built on a wooded rise, its stone gables visible from a good distance, pinnacles of desire to Erasmus as he saw them now, sunlit, rising clear of the trees. As he followed the long curve of the carriageway he knew in some part of his being that these were the last moments of his true selfhood: he was about to reveal a need, and therefore an insufficiency. But what hurt him in this thought also spurred him on. His will was fixed on the girl. In obsessive natures the prospect of pain too becomes an incentive, just as fear of wounds inflames the warrior. In this gentle, windless May weather, with the new green along the beech avenue, songs of warblers falling with their strangely secretive trickle through the foliage, Erasmus found himself gritting his teeth with the violence of his intention.

The ancient footman Andrew came in answer to his ring and stood peering, dishevelled as usual, wigless, his scant remaining hair standing in tufts above his bloodless ears. Erasmus asked for Charles in a voice that nerves had made sharper.

'They'm at their reharsings,' the old man said in mumbling tones, blinking around him as if affrighted by the daylight.

'I wish you'd learn to speak up,' Erasmus said. He had always thought it an unaccountable indulgence on old Wolpert's part to keep such a witless fellow in service. 'Did you say horses? Are they from home?' He was divided between disappointment and relief.

'They'm at their speeches. Practisin'. *Reharsing*.' There was a touch of reproof here at Erasmus's misprision. He pointed an arthritic finger towards a coppice of mixed oak and elm some

34

three hundred yards off across the lawns that lay below the house. Through the trees Erasmus saw gleams of water. There was a small lake down there, he remembered.

'Do you mean to say they are rehearsing a play down there? Who? Miss Sarah too?'

'Miss Sarah an' a young leddy from Stanton an' Master Charles an' Master Robert an' a clargyman name of the Reverend Mister Parker an' the schoolmaster from –'

'Very well, you need not make a catalogue of it.' He looked in amazement towards the coppice, where the trees grew thickly together. The yellow of the new oak leaves and the pale green of the elms swooned together in the sunlight to make a delicate haze, fiery round the edges, with a fierce, pure line where foliage touched sky. Abode of angels. Somewhere within this pure empyrean Sarah Wolpert was rehearsing a play. 'I'll go down to them,' he said after a moment, and nothing could have marked his confusion more than this confiding his intention to a servant.

'The clargyman is performin' as a savvidge.' Andrew's pale mouth drew down. 'There is some as don't think it befittin'.'

'I don't know what you are talkling about,' Erasmus replied briskly. He had made a sort of recovery. 'See to my horse, will you? Or get someone to do it.'

He began to make his way towards the coppice, a certain offendedness growing in him as he did so, a sense of having been excluded. Though so far locked within his breast, his love, he illogically felt, gave him rights.

When he reached the trees he did not know which way to go; Andrew's clutch at the landscape had given him no very precise idea. The lake was no longer visible. After a moment's hesitation he decided to go straight forward. He startled a blackbird, which flew off with a low, reproachful fluting. The wood was more extensive than it had looked from the house and it had clearly been neglected of late years; the oaks had bushed out at ground level and there was a thick undergrowth of saplings and bramble and straggling clumps of rhododendron. Erasmus was obliged to make detours. He should not have come through the wood, he realized now, but skirted round it. Glancing up, he had a swift impression of scarlet – the sun was piercing through

35

the red casing of the elm leaf buds. He could hear nothing. He had no idea in which direction the lake lay. He felt uncomfortably hot inside his satin suit. It came to him that he was – not seriously of course but for the moment indubitably, and quite absurdly – lost.

He moved forward again. After some moments he thought he heard voices and he turned in the direction of the sound. The trees were thinning out. He caught a glimpse of water. Ahead of him and to his right a man's voice was raised, sonorous and loud.

> Beware all fruit but what the birds have pecked,
> The shadows of the trees are poisonous too;
> A secret venom slides from every branch.
> My conscience doth distract me, O my son!
> Why do I speak of eating or repose,
> Before I know thy fortune?

Erasmus had come to an involuntary halt. There was a brief pause, then another voice, which he thought he recognized as that of Charles Wolpert, said, 'If you don't mind my saying so, the second part of that speech is supposed to be delivered aside. The others are not supposed to hear it, you know. It is marked "aside" on your copy. The part beginning, "My conscience doth distract me".'

Some words followed too low for him to catch. Then the first voice came again: 'But they are bound to hear it if the audience is to hear it.'

'There are theatrical conventions, Rivers.' A different voice this, higher-pitched, slightly nasal. 'What Wolpert is getting at is that you are delivering the whole speech in the same tone and at the same pace. You could make a pause by advancing to the foot of the stage and addressing the audience directly.'

'Thank you, Parker, thank you.'

There was very little gratitude in the tone of this. Erasmus stood transfixed. He would seem ridiculous, blundering out of the wood into the open, into full view. Other voices came now, lower, blending together so that he could make nothing out. These fell away to silence and a moment later, without warning, he heard a girl's voice, plaintive and sweet, raised in song:

36

Come unto these yellow sands
    And then take hands.
Curtseyed when you have and kissed,
    The wild waves whist . . .

Erasmus gave one wild glance upwards towards the scarlet
blaze of the elm leaves, then one down as if to see where his feet
had led him. The new curls of the bracken were red too, he
noticed in this moment of vivid particularity, the folded serrations of the fronds rust-red in colour. For a moment he felt on
the verge of some momentous discovery. Then the voices joined
together, male and female, in a ragged, barking chorus, '*Hark-
hark! Bow-wow!*' It was like some savage incantation and
Erasmus, as if summoned by it, moved forward through the last
of the trees out into the open, where he came again to a halt,
checked by the sudden enlargement, the openness of the sky, the
gleaming oval of the lake and the wide view beyond it.

The lake was reedy at the edges and rimmed with pale artificial shores of sand. A rowboat lay tethered on the far side.
On the shore to his right, between the water and the trees, a
structure to represent a cavern had been made with branches
and canvas. Before this, on the sand, a group of people stood
close together. One of them was Sarah. She was in a blue dress
and a broad-brimmed sunhat tied below the chin. No one had
seen him yet. Sarah said, in a clear, excited voice, 'I'll read
Ferdinand, if you like.' She took a pace forward, holding up her
book:

Where should this music be? i' th'air or th'earth?
It sounds no more . . .

As she glanced round to catch the dying echoes, her gaze fell
upon Erasmus, who was still standing motionless at the edge of
the trees. 'Heavens,' she said. 'It is Erasmus Kemp. Where did
you come from?'

'I came to see Charles.' Erasmus shouted the lie across the
water. His heart was beating heavily. He made a gesture towards
the trees.

'Pat he comes, right on cue.' This from a portly, loud-voiced

37

fellow who alone among them had made an attempt to dress for the part: he wore a red calico morning-gown and had a sort of wizard's turban of the same colour on his head. The schoolmaster, Erasmus thought, seeking with immediate jealousy to identify all around her. The curate, Parker, was easy enough to pick out – he had retained his clerical collar.

Sarah quitted the group and came round the lakeside towards him, over the sand, lifting the skirts of her dress. Watching her, not moving, he was briefly aware again of the setting, the water, yellow of broom on the rising ground beyond and scattered sheep grazing; and the strangeness of it came to him: the actors had become spectators, they were all watching him and Sarah. Then his vision narrowed to the young woman approaching him and he felt a pang at the beauty of her present slight disablement, the way the long dress and the soft sand impeded her.

'Oh, Erasmus,' she exclaimed, while still some yards off. 'I am so glad you thought to visit.' Excitement had dispelled constraint, she was regarding him boldly. 'Just when we needed someone,' she said, with a smiling air of wonder, 'you appeared like a spirit.'

Erasmus cleared his throat. 'Well, I am mortal,' he said, and she may have seen something in his eyes to corroborate this, for her look became cooler.

'Jonathan Rigby fell off his horse and he has broke a leg,' she said.

'I am sorry to hear that.' He was bewildered. This Jonathan Rigby was someone he knew only slightly. 'I hope 'twas not a bad break.'

'No, it isn't that. You see, we are doing a play called *The Enchanted Island* and he was our Ferdinand, but he can't do it now. You could take his place if you liked.' She looked him in the eye for a moment and said in lower tones, 'If you liked to please me, that is.'

SIX

'So that is satisfactory to you and all agreed? We are allowing you five pounds per month wages and four pounds out of every one hundred and four pounds net proceeds of negroes, gold, ivory etc., and in lieu of your private adventure we admit you to be concerned with us two hundred and twenty-five pounds in the cargo. Your chief mate is to have three negroes privilege, your second mate two. There is to be a surgeon with the ship and he shall have three negroes privilege.'

'Surgeon?' It was not Saul Thurso's habit to inflect his voice much; years of bawling against the wind had reduced it to a single hoarse and grating level. 'We are not bound to carry a doctor with us.'

'Well, of course I know that,' Kemp said. 'I do not send him because I am obliged to do so. I send him for reasons of humanity.'

Thurso considered for some moments, looking out from the square cage of his brows at this flushed fellow who was to be his employer, thence across the narrow office where they were sitting to a section of the warehouse beyond, where bales of cotton rose to the ceiling. He felt the beginnings of rage, always his willing confederate. He said, 'I do the examining of the blacks myself. I know what to look for, I know the tricks they get up to, I am an old Guinea hand, sir. I have never bought a bad negro.'

'I know it. You have been recommended to me, Captain Thurso, by those whose opinion I respect. I know you are well qualified. But then, so is the man I am sending with you. He is a fully qualified medical man.' Kemp paused for a moment, then brought out, as if it were the most significant qualification

39

of all, 'In point of fact, he is my nephew.' The knowledge that this would not be welcome news to the captain hastened him into further speech: 'He will be here any minute now. I asked him to call so as to effect a meeting between you. He starts back for Norfolk tomorrow, where he will stay until we are ready to sail.' He paused a moment, then said, with something of appeal in his voice, 'I intend to leave no stone unturned, nothing that could assist the enterprise.'

Thurso looked fixedly before him without speaking. If this had indeed been an appeal he showed no sign of being moved by it. A relative of the owner on board! He felt the fury gain ground on him, made worse by the necessity he was under to be civil. He clenched his fist below the level of the desk. All Thurso's stoicism lay in enduring these dark rages that would come to him, increasingly of late, all his patience in waiting for the moment, the appointed victim, God's signal for release. Long, cunning habit made him seek now to cover the traces, conceal himself in secondary matters. 'Perhaps you were thinking of the branding?' he said. 'As to that, we don't need a doctor, what you need for that is an experienced man who knows the way to go about it. My first officer, James Barton, who has sailed with me before, he is used to doing that side of it. You need a light touch, especially for the women. Barton is an artist at it. I can swear by Barton.'

'No, no, you misunderstand me,' Kemp said. 'I don't speak of this particular thing or that, it is the general well-being that I am interested to promote.'

Thurso's face had never been remarkable for its mobility and with the years it had set very hard indeed; but his impassivity seemed now to have a quality of consternation about it, as if rock had been able to realize at last what the weather had done to it. 'Well-being,' he repeated in his hoarse, toneless voice. 'Well-being.' It had the effect of a wondering interrogative.

'Here he is.' Kemp spoke with quick relief. His voice, unlike the captain's, was a direct register of his feelings, and he had not been finding this interview easy.

The two men watched the tall figure make its way down the length of the storeroom between the stacked bales. They heard him give good-day to two aproned men loading a handcart. He stooped through the doorway, taking off his low-crowned, countryman's hat as he did so. 'I find you at the heart of your empire,' he said to Kemp.

'Hardly empire, hardly empire. Allow me to present . . . Captain Thurso, Dr Paris.'

Thurso had got up and the two men bowed slightly.

'Your servant.'

The voices overlapped, mingled briefly, one deep and vibrant, the other a bare mutter, hoarse and abrupt.

'I have just been telling Thurso what a welcome addition you will be to the crew.'

'An addition I can't help but be.' Paris smiled slightly at Thurso but failed to detect any answering expression. 'Whether welcome is another matter,' he added after a moment, in the same tone. He thought he saw some struggle for amiability on the other's face, which was broad and brick-coloured, with prominent ridges of bone at the temples and wide, heavy jaws, a fortress of a face that yet failed to give shelter enough to the short-lashed blue eyes. These were full of fury, he noticed now, though whether caused by present emotion or their own inability to creep further into the fastness of the skull he could not determine.

'You will be welcome aboard,' Thurso said at last. 'All according.'

'According to how we agree together?'

At this, Thurso drew his brows forward in what seemed the intention of a smile, and now the eyes did succeed in retreating for a second or two. 'There is only one way to take aboard ship, Mr Paris, and I think you know whose way that is.'

This was not very jocular but it was as near as the captain seemed likely to get, and Kemp fastened on it with some gratitude. 'Well, gentlemen,' he said, 'we'll have a dram on it. I've got some brandy here that I dare say you'll find to your taste. And I suppose you would not be averse to a good Havana cigar? Brought in without benefit of the Spanish, naturally, but none the worse for that – some might say all the better. Here you are. Just try that. I give you good health! Captain Thurso is an old hand in the Africa trade, you know. He has made lord knows how many voyages. Your health again, sir!'

Kemp drank and paused, as if waiting for confirmation. Thurso, however, said nothing, merely sat looking before him, the glass of spirits engulfed in his sunburned grip. Nobody knew exactly how many times Thurso had sailed the triangle. Some said more than twenty. He himself gave out no statistics, this being part of his private pact made long ago never to advertise God's favours to him. He had gone to sea at twelve as a cabin boy on a Bristol slaver in the early years of the century and had been given his first ship at the age of thirty-six. He was fifty-three now. He had survived every hazard of the trade: tempest, fever, slave uprisings, French privateers. Time and again he had returned to his home port with full cargoes, making good profits for his owners, his crews reduced by desertion and disease, himself steadily thicker-set and squarer-faced, his eyes seeking still to withdraw and failing.

Paris, who did not fully appreciate the odds against such survival, nevertheless found him amazing. All his teeth still in place, by the look of him. Limbs a bit stiff perhaps but he had risen on the introduction without the smallest appearance of effort. Stomach doubtless in good order too. Only the windpipe seemed affected; and the eyes, which did not seem to have weathered as well as the rest . . . 'Well, Captain,' he said, raising his glass, 'here is to our good success.'

With habitual caution Thurso glanced away from the surgeon's pale, impertinent regard. The man was spying at him already. A landsman if ever there was one and cackhanded into the bargain – he had noted at once Paris's slightly awkward gait, the way he seemed to step short as at some threat to balance. And a gentleman, too. What was such a man doing, signing for a slaveship? Who had set this in train? Thurso felt forces ranged against him. He heard the voice of his counsellor. *Talk to him. Disarm his eyes. Set him down lower.* 'So, Mr Paris,' he said, 'you have not been to sea before, I believe?'

'No.'

'It is a long voyage. You will have time enough to discover whether you are meant for the life or no. There is a kind of temperament which takes to it.'

'I do not go for that reason,' Paris said, and was warned by a sudden leap of interest in the other's eyes. 'The crew,' he continued in a different tone, 'are they enlisted yet?'

'Crew? We are still some weeks off sailing. No one in his senses would engage a crew so far in advance, not for a Guinea ship.'

'I do not doubt your judgement,' Paris said mildly. 'But is there not some danger that we shall find ourselves short-handed?'

Something between a smile and a grimace came to Thurso's face and he glanced aside at the merchant. 'We generally take care of that the night we leave the Pool,' he said. 'We shall gather some likely lads, never fear.'

'I believe you need more than the usual number of crew on a slaveship, so as to manage the negroes?'

'Manage them? Aye, you are right, sir. I see you have been going into the matter. Tell me then, how do you suggest we could secure the men, if we took them on so far in advance?'

'Let me see now.' Paris affected to consider. He had heard the sarcasm, had noted the sly way Thurso smiled upon his uncle. The balance of pride and humility in him was always uncertain and never more so than in these days of his self-contempt. Whatever he privately felt he deserved, when meeting hostility his first impulse was to fatten it with feeding. 'Give them an advance of pay,' he said with deliberate carelessness.

'Advance of pay, advance of pay?' Thurso turned with a stiff gesture towards Kemp, as if the latter must see now how ill-advised it was to have confidence in such a man. 'Do you mean we should give them money without securing their persons? That would be utmost folly, Mr Paris. You would never see them or your money again. The men who sign on for the Africa trade are the lowest of seafaring men. They are scum, sir.' He paused, looking closely at Paris. He had seen or sensed some indefinable change in the quality of the other's attention. Pre-destined foes will find each other out, though signs of weakness may at first be only dimly perceived. Nothing changed in Thurso's expression or his posture but when he continued it was with a vigilance half instinctive. 'Scum,' he repeated. 'The very dregs of the trade. Some landsmen and simpletons among 'em, looking for a change of circumstance, but they are men in hard case for the most part, men with something to run from.'

'Aye, poverty,' Paris said hastily. 'Otherwise they would choose better.' He saw Thurso bristle his brows at this and was warned again by the sharpness of interest in the small eyes.

'My nephew is going for instruction and experience,' Kemp said.

'That is a worthy aim,' Thurso said in a lighter tone. 'Of course, I was speaking of the common seamen.'

'So was I. I do not doubt there are bad men among them. All the same, it is not beyond them to mend, I suppose, these sweepings of the prisons. Those who have remained unpunished may often be more wicked.' He paused in some confusion. Thurso had not mentioned prison, he now recalled. He felt the blood rise to his face. Without quite knowing why, he said in low tones, 'Something in us dies so the rest can live on, but it must not be the heart.'

'The heart.' Grating and toneless, it came with the effect of a contemptuous question. Thurso craned round at Kemp as though looking for some saving intervention.

'Mr Paris has heart on the brain,' said the merchant, laughing more heartily than seemed warranted at this joke. 'He was telling me only last night that he has been busy making a version from the Latin of a work on the circulation of the blood. You'll take another glass, won't you? We will not all meet again till close on sailing. Let me give you a toast, gentlemen. Perdition to the king's enemies. Success to our enterprise.'

Thurso and Paris touched glasses and drank, but it was the spirit of enmity they imbibed that afternoon, and both of them knew it.

SEVEN

Bulstrode was apoplectic, with a thick neck and protuberant eyes and a gusty habit of breath. As Prospero, in the grip of histrionic excitement, he reddened and swelled in a way that was alarming to some members of the cast. He was winding up to it now, in his morning-gown and wizard's hat covered with yellow stars, which everyone suspected he had set some of his pupils on to making.

Caliban was still venting his mirth at the notion of breeding a race of monsters on Miranda. As usual, Prospero could hardly wait for him to draw towards the end of this – as he viewed it – unnecessarily protracted bout of chuckling. And in fact his impatience had already been a cause of altercation between the two, the curate complaining that he was not being given time to do justice to this laughter, which was, as he pointed out, a very important element of dialogue, highly significant, though not expressed in words. 'All the more so for that very reason,' he would point out to them, his fair hair standing up with electric tension all around his head.

But now Prospero swelled up and did exactly the same thing again. 'Abhorred slave!' he shouted, before Parker could get far into his ho-ho's, then went on at a spanking pace:

> Which any print of goodness wilt not take,
> Being capable of all ill! I pitied thee,
> Took pains to make thee speak, taught thee each hour
> One thing or other. When thou didst not, savage,
> Know thine own meaning, but wouldst gabble like
> A thing most brutish, I endowed thy purposes
> With words that made them known. But thy vile race –

A pause, however, was obligatory here and Parker was quick to seize on it. 'No, just a minute,' he said. 'Upon my soul, you did it again, Bulstrode. You do not seem able to forbear. I must be given time to carry out that laughter.' The curate's hair had bristled delicately up. His face was pale with vexation. 'Caliban has no words, you see. They have taught him language but he has no words. That is the paradox of it.'

'Caliban is a malignant savage,' Bulstrode said loudly. 'He is beyond all reach of good. I say it in my speech. Damn me, man, it is here in my text, before my eyes.'

'No need for oaths,' the curate said. 'My profession does not allow me to believe that there can be a soul which will take no print of goodness. Ergo –'

'No words, Mr Parker? Did you say no words?' This sharp question came from a girl called Elisabeth Jane Edwards, who was playing Ariel. She had a beautiful voice – it was her singing that Erasmus had heard the previous Sunday when he had blundered through the trees into the open and been ensnared. 'He has some of the best speeches in the whole play.'

'Ah, yes.' The curate wore an air of pale triumph. 'Quite so, but may I ask when those speeches are delivered? Allow me to answer. They are spoke when Caliban is intoxicated or in fear or pain, are they not? When he has to *argue* his case, he has no words, he is lost. He has no language for debate.'

'Caliban is no more than a buffoon,' one of the shipwrecked mariners said. People were getting rather tired of Parker.

The curate smiled with superior wisdom. 'If he were no more than that, why should Prospero rant at him so?'

'Prospero does not rant,' Bulstrode said. 'I repudiate the aspersion. I deliver that speech with –'

'As a matter of fact,' Sarah Wolpert said, 'I think I should have the speech.'

Both curate and tutor turned to regard her with expressions of surprise and displeasure almost identical.

'Which?'

'The one you have just uttered, beginning, "Abhorred slave". I think Miranda should have it, not Prospero.'

'But that is my speech.' Bulstrode had an air of swollen and furious bewilderment. 'It is set down so in the text.'

'It comes better from Prospero,' the curate said. 'A great gust of rage is needed after my laughter, otherwise the point is lost.'

'I think Miss Wolpert ought to be allowed to state her case.'

This came out more loudly and emphatically than Erasmus had really intended. He had said almost nothing so far, remaining on the edge of the group, conning his lines, looking occasionally in private anguish across the narrow expanse of the lake to the sunlit fields beyond. The moment he dreaded was approaching, when in response to Ariel's first song he would have to walk forward, round the lakeside, holding his head up, glancing to find the invisible source of the music. He found this a terribly difficult thing to get right. He rehearsed the words constantly in his mind: *Where should this music be? I' th' air or th' earth? It sounds no more . . .* He knew the speech by heart, but that made no difference to the quality of his performance, which was lamentable. He had had time in these few days to learn that he was a hopeless actor. Apart from anything else, he felt idiotic, talking to thin air. The prospect of a reprieve cheered him, however brief. 'She would hardly claim the speech for hers without good reason,' he said.

'Thank you, Erasmus.'

He glanced at her, suffered the usual blow at her beauty, the composed, fair-complexioned face delicately shaded by the brim of her hat. Her colour came and went with her feelings, he had noticed, but this porcelain composure never changed. Her lashes were pale silk and they were wide now, as she fixed on Prospero a look of serious determination.

'After all,' she said, 'it is about Miranda, is it not?'

'I cannot for the life of me see what you mean.' Bulstrode had puffed himself up in an intimidating manner. 'I cannot tell what you are talking about, Miss Wolpert. The speech is about Caliban, not Miranda.'

'Miss Wolpert is not referring to the speech,' Erasmus said with a perceptiveness sharpened by his desire to acquire merit in Sarah's eyes. 'She is talking about the laughter.'

This time he was rewarded with a smile before she transferred

47

her gaze back to confront the indignant wizard. Her next words, however, made clear how little she really needed help. 'Of course I am,' she said. 'It hasn't anything to do with Prospero, so why should he be so vexed? I mean, it isn't Prospero that . . .' Sarah paused and blushed, then went on with increased energy: 'It isn't him that Caliban tried to ravish.' She looked from face to face with a sudden, surprising openness of regard. 'He was laughing about his attempt on *me*,' she said. 'Or have I not properly understood the matter?'

There was a short silence among the rest of the company, perhaps at this notion of ravishment, perhaps at her forthrightness, though they knew by now what she was capable of: had she not marched up to Erasmus Kemp and enlisted him on the spot? And then, she had a way of holding herself, an unusual habit of emphasis: as she drew to the climax of what she was saying, her voice would quicken, she would raise her head and lower her lashes and a delicate shudder, slight but perceptible, would pass over her like a throb of delivery or release. It was this the men waited for, as Erasmus had jealously noted. They attended on it now, Caliban, Hippolito, Alonzo, the three mariners. Only Prospero, armoured in egotism, was immune. 'It is the father that should speak for the child,' he said. 'She is obedient, as befits a young girl. Besides, she is too well brought up to burst into the conversation in that manner.'

'I verily believe,' Erasmus said coldly, 'that if you could contrive it, Prospero's would be the only speaking part in the play.'

Bulstrode swelled even redder. 'That remark is totally unwarranted. Miranda can have the speech for all I care. She can have all the others too. The father can sit dumb while the child explains how she has contrived the shipwreck.' And with this he stalked some paces off and presented an offended back.

Set on her rights, however, Sarah was relentless. 'As for obedient,' she said in her high, clear voice, 'she contests with her father to prevent him ill-using Ferdinand.'

'Yes,' Erasmus said, with a sense of brilliant improvisation, 'and at the beginning of Act Four she goes against his orders when she visits Ferdinand in his confinement.' He knew the play in every detail, having sat up half his nights studying it in the hope of improving his performance.

'So she does.' On Sarah's face there was the glowing, slightly inward look of one who has just had the better of an argument. And in fact no one offered further objections; Prospero allowed himself to be cajoled; the rehearsal was resumed and not much later Erasmus found himself once again regarding Miranda's face from close range. He had heard Prospero promising Ariel his freedom and on this cue had stepped forward, altogether too briskly, like a soldier, shoulders braced for the encounter, only to find himself at once marooned in the limpid depths of her eyes.

'Fair excellence,' he said in a voice not altogether under his command, 'if as your form declares, you are divine, be pleased to instruct me how you will be worshipped . . .' He glanced beyond her for some desperate seconds. He knew the view well by now: across the lake, continuing parkland, then a low stone wall with a gate in it, beyond this the upward slopes of the pasture, dotted with yellow clumps of broom and hawthorn bushes in their first delicate suffusion of flower. All the dreams of escape he had ever had lay in the sunlit ground beyond that gate; escape for both of them – together they could go there and climb the slope and he could say his own words to her, not these stupid words he was obliged to repeat. Since agreeing to be Ferdinand he had not succeeded in having a single moment alone with her. He met her eyes again, seemed to see disquiet in them, though of a kind unlike his own. 'So bright a beauty,' he said, huskily and too quickly, 'cannot sure belong to human kind.'

This had all to be done over again more than once while Ferdinand strove to keep his temper before the comments of his colleagues, and to master his tendency to race his words together. It was late in the afternoon when he set off for home. The sun was warm still, the fields bordering the road were green with young corn and the air was full of the song of larks. He felt weary with his efforts at discipline and divided in his feelings – it was the paradox of his condition during these days that he was happy to be released yet sorry to leave. What comfort there was lay all in retrospect: he combed the scenes just past for smiles, words, glances of encouragement. These had not been lacking, but she was so confoundedly set on the play that he could not tell whether her encouragement was for Ferdinand's suit or his own.

He had entered the town and was riding at a slow pace towards the area of small market gardens and brick kilns that lay around the entrance to Sweeting Street when he found the way blocked by spectators of a fist-fight – two men stripped to the waist and both showing marks of blood were facing up to each other, though whether they fought on a quarrel or for a purse he did not pause to enquire, but turned off down an alleyway to avoid the crowd and found himself after some minutes in a maze of close and evil-smelling lanes and courts in the vicinity of the docks.

The approach of night was already to be sensed in these narrow, airless confines. There was room for not much more than the passage of his horse. A bedraggled woman called to him from a doorway and two ragged children ran alongside, whining for coppers, plucking at his boots. He knew the river was to his left and tried to keep in that direction but it was impossible in this warren to maintain any consistent course.

He was impatient rather than afraid – Erasmus did not feel fear easily and knew how to use the sword at his side; but the dark was not far off and his calfskin boots alone were prize enough for the wretches that inhabited here to risk hanging for. He was resolving to find someone and ask directions while still some light remained when he heard a harsh sound, like a painful breath, and saw as he reined in his horse a dark heap against the wall some yards down a narrow entry.

For some moments he hesitated. He had heard of this sort of trick too. But there had been too much suffering in the sound for him simply to ride away. The harsh aspiration came again as he sat there and again as he dismounted but with the first scrape of his steps it sounded no more. He saw the heap start against the wall, with a sudden movement almost violent. Then as he drew near, it was absolutely silent and still.

Matted hair obscured the face but he saw blood on it, still

glistening fresh, and as he leaned closer he made out the puncture marks of small teeth: one side of the man's face had been bitten at by rats while he lay helpless there. But it was not this that held Erasmus, rather a kind of puzzlement: why, at the first sound of steps, had he fallen so silent and still?

Erasmus leaned closer and looked into the man's eyes. They were wide open, staring up at him or at the night beyond him and the awaited end the night contained. And Erasmus knew himself in that moment for an intruder, knew this creature wanted him gone, was with the last energy of his life holding himself still against being touched, being moved. That recoil against the wall had been an attempt at concealment. He had crawled into this runnel as if dying were a sin he did not want to be caught at.

The stench of long neglect rose from his rags, a nauseous reek of old cold dirt and grease and excrement and fever. Erasmus felt his gorge rise. He turned away and went back to his horse, unaware yet, as he rode on, as he found his way eventually into wider, better-lit streets of shops and taverns and people, that he too had been violated in some narrow place where he had crawled. There are no stronger fetters than those we forge for ourselves. Because he had ridden away, because he might have been mistaken, Erasmus told no one of this encounter. It was never disinfected or treated in any way. The memory festered and in the course of time rotted its container and leaked into his father's death and into the smell of the ship's timbers.

EIGHT

Work on the ship continued; she rose on her stocks from day to day, proceeding by ordained stages from notion to form. Like any work of the imagination, she had to maintain herself against disbelief, guard her purpose through metamorphoses that made her barely recognizable at times – indeed she had looked more herself in the early stages of the building, with the timbers of the keel laid in place and scarphed together to form her backbone and the stem and sternpost jointed to it. Then she had already the perfect dynamic of her shape, the perfect declaration of her purpose. But with the attachment of the vertical frames, which conform to the design of the hull and so define the shape of it, she looked a botched, dishevelled thing for a while, with the raw planks standing up loose all round her. Then slowly she was gripped into shape again, clamped together by the transverse beams running athwart her and the massive wales that girdled her fore and aft. She was riveted and fastened with oak trenails and wrought-iron bolts driven through the timbers and clenched. And so she began to look like herself again, as is the gradual way of art.

William Kemp was present at every stage. Garrulity grew upon him. With his tricorn hat tilted back, his sober, expensive, negligently worn clothes, his short wig emphasizing the dark flush of his face, he held forth to the people of the yards, the shipwrights and their labourers, the fitters, the rope-makers – he would talk to anyone connected with the ship, down to the lad heating tar to calk her seams.

With business associates he was voluble about the op-portunities just then afforded. There was no shortage of examples among their common acquaintance. Old Jonathan Horstmann who, as everyone knew, began as a tallow chandler in a back-street shop and bought a thirtieth share in one of the first slavers to sail out of Liverpool, had just died, leaving near a quarter of a million. Less than three years previously, the Wyatt family had fitted out four ships for the transport of twelve hundred negroes to the Caribbean. They had made no less than six voyages since, on the regular circuit. 'I was talking to Ned Wyatt only last week,' Kemp said. 'It brought the family return enough on those six voyages to stock another dozen vessels in the West Indies with rum and sugar.' He raised his hands to make a quick shape of wealth. 'Now I ask you, where else can you get profits like that?'

In part it was superstition; much of that talking was like the babble of a spell to keep off demons. He was not desperate, however, during these days, merely rather feverish and talkative. Those who afterwards asserted otherwise did not know him. Poverty was distant, his success had been complete. His life was miraculous to him. He had limped into Liverpool as a boy of twelve, barefoot and penniless, and picked up a sort of living along the docks until he was big enough to get work as a labourer. He had put his pennies together. With his first five pounds he had bought a share in a consignment of hayforks and scythe-blades for the colonists in Virginia. The profits from this bought sugar in Jamaica which was then resold on the Liverpool Exchange. This trebled his capital. He repeated the venture with a larger stake and went on repeating it until he was strong enough to go into cotton. Markets for English printed cottons were opening every-where. With luck aiding energy he had grown rich beyond his dreams. Perhaps it was this, the sense of his career as miraculous, that was ultimately his undoing. Miracles are not subject to reversal. Crutches can be thrown away, the wine will not run thin again; Kemp had been raised from the pit and he could not believe he would fall back into it, any more than Lazarus into his. He could fear it but he could not believe it. And so he could not adapt to the losses he had taken, the blockades of the war years, the plunge in prices, his heavy expenditure on attempts to find a fast red dye that could compete with Indian cottons.

53

The *Liverpool Merchant* was part of the miracle. It fascinated and consoled him to watch the building of it from day to day, to see the gaunt-ribbed hulk wrought to a shape of beauty and purpose. He had other interests; his dealings were diverse, like those of most Liverpool merchants of the day. In Welsh quarries men toiled to bring out the dark slate for him; colliers under his charter shipped coal down from Carlisle for the Birmingham furnaces; settlers in remote places boiled their water in kettles he had exported. But the ship was something of his own.

For Erasmus too this was a time unlike any other. Changes he noticed in his father seemed to reflect his own state, symptoms of his own – and Ferdinand's – disorder. His life during these days was lived at quite distinct levels of intensity. There was the business, in which he had as yet a relatively small part, being mainly responsible for the transport by mule train of various manufactured goods from Warrington to the Mersey docks and for buying up small lots along the route against the day, which he felt sure could not be long delayed, when the present track would be made fit for coaches. Then there was home, his mother's complaints and his father's certainties, fencing practice at the academy, nights on the town with friends, drinking bouts which he did not enjoy greatly, disliking the sensation of being other than himself – it was this that made him such a bad actor. Nevertheless, it was the acting, the scene of his rehearsals, where his true life lay at this time – the lakeside, the pale sand of the shore, Caliban's cave, Prospero's cell: these formed a territory where Erasmus endured for love's sake what was worse than any labour, the twice-weekly parade of his ineptitude, the ache of not knowing who Miranda's smiles were for.

Once or twice at the beginning the rehearsals had to be held indoors because of rain; but then the weather settled down to a long succession of warm, clear days, identical save for the gradual advance of spring, the deepening colours of the hawthorn blossom on the slopes above the lake, the appearance of soft spikes of flower on the chestnut trees in the grounds. Amidst this slow flushing of the season experiences took on an importance for Erasmus that somehow belonged rather to their associations than to themselves and made odd fusions in his mind. Already there, the virulent speck that would curdle his memories, already working among the impressions of the time, a man sniffing at timber, another the sport of rats in an alley, a haunting song of deep seas and dead fathers that came to him while he waited for his cue.

Sometimes he went with his father to the yards to see how work was progressing on the ship. One of these visits was towards the end of May and it stayed long in his mind because of an accident that happened then.

She was framed up by this time, with all her cross-beams in place, and the oak timbers which would support the bowsprit, and the flexible ribbands of fir nailed along the outside of the ribs so as to encompass the body lengthways and hold it in frame. On this day they were putting in the first of the long single planks that ran the length of the vessel from stem to stern. Erasmus stood beside his father on the bankside, following with his eye the curve of her hull as it bellied out away from him – she would slide down into the water stern-first when ready.

The vertical timbers shoring up the scaffold at her sides rose sheer above. Erasmus looked up but his eyes pained him, he could see little beyond the gunports. The air was full of sunshine and smoke. Higher up the bank, but still quite close to the slipway where the ship rested in her cradle of scaffolding, three men had overturned a barge and they were burning the crusted filth of the river off her. There was an acrid smell and smoke hung in the air, blue from the faggots, black and oily from the melted pitch of the boat's bottom.

'They are putting in the first of the strakes,' Kemp said. 'They have marked out where the next plank is to go, you can see the line of the batten.'

Erasmus narrowed his eyes to see through the bright haze the pale line of the batten that ran a good third of the vessel's length. Nearby, running alongside the slipway, was the long kiln for steaming the planks – the oak had to be softened until it was pliable enough to be moulded to the shape of the hull. Erasmus could hear the hiss from the copper boiler housed inside; steam rose from it, adding to the sunshot haze.

'Here's Thurso now,' Kemp said. 'He mentioned that he

would come by to see how things are going forward. He has got someone with him.'

They came from beyond the ship, passing through the deep shadows under her bows and out again into sunlight, the square-built, deliberate captain whom he had met already and a lean man, rather dandified, with a sailor's walk and his hair in a short pigtail. As they came out from the shadows into the sunlit space between the ship's hull and the beam-sheds, there was a sudden ruffling breeze over the water and Erasmus saw the man with Thurso raise a sharp face and sniff like a dog.

Thurso raised his short black cane to the corner of his cocked hat. 'I thought I'd bring Mr Barton along with me,' he said. 'I have spoke of him before, I think. He is to be my first officer.'

'Humble servant, sir.' Barton gave father and son a look and a bow in turn, then took two deferential paces back and stood with his hands at his sides. He had restless black eyes and a thin mouth that smiled easily.

'Well,' Thurso said, in his hoarse, uninflected voice, 'she lies sweetly in the slip. She has been well framed, Mr Kemp.'

'I am glad to hear you say it.' The merchant's look of pleasure was testimony to this. ''Tis true she sets well, she is broad enough in the beam.'

'I don't trust a ship with a narrow bottom,' Thurso said. 'Eh, Mr Barton?'

'Right, Captain, right, hunnerd per cent.'

'Or a wench either,' Kemp said. 'All the same, between you and me, Captain Thurso, I have sometimes repented that I did not have her made bigger. There are Bristol ships that will hold you six hundred negroes, so I am told.'

'Aye, but how long must they stay on the Guinea coast before they are full-slaved? Why, sir, flux or fever will do for half of 'em before you are ready to sail. We will be home and dry while they are still rotting there. No, take my word for it, a ship the size of this one is what you need, around a hundred and twenty tons' burden. You'll get two hundred blacks between decks on the *Liverpool Merchant*, clean as a whistle, and off again in three months. You'll see that I am right, sir.'

'A man can see a deal of things by lookin',' Barton said

unexpectedly, 'pervided he knows how to use his lamps.' His voice was quick and fluent, unhesitating.

'The strakes they are putting in now will need to be laid right,' Thurso said. 'It is the planking lengthways that makes the difference to a ship.'

'Those already laid fit snug enough. Come down nearer, Thurso, and take a look. You will scarce see the joins between them.' Face glowing, Kemp drew the captain towards the ship's side, to where a ladder led up to the work platform high against the hull. A group of workmen waiting at the foot of this for the next piece from the kiln made way for them respectfully.

Erasmus did not follow immediately but turned instead to look out towards the glimmering, slightly ruffled water of the river. On the wharf before him men were hoisting down barrels into a lighter. Out in midstream a skiff with two timber-rafts in tow was making towards the Pier Head. When he turned round again he saw that Barton had remained beside him and felt constrained to speak. 'It will be a delicate business, I suppose,' he said, 'fitting those heavy planks on to a curving surface.'

He saw Barton raise his head in the same alert, dog-like way, as if sniffing for the right line to take with the owner's son. The movement raised his throat slightly clear of the red silk choker he was wearing and exposed the upper part of a pale, puckered scar, which ran for some four inches along the side of his neck, revealing with an ugly fidelity the curve of the cut that had made it. 'The hull curves two ways, sir,' he said, 'beggin' your pardon, that is what makes the job ticklish-like, as you rightly say.'

'How do you mean?'

'Well now, a ship's hull.' Barton's voice had a sudden energy of pleasure in it. He raised a brown hand, palm upwards, fingers slightly curled. 'Think of a fourth portion of a orange what you have took the peel off it all in one piece, if you think of that portion of peel, sir, the edges will curve inwards top and bottom and at the same identical time that peel will curve along its length, fore and aft. It is the same thing with a ship's hull. Every blessed one o' them planks has to fit snug against the next along its length and by its depth.'

57

It was clear that Barton had a way with words; there had been a savouring, lingering quality in this; he was smiling still with pleasure at the comparison. 'That is what makes it ticklish-like,' he said.

Kemp and Thurso had turned back towards them. Four of the men had begun to climb to the platform, a double plank in width, slung against the battens. The men by the kiln were wrapping rags round their hands.

'They are fetching the next pieces out,' Kemp said to his son. 'They have been steaming long enough – near eight hours. We shall stay and see them laid in place.'

Erasmus saw the great oak plank drawn smoking from the kiln. It must have been thirty feet long. Six men, their hands swathed in rags, went at a crouching walk with it across the dozen yards to the ship's side. Here it was roped and hoisted from above – men had been waiting on the cross-pieces of the unfinished deck, high up in the smoky brightness, difficult to see. He watched the plank hauled to the level of the platform, saw it manhandled into position against the batten markers, saw it driven into place with heavy mallets, the blows sounding in ragged unison as the men forced the heavy timber to bend in obedience to the curving shape of the hull. Once in place it was held there against the strain of its cooling fibres with thick wooden billets that fitted flush against the plank and were bolted through and locked on the inside of the vessel.

'By God, those two fellows are putting their backs into it,' Kemp said in tones of approval.

It was not quite flush, Erasmus noticed: the billets amidships, where the convex curve was greatest, did not seem long enough, and had to be lashed to the bolt-heads; the two men his father had referred to were hauling at the short ropes, leaning back on their narrow platform to get a better purchase.

Kemp took out his watch and consulted it. 'Less than fifteen minutes to get that timber in place.'

Thurso was beginning, in his laborious, impeded way, to say something in reply, when there was a wrenching sound from the ship's side, followed at once by a strangely tuneful twanging note, like a single vibrant beat of pinions. Erasmus glimpsed a flying shape of white caught in the sun like a flash of wings, saw the gap where the timber had sprung free, sweeping the two men working there off the platform, one to slide down between hull and slipway and lie groaning out of sight, the other, whose fall his eye had caught, flung clear on to the wharfside, where he lay broken and still.

The pause of shock, before the men's mates moved towards them, was of the briefest; but to Erasmus, when he thought later about it, it had no limits, extending without dimension of time into the blank afternoon, the hazy light, that twanging note of death. He was young enough still to glance at the others' faces for guidance in composing his own; and what he saw there had no end or beginning either. The only face on which he could detect any expression at all was Thurso's, whose small eyes contained a look of satisfaction, as at some promise fulfilled.

NINE

From a man maimed and a man dead and a look in another man's eyes, his memories of the ship took a sweep over a void and only found lodgement again in the week before she was launched. There were difficulties with the figurehead, which continued almost up to the last minute, due to his father's wish for changes and his consequent altercations with the carver, Samuel Oates.

Oates was a notable craftsman, famed for his execution of figureheads, quarter figures and all kinds of ornamental scroll-work for the timber heads. He had been a shipwright till a fall from scaffolding had lamed him and sent him back to his boyhood passion for carving wood. With the expansion in ship-building he had prospered greatly and now employed two journeymen and several apprentices. These days he did not take kindly to customers who pestered him over details.

Kemp, however, was adamant. He knew the importance of emblems; and he knew what he wanted. For the rudder he wanted the bust of a man in a plumed hat and full wig, to epitomize the newly formed Company of Merchants Trading to Africa, of which he had become a member. For his figurehead he wanted the Duchess of Devonshire as the Spirit of Commerce, flanked by two small lions. He had seen the duchess once and thought her splendid. It was she now who was causing the difficulty. Either Oates had misunderstood his instructions or – as Erasmus suspected – his father had changed opinion, which he more frequently did these days. In any event the carver had fashioned her bareheaded, whereas Kemp had decided that he wanted some regal adornment, something like a diadem or coronet. 'Not a crown,' he said. 'It would not be seemly for her to wear a crown. But if she is to represent the enterprise that creates the nation's wealth, she must have a coronet at the very least.'

It was here, in Oates's workshop, that Erasmus came nearest to a sense of wonder at what they were setting in motion, felt something of the spirit that emanated from his father, among these staring effigies in this long gallery of a room, amidst smells of paint and wood shavings, viscid brews of varnish and oil, resinous bubblings from the open jars where Oates distilled his turpentine. A naked, waxy nymph, her lower regions concealed in bright green foliage, a turbaned Turk, two gilt cherubs and a prancing unicorn looked down at them through the vaporous air. Oates stumped among his creatures, limping and irascible. 'You must understand, Mr Kemp,' he said, 'I have other work in hand, I cannot begin her over again and have her ready in time for you.'

The huge, brightly coloured duchess loomed above them, her blue eyes fixed in a wide stare. She was sealed and waxed and shining, ready for all weathers. Her long yellow hair flowed down her back. Her royal blue gown, voluminous at the skirts, left her white shoulders bare, and her great smooth breasts with their brilliant crimson nipples. Her arms were drawn back behind her, disappearing in the folds of her dress, and this gave her a poignant look, like a captive giant pinioned for sport or sacrifice.

Kemp turned passionate eyes on Erasmus. 'By God,' he said, 'she makes a fine figure. But I must have a coronet for her.'

'I can fashion you a gilt coronet in best elm,' Oates said, with a sort of irritable resignation, 'I can set it on her brows and fix it into quarter-inch panels round the head and glue it in place – I make a glue here that will stick you till the last trump, Mr Kemp. It will be a separate piece but there is no stress on it to speak of.'

This was the solution finally agreed on; but because of the delay the installation of the duchess had to be done almost at the last, the shipyard carpenters hoisting her into place and setting her on the prow amidst other last-minute tasks, finishing

61

the hatches, mounting the swivel guns on the bulkheads of the quarterdeck, coating the ship's bottom with the mixture against ship-worm newly recommended by John Lee, the master-caulker of the Royal Dockyard at Plymouth, composed of tar and pitch and brimstone.

The launching itself was a quiet affair. It had come to Kemp that he would be tempting fate to make a show. In the event there was just father and son and a few bystanders and the people of the shipyard to see her into the water. Kemp had champagne served at the dockside and he made a short speech, thanking the men who had worked on her. They cheered him with full throat; he had always been popular with them and it was known that he had dealt generously with the widow of the man who had been killed and the family of the disabled survivor.

There was the customary silence as the last of the scaffolding was removed, the shores knocked away and the ship eased up from her blocks. She seemed at first undecided whether to settle again, then she moved massively forward down the greased slipway, the timbers that cradled her keel moving with her. For those few moments she glided resplendent, all below the water-line new-painted white, her clean plank above shining with resin, her mainwales and the lettering of her name picked out in dapper black; but she lost this gliding grace when she touched the element she was made for, ducking her rear into the dark water, wallowing there while the timbers of her cradle, freed at last, floated up alongside.

The last Kemp saw of his ship was the duchess yearning away from him, as the *Liverpool Merchant* was towed out stern-first into midstream, where her masts would be fitted. It is true that on the eve of her sailing he would stand at the dockside, peer across the misty water, see, or have the illusion of seeing, the masts and spars of his ship where she lay anchored out in the Pool; but this was any ship now, a shape become generic, universal. His last real sight of her had been that swanning glide, that brief, ungainly wallowing, that yearning retreat of the figurehead. It was the last of her he would ever see.

PART TWO

TEN

Matthew Paris's last night on shore was spent at an inn in Water Street, not far from the docks. He had called earlier at Red Cross Street to make his farewells, declining all hospitable urgings, deeming it easier for himself as for his patron if he did not impose himself for such a short stay. His wish was for solitude; more of his uncle's ardent prophesying he did not feel able to endure and he might have been constrained to show it.

He was ready for the voyage, as far as concerned physical readiness; he had the bare wardrobe he thought would suffice, together with his medicine chest, instruments, bandages and dressings and a large store of medicaments and drugs: not knowing what to expect, he had brought everything he could think of, from mustard to eucalyptus oil. In the lacquered box his aunt had given him he had his writing materials and in a larger one of tin plate lined with wood his books, which for reasons of space were few and carefully chosen: Pope, Maupertuis, Hume, Voltaire. These four he had rescued from the bailiffs, who had taken almost everything else. On the fifth, Astley's *New Collection of Voyages & Travels*, he had spent some of his uncle's money, having been assured that it was a mine of information for anyone wishing to learn about Africa. Alongside these, in that same stout box, was the unfinished translation of Harvey's *Treatise on the Movement of the Heart & Blood*, which he had begun in prison, when with his uncle's help he had been able to afford a private room.

Books were a habit and so a need. But whether or not to include Harvey was something he had hesitated long over, caught in a contradiction he could not resolve. Stepping on to a slaveship, sailing with her, was as near to cancelling his former life as he felt he could come. And that was what, when he interrogated himself, he believed he most wanted – he wanted to cauterize the nerves that held him to the past. And yet he had not felt able to leave Harvey behind. Ambition, the wish for some lustre to fall on him from this great and revolutionary work? But how could that live in one breast with a desire to kill the self, to smother it in darkness, a desire so urgent at times that it came to him like an impulse of violence? And why, in spite of this, did the past lie in ambush for him at every un-guarded turning of his thought? His desolation bristled with such questions, like blades.

There were reasons more immediate, and these also he gave weight to. The voyage was likely to take eight months at least and he did not expect to be occupied with medical duties for the whole of the time; there would be vacant hours to contend with. Eight months, he thought, sitting at the window of his upstairs room, looking out at the light rain which had just begun to dampen the cobbles. Perhaps longer, perhaps a year – all accord-ing, as Thurso no doubt would say. Perhaps in that time, among those new scenes, he would become somehow different. But it did not seem likely. He felt fixed for ever in his shape, impervious to change, whatever lay before him. It seemed to him that he had reached this final shape quite quickly: a few random blows had been enough. All the years before, his studies, his practice, the happy years of his marriage, he had remained unformed, impressionable, he had thought of himself as flowing towards something in a kind of pursuit. Quite suddenly this had been reversed, he had become an object of persecution. Was this the rescue, this shape of stone he was now? Those in pursuit did not turn to stone, only the pursued were wrought into shapes beyond change . . .

In the late afternoon he had writing materials brought up to him and sat down to write a letter to a friend and colleague in Norwich, to whom he had entrusted his collection of fossils, all he had, really, to leave or care about. He hesitated for a little while, looking from his blank page to the thin slant of rain outside. He had said goodbye before he left – this was a mere

66

indulgence of his solitude. Almost he decided not to write at all. Then, with an impulse of impatience, he dipped pen in ink and began:

My Dear Friend,

I write on the eve of departure, to say my farewells over again and to thank you once more for all your acts of kindness towards my Ruth and myself.

A blurring of his page obliged Paris to pause here, though having only just begun; gratitude to his friend released tears in a way that thoughts of his wife could not – her name in his mind was all desolation. Clear-eyed again now but with throat painfully tightened, he resumed:

I do not in the least know what awaits me on this voyage and – though this need not at all distress you, my dear friend, and I am not seeking to make a parade of it – I am quite indifferent to what becomes of me, at least so I think at present, though if it came to a danger to my person, I dare say I should scramble with the rest, that being our nature.

If I should not return, please keep for your own use the collections you have been kind enough to house for me all this while. They are all I possess of any value. I mean to say by this that you should keep them whatever happens and regard them as yours; since even in the unlikely event of my ever returning to Norwich, I shall not want to set eyes on them again – they would recall the past too painfully. I hope the specimens will be of use in your own investigations, and in particular those preserved parts of sea animals, by which we learn of the changes of place in the waters which otherwise could not have been supposed.

I am giving up the work, because it belongs to a part of my life that is over now for ever, but I have not changed in my convictions. I can only recognize one vital principle throughout animate nature: by natural gradation of species we must always be led to an original species, and this must be the same for man. Though life may appear very compounded in its effects in a complicated animal like man, in my view it is as simple in him as in the most simple animal. I think we have reason to suppose that there was a period in time in which every species of natural production was the same, and this could square with the account of creation given to us in the Old Testament. But over great spans of time and with the earth and water changing situations, there have been many sorts of transmutation. It is not true, as they said, that I denied God's creation and promulgated atheistical notions. But I cannot agree, my reason will not allow me, with those who would have us believe in a fixed immutable species or in successive acts of creation and extinction . . .

Self-contempt had been growing steadily in him and he ended abruptly, with good wishes and renewed thanks. As he chalked the page dry he was swept by a despairing sense of his incorrigible vanity and folly. Even now he could boast of his constancy, could stand up on the ruins of his life and crow with his doctrines like some vainglorious cockerel on a dung heap. He had maintained an abstract truth and published it abroad at the expense of all that was dear to him – and he sought still to make it a cause of pride. It was appropriate that dry bones and dead beetles should be his only legacy. The rabble set on by the Church Party had smashed his press and thrown his furniture out into the street; but by an unerring instinct of contempt they had ignored the cases of fossils in his study . . .

If I could have the choice again, he thought, if I could keep my Ruth and the child inside her, I would make any grovelling recantation, on my knees I would confess to all error since time began . . . But this was another proclamation from the dung heap. If he could not claim all truth, he would embrace all error. Never the common mixture of mortality . . .

In shame he would have torn the letter across but checked himself; it was well that Charles should know the specimens were for his unrestricted use. He would be more cautious in that use since such was his nature; he would continue to collect evidence, make his observations, write notes; but nothing would be published until he was safely dead. Some day these obscure researches that men all over Europe were making would find a synthesis in one brain and then the age of the earth would be stated boldly and it would be shown how the creatures had changed . . .

A little later, when it was getting dark, he went out and walked towards the Pier Head. The rain was still falling. He saw a woman lying sodden against a wall in a fume of gin. One or two taphouses showed gleams of light and he saw a farrier

68

hunched at work still inside his shop. But the streets near the waterfront were for the most part deserted.

Paris stood in the rain looking towards the open sea. Lanterns of ships out in the road winked through the moist air. The *Liverpool Merchant* was there with the others, riding on the dark water. For some moments, as he stood there, the night was hushed around him, there were only the winking lights across the water and the silent rain. Then he heard the running of the tide, the scream of a late sea-bird, voices raised and lowered again from a tavern further along the quay.

He tried to think of Africa, tried to imagine the lives of Africans, lives that would be changed, more even than his own, by the ship. But it was too far away. There was only the rain on his face, the sense of solitude. The door of the tavern opened, two men came out and stood talking there. In the yellow light from the open door the rain had become suddenly visible. Paris saw the glint and swarm of it and without warning was transported to summers of his childhood, insects round lamps at night in the garden or over river water in dying sunlight, rising and falling as regular as breathing in the last warmth of the day.

The door closed, the bright swarm was extinguished. But the vision of those lost summers remained with him, like the sum of all loss. Standing there, looking across to the lights of the ships, one of which was to take him to a future of sorts, Paris could think only of the past.

ELEVEN

Seated in his cabin, Thurso listened with satisfaction to the sighing and creaking of his ship as she felt the movement of the tide beneath her. She was a good one, he knew it. The sign had been given, the seal of blood was on her. He looked for some moments without speaking at the faces of the three men he had asked to step up here. Barton he knew of old. His second mate, Simmonds, sat opposite, directly under the lamp. He was younger, with fair hair and calm blue eyes and a nose that had been broken once and mended badly. Haines, the bosun, was brawny and dark-complexioned, with a mass of oiled curls and glittering, close-set eyes.

'Now listen well,' Thurso said at last. 'It is but a few words I have to say but I want them remembered. As you know, we are all but ready for sailing. We are light of some of our salt beef still and all the fetters have not been taken aboard, but that will be seen to shortly and then we need wait only on the wind. I don't want any of the crew mistreated in the meanwhile. They cannot be allowed off the ship but they can eat their fill and while we are in harbour they can be served a half pint of grog per day for each man – no more, or they will fall to fighting. Keep 'em busy as far as possible, but there is to be no use of the rope's end till we are under way and out past the Black Rock.'

The harsh whisper of the voice ceased for a little while and Thurso seemed to consider. When he resumed, it was on a note that seemed intended to be more jovial. 'I don't want any of the beggars jumping overboard and swimming for it, as I have known happen on other ships. Whether they sink or swim, it is the same loss to us.' He paused again, looking closely at each face in turn – an old, disconcerting habit. Raising a thick fore-finger, he said, 'Anything untoward and you will answer for it. That is all I have to say, gentlemen. Mr Barton, you will stay behind, if you please.'

When the others had gone both men relaxed in their different ways, one moving less, the other more. Barton shifted in his seat and raised a narrow, watchful face. 'They have done you proud for a cabin, Captain Thurso,' he said. 'Hoak panels, mahigonny table.'

'Don't you concern yourself with my cabin, Mr Barton. I can see for myself how my cabin is appointed. My cabin is not in your province.'

'No, sir, a' course not, only remarkin'.' Barton risked a note of humorous alacrity only possible when he judged his captain to be in the best of moods. But his eyes had narrowed at the rebuke and there was nothing humorous in their expression.

'You keep to your side of things and I will see you all right,' Thurso said. 'You can leave the sea for good. You know what that side is, don't you? You will do my shouting for me when we are at sea. When we get to the Slave Coast you will go upriver with me and you will deal together with me for the gold dust on the proportions we have agreed, and you will say nothing about this private dealing to any man either aboard ship or on land. You keep to this and I will see you all right.'

'You know me, you know Barton. We have dealt this way before.'

'Aye,' Thurso said grimly, 'I know you well. Take some brandy. You know me too, don't you? You know the Guinea Coast too, don't you? If you don't keep faith you will not see Pool Lane again, nor the ladies of Castle Street. You will not dip your wick there again, I tell you.'

Barton made no reply to this, merely swallowed some of the contents of his glass, then worked his lean jaws appreciatively. 'This is a excellent brandy,' he said. 'First class.'

'Never mind the brandy, damn you. You are getting too familiar. This is my last voyage, as you know. I intend to run a tight ship, same as always. Better than ever, for the last. Try to abuse your position and you will soon discover that Thurso has no favourites at sea.'

'Aye, sir.'

Thurso raised his head. 'I feel her straining,' he said. 'She is pulling at her moorings. I am going to take care of my owner's profits too, same as always. I will trade on the best terms I can get.' He kept his head raised, as though listening for something from the night outside. Light from the lamp lit his heavy brows but his eyes were shadowed. 'He sets me on again,' he said. 'I will do my best for him, same as always. It is in my compact.'

Barton, who had been regarding the abstracted captain with a look of stealthy dislike, said, 'What compact is that, Cap'n Thurso?'

'Never mind, never mind. I have kept my square, I am still here.'

'Some owner, he is,' Barton said after a moment. 'He is all over the place. Still, we have taken on a fair mix of cargo, I will say that for him. He has ordered everything just right for the trade.'

Kemp had been diligent in this as in all else, and he had taken counsel. In these last few days, in addition to victuals, they had stowed away muskets, flints, gunpowder, glass beads, iron bars, bolts of brightly coloured cottons, bales of taffeta and silk, gold-braided cocked hats, knives of various sorts, copper kettles and basins, casks of brandy and rum, five hundred looking-glasses. Together with this were articles not intended for sale: whips, thumbscrews, branding irons and a quantity of manacles, fetters, chains and padlocks, all of good substance and well wrought.

'All the same,' Barton said, 'three negroes privilege for a second mate, that is unheard of, that is carryin' phalinthroppy beyond what is warranted.'

Thurso drank and mused, head lowered now. He had a way of removing his attention, as if others were no longer in the room with him. The tide was on the ebb, he had felt the change in the way the ship rode at her anchor. The lamp was turning through a slight arc and light from it moved over the oak panelling, which still smelled of varnish, and over Thurso's lowered head and the suddenly indignant face of his first officer.

'No, it ain't right,' Barton said. 'He could give somethin' to

72

the carpenter or the gunner, they are vallible people aboard. We know what a second mate is, on the Guinea run.'

Thurso raised his head and fixed the other with a sombre stare. 'Don't you concern yourself with that,' he said. 'Who knows where the second mate will be, or the gunner or the carpenter, by the time we reach Jamaica? When were you last on a ship that brought all her crew back from Africa?'

'Then there is the doctor,' Barton said in the same tone of indignation. 'Relative of the owner, never been to sea before, what the jig is he doin' aboard of us?'

'Aye, there is something there,' Thurso said. 'There is something pressing on him that he might be ready to talk of to the right man. Try to smoke him out, Barton. Do it friendly like, you will know how.'

'I will do my best.' Barton looked earnestly at the bottle. 'My level best, Cap'n Thurso.'

'Have some more brandy. After that I will require you to go ashore.'

'Tonight?'

'Aye, tonight,' Thurso said irritably. 'Are you afraid you will melt in the rain? The sailing has been posted for three weeks now but we still have only twenty-two men signed. Homeward bound, with the blacks discharged, it will not matter if we are light. But we cannot set out with less than twenty-five. Take Haines along with you, he looks a handy fellow. See what you can find along the waterfront.'

'Can I take a third man, in case of things turnin' out unreasonable? Libby, say, him with the eye-patch? He is friendly with Haines, I see them talkin' together.'

'Mr Barton, I am surprised at you. Set an ordinary seaman on a slaveship to press men on to the same ship? There would be blood all over the deck before we were out of the Formby Channel. From the officers they will take it, not from one of themselves. No, if you and Haines need help you will have to pay some scum there to help you. You can split up if you like, when you get ashore. Get back here about nine. I will leave Simmonds in charge and we will go over together to see what the posters have done for us. You had better stir yourself. You and Haines stay sober, or it is on your head, you being the senior. We need more crew, Mr Barton, and it is a matter of indifference to me how we come by them.'

TWELVE

Half a mile away and half an hour later a seaman in a medium state of drunkenness named William Blair was entering an obscure ale-house in a narrow lane close to the docks. He had been paid off two hours previously after eight months at sea. In those two hours he had travelled some three hundred yards from the edge of the water. He was in his best shore clothes, still had most of his money and was poised precariously between jollity and truculence.

As he swaggered up between the tables he tripped over feet that hadn't been there before and stumbled slightly. 'Stow them trotters, bonny lad,' he said, more for the sake of dignity than anything else. Blair was always careful of his dignity, which led him sometimes into quarrels. He was short of stature but very quick. And he was fearless.

The man thus addressed made no answer but he kept his feet where they were. Looking down, Blair saw bright dark eyes set close together and a bitter mouth. Most of the man's face was shadowed by his hat, which was high in the crown, varnished and polished in sailor's fashion.

'Well,' Blair said, coming up to the counter, brushing the rain from the front of his buff nankeen jacket, 'still gans on spittin', I wish to God it would rain and be done.'

The landlord was bald and corpulent, with a greasy apron and an impassive face and dull brown eyes. 'Yes,' he said, 'that is looking at it one way, but a drizzle is good for trade, brings 'em in.'

'Anythin' is good for this trade. All weathers. You canna gan wrong, man. Gie us a gill o' best Jamaican, an' let us see you fill it up.'

'Hey, Scotch!'

The voice, rudely peremptory, came from behind him as he was taking out his purse to pay. He knew without needing to look that it was the man whose feet he had tripped over. He noticed another man, in a long, ragged cloak, go out through a door behind the counter, but thought nothing of it, being again concerned with dignity, which did not allow him to glance round. It did not permit him, either, to put away his purse other than very slowly. 'Iggerant,' he said regretfully to the landlord, loud enough for the other man to hear. 'The majority o' persons learn to tell the difference between their arse an' their elber, but there will allus be them as cannot. There is a class o' lad that will still gan on tryin' to shit through his elber joints.'

He listened for the scrape of a chair, some sound of movement behind him, but heard nothing. He drank deeply, felt the heat of the rum in his throat and chest, knew he was on the way to getting good and drunk. 'I'm fra Sunderland,' he said loudly. 'Gie us another, if you please, landlord. A exact copy.'

The landlord nodded. His eyes had been on the purse and its contents and on the pocket to which it had been returned. 'Just off a ship, are you?'

'Docked this afternoon. Seventy-five days from Caracas. The Brig *Albion*, Captain Josiah Rigby. I am bleddy glad to be off her, the first mate was a cannibal in human form.' Blair fixed the landlord with a belligerent stare. 'If we meet ashore I will spill him out,' he said.

The ragged man reappeared and a few moments later two young women came in laughing together, hair wet from the rain. They came directly up to the counter.

'Goin' to buy us a drink, my chuck?'

'I will buy you a drink,' Blair said handsomely. 'Billy Blair is not a man to say no to the ladies. But don't get up yor hopes, as he is not purposin' to gan on wi' it all bleddy night long.'

'Speaks pleasant, don't he?' the same woman said. She had an Irish accent, hair the colour of pale carrot and a pretty, anaemic face, darkly bruised on the right side, over the cheekbone. 'I like a good-spoken man,' she said. 'Yer can keep these foul-mouth gits. Gin please, Captain. How about you, Bessie? This here is Bessie. I'm Eve.'

'Gin,' Bessie said.

'Gin for the ladies, rum for me,' Blair said. 'By God,' he added to no one in particular and passed a hand over his face.

'It goes down on the slate,' the landlord said. 'No need to pay every time round. In this type of occupation you gets to be a judge of human nature, you gets to know who you can trust.'

'Sure, it is not often you find a open-handed feller in these parts,' Eve said.

'What about these parts?' Blair leered and pointed down at himself.

Eve uttered some high mirthless laughter. 'Well, I don't know, do I?' she said. 'What parts you hail from, Billy boy?'

'He's a wee cockalorum from Scotland.'

Blair turned to meet the dark, close-set eyes and thin smile. The man was still sitting sprawled there. He had taken off his hat, revealing a mop of black ringlets glistening with oil. He was strong-looking, with broad shoulders and thick legs. 'You again,' Blair said. His hand strayed a little towards his right hip. 'Been curlin' yor hair, haven't you?' he said. 'Bleddy scut-head.'

'Take no notice, darlin' Billy,' Eve said, pressing close against him.

'I will mince him up,' Blair said with extreme ferocity. 'I told him once I an't a Scotchman.'

'Have another drink,' the landlord said. 'I will stand it. It is not often I take to a man. We got meat pies in the kitchen. Prime beef. You,' he said to the seated man, 'you hold your gab or you will go out on your arse.'

The place was more crowded now. The woman called Bessie had gone off to join some others round the table. Billy allowed himself to be pacified. He had more rum and a plateful of pies. He was having some difficulty now in seeing clear across the room and was tending increasingly to reduce the range of his focus. Standing up close against him, Eve gave him a gentle squeeze of his balls.

'Full o' grape-shot, them,' Billy said boastfully, through a mouthful of meat pie. 'England's finest.' He had taken a definite

77

fancy to Eve, with her blue eyes and delicate pallor of under-feeding. 'Some bastid been cloutin' you?' he said, looking at the disfiguring bruise on her cheek.

She laughed on the same high, careless note. 'I was runnin' round in circles an' I bumped into meself.'

'Have you somewhere we can gan together, just the two of us?'

'I have got a love-nest all me own, darlin' Billy. But let's have a dance first, let's have a bit of fun for God's sake, we might all be dead tomorrer, Jemmy, mightn't we?'

This had been addressed to the landlord who agreed with every appearance of fervour. 'Where the devil is the fiddler?' he said. 'Where is Sullivan?'

The cry was taken up by others – several people wanted to dance, it seemed. The fiddler was found in a dark corner, sleeping with his head on the table. Roused, he came shambling out into the centre of the room, clutching fiddle and bow, a tall, ragged figure with glinting stubble on his cheeks, a dark shock of hair and dazed green eyes that seemed lately to have looked on wonders and to be glancing after them still.

'Give us a reel!' somebody shouted.

'I'll not play without a drink,' Sullivan said. 'Niver a note.'

'Give him a drink.'

'I seen you before,' Billy said. He steadied himself against the counter, took a careful pace forward and looked closely at the long face and beautiful, bemused eyes of the fiddler. 'We was on shipboard together somewhere,' he said. 'Michael Sullivan. Always arguin'.' He paused for a moment, swaying slightly. Then he had it: 'The *Sarah*, Captain McTavish, 'bout five, six years ago, cargo of hides fra Montevideo. Am I right or am I wrong?'

Sullivan paused a long moment as though gathering his wits. 'I was on that ship,' he said at last. 'I will not say that I wasn't. It was you done all the arguin', not me. McTavish was for iver blasphemin'.'

'Dead now. He overdone it on the bottle.' Feet planted for balance, Billy looked proudly about him. 'By God,' he said, 'there canna be many that has a memory like Billy Blair. Drunk

78

or sober, Blair is razor sharp. You remember me? Come now, you canna have forgot Billy Blair?'

'I do an' I don't,' the fiddler said. Some change had come over his face. 'Listen, Billy,' he said, 'you don't want to be dancin', 'tis a idle pursuit an' the Pope has frequently spoke out agin it as leadin' to all manner of sins.'

'What's wrong wi' you?' Billy screwed up his eyes in order to see the fiddler's face better. 'Why you switchin' yor lamps about?'

'Stir yourself, Sullivan, give us a reel,' the landlord said. 'What do you mean by talking?'

'He needs another drink,' Billy said. 'Once a shipmate always a shipmate, wi' Billy Blair. Gie us yor hand, man. Have you follered the sea since?'

'I follered the divil. Listen –'

But then Eve was standing close again and there were two men between Billy and Sullivan, one of them he of the ragged cloak. 'Stow your gab,' this man said roughly to the fiddler.

'Come on, Sullivan darlin', give us a reel,' Eve said.

After that events became confused in Billy's mind. Sullivan made no further attempt at conversation. He played 'I'll Away No More' at a brisk pace and followed it with 'Sweet William'. There was dancing; the small space was crowded with people jostling together. Eve laughed a lot and touched him intimately. The drink and the dancing had brought colour to her face. After a while she excused herself with a tender smile. 'I'll just be away for a piss, darlin',' she said. 'I'll be with you again before you can shake yer peg.'

But she did not come back; and this defection changed the quality of everything in a strange and sudden way. The fiddle fell silent. There were fewer people in the room and these only men. The landlord's looks grew sullen and disdainful. Billy was sweating and asked for ale but this came slowly and when it came was sour and thin.

These various factors combined to turn his mood ugly. Such sudden lowerings are difficult to take with equanimity, even for milder temperaments than Billy's. It is one thing to know that pleasure is fleeting, youth ephemeral and the grave just round the corner; it is quite another to have it brought home to you all in the space of five minutes. 'What taplash piss is this?' he said. 'You have served me wi' the washings o' the casks.' And he splashed the rest of his beer down on to the stone floor.

'Now that was the act of a out-and-out swine,' the landlord said. 'I see I was mistaken in you. You can pay up your score and get out. There is three shillings and four pence on the slate.'

'That is robbery, you fat bouger,' Billy said. 'If I come round that bleddy counter you'll be right sorry. Where is Sullivan? Shipmate, let's you an' me cast off from here. I have got money, I will stand treat.'

But it was precisely at this lordly moment that Billy found he had no money, none at all: the purse was gone from his pocket. And when in the shock of this discovery he looked at the landlord's face and saw the ugly complacency on it, he knew with that power of divination that descends on the cheated, instant and terrible, like a dark afflatus, that from the moment of walking into this ale-house he had been among actors. 'My purse,' he said. 'That Irish crack has stole my purse. We could catch her yet, before she gets it to her scully.' He made a movement away from the counter.

'No you don't,' the landlord said. 'Cover the door. What purse? I never saw no purse. Anyone here see a purse? Catch a hold of him, lads.'

He had started round the counter. Two men moved on Billy, one from either side. He put a hand to his hip pocket but the knife was gone too. Drink and shock had slowed him but he had time to throw his tankard into the first man's face and hear it strike against the teeth, time to take two steps and land a hard kick on the landlord's kneecap. He was staggered by a wide-angled blow to the side of the head, evaded another by some instinctive cunning of the body, struck back and missed, slipped on the wet flags, recovered. A body fell against him and he struck at it, only to realize it was on its way floorwards anyway, and not by his doing. He took another jolting blow to the face. Someone caught at his arms from behind.

'Well, my mannikin, how goes it now?'

Billy could feel blood running into his mouth. Someone was

groaning behind him. There was a man lying on the floor. Through a bitter film of moisture he saw the smiling face of the man who had baited him. He had a gold band in one ear and smelled of coconut oil. 'Scut-head,' Billy said. He made a violent effort to free his right arm so as to strike at the face before him. Without ceasing to smile the man gave him a blow in the stomach which cut off his wind completely.

'All right,' he said, when he could speak. 'I'm done. Let me sit down.'

'Scut-head, is it?' the other said softly. His eyes were shining. With the outer edge of his hand he gave Billy a light, almost casual blow across the bridge of the nose, blinding him with tears. When these cleared he saw that the man on the floor was Sullivan; there was blood in his hair. 'Give the fiddler a sousing,' someone said.

Billy did not see this done as he was hauled off now into a smaller room and seated on a stool. The same two men stood beside him. One of them had a badly split lip, he noted with satisfaction. 'There's yen blaggard earned his shillin',' he said. His right eye was half closed up.

'Now then, Billy boy,' the dark-complexioned man said. 'We have had our little difference. It is a simple enough matter I have to put to you. My name is Haines, you will get to know me well. I am bosun on a fine, new-built ship an' we finds ourselves needing one or two likely lads. Now you are a likely lad an' no mistake, a fine little strutter, you are. You owe money here that you cannot pay by any manner of means. Where are you going to get three shillings an' four pence, darlin' Billy? You signs for the voyage all fair and square, or the landlord calls the officers an' lays charges agin you. There is plenty of people to swear you never had no purse when you come in. He will swear debt an' assault agin you, an' he will put his heart into it – you have near crippled him.'

Billy spat some blood on to the floor. 'I'm right sorry to hear that,' he said. He was caught and he knew it. What Haines was telling him was an old story. 'I walked in the wrong door, didn't I?' he said. 'That gang o' thieves shares out my purse, you pays the score here an' docks it out my wages. What manner o' ship is she? Where is she bound? You are never a bosun of a navy ship.'

'What difference does that make?'

'If she is not a navy ship,' Billy said slowly, 'she must be a Guineaman – you wouldn't get up to this for a ordinary merchant vessel.'

'Well, my game cock, which is it to be? It will be proved agin you, never doubt it, you will go to prison till it is paid. An' how long will that take, my bantam? Men have died in prison for the sake of a shillin'. You been in prison before, Billy?'

Billy looked at the bosun's face. The narrow-set eyes were observing him with close interest. There was not much cruelty in Billy's nature and it came to him now, with naïve surprise, that Haines was getting pleasure from this. Spattered with blood as he was and still half dazed, he had his dignity to think of. He sat up straight on his stool, gripping the sides for balance. 'Blair is the name,' he said. 'It is only my mates call me Billy.'

Not very far away, in Mount Street, Daniel Calley came in from the rain. He had been working since first light, carrying sheep carcasses and crates of fish up from the quayside to the top of the market in Stone Street. He had ninepence in his pocket and he was wet through and hungry. Also, in an obscure way, he was distressed. As usual the bargeman and stallkeepers between them had cheated him and as usual he had not been able to understand how. The shift to symbolic modes of reasoning, the essential transfer from concrete to abstract normally occurring in the course of childhood, had never occurred at all in Calley's case. He could not work out what was due to him. He puzzled at it as he toiled back and forth but the figures would not lodge in his head. Sometimes he was driven to ask, but he could not understand the glib explanations. He would clench his big fists in misery – not so much at thoughts of the money but at being derided and treated unkindly. A simple sort of joking was the best way with him then; the men who cheated him knew that. Like a child he could be confused and softened by jokes; but a wrong word to Calley when he was excited or disturbed could have dangerous consequences.

82

He entered the pothouse where he usually ate when he had money and often slept – they let him sleep in the yard in a little covered space behind the chicken coop. He took off leather harness and back-pads and fish-slimed apron and shook the rain out of his hair. He was squat and very muscular, broader in the nape than the skull, so that his head was tapering and blunt like a seal's – a resemblance that the rain, by sleeking down his brown silky hair, had made more obvious. In the close, low-raftered room he gave off a steam of wet clothing and sheep's blood and fish oil, enriching the effluvia of boiled mutton and stale beer already resident there.

He asked the serving girl, whose name was Kate and who was fourteen and had one leg shorter than the other, to bring him mutton broth – all the place offered. While it was coming he thought about his entertainment for the rest of the evening. He knew the cost of certain basic things and on his fingers he could balance accounts. He knew he could have his mutton broth and then some treacle tart from the pastry-cook's on the corner – he was fond of sweet things – and that Kate would come out into the yard with him for two of his pennies and that he would still have enough for a pancake next morning . . .

These thoughts were producing a simultaneous salivation and erection, when a man came and sat at his table, a tallish, wiry, sharp-featured man in a blue pea-jacket and wide-bottomed trousers and with his hair in a pigtail.

'Clammy night,' this newcomer said. 'Keeps on rainin', don't it?'

Calley smiled but said nothing – he was always shy with strangers. The saliva of his anticipations made little, stretching webs at the corners of his mouth. His eyes held an unchanging radiance, as at some remote delight whose source was long forgotten. He had a complexion a woman might have envied, clear and pale, without the smallest blemish. 'I got wet,' he said.

'Aye, did you so?' The stranger cast a brisk eye over the harness and the thick leather pads against the wall. 'Been porterin'?'

The broth arrived and Calley launched a noisy assault on it. 'I been workin' in the market,' he said between mouthfuls.

83

'I see it has give you a happytite. You must of got two shillin'
at least for a heavy day like that.'

Calley looked up defensively. Some of his earlier feelings of
frustration and distress had returned, but it did not occur to
him to lie. 'I got ninepence,' he said.

'What? You have been labourin' all the livelong day with a
saddle on you like a horse an' you gets ninepence for it? I can
scarce believe my ears.'

'I ain't a horse,' Calley said.

'That is a utterly pernacious state of affairs, it is scandalous.'
The stranger was looking round the room and shaking his head
in amazement. He had a peering, sniffing way of seeming to
interrogate his surroundings. 'It is enough to freeze the marrer
in a man's bones,' he said.

Calley rested his spoon in his broth. 'You sayin' I am a
horse?'

'You're a man an' a fine strong one an' good-lookin' – I'll
wager the ladies is after you, ain't they? Linin' up for it, ain't
they?'

'Kate likes me.'

'I dare say she does, an' who would not? I have took to you
myself. Here, try this.' The stranger drew a bottle from the
capacious side-pocket of his jacket. 'Take a swig of this, then tell
me if you have tasted a better brandy.'

Calley drank and the liquor coursed through him, bringing
with it the knowledge that this man wished him well. 'Good
brandy,' he said.

The stranger drank and smacked his lips. 'Nectar of the gods,'
he said. 'Here, have some more, that's right. What's your
name?'

'Dan'l,' Calley said shyly.

'Tell me, Dan'l, what is a man like you doin', slavin' up hill
an' down dale, for a few pennies? You are not a horse, but they
are saddlin' you up like a horse, they are workin' you like a
horse, see what I mean?'

'Kate comes out in the yard with me,' Calley said. He did not
want this new friend to think that his portering was the only
thing about him.

'An' well she might. I expect you show her a good length, don't you?'

A moment of inspiration came to Calley. 'Like a horse,' he said. He saw with delight that the other was laughing at this and he began laughing too.

'That's a good 'un. Listen, I have took to you, an' I want to do you a favour. I am mate on a fine new ship that is bound for Africa an' I have got the idea that I can obtain you a berth on her by exertin' my influence with the captain. I wouldn't do it for everyone, but we are mates, ain't we?'

Calley smiled. His mouth shone innocently with mutton fat. 'That's right,' he said.

The mate pushed the bottle over. 'Have another swaller,' he said. 'Africa, there's a place for you. Sunshine, golden beaches, as much palm wine as you can drink, trees loaded with fruit, thick with it; all you have to do is reach up an' take it. I tell you, it is a earthly paradise. An' the wimmen! Bigob, they are hot.' He kissed his fingers with an extravagant gesture and a smacking sound very fascinating to Calley. 'Sable Venus,' the mate said. 'They will do anythin' you want. Hot – they are always on fire. It is the diet, all them peppers, it is the climate, it is their nature.'

'Sable Venus,' Calley repeated softly. Neither of these words meant anything to him, but pronounced together they had a deeply suggestive sibilance that fell on his ear like music. He drank some more from the bottle. 'What will they do?' he said.

'I am goin' to tell you somethin' now that I have varrified from personal experience. They have got these highly developed muscles in their cunnies, they can fuck you just by squeezin'. They are trained up to it from earliest infancy.' He paused for a moment, observing the effects of the brandy. Then he said, 'You can try them wimmen if you want, Dan'l. Why don't you come along with me? You gets twenty-five shillin' a month an' your vittles. You can leave that harness standin' there agin the wall an' come along with me. You will stand up like a man, you will not go creepin' about with a saddle on your back.'

'Not like a horse.' Eagerly Calley waited for his friend to laugh again at the joke. 'I got two legs, not four,' he said.

85

The mate got to his feet. 'Let's be goin' then,' he said. 'You needn't fetch an' carry for them bastids any more.'

Calley got up too, caught in a wave of enthusiasm. 'Them bastids,' he said. 'They can carry their own sacks o' turnips.'

'No more sheep guts for you,' the mate said. 'They can get someone else to do it.'

'Someone else can do it,' Calley said. He was still laughing but rather uncertainly now.

'You come along with me, I will see you all right.'

But the mirth had left Calley's face, to be replaced by a look of anxiety. 'No,' he said, 'I can't come now.' He felt unhappy to be disappointing his friend but he had thought suddenly of Kate and the treacle tart.

Barton was a sensitive man in his way and he had noted the change of expression. He put an arm round Calley's shoulders. 'I'll tell you what,' he said. 'We are only out in the stream. You come along with me now an' look the ship over. If you don't like what you see, you can be back again within the hour.'

The knowledge that Deakin was worth money had been in Jane Britto's mind for some time, but she did not know that she intended to sell him until he spoke of leaving.

She had been waiting in the cellar where they lived for her husband and Deakin to get back, standing half stupefied in the steam of washing, with the gasping cries of the baby in her ears and no drink and no money to send out for any. But it was only when she heard them that she felt the clutch of rage at her throat.

First came the scrape of their boots in the alley above, then the clatter down the cellar steps. The two of them came through the door, filling the low room with their voices and bodies. Perhaps the rage sprang from this, the intrusion, though there was little here she could have wanted to defend, in this dank place with the mangle and tub against the wall, smells of rank bacon and tallow fat, the sick baby, the two children squabbling together on a mattress in the corner. But there is no world so wretched that it cannot be violated and Jane felt her body stiffen as she looked at the two men. They were wet and smelled

86

of drink and Britto was jovial and Deakin, as usual, serious –
this much she took in.

'What have you got for us to eat?' Britto said, almost as soon
as he was inside the door. 'Me and Jim in famishin', ain't we,
mate?' He was a stocky, dogged man with bad teeth and steady
eyes and too much suffusion of blood in his face. The abruptness
of his speech she knew for a sign of failure – they had been
looking for casual work on the docks.

'Me and Jim is famishin',' she repeated, with a sudden strident
mimicry that astonished them. 'Me and Jim is a pair o' pisspots.'
She would have liked to go on longer in this oblique, ironical
vein, but rage got the better of her. Her voice rose and shrilled.
'Proud on yerselves, are you? Think you are men? Where is the
rest of it?'

The smile left Britto's face. He looked uncertain for a moment,
then angry. 'Where is what?' he said. 'What are you talking
about?'

'The money what you have kept back for yer fambly. The
penny-worth o' juniper-juice what you have brought home for
yer wife.'

'We didn't find nothin',' Britto said sullenly. He glanced at
the silent man beside him but found no support there, in the
tanned face, the serious, reckless eyes.

'No good looking at him. You'd do better to look at them.' She
motioned violently towards the mattress in the corner, and at
once, frightened by the gesture or by the prospect of blows to
follow, the white-faced little boy and girl began gasping and
crying.

'You trollop, stow your noise. I ain't got nothin' to give
you.' Anger at being obliged to state the fact thickened his
voice. He took two steps towards her. 'You loud bitch,' he said.
'You better mum your dubber.'

'My arse.' She felt rage and fear together. He was not less
likely to strike her with the other man there. 'Where'd you get
the drink then? Think I can't smell it on you?'

'We went up town,' Deakin said, in his light, dispassionate
voice. 'We were holding horses' heads for some gentry. They
gave us threepence between us an' we drank it.' He paused

87

briefly, then in the same tone said, 'I'll be leaving tomorrow – early morning.'

He was taken by surprise himself at the announcement – he had intervened only to avert a row. But the main decisions of his life had been like this, recognitions of some truth, something self-evident, that had to be acted on. 'Devon,' he said. 'That's where I am going.'

'Well, there's a piece o' news,' Jane said. 'More'n two weeks you been here, takin' up space.' Once in that time, when she had been drinking alone, Deakin had come back in the afternoon and they had lain together on Deakin's pallet and coupled without tenderness and she had clutched at his hard body and felt the welts of old floggings on his narrow back. 'Then you go waltzing off,' she said, 'without so much as a kiss my bum.' Her rage was rising again, directed now at Deakin's uncluttered life. Casually, just like that, he could walk away, disappear – and the money with him, she thought suddenly: within half a minute of his leaving the price on him would be lost to them for ever . . .

'You leave him alone,' Britto said. 'He has got the right to go when he likes.'

But she could tell that Britto hadn't known either. 'Don't you talk about rights,' she said. 'What is it to me that you was shipmates? Very fine, ain't it? He's run from a navy ship, you tell him he can stay here. You does the favour, I gets the extra work.' The idea expanded steadily in her mind while she was talking. It might be as much as three pounds that Deakin was worth. For twopence a day and keep she could get a girl to mind the little ones. She could buy a grinder, get scraps from the butcher, make sausages and sell them in the street. There was profit in sausages. Perhaps they could save the baby . . .

'Little place called Sheepwash,' Deakin said. 'That's where I am going.'

'No one is askin' where yer goin'.'

'You aren't asking but I am telling you,' he said mildly. 'I was born there, see, an' I've not been back since I ran away when I was twelve.'

'You done some runnin' in yer time,' she said bitterly. She

paused, looking at Deakin's composed, fair-browed face, the remote blue eyes that always seemed to look beyond people. The intention to sell him had come to her like sudden hope and blossomed with her rage. Without rage to keep it fresh she was afraid it would wither. 'Never bring a penny in!' she shouted. 'Catch a few bloody fish in the river. I'm killin' myself at this mangle. They are callin' me a whore in the court because I have got two men in here. An' you spent it all, didn't you? Call yerselves men?'

Britto moved towards her. The voice of the little girl on the bed rose in remonstrance or fear. The woman moved back sharply, felt round behind her for the long-handled pan on the stove. 'Keep off,' she said.

'The bebby's sick,' she said. 'It can't hardly cry any more.' A storm of weeping shook her suddenly, even while she felt for a weapon. 'I dunno,' she said. 'I dunno. You could of brought a drop o' gin back.'

Britto went to the crib in the corner, looked down at the bloodless, crumpled face, with its inflamed lids, the glaze of vomit on its chin. The baby looked up at him with an impersonal solemnity, its hands curled against its breast like tiny, shell-less crabs. After a moment Britto turned away, raising his own hands in a clumsy gesture of helplessness, and he was again the man she knew, dogged and ashamed.

She felt something like pity for him then: he had tried for work all day and come back to this. 'It has got somethin' wrong with its stomick,' she said. 'It can't keep anythin' down.' She could not tell him what she was going to do. Not then, because she knew he would prevent her; and perhaps never – not only because of the thrashing, but because such a hurt to his pride would make him unpredictable and she was afraid he might leave her. She could conceal the money, she could say it came from somewhere else, she would think of something. 'You goin' out again?' she said, looking at both men.

'Not me,' Deakin said. 'I'll get my gear together. I want to get an early start. Not that I have got much,' he added with a faint smile.

'There is cockfightin' over behind the Pickerel,' Britto said. 'I had a hand in trainin' two of them. The owner might put somethin' on for me.'

She knew this indirectness meant he wanted to go but would stay if she liked – the look of the baby had softened him. 'When's that then?'

'Ten o'clock. They're fightin' our birds first.'

'You go,' she said. 'You might win somethin'.'

Britto grinned, relieved at her change of tone. 'That would make a change.'

'I'm goin' out to see about some washin'. There is a bit of bacon an' some 'taters in the stove. You could hot 'em up.'

She put on bonnet and shawl and went out quickly without looking any more at Deakin. The Bell was the inn named on the poster. It was a mile off but the rain had stopped now and the moon rose clear in the sky. At the inn she was directed upstairs, where she found two men at a table.

'You the ones takin' on crew for a slaver?'

'That's right, my pretty. Hunnerd per cent.' The man who answered her was sharp-faced and smiling and had an alert, peering sort of way with his eyes. '*Liverpool Merchant*,' he said, 'a spanking new ship that anyone would be proud to sail with, only we ain't takin' any ladies on, not this partikkler voyage.'

'Mr Barton, you go too fast,' the other said in a hoarse monotone. He was in a grey wig and a stiff blue coat with brass buttons and his cocked hat lay on the table before him.

'You the skipper?' she said. 'I know where there is a man for you. I can tell you where you can find him. Once you get a hold of him, he can't choose but go. He's run from the navy.'

'Has he so? Been treating you badly, has he? You tell us where he has put into, my dear, we will take him off your hands.'

'I can take you,' she said. 'I can show you the place. If we was to go now we would find him on his own. How much will you give me for him?'

'Able seaman, is he? Fore the mast? Sound in wind and limb, is he? How old is he?'

This hoarse questioning caught her unprepared. She met the gaze of raw-looking blue eyes. They were small in the dark red square of the face and they held no kindness for her. ''Bout twenty-five,' she said. 'I dunno. He's been on an' off ships most of his life. I want three pound.'

'If we can secure him, and if he has got all his arms and legs attached to him, I will give you two pounds. That is the going rate and that is what we are paying.'

'Haw, that's a good 'un, arms an' legs,' the other man said.

'I want three pound.'

The man in the wig sighed harshly. 'Explain to the woman, Mr Barton,' he said.

'My pretty, I am afraid you do not unnerstand the finances of it. To take in hand a able-bodied man what has his full copplement of arms and legs and what doesn't see eye to eye with you as to the tack he should foller and is inclined to be disputacious, that needs three stout men. Them men has to be found and them men has to be paid and that pay has to come out of the price. That leaves two pound for you, or there's the door.'

She had not wanted to think about Deakin, but now something resigned about his face came into her mind and she remembered the scars she had felt upon his back. Her resolve did not change but the composure that had sustained her so far began to break at last. She felt tears gathering. She wanted gin so badly now that she could hardly keep her limbs still. 'Blast yer livers an' yer eyes,' she said with a sob. 'You neither of you worth him pissin' on. Make it guineas, for God's sake, give me two guineas for him.'

Having assembled his few possessions and made a bundle of them, Deakin lay down on the pallet in the narrow space against the wall at the far end of the cellar. The damp from the wall came against his face. He heard a catch of breath from the exhausted baby. The children on the bed were silent, perhaps sleeping. He began to think about the next day. He had no money and no plans, no sense even of a likely sequence of events. All his programme was imagined sensation, the silent street he would step out into, dawn coming slowly over the tips and brick kilns and dirty pools on the outskirts, then the open fields, and himself moving through luminous spaces, with the sun rising and the fields filling with light and himself always moving, unimpeded, totally free and yet awaited – he knew the impossible ambition of the escaper to find welcome horizons.

He had not been back for fourteen years. He did not know if his mother was still alive. He wanted now to know – she had pleaded for him as far as her fear allowed. Whether his father was alive or dead he did not care. He had a memory of the place he had started from, as simple and brightly coloured as a child's picture book, soft green folds of hills, lush grass, red earth, brindled cows grazing knee-deep in buttercups. Embedded in this like a splinter was the stone farmhouse on the coomb-side, the dark little shed where his father locked him up after beatings for tasks neglected or badly performed, though this was a dark mystery as the beatings came regularly in spite of all effort, and pardon did not depend on anything he could do or say but had to be wrought by the darkness of the shed – sometimes an hour or two, sometimes whole nights he had spent in the dark, the pain of his stripes receding to make way for fear.

The shed itself had no place in the picture, no shape or form, only the darkness within it and the plenitude of light he had stepped out into the morning of his escape, that dawn he had found a short bar inside and used it to wrench the door off its hinges. He had never forgotten this violent conquest of the dark, the feel of the metal, the joy and fear of the splintering wood, the revelation of light that cold morning with sheep coughing in the field above and the distant sound of a dog barking. Within half an hour he had been on the upland road and begging lifts to Bristol.

He had run away often since then, but all flight had been attended by the radiance of that dawn. He was thinking of it now, when he heard steps on the stairs coming down.

THIRTEEN

Billy Blair woke from stupor to find himself lying in fetid darkness in the hold of some old flat-bottomed hulk like a barge. She was moored in deep water – he could feel how she moved in her chains. His face was stiff with dried blood and his right eye gave him pain. Someone not far away was whimpering tearfully. 'Wha's that snufflin'?' he said. Faint light came through the ill-fitting planks of the deck above and he heard sounds of movement there. 'Got any grog up there, shipmate?' he called up. 'I am parched.'

Someone brought a face down close to the deckboards and spoke through: 'You can have water.'

'Water's no bleddy use, man. My throat is on fire.' He paused, casting round for further arguments. 'The bastids have cooped us up down here,' he said, with pathos.

After a moment or two longer the hatch was raised and he saw the tousled head of a man looking down at him. 'You keep yer napper stowed below there and don't try no tricks. I have been set over you till we gets aboard an' I will do it. I ain't riskin' the bilboes for you, so you better not think of tryin' to cut loose.'

'Now there's a friendly soul,' Billy said. 'All I am askin', from yen Christian to another, is have you got any grog?'

There was a short silence and then to his delight Billy saw a bottle swinging down to him, tied with a cord round the neck. 'God bless you,' he said, grasping at it. 'I will overlook them former threats. What's yor name?'

'Cavana,' the man said. 'The other one here with me is Hughes.'

93

'I am Billy Blair.' He took a drink from the bottle, felt the spirit take its fiery course down his throat. 'Ah, by God,' he sighed, 'that's better.'

The hatch was lowered, leaving him once again in darkness. A melancholy voice spoke from somewhere near him. 'Give us a drop, Billy, for the love of God.'

'Wha's that?'

'It's me. Michael Sullivan.'

'Sullivan! How the pox did you get here?'

'Same way as you. They knocked me senses out of me an' brung me over an' threw me down in this floatin' stink-hole.' The voice paused a moment, then said with deepened sadness, 'An' me givin' them no cause for offence at all.'

'Were you whimperin' an' crying just now?'

'No, I was not. I was lyin' quiet here, thinkin' of me troubles.'

'Well,' Billy said, 'it serves you right. I am passin' the bottle to you, because it is a charity, but I don't know that I would choose to drink wi' you in other circumstances, now that I see what you have come down to, playin' the fiddle in a whorehouse an' helpin' to sell poor sailor lads.' He saw a dark form raise itself in the dimness of the hold, made out the pallor of the face. He extended the bottle, felt it taken from him, heard Sullivan take a long swallow. 'That is not work to be proud of, Michael,' he said. 'An' just gan easy wi' that bottle, will you? Here, let's have it back.'

'I was doin' fine till you come on the scene,' Sullivan said, in a stronger voice.

'Now it's my bleddy fault, is it?'

'You had to come into that place, didn't you? An' just the time when I was in it. Sure, the divil directed your steps. That wasn't the only place I played in an' they wasn't all whorehouses an' snuffle-dens. If a man finds himself in bad company he keeps mum. That is a first rule an' I broke it like a idjit. I could get a bite to eat an' a dram an' a place to lay me head an I could play me fiddle. Then you come in, full of piss an' wind, an' I remember you straight off because you always was full of piss an' wind, you haven't changed one iota, an' I does my best

94

to warn you but you are too drunk to understand anythin' at all. Like a idjit I get in the way of the fightin' and get knocked off me feet an' end up here.'

'Well,' Billy said, after a pause for reflection, 'I see how it was. You played the part of a friend to me an' Billy Blair does not forget his friends. Here, I forgive you, have another pull at the bottle.'

'You forgive me? Holy Mary, that's rich.'

'There is someone else here has a thirst,' a quiet voice said from the darkness forward of them.

Raising himself on one elbow, Billy peered through the dark, made out a man sitting upright where the boat narrowed at the bows.

'Wha's that?'

'The name is Deakin. I been pressed here, same as you.'

'Pass him the bottle,' Billy said, in a tone of resignation. 'Was that you snufflin' just now?'

'No, there's another feller here alongside of me.'

As if this were a signal, the whimpering began again. Deakin hesitated a moment, then reached out and touched the shoulder of the man lying near him pressed against the boat's side. 'Hold your noise,' he said. 'What's your name?'

'Dan'l Calley.' The voice came choked with mucus and tears. 'I don't want to stay here.'

'Be jabers,' Sullivan said in a tone of affected surprise. 'You up there!' he called out. 'There's a man here says he doesn't want to stay. I think he should see the capting.'

A different voice answered this time, harsher, more violent than the first. 'Damn you, stow your gab. There's no more rum. You get a bucket of bilge-water if you don't keep quiet.'

Deakin kept his hand on the man's shoulder a few moments longer. The choked voice had touched something in him. He had heard men cry for pain before; and he had stood at the guns, on decks strewn with bodies and running with blood, and wept with exhaustion; but he had never heard a grown man whimper with misery like this. Now, in his despair, it was as if he heard his own tears of the past, heard his own voice in the dark nights of long ago and found a comforter. 'Keep your

95

spirits up, Dan'l,' he said. 'Be a man. There's nothing to do but wait for the morning.'

'Aye,' Billy said, 'a man has to look on the bright side. I got a few drams an' a plate o' meat pies before that screw took off wi' my purse. I wish I could of fucked her an' all,' he added wistfully.

'You will lose more than that again,' Sullivan said. 'Whativer they have give the landlord for us comes out of our wages, mebbe two guineas apiece.'

'God will find out that fat buggeranto of a landlord. An' in case not I will find him out when I get back an' I will slit him up the nose. Here, lads, let's have the bottle back this end.'

'Don't you be mentioning God to me. I stopped believin' in him years ago, but now I am goin' to give him up for good. He has shipped me on a slaver only for tryin' to stand up for a shipmate.'

'Aye, that's right.' Gloom descended on Billy. 'Took for the Africa trade,' he said bitterly. 'An' looka that, there's nowt left in the bottle. Them fellers down there have supped it all up.'

After a long silence, during which Billy thought Sullivan had fallen asleep, the mournful voice came out of the darkness. 'I hope me fiddle is all right. If they have broke it, I will have the law of them, sure as me name's Michael Sullivan.'

'Law of them, you daft bumbo? They have threw you down here, they are goin' to send you chasin' quashees up an' down all the pox-ridden rivers on the Guinea Coast, an' you talk about gettin' the law of them for the sake of your bleddy fiddle.'

'I see well that you know nothin' at all about the law,' Sullivan said. 'Me fiddle is property. It comes under a different headin'.'

Sitting above in the ramshackle shelter they had built aft of the hatchway, with Cavana asleep beside him, Hughes heard the voices below and the silence that surrounded the voices and both sound and silence were of the same quality to him and had the same degree of meaning. The sky was clearing now, after the rain, and the wind was veering south-west and freshening – he could hear the strengthening slap of the wash against the buoy to which the hulk was moored. While the wind stayed in that quarter they would not clear the river.

He sat hunched against the chill, his cloak over his shoulders. He did not like the proximity of Cavana, breathing heavily beside him. But there was no other shelter on the hulk. Human beings too close constricted him to the point of violence sometimes – on board ship he never slept below except in the worst of weathers. Neither did he like the job of guarding pressed men, it made for bad blood at sea, but he had been detailed for it and had no intention of getting a flogging for their sake, so he kept awake; men determined enough might start the hatch or the rotten planking of her sides, and try to swim for it.

He was impatient for the sea again. At forty-three, Hughes was a stranger on land. Brief, violent debauches at her dirty edges was all in twenty-five years he had known of her. When there was nothing left to spend there was no reason for being ashore. Penniless, light-headed with drink and venery, Hughes signed for the first ship he could get, so long as she was an ocean-going vessel. That this one was a slaveship made little difference – he had been on slaveships before.

He looked towards her now, where she lay out in the road. He could make out her deck lamps, their lights softened and diffused by the vaporous air surrounding her; she was enveloped in the mist of her own breath. She was a new-built ship and her timbers were breathing – Hughes knew this well enough. New timber would always steam on a cool night. But there are different sorts of knowledge and he had no doubt either that the *Liverpool Merchant* was panting for the open sea.

FOURTEEN

Late on the following day the wind changed direction slightly, veering between west and south. Thurso, checking stores with his gunner, a lanky man named Johnson, between decks in the after part of the ship, felt the change at once, in the way she settled between wind and tide. He felt it in the balance of his body, as one might feel a change in the rhythm of music, though nothing showed in his face or changed in his voice.

'Wind coming round ahead of us, Capting,' the gunner ventured, and received the full glare of the small eyes.

'When I want your opinion of the weather, or anything else, I'll ask for it.'

'Aye-aye, sir.'

Later, in the forecastle, Johnson was to relate, with suitable embellishments, this brief exchange, laying the first strand in the tissue of gossip, bravado, calumny and indirect abuse which is spun hour by hour and breath by breath among the crew of a ship and is that ship's unwritten journal, voluminous, untrustworthy, dissolving like a dream when the ship reaches port and the crew is disbanded. 'Turned on me like a tiger, he did, only because I spoke first. I tell you, he is goin' to be a tartar, this one. It wasn't just lettin' me know who is skipper. He was savage like, as if he would have had me seized up straight away for a good dozen.'

Shortly after midnight they cast off from the Pier Head. Running under her topsails against the flood, obedient to the cables that towed her, the *Liverpool Merchant* headed slowly towards the estuary. On the ebb she moored at Black Rock and waited for a change in the wind in company with two small brigs and a Danish schooner bound for Dublin.

They were obliged to stay here for the two days following. The pilot-boat came in from Liverpool with supplies of powder and bread and two sides of beef. Simmonds saw to the hoisting in of these, with Thurso's eye upon him; the ship was fully loaded now and there was need for care in the stowage if she was to handle properly in the seas she would meet.

There was work enough apart from this to keep the crew busy. Barton, his ear always alert for the hoarse voice from the quarterdeck, saw to the rigging of the jib boom and had the sails fixed on the longboat. Men were set plaiting rope yarns for cordage and making deck swabs out of old rope. Calley could not master this so soon and had to begin with something simpler; as a first step towards the delights he had been promised he found himself, in company with a ragged, shivering runaway of fourteen named Charlie, untwisting old ropes to make oakum for caulking seams and stopping leaks. Libby, the big, one-eyed Londoner, veteran of several slaving trips, was given a special task – one which he was well qualified for, having once been bosun's mate on a seventy-four-gun frigate. He was set down on the main deck, in full view of all, to fashion a cat o' nine tails. This was a longstanding practice of Thurso's, it being the captain's fixed belief that it did the men good to see, as they went about their tasks, the plaiting of the stem, the drawing-out one by one of the nine logline branches of the whip, the ritual tying of the four knots in each. It convinced them from the start of the seriousness of his intentions.

Paris, pleased to find himself so far clear in mind and untroubled in stomach, passed the time in reading, writing the first pages of the journal he had resolved to keep and walking about on deck, where he was able to follow Libby's progress with the fearsome whip more closely than he liked. He had discovered that the small, malodorous room below the water-line which had been allotted as sick bay was taken up with rope and tackle and spare sail-cloth. Twice he had attempted to speak to Thurso about this but the captain had bitten him off short. Nonetheless, he was determined to take the matter up again at the first favourable opportunity.

On the third day, at a few minutes after four o'clock in the morning, Simmonds, whose watch it was, felt the wind turn fair against his face. As instructed, he roused Thurso immediately. The captain waited for the top of the high water then gave orders to weigh anchor.

Paris woke to the wailing cries of Haines, the bosun. He dressed quickly and came up in the first light to a scene of uproar and apparent confusion, shouted orders he could not make out, bewildering movements about the deck. Thurso stood above, on the quarterdeck, the only motionless element in this violent pandemonium. Then Paris began to see the division of tasks among the crew as they worked to spread and loose the great square mainsails. He heard the strange, drawn-out lamentation of men heaving at the windlass and in a few minutes knew that the ship was under way, knew it from the noise of the water thrown from her bows, from the way she leaned over in the damp dawn breeze and rolled with the heavy ground swell.

And so, in the course of that morning, the *Liverpool Merchant* was turned loose into the Irish Sea. With her mainsails set and a fair wind from the south-east, released from tethering rope and umbilical cable, she was for the first time in her life unfettered, free – save for her own groaning tensions – between wind and current.

PART THREE

FIFTEEN

Erasmus Kemp stood by the lakeside. The scene he looked forward to and dreaded was almost upon him. Recently, between his public and private performances as Ferdinand, a yawning gap had developed. He had his lines by heart and could recite them perfectly when alone; but once in her presence his tongue stumbled, his throat dried. It was not timidity; he was not by nature timid and would have welcomed the opportunity to speak his love in his own voice. What disconcerted him so terribly was having to pretend, as the price of being with her, that both of them were other people.

Nevertheless, he went on trying. Practising before the mirror in his bedroom he had achieved fluid and graceful motions of the hands and body and even dazzled smiles as at blinding beauty; but when it came to the rehearsals he moved like an automaton about the shores of the lake. He nursed the hope – and into it went all the passionate tenacity of his nature – that by endurance the gap would be closed and the accomplishments of his solitude win the day.

Of this there was small sign as yet. Meanwhile, though he was too locked in his travail fully to notice it, he was having a subtly demoralizing effect on the others. Miranda's performance had lost sparkle, partly through the infection of his awkwardness, partly out of awe at the intensity of his regard, and this central uneasiness between the lovers was exacerbating the strains and divisions already existing among the cast. Prospero's headlong, domineering style was continuing to cause resentment; Miss Edwards sang beautifully but was felt to be too sardonic for Ariel, especially when addressing Prospero, whom she disliked;

and doubts concerning the curate's interpretation of Caliban were felt by just about everyone.

Now they were nearing the end of Act Three. Hippolito, who was played by a friend of Charles, had reached the final lines of the soliloquy in which he declares his intention of having as many women as he can, now that he has discovered that the creatures exist. He was doing rather well in the part, combining a certain foppishness of style with the erotic innocence of one who, kept in solitary confinement by Prospero on the Enchanted Isle, had never till now seen a specimen of womankind. Erasmus, who could not remember envying anyone anything before, found himself envying Hippolito's assurance as he moved across to exit with the final words of the soliloquy:

> I now perceive that Prospero was cunning;
> For when he frighted me from woman-kind
> Those precious beings he for himself designed . . .

Erasmus knew that he must go directly, before the entry of Prospero and Miranda, and conceal himself in his cell. But he hesitated some moments longer, looking towards the parkland on the other side the lake, at the yellow of the new oak leaves, the stiff white cones of flower on the chestnuts, more vivid still for the lustreless surface of the leaves. Beyond was the gate in the wall, the ground sloping upward, a hawk wheeling high above . . .

'Time you were creeping, Kemp.' One of the several things about Bulstrode that others found irksome was his habit of trying to direct the play and the way he sought to disguise this under a cloak of facetiousness. 'Into your *den*,' he added now with a false smile.

Erasmus gave him a glance of disdainful surprise before moving forward and ducking into the low structure of canvas and lath they had put up some yards back from the water. Sitting a little way inside it, he was invisible to Prospero and Miranda, who had now appeared by the lakeside. He heard Prospero utter the opening words of his speech with the gusty grandiloquence the tutor brought to the role:

Your suit has pity in't, and has prevailed.
Within this cave he lies, and you may see him . . .

Erasmus waited for this to come to an end, then counted to
twelve, took a breath and began: 'To be a prisoner where I
dearly love is but a double-tie . . .'

The first lines did not tax him much, as they were addressed
to himself and uttered within the solitude of his cave; he even
achieved a certain declamatory force in their delivery. They
were the truest of all his lines, the most truly expressive of his
condition: Ferdinand's captivity exactly coincided at this point
with his own. He was a prisoner of the play itself; these rehearsals, so chafing to the natural haughtiness of his spirit, his
subjection to the condescension of Parker and Bulstrode, these
were labours he suffered for his jealous love. No one must replace
him, no one else get a chance to play Miranda's lover.

Now her voice came, asking his whereabouts. From within
the crumbling security of his cave he called to her: 'Is it your
voice, my love, or do I dream?'

On learning that it was indeed her voice he was obliged to
come scrambling out. She was wearing a peach-coloured camlet
gown this afternoon, opening over a stiffened petticoat of the
same colour. A lace fichu covered her shoulders but allowed the
skin to glow through. Her hair was drawn back softly over her
ears and tied in a knot behind. 'O Heavenly creature! Ten times
more gentle than your father's cruel . . .' He had now somehow
to cover the space between them, take her hand and gaze into
her eyes: 'While I stand gazing thus, and thus have leave to
touch your hand, I do not envy freedom . . .'

It was a scene that left him feeling strangely weak. Of its
effect on her he was not sure, but these days he read an expression of trouble in her eyes. There was a momentousness in
these exchanges, conducted always before spectators, that was
beyond anything in his experience, a curious tension between
avowing and dissembling, in which real feelings chased pretended ones and the studied movements about the stage cast all
in doubt until the naked exchange of looks brought a kind of
certainty back. Eyes locked together, hands clasped and breaths

intermingling, Ferdinand and Miranda played their allotted roles while Erasmus Kemp and Sarah Wolpert had thoughts for which they had as yet developed no dialogue.

It was a lack that came mainly from want of occasion. So far he had not succeeded in being completely alone with her for more than a few minutes at a time. By contrast, he had seen more of Charles Wolpert in these few weeks than during the previous ten years. He was not particularly drawn to Charles, but he was her brother after all, the same parents had engendered them both, the same blood ran in their veins – something of her might be shed on him, though it seemed unlikely, Charles taking after his father, with the same dark eyes and prominent nose. However, it was the nearest he could get. So he went riding with Charles, accepted a spaniel bitch that he didn't really want from Charles, dined out with Charles and other young men of Charles's acquaintance.

On the few occasions when by accident or contrivance he had found himself alone with Sarah, he had floundered rather, the time had been too short, he had failed to find words that without startling her would do justice to his feelings.

In this she had not given him a great deal of help. That she knew what his feelings were he had no doubt whatever; it was the nature of hers he was not sure of: off-stage, in her real person, she was considerably less frank about them than Miranda. He garnered what crumbs he could get, smiles or words that were for him alone, glances they had exchanged one evening when he had dined there and she had played on the clavichord and sung for them, while old Wolpert sat heavy-lidded and the mother stitched at some eternal embroidery. So far, this had been all.

Today, midway through the rehearsal, refreshments were brought down from the house in an operation that involved the ancient footman, Andrew, two kitchen maids with trays and the stable-boy with a card-table. Tea and wine and sweet cakes were laid out on this. Erasmus was making towards Sarah, who was for the moment alone, when he found Parker in his way. The curate's face had the pale, ardent look it always wore when he was about to offer advice. He was dressed in his best clerical garb today, black silk stockings, a suit of black broadcloth and an immaculate white neckband. He had come from a baptism – the vicar had been away from the parish for some weeks now and Parker had much to do.

'I hope you won't be put out by this, Kemp,' he said, 'but I think – and I am not alone in this, in fact I have been delegated to speak to you – that you emerge from your cave in too soldierly a style, almost as if you were answering the call of the bugle rather than the voice of one whom, er, your soul cherishes. Try relaxing the shoulders.' Here, as if in illustration, Parker moved his own narrow shoulders up and down in a series of shrugs. 'I know you will take this in good part,' he said. 'To assist me with Caliban I am constantly practising the sinuous movements of the savage.'

Erasmus hated advice of any kind as an unwarranted and impertinent comment on his activities. It was particularly displeasing just at present, as it had cost him his chance of a few moments alone with Sarah, who he saw had now seated herself on a bench and had Trinculo on one side of her and Hippolito on the other. 'You may be right,' he said coldly. 'Can I by the same token bring to your attention what is generally considered an imperfection in your portrayal of Caliban? I am referring to that part in the second Act when Trinculo plies you with wine and you take him for a god. It is not felt that you are totally convincing as a drunken monster. You do it more as if you were taking the Sacrament, if I may say so.'

A flush had risen to Parker's face. His excitable hair was glinting round his head like an aureole. 'But you have totally failed to understand that scene,' he said. 'Caliban is not drunk, he is exalted. He says it himself, it is celestial liquor that he is given to drink. It brings out all the poetry of his nature. His new master offers him freedom and enlargement, a new world is opened up before his eyes, all he has to do is lay down his burden and –'

He was interrupted here by the tutor, Bulstrode, who always assumed he would receive immediate attention. 'What do you think, Parker?' he said, advancing on them, glass of wine in hand, some remnants of cake in his mouth still not fully masticated. 'As the speech stands it is quite out of character for Prospero, at least as I conceive him. As I conceive him, he cannot err, he is infallible. I am talking about the scene we have just done, where he sends Miranda to talk to Ferdinand. It is a most egregious blunder for Prospero to tell her to speak for Hippolito, as this only arouses Ferdinand's jealousy and brings about the duel, the very thing that Prospero –'

Erasmus saw Sarah get up from the bench and settle her skirts in a way that suggested she was not going to sit down again. Perhaps he could intercept her somehow, contrive a tête-à-tête, however brief. 'I think we have difficulties enough, without starting to rewrite the play,' he said to Bulstrode. She was coming towards them with the apparent intention of joining her brother and Miss Edwards, who were standing together further along the lakeside. He excused himself and moved away, timing the manoeuvre so that he and Sarah came face to face as she was passing between the water and the edge of the trees.

Both stopped. There was no one else within the space of several yards. Erasmus was awkwardly silent for some moments – he had not thought of what he would say. Absurdly, he found himself tempted to echo Ferdinand. 'While I stand gazing thus . . .' But she did not, as Miranda did, sustain his gaze for long. 'How did our scene go, do you think?' he said. 'Any better?'

'Yes. I think it was better this time.'

Erasmus hesitated. She was looking away from him still. Some grace bade him tell the truth. 'It was no better,' he said. 'And it is all my fault. I cannot act – I cannot stop thinking of Erasmus Kemp for long enough.'

She had smiled at this. 'And Mr Bulstrode, for example, does he not think about himself?'

'Aye, but he thinks of himself and his part together. I cannot think I could have the luck to be Ferdinand.'

'Luck?'

'Yes. His Miranda loves him . . . She returns his love. He can speak to her when there is no one else nearby.' He paused again, confused by the rush of feeling his own words had brought. He said precipitately and almost violently. 'That would be a welcome prison to me too, in the like case.' He saw her bring a pale hand up to her neck to touch the small locket there, in a gesture that seemed like one of self-protection or alarm. But her eyes rested on him steadily. 'May I come to visit, to the house?' he said, and felt the blood leave his face with the question.

As he whitened she had blushed. 'My brothers,' she said, 'will always –'

'No, it is to see you.'

She surprised him now with a smile in which there seemed genuine amusement. 'To practise our scenes?'

'If you like.' He had little humour and certainly saw nothing at all humorous in the present situation. That she could do so, that she could have this difference of sensibility, came as a shadow on his sense of her perfection. Other girls he had known took their tone from the man. And he was to remember later how, even at such a moment, the play was uppermost in her mind. There was a firmness of self-possession about her which he felt fully now for the first time. She was fair-skinned and the motions of her blood betrayed her, but whatever agitation she felt was mastered quickly. Her face as she regarded him now had returned to its flawless and delicate composure, her blue eyes were fixed on him with a candidness he found difficult to match. She was *seeing* him, he felt suddenly; and something within him quivered at being seen. 'Will you allow me?' he said.

'I shall have to speak to my parents.' There was a quality in this almost childish, as if it concerned permission for some treat.

'Yes,' he said, 'of course, speak to them.' He found he had some trouble in controlling his breathing. He did not know what her sentiments were, his own agitation obscured what indications she had given him. 'But *you*?' he said, and hesitated, and everything waited with him, the sky, the pale gleam of the lake, all the marks of the season around them, the candled domes of the chestnut trees, the meadowsweet along the edges of the wood, half choked in the long, flowering grass, all the musky secretions of May enfolded his question, endorsed with the promise of summer her continuing silence, which he read now as consent, or complaisance at least. He might have demanded more from her, but at this moment Charles Wolpert, who without his noticing had moved to a central position among them, began to make a speech.

It was some time before Erasmus could collect himself sufficiently to take in the words, though he understood the matter was grave, as all matters touched on by Charles seemed to be. At twenty-one he had acquired already his father's habit of weighty pauses. This natural solemnity made him effective in the role of Stephano, endowing the drunken mariner with a comic sort of ducal dignity.

There was general dissatisfaction, he was saying now, at the way these rehearsals were progressing. It was felt – he had felt it himself – that there had been a loss of direction. Apart from anything else, there were too many conflicting opinions, he would not say squabbles, about the way things should be done. He had began to fear – and he was not alone in this – that at this rate they would never arrive at the point of an actual performance. He felt responsible for the business because it had been his and Sarah's idea in the first place as an entertainment for their father on his sixtieth birthday, and they were acting as hosts to the rest. In view of all this he had taken it upon himself to invite an acquaintance of one of his London cousins to come up and spend a few days as his guest and give the company the benefit of his advice. He trusted this would meet with general assent. It was a bid to save the enterprise, which otherwise was in danger either of breaking down in disorder or petering out altogether.

'He is a London man,' Charles said with utmost gravity. 'He comes highly recommended. I understand from my cousin that he is a man of the theatre to his fingertips, a playwright and critic. He is a man fully qualified to oversee our efforts and give us the benefit of his counsel. Naturally a man of that calibre has demands upon him, but he has made the time for us. He has said that he can come; I expect him within the week.'

In short, they were to have a director.

SIXTEEN

When the *Liverpool Merchant* was three days out and rounding to clear the island of Anglesey, the weather thickened and squalls began to build up from the south-east. Through the night they grew in strength and by mid-morning of the next day it was blowing so hard that the trysail and topsails and later the foresail had to be handled and the boats lashed to the scuppers. The ship plunged under mainsail alone in a high, irregular sea.

These were dark hours for Paris. Feeling the disquiet of approaching seasickness, he took some powdered ginger-root as a preventive and afterwards went up for air. But the shriek of the wind in the rigging, the tilting deck, the unaccustomed difficulty of the footing and the rapid movements of the men as they worked to take in the topsails bewildered him. Despite the ginger, his anguish grew on him with dire speed. Clutching at the gunwale he vomited wildly to leeward in the dark and when the spasm was over went below. Here, on his narrow bunk, in the close confines of his cabin, he rolled and groaned with the shrieking ship, prey in the darkness to shuddering waves of nausea the like of which he had never known and which excluded all other sensations save a sort of feeble astonishment at his capacity for suffering. Long after all contents of the stomach had been voided, the miserable body kept up its writhing and retching until the thin bitter stuff he dribbled out seemed like the curds of his own rotted substance, the very taste of dissolution. Above him, at intervals that seemed as arbitrary as the bouts of sickness or the spurts of dreams that visited him from time to time, he heard the sound of the ship's bells; and there were moments, either in his dream time or the real life of the ship, periods of lull, almost of silence, when he would hear a swift patter of rain on the deck, creaking of blocks, shouted orders and the hoarse, peculiar singing of the sailors at their ropes. Then all was swallowed in the loud impact of the heavy head sea on the ship's bows and the rippling detonations of the sails as they filled out and backed. All-pervading, adding inexpressibly to his nausea, was the stench of the bilge-water shaken up in the depths of the hold below him like some excretion of the labouring ship. For a maiden, her breath was atrocious.

This purgatory lasted most of the night. On the following morning, weakened but feeling light and purged – and ravenously hungry – Paris went up on deck. The weather had cleared. The light seemed strangely pure to him, like the primal light of the world. The sea was still choppy and seamed with white but the sky looked as soft as some small bird's breast. He saw two men high up on a cross-piece of the mainmast. Others were hauling on a rope immediately below, to sway up the yards. Thurso stood on the quarterdeck with the helmsman directly behind him.

Paris gave the captain good-morning, heard no reply and went directly to the galley, where he found Morgan, the cook, stirring with a long ladle in a deep and narrow-necked iron cauldron.

'What is that?' he asked.

Morgan removed the short, foul-looking pipe from his mouth. 'Lobscouse, sir. That is what they call it.' Morgan's face had a shine of sweat that seemed permanent. He wore a calico apron greasy with the wipings of his hands, and a ragged bonnet of dark red wool sat on top of his head. This cap was his badge of office on board. No one ever saw him take it off.

'What is lobscouse?'

'That is according to what goes in it.'

There was something sullen in this and Paris realized after a moment that the man distrusted him and perhaps thought his question some kind of a trick. 'No,' he said, 'really I do not know. What is in this particular one?'

'Salt beef, potatoes and onions in this.'

'Please go on with your smoking. It is not ready now, I suppose?'

'No, sir. Only just got the fire up, after this dirty weather. It will be given out to the men at dinner-time – eight bells.' Morgan paused. He still had not looked directly at Paris. 'There is burgoo left over from breakfast,' he said at last.

'Burgoo?'

''Tis only boiled oatmeal, sir, with a bit o' sugar.'

'I will have a good bowlful of that,' Paris said. 'Make it up thick, will you?'

'Very good, sir. I will get the boy to bring it below.'

'No,' Paris said. 'I am unwilling to wait so long. I will have it here and now.'

'Here, sir?' Scandalized into directness at last, Morgan permitted himself a stare. 'In the galley?' He saw a smile come slowly to transform the surgeon's white face.

'Yes,' Paris said. 'And as soon as may be.'

From his place by the helm Thurso had watched the emergence of his surgeon with an ill-will tempered only by his weariness. He had slept hardly at all since the onset of the squally weather, undergoing the travails of storm baptism for his ship, a kind of agony commensurate with that endured by Paris, though on the plane of spirit rather than flesh. He had felt the gallantry of the vessel – she would strain and tear her own ligaments if kept too close-hauled. But to turn her away from the wind meant detours and delays, and this conflicted savagely with his wish to make good time on the voyage. Standing in the roaring darkness, hands fast to the rail of the quarterdeck, he issued his orders, heard Barton transmit them, heard the human voices blend with the voices of the wind. Rising from brief slumber he thought he saw the running glimmers of Aurora Borealis in the northern sky, fugitive traces of crimson and gold, gone as soon as glimpsed. It was earlier in the year than any man had reported seeing the Merry Dancers in these latitudes and Thurso knew it for a sign to him and had the cables clinched round the mainmast and the topgallant masts lowered.

Sure enough, this morning the wind had abated and veered to the west, and the sea had calmed. The masts and lower yards were swayed up again and by noon they were making good progress with an easy breeze from westward. But the weather made sport of them still. Two miles round the head and just out of the road a whispering calm descended. The ship loitered, drying her sails in pale sunlight. Then the wind sprang up again but from the wrong quarter, from the south-west. Darkness fell as they made slow way southwards over a sea split with low ridges to the horizon.

Next morning, savagely out of temper at these perversities of the wind, Thurso was approached by the boatswain with a complaint that one of the men had made to strike him.

'James Wilson, the man's name,' Haines said. 'Others saw him raise his hand to me; it is not on my report alone.'

'No matter if it was.' Thurso considered the bright, narrow-set eyes and the bitter mouth of the man before him. 'I take your word until I know different,' he said. This was untrue – he trusted no one and least of all a man who offered to call witnesses before he was doubted. There were the lineaments of cruelty in the boatswain's face. Thurso had seen them too often before in men of every type and cast of feature to be mistaken now. This was not necessarily a bad thing; if the men feared the boatswain they were likely to put more into the work; and they were at the beginning of a long voyage, the authority of the ship's officers must be upheld. Thurso despised cruelty, as he did compassion, and all other redundant shoots of the human spirit. He knew he was not himself cruel but merely practical and obedient to the counsels of necessity. They came to him now: *Reduce the man. Slight his grievance. Above all, do not seem to share it . . .*

He took two paces forward to the quarterdeck rail, presenting Haines with his back. From here he looked down over the deck below for some moments in silence. The half-witted landsman that Barton had netted sat cross-legged amidships surrounded by piles of junk rope, drawing out yarns and knotting them together. His mouth hung open with the effort of concentration. Useless aloft, but Simmonds had said that hauling on a rope he was worth two. Beyond him, well forward, people were getting up tackle to brace the foremast stays: some of the standing rigging had slackened under the assaults of the gale. He made out the hulking Libby with his black patch, the starveling boy and the little Tynesider – this last was a handy one, he noted with sombre approval, he was shaping to the work well. There was blood down the front of his nankeen jacket. 'What is his name again, the little one there?' he said, keeping his back still turned on the boatswain.

'Him takin' up the slack? Cocky little devil.'

'I asked you for his name, not his character.'

'His name is William Blair, sir.'

'And that milk-faced fellow beside him, the tall one who always seems to be looking through the air for something?'

'That is Michael Sullivan, sir, the fiddler.'

'Aye, we shall find a good use for his fiddle when we have the negroes on board. His clothes are falling off him. I cannot have a man walking about my ship in rags. I warrant he is verminous too. We will have vermin aplenty before we are done, we can try for a clean start at least.'

'Yes, sir.'

'He is not alone. I have seen others in the same case. That filthy little Scotchman –'

'McGann, sir.'

'When time affords, I want those men taken to the heads, stripped off and sluiced well down and their clothes burned. They can be given slop clothes from the stores and I want it charged against their pay.'

'Aye-aye, sir.'

'Come forward to me here,' Thurso said, turning slightly round. 'Now regarding this Wilson, he is an able seaman, if I mistake not, a fore-the-mast man?'

'Yes, sir.'

'What took place?'

'It was early today, the wind was just comin' round fair an' we was swayin' up the gallants. We had to look alive, every man of us, to get the benefit – them was your orders, sir. It seemed to me that the men were not puttin' their backs into it, so I started 'em up a bit in the normal way an' he turned sharp round on me.'

'You are saying you gave them a stroke of the rattan to smarten them up?'

115

'Yes, that's right, sir.'

'One stroke, or more than one?'

'One here, one there.'

Thurso observed with rising malignity that the fellow was permitting himself a slight smile. 'And the same to each man?'

'I don't well remember, sir.'

Thurso looked closely into the boatswain's face. The dark eyes were unabashed, alight with an energy of their own. 'You don't remember?' he said. 'Can you not count? You had better learn. He saw it was you and he raised his hand?'

'Aye,' the boatswain said, with a sort of bitter pride, 'he knew it was me right enough.'

Thurso considered for some moments longer. The man Wilson would have to be punished, so much was certain. A day in irons would meet the case. But was it enough? He thought again of the sign he had been given in the night, in the worst of the gale, those glimmers of crimson among the scudding clouds. And now these contrary winds and calms. Eight days out and they were not yet clear of the Dungarvon high land. A square-rigged ship in narrow waters ... With unlucky weather they could be caught in this channel as long again, or longer. Something was clogging, preventing ...

'Have the man brought up on deck and put in irons,' he said. 'I will make an example of him.'

'Aye-aye, sir. Thank you, sir.'

'Damn you, I don't want your thanks.' Thurso turned his eyes on the boatswain and saw the man's head retract slightly and the dark eyes open wider. 'Hark to me, Haines,' he said. 'Do not try to come too near me or you will get scorched. You take that tack and you will find your mistake soon enough. And you had better learn to count. Driving the men is one thing, but I don't want bad blood on the ship, more than I can help. Now get off my deck and go about your work.'

Billy Blair, hauling on the larboard tackle to set up the stays, saw the raw-boned Yorkshireman Wilson brought up on deck and the heavy leg irons fastened on him. 'Christ save us,' he said. 'We are not oot o' Georgy's Channel yet an' they are startin' already. What has that poor lad done?'

Sullivan's dazed and beautiful eyes regarded him through the mesh of the rat-lines. 'What has he done?' he said. 'He has committed the wrong-doin' of bein' aboard of this ship.'

'Ye daft twist,' Billy said irritably. 'How could he have knowed it when he stepped aboard?'

'Anyone who knows anythin' about the law knows that ignorance is no excuse. We got a flogger for a bosun an' a hound for a mate an' a divil for a skipper an' a year o' hell to look forward to an' you ask me what the lad has done.'

'Yor argument doesna' hold water,' Billy said, after some moments of reflection. 'They canna put a lad in irons only for existin'.'

'Can they not?' Sullivan said. 'Holy Mary, I wish it was dinner-time. Me hands is all comin' to pieces with these ropes, bein' out of the way of it these days. Well, 'tis me own fault, sure enough, I should have minded me own business, I should niver have taken your part.'

'I wish you'd give over on that tack,' Billy said.

Libby was passing by them, his arms full of chafing gear. 'I heard you're goin' to get a nice new suit o' clothes,' he said to Sullivan and gave a yellow-toothed grin that was too prolonged for friendliness.

'I don't know what you are talkin' about,' Sullivan said.

'Shag off, blob-eye,' Billy said pugnaciously. Neither of them trusted Libby, who was rumoured to be on close terms with Haines.

'Prick-ears.' Libby was searching for further insults when the second mate came up to them.

'I don't want to hear so much talking,' Simmonds said. 'You – Libby – get aft with that gear. There is a man in irons already, do you want to keep him company?'

'Thank you for sendin' that man about his business, mister mate, he was hangin' about an' impedin' our work,' Sullivan said, displaying a smile of gap-toothed charm.

'That's enough, get on now.'

Eight bells were sounded shortly afterwards but before anyone could move to go below there came the boatswain's whistle and his long-drawn cry summoning all hands on deck. The men of

117

Barton's watch came tumbling up. Barton himself took up a position on the quarterdeck a pace or two behind Thurso. Simmonds remained with the men on the deck below. Haines tilted his head to give his lungs free play. 'All hands to witness punishment!' he shouted at the top of his voice, as if to include the sky itself and whatever beings might be dwelling there. The crew lined up against the rails to starboard or port according to watch.

Thurso turned to Barton. 'Everybody present?'

'The doctor is not here yet, sir.'

The captain's heavy jawbones become more prominent and he paused for a moment before speaking. 'Haines, I want Mr Paris up here as soon as may be.'

In the interval no word was spoken; no sound came from those waiting in line at the rails or from the sullen man in his fetters seated between them, who kept his head down, looking at no one. The wind had dropped again to a faint breath from the west. There was not sea enough to slap the ship's bows. She dallied there, sails set to the topgallants and scarce enough breeze to give her steerage way.

Paris emerged to this silence, climbed the companion ladder to the quarterdeck and took up a position alongside Barton. He knew what was going to happen without needing to be told, some blend of experience and instinctive knowledge informing him that this silent assembly was there to do or witness hurt to a fellow-being.

'Glad you were able to get here, Mr Paris,' Thurso said with malignant sarcasm. 'Strike off the man's irons and rig the grating,' he said to Barton.

The fetters were taken off by Haines, with Libby assisting. Wilson got stiffly to his feet. Hughes and the cooper, a man named Davies, dragged aft one of the wooden gratings used to cover the hatches. This was laid upright and secured to the bulwarks by the lee gangway.

'Grating rigged, sir,' Davies said.

'Mr Barton, ask the man if he has anything to say.'

But Wilson had heard this; before the mate was finished speaking to him he raised his head and looked up steadily at the figures on the quarterdeck. He was a big-boned, powerful man with a gaunt face and pale, washed-out eyes. 'Nowt that can help,' he said.

'Aye,' Thurso said grimly, 'your help comes when I stay my hand. Seize him up.'

Haines and Libby were holding him still, but lightly. They would have stripped off his shirt but he drew back sharply, pulled it over his head and dropped it from him. Then he walked alone to the foot of the gangway and raised his arms so his wrists could be lashed to the grating. He was deeply tanned at the neck and arms but his back was pale and the scars of old floggings were visible on it.

'Seized up, sir,' Haines reported.

Deakin, standing to starboard with the others of his watch, witnessed these preliminaries with a familiar sickness, compounded of his own old fear and pain. He knew that pride of refusing to be manhandled to the grating – doomed pride, because the flogging always brought a man to his knees. Deakin had been beaten and seen men beaten for almost as long as he could remember and he knew that the Yorkshireman would be given extra for raising his head and looking steady – not for spite, but because flogging was meant to reduce a man. On a slaveship it would not be the boatswain that would deliver the lashes, or either of the mates – the grievance would be too strong for this looser discipline. Officers and men had often to work side by side with their hands dipping in the same grease-tub. Things could happen that looked like accidents. Or a knife between the ribs and over the side and nobody the wiser . . . No, it would be the skipper. He was talking now, in his hoarse, unchanging voice. Deakin took in the sense without paying much attention to the particular words. He had heard similar speeches on a dozen ships. Wilson had raised his hand against one of the appointed officers. This was to raise his hand against the captain himself. He, Thurso, was not the man to stand this. They did not know him yet. They would get to know him, by God. He could be a devil incarnate to them if they crossed him. If they went his way he could be sweet as honey. Let everyone see and take note what would befall them at any failure of duty or breach of discipline. . . .

Thurso divested himself of his coat and waistcoat, handing them to Barton, who came forward for them like a valet. Haines was undoing the red baize bag in which the cat was kept. To Paris, already bracing himself for what was to come, there was a horrifying elegance in this ritual disrobing, despite the incongruities of the captain's thick figure and his big, square, weatherbeaten face. He might have been in his changing-room at a levee, his attendants about him, his petitioners below.

He took the whip from Haines and stepped down the companion. He measured his distance, took two short steps and struck with full power of his arm. They heard the swish of the tails and the pattering crack of the impact. A loud, deep panting sound came from Wilson as the breath was driven from his body by the force of the blow. Paris saw the tendons of the man's neck tighten with his effort to make no sound. The first blow had opened his back and a broken line of blood showed where the knots had cut. Thurso delivered stroke after stroke with unfaltering ferocity and astounding energy, his eyes staring and his face dark red and swollen-looking. Wilson still made no sound but he writhed against the grating. His back was a red slough from neck to waist. Drops of blood were scattered over the deck with each stroke. At the tenth, and each one thereafter, Thurso was obliged to pause in order to run his fingers through the tails of the cat to free them from blood and bits of flesh. The fourteenth blow broke Wilson's resolve. His knees gave and he hung by his wrists. 'Oh God,' he shouted thickly. 'God help me.'

'Aye,' Thurso said, shaking drops over the deck. He had stains of blood on the sleeve and shoulder of his shirt. There were beads of sweat on his face and his chest was rising and falling heavily. 'You are singing now, are you? You had better call on Thurso, he is nearer.'

It was what he had been waiting for. Wilson was a hardy ruffian but he had known he must give way. He took the count to eighteen, however, before throwing the whip to the boatswain. 'Clear the thongs well for the next man that forgets himself,' he said, and stumped back up the companion. 'Cut the man down, Mr Barton, and send the crew about their duties. Tell Morgan I want hot water brought to my cabin on the instant.'

Freed from the grating, Wilson collapsed at once upon the deck, his eyes fixed and his face darkly congested, Paris saw him half led and half carried below by two men. He stood for some moments struggling to master his disgust and indignation. It came to him that he could assert his will against this brute in a way that poor Wilson, with no privileged exemptions, had not been able to, and so give some dignity to those lacerations. He stepped forward to face the captain. 'Excuse me, Captain Thurso,' he said. 'I should like the favour of a word with you.'

He met the captain's eyes and saw something vacant in them for the moment, the sort of vacancy that sometimes comes after strong effort or emotion. 'It is not convenient at present,' Thurso said.

'Sir, this is the third time of asking and I have a right to be heard.'

'A right?' Thurso said. 'What do you mean?' His tone had quickened. 'Do you talk to me about rights, here on my deck?'

Paris felt a violent contempt rise in him as he met the renewed glare in the other's eyes. So strong was the feeling that he had consciously to caution himself, discipline himself physically. He clasped his hands together behind his back. 'Yes, sir, I do,' he said. He rested his eyes steadily on Thurso and saw something change in the other's expression as the antagonism was registered. 'I am referring to the question of the sick bay. It has not been cleared yet, in spite of my former requests to you. Now there is a clear case of need for it.'

'Sick bay?' Thurso glared up at his listless topsails for a moment. 'Are you mad, Mr Paris? What need is there now for it when we have no sickness aboard?'

'I intend to treat that man's back,' Paris said. 'His lacerations could easily become putrid if not attended to.'

'Wilson? God damn my blood,' Thurso said violently. 'I don't know whether to laugh or cry at you. I have seen a hundred like him treated well enough with a handful of salt.'

Paris hesitated. He had not wanted to use his uncle's name, but he was set on winning the day – and not for his own sake only. He said, 'You compel me to remind you that Mr Kemp intended me to have the use of that room. He so stated and in your hearing.'

He saw that Thurso had clenched his right fist so that the knuckles whitened. At the sight, with a reciprocal impulse of violence he did not know he possessed, and which he was afterwards to think of as some infection of madness, he advanced his face and brought his hands to his sides. 'I want that sick bay cleared, sir, if you please,' he said.

'Yes, I thought we should hear of your uncle before long.' Thurso seemed about to say more, but suddenly his expression changed and he lifted his head. 'There, can you hear it?' he said.

'Hear what?'

'The wind, you fool.'

Listening now more intently, Paris heard a tune in the rigging that he did not think had been there before, and a moment later he felt a breeze against his face. There was a series of rippling sounds as the canvas began to fill out.

'You can have your precious sick bay if it matters so much,' Thurso said with contempt. He felt the wind increasing, felt the responsive gathering of the ship. It came again, stronger, singing through the ropes, a harmony of high-pitched tones, transmitted to the chains and thence through all the timbers. And it was coming from the west. 'You see, it is answered,' he said, turning away. 'We have freed the wind.'

'What do you mean?'

No answer came to this. The captain's face had relaxed into lines of fatigue. He was looking down to the foot of the gangway, where drops of Wilson's blood still glistened.

SEVENTEEN

Erasmus waited for an occasion when his father was in relaxed mood – occasions rarer these days than he had ever known them to be. He chose one evening after supper when his father, at ease in skull-cap and dressing-gown, was smoking a pipe or two in the small, oak-panelled sanctum he called his study.

'Can you spare me some minutes, sir?'

Kemp, observing for a while in silence the military posture that his son had adopted, head up and shoulders braced back, was brought to mind of other occasions, going back to earliest childhood, when Erasmus had stood before him thus. Un-expectedly, and in the midst of his anxieties, he found himself visited by compassion for this self-willed son of his, for whom life had always been a succession of self-imposed tests and ordeals. Just in this way, he thought, Erasmus will bear himself at the news of my ruin, if it comes.

'Yes, of course, my boy,' he said. 'What is it?'

'I want to ask Sarah Wolpert to marry me,' Erasmus said, looking straight before him. 'That is, I want to ask her father . . .' He stumbled a moment. 'I want to ask for her hand. I wished to know if you had any objections to such a course, sir.'

'Wolpert's daughter?' Kemp was taken aback. He had noticed an increased interest in clothes on his son's part; the boy took longer over the dressing of his hair and the tying of his neck-cloth; but Erasmus had always been fastidious about his linen and careful of his appearance and was now at a foppish age. He knew his son had been going a good deal to the Wolpert house but there was the play to account for this and Wolpert had a boy only slightly younger than Erasmus.

'I suspected nothing of it,' he said. 'I have been much preoccupied of late. Besides, you are secretive – you always have been so. You do not come to me with your feelings, only your decisions.' If there was reproach in this it was mainly for himself, for his failure to notice. Nevertheless, he felt immediate compunction for it. 'Well, it is your way,' he said.

'Are you displeased with me, sir?'

'No, I am not displeased. Our natures are different in this respect. I would stop to look at something, take soundings, before my course was so far set. Now I see this business is screwed to such pitch that I could not oppose it without damage.' He saw nothing on his son's face to indicate any appreciation of this. The boy still stood braced there. 'Come, sit down,' he said. 'Here, by me. You keep to your purposes, that is not so bad a thing. But you are young to be married. And the girl cannot be more than eighteen.'

'She is not yet eighteen, sir.'

'It is young,' Kemp said slowly. Something had changed in his tone, now that surprise had faded, giving time for a glimpse of the implications. These expanded in his mind as he looked at the level-browed, intensely serious face close to his own. 'On the other hand,' he said, 'your mother was barely seventeen when we were married. I cannot spare you from the business,' he added after a moment.

'There would be no need,' Erasmus said. The interview was not proceeding as expected – he was surprised to find his father so amenable – but this last objection he had anticipated. 'The match would do good for us. The combination of the families would make a powerful force, with the town growing so fast.'

Kemp nodded, as if this thought had only now occurred to him. 'That is so,' he said. 'The connection would be of benefit to both.' With some appearance of effort he met his son's eyes, so like his own. 'It is what you want?' he said.

'I am set on her.'

Kemp was silent for a long moment, looking down. Then he raised a face grown suddenly haggard. 'You have my consent,' he said.

It took a further week for Erasmus to discover the right

circumstances, poise and apparel for his interview with Sarah's father. It was not nerve he had to summon – he had enough of that at his command – but humility, the readiness to demean himself, as he saw it, by stating his desires and seeming to petition for their legitimacy. He would have felt this whoever the man had been; he had felt it, to some degree, even with his father.

Love had not so far made him happy. His intention, the fixing of his will on the girl, he experienced as an affliction. His whole being seemed tender, painful to the slightest touch – even at times, the touch of air itself. The impressions of his senses came as blows to his heart, strangely similar to those of loss or violation. In this vulnerable state he experienced the burgeoning of the season like a man set on bruising himself. Never had he noted the symptoms of summer with such particularity. As he saw to the unloading of the pack-trains on the waterfront, or the weighing and recording of cotton bales in the yard behind the family warehouses, he heard the cuckoos calling from the market gardens of Wallasey across the water, all regret and all promise mingled in their notes. In the wood by the lake the bluebells came in swathes and the ash trees emerged from winter over-night, as it seemed, and were hung with reddish, plumy flowers.

He took particular care with his dress the evening of his visit: an immaculate exterior reduced the appearance of suing. He chose a suit of dark satin, short in the sleeve to show the plaited linen of his shirt cuffs, a white waistcoat and black, pointed-toed shoes in the latest fashion. He had powdered his hair lightly and tied it behind with a long black ribbon; and instead of the usual short hanger, he wore his best sword with the silver chasing on the hilt.

'I love your daughter, sir,' he heard himself saying, sitting bolt upright on his chair. 'I want to marry her.' It sounded angry, almost. He had been unable so far to see any reaction on the broad face before him or in the shrewd, deliberate brown eyes which regarded him now for some moments in silence.

'Do you so?' the merchant said at last. He had come from business and was still in outdoor attire, full-skirted cotton summer coat, buff waistcoat, old-fashioned wig with a roll of curls above the ears. 'And she, how does she view the matter?'

125

'I think she is not averse to me.'

'Is that a way of saying there is already an understanding between you?'

The question was deliberately disingenuous; he knew already of the young man's interest: it had been expressed to him by Sarah herself. And he knew to what extent the girl had responded. But Erasmus's hasty manner inclined him to temporize, partly from the long habit of bargaining, partly because he had been roused to some hostility by it. 'I am asking if you have spoken together,' he said rather sharply.

'There is no understanding, sir,' Erasmus said. 'But she has given me reason to hope.'

Wolpert considered for some moments. Though phlegmatic in manner, he was acute, particularly where it concerned him nearly. His daughter was a source of delight to him and he treasured her deeply. There was no timidity in the bearing of the young man before him, no personal deference towards himself. This first suitor of his daughter was no doubt suffering, but it seemed from arrogance as much as love. He had known Erasmus for many years, had seen him from time to time as he grew up. It was with a feeling of surprise now that he met the dark eyes and realized that the youth had become formidable. 'How old are you now, Erasmus?' he said.

'I shall be twenty-two in December, sir.'

'You have spoken of this with your father, of course?'

'Yes, sir.'

Wolpert permitted himself a smile. Erasmus was the only son and he knew the extent of Kemp's ambitions for him. 'And how did he take it? With a pinch of salt, I suppose, eh?'

'He has given his consent.'

'Aye, I dare say so.' Wolpert was still smiling. 'Why would he not? But as a distant prospect, no doubt? He will want to keep you by him some time yet.'

'No, sir, he has made no condition regarding the time.' Erasmus had great pride of family and as far as he had pondered his father's response, apart from his own relief at it, it had seemed to him like a condescension to the Wolperts, something they ought to be pleased at. But now he saw the indulgent smile on the heavy face fade quickly, and for a space of some moments he found the older man's eyes turned upon him as they might have been on some not fully trusted associate – not unfriendly exactly, but appraising and rather cold.

'How?' Wolpert said in a quieter tone. 'Are you saying your father has given immediate consent to the match?'

'I have said so,' Erasmus returned, rather brusquely.

Wolpert appeared to muse for some moments, then he said, 'Listen well to me, my fine young man. My daughter is not yet eighteen years of age. She is too young to be saddled with promises. You may say to her what you like and she may answer you as she pleases – I cannot be present at it, so I can have nothing to say about it. But I will countenance no special arrangements, at least for the time being. You may continue to see my daughter as you see her now, as a friend among other friends. She will be eighteen in some months, then we shall re-consider.'

Rising to terminate the interview he caught a blaze from the young man's eyes such as might have been reserved for a rival. 'I expect you to abide by this on our words and my wishes alone,' he said with an involuntary response of severity. 'And I will make both known to my daughter.'

This he did, in gentle terms, and had an impression the girl was relieved at it. That same evening he consulted his wife, who had been aware of the situation for some considerable time, he now discovered, and who had sounded the girl in ways that would not have entered his head. Of the strength of the young man's feelings there could be no doubt. 'He cannot keep his eyes off the girl,' Mrs Wolpert said placidly. 'He watches her every movement.' Embroidery in lap, eyes mild, hair tucked under her close-fitting lace coif, she seemed at a long remove from such devouring regards, but managed nevertheless to convey an idea of them to her husband's mind. Young Kemp's feelings were written in his eyes. And what eyes they were, full of fire! There was no denying he was a handsome young man, though far from smooth-mannered, and Sarah of course was aware of it, looks and manners both; there was growing up a fashion for wildness . . .

'If it is a fashion, it cannot be so wild,' Wolpert said drily. 'And Sarah, with what eyes does she look at him?'

'It is bound to make an impression on a young girl to be the object of so much attention. She is very much aware of him.' Mrs Wolpert paused for a short while, though without looking at her husband. 'I think she is rather frightened of the young man,' she said at last, 'though she would laugh at the notion.'

'Frightened, you say? She is not easily daunted.' Wolpert considered for a moment, then he said, 'If she is frightened, she cannot have much tenderness for him.'

Upon this his wife favoured him with a look of pity for his understanding; and as usual, in response, he showed himself aggrieved. 'Why are these things kept from me?' he demanded. 'Why am I always the last to learn of a thing? I wager old Andrew knows more of the business than I do. A fine thing for a man's wife and daughter to plot together to keep him in the dark.'

But he kept wife and daughter and everyone else in the dark concerning the step he took next in the matter. He might or might not be obtuse, he told himself, regarding matters of the heart; but he was certainly not so where material interest was concerned, and his suspicions had been roused by Kemp's alacrity. The following afternoon he called on a man named Partridge, whom he had used once before, some years previously, on a delicate investigation into the extent of a client's credit, and whose thoroughness and discretion he had not forgotten.

Partridge was accustomed to describe himself as an attorney. He had a close and cluttered office on the upper floor of a house in Limekiln Lane, invaded by the fumes of a nearby tannery; but most of his business was conducted elsewhere: in registry offices, counting-houses, copying-rooms, the taverns and tap-houses frequented by clerks and warehousemen and the small functionaries of business houses. He belied the associations of his name, being lantern-jawed, gimlet-eyed and scrawny, dressed in rusty black, with an ancient, dishevelled goat's-hair wig.

'Remember,' Wolpert said, 'the most absolute discretion is essential, not only as concerns the dealings between the two of us but in all that affects Mr Kemp. I do not want anything noised about, no suspicion attaching anywhere – people are always ready to say that when there is smoke there must be fire. Mr Kemp is an acquaintance of many years, for whom I have considerable regard. There must be no damage to him or to his interests. All I want is the facts of his present situation.'

'You shall have them. Have no worry on that score, my dear sir.' Patridge nodded and glanced aside through his small, smeared window at the tannery yard below, as if witnesses lay out there, among the malodorous hides. 'Joshua Partridge is the soul of discretion,' he said. 'Discretion is his strong suit. He is noted for it, famous for it.'

'Famous for discretion?'

'That is not the contradiction it seems, sir. I mean of course among those who have honoured me with their commissions. Without that reputation I could not continue in employment one day longer. In short,' Partridge added with one of the sudden bursts of frankness which characterized his speech, 'I should be on the rubbish heap in no time.' He paused for a moment to investigate an ear for wax. Then he said, 'I shall require, in addition to the fifty per cent advance of fee we have agreed on, a sum of ten shillings a day while enquiries last. This is to cover all necessary expenses I may incur in the furtherance of my enquiries. In short, sir –'

Wolpert was ready to pay but it was against his engrained habit to pay without discussion. 'That is considerably more than I remember paying the last time I had the honour to employ you, Mr Partridge.'

'Sir,' Partridge said, 'this is an expanding age, the nation is prospering, our voice is heard in the councils of Europe. As a result of this the cost of everything goes up daily and that must also include gifts, rewards and all manner of pecuniary inducements. Numbers of men are getting richer and greater numbers are getting poorer. Alas, both classes have higher expectations these days.' The attorney permitted a lean smile to move his jaws. 'In short, sir,' he said with a burst, 'there has been a leap in bribes.'

EIGHTEEN

Day by day the *Liverpool Merchant* made progress southwards. Under full sail, propelled by fair winds, she dipped and rose through the heavings of the sea with a profound regularity. On the line of the horizon there would sometimes appear the brief stain of another ship, like a breath on a distant mirror; but most of the time she could feel herself alone on the ocean, the sole trader of the world, instead of what she was, a member of a vast fleet sent forth by men of enterprise and vision all over Europe, engaged in the greatest commercial venture the world had ever seen, changing the course of history, bringing death and degradation and profits on a scale hitherto undreamed of.

That the ship was a mere corpuscle in this nourishing bloodstream was not easy to imagine for the men aboard her. To them she was a universe of routine tasks and routine sounds – the bell marking the half hours, shouted orders, the wash of the waves, the wincing tune of the timbers as they were exercised by the sway of the sea. Forces less tangible but equally determinate worked on the men and they were set in relation to one another in sympathy or antipathy, as happens in all communities.

Fourteen days out they began to be sensible of a change in the climate. Hughes felt it high up at the main topgallant masthead, standing by to loose the sail. He was always happiest when alone and high up, past the timbers of the mast-heads; only here, apart from corners of the night-time deck, could he be sure of finding no others close by him. He climbed to solitude hand over hand, looking up towards it where it lived in the sky, bare feet sure in the rat-lines, body moving to the sway of the ship. Most of the crew could work aloft if need be, and men like

Blair, Wilson, Libby and Deakin were proficient seamen; but there was no one to match Hughes when it came to working in the tops, no one with his speed and balance in climbing. He could go from deck to cross-trees quicker than men half his age and keep nerve and footing and hand sail in storm and dark when the gail tore at him and the ship bucked like a maddened charger to throw him off.

This sunny morning, leaning to brace in the yard for a free wind, the scent of the south came to him across the water. Some quality of balm had come into the air. The ship leaned to starboard and Hughes saw dolphins swimming alongside, directly below, close to the surface. The sun struck down to them and in their rapid motions the creatures formed and dissolved themselves, dark grey, silver and blue by turns, then shimmering and streaming into sunlight. And Hughes, who from adolescence had been unsettled by people coming too close, who had once scarred a man terribly in the hysteria of contested space, was happy to be in this clear weather, above the clouds of sails, with these rainbow bursts of dolphins following the ship.

Paris, taking his paces on the after part of the deck, felt the change in latitude as a softer quality in the sky and a gleam of pearl at times on the undulations of the sea. He saw flying-fish for the first time in his life and wrote about them in his journal. He had found unexpected solace in this daily recording of observation and impression; it had come to seem a contrivance for talking still to Ruth, telling her of things she might not know, submitting his thoughts to her, to share them and in a way to have them judged, as he had delighted to do when they had been together.

The translation of Harvey, too, he persisted with, as a focus for the mind, something, in the monotony of these southward-sailing days, to give him a sense of choice, of independent being, some relief from the oppression of passivity which stalked his days and nights. He felt as subject to external forces as the ship was, or as the sea itself, whose every twitch was determined, whose rages and calms were equally docile. Docile too the vast forces that ruled her and the shores she nibbled at. Paris thought

131

of it as a maze of concentric circles on a single plane, each continuous with the next, like a flattened spiral, with himself a speck on some interior rim. Somewhere beyond and above was that principle of harmony eloquently espoused by Mr Pope in his 'Essay on Man'. The couplet ran through his mind now:

> All discord, harmony not understood.
> All partial evil, universal good.

The followers of this harmonizing God, in a spurt of partial evil, had killed all his hopes and ruined his life. And now, at some other rim of the maze, there were flying-fish, which Ruth had never seen.

They are, as far as I can judge, some eighteen inches in length, with tails forked like a swallow's, but one side is shorter. They have two wings, which are not properly speaking wings at all but which I take to be the fins of the breast enlarged and shaped to this purpose of flight. (It is a large question how this shaping came about.) I did not observe the fishes to flap their wings, but to glide rather. They appear to build up speed under the water and, on gaining the surface, make rapid beats of the still-submerged tail, and it is this which gives them the final impetus they need to rise up into the air. Once airborne thus, they are capable of performing several consecutive glides over the water, the tail propelling them up again each time they sink below the surface.

These creatures are fashioned precisely to their purpose. The fashioning is open to observation, but the purpose remains obscure. Why should these fish alone, among the denizens of ocean, be equipped for flight? Can there be aspiration among fishes? A question I could put to our good captain, if only to see him struggle with the furious contempt it would cause him. If aspiration determines development, the eagle would be judged superior to the wren ... It occurs to me as a legitimate question, whether these flying-fish could replace their fins if damaged. We now know a lizard can do so with its tail; and Réaumur has demonstrated beyond any reasonable doubt that a crayfish can grow a new claw. These are strong arguments against a fixed creation and an unchanging order. If a crayfish can grow a new claw, why cannot a bird? If a lizard was given this particular attribute at the moment of creation, why were other creatures not given it?

Paris paused. The door of his cabin was open and from where he sat he could see the stern of the punt, which was hoisted amidships just forward of the mainmast. It made a beaker-shaped angle with the boom on which it rested, and the beaker filled and drained with exact regularity as the ship dipped her bows and raised them. The liquid, pale cobalt in colour, was not at first associated in his mind with the sea at all; for some moments, seeing this calm filling of the beaker, he was back in his student days, at a long, stained bench with others, testing for acids with litmus, holding up the glass vessel to see the obedient stain. He was distressed now at the memory. Those days were like a time before a fall; the ruin of his life lay between. How wonderful he had thought that suffusion of red . . . The memory of Wilson's flogging came suddenly to him, the start of blood across the man's back, the pattern of drops on the deck, Thurso's expression of fulfilment . . . Conviction pierced Paris before he could summon any customary defence: this was not some other point in that maze of circles, he and Wilson occupied the same point. *My back, my blood, me sullen in chains, me calling for help* . . .

He started away from this as from some appalling temptation, hastily closing and stowing away his journal and taking out, as antidote to such poisonous abasement, Harvey's treatise and the pages of his translation.

After some minutes the plain and closely argued Latin text succeeded in putting other thoughts from his mind. It had fascinated him and struck him as paradoxical from the start that this treatise, destined to change beliefs held since Galen's time and assert a new path for the blood, should still be couched in the strict form of scholastic disputation unchanged since the Middle Ages.

He had got as far as chapter eight, in which the author explains his reasons for the forming of his famous hypothesis. To restore himself he looked at the beginning of the third paragraph, one of the most profoundly influential in the history of medicine, and marvelled once again at the miraculous tentativeness of it, almost casual, like a man working from dream to truth: *Coepi egomet mecum cogitare . . . I began to bethink myself whether it might not have a kind of movement as it were in a circle . . .*

He was interrupted by the appearance at his door of McGann, a small, tight-faced Scot, one of the men who had been deloused and hosed down on the captain's orders soon after sailing. The working rig he had been issued with was too big: his canvas smock hung round him and he wore the baggy breeches rolled up to his knees.

'Beggin' your pardon, Doctor,' he said, removing his woollen bonnet to show a cropped head, 'I hae been pissin' pins an' needles again, an' 'tis unco' painful.'

'I have told you why it is,' Paris said. 'And you knew it well enough before.' Nevertheless, he was glad in a way to see the man there. His medical duties had so far been less than onerous. He had seen to the lacerations on Wilson's back; he had pulled a tooth for a man called Bryce, which had been broken in some shore fight and subsequently rotted; he had dressed a burn for Morgan, the cook, and given a course of mercury to McGann for his gonorrhoea. It was not much, in more than two weeks at sea. 'You are past the worst of it,' he said. 'You have no venereal chancres. Your general health is not impaired.'

McGann glanced up at this. His eyes were watery grey beneath sandy brows and they possessed a kind of spurious alertness. The nature of his disease gave him no apparent disturbance. It was no more then an item in the sum of difficulties and small stratagems that his life represented. ' 'Tis unco' painful,' he said again.

'No doubt it is,' Paris said. 'They talk about the pains of love, don't they? But it will pass.'

McGann made no immediate move to withdraw, but remained where he was, cap in hand, eyes lowered, as if waiting for some gift of words that he could carry away with him. Or possibly something more tangible, Paris thought. He had grown more sensitive to faces of late and he had seen in McGann's a sort of ultimate reduction to the necessities of survival. Everything possible in the way of misfortune and abuse had been endured by the small-featured, freckled face before him, with its pursed-up mouth and spurious shrewdness of expression. McGann's life seemed entirely a matter of improvisation, of seeking advantage, however small, from every occasion.

'I don't know what you want from me,' the surgeon said. 'You are quite fit for duty. All you are now suffering from is a slight inflammatory discharge of mucus from the membrane of the urethra.'

134

McGann seemed impressed by this, though he kept his eyes respectfully lowered. 'Jimminy-jig,' he said. 'I've got a' that too, have I? Where is it situated?'

Billy Blair, hoisting out the punt to try the current along with Sullivan and the taciturn Wilson, felt the change too, some essence of scent dissipated by distance. He raised his blunt nose and sniffed at invisible shores. 'We are gettin' south,' he said. 'Soon be up wi' the Canaries. I can smell them bleddy pine trees an' spices. Blair has the keenest nose of anyone. I can smell them African wimmin already. I can smell the palm oil in their cunt-thatches.'

It was said, as much as anything, as an attempt to deflect Sullivan from the grievance of his forcible ablution. After a fortnight at sea any mention of cunt was likely to cause a diversion. However, on this occasion it failed to do so. 'No,' the fiddler continued, 'look at it howiver you like, to take a man an' strip him an' throw water over him an' burn his clothes an' give him clothes he niver asked for an' wouldn't be seen dead in an' cut his hair close enough to draw blood an' all against his consent, mind you –'

Sullivan paused to take breath, gazing at Billy over the bows of the punt. His long bony face, dark eyebrows and bemused green eyes were more evident for the shearing away of his hair. ''Tis a blow struck against the liberty of the subject,' he said, 'an' it bears on ivery man aboard of this ship.'

'It doesna' bear on every man aboard o' the ship,' Billy retorted. 'Every man aboard o' the ship is not full o' bleddy fleas. I an't for one. How about you, shipmate?'

This was to Wilson, who pondered for some moments darkly, then gave it as his opinion that there was many a worse thing than fleas.

'Well, 'course there is,' Billy said impatiently, 'there is crab-lice, there is rats, there is bleddy lock-jaw, but that is not the point I am seekin' to make. That coat was rotted, it was fallin' off him, it's no use him denyin' it.'

'That coat could have been mended,' Sullivan said. 'That coat only needed a lovin' woman's hand. An' another thing, that coat had six brass buttons on it, good as new. Where are thim brass buttons now? I am goin' to ask Haines one of these days about thim buttons. I am waitin' for the right moment. An' they have took it out of me pay, they have took another three shillin' off me for this linsey-woolsey stuff I niver asked for.'

'Well,' Billy said, 'they have took less fra you than fra me.'

'They are takin' two months wages off the both of us to pay back what they spent to get us,' Sullivan said.

'Aye, but I am signed for an able seaman an' you are signed for an ordinary seaman an' the difference between us is four shillin' a month. So the bastids are takin' eight shillin' more from me.'

'That's another thing that is woundin' to the spirit,' Sullivan said. 'Why should you be worth four shillin' a month more than me? We are both men, aren't we? An' I am gifted for the music.'

'Curse me,' Billy said, striking at the gunwale of the boat with the flat of his hand. 'I have seen some cuddies in my time, Sullivan, but I never saw anyone the like o' you for gettin' hold o' things the wrong bleddy way. You should be glad to be losin' eight shillin' less than me.'

'We are both losin' the same,' Sullivan said. 'They are takin' the same off the both of us.'

'Now just a bleddy minute.' Billy's tone was irate but his face was beginning to wear a baffled look. 'God-amighty,' he said, 'if they are takin' eight shillin' more from me than they are from you, how the pox can they be takin' the same from both of us?'

'That eight shillin',' Sullivan said patiently, 'that is just a idea in your head, Billy. That is the different value them miscreants have set on us. But we are both goin' to work two months for nothin' an' risk our lives among them heathen blacks . . .'

Sullivan appeared at this point to lose the track of what he was saying. He was gazing forward to where two or three men, Libby among them, were sitting up against the windlass, working on some cable; in anticipation of long anchorage off the Windward Coast, Thurso had ordered the cables to be rounded so as to protect them from chafing in the hawse.

136

'Come on then,' Billy said irritably, 'finish what you are sayin', man, give over dreamin'.'

'I have finished,' Sullivan said. 'At the end of two months we have got nothin', so they have took the same from the both of us. How do you think he knew?'

'Who?'

'That miscreated mortal down there, Libby. I just remembered somethin' he said to me about gettin' a new suit. He knew they were goin' to take me clothes off me.'

'I an't surprised,' Billy said after a moment. 'He is Haines's catch-fart.'

'They knew each other from before,' Wilson said. 'They have been together on a Guineaman before.' The morose and saturnine cast of his face brightened with a sudden radiant intention of violence. 'Haines,' he said. 'Son of a whore. He picked the wrong cull this time. After this voyage he'll never walk straight again. I have swore it.'

Unaware that he was under discussion, Libby was enjoying a joke of his own, of the kind he liked best, bringing present ridicule and future misfortune for the victim. He and a man named Tapley and the boy Charlie had been set to binding a length of the ship's cable upwards from the anchor ring to protect it from chafing. Each had taken up a section and was winding old rope-strands firmly and closely about it. Calley, sent forward to join them, had come upon a length of hawser lying there waiting to be spliced. In his eagerness to do his work well and correctly he did not notice the two-inch difference in circumference and set to work at once, head lowered in utmost concentration.

Charlie seemed about to point out the mistake but Libby stopped him with a quick gesture. Tapley he merely winked at. He waited until Calley was well into the work, then he said, 'Gettin' on well, ain't he?' and grinned at Tapley and the boy, both of whom he knew, with the bully's infallible instinct, to be afraid of him. 'They will make a sailor of yer yet, Dan'l.'

Calley smiled without looking up. His mouth hung open a little and his blunt pink tongue protruded slightly in the unremitting attention he was giving his task. A dribble of saliva had escaped its soft crease of containment at the corner of his mouth and made a silver thread like a snail's track on his chin. There was a bright shine of snot on the short slope of his upper lip. Everything exuded by Calley had a magical shine and purity about it, the beads of his sweat were like small pearls. Without saying a word to anyone he had been filling with the pride of achievement. He tied the strands round and round as he had seen the others do, in his big, calloused hands, keeping the tarred threads of the yarn tight and close together, making sure not to cross them or leave any gaps, the thick hemp rope lying warm and heavy across his thighs.

'Yer'll not only be the best man aboard at jerkin' off,' Libby said, 'yer'll be the best at servin' a cable. Have yer seen him?' he said to Charlie. 'Every night he goes out to the heads an' jerks hisself off, reggler as clockwork. Yer too busy doin' it yerself to take notice, ain't yer? I'm talkin' to yer.'

The boy turned his sun-freckled, undernourished face towards Libby. 'Yes,' he said, 'that's right.'

'Too busy juicin' yerself, ain't yer?'

'That's right.'

Libby stared at him for some moments. The frozen lids of his blind eye hung a little open, showing an ambivalent gleam. 'Pity to waste it,' he said.

'Waste what?' Deakin had approached soundlessly on bare feet. 'Give us a bit of cable,' he said, making to get between Calley and Tapley. 'Haines sent me to give a hand. What the jig do you think you are doing there?' he said to Calley.

'Dan'l is servin' cable an' he is doin' well, we are proud of him.' Libby gave his droll wink, the dead eye briefly doing duty for the living one. 'Now don't you go spoilin' his concentration, that wouldn't be right.'

Deakin said quietly, 'Dan'l, look up a minute, will you? Don't you see, you are working on a loose piece of hawser, not on the anchor cable. You are wasting your time and if someone comes and catches you at it you will get in trouble. Who told you to bind it there?'

'One o' them.' Calley pointed at the others. 'They said do it here.'

138

'Stab me if we told the half-wit anythin' at all,' Libby said. 'Why are you interferin'?'

'You will have to unpick it,' Deakin said. 'Then you come further down here and I'll show you how to do the worming on the cable and then the binding.'

'I don't want to unpick it,' Calley said. 'I done it right.'

'You have done it right as far as the work goes, but you have done it on the wrong rope. That piece doesn't need chafing gear on it.'

Calley looked down at the rope in his lap then up at the grinning Libby. Some sort of suspicion was beginning to dawn in his eyes.

'You should have told him,' Deakin said to Tapley and Charlie. He did not look at Libby. 'Men on a ship should stick together. Don't make any difference what kind of ship she is.'

'We have got a preacher here,' Libby said. His mood was turning ugly. The joke had misfired and he felt his authority was being undermined. 'You don't stick,' he said. 'You run.'

Deakin looked at him without expression. Someone had talked, then. 'Do you think I would run from you?' he said. 'You are big, but your bollocks hang by a string, same as anyone else's.'

'You shit-sack,' Libby said. 'I will spill you out.'

At this threat to his befriender, something mad looked out of Calley's eyes. 'No, you won't,' he said. With astounding speed and agility, before Libby had so much as registered the threat, he had come from a sitting position on to his haunches, had his left hand planted on the deck to take his weight and his right clenched and drawn back.

Leaning sharply forward, Deakin was in time to catch at his shoulder. 'They will flog you if you start a fight here,' he said. He kept his grip, feeling after some moments the muscles of Calley's arm relax. 'He is not worth getting a flogging for,' he said more quietly.

Calley, in the red mist of rage, felt the hand on his shoulder and knew the touch. This was Deakin, who had spoken words of comfort to him and touched him in the darkness of the hulk. 'Deakin is not a shit-sack,' he said.

139

Feelings of loneliness and distress had accompanied Calley since the first day out. Barton had proved a false friend, giving him nothing but abuse and kicks once he was on board. The vision of Africa and the hot lewd women had faded now; it was lame Kate from the taphouse that he mostly thought of at night when he crept to some deserted corner of the deck and rubbed himself for comfort in the dark and whimpered with brief pleasure. Now he smiled as he glanced up, and the traces of his rage shone with pristine glory on the smooth skin below his eyes. 'Deakin is my friend,' he said.

NINETEEN

Hag-seed hence!
Fetch us in fuel and be quick
To answer other business: shruggst thou, malice?
If thou neglectest or dost unwillingly what I command
I'll wrack thee –

'No, no, Prospero, no, no, egad, pray allow me, I really must interpose.' The director spoke with customary languidness, but his words were enough to bring the headlong wizard to a halt, though swollen with pent speech and frothing slightly. They were rehearsing in the library, the weather having turned rainy. 'No, no, you see,' the director said, 'you are in too much haste, you absolutely must give Caliban time to do a proper shrug. It serves no purpose to ask him if he is shrugging and menace him with cramps before you have allowed him the time to do it.'

His name was Henry Adams – a well-known one on the London stage, as Charles Wolpert had assured them all. He was a sallow, long-shanked man with fine eyes and bad teeth and a fashionable limpness of manner.

'It is what I keep telling you, Bulstrode,' the curate said. 'It is what I have often complained of. I must be given time to perform my shrugging.' His face was pale as always in the stress of these rehearsals and his fair, fine-spun hair showed the usual startlement.

'Why, sir, as to that,' Adams said, 'if you will permit me, you are not performing a suitable kind of shrug for a monster, you are drawing yourself too much upright, you are making Caliban too damnable proud.'

141

'But, sir, excuse me, that is exactly why I do it in that way,' the curate said excitedly. 'I see Caliban as a proud and rebellious character.'

'There is only one way to see Caliban, reverend sir,' Adams said without heat, 'and that is my way, so long as I am directing the play. I want a more abject shrug. Like this.' He crouched slightly, half turned his body and made a long, writhing motion which seemed to start at his thin knees. 'A touch more sinuous, my good sir,' he sighed. 'Try it once again.'

Standing alone in a corner of the big bay window, Erasmus observed this demonstration with wondering distaste. That a man should speak in his own voice one minute and someone else's the next, that he should slip so easily into mime and alien gesture, struck him as bordering on the obscene. There were other things too about the new director that he disliked, quite a number: the exaggerated cut of his coat, the tightness of his trousers, the rouge on his cheeks, the pimple painted black to make a beauty spot, the languid manner, the airs of a town man among provincials, the less than pristine cleanliness of the lace at his cuffs. But these were minor irritants, which under normal circumstances would have done no more than confirm Erasmus in his prejudices. What roused his rage was Adam's freedom with his hands. A man of the theatre to his fingertips, Charles Wolpert had called him. These, along with the fingers that went with them, were all too frequently laid on the persons of the female players – particularly Miranda's, or so it seemed to Erasmus. And – most distressing of all – Miranda showed little sign of resenting the freedom. She was there now, beautiful in pale blue taffeta, but she had no eyes for him – she was waiting for her scene.

'Exeunt Prospero and Caliban, shoo, shoo, off you go, don't overdo that over-the-shoulder snarling, Mr Parker, if you please. Caliban is daunted, he should cower more. Now we have the scene with the sisters. Come forward, Dorinda. Could I prevail upon you to abandon the window for a while, my dear young sir? They must look out that way while they talk of the ship. Thank you. Now, Dorinda.'

Dorinda was being played by the daughter of a neighbouring

squire. She was a rather heavy-faced girl but of good complexion, enhanced now by the excitement of performance. 'Oh, sister!' she exclaimed, moving towards Miranda with a rustle of skirts, 'what have I beheld?'

'What is it moves you so?' Miranda asked, and Erasmus felt his heart lurch at the sweet enquiry of her voice.

Dorinda gathered herself, gestured towards the window, took a breath and began:

> From yonder rock
> As I my eyes cast down upon the seas,
> The whistling winds blew rudely on my face,
> And the waves roared; at first I thought the war
> Had been between themselves, but strait I spy'd
> A huge great creature.

Miranda waited a moment or two then uttered the short line Erasmus knew she hated most in the play and found most difficult: 'Oh, you mean the ship.' It always sounded so flat, coming after Dorinda's vivacious description.

'Is't not a creature, then?' Dorinda widened her eyes. 'It seemed alive –'

'No, ladies, no.' Adams minced forward between them. 'I swear,' he said, 'one might suppose you were talking in your sleep. Rot me if I tell a lie, you will cease altogether from petrifaction if you do not impassion your good selves more. There is Mr Bulstrode who gallops too much and you two sisters who are far too stately, my dears.'

He took Dorinda by the hand and led her back into the centre of the room. 'Dorinda should look raptly towards the sea while she is making her speech. She has never beheld a ship before, she has no idea what it is. She is lost in amazement. On the word 'creature', Miranda counts three to herself, one-two-three, then turns. So.' Here he set a hand at either side of Miranda's waist and half turned her. '*You* know it is a ship, my dear, because Prospero has told you so. This is a little moment of triumph for you, and that is cosmic, is it not? It is a ludicrous descent from Dorinda's high-flown description. That is the way to save the line, point up the comedy of it.'

With rising fury Erasmus saw that Adams kept his hands on the slender stem of Miranda's waist for an appreciable time after she was in the right position and that he moved them just a fraction up and down. Her face looked absorbed but there was a small flame of consciousness in her cheeks.

'Of course,' Adams said to the cast at large, 'they are also talking about men. Neither of them has seen a man before, other than Prospero. Caliban does not count as a man, being a creature of a lower order.'

'I dispute that, sir,' the curate said.

'You may dispute it, sir, till you are blue in the face. If we go by the indications of the play, these two charmers have never clapped eyes on a man before, never flirted, never known the sweets of love. That is the brilliant new feature of the piece as Davenant has given it to us. He has taken the original, not generally regarded by our cognoscenti now as more than indifferent good, and he has brought it to the point of genius. By introducing a sister for Miranda and bringing in Hippolito as a counterpart to Ferdinand, he has given us two couples to play out the comedy instead of just one. So you get all the complications of jealousy among 'em.'

'All the complications of jealousy, aye, there it is,' Bulstrode repeated, nodding his head. He had become very sycophantic towards the director and often repeated his words. 'Twice two is four,' he said. 'They have doubled the comedy.'

'Egad!' Adams said. 'I have seen Mrs Belmont do Miranda to a miracle, that turn of the head and swirl of her skirts, you know, and that sly look at the audience. These two innocents know a deal more than they are supposed to; the thing is full of double meanings, it is all brilliantly paradoxical. It is a play exactly suited to the age, full of raillery and sensibility and refined manners. Mrs Belmont is shortly to appear in a trifle of mine.'

He had looked rather deeply into Miranda's eyes as he spoke of the play's ambiguities, or so at least the feverish Erasmus fancied. And not much later he was making remarks about Ferdinand that added insult to injury. 'Lord love me,' he said, 'you are supposed to be charmed by wandering airs, bemused

144

yes, bewildered perhaps, but not, my dear young friend, as if struck by a butcher's axe.'

As this was not said to him personally but in his character of Ferdinand, there was nothing Erasmus could reply, resent it as he may; and the words had a spiteful aptness that made several laugh, the tutor with sycophantic loudness. Miranda did not laugh, but she looked vexed, which Erasmus thought almost worse. Later, for no good reason that Erasmus could see, Adams placed a hand in the small of her back, in the elegant concavity just above her bustle, and kept it there for at least fifteen seconds while he spoke quite close to her ear.

It was at this moment that Erasmus, smarting with humiliation and furious with jealousy, formed his intention to depose Adams and ruin the proceedings. Though hardly at first so definite as this to his mind, he saw soon enough that the thing brooked no delay. He knew that he was living on borrowed time. From the first the director had regarded him as an unmitigated disaster in his role of Ferdinand. He now suspected that Adams had designs on Miranda. With both these factors combining, it was only a question of time before he was put out of the play altogether and someone else brought in to look into her eyes and declare his love. Perhaps even Adams himself...

The idea was intolerable. The very thought of it made him flush and clench his fists. He thought of sounding the rest of the cast for support, attempting to incite a mutiny among them; but he was not sure of finding immediate support and there was no time for persuasion even if his pride had allowed it. No, he would have to act alone.

Intimately joined with these thoughts was the pain of Miranda's complaisance. As the last days of June passed into the first of July and the open land around the town was deepened and made vivid by the colours of the young corn, he struggled to understand why she showed no repugnance, why her face had no shadow on it when that posturing jackanapes issued his vinous breath close beside her, made his insinuations, put his reprobate hands upon her...

Finally, in order to bind himself and guarantee success, he translated his intentions into a solemn vow. He had carried from childhood the belief that if one promises hard enough anything can be brought about. At home, in the silence of his room, in the midst of objects sanctified by familiarity – a pair of silver cockspurs, a framed embroidery of the Eighth Beatitude, done by his mother in blue and white, the silver-mounted duelling pistols that had been a present from his father, his washing basin and matching jug with the design of daisies – before these silent witnesses he uttered aloud his vow to put paid to the director, even if it meant wrecking the play.

After this, he felt, it could only be a matter of tactics.

TWENTY

At the beginning of July the ship came into hazy weather with light falls of rain in the night and a small northern swell. At sunrise on the morning of the second, Thurso took an observation of the amplitude and was surprised at the extent of the compass error – it was customary to allow no more than a half point of deviation in these waters. He began to suspect that he was on a course eastward of the Grand Canaries but found it difficult to believe that he could be so far out in his reckoning on a relatively short run and in this continual fine weather.

Some degree of uncertainty he was long accustomed to, navigation being a chancy business at this time. Latitude could be known with reasonable accuracy by measuring the height of the sun at noon; but to establish longitude Thurso had to depend for direction on his compass and for distance travelled on the log – a small board drawn astern by which the ship's speed could be measured. This was not an accurate instrument, allowance having always to be made for drifting to leeward and for the action of currents, so the reckoning was frequently wrong. It was seldom that the master of a ship at sea knew exactly where he was. But the error here was greater than usual. It began to seem to Thurso now that they had come between Madeira and Port Santo, though without seeing either. If that was so, he was a good fifty leagues eastward of his reckoning. The suspicion troubled Thurso and darkened his mood. He sat alone in his cabin with a bottle of brandy, brooding on the malignant current that had carried them thus far out, seeking to understand whence it had come and to guess what offence on the ship had set it in motion.

Another man flogged today, Paris was writing in his journal some hours later. *This for fouling his bedding after due warning by Haines, the boatswain, who I believe is generally hated. Thomas True, the man's name. He was given a dozen lashes by our accomplished captain and unlike Wilson cried out almost from the beginning. When it was over he was not able to stand unsupported. That such cruel punishment can overcome engrained habits of uncleanliness or perhaps symptoms of some deeper disorder of mind, I do not believe. Indeed, it seems too savage a question even to speculate upon; and it is one in any event I could not pursue with anyone on board the vessel, my position as an officer of the ship preventing frank speech among us.*

I went forward to do what I could for True's lacerations. I have also lately treated a member of the crew named Cavana for an inflamed condition of the eyelids which I suspect is venereal. I got it from True that he had come as a youth to Liverpool, to better his condition, as he says, after working from the age of ten in a stone quarry in north Wales. Having spent what money he had, he was given credit by a tavern-keeper and afterwards threatened with the magistrates unless he signed on for a slaver. He was also obliged, in the event of his death, to bequeath his wages for the trip to this same tavern-keeper.

Since then he has been on several slaveships. He says he would not choose a Guineaman, notwithstanding the higher wages – it appears the men get two shillings a month above the normal rate as an inducement. This does not seem much to me in view of the bad conditions on these ships and the dangers of disease on the Guinea Coast. But the fact is, they cannot choose. All these men are driven by the direst poverty. I do not think there is one of them who would not quit the sea tomorrow if they could, except perhaps Hughes, who is savagely misanthropic and seems happiest when up in the rigging alone. He too has been on slaveships before, or so I think. It seems to me there is a difference, in the aura they carry about them, between these men who have sailed on Guinea ships before and those who are new to it, however experienced they may be as seamen. I would be hard put to describe this difference; they are rough and reckless men almost all, yet I feel that it exists, and is indeed one of the elements determining the constitution of this floating commonwealth. Some are always alone, like Hughes and a man called Evans, who never speaks; but most have made alliances of one sort or another. The strong have their satellites who also have theirs, in a chain of being like the order of creation which we are told governs the universe. Haines has Libby for attendant and Libby a man named Tapley, a most unpleasant vicious fellow to all appearance, who in his turn lords it over poor Charlie, the cabin boy. At the apex there is Captain Thurso with Barton as his messenger and voice; and Thurso carries a passenger nobody sees but himself, a kind of divine supercargo who relays messages from some more abstract deity, some wielder of wind and current. I am growing convinced that

148

our captain interprets the universe as a system of signals addressed to himself, which is what many do who end in Bedlam; but he has this world of the ship to govern, he has people to judge and punish, he can force the shape of things to suit his sickness. How many of our governors and judges would end poor frothing Bedlamites without this resource, I wonder? And perhaps it is natural so to force the world, if one has the power to do so. We know so little of it in any case – we are so little skilled at reading the evidence. We see appearance only. Then, if we are in a dream, why not be our own interpreters, like Thurso, and turn madness to good account?

Paris paused, and laid down his pen. Perhaps it was wrong to think of systems, to seek coherent principle in this random human community of the ship. The words of his revered Maupertuis came back to him: *One constructs for oneself a satisfactory system only when one is ignorant of the characteristics of the phenomena to be explained* . . . What was one left with then but isolated phenomena, fast losing distinctness – the look in a man's eyes, the start of blood on the pale skin, the patter of drops on the deck. So to what end do I pass distractedly from observation to speculation to some wild call to take on sufferings not my own? I have enough with my own. As if in the duress of a dream it came to him again: *my blood, my pain.* And now, clamouring for inclusion, there was Thomas True, who soiled his bedding and was flogged for it, and Cavana, with his confiding air and the putrid discharge of his eyes . . .

It was with a sense of fleeing that he rose, passed out of his cramped cabin and mounted until he could see the rail of the quarterdeck and the dark figure of the helmsman beyond and a scattering of stars. He became aware again of the ploughing ship, the endless complaint of the timbers. With this the familiar sense of unreality descended on him; he was adrift among strangers, set on no purpose that he could call his own. And yet they were not strangers, like him they were captives here; fellow-captives can never be strangers though one knows nothing of them but this – it was one of the lessons of his prison days.

As he stood there he heard eight bells sounding, signalling the end of the watch. Mounting to the deck, he saw a figure he thought was Barton come down the ladder and disappear below. Two or three men stood talking in low tones at the forecastle, having just come off the watch. It was time for him to present himself in the small stateroom adjoining the captain's cabin where, in company with Barton and Thurso when the business of the ship allowed it, he was accustomed to take his evening meal.

He found the two men at table already, presenting the attitudes that in the course of these weeks at sea had come to seem heraldic to Paris, the one heavy-set and fearsomely immobile, with a face the colour of dark brick and eyes that looked always furious at not being able to burrow further in; the other servile, watchful and jaunty, with a habit of raising his narrow face as if sniffing.

'Well, sir,' Thurso said, 'I believe you have had a busy day.'

Paris saw a faint grin come to Barton's face, just enough to show the edges of his sharp upper teeth. It was a regular joke with both captain and mate that his days were not much occupied; but in this present remark he thought there was a hint at his ministrations to the man who had been flogged. 'I do what comes in my way,' he said.

'Aye, do you? More will come in your way yet.'

Paris made no immediate reply to this and so was saved from having to reply at all, as Charlie entered at this moment with a tray from the galley. Morgan had that day killed one of the pullets they had brought on board with them and boiled it with onions and black pepper – his invariable way with a winged creature. It lay glistening on its platter now, flanked by a mash of turnip and potato and a jug of oily gravy of Morgan's own devising. Charlie, who had been promised some of the soup, was bearing himself – and the food – with some ceremony until Thurso growled at him to look sharp, which put him in such sudden fear that he set the tray down too hard and spilled a little of the gravy, for which he was sworn at by Barton and threatened with a caning.

'Aye, aye, the boy is a born fool, let him go,' Thurso said with surprising mildness. 'Mr Barton, be good enough to carve the bird for us.'

'Why the fatted calf?' Paris asked, risking a note of levity; he knew the captain's moods by this time and sensed an air almost of jocularity about him, though the small eyes still ranged over objects as if searching for the cause of what made them less than satisfactory. 'Is there something to celebrate?' he said.

The mate, having carved and served with remarkable dexterity, had a mouth now bulging with chicken and mash, and a fork freighted with more of it already moving upward – he was a neat and voracious eater.

'Explain the situation, Mr Barton,' Thurso said, in his hoarse monotone.

Barton lowered his fork with visible reluctance. 'This will be our last evening for supper in here till we have our full copplement of quashees an' are under way for Jamaica. We are to have the samples hoisted in here tomorrow an' laid out.'

'Samples?' Paris had still not understood.

'Stock the place out,' Barton said indistinctly – he had resumed eating while Paris hesitated.

'We are approaching Africa, Mr Paris,' Thurso said. 'Within ten days or so I expect to be sighting Sierra Leone. This room will be our showplace, our shop, sir. The caboceers who come aboard with slaves for sale will be able to see a selection of our goods. It is important they get a fair view of what we are carrying. The negro is appealed to through his eyes, Mr Paris. I know these people. I was dealing for slaves before you were born.'

'Their eye is caught by shine an' shimmer,' Barton said, pausing to wipe his mouth with the back of his hand. 'Bright colours is what they likes, an' jewelly, glittery things. It is no use in the world to explain or describe anythink to them – they have no patience to listen, they cannot hold it in their minds.'

'Perhaps it is that they don't believe us,' Paris said, and was surprised to see a sudden gleam of humour come to the mate's face.

'Not believe us?' Thurso said. The idea seemed completely new to him. 'I am known on that coast,' he added after a moment.

'Bigob, sir, I believe you are,' Barton said. 'So the captain thought,' he added, turning to Paris, 'since this is our last occasion here for a good bit, we had better have one of the fowl. An' a very good thought, say I.'

Thurso turned his head slowly. 'My thoughts are not in your province, Mr Barton. Good or bad, they are beyond your ken.'

'Aye-aye, sir.' The mate looked aside with his accustomed expression of wariness. He did not, however, seem particularly chastened by the rebuke, though he had fallen silent.

'So they come out to the ship, then?' Paris asked. 'Those selling slaves, I mean. We do not go into harbour?' But he saw instantly that he had once again given occasion for the conspiracy of contempt Thurso had such relish for, saw it in the way the captain leaned stiffly forward in his chair and glanced to include the mate.

'Harbour?' Thurso said. 'Off the coast of Sierra Leone? Where is your geography?'

'Haw, that's a good 'un,' Barton said, permitting himself a subservient echo. 'Show me a blessed harbour there, I would like to see one.'

'We may get through the surf with the longboat to trade downriver,' Thurso said, 'but we cannot stand inshore, not in those seas, Mr Paris. You are talking about the Windward Coast of Africa.'

'I see, yes,' Paris said. 'My ideas of the coast are vague, I will admit.' He looked from the one to the other. They were united now in knowledge, but he sensed an understanding between them much older. They had known each other before this voyage, his uncle had said so. Thurso had asked for Barton as his mate. Something there was between them, though friendship it could hardly be called. It seemed more in the nature of a shared secret . . .

'You and Mr Barton have sailed together before, I believe, sir?' he said. He saw the look of satisfaction disappear from the captain's face and his brows draw together suddenly.

'Sailed together?' Thurso looked at the man before him, noting again the big, slightly awkward frame, the deeply marked face, touched by the sun now, showing the paleness of the eyes by contrast. These eyes were regarding him steadily and they did not turn away from his frown. He was being stared at aboard his own ship and with eyes that contained some impertinent, some hateful quality of perception, of understanding. He caught sight of Barton nodding and turned his rage that way. 'Damn you, do you sit there agreeing against me? I sail together with nobody.' He turned his eyes back to Paris and said less violently, 'The captain sails together with nobody. Mr Barton has been my first officer on a previous voyage, so much is true. You have a lot to learn, Mr Paris.'

'I know it, sir, and I am doing my best,' Paris said.

'I fancy you will understand things a deal better when we have slaves aboard. At present you think yourself superior to the business, I can tell. You are one of those who despise the money that is made from it. But mark my words, sir, you will go with a whip in your hand and a pistol in your belt like every other man aboard. Depend upon it, the keeper will very quickly decide which side of the cage he is on.'

'Will he so?' Paris spoke without pause for reflection, impelled by pride and a passionate sense of opposition. 'You are admirably clear in your mind, if I may say so, as to who is caged and who is free. I know something of the matter, having seen both sides, but still cannot always see the difference.'

'Both sides?' Thurso's voice had no register for feeling; it came as hoarse and uninflected as ever; but his eyes were fastened on the surgeon's face. 'How do you intend that remark?'

Not caution but enmity restrained Paris now. He was silent for some moments then said more calmly, 'There are many would think the keeper is behind bars too, sir, for all his pistol and his whip.'

Thurso compressed his lips and looked aside. It was clear that he regarded this as not worth answering. Delivered now from the rage that had possessed him, he maintained an unbroken silence for the rest of the meal and Barton, out of prudence or inclination, followed suit, though Paris felt the mate's eyes on him from time to time.

He was relieved when he was able to get to his feet and bid the others goodnight. Somewhat to his surprise Barton rose with him and the two men left together. Up on deck they stood for a while at the stern. The moon had risen and stood clear of the sea to eastward in faint wreaths of cloud.

Barton seemed disposed to linger. He took a short-stemmed clay pipe from his pocket. 'Fair weather,' he said, nodding towards the faint track of moonlight on the dark sea. 'When the clouds look singed-like round a low moon I allus find it follers with good weather. I don't know why it is, but I have allus found it so.'

'Well, I hope it proves so this time again,' Paris said.

There was silence between them for some moments, then Barton said in accents of sympathy, 'By God, he is a tartar, though, our captain. The way he shot up at you tonight! An' you give him no cause. He has done the same with me, many's the time, but you are a man of learnin' an' scallership, so you are bound to feel it more.'

'I did not mind so very much.' Paris spoke coolly, warned by Barton's flattering tone. He knew the mate for a cunning fellow and in a way dispassionate – a dangerous combination. He said, 'He seemed in good enough spirits to begin with. Something in my question annoyed him.'

Barton puffed at his pipe in silence for some moments, looking down at the track of the moon, which was broader and brighter now. 'It was not in the question,' he said. 'It was in the way you looked at him. Captain Thurso does not like to be looked at. He sets himself above it, if you get my meanin'. But 'tis all bound up with the ship. He was put out of temper by our bein' so far eastward of the reckonin', which as we have had fair winds and weather, must be owin' to a demon of a current settin' to eastward, an' out of all nature strong, sir, it cannot be supposed less than twenty mile per diem from the time we passed the parallel of Cape St Vincent. That is what put him out, Mr Paris. Men like you and me, we take a broad view. Rain or shine, what's the difference?' Barton paused, raising his face and smiling. The moon was clear of the cloud now, less blanched, more radiant. Light from it fell on the mate's face. 'What is a current?' he said. 'It is just a settin' of the water. It is like anythin' else in this world, tempery. Everythin' is tempery in this world, whether it is the toothache or the love of wimmin. But he takes it all personal. Now we have had a sightin' of Tenerife to the west of us, so we knows where we are again.'

154

'Well, it is strange,' Paris said. 'We can observe the movements of the heavenly bodies, we can chart the course of the planets, but not that of our own ship in a little stretch of water.'

'By God, that is true.' Barton spat over the rail and laughed with apparent delight. 'It never come to me in quite that way before,' he exclaimed. 'That is wit, that is what it means to be a man of education. But you have been in the school of life too, haven't you, Mr Paris? You have seen both sides of the cage.'

Paris remained silent for a short while, looking out to sea. The African coast lay somewhere to the east of them, in the direction of the moon – it seemed to him now that the ship was keeping to the broad track of moonlight. The sails were blanched. He made out a dark figure sitting alone in the cross-timbers of the mainmast and wondered if it were Hughes, who often sat there at night. He sensed the attentiveness of the man waiting beside him. The mate's question had come concealed in praise. Barton had a nose for weakness, for the festerings of spirit; and he was subtle enough to know that dislike is no impediment to confidences, that men of a certain cast of mind will confide even where they distrust, because not to do so shows fear or shame.

'Them was your words, I think,' the mate said softly.

'Yes,' Paris said, 'a physician sees a good deal of life, you know.'

He saw Barton relax his shoulders as if in some release of tension. The mate paused a moment, then said in a different tone, 'All the same, he was right, the captain was right.'

'In what way?'

'There is nothin' like fear for keeping men together. Nothin' else will do it, not on a slaveship. It is one of the chief snags of the trade that the merchandise has a tendency to rise on you. You wait till we have got upwards of two hundred negroes chained between decks, all of 'em ready to dash your brains out if they gets a chance, an' twenty men to guard 'em, feed 'em, wash 'em down, exercise 'em up on deck. By God, Mr Paris, then you will see what fear can do to a man of learnin' an' scallership. It will bring him down to the level of the lowest scum aboard what can't write his own name.'

155

Barton's pipe was finished. With a gesture curiously dandified he took a silver thimble from his waistcoat pocket, fitted it on his little finger and pressed out the last spark in the bowl. The tone of these last words had been hostile – perhaps through disappointment at his failure to draw Paris out; but he now raised his face again in the peering way characteristic of him, almost benevolent-seeming. Moonlight caught the thimble in a running gleam as he returned it to his pocket. 'Yes,' he said, 'you will know which side you are on, whatever you meant in there. You will live in fear like the rest.' He nodded, still smiling, and turned to go below. 'It smells of hexcrement,' he said. 'You will get to know the smell, because them two hundred or so blacks will be shittin' in fear too.'

Paris stayed alone on deck some minutes longer, then returned to his cabin. He was too disturbed in mind to think immediately of sleeping. It seemed to him that he had grown more impressionable in these last weeks, more easily affected by what he felt emanating from others. He looked more closely and saw more – not by conscious intention but somehow helplessly. Increasingly of late he had felt drawn into conflict with Thurso, a struggle too mortal for their short acquaintance: it was as if they had recognized each other as heirs to some ancient feud. Just now, on deck, Barton's rhetoric had oppressed him, and the moral vacancy he felt behind it. The mate had a sort of degraded subtlety about him, a scavenger's instinct for scents of weakness. And Paris felt himself that it was a weakness, this vulnerability to impression, this too-strong sense of other human beings – almost like a failure of manhood. He blamed it on his isolation. In the removal of all that was customary in his life, some customary skin of protection also had gone, it seemed.

He found solace for the spirit now in *De Motu Cordis*. The Latin text acted on him these days with the power of incantation. He had earlier been labouring to do justice to Harvey's paean to the heart's pre-eminence towards the end of chapter eight: *Just as the sun deserves to be called the heart of the world, so is the heart the sun of the microcosm and the first principle of life, whose virtue quickens the blood and keeps it free from all taint of corruption . . .*

It was not, he reflected, that the analogy was original; the

156

notion of the heart as the sun of man's being was an ancient one, deriving from Aristotle; but if you are about to demonstrate, for the first time, the difference between veins and arteries and explain how the blood is transferred from the *vena cava* to all parts of the body, you may be allowed to borrow your comparisons at least. There were other great men, of course, who didn't. Paris thought while preparing for bed of Newton and that confession of ignorance in which he compares himself to a small boy playing with pebbles by the shore of a great unknown sea.

This led him, by a leap he did not pause to examine, to thoughts of his cousin Erasmus and that lonely struggle of the eight-year-old boy to make the elements conform to his will. Memory of it came first in a wide perspective – the empty beach, the grey sea, the small, intent figure. Then, in one of those swooping approaches sometimes experienced in dreams, he drew near, saw the white face, the bloodied fingers . . . There was nothing in common here with Newton's image of human limitation. Erasmus had wanted to subdue the world. Paris recalled what Barton had said of Thurso a short while ago: *he takes it all personal.* But that staring child had no world to command, no ship, no community of men to wrench to the shape of his obsession.

Perhaps because of his quickened thoughts, sleep did not come to him, despite the cradling motion of the vessel. He lay staring up through a darkness so profound that it cancelled all sense of confine; the deck above him was no nearer than the spaces of the sky beyond and the planets in their obedient courses. Docile these too, he thought, as subject to law as the motions of my heart, the flight and homing of the blood. Even in its rages nature was always captive. Man too, led in shackles from the womb. Death is a corruption which befalls by defect of heat, so Harvey defined it. Between the warm and the cold the body flushes a certain number of times. Ruth's body corrupted by defect of heat prematurely. Again he was harrowed by the thought that it was the unborn child that had nourished the mother.

In prison I was subject also to defect of heat, he thought,

remembering the stone floor, the bare walls. At this interval of time Norwich Jail had assumed the shape of a pit in his mind, with descending levels of damnation. At the lowest level were those who had no money at all and small means of obtaining any. He had been one week here, on the orders of the outraged cleric who owned the prison, as punishment for printing seditious views concerning God's creation. Here men and women fought with rats in damp cellars for scraps of food thrown down to them through a trap-door, and huddled together for warmth upon heaps of filthy rags and bundles of rotten straw. Lunatics stumbled about here, women gave birth, people died of fever or starvation.

These were people yielding no profit. Higher in the scale were those who could pay for food and a private room and it was here that Paris, until redeemed by his uncle, had found lodging. Two shillings a week had provided him also with writing materials and given him access to the prisoners' common-room, where there were newspapers, and a fire in the coldest weather; but it had not been enough to free him from the stench of the place, nor the brutalities of some of his fellow-inmates – thieves and pimps mingled with debtors here. Higher yet, serenely above all this and freed from unpleasant associations, were the rich prisoners, who lived as the bishop's guests and entertained on a lavish scale.

Norwich Jail had given Paris his notion of hell, and its workings afforded an example of docility to law every bit as absolute as the motions of the blood postulated by Harvey. Money regulated every smallest detail of the place, from the paupers in the cellars to the profligate feasters above. All rents went to the bishop, who had spent a thousand pounds to acquire the prison and was laudably set on making his investment as profitable as possible, this being a time when the individual pursuit of wealth was regarded as inherently virtuous, on the grounds that it increased the wealth and well-being of the community. Indeed, this process of enrichment was generally referred to as 'wealth-creation' by the theorists of the day. The spread of benefits was not apparent in the prison itself, owing to the special circumstances there and particularly to the very high death-rate.

158

The keepers at their lower level sought to emulate the governor, pursuing wealth diligently through the sale of spirits, the purveying of harlots and the extortionate charges to visitors. The visits had been an ordeal for Ruth, he remembered now. She was prone to nausea in the first period of the pregnancy and the smell of the place had sickened her. She came with a handkerchief soaked in vinegar and held it from time to time to her nostrils. He remembered her face on the last of these visits, angry and distressed: she had been searched and subjected to indignities by the foul-mouthed viragos in the prison lodge on the pretext she was a whore, and robbed by them of a scarf. He had told her to keep up her courage, told her he would be free soon.

Wide-eyed in the darkness, he saw, or feared to see, the distress on Ruth's face turn to reproach. He sought for a shield and found one in the absurd and terrified appearance of a young debtor called Deever whose head had been thrust through the legs of a chair by his fellow-inmates of the common-room for his inability to pay chummage – the obligation to buy spirits for the company that was laid on all new arrivals. In this place of misery and shame, they aped the manners and adopted the ritual of those who had condemned them. Witnesses were sworn with due ceremony, counsel made their pleas on one side and the other. A burly thief with a towel tied up in knots in imitation of the judge's wig solemnly pronounced the sentence . . . It was Deever's face that Paris saw now as a refuge from Ruth's, ashamed and fearful, looking from his cage at the tormentors who were his fellow-prisoners too . . .

So he lay sleepless, trying out versions of the past that might be tolerable to his imagination, while the deck above him lay awash with moonlight and the ship made steady way with all sails set and a following sea. In this warmer weather some of the crew found sleeping space on the deck. Calley, huddled in his blanket amidships, groaned in his sleep, beset by horrors. He started up at last, to stare affrighted across the moonlit deck, his face dewed with sweat. He had woken Deakin, who hissed at him, but Calley was still in the toils of nightmare and could not properly hear.

159

'What is wrong with you?' Deakin asked. 'Why don't you sleep and give us some peace? There, get under your blanket.'

'It came out my mouth,' Calley said. He was shivering. 'Comin' out an' never stop.'

'What are you talking about?'

'This white worm come out my mouth.'

'What worm?'

'Africa worm. Long white un'. You swallers it in the water; you can't see it when you drinks, it is too little. It gets bigger in your stomick an' it fills up with eggs an' it comes out to lay the eggs in the water. It can come out anywhere, it can come out your nose, it can come out your belly-button.'

'Who told you that?'

'They tol' me.' Calley never mentioned names. His eyes started round the deck. 'It knows when you go near the water,' he said with wonder – he was calmer now. 'One come out his eye, that's why he only got one eye. It can come out your ear, it can –'

'Keep your voice down,' Deakin said. 'You ought to have more sense, Dan'l. They were only trying to frighten you with them stories. You don't drink standing water anywhere in those parts where we are going. You stick by me, you won't get no worms.' He looked across the deck for some moments in silence. Then he said, 'We will run, Dan'l. You and me. First chance we get. We will get clear of this ship.' He had never included anyone else in his plans before. Since the day of his quarrel with Libby he had known that he would have to run. No ship ever left harbour with a crew that could all be trusted. Haines or Libby or someone else would turn him in for the bounty as soon as they came up with a navy ship. Or the captain would hand him over in the West Indies to save wages on the voyage home. Once they had unloaded the negroes there would be no need for so many men. There might be a naval frigate at anchor in Kingston harbour. In any case, he could not wait to find out. For desertion he could expect two hundred lashes and he did not believe he could survive so many. He would rather take his chance ashore. 'When we get the chance,' he said. 'When we get to Africa, you and me will run. But you must keep mum about it.'

'It can come out your arse,' Calley said. Fear had receded now but he was unwilling to part with the horror of the worm altogether. 'It can come out your nose,' he whispered, round-eyed in the moonlight.

'Leave off that tack, will you? You and me will run. We will wait for our chance. Don't you talk about this to anybody.'

'Will we get some o' them black cunnies?'

'You'll get nothing if you blab. You will get a flogging. Do you hear me, Dan'l?' As always he saw himself breaking through. But this time not alone. There would be a place, dark among trees, where they could hide until all search was over. This would part like a screen and they would pass into the open, into light ... 'I will look after you,' he said. 'But you will get nothing if you blab. You will get a flogging.'

'I won't blab,' Calley said. He struggled for a moment with the idea of it. 'What will we do there?'

'Do? We will get into trade, we will set up for ourselves.' He did not care, really, he was occupied only with thoughts of parting the screen, stepping through into the open, taking possession of the space. He spoke in whispers to the round-eyed Calley. There was a trade in ivory and camwood and gold dust. With money they could take passage from Sierra Leone to Georgia or Carolina ...

His whispers went on, lulling Calley to sleep again, becoming briefly part of the life of the ship, the play of shadows over the decks, the slow creak of the boom, the faint language of the canvas and ropes. To these sounds the captain, released for a while from his demon, slept in his cabin; Hughes the climber slept wrapped in his blanket in the fore topmast staysail and Thomas True in his hammock in the forecastle, lying face down to save his torn back. Sullivan dozed under the punt and was discovered and kicked awake by the second mate, whose watch it was. Wilson, ordered forward on lookout, set his saturnine face to the glimmering horizon and thought of ways of broaching the rum in the storeroom. In the darkness between decks Evans and Johnson found each other.

The moon rode clear in the sky now and the ship's sails were the colour of bleached bone. Moonlight, falling through this high pyramid of sail, made of the deck another sea, with a trailing, glinting weed of rat-line and shroud, and shoals of moonbeams flickering across her as the ship rose and fell. The real sea was unbroken, luminous to the horizon. With the utmost regularity, like a sleeper breathing in the deepest vale of sleep, the *Liverpool Merchant* dipped into her moonlit reflection and rose and dipped again, as if she could never have enough of her own image, the curving headrails, the full cheeks of the bows, the bosomy wraith of the Duchess of Devonshire yearning up to meet her and endlessly falling away.

PART FOUR

TWENTY-ONE

From where Erasmus was standing he had a view across to the open farmland rising beyond Wolpert's estate. The day was slightly fluffed with mist and in this moister air colours were deepened, the distant corn fields flat jade, the hedges of the beech walk, from which the director would shortly emerge, soft emerald. Somewhere nearby a chaffinch was singing. Though waiting here in ambush, Erasmus felt a little drowsy.

There are moments in anyone's life when some blend of circumstances, some consonance of surroundings and situation and character, show him in a light peculiarly characteristic, make him seem more intensely himself – to the observer, that is: the subject will not be aware of it. He seems to us then to be immobilized, taken out of time – or he steps, rather, into some much older story. So the blind mulatto, sitting among shadows, talking of paradise. So – to take an example among many – the first mate, Barton, extracting from a waistcoat pocket his dainty thimble, standing on the moonlit deck, explaining the nature of fear to Matthew Paris. So Erasmus waiting there, near the beginning of the alley that goes down between tall hedges of beech, waiting for the rival he has fashioned for himself to give grievance to his love. He is there imperishably, wild with his jealousy, vague with the peace of the day. He is always, always to be found there.

He had watched Adams go up to the house for his snatch of repose, as the director was accustomed to term it; Madeira and biscuits were set out for him in a small room adjoining the library. He would return by the same path, ever more offensively free in his manners, or so Erasmus considered. He knew now that this confrontation was the only way. There had been no time for manoeuvring. He was convinced that Adams was plotting to expel him from the cast and bring in another Ferdinand to take his place and usurp his love. I had rather force it to a fight, he thought. I would kill him rather. With this he came awake, experienced an increase of purpose. But the readiness to shed the director's blood was not new – it had been there already, implicit in his vow.

He saw Adams, in his pale blue coat, descend the steps from the terrace, cross the short lawn below and disappear between the hedgerows. He waited where he was for a minute or two longer, then took the few paces that brought him within the line of the alley. The other was approaching, the sunlight twinkling on his silver buttons. He was not more than thirty yards off. There was no way now that a meeting could be avoided, short of one of them turning abruptly about and retreating in the opposite direction.

Adams's face showed small pleasure at the prospect of the encounter. On Erasmus, watching the director approach, waiting these final moments before speaking, the white gravel of the walk, the clipped green walls of the hedges, made an impression of neatness and order almost dizzying.

'A word with you, sir, if you will be so good.' He encountered the insolently languishing dark eyes. This was perhaps the first time he had seen the director's face completely in repose, the first time certainly they had spoken together outside of the rehearsals.

'Your servant, sir,' the director said. 'I am awaited, as you know.'

'It will not take long.' He paused still, however, seeking to control his breathing. Adams's face at close range and in the intimacy of this narrow space had brought back with a rush all his detestation, which for a while had been submerged in the business of contriving the encounter. This suddenly renewed sense of the other man's physical being, the eyes, the pimple converted into a beauty spot, the smell of attar of roses and ingested wine, confirmed, touch by touch, lechery, treachery, all sins.

'Well, what is it?' Adams was impatient. It was hot there, in the enclosure of the hedges. 'You might do better to be practising your lines. You have some way to go, sir, yet, before you can be deemed proficient in them.'

'These lines I have rehearsed,' Erasmus said, and even smiled a little. 'I am perfect in them.'

Adams failed altogether to catch the emphasis of these words or hear the faint tremor of control underlying them. He was not a man who noticed others much, unless it was in the way of business. Moreover he was at present rendered somewhat distrait with wine, as he might himself have put it. He had observed the unnatural straightness and stiffness of Erasmus's posture and the fixity of his regard; but these he was familiar with already, they were characteristic of the young man in his role of Ferdinand, mere aspects, to the director, of Erasmus's general uncouthness and lack of talent as an actor. 'Well, I am glad of it,' he said. 'Is that what you waited here to tell me? But there is more to it than being able to recite your lines. There is the whole management of your movement on stage. There is the language of the body. This is between ourselves, my young sir, but I swear I never saw an actor so block-like in performance, so little in command of himself, and by God I have seen some inept performers in my time. It is not a matter of the state you are in beforehand. There is Mr Keith, presently at the Queen's Theatre – he was recently in a trifle of my own – you will not get him to go on at all without a pint of Burgundy inside him, but an immaculate performance, sir, immaculate. Why, I remember Mrs Bellamy, she would shake all over with nerves like a damn jelly but cool as ice the moment she was on the boards. Dead now, alas, a great loss to the stage. But you, sir, if you will forgive me, you are a well-fashioned fellow and you have a good face, but you might as well be made of wood. You can't walk on with any grace, you don't know what to do with your hands, you don't know which way to look. Tell me, have you not thought of resigning from the play?'

'I may not know what to do with my hands as Ferdinand, but I shall know well enough what to do with them as Erasmus Kemp, if you cannot learn to keep your own hands to yourself.'

This, now that he had finally come out with it, he felt to be well phrased; and the feeling did something to lessen his fury at the director's humiliating criticisms.

'I beg your pardon?' For a moment or two Adams was slack-jawed with astonishment. Then he drew himself up. 'Here are rustic manners indeed,' he said. 'We have awaked the boorish Daphnis, have we?'

'You will know what you have awaked, sir, if you persist in your insolent freedoms with these ladies.' Erasmus, who had not understood the reference to Daphnis, felt his rage begin to rise again. 'I will make you know it,' he said.

For the first time Adams looked directly into the younger man's face, something that disdain had hitherto prevented. His own face had whitened, but his voice was firm enough. 'It is not the ladies you are concerned for,' he said after a moment. 'It is the pretty one, Wolpert's sister. Did she ask you to speak on her behalf? No, I thought not. Are you affianced? No again. Well, sir, in that case it is for the lady herself to make her wishes plain. She has not protested to me.' Adams made the mistake now of permitting himself a certain kind of smile. 'Quite the contrary,' he said.

Erasmus took a pace forward and his hand went to the hilt of his sword. 'You beastly popinjay and sponger,' he said. 'If you touch her again, I will kill you.' His throat was dry and his voice sounded remote and strange to him.

Adams stepped hastily back, the rouge on his cheeks standing out in irregular patches against the pale skin. 'Do you offer to murder me?' he said. 'For the sake of touches in a rehearsal, where such things mean nothing at all, things I have hardly noticed and can scarcely remember and she no doubt even less? You are mad. Stand away from me. I am not wearing a sword.'

'You will have one in the house. I will wait for you here.'

'Fight without witnesses and risk a capital charge? You are out of your senses. Stand out of my way, I wish to pass.'

'I will wait to hear from you,' Erasmus said, and stood aside at last to let the other pass.

He watched the thin-legged, agitated figure of the director recede, disappear finally. The tumult of his heart quietened slowly, but this brought him no peace. Adams had not behaved as expected. It was not so much that he had shown no smallest trace of guilt or defensiveness; in such a reprobate this was hardly surprising. But he had been taken aback, he had been astonished as well as indignant. Of course, the fellow was an actor . . .

At the moment that the son was threatening a fellow-being's life on grounds that to anyone else might have seemed flimsy, a report on the father's financial affairs, provided by the indefatigible Partridge, was being digested by old Wolpert in his place of business on the waterfront.

'Time and money, sir,' the scrawny, sharp-eyed lawyer had said, in the course of collecting the balance of his fee. 'It generally comes down to that. The right relations between 'em is as important for the man of business as winds and tides for the mariner. And of the two it is the time that matters most. A man is rich so long as his creditors are patient.'

It was surprising what Partridge, by means of innumerable small and grubby enquiries, had been able to find out. Much of it came as no surprise. Kemp, in company with others that Wolpert knew of in the cotton trade, had suffered heavy losses in the disruption occasioned by the recent wars with France. On the ceasing of hostilities he had, again like others, imported quantities of raw cotton on credit in anticipation of a boom in prices which had yet to materialize. Some of this he had sold at a loss to meet short-term bills; much of it clotted his warehouses still. The Manchester dealers with whom he had been accustomed to do a large part of his business relied on resale to the manufacturers within a few days of purchase; their profit margins were too low for them to buy at prices over the market. In this pass, Kemp had turned to printed cottons, entering into partnership with the textile firm of Barfield Brothers. For a while, according to Partridge's informants in Lancaster, they had done well; but printed cottons of Indian manufacture, transported in bulk in the huge East Indiamen, were daily increasing their share of the African and South American trade.

'Unfair foreign competition, sir, as any true patriot would

169

agree,' Partridge said. 'These confounded Indian cottons are not only superior in the quality of their dyes but they come cheaper on the market.'

It seemed that Kemp had also laid out money to finance a dyeworks in Warrington, in an attempt to find faster dyes. It was Partridge's general view, expressed in spidery writing and with all his customary discretion of phrase, that Kemp's resources were stretched, perhaps dangerously, but that he might have private means (outside the scope of the present enquiry though open to investigation at a renewed fee if required), which might be enough to carry him through to the upturn in the cotton trade confidently expected on all sides.

Wolpert mused on this awhile. He saw in it no great cause for alarm, certainly no grounds for suspicion. If Kemp could wait, he might do very well. Legislation was under way to impose tariffs on Indian cottons and protect the home industry. The bill might be delayed – there were powerful interests opposed to it; but it would go through. Newcastle was for it and he would play the patriotic card in the House. With Indian competition choked off, there would be big profits for local dealers. Kemp might be short of ready money. He had built and outfitted the *Liverpool Merchant* on notes of hand at eighteen months' date, through merchant houses in Warrington and Preston – a total of some twelve thousand pounds by Partridge's computation. But this was common practice, especially in slaving enterprises; even banks were ready to offer credit to slavers these days, for the sake of the high interest.

It was a kind of investment that made no appeal to the cautious Wolpert. He sometimes made use of ships returning from the West Indies to carry his freight, but trading in slaves was too risky. Rewards were high, of course, on a prosperous voyage; Kemp stood to recover his twelve thousand and make as much again in net profit – and that within the year.

It came to him now that he knew very little about Kemp, though they had been acquainted for more than twenty years. A good man in company, fond of a glass, shrewd enough to all appearance, though too flamboyant and hasty for some, with those flushed good looks and that habit of eager gesture. Something extreme in him, a tendency to excess. In the son it was more pronounced, almost fanatical. The merchant still remembered the young man's statement of love and intention – he had thought it enough to make his wishes plain – and the blaze of his eyes on being rebuffed. Too much pride there, not enough sense of other people. But that would be supplied by commercial dealing, the best school there was for a study of human nature, so Wolpert thought. Erasmus would not make such a bad son-in-law, if it came to it. He had energy and determination, more of both than his own son. Charles had a good manner and a proper sense of occasion, but he showed small aptitude for decision. He was obstinate though, which was something different. Wolpert sighed. The boy could not be budged on the matter of this actor fellow who was badgering the maids, drinking his way through the wine-cellar and wearying his host each supper-time with chatter about the theatre. I would give something to be rid of that fellow, Wolpert thought. He couldn't himself say much because he had discovered that the whole thing was in honour of his sixtieth birthday, due the following month . . .

TWENTY-TWO

The *Liverpool Merchant* had crossed the latitude of Capo Blanco and was making steady way south-westward towards the Cape Verde Islands. As the air grew more languid, preparations for accommodating the negroes grew the more brisk. Men were set to work splicing the hawsers for a long anchorage and serving the ropes of the longboat; the hold was rummaged to make space between decks; the open woodwork of cross-battens and ledges that formed the covers of the hatchways had to be raised so as to give more light and air to the lower decks. The carpenter's name was Barber and he had picked out Blair and Sullivan to help him with the gratings; it was customary now to employ these two together.

'Well,' Sullivan said, squatting to raise the framework on the starboard side, 'a good deed lights a candle, as me sainted mother used to say, an' God will spy it shinin'.'

'I thowt you'd given God his last chance the day they pressed you on to this here ship,' Billy Blair said. 'Lift yor bleddy end a bit, will you? I never seen anyone like you for husbandin' his strength. What good deed are you talkin' aboot?'

'By raisin' up these hatches we are deliverin' parcels of light an' air to the heathen below an' sweetenin' their passage. Some of thim fellers, a certain proportion of thim black fellers, will live to cut the sugar because of what we are after doin' now. Isn't that right, Mr Barber?'

The carpenter, a morose, squat, long-armed man, said, 'If talkin' was rated high, you would be Admiral of the Fleet by this time, Sullivan, instead of a ordinary seaman. We'll have to take this right off altogether, so I can put a trim on it.'

172

'You are wrong anyway,' Billy said. 'As bleddy usual. We are just doin' what we was told to do. If they had said to lower the gratin's an' leave the beggars in the dark, we would ha' done it just the same.'

Sullivan glanced up at the bright sky as if for patience. His hair had grown again after that drastic cropping. It stood up from his head in a thick, black, softly bristling mat. His long-jawed face had darkened with the sun, making the eyes seem more bemused than ever, straying after some vision just lost. 'In that case,' he said, 'since it would be a wilful act an' contrary to practice an' with no grounds in reason or law, it would be a dastardly bad deed an' ould Nick would make a note of it.'

At this flagrant illogicality Billy felt the onset of a familiar baffled fury. 'I dunno how it is,' he said, doing his best to disguise this while at the same time holding up his end of the grating, 'but any attempt at conversin' with you gets a man in a deadlock in no time.'

'It is you, Billy,' Sullivan said mildly. 'I niver arrive in dead-locks with nobody else.'

'Listen to me, for Christ's sake.' Billy shifted on his haunches and spat over the rail. 'If it is a good deed to raise the gratin's on these hatches,' he began slowly and laboriously, 'what are we doin' puttin' the quashees down there in the first place? Them fellers gets light an' air enough in the forests where they are.'

'This is commerce we are talkin' of now,' Sullivan said. 'It comes under a different headin' intirely.'

Billy felt the heat rise to his head. 'Now just a bleddy minute –'

'You are both of you iggerant beggars,' the carpenter said. 'You ain't been on a slaver before, have you?'

Sullivan assumed a smile of patent falseness. 'No, Mr Barber, we have not,' he said. 'But we are dyin' to learn, ain't we, Billy? I was just sayin' the other day, I think it was to Dan'l Calley, who you see pickin' yarn down there this very minute; he might seem slow, Dan'l, but he has an enquiring mind, an' he was askin' me somethin' to do with the trade an' I says to him, you better ask one of the officers, you better ask Jack Barber, I says, someone who knows the slavin' business inside an' out.'

The carpenter looked at him darkly for some moments, then he said, 'You were both talking as if it is the men that will lie below here, but this grating is the one over the women's room, not the men's. We allus puts the men in the forward room, the boys in the middle and the women in the after part.'

'Now that is somethin' we niver had the slightest inklin' of,' Sullivan said.

Billy Blair sat back on his heels and pushed the red cotton kerchief up over his heated forehead. He looked towards the waist where Calley and McGann were working together. Calley was sitting up against the gangway ladder, pulling out yarns, his big hands picking at the strands with surprising nimbleness, his blunt, seal-like head lowered in absolute concentration. He was naked to the waist, his powerful torso a smooth red-brown. The skinny McGann was working the hand winch to twist the yarns into rope. The doctor was beyond him, taking his walk on the weather side of the deck. Thurso and Barton stood talking together on the quarterdeck. The dry rattle of McGann's spindle resounded through the ship — all the sound there was. Billy thought of the women and felt the rage of argument recede. 'It hadna' come into my mind they would be separated,' he said. 'The wimmin are below here, then?'

'Aye, that's right. You can get up to a hundred in there, if you stow 'em spoon-fashion, arse by tit.'

'Bigob, a hundred black fannies,' Billy said.

The weasel-faced Tapley, passing with a bucket of hot pitch, heard this and paused, grinning. 'He thinks he's goin' ter creep down when no one is lookin' an' shag hisself silly,' he said.

'You shag off yourself with that bucket,' Barber said severely, jerking his thumb. He did not like anyone much, but Tapley less than most. 'Nah,' he said to Billy, 'you have to get them on their own if you want anything. On the deck maybe, or get one down in the room while they are exercising up here. No good going below, 'cept with a whip. They get into states, they get shrieking wild sometimes, specially when the weather is bad. They would have you down and chew your bollocks off.'

'Persuasion is best in any case,' Sullivan said. 'I know women,

174

they are sensitive. A little bit of kindness goes a long way with women.'

Paris, turning at the end of his twenty paces, had observed Tapley's brief pause with the bucket and his unpleasing smile. A distasteful fellow, Tapley. What was it? He seemed to have no nature of his own. In moral terms a rudimentary worm indeed, eyeless in the dark. Many of the men on board he had felt to be stricken in some way, made brutal or heedless by the circumstances of their lives; he had sensed some loss, something visited on them, feelings cauterized. But Tapley was without this emanation of a hurt or dispossessed creature: he writhed complete, his evils effortless. Or so, Paris thought, it seems to me. And what, after all, gives me the right to judge? And if indeed I have the right, what persuades me I can see the truth of another human being, and one with whom I have exchanged almost no words? Nothing persuades me in reason, and yet I *know*. Once again he was swept, desolated almost, by the lonely certainty of his perceptions.

He paused at the rail, looking eastward towards the invisible coast of Africa. Sight of land, when it came, would reduce them, set them once again on the margin of existence. Here, ringed round with the ocean horizons, one felt at the centre of the world. The land, so much longed for, signifying the end of exile, would make them mere loiterers again. It came to him now that this paradox lay at the heart of all desire, as true for himself, standing perplexed at the rail, as for every other man on board, whatever Africa represented to him.

Not that all points of the horizon appeared equally far away, even to the casual and naked eye. He knew, he had seen in this succession of days, how there is always a point more distant in seeming than all others. Depending on the position of the sun and the distribution of light in the sky and the bulk and drift of cloud, one part of the rim will always be notched with remoteness.

Is this a notion of infinity? Paris wondered rather wildly, glancing round for it now, holding to the rail, feeling his body move with the sway of the ship. Can such a notion derive from sense impression merely? So Locke would have it, with his denial

175

of innate ideas. But the consolations of philosophy were limited, he found, aboard this ship. Locke defined pleasure as the reward of the just. What then should one call the emotion that lightened Libby's face or brought a glint to the eyes of Haines, the boatswain?

He could hear the rattle of the winch from amidships. A smell of hot pitch lay over the ship. Simmonds was shouting orders for the fairweather sails to be hoisted. Paris found his remoter point and fixed his eyes upon it. The sun, concealed in cloud and low in the sky, made shafts and corridors and vaults to give infinity a baroque ornamentation, but it was there; random impurities swam in the depths and were dissolved.

Next day the slave rooms were marked off and work was begun on the forward bulkhead. The stateroom had already been stocked with an assortment of goods from the hold; now a new main topgallant sail was bent and the old one primed as soon as taken down with resin and oil, so as to make an awning for the quarterdeck, where the shipboard dealing would be conducted. Johnson, the gunner, began making cartridges for the swivel guns. Two hogsheads of spirits were drawn off, to sweeten the native dealers.

'Them fellers has got holler legs for the stuff,' Barton said to Paris, with the peering relish characteristic of him. 'All the marrer has been lickified out of their bones, I do believe. An' there will be work to keep our lads off it, once it has been broached. A flogging won't keep 'em off drink, when the smell of it is about, any more than it will keep them off the women, Mr Paris. That is only human nature.'

And still Thurso did not know precisely where he was. He had seen no land since sighting the highlands of Tenerife. There was no means known to navigation, in that summer of 1752, which could have helped him to determine his longitude. The water continued a deep-sea colour, giving him hope he was not too much out in his reckoning. According to this he should have been at least fifty leagues north-west of Cape St Ann. All the same, he was anxious. The banks lying off the cape were the dread of all Guinea traders. Thurso had encountered powerful indraughts there on previous voyages and he knew cases of ships drawn into the shallows, sported with by fickle breezes for days or weeks or grounded in the shoals. He took soundings in thirty fathoms and the lead showed coarse red sand and fragments of shell, indicating they were further eastward than he had expected, nearer the coast. To make matters worse, the weather was thickening to the west. He gave immediate orders for the ship to be put about.

Hughes the climber, on lookout in the crow's nest, heard the shouted orders and felt the ship quiver through her length as she was brought closer to the wind. A mackerel sky was building to westward, with dark banks of stormbreeders low on the horizon. But there was some sun still, lying flat on the sea. He watched the gulls which earlier that day had found the ship. They were following on the starboard side, fewer now, but in good number still, which made him think they were in for no more than light squalls. He tried to count the birds, but lost himself in the rising, dipping dance of their flight, the constant changing of position among them. Thirty at least, completely silent. Sea-birds were mute at the approach of bad weather, he knew that about them and much else besides – whatever could be understood from close watching. Animals and birds, any creatures other than human, he had always liked to watch. He noted again how the birds rode the wind, how the dying sun flashed on their breasts. Below them the sea was riven with gashes. The wind was rising. He looked away from the birds at last, to eastward. The horizon on that side was pale and clear still and Hughes saw, faint and ragged but unmistakable, the shapes of land. He cupped hands to mouth and bawled the fact to the darkening sky.

Thurso, standing forward of the helm, heard the cry from aloft and the boatswain's long-drawn lamentation of response. 'Whe-e-re aw-a-ay?' He did not wait for the lookout to answer but at once raised his glass. When the answer came, with a rough bearing to larboard, Thurso had already found them, shifting, evanescent, but no shapes of cloud or sea, a line of deep, irregular serrations. A rippling swell swept the ship up and dropped her and he lost his view. But he knew he had seen

177

the mountains behind the Sherbro River; and in these moments of pause, in the cool breath before the onset of the squall, Thurso made proper acknowledgement to his counsellor for having brought them so far eastwards in deep water, beyond the sucking evil of the shoals.

TWENTY-THREE

Throughout the day the wind had been rising, smelling of rain on the way. It sent ruffles across the lake and swept up the spent May blossom into miniature storms. The cast of *The Enchanted Island* had assembled in the library, where a fire had been lit.

'We are all here, I think,' Charles Wolpert said, his accustomed gravity of manner contending with a certain visible embarrassment. 'Except for Parker, that is. He had duties in the parish – it seems the vicar has returned. And of course, Mr Adams.' He paused on this to clear his throat before continuing. 'I don't want to beat about the bush. Mr Adams is threatening to leave us. In fact he talks of decamping on the spot. It appears that dissatisfaction has been expressed with his manner of directing the play. He doesn't go into details but he names the person. I see no reason why we should not all know who it is. It is Erasmus Kemp.'

Several people glanced at Erasmus now. He looked straight before him. His face wore a slight frown but he was otherwise impassive.

'Good heavens.' Prospero had passed instantly to red-faced, swelling indignation. 'That is a piece of barbarity,' he said. 'What, did he presume to speak for us all?'

'It seems that Mr Adams was intercepted,' Charles said. 'Is there anyone here you consulted beforehand, Kemp?'

'No,' Erasmus said after a moment; he had had to struggle with himself to answer at all, in face of this public questioning. 'It wasn't the business of anyone else. I didn't speak to Adams about his direction of the play. That is a lie. It was a personal matter. He had no business to complain to you.'

'No business to complain to me?' Charles paused for a moment or two as if at a loss. Then he said more loudly, 'He is a guest in my father's house, at my invitation. He has received discourteous treatment. Who else should he complain to? I must tell you, Kemp, I think you have behaved strangely, and you may make of that what you like.'

For the first time Erasmus turned his head to look at his interlocutor. Resentment at this public rebuke showed in his suddenly heightened colour and fixity of gaze. This was her brother, a quarrel was out of the question. All the same, it came to him now that he had suffered discomfiture enough from the Wolperts, father and son. When we are married, he thought, I will keep her from them. There was a keenness of pleasure in this thought which he did not pause to examine. For a moment he allowed his gaze to fall on Sarah. She was standing in the recess of the window with her back to the light. She was looking at him steadily but he could not detect any change in the normal composure of her expression.

'I am fair sick of the whole business,' Charles said. 'I am sorry now that we thought of it in the first place. Jonathan Rigby was well out of it when he broke his leg. I swear I'll never be in a play again.'

'Me neither,' the young man who played Hippolito said. 'We have given up hours to it. To speak frankly, I don't care for Adams much. I don't think he has furthered the play. And he takes us for ninnies. I don't care if he goes.'

'Nor do I,' Dorinda said suddenly and unexpectedly, tossing her head, perhaps remembering some slight or belittlement.

'Well,' Charles said unhappily, 'now we are coming to the point. Adams has made it a choice. It is either Erasmus or him, he says. Either Erasmus withdraws from the play and ceases to attend rehearsals or he takes post from Warrington tomorrow morning.'

There was a short silence, then Erasmus said, 'I won't be forced out by Adams. I will resign from the play if everyone is agreed they want me out of it.'

It was the only card he had to play but it was a strong one. He could not believe Sarah would vote against him, even to save the play; and there was a good chance that dislike for Adams would keep some of the others on his side and that deliberations about expelling him would collapse in disorder, along with the play itself.

He gave the company a short bow and left the room, passing through the house and out on to the terrace. As he descended the steps and walked towards the lake he heard the wind in the high branches of the trees and saw the rapid scud of clouds in the sky. Once among the trees he stood still and breathed deeply, as if he had been running. The humiliation of that public interrogation, the rein he had kept on himself, brought their sharp reaction now. For her sake he had suffered it all. The words ran fiercely through his mind again: *When we are married* ... Once more he became aware of the wind in the trees above him. He raised his face and saw the branches swaying and rooks flung across the sky beyond.

When the battle is equally poised, the outcome will often depend on chance. Victory, had Erasmus known it, was being achieved for him not very far away.

The curate, Parker, seated in the vicarage drawing-room opposite the vicar himself, in a chair that was neither easy nor upright but partook of the awkward qualities of both, saw through the casement window how the wind agitated the yews in the garden, shaking them until they lost all resemblance to trees and became like dark, tossing plumage. With them he seemed to see his role as Caliban in *The Enchanted Isle* dislodged, shaken loose, blown away for ever.

'We live in dangerous times, sir, perilous,' the Reverend Edward Mansell said. 'And crucial for the Church.' He was a robust man, well rounded out, with a full gaze and a high, pale forehead and abundant auburn hair, of which he was proud. His black broadcloth suit was of best quality and his collar was of a snowy whiteness amazing to Parker. He said, 'It behoves the clergy to be particularly careful in all matters affecting their repute. I go away on essential business, leaving you in charge of the parish, and what do I find on my return? I find you preparing to portray, on the public stage, an uncouth savage given over to lechery and drunkenness and I know not what.'

The curate leaned forward eagerly, raising reddish hands. His fluffy, light-coloured hair had some energy stirring in its roots which caused a permanent startlement. 'Allow me to explain, sir,' he said. 'My motives are of the best. I am seeking to portray Caliban as debased, not in himself but by others. He is first unjustly subjected by Prospero, afterwards corrupted by the bad example of the mariners. The evil of strong liquor is also at the heart of my performance, sir. It is an evil of great magnitude in all parts of England now.'

The vicar sighed and pursed his lips and smiled upon his curate's writhings in the spindly, armless chair. 'So the savage is noble,' he said, 'leading a moral life by the light of pure reason, without benefit of scripture, until we Christians come to lend him our wickedness. This is not good theology, Mr Parker. I am sorry you have been infected by these radical ideas. You would say then that Caliban has a soul which renders him capable of receiving the message of redemption?'

'Yes, most certainly.'

'In that you go beyond the councils of the Church. The baptism of savages is not yet established, it is still subject to debate.'

'The main voice in the debate, sir, at present,' Parker said excitedly, 'is that of the slavery lobby, who seek to deny –' Belatedly he remembered that the Mansell family had holdings in the West Indies. In agitation he thrust his hands between his knees and held them there, as it were by force. 'We are all children of one father, sir,' he said.

'No doubt, no doubt.' The vicar remained silent for some moments. He was not sure of the best line to take. He did not want to embitter the curate if he could help it. Parker was an ideal assistant in the main: he had neither money nor connections to reduce his dependence and he was diligent and enthusiastic, ready to do all that was laid upon him. 'Well,' he said at last, 'I cannot allow it, and I am sorry indeed to see that you have elevated yourself in this way. There is only one Revelation, Mr Parker. They invite the fate of Lucifer who presume to weigh eternal truth in the balance of their own judgement.'

The doomed and flaming angel seemed far to Parker at this

moment from the sadly nodding plumes of yew he could see outside the window, waving farewell to his stage career. However, as he sat there, still pressing his hands between his knees, a serious spirit of rebellion was born in him that afternoon. Somewhere under the skies there was, there must be, a place where a man of the cloth could play Caliban. With a last hope that the matter might still be saved by dispute, he began, 'I do not deny to Caliban original sin –'

But Mansell had raised a shapely hand. 'No more, sir,' the vicar said. 'This debate has been protracted long enough,' and indeed he had seen from the clock that it had gone past his tea-time. 'I see I shall have to be plain with you. I cannot countenance this performance and I must request you to withdraw yourself from it now, today.'

'Without Caliban the whole play collapses, sir, all the work we have put into it . . .'

Looking at the disappointment writ large on his curate's fair-skinned, rather equine face and at the convulsive way he seemed to catch at his limbs to keep them in check, Mansell wondered briefly if the man might not be something of a hysteric. Too uncontrolled a sensibility there. Parker would not get far in the Church. He thought of his tea, which he would ring for immediately on his curate's departure, and of his study fire. 'Let it collapse,' he said. '*Ruat coelum*, Parker. Principle must be served first.'

Erasmus paused at the lakeside. Wind stroked the surface of the water and stirred the willows on the other side. He had never been here alone, never, he felt, really seen this stretch of water, this sandy foreshore – it had been merely the scene of his ordeal as love-sick Ferdinand. Now he was surprised by its forlornness, its air of an abandoned encampment. The awning of Caliban's cave was lifting in the wind and the fabric at the sides of Prospero's cell was rippling continuously, with a sound like pigeons' wings.

He began to make his way round the lake, towards the gate in the wall, which he had so often looked longingly at while chained to the play, waiting to make his appearance, pretend

183

that wonderment at Ariel's song. Snatches of his lines came back to him now: *Sitting on a bank, weeping again the Duke my father's wrack* . . .

Glancing back across the water he saw Sarah and her friend Miss Edwards approaching the lakeside. She gestured to him to wait. The two girls advanced together until they were some twenty yards away, then Miss Edwards fell back a little and Sarah came on alone. She had put a dark cloak over her dress and wore a felt hat with a scarf over it, tied below the chin. As she came up to him he saw that her eyes had an angry fixity of expression and that her small, full mouth was now tightly compressed.

'I should like some words with you, Erasmus Kemp,' she said.

He nodded. 'We could walk through that gate,' he said, as if obeying some compulsion in a dream, 'and up the hillside a little way, if that is agreeable to you.'

'Anywhere you please, it is immaterial.' Her voice quivered. He knew it was anger that possessed her but she was framed so gently that it was indistinguishable from distress.

They walked for some time in silence. Beyond the gate was pasture land, ridged and hummocked, rising to a line of ancient, racked beeches on the horizon. They kept to the path, Miss Edwards dutifully following at some distance behind. As they rose higher the wind grew clamorous against them, plucked at their clothing and their eyes. Sarah was obliged to turn more towards Erasmus than she might have liked, so that her words should not be blown away.

'I want you to tell me the truth,' she said. 'It was me you talked of, was it not? Charles has hinted so much.'

Erasmus had little humour in his nature, no resources that might have lightened the terrible seriousness with which he now made his simple assertion above the wind: 'I defended you.'

'Defended me?' She stopped at this and turned to face him. The brim of her hat, pressed down on either side by the scarf, made a frame for the narrow oval of her face. She was flushed, her eyes bright with tears of vexation. 'Cry mercy,' she said, with angry sarcasm. 'And to think I never knew I was being attacked. Defended me from what, pray? Who was harming

184

me? And besides, and besides . . .' She fell silent for some moments, as though helpless, looking down to where her friend had also stopped. 'Nobody asked you,' she said. He saw the movement of her throat. She was too tender, he thought, too delicately constituted for such strong displeasure. He would protect her from such feelings, he would be careful with her. That she might have just cause did not occur to him. *When we are married*, he thought again – it was like a refrain.

'Who appointed you?' Sarah said with renewed energy. 'How did you dare? You have ruined the play. We shall not be able to go on with it now. I believe you intended to do it from the start, because you could not shine.' She paused, in search of further wounding phrases. 'You are an exceeding bad actor,' she said. 'I am heartily sorry now that ever I asked you to be Ferdinand.'

Erasmus said, 'I don't care anything about the play. I only stayed in it for you.'

She made some incoherent exclamation at this and turned from him and began walking upwards again, Erasmus keeping by her side. And now the path they were following curved sharply and they passed into a fold between low hills, where there was suddenly no wind at all. Surprise at this brought them again to a stop.

'You had no right to do it,' she said. 'I have a brother already who is watchful of me – too much so. Even if we had been engaged, you had no right, not without speaking of it first to me.' But she had lost some vehemence, suffered an abatement of her anger, here in this sheltered place. 'The reason you didn't,' she added in low tones, 'speak of it to me, I mean, was that you knew I would tell you there was nothing in it. You meant to ruin our rehearsals.' She looked at him and her eyes widened with an expression almost of awe. 'You meant to do it,' she said.

'He made too free with you. He allowed himself liberties.' He was blind to all other questions but this. He wanted her to understand that he was older, wiser, a better judge of what she should permit. Below this there was an intense wish that she should see and acknowledge her fault. If only she would do this, it would put him in the right – it was the very least she could do to repair the hurt she caused to him.

'Liberties?' Sarah's voice sharpened. 'Who is to be judge of that? Do you stand there and say that I have been too careless of myself?'

He hesitated on this and saw the girl's chin rise and her eyes narrow slightly. She was more wilful, more defiant, than he had believed possible. 'No, no,' he said at last, 'but you are innocent. A man like that –'

'I found nothing to complain of in him,' she said simply.

This bold, unfaltering statement of what lay unvoiced at the heart of his complaint against her dumbfounded Erasmus. He could only stand there looking at her, in this hushed enclave they had found.

'He was perfectly polite,' she said. 'He often complimented me on my playing of Miranda.' Her tone had changed, some note of provocation or challenge had come into it now.

'Can you not see anything except in the terms of this play-acting?' Erasmus demanded.

She raised her brows at this in surprise real or assumed. 'But all that you complain of happened in the rehearsals of a play.'

A sense of being caught in toils came to Erasmus. 'There is a wider view,' he said, but no words with which to enlarge on this came immediately to him.

He was looking aside, thinking how he could proceed, when he heard her say, 'No, I found him quite agreeable. He is a handsome man, I think. He is famous in London among people of the theatre there.'

'Famous as a parasite and poseur, I make no doubt,' Erasmus said, forgetting everything in the immediate promptings of his jealousy. 'He would be famous anywhere for those qualities.' He paused a moment. He knew she had praised Adams only in order to wound him. He said with bitter accusation, 'He touched you.'

There was too much force of feeling in this for the loneliness of the place, and he saw the consciousness of it reflected instantly in her face. On the way here the boisterous behaviour of the wind had kept them separate. Now this magic calm, like a descent, a hush imposed on them from above, brought a greater closeness than being alone in a room could have done. In a room there is walking to and fro, there is looking at objects, there is glancing at the different world outside the window. Here there was only one world, at once vast and narrow, and they were enclosed in it, with nothing to look at but further evidence of the fact. All movement and sound further off – the violent agitation of the trees on the skyline, the distraught cries of lapwings plunging in the wind – deepened the silence they were sharing.

'We must go back,' Sarah said. Only rage with him could have brought her this far; and all rage had gone, short-lived as always with her, succeeded now by apprehension at the passion she saw in his eyes and a sort of pity for his tenacity. All his being was there together – he never flickered, never faltered, he had no reserve. She was swept by a sense of his physical splendidness and the doggedness of his desire for her. This, though not quite an acknowledgement of his merit, came the more keenly for her recent upbraiding of him. An instinct of subterfuge, a desire to reduce the level of feeling, led her to say, almost as if in commiseration, 'Of course, I know he did not have a high opinion of your acting, but I often heard Elisabeth say he was too severe in his judgement, and Mr Parker said so too.'

'Good God,' Erasmus said violently, 'I don't care what he thought of my acting. Do you think I would have killed him for that?' He paused for a moment. His throat pained him with the sudden onset of his love. He knew, with the perception of the stronger, that she was improvising now, that she was spent, in retreat. 'He touched you,' he said. 'He touched you and I mustn't, that is why.' The injustice of it released him. In vibrant tones he said, 'And yet I have more right. I love you. I cannot rest for thinking about you.' He moved towards her awkwardly, clumsily. 'You are my life,' he said. He was half blind with the force of his feeling and the terrible exposure of the declaration.

She started back a little, then stood still. The flush his words had brought faded, leaving her paler than before. Her breathing had quickened, but her eyes rested on him steadily. 'Elisabeth,' she said. 'She will be watching us.'

'I don't care who is watching,' Erasmus said.

Not to deter him, but for the sake of saying something in face of the advance upon her, she was beginning to speak of Elisabeth again when she felt herself taken in a strong embrace and urgently kissed on the mouth. Briefly, but with an unmistakable warmth, she returned the kiss. She felt a strange leaping motion within her as she was pressed against him. For some moments there was a sense of precariousness, as if she might fall if he let her go. Then she pressed her hands hard against him and broke free.

Neither of them said anything for some moments. Erasmus's breathing was clearly audible to both. He glanced away from her, back the way they had come. The lake, scene of his tribulation, was not visible from here, but he could see a section of parkland and the upper part of the long-fronted house. It looked unbelievably distant. He felt the warmth of Sarah's kiss still on his lips. 'We had better go back,' he said, looking steadily and unsmilingly at her.

Now it was she who seemed disposed to linger. 'Look at the sheep there,' she said. 'They have found a place out of the wind.'

Slightly above them, a little further into the fold between the hills, enveloped in the same hush as themselves, sand-coloured sheep were grazing together, their fleeces unstirred by the wind which only a few yards beyond them was sweeping the grass.

'They have found the one sheltered place,' she said. She knew that this was a moment she would remember all her life. 'Just like us,' she said. Wonder at this caused her to meet his eyes, this time with a gaze protracted.

'Say you will marry me,' Erasmus said. 'Say it.' It sounded harsh – more a demand than a plea. 'You will kill me if you don't.'

'We must keep to what my father said.' Sarah was pale still, but she was smiling and her face wore an expression he had not seen on it before, of promise or perhaps only a new boldness, he could not determine. 'We must wait till I am eighteen,' she said.

TWENTY-FOUR

The *Liverpool Merchant* crept nearer to the coast through repeated, violent squalls of rain, a suitor drawn by obstinate attraction to brave all rebuffs of the beloved. From time to time the distant arc of the Sierra Leone mountains was glimpsed, only to be lost again in the low banks of cirrus constantly building to eastward. After three days of this, the weather clearing, they came to anchor in eleven fathoms. At daybreak the following day they weighed again but now, after all the buffetings they had suffered, there was not wind enough to overhaul the ebb and so they languished under full sail until a fuming Thurso ordered the yawl hoisted out to tow athwart the tide. Late in the afternoon a sea breeze sprang up and with it they gained upon the tide enough to make anchorage that night in nine fathoms, just south of the Bananas, leeward of the shoals and near enough shore to hear the incessant crashing of the breakers – as near as any merchantman of the time dared go.

Early next morning, from the deck, Paris had his first steady sight of Africa. Beyond the stretch of sea and the boiling of the surf, a low, forested horizon, pale green, unbroken, giving an immediate sense of subterfuge, of a deceitful sameness. There were no mountains in view now; they were concealed behind the wooded promontory of Sherbro. The sky was pale crimson in the aftermath of sunrise, as if with the glow of some distant conflagration. The land itself, where the creatures dwelt that they had come for, was hidden behind the green wall.

Flecks of white wavered above the line of the shore – sea-birds of some kind. It was not a single line, he now saw. There was an interplay, bands of colour or light, sea-water paling as

189

the depth lessened, the mist of the breaking waves, the wet shoreline, the haze of green where shore and forest met. The zones lay side by side, blending at the edges but quite distinct. Some memory tugged at Paris, an obscure sense of recognition.

Perhaps it is merely the fact of arrival that seems always the same, whatever the look of the place, he wrote a little later in his journal, seeking by compulsive habit now to confide his sensations. *That is, if this can be called an arrival. To arrive, in any happy sense we give it, is to be restored to oneself, to be taken back into community, for whatever that holds of good or ill. But we carry our community with us, like all ships, and it is one that seems unwelcome to the land; we have had this battering of squalls in these last days; and now there is this fearsome surf, which does not let us approach nearer, and the barricade of forest beyond it.*

Meanwhile, we continue to make preparations, and beautify ourselves as if for a bridal. The booms have been lashed up to the masts, the decks cleared and scrubbed and scrubbed again and the ship's complement of cannon run out – Thurso means to announce our presence here with a salvo. There are men fixing the awning on the quarterdeck and others busy fitting out the yawl. This yawl, or longboat, as I learn from Barton, is very essential to our purpose here, where the ship is prevented from coming in close. They have furnished her with spars and sails and the gunner is to mount a swivel cannon in the bows. Being flat and high-built she can bring stores aboard through the surf; but her chief employ is cruising the coast for slaves and getting downriver to the small trading stations.

Amidst all this activity there are two men conspicuously idle: these are the hulking, one-eyed man Libby, and the little man named Blair, more likeable, but a great boaster and violent in his disposition. These two have been on deck since yesterday in leg irons, on the captain's orders, for fighting on board ship. Both their faces show the marks of it. I feel a tension among the men these days, which seems to mount with the pace of preparation and the expectation of having slaves aboard; or it may be no more than the nearness to land after these long weeks at sea. Enmities flare up among them, violent disputes and sometimes blows; these two now are sitting together against the windlass in an enforced proximity that must be in the highest degree –

It was at this point that he heard the sudden thunder of the ship's cannon. He left the sentence unfinished. Almost before the reverberations had died away he had closed his journal and was making his way above. There was no sign of either the captain or the first mate. Among those on deck the discharge appeared to have aroused small interest. Curls of blue smoke lay over the deck and there was a sharp smell of burnt sulphur. Wilson, Sullivan and Cavana were still at work on the quarter-deck awning. He saw Deakin and Calley wringing out swabs at the starboard head – these two had struck up a friendship, he had noticed. They generally worked together now, the big simple one, whose face wore often a shy and vacant smile, following the smaller like an enlarged shadow. Paris made his way forward towards them.

'That was loud enough to wake them,' he said, nodding towards the indifferent line of the horizon. Nothing changed in Calley's face or posture but he saw Deakin straighten himself and come to a position of loose attention. He was wearing only a singlet and wide-bottomed nankeen trousers. His body was narrow and sinewy, straight-shouldered, deeply burned by old suns.

'That will let them know we are here, I suppose, if anything will,' Paris said, giving to the words the tone of a question. He had from the beginning, almost, used his ignorance – of the sea, the routines of the ship, the procedures of trade – to incline the men to talk more freely to him, break down their sense of the difference in station that made them distrustful.

'Yes, sir,' Deakin said. 'Well, that is, they already know we are here, but by the cannon they know we are ready to trade.'

The voice was level and flat, rather toneless, conveying a sense, odd to Paris, of dissociation from the mind behind it. With the almost helpless acuteness of perception that descended on him nowadays in any exchange with his fellows, Paris met the blue, rather deep-set eyes. Deakin's regard was very steady and direct, though without insolence. There was something stark in it, as of a secret to be communicated, some unique idea that had been long suppressed.

'To trade for slaves, that is?' Paris spoke carelessly, at random almost, seeking to recover distance, to dispel his too-intimate sense of the other's being. He glanced at Calley, who was looking down, licking slowly round his mouth with a blunt tongue. 'Not other trade?'

'Aye, there is ships come in here for all manner of things.

Camwood, pepper, palm oil, elephant's teeth. The slavers take teeth often enough, and they will take gold dust further down the coast, but mostly this is to spend for negroes, when they get the chance. It is slaves that make the trade nowadays. That is what they say who have done the voyage regular.'

'And you have not? But you have made the Guinea run before, haven't you? This is not your first time on a slaver?'

'Once before, yes.'

'And how did you find it?' He at once regretted this question, which he thought must seem frivolous. It had been the result of processes too complex for explanation, even had they been clear enough to him: his own sense of impending ordeal, brought out by the crash of the cannon; curiosity about a man obviously decent, for Deakin seemed that to him . . .

'Find it?' Deakin repeated wonderingly. It struck him as a strange question. His life was a pool not so easy to fish in. Only one of higher station could so carelessly try to do it. He met the gaze of the man talking to him, noted the strongly marked brows, the furrowed lines running to the corners of the mouth. The surgeon's eyes were a strange colour – they looked silver against the sun-darkened skin. Neat and quick in his own movements, Deakin had noticed from the first the surgeon's ungainliness of posture and movement. He seemed not fully at ease with his own body now, as he stood there in the full-sleeved white shirt and dark breeches. 'When I was younger,' Deakin said steadily, 'when I was first going to sea, I made a voyage on a slaveship. The negroes rose on us while we lay at Calabar with the crew all drunk. They knocked the brains out of the first mate and two of the men on watch. We had to kill twenty-three before we could get them below. They all but took the ship.' He was silent for some moments, then he jerked his head towards his companion. 'Dan'l has never been on any kind of ship before,' he said.

'He is learning well,' Paris said. He had noticed Calley's devoted application to the ropes.

Calley was flustered at being so suddenly the centre of attention. This man expected something of him and so did his admired Deakin. 'I used to work in the market,' he said. 'Porterin'. You gets a saddle to put on.' He looked with a mirthful expression at Paris.

'You have to harden your heart against them or you cannot do it,' Deakin said. He was still struggling with Paris's question. 'A man doesn't expect to like things,' he added, half to himself.

'At all events,' Paris said, 'here you are.'

'Yes, here I am. Dan'l and me must get on, sir. We are wanted to lend a hand with the longboat. You see, they have heard us.' He gestured towards the land.

In some indeterminate zone between the bright surf and the wall of forest Paris saw pale feathers of smoke rising. They uncurled slowly in the milk-blue haze.

'That is their fires, is it?' He watched with some fascination these thinning puffs from a hidden continent. No human agency was evident. It was like some breeding of vapours out there, where the spray made the atmosphere vague.

Haines, the boatswain, came quickly towards them. 'What are you doing here?' he said fiercely to Deakin and Calley. 'How long does it take you to wring out a few swabs? You pair of lazy sons of whores, wasn't you ordered aft to lend a hand with the boat?'

'I detained them in talk,' Paris said quickly. There had been insolence towards himself in this violent incursion – Haines had addressed the men without a glance in his direction. 'Do you hear me, Haines? I say it was I who kept them there.' He encountered the glittering, close-set eyes of the boatswain and caught the slightly rank odour of the oil he used on his abundant ringlets. Haines was wearing a sleeveless calico waistcoat and the muscles at his shoulders and arms flexed smoothly as he struck lightly with the side of a hand against the gunwale. There was a constant bitter energy about him, as if – or so it seemed to Paris – the boatswain was recharged by the abuse and blows he distributed.

'Talking is for below, not for men on deck,' he said. 'There is work still to be done, Doctor. We shall have visitors before long, judging by the smoke they are sending up.'

'I know it. I was only intending to say that it was my doing that these two were delayed.'

193

With the barest of nods, Haines turned away and went aft again, to where the longboat was hoisted out between the fore- and mainmasts. Cavana and Sullivan were packing oakum into her seams and ramming the yarns home as close as they could with fingers and short chisels, Wilson following behind with mallet and spike to drive the wadding in tighter. McGann was tending a small iron brazier, which stood alongside on the deck with a cauldron of steaming pitch on it. The air above the brazier rippled with heat and the flat, muffled blows of the mallet echoed over the ship.

With Haines's eye upon them they worked in silence, but he was summoned by the captain after some minutes. On the strength of the signal fires and the absence for the moment of rival traders, Thurso had decided to moor with the sheet anchor and stay some time here.

Sullivan straightened himself up as soon as the boatswain had turned his back. 'McGann has the best of it,' he said without rancour. 'I am destroyin' me finger ends on this rope. I'll niver be able to play the fiddle if me fingers is reduced to stumps. I will have the law of thim for takin' away me livelihood. McGann has the best of it, he is just sittin' there. Tendin' fires is an easy lay, as the black spy knows well.'

McGann, from his position beside the brazier, exposed appal- ling teeth in a grin which contained no smallest element of sympathy. 'Get your misbegot backs into it,' he said in what seemed an attempt to imitate the boatswain's menacing utter- ance.

'Who is the black spy when he is at home?' Cavana said. 'Are you talking about that pissfire Haines?'

'I'm talkin' about the divil,' Sullivan said. 'All he needs is a poker an' tongs.'

'I have sworn to cripple the bastid,' Wilson said.

'No use nursin' a grudge,' Sullivan said. 'I know Haines got you a floggin' but broodin' on it will only shorten your life. I niver bear a grudge meself. They took me clothes off me against me will but I don't let it darken me days. Haines took six brass buttons off me coat, an' that is property we are talkin' of now. A floggin' heals up, but thim brass buttons is worth money, it

194

comes under a different headin' intirely. One o' these days I am goin' to walk up an' ask him what he done with thim buttons. I am waitin' for the right moment.'

McGann raised himself to look towards the land. 'That smoke is comin' from inside, by the look of it,' he said. 'They hae got slaves there for sure. The captain will be sendin' the boat up-river, like as not. But you are better off stayin' aboard if you can. It is killin' hot inside there, out the wind.'

The first to see the shore fires had been Hughes. He reported it to Simmonds, who went with the news to the stateroom where captain and first mate were checking trade goods. Thurso nodded, without change of expression. 'Send someone up to the mainmast trestles,' he said, in his hoarse and penetrating voice. 'Send Hughes. Tell him to keep his eyes peeled. I want to know the moment they put out from shore. Those two men in irons, Blair and Libby, they can be released now. I don't want men in irons sitting about the deck when any of these local chiefs come aboard. It gives a bad impression. They don't understand any process of law or proper punishment, they think it is all done on a whim, as they do things. I know these people, Simmonds.'

'Yes, sir.'

'And you may tell Blair and Libby that they are lucky to get off so lightly. They can do their blood-letting on shore. If there is any more of it on board my ship I will take the skin off their backs.'

'Aye-aye, sir.'

'That little 'un is a goer,' Barton remarked, as soon as the second mate had left. 'He landed one or two good'uns on Libby.'

'Why do you talk to me of that?' Thurso said, turning sharply upon him. 'What is it to me? They will be here shortly. We have hit upon a good moment. There are no other ships any-where in the offing or to seaward of us, which cannot long be the case. I believe they will have prime slaves in their pens there. We shall have to do what trade we can as speedily as may be. But hark you, Barton, I will not pay over the odds for them.'

'No, Captain.'

195

'I will not go a penny over the market.'

Barton raised a thin and cautious face among the bales of brightly coloured fabrics and the shining rows of pans and kettles. The captain was becoming a talker these days. He glanced with accustomed stealthy dislike at Thurso's impassive face and raw-looking blue eyes. Barton was sensitive to impressions and it seemed to him now that the captain was making assurances to somebody not in the room at all. 'It would not do to pay over the odds, sir,' he said softly.

'I am up to their tricks,' Thurso said. 'There isn't a man knows these waters better, nor the quality of the blacks here. They are rascals but I will be too much for them as I have always been before. They will find Saul Thurso always a jump ahead. I have never sold my owners short and I am not going to begin now, with the last one. He sends his nephew to spy on me, but I will do my best for him just the same. This is a hard trade and there are disappointments in it that could break a man's spirit and blight his hopes who is weak enough to allow it.' He fell silent here, looking in dark abstraction at strings of glass beads hanging before him.

'It has broke men's hearts, Captain, to my sartin knowledge,' Barton said after a moment. 'But we have a first-rate selection of goods here, upon my soul, there is what would please the most contrary and pernacious animal among 'em. An' some of 'em are pernacious difficult to please, as you an' I both know, Captain, havin' been –'

'What I know is not in your province,' Thurso said, rousing himself. 'You keep to your place and I'll keep to mine. I am just talking to you at present, Barton, that is all. We are in business together for the gold dust, as agreed. That is as far as things go between us.'

'Yes, sir.' Seeing Thurso's head lowered again in a return of that dark musing, Barton allowed his face to fall into an expression of faintly smiling indifference.

So the two men stood for some time in silence in that festooned and cluttered emporium, surrounded by goods of extraordinary variety: hanging strings of yellow glass beads, copper bands threaded together, rolls of tobacco, cases of muskets, brass basins and copper pots, iron bars, linen handkerchiefs, pewter mugs, silk ramalls, bright red and deep blue bafts, chintzes, checked cottons, knives and cutlasses and gold-laced hats.

Paris, approaching from the hatchway, glancing round the open door, saw them thus – standing silent in this cave of treasures, among coloured stuffs and shining surfaces – and he had an immediate feeling that these two also were on display, among the objects of commerce. This lasted only a moment. Then Thurso raised his head and saw him and said, 'Well, it is our doctor,' with the usual intonation of sarcasm.

But Paris could not return so soon to the tone of their everyday dealings. Whether he knew it or not, Thurso for the moment was transformed: bareheaded here, with his square-set figure and greyish poll, his attention momentarily disabled or distracted among sheen of cloth and gleam of metal, the reflecting surfaces of knife blades and mirrors and beads, it was possible to think of him as a stout and deferential ironmonger or draper – almost Paris expected to see an apron on him. Then he turned his head, the light fell on the square cage of his temples and jaws and the trapped and furious eyes within it, and the impression vanished.

Paris began to speak, but he was interrupted by a sharp, wailing cry from above.

'There they are,' Thurso said. 'Mr Barton, I want the brandy we drew off hoisted below the quarterdeck awning. I want you to speak to Johnson and make sure he primes the swivel guns. The small arms will remain under lock and key, but you and Simmonds and Haines will carry pistols, if you please.'

'Aye-aye, sir.' Barton was already out of the room and making for the hatchway.

'As for you, sir,' Thurso said, 'I shall want you up on deck with me. You had better wear your hat. Hats always impress these people. A naked-headed man is not rated so high with them.' He had himself donned a cocked hat. Under its shadow his eyes seemed to have retreated further. Something like a smile touched the corners of his mouth. 'You may find yourself with something to do at last, Mr Paris,' he said.

Paris went back to his cabin to fetch his hat. He had only the low-crowned black one which he had worn on his visit to the Kemps and which had, unknown to him, aroused such antipathy in his cousin Erasmus. He put it on, for lack of anything more imposing, and ascended hastily to the deck.

Here for the moment there seemed only what there had been before, the hot sun, the welcome breath of the northern trade wind, the distant thunder of the surf. The tapping of Wilson's mallet continued to be heard, there was a smell of hot pitch and black fumes of it were hanging everywhere. Standing on the afterdeck some yards from Thurso, he heard the boatswain order McGann to take the cauldron off but leave the brazier in place and keep it fed.

Looking towards the shore, he saw at first nothing different. There were the changing depths of the water, marked by shifts to paler colours; the plunge and seethe of the waves as they broke on the shore and the distant iridescence of the spray, which was flung high – higher than the level of the deck, as high as the ship's cross-trees, it seemed. Beyond this was the veiled forest.

Straining his eyes through the dazzle of the surf, he saw at last the dark shape of the canoe, rising up to the line of sight like a piece of sediment in a shaken bottle. It rode a crest for appreciable moments on a course slightly athwart the ship. He heard or seemed to hear the blare of some instrument like a trumpet and a rapid pattering of drums. Then the canoe had plunged into a trough among the waves and vanished from view as completely as if it had never been, as if the sight of it had been mere illusion, product of strained eyes, trick of light.

It was in this dream-like interlude that Paris knew suddenly why this coast had seemed in a way familiar amidst all its disturbing strangeness, why he had felt at first sight of it something tug at his memory. Those parallels of colour and light had reminded him of his boyhood in Norfolk, fishing from a rowboat, looking shoreward when the tide was on the ebb, the pale striations of the shallows, the constant fret of surf and strips of half-dried sand beyond, pale gold, with stretches of gleaming wet between, layer on layer, always merging and always distinct. Like the plumage of a bird, he thought, like wing feathers . . .

198

He felt homesick, desperate for a refuge. In these few moments, with the canoe still lost to sight, an urgent desire for escape came upon him – not only, he realized, from the thraldom of the present and the ordeal he sensed coming. The scenes he had remembered belonged to his youth, to the days of his courtship; he had come with Ruth to those beaches in the early days of his marriage. It was what had happened to Ruth that he wanted to flee from, his part in it, the desolation of his life. These seemed connected, in a way he could not properly understand, with what he now stood waiting for. Somewhere within him words of a prayer formed, drop by drop, as if by some process of distillation independent of his will: *Take this from me, let nothing more be required of me, let me go back to the time before such things were done, such things were possible* . . . But he knew there was no such time.

The canoe rose to sight again, nearer now and more distinct, broadside to the ship, and Paris saw that it was indented or fretted with heads. He had time to notice, before the craft bobbed down again, the processional, frieze-like effect of this, enhanced by what seemed some shared and ceremonial burden. At the prow a man was sitting upright, wearing a high-crowned hat. One of that frieze of heads raised a tubular object as though to drink. The bugle blast came again over the water.

They watched as the long canoe was steered through the zone of the surf with amazing dexterity. In the calmer water her progress was swifter and more direct. Soon she was lying alongside.

The hatted figure at the prow had got to his feet, holding to the ship's accommodation ladder for balance. He was a tall, obese man, the colour of dry clay. In addition to his gold-laced tricorn hat he wore a pair of linen drawers, a cutlass and a necklace of feathers. He was flanked by several men armed with muskets. One of these had also a drum between his knees and another a small bugle round his neck. All of them, chief and escort, were smiling broadly.

Paris looked down at the bound figures in the waist of the long canoe. That frieze of heads had been theirs. There were ten of them, five men, two boys, two women, and a girl, all completely naked. They sat in silence, their arms bound behind

199

them and their heads forced upright by means of a common yoke: it was the projections of this that had looked so strangely ceremonial at a distance. They were lighter in colour than the boatmen, who were coal black and heavy-browed, and had a muscular development of chest and arms such as Paris had never seen before. He could see the deep rise and fall of their breathing as they rested on the long paddles. He saw that Barber, the carpenter, was standing near and remembered he was an old hand on slaveships. 'The boatmen seem a different people from the captives,' he said.

Barber had lit a pipe in the interval of waiting. 'Aye,' he said, 'they are Kru people, they belong to the coast; no one else can get these skiffs through the surf. The slaves are from inside the country.'

'And are they never made captive themselves?'

'The Kru?' Barber grinned round the stem of his pipe. It was clear he found this question funny. 'Who would do the paddlin'?' he said. 'Not those other beggars – they prob'ly never seen the sea before.'

'Never seen the sea?' Paris peered down over the side again. 'But in that case –'

The man standing in the canoe was still grasping the narrow accommodation ladder. He looked to Paris now as if he might have mixed blood. He made a kind of military salute with his free hand and turned a beaming face upwards. 'Welcome Libberpool!' he called. 'Cap'n Thursoo! Haloo! You 'member me? You 'member King Henry Cook?'

'It is that fat scoundrel Yellow Henry,' Thurso said to Barton. 'One of those women has got fallen breasts, I can see it from here. I 'member you fine,' he called down. 'Come up, and welcome aboard.'

Yellow Henry was beaming still but he made no immediate move to accept the invitation. 'Ten prime slave,' he shouted. On the words, the drummer struck his drum a number of times and the bugler tilted up his instrument and elicited a short series of ear-splitting notes. Yellow Henry smiled through this, holding his hat. Still he made no move to mount the ladder.

Thurso nodded his head as if in appreciation of the music.

'Bring up you slaves for look-see,' he said. 'You know me, you know Thurso, no panyar with Thurso.'

'What is panyar?' Paris said quietly to Barber.

'That is kidnappin', stealin' people for slaves.'

'But that is what we are doing, isn't it?'

'No,' Barber said. 'What we are doin' is buyin' slaves. There is some skippers go in and take their own slaves, without benefit of dealers. They even takes the dealers for slaves sometimes. That's why these fellers are grinnin' so much. They are afraid of being took themselves.'

Paris watched the slaves unbound and the halters taken off them, watched them forced up the ladder one by one, Yellow Henry's attendants, all steadily beaming, prodding them on with their cutlasses. The girl was very young, he saw now, hardly out of puberty, with high, small breasts and a thin down of pubic hair. He saw that there were tears on her face, though she made no sound. The faces of the others were fixed and expressionless – from exhaustion, it seemed to Paris. But their eyes showed too much white as they came on to the deck. Some final, useless reluctance made him move away from the opening where the ladder was let down.

Last on board was the king himself, his arrival signalled by a fanfare more prolonged than any yet. He shook hands with Thurso, smiling still, breathing heavily from the climb. His attendants formed up on either side of him, clutching their muskets loosely. They were a motley band. All wore cartridge belts across their bodies. One or two sported cocked hats, though not so magnificent as their chief's. One wore a dishevelled grey wig, another a lace shawl. All cast uneasy glances round them.

'Ah, Bartoon,' the king said. 'You keepee strong?'

'Can't complain.' Barton raised his narrow face and grinned. 'You have got a memory for names, ain't you? This here is Mr Paris, our doctor.'

'Ah, Paree! Dat a good hat.'

Yellow Henry smelled strongly of rum but he did not seem unsteady. There was spray on his gold-laced hat and on his sparse grey chest hairs and grossly swollen belly. The slaves, whom he affected now to ignore, were huddled behind him

201

against the rail, guarded by members of the crew armed with whips. His own people stood in a semicircle around him. 'You Libberpool?' he enquired of Paris.

'Norfolk.'

'No fuck. Haw-haw.' Yellow Henry glanced at his followers. 'You no fuck now, we got biznez.' There was a general guffaw at this, in which some members of the crew took part. 'Fuck later,' Yellow Henry said, encouraged. 'Bristool trash place,' he added after a moment. 'Bristool shippis no give dash.' He took a pace and spat with delicate contempt over the side. 'You got dashee for Kru mans?' he said.

'I am goin' ter bust that one,' Paris heard someone say behind him. Turning, he saw Tapley and McGann standing together. He did not know which had spoken – he thought Tapley. Both wore a similarly gloating expression. They were looking at the girl slave, who had not changed position since being thrust on to the deck. Her head was lowered and sun glinted on the tight springs of her hair. She stood in a position of frozen modesty, shoulders hunched forward and wrists crossed over her genitals. It came to Paris, with a certain surprise, that she, and all these people probably, the men too, were accustomed to being clothed below the waist.

'We will talk about dashee when we have had a proper look at the goods,' Thurso said, in a tone almost jocular. 'Have a seat here in the shade. Will you take a dram while the slaves are being looked over?'

'Brandy,' Yellow Henry conceded. He settled his bulk with dignity, at the same time darting looks to left and right of him. 'Dese chiefs also like dram,' he said, indicating his escort.

'Mr Paris,' Thurso said, with a sort of ponderous and malignant courtesy, 'go forward and take a look at what they have brought, if you please. You had better go with him,' he added to Barton.

'Aye-aye, sir.' Barton's eyes had been on the barrel. With visible reluctance he stepped alongside Paris towards where the slaves were clustered. He had pistol in his belt and a broad-thonged whip of plaited leather in his hand. 'It is teeth and eyes you looks at first,' he said moodily. 'These beggars is up to all manner of tricks.'

Paris thought he must mean the traders – the captives looked past all tricks save that of endurance. He had taken himself in hand: this was a medical examination he was about to conduct, not different in essence from others he had conducted. Nevertheless it was with a continuing sense of not being fully responsible, of acting under duress or in some sort of preordained ritual, that he now approached a tall negro on the outside of the group, took him by the wrist and sought to draw him forward a little. Why he began here he could not have said. The man had raised his eyes at their approach, unlike the others; and Paris had seen him hold back on the climb up the ship's side – he had been struck several times with the flat of a cutlass. He hung back now; Paris had to use some force. Seeing it, Libby stepped forward with an oath and struck with his whip at the negro's flank. The man gasped and started at the blow and his head shook, but he uttered no other sound. Libby would have repeated the blow but Paris raised his left arm as a barrier.

The man came forward now without resistance. Across his chest and shoulders Paris saw the weals of some earlier beating, edged with blood. The arm he held was trembling through all its length with a continuous vibration, like a leaf in a faint current of air. Again, like a refuge, memory came to Paris: an exhausted swallow on the beach; he had warmed it between his hands, felt the pulse of fear pick up with the return of warmth, until its whole body was a single vibration of the terrified heart. But not terror only, he thought – there had been some indomitable hope of life in the bird . . .

With the same sense of compulsion, like that attending some quest or mission in a dream, he met the dark and somehow impersonal regard of the negro, the eyes at a level with his own, fathomless and shallow in the bony sockets. He faltered for a moment at the gaze of these eyes that did not see him, did not know what they were seeing – the man was stricken with the openness of the place, he was sightless at his own exposure. Paris felt sweat gathering inside the band of his hat. The enveloping glare of the noon sky was all around them. With a slight grinding of the teeth, a simulation of savagery without which he could scarcely have proceeded, Paris seized the negro's lower jaw and

203

forced it open. There was no trace of saliva in the mouth, but tongue and gums were perfect, the teeth immaculate.

'Good mouth,' Barton said in his ear. 'They chews on a piece o' bark.'

With Barton murmuring at his side like some confidential assistant, full of hints and instances, he peered at the negro's eyeballs and into the pink whorls of his ears. He prodded his chest and listened to his heart and felt the glands of his throat. He examined the surface of the body for evidence of disease but found only the whip marks and extensive contusions in the upper arms caused by his bonds; he had been bound very tightly and for considerably longer than it had taken to ferry him from shore.

'Don't forget the cock, Mr Paris,' Barton said. 'Seat of pleasure. Lay hold his arms, Libby. They sometimes strikes out. Big 'un, ain't he?'

The man was circumcised. Paris drew the loose skin back to look at the whole crown of the penis. He was aware again of that light, continuous trembling. He spread the man's thighs to look for venereal lues in the region of the groin. There was nothing. Straightening up, he saw the fluttering of fear or shock at the base of the negro's throat. The man panted suddenly, a single deep gasp. His eyes were unseeing. 'He is in good condition,' Paris said. He experienced a momentary giddiness. I must have got up too suddenly, he thought. There was a sweetish, musky odour in his nostrils.

'Let's have a look at his arse,' Barton said. 'Get him down on his knees. Get his head down, Deakin, will you? And you, Calley – press him by the nape. You fool, what are you doing? I want his head touchin' the deck an' his tail in the air. That's right. You have got to be up to their tricks, Mr Paris. I have known these rogues of dealers to plug up slaves' arses with corks to keep in the bloody flux long enough to sell 'em. You wouldn't credit what they will stoop to.'

'I think I would,' Paris said. The examination seemed to have passed out of his hands. He looked away from the bowed form of the black man, still as stone on the deck, to the sea, the distant wildness of the surf, the wall of forest beyond. They had come from somewhere behind there, perhaps from far inland. They were forest people. It came to Paris, like so much these days, as a shaft, a missile that found him, which he would have avoided if he had been able – broken sunshine, river banks, clearings of villages, always cover somewhere near, always enclosure. And now this terrible openness of sea and sky . . .

'We have got to make him caper,' Barton said, cheerfully. He was his usual loquacious self now, having apparently recovered from his disappointment over the rum. 'Make sure he has full possession of his limbs,' he said. 'Step back, Mr Paris, out of the line of the whips. Let us see the brute jump a bit. They are idle devils. Here, you beggar, like this.' He jumped up and down and kicked out sideways. 'Like that, you sabee? Quashee do same-same ting me. Jump, damn you. Here, Cavana, wake him up with your whip, will you?'

The negro panted when he felt the lash, and seconds later cried out on a high-pitched note that sounded more of despair than pain.

'He is givin' us a song when we wants a dance,' Libby said with a grin, turning his good eye round on his henchman Tapley.

'That's it, oopla!' Barton clapped his hands.

The negro had begun a shuffling motion, kicking out his feet and flapping his arms. Paris, again with a sense of being impaled on his own perceptions, saw that thick tears had gathered in the man's eyes.

'We have one to start with, Captain,' Barton said, going up to Thurso where he sat under the awning with the king. 'Prime male, 'bout thirty years old, no pox, no flux, clean as a whistle.'

'We'll start with him then,' Thurso said. 'Tell Mr Paris not to waste his time on the older woman, she's got fallen breasts, I won't buy her. You sabee Thurso,' he said to Yellow Henry. 'We do trade mebbe five-six time. What for you bring me woman dugs down her belly? You sabee damn well I ain't go buy dat one.'

Yellow Henry's smile disappeared and his face settled for some moments into lines of sullen savagery. 'She one fine-fine slave,' he said. 'Worth fifty bar. She cotched together with de girl. Turns out she dat girl's mudder.'

'What is that to me?' Thurso said. 'She is not worth transporting. You can't get any sort of price for a drop-breast woman. No, she goes back to shore. I'll keep the girl, if she is sound.'

'She sweet-sweet.' Yellow Henry belched and began to smile again. 'One more drams,' he said, holding out his glass. 'She sweet cunny, dat one. Look how she holding it. She not bambot ooman – nobody bin inside. Keep her han' over it like a bird fly out.' He rolled his bloodshot eyes roguishly. 'Bird go fly *in*,' he said.

The king's bugler laughed loudly at this witticism and half raised his bugle as if to deliver a blast, then appeared to think better of it. 'Whoosh!' he laughed. 'Bird fly in.'

Thurso had not smiled at the sally. 'We go below now, look-see goods,' he said. 'We got plenty fine-fine thing. Yes, you can take some men with you but they'll have to wait at the door, there's no room inside. You had better come down with us,' he said to Simmonds. 'Barton stays up here with the doctor. Haines, stand by the brandy.'

They were below a considerable time, during which Paris, with his mentor always at his side, proceeded with the examination of the slaves. The last of the five men had a hard crust on the pinnae of the ears, a concretion oddly similar to the deposit Paris had known to form on the surface of the joints in cases of gout. There was also a tumour-like swelling in the groin which had broken at the surface to excrete a gum-like substance. 'Do you see that, Barton?' he said. 'See how hard it is along the edges – it has made a kind of rim round the ulcer.' In the interest of this, he forgot for a moment where he was, what he was doing. 'The wound is like a crater,' he said. 'I have read of this somewhere.' He began a careful palpation of the arms and legs, the short and thickset negro submitting with a sort of exhausted docility. Close to the surface, quite distinct to the touch, he found a number of small, tumour-like swellings. Beneath the dark skin he could discern a reddish colouring around them.

'Been eatin' dirt, ain't you?' Barton looked bored. 'They eats dirt,' he said.

Paris took off his hat at last and felt a reviving breeze on his

206

head. 'Nothing to do with what he has eaten,' he said sharply. 'This man has yaws. I have never seen a case before but I remember now to have read of it in Jacobus Bontius, in his book on diseases attending the negroes. He describes exactly this raspberry colouring of the tubercles and the hard bony edges of the ulcerations.' Paris broke off. His voice had begun to sound strange in his ears, at once remote and insistent, as if he were reciting in an echoing room. He looked briefly down at his hat. On a sudden violent impulse, inexplicable to himself at the time and terribly startling to the diseased negro before him, he took it by the brim and pitched it like a quoit with all the strength of his arm clear over the side, where it went skimming with a long and graceful trajectory into the sea. 'Unfortunately,' he continued with unmoved countenance and quickened breath, 'there is some confusion in Bontius's treatise, as he uses the same word to describe the papules of yaws and those of syphilis, whereas as far as is presently known yaws is not necessarily transmitted by sexual intercourse, but by direct contact at the infectious –'

Glancing round, he found himself an object of general scrutiny. Even the slaves had raised their eyes to follow the bird-like skim of his hat. Barton was looking at him with an expression of particular attention. 'I would need to keep this man under observation,' Paris said.

'Under observation?' the mate said. 'That's a good'un. Why'd you pitch your tile overboard, Mr Paris?'

'To tell you the truth, I don't know,' Paris said. He met the eyes of the diseased negro. They were muddy and there was a sort of remote terror in them. 'It was mine to dispose of,' he said heavily. He felt again the hot clutch of the sky.

Barton raised his face in the peering, sniffing, jocular way he had. 'Well,' he said after some moments, 'whether this quashee has got pox or whatever it is, we can't take him. We would have the whole shipload sheddin' their skins before we get sight of Kingston. An' one of them boys is too young, not more 'n nine or ten, by the look of him. The captain won't take 'em so young, on account of they needs extra lookin' after an' then generally dies anyway. So that leaves the two wimmin.'

The procedure with these was the same as for the men, except that they were made to lie down on their backs and open their legs for the more convenient inspection of the genital parts, a spectacle arousing much ribald comment from the crew, though there were those who observed it in silence and one or two who, with feelings of uneasiness they might not have recognized for compassion, contrived – though inconspicuously – not to look closely on.

The woman was full-breasted, with high muscular haunches and slender legs. Pushed down to the deck, she yielded to the gross inspection, merely turning her head to the side and laying an arm over her eyes. The girl uttered some sounds of no more meaning to the men around her than the cries of gulls, and she stiffened involuntarily against the pressure of Paris's fingers. Her arms had to be held, or she would have covered herself. This agony of resistance was brief. With surrender the girl's body collapsed into inertness on the deck, though her eyes remained open and fixed as she stared directly upwards.

'Nice bit of flesh, this 'un.' Barton flicked his fingers at the small nipples with casual brutality. 'Hot little bitch too, I 'spect, when she gets over this. Like all of 'em. But I would rather rattle the older one. I like 'em matoor, they knows more tricks. Not that there'll be much joy on this voyage, not if I know anythink, not without payin' for it with the skin off your back. With Thurso it is hands off or a floggin'. Our skipper takes a moral line with wimmen slaves.'

Before Paris could inform himself further as to this, the captain himself reappeared from below with King Henry by his side. They reseated themselves under the awning, where the king's motley entourage once more assembled around him.

'More brandy for our guests,' Thurso said briskly. Paris had not seen him before in such festive mood. 'Morgan,' he shouted, 'damn you, look alive, serve it out. Mr Barton, I want you by my side here. Haines, go and see to the fire. I want them branded as soon as purchased.'

'There are three we don't take, sir,' Barton said. 'There is the woman and a boy who is too young and one of the men who our doctor will give you a full report of when you are more at leisure, but it looks like a case of Spanish pox to me.'

'I want them off the ship,' Thurso said. 'They can go back down over the side. Tut-tut, sir,' he said, turning to Yellow Henry. 'You tink Thurso go buy pox man?'

The king was looking graver now, though squinting slightly as a result of the liquor. 'You no got green baftee stuff,' he said. 'I very sorry bout dat. You got blue, you got red, you no got green.' He shook his head sadly from side to side. 'I hopin' for green,' he said. 'Plenty trade for green baftees. You no got sletas, neether. Dat bad, Cap'n Thursoo. Plenty trade silk sleta stuff.'

Thurso nodded. He had expected that the mulatto would start with complaints. It was always what you hadn't got that they claimed most to want. But he had noted the scornfully cursory way Yellow Henry had glanced at the pans and kettles and the gilt-framed looking-glasses. It was these he really wanted, not bafts or chintzes. And muskets, probably – without arms they could not make forays for slaves. 'For dat tall feller there, I make you bargin,' he said. 'I give you fifty-five bar for dat one.'

Yellow Henry's broad face, liberally moistened now and resinous-looking, sagged into lines of disbelief. He pressed a large palm the colour of dark butter against his nose in an apparent attempt to flatten it further. 'Dat prime slave an' fust clas' charakker,' he said, when he had to some extent recovered from his surprise. 'He Mandingo people. Price all long dis coast sixty-two bar for prime man slave.'

'Come now,' Thurso said. 'We both sabee dat too high. I can't go above fifty-seven.'

'How you make up one bar? What you go give me make up one bar?'

'I make you two pound gunpowder, one bar. I make you one pound fringe, one bar. I make you one ounce silver, one bar.'

'An' you make dashee, put to dat?'

'I make dashee six pewter tankards with each slave.'

'No take tankids,' Yellow Henry said sullenly. 'You tankids trash, they no got handuls.' His temper seemed to be deteriorating. 'I take dashee two bras' ketuls,' he said. Suddenly he started forward, his eyes rolled fearfully and his hand went to the hilt of his cutlass. 'Keep dat man back,' he said.

'What the devil is it?' Thurso turned sharp round. 'Where are your wits, Haines?' he said. 'Keep our people back.'

Calley, either curious to see more closely what was taking place or in eagerness to get within touching distance of the women, had blundered too near.

'Stand clear, you clod-poll,' Haines snarled. Annoyed at being found wanting, he struck back-handed at Calley, catching him across the cheek. 'Do you want to start them shooting?' he said.

Paris, leaning back against the gunwale, taking deep breaths of air, observed the bemused and rather frightened expression on Calley's face as if from a great distance. He felt remote from the proceedings now, like an accidental bystander, and strangely open to the space of the world beyond the ship, swept, blown through with it. At the same time he was intensely aware of his physical being, aware of thirst, of his lungs breathing, of his hands, in which he still seemed to feel the warmth and shape of the women's knees. In his hands too, not yet acknowledged in his heart, the throb of lust and jubilation he had felt at her abandonment . . .

He ceased after a while to follow the bargaining, which was extremely complicated. To establish the value of the slave in bars, which he had thought at first to be the whole purpose of the proceedings, was in fact only the beginning. This bar, it seemed, was merely a value given to a certain quantity of goods. It could be half a gallon of brandy or a bag of shot or two dozen flints or a length of printed cotton. It was in order to obtain small concessions and adjustments in these values that Thurso and Yellow Henry, facing each other in their respective hats, wheedled and blustered and simulated mirth or astonishment or disgust.

The tall negro whom Paris had examined first was purchased finally for six brass kettles, two cabers of cowries, four silver-laced cocked hats, twenty-five looking-glasses and an anker of brandy, with a bonus of six folding knives and a plumed hat offered by Thurso for the goodwill of the king's trade. As soon as the deal was struck and the goods brought up, the man was dragged forward into the waist of the ship, where the branding irons had been heating all this while in the brazier.

210

Some fixity of the will kept Paris gazing after them. The slave was concealed from view by the men holding him down. But Paris saw the equable second mate, Simmonds, take out the bar, saw him hold it up and spit on the red-hot device at the tip, caught for a moment, against the white hull of the yawl beyond, the glowing, angular design of the brandmark – it was the letter K. Simmonds's face wore a look of concentration, a recognition of the need for accuracy, which suddenly recalled to Paris his student days, assisting at dissections. Almost, for a moment, even now, it seemed that he might find some retreat in the memory of those days, the intent circle of students clustered round the table in the lamplight, the precise and somehow stealthy approach of the knife to the cadaver. Faces too, there were, in this present circle, which showed signs of distress, like those novice anatomists of long ago. He saw Blair's face, marked still from his fighting, staring down with jaws rigidly set. The tall, dishevelled fiddler had a similar fixity of expression.

These men briefly aided Paris, abetted the illusion. But from a living man, not a drained simulacrum, the sound that came now, the single cry from below, throat-formed and pure. He saw the brief tension in the group of men holding the negro down. Barber, with the boy Charlie to help him, moved forward with the shackles for the legs. A smell of burned flesh hung in the air. My uncle has acquired his first slave, Paris thought. Through what seemed still the ripples of the cry he heard Yellow Henry's voice raised in a tone more plaintive than angry: 'For why you no got green baftees? For why you tankids no got handuls?' Bargaining had commenced over the second negro.

'Stow dat palaver,' Thurso said, leaning back with affected carelessness. 'You take dashee two brass pan?'

'Man here no want sospens. Dey say you sospens trash.'

'We got muskets, made Brummagem.'

'Muskits, haw-haw.' Yellow Henry raised a face distorted with false mirth. 'We know you muskits,' he said. The men around him laughed in a whooping chorus.

It was death of course that made the difference, Paris told himself carefully, as if reciting a lesson. You can work your will on a dead body. Those laid out for dissection had been men and women dying destitute, stolen from paupers' graves, or criminals cut down from the gallows, with no rights whatsoever over the disposal of themselves in death. And in life? As he stood there the distinction grew blurred in his mind. Was there really so much difference?

Glancing up, he saw Hughes high in the cross-trees of the foremast, white sea-birds wheeling beyond him. From so high above what must this business seem like? What sense could someone unacquainted with the trade have made of it? Too far away to smell the scorched flesh. A brief contortion of the face, which might have betokened laughter or even merely dazzlement. A cry thinned out to a voice of the wind. And all the while these goods steadily piling up on the quarterdeck, shining kettles and pans, cut glass beads, the jumble of vividly coloured cloths. From the perspective of the cross-trees inexplicable, unless you knew. From the office where his uncle sat even the mystery was gone from it, reduced to an entry in a ledger.

Banks of white cloud were building to the west. The sun struck through them in shafts of silver. Paris stood against the rail on the weather side of the ship, taking advantage of what breeze there was. The boy went for thirty-five bars – the last of the males to be sold. He began to cry out as soon as he was seized, and screamed repeatedly while he was branded. Afterwards he wept, with an isolated and persistent sobbing in which there seemed all childish heartbreak and loss. It was not even this, however, but a kind of joke about the muskets, which finally drove Paris below.

In the course of bargaining for the female slaves Thurso had ordered two cases of muskets to be brought up on deck. One had been opened to show the oiled barrels. He was hoping to seduce Yellow Henry with the sight, having been privately surprised that the other had not so far made any mention of firearms. The mulatto's rule depended on his ability to reward his followers, which in turn depended on his ability to maintain a supply of slaves for the visiting ships. This he did, as Thurso knew, by fomenting small wars in the interior and sending raiding parties to make captives in the confusion. It was a profitable trade and the mulatto had rivals – Thurso knew of several. The more men Yellow Henry could enlist to his cause, the safer he was. But recruits had to be attracted with the promise of muskets ... 'See,' Thurso said, pointing at the cases. 'These fust-class muskets. Brummagem goods. Look here, it is printed on the case.' He pointed to the black stencilling on the lid.

Yellow Henry sighed and rolled his eyes disdainfully. He barely deigned to follow the direction of Thurso's pointed finger. He was not a proficient reader in any case. 'Las' time all same-same,' he said. 'Brumgem trash place, muskit no good.' His face fell suddenly into an expression of angry truculence. 'We buy Dutchee muskit,' he said.

'Dutch muskets?' Thurso was clearly scandalized at this. 'English workmanship is the best in the world,' he said. Despite his attempt at equanimity some rage had crept into his face and voice at the insult.

Yellow Henry appeared to meditate for some moments, stretching his mouth and distending his nostrils in an expression half savage, half humorous. His face glistened. Some quality of stillness had invested the men flanking him. 'Brumgem muskit take off man fingah,' he said at last. Apparently deciding to make a joke of it, he pouted and puffed explosively into the air, blinking rapidly and raising a hand to follow the track of his breath. 'G'bye fingah,' he said. There was laughter at this among his men. He turned his heavy shoulders to look round at them. 'Show dem Brumgem muskit,' he said.

Two of the men, smiling radiantly, raised their right hands. Each had a forefinger missing and one had lost also the first joint of his thumb. At the sight there was a whooping clamour of merriment from the king's retainers.

Yellow Henry himself was overcome by laughter. When he looked up there were thick tears in his eyes. 'Why you laughin'?' he said. 'Why you make big yai? Dey lucky, still got hans.'

Paris looked from the grinning faces to the mutilated hands. It seemed suddenly swelteringly hot, as if the clouds had hushed the wind. A sensation of nausea came to him, like the onset of some long-suspected disease. Taking advantage of the general release of tension in the wake of Yellow Henry's joke, he passed down on to the main deck, where the slaves already branded and shackled were grouped together, and thence to his cabin.

Once there, he bathed face and neck and hands in the water it was Charlie's duty to fetch for him each day. He tried not to smell it, as it had become malodorous with this long time in the butts; but it was blessedly cool. The nausea receded. In an attempt to reach some degree of the detachment he felt was needed now to save him, he had his usual recourse to Harvey, turning quickly through the pages until his eye was arrested at the celebrated argument from quantity, the first of its kind in the history of physiology: 'The heart in one half hour makes above a thousand pulses; indeed, in certain men and at certain times, two, three or four thousand. Now if the drams be multiplied, it will be seen that in one half hour there is a greater quantity of blood, passed through the heart into the arteries, than can be found in the whole body . . .'

But for once Harvey failed to provide solace. It was too closely argued, too logical, it resembled too much what was happening on deck at that moment: Thurso and Yellow Henry were using the argument from quantity too, and every whit as rigorously. Perhaps he needed some more personal and passionate statement. He opened his volume of Pope and began to read at random:

As Man, perhaps, the moment of his breath,
Receives the lurking principle of death;
The young disease, that must subdue at length,
Grows with his growth, and strengthens with his strength:
So, cast and mingled with his very frame
The Mind's disease, its ruling Passion came . . .

This was beautiful, but too measured for him in his present disturbed state, too neat in its elegant contrivance of the rhymes and precise balancing of analogies. He abandoned it in favour of Astley's collection of travellers' accounts of Africa:

They have continual warre against Dragons, which desire their blood, because it is very cold: and therefore the Dragon, lying awaite as the Elephant passeth by, windeth his taile (being of exceeding length) about the hinderlegs of the Elephant, and so staying him, thrusteth his head into his tronke and exhausteth his breath. When

214

the Elephant waxeth faint, he falleth downe on the serpent, being now full of blood, and with the poise of his body breaketh him . . .

He continued to read with obstinate attentiveness, through the cries that came to him as the women were branded, through the prolonged and cacophonous fanfares of Yellow Henry's departure. Then there was an hour with only the faint washing of the waves for sound. He read of the inhabitants of Guinea, 'a people of beastly living, without a God, lawe, religion, or common wealth, and so scorched and vexed with the heat of the sunne, that in many places they curse it when it riseth'. He read of the Queen of Saba who went to Jerusalem to hear the wisdom of Solomon, and of Prester John and the peoples of the interior of Africa, the satyrs who resemble men only in shape, the Troglodytes who dwell in caves and live on the flesh of serpents, and the Blemines, a people without heads, who have their eyes and mouth in their breast . . . At the change of watch Charlie came knocking at his door with a request from the captain for his presence up on deck.

He went up to a spectacular sunset with great rafts of fire smouldering among the dark ash of the cloud. Thurso was on the quarterdeck already, standing at the forward rail, with Barton and Simmonds behind him. The crew were mustering below on the afterdeck. Paris mounted by the companion ladder and took up a position some yards from the first mate. The slaves were sitting in the waist, the men chained, the woman and the girl free.

As soon as the men were assembled, Thurso began speaking directly down to them in his hoarse, barely inflected voice. They had taken their first slaves on board. Any man who had sailed on a slaver would know that now the real business had begun. They had all been on a holiday before. Now they would start to earn their wages. Negroes were valuable merchandise. Every care had to be taken to make sure that each slave purchased was delivered in first-rate condition, so as to fetch best prices at Kingston market. They were to be kept under constant watch while on deck to prevent them from jumping overboard or doing themselves some other mischief. Any man found sleeping on watch could be sure of a dozen lashes for the first offence, doubled for the second.

'I will not have the negroes damaged,' he said. Rage at the notion whitened his knuckles as he gripped the rail before him. 'By God,' he said, 'the man will be damaged who tries it, I promise you. He will wish he had never been born. Use of the short whip against 'em is permitted to all members of crew for purposes of making 'em move and keeping 'em in order. But I will not have 'em cut or struck about the eyes or mouth.'

Relaxing his attention somewhat, Paris looked to seaward, where that first fiery splendour of the sunset was softening now to drifts of dusky, luminous gold. The sky to the east, empty of cloud, was a single bright bruise of violet and rose, draining on the horizon, above the darkening line of forest, to the colder blue of night. The plunge and crash of the surf still sounded without abatement. The spray showed a dim radiance of watered blood before it rose and was lost in twilight.

'One more thing,' Thurso said. 'On no account will there be fornication with the women. I will have no foulness of that sort aboard my ship. Any man found lying with a female slave will be first flogged and then stapled down to the deck. And I will know of it, never fear, because I am purposing to bring a linguister aboard tomorrow who will understand the language of these people. We will be trading ashore in the longboat in these next days. What you do ashore is your own business. I will not have my cargo damaged, I tell you, and I will not have my ship turned into a sink of iniquity. A girl still intact is worth a good ten guineas more in Jamaica. Which man of you will step forward now and put ten guineas into my hand?'

There was silence from the men below. Thurso raised his face to the darkening sky. 'I made my promises long ago,' he said. 'Before most of you men were born. That is why I am still here talking to you. I will keep a clean ship while I live.'

PART FIVE

TWENTY-FIVE

The departure of Adams and subsequent collapse of the rehearsals brought happier days for Erasmus. He became an
accepted visitor at the Wolpert home. His handsome, glowering
silences, the evident force of his attachment, had ended by
disposing Sarah's mother towards him, had even in some degree,
if not softened the father's heart, at any rate relaxed his severity.
Wolpert did not like the young man any better for being in love
with his daughter – rather the contrary. Strong-willed and pro-
prietorial himself, he found these qualities difficult to stomach in
another; and the saving irony which he was sometimes able to
direct at himself was a quality his prospective son-in-law showed
not a glimpse of. Moreover, with that perceptiveness he had for
all concerning his daughter, Wolpert noted still the oppressive
effect on her of the young man's visits, the way he seemed to
overshadow the girl, to work a reduction of brightness in her.
Nevertheless, dimmed or not, she sought to be with him, she
went running to meet him. It was clear to Wolpert that his
daughter wanted Erasmus Kemp and he could no more refuse
her this than anything else she had ever wanted that had been
in his power to grant.

So without any official change in his position or status
Erasmus was allowed to visit, to walk with Sarah and talk to
her, alone sometimes for short periods, more often with someone
in discreet attendance – generally an unmarried second cousin
of Sarah's mother, a Miss Purdy, who lived in the house.

His nature expanded with this sense of occupying a privileged
position. He talked much and confidently about the future,
their future, when they were married, and that of the city,

which he saw as intimately connected. 'Transport and the carriage trade,' he would pronounce, with glowing eyes. They were words of love and promise, containing all that he meant to work for, all that he would offer her. 'That is where the future lies. Money is flooding into Liverpool, more every day. The best use that money can be put to is extending the docks, cutting new canals, improving the roads so as to give better access to us from the interior of the country.'

The fervour sprang from a source not altogether pure: on his father's instructions he had been buying up a good deal of the land bordering the approach roads to Liverpool; the value of this would increase dramatically with the sort of development he was hoping for. But his enthusiasm was due only partly to this. The idealism of his nature was roused by thoughts of material progress. He saw a beautiful and prosperous city rising. Liverpool would be the greatest port in the land, greater than London. She would take over the Atlantic trade. All the manufacturing wealth of Lancashire would flow through her. Wolpert, he knew, had interests in coal and in the Cheshire salt mines. Taken with the Kemp shipping and import business, it made a formidable combination.

The future he thus envisaged was a palace of marble and Sarah was queen of it, enclosed within, securely his own. About the present he could never feel this confidence. The present was curiously porous, it had no containment, things leaked away from him in all directions. Sarah's affections were offered too widely: they extended beyond her family, to friends, servants, even her pets – there was no end to it. In the presence of others, among people who had knowledge of her out of his reach, he was never at ease. He took greater pains than ever with his person and his clothes and was agreed among Sarah's acquaintance to be well favoured enough but disobliging and too proud.

One habit of hers, first noticed during the rehearsals for *The Enchanted Isle*, troubled him greatly and he was resolved to eradicate it as soon as he had acquired the authority of a husband. She had a luminous way of recounting, or confiding – he knew not what to call it – a way of commanding attention when talking in a group, by spacing out her words rather deliberately and punctuating them with small climaxes. She would say, 'That was a great disappointment to everyone,' or 'I simply adore strawberries,' and she would raise her face and smile slightly and just for a second her eyes would close and there would pass over her a sort of slight shudder or pang, like the faintest of pleasurable spasms. Those around her, and especially the men, as it seemed to Erasmus, were held in thrall to her as they first awaited, then sympathetically shared, these climactic moments.

It was charming, no doubt, but there was something unseemly in it to Erasmus's view. It might be permissible in an unmarried girl, and one who had been much indulged – too much, he sometimes thought these days; but it would not do for a wife, who after all is guardian of her husband's dignity. He would have liked to speak to her immediately about it but hesitated to do so, being afraid that she would misunderstand his motives. She was wilful and did not take kindly to correction. But he was resolved to make his views plain to her when they were married. Small resolves of this sort were mixed inextricably with his larger ambitions for the future.

Finding himself unable to control the present, as he could the future, by excluding anything unpalatable, he tried to do it by grasping for the essence of Sarah's life before he had appeared in it. He would question her in a painstaking fashion, but his questions always failed to elicit what he sought; and any information she herself volunteered was somehow unmanageable. Her catechism dress, a pet pug, visits to Chester with her mother – his mind could not work on these things, he could not take them over. Trying to imagine a past for her, a separate existence, a time when he was not present, this was as painful and difficult as trying to be Ferdinand to her Miranda, and in fact not much dissimilar.

What came more easily to him was a sort of appropriation; he was happiest when he could take her experience and reinterpret it for her. One morning in early August when they had arranged to go riding together, as he was waiting for her in a small room adjacent to the salon, his eye fell on a painting hanging there, set in an elaborate, scroll-gilt frame. It was a picture of a landscape with lords and ladies in fashionable dress of some former period. The men were handsome and proud, the ladies slender and exquisite. Accompanied by servants and long-legged, elegant hounds they strolled through orchards, where fruit glowed among dark leaves and the turf beneath their feet was spangled with white flowers. Erasmus gazed for some time at the painting, struck by the sense of serene enjoyment contained in it. It was obviously old; the pigments had thickened and darkened, and the glaze showed through here and there. But there was a brightness still about the faces of these fashionable strollers; they had a charmed, invulnerable air, as if blessings were raining invisibly down through the strangely rounded, clump-shaped trees.

When Sarah came in, dressed for riding in a dark green habit, he asked her where the painting had come from.

'It belonged to my mother's family, I believe – so I have heard tell.'

'You are not sure?' He smiled, thinking it odd that she should be vague about such a thing; he knew the exact provenance of every article in his own house.

'It has been here for as long as I remember,' she said, with something defensive now in her tone. 'Always in this same place.'

'Do you not know who painted it?'

'I have no idea. Is that so strange?'

'When it is known who painted a picture, the value of it may thereby increase.' Erasmus said this rather loudly and sententiously, secure in his greater knowledge of affairs.

'Value?' Sarah arched her brows at him as if in some surprise. She paused a moment, then said, 'If I ever knew the name of the painter, I have forgot it. It will be some foreign man who lived long ago. I do not know how it is titled, either. I mean what *he* called it. But I do know what it is about.'

Erasmus recognized the distinctness with which she uttered these last words and the luminous smile that came now to her face. With absolute certainty she said, 'It is a picture of people in paradise,' and for the briefest of moments her eyelids flickered together and the slightest of shudders went through her.

For a short while Erasmus considered her gravely. Then he looked back at the painting, but with a sharper and more deliberate attentiveness now. 'Paradise?' he said after some moments of scrutiny. 'Who has servants in paradise? Those are servants, aren't they?'

'No, no,' she said quickly and somehow urgently, as if a word in time now could prevent serious misunderstanding. 'No, people would see it in the light of their own lives. If you have servants while you are alive, you would naturally think of having them in paradise too. I have known this picture all my life. It used to fascinate me when I was a little girl, the expression on their faces. They are in paradise. You see how blessed they are. Nothing can touch them, they command everything.' She had spoken volubly and with the same note of urgency, a tone almost of pleading, childish and insistent.

Erasmus looked at her with the same deliberateness with which he had regarded the painting. His face wore an expression she had never seen on it before, patronizing and almost contemptuous. 'And dogs?' he said. 'And fine clothes? Those are hunting dogs, you know. Do folk go hunting in paradise?'

In her expression now as she looked at him there was a kind of bewilderment. 'But I have explained that to you,' she said. 'People have to see things in their own way. If it is happiness on earth to wear beautiful clothes and be at leisure, then they think it must be the same in heaven too.'

'Explained it to me?' Erasmus was smiling still but his eyes had narrowed. He said, 'I believe you see yourself as one of those fashionable ladies, Sarah, don't you? That must be why you like the picture so much. You think paradise is a place to dress up and act a part in. It is like being on a stage, isn't it, like *The Enchanted Isle?*'

'That is not how I feel at all, it is just the contrary,' she said, regarding him more narrowly. 'I always felt that they were in another world from mine, that is why –'

'No,' he said. 'That is what you may think you felt but it is not the truth of the matter. Children make up stories. You must always have known it was really just a picture of people walking about in a garden, but you made up a story about them. I tell you, Sarah, I know you better than you know yourself.'

The shaft of perception had restored his good humour. He gestured towards the painting. 'These are just people walking about in a garden,' he said. 'If you will only look properly at the picture, you will see that I am right.'

Turning back towards her, he was surprised to encounter a face set against him, blue eyes that looked antagonism. 'Well, well, what a long time I have been mistaken!' she said, in the tone of angry sarcasm with which she nearly always began quarrels. 'And just imagine, I might have continued in error if one fine morning Erasmus Kemp hadn't condescended to take a look and tell me what opinion I ought to have, which of course turns out to be just exactly the same as his. In fact it seems I have always been of his opinion really, but without knowing it.' She had begun steadily enough, but her voice quivered now. 'You don't know me at all,' she said. 'You don't see me as I am. When you say what I am like, I don't recognize myself. You don't want me to have anything of my own. You don't want me to have anything to give you. You are not in the least bit interested in the painting.'

'Not interested?' Erasmus repeated slowly. He could not understand what she meant. He was hurt and astonished at this resistance to his knowledge of her – it was like a rejection of his love. 'Sarah, consider a moment,' he said. 'Reflect on what you say. Can people not discuss an old painting together?' He drew himself up and looked at her with a sort of gloomy remonstrance. 'If we are to fall out over small things, how shall we agree on the great ones?'

This was, he felt, an important question, and one she should have tried to answer. However, she said nothing. She kept her face still turned from him. The ride together did not promise well and they might have decided against it, had not Miss Purdy, dressed and ready, now put in an appearance. If she saw anything amiss between them, she did not remark on it; the morning was fine and she was looking forward to her ride.

It was a day of pale sunshine and light cloud. They rode together in silence, through meadows thick with vetch and buttercups and clover, Sarah in front, then Erasmus, prey to conflict still, dignity preventing him from riding alongside, love from falling too far behind. Miss Purdy kept further back on her stout, short-legged mare.

Unhappiness in Erasmus was compounded with resentment. She had been perverse and unjust, he felt. Was he not allowed an opinion? To be misappreciated is never one's own fault; it must therefore be Sarah's if he had failed to demonstrate his true worth. He wanted her to see that it had been a disinterested quest for truth that had led him to discuss the painting with her. She expected still the indulgence accorded to children. He had shown her the respect of treating her as an adult – that was all his offence.

He marshalled this in his mind as he rode along. He knew it to be true by the infallible sign that the alternative to thinking so involved self-reproach. He had never been much given to introspection. He knew what he wanted, and that was motive and reason enough. He knew he wanted to marry Sarah Wolpert. He knew he wanted to be rich. Some deep unease, something akin to fear, would come to him at any attempt, whether made by himself or others, to root about below the level of his conscious will. Virtue lay in achievement. It was this that since early childhood had led him to sanctify his desires by taking them to the high altar of his room and giving them the form of solemn promises.

Their way wound upwards, at first through stands of mixed woodland, then out into more open country. After some half hour, as they were approaching a point where the bridle-path curved round a low spur, Sarah turned in her saddle to glance briefly over her shoulder at Erasmus, then urged her mount into a trot. He followed suit, as it was clear he was intended to, and found her reining in broadside across the track at the far side of the spur. She looked at him with the expression of conspiratorial glee he had come to recognize and rejoice in – they had achieved by this stratagem a minute or two out of sight of Miss Purdy.

He had the grace at once to realize that with generosity greater than his own she had contrived this occasion for them both. He saw too, almost as quickly, that though an exchange of smiles might have been enough for reconciliation, a kiss would be considerably better. He urged his mount forward. The two horses drew close, rubbed hot flanks together; and their riders leaned forward in the saddle and kissed with a warmth the more eager for the fact that they could touch nowhere but at the lips.

Other kisses there had been between them during the foregoing weeks; but in the isolation of this moment, the overwhelming sense of love restored and faults forgiven, Erasmus seemed for some moments to achieve the dream of containment he was always pursuing; sky and land formed a bubble of thin crystal shot through with light and he and Sarah were caught and held in it beyond the touch of change. It came with a shock almost, as he drew away from her and the walls of their bright capsule dissolved, to find himself exposed again to the touch of air, the world of colours, the attention, possibly reproachful, of the approaching chaperone. 'I am sorry I hurt your feelings,' Sarah said in low quick tones. 'I did not mean to.'

Love does not stand still, as everyone knows; it is always adding to its own shape whether by advance or retreat. Wounds can be absorbed, but only like elements embodied in a story; they are always there, part of the meaning. Sarah was spirited, quick to resent wrongs and slights, to herself or any creature she was attached to; but no resentment could last long with her — she did not bear grudges. Nevertheless, she was accustomed to kindness, especially in her home; she would always remember the look that had come to Erasmus's face when she had confided the meaning of the picture to him, and she would always know that she had been treated with cruelty that morning.

As for Erasmus, even while, in the moments before Miss Purdy came up with them, he was assuring Sarah that he loved her more than anything in the world, somewhere within him he was registering a private displeasure at the terms of her apology. This too, though vague at the time, was destined to take root in the formal garden of his future resolves. It had been right for her to ask his pardon, but not for the hurt she had given him, that was neither here nor there. Wounded feelings did not matter, but there was a principle at stake. Her apology still left unresolved the important question of whose fault it had been.

She should acknowledge that she had been wrong about the picture. Perhaps some day, he thought, there would be an opportunity for him to return to the question. The present moment was clearly not appropriate. But she was fond of the painting and when they were married it might quite possibly be one of the things from home that she would want to bring with her . . .

With Charles Wolpert he was quite often at loggerheads these days. There had been a certain coolness between them since the abrupt end to rehearsals of *The Enchanted Isle*. Charles largely blamed Erasmus for this fiasco, even to the extent of privately holding him responsible for Caliban's defection as well, though the unhappy curate had long since explained to them the real reason. Moreover, he could not forgive Erasmus the lèse-majesté of waylaying a Wolpert guest on Wolpert ground. There were, besides, temperamental differences between the two young men which would probably have led to disagreement in any case. Charles had his father's physical bulk and gravity of address, but little of his business acumen. He was diligent and conscientious and sought to conceal his chronic irresolution behind a manner that grew daily more magisterial. Erasmus, possessed by the twin ardours of love and ambition, and with a vision of the towers of Liverpool rising lovelier than those fabled ones of Ilium, besides offering much better rates of compound interest, grew impatient with the cautious and legalistic habit of Charles's mind and with his long-windedness.

One afternoon, when Erasmus was taking tea in company with Sarah and her mother, Charles returned from the courts in considerable ill-humour and proceeded to complain at length about the protracted course of some litigation the family were involved in, which his father had made him responsible for. As Erasmus knew, there had been recent Acts of Parliament seeking to limit damage to the roads by restricting the number of horses to the wagon and the breadth of the tyres of the wagon wheels. The Wolperts were seeking a ruling on permitted loads per wagon, and it was taking an unconscionable time, according to Charles.

'They talk about horses, they talk about wheels, but they won't come round to the question of loads,' he said. 'It is exasperating in the highest degree.' He had taken to wearing a curled wig lately, which increased the resemblance to his father. He was booted still from riding, having entered in haste for his tea and the sympathetic attention of his mother and sister – it had not much pleased him to find Erasmus ensconced there. He sat back frowning, legs stretched out before him, thumbs looped into his waistcoat pockets. It was a pose Erasmus recognized as the prelude to a great deal of tedious prosing.

'If we could only get a ruling on it, you see,' Charles said, 'we might then be able to turn the tables, as we could retort upon them that with loads of that order it is nonsense to forbid extra horses or they will simply burst their hearts between the shafts. If we can once carry that point, we might be able to press for a change in the regulations concerning the wagon wheels. But these lawyers talk endlessly and get nothing done and charge confounded high fees.'

Erasmus had felt antagonism merely at the way Charles sprawled there, the space he took up. And then these tedious and pointless squabbles over pack-trains . . . 'Wrangling in the courts is a waste of time,' he said. 'You will take six months over it and get an inch or two added to the width of the wheels. For the life of me I cannot see what good that will do. Your costs are not thereby much reduced, the amounts you can transport not much increased and the roads remain in the same state, all ruts in the dry weather and streaming with mud when it rains. It is the roads that need attention, not the wagon wheels.'

These remarks and the manner of their delivery were irritating to Charles, who had been embroiled in the business for some time now and so felt entitled to be listened to, especially on his home ground. 'It is no use trying to run before you can walk,' he said. 'That is a besetting fault of yours, Erasmus, if I may say so. The coal is lying there, in the coalfields. It is needed now, today. We have to bring it on the roads we have got. What do you think will be the consequence to our salt works if we let the coal pile up thirty miles away while we wait for this Utopia of yours?'

'I am not talking about Utopias.' Erasmus's eyes had kindled. 'I am talking about known facts. The road between Liverpool and Prescot was metalled and tolls charged for the upkeep and that led to vastly improved supplies of coal from the south-west. Now they have extended it to St Helens and in time they –'

'It is time my son is talking about.'

For some moments the heated Erasmus could not quite determine where this gentle female voice had come from. It seemed to fall on his ears from some unlocalized source somewhere up towards the ceiling. Then, with intense surprise, he realized that it was Sarah's mother who had spoken: in her mob cap and lace shawl Mrs Wolpert had leaned forward and actually interrupted him.

'That road was turnpiked more than twenty-five years ago,' she continued placidly. 'That is before you were born, Erasmus. I remember it well, it happened in the year I was married. It has taken all these years just to carry the road on to St Helens, in spite of all the great advantages you speak of. I hope you don't mean to say that my husband has to sit twenty years and wait for better roads while they make their laws against him in London?'

Erasmus could find no immediate response to this. He had felt his jaw slacken with astonishment. Never in his whole life had he heard a woman intrude her opinion into a conversation on business matters between men. It was inconceivable that his own mother should ever do so. Wolpert must permit it, he thought, divided between wonder and contempt. Perhaps he even consulted her – her tone had betokened intimacy with her husband's affairs. No wonder Sarah was so ready with opinion, with this model before her eyes. 'No, madam,' he said at last, staring straight before him, 'I did not mean to suggest that. How your husband fetches his coal to Liverpool is entirely his own affair.'

The reproof rankled long afterwards as a setback, a blow to his self-esteem, made worse by the vindicated complacency that he had seen come to Charles's face. But when he was alone and safe from such pettifogging objections, when he was at home or riding to and from the Wolpert house or occupied with family business, his mind expanded with a sense of the glorious opportunities the future afforded and the certainty of his place in it – his and Sarah's.

Coal was the key, so far Wolpert was right. The population of the town was more than twenty thousand now and rising rapidly, and the domestic demand for coal was rising with it. In Cheshire the boiling of brine and refining of rock salt called for coal in ever larger quantities, as did the other new industries springing up on every hand, metal-working, glass-making, sugar-refining: all were hungry for coal – and all were obliged to use the port of Liverpool to ship their goods.

It was clear to Erasmus that wagon trains could never bring the quantities needed, even if the roads were improved. The coal would have to come by water. Already the Mersey was navigable by small ships as far as Manchester, and the barges were plying back and forth from Stockport. This had been achieved in the teeth of scoffing unbelievers, by deepening and straightening the river channels. A great feat of engineering – they had reconstructed the river, no less. The skills thus learned could be – must inevitably be, and soon – applied to man-made waterways, which would carry a vastly greater tonnage at a fraction of the cost. Erasmus felt energy course through him at the thought. His imagination might remain untouched by Ferdinand weeping for the king his father's wreck, or Sarah clinging to a cherished notion of childhood; but it became incandescent at thoughts of transporting a hundred thousand tons of coal a year in your own barges. The future lay in coalfields and canals. He knew it beyond any shadow of question. The men who gained control of these would be the new princes of the city, eminent, powerful, rich beyond the dreams of avarice . . .

He was happy during these summer weeks. It was to be, in his recollection, a golden time, instinct with a promise and hope that he sensed at many different moments of his day, at home in his room or in the streets of the city or at work, where in addition to the duties normally falling to him – he was responsible now for all the coastal shipping business of the firm and for the movement of raw cotton to Warrington and Manchester – he was applying himself diligently to the study of accountancy and mercantile law.

The season seemed to contain the same promise. It was full tide of green now in the hedges and wasteground on the outskirts of the city, where herons flapped above the marshes and cows grazed and vagrants slept in the long grass among the brick kilns. The willowherb came and the berries began to redden on the rowan trees. The meadows were scythed, the grass lying in long, slightly darker swathes. The slopes of the hills and the edges of the wheat fields echoed to the stuttering song of the yellowhammer, with its mournfully protracted final note. Then the birds fell silent and the stubble lay crepitant and hot, emitting odours of slightly stale sweetness. Summer reached its apogee and began insensibly to wane; and it would have no more been possible to say when this waning began than it would have been to say when William Kemp admitted despair as the companion of his days and with it the lure of death.

TWENTY-SIX

Hunched in his cabin over his journal, Paris contended with sultry heat and general feelings of lassitude. In a way, these discomforts helped his resolve to complete his notes for the day; they were, together with the words themselves, details in the belated evidence of love that he was always offering to Ruth. The entries, however trivial or commonplace, had become links in a chain of communion. He spared no distressing matter, feeling that this too, all that he was enduring on the ship, could somehow be offered to her in terms of love and contrition.

Our privileged position for trading has not lasted very long. We have now been anchored here ten days and woke this morning to find two ships in the offing, a Frenchman and a Bristol slaver named the Edgar, *whose captain Thurso is acquainted with – a man named Macdonald.*

The presence of the French ship put our good captain thoroughly out of temper at once. It seems that the French are notorious for paying high prices, and this because they can sell their negroes dearer in their own colonies than can we in ours. And so they ruin the trade for the English. Thurso clenched his fists when he spoke of it and flushed up very dark, and those strangely unprotected-looking eyes of his that I have spoke of before went glancing all over the deck as if he hoped to find a Frenchman handy whom he could seize up to the grating and exercise his wrath upon. His deepest rages are always reserved for crosses to his will and especially when this involves any loss in trading – I have often remarked on it; but it is nevertheless strange to hear a man abuse a whole nation, as he did the French for several minutes on end, for popery and cowardice and poor seamanship and I know not what, when the true cause is only that they can obtain five pounds a head more for their negroes than you can for yours.

He seems lacking in any sort of perspective beyond commercial advantage and

232

without imagination for how others might see things. Barton, though I think him a wickeder man, at least in the sense of conscious wickedness, has greater perception of others and even humour of a certain kind, as I saw once again in the matter of the muskets. These, or rather the mutilations resulting from them, lived on in my mind with some special horror, I think because of the ludicrous display the men made of them. This was so much the case with me that I took the step – unusual these days, as he and I rarely have much to say to each other – of asking the captain directly if it were true that we sold defective firearms to these people. He denied it fiercely, being, I really think, incapable of admissions that might be weakening to his commercial prospects; but Barton later told me, with a good deal of chuckling and peering about, that English slavers have for many years been including inferior goods, bought at cheaper rates from the manufacturers, in their trade cargoes – not only weapons but metal goods generally and textiles too. 'They cheat us and we cheat them,' as Barton put it, 'that is the way the world goes round.' I dare say it is, but I cannot help suspecting that it was we, rather than the Africans, who gave the globe its first spin in that direction.

In the time we have been here we have acquired seventeen more slaves, bringing our total now to twenty-four, of whom eight are females. Several of them have inflammations from their burns and I have treated them as well as I can with dressings. There is a difference in the way they are branded, the men being marked on the breast, the women on the buttocks. They have been kept mainly on deck so far, under an awning that has been rigged amidships.

Tapley was punished this morning for spitting on the deck. He received a dozen strokes with a rattan cane. He is the second to be caned since we came here; the other was Calley, who apparently tried to take hold of one of the women but she set up a shriek and prevented him. He escaped the heavier punishment of flogging, as it was seen he had done no harm. It is doubtful, I think, whether he meant any; he is in some dream of his own much of the time. The woman's cry had so frightened him that he fell headlong on the deck and half knocked himself out. Thurso had him hauled up and caned there and then, as a convenient example, with the blood still running down from a cut in his scalp. Even thus dazed he struggled violently and four men were required to tie him. What the negroes think when they see their captors being thus treated, I have no means of knowing. The interpreter Thurso threatened the men with has not yet appeared.

I was told by Simmonds, on whose watch it occurred, that there was an eclipse of the moon in the early hours of the morning. He says that he perceived the shade enter upon the moon's disc shortly before four o'clock and it was wholly darkened by five, soon after which he lost sight of it in the haze, it

233

being by then very near the horizon. I was sorry not to have been present at this, as I think I have only once before seen the moon totally shaded.

Captain Thurso is not aboard at present. He has left Barton in command with orders to keep a good watch and to buy any likely slaves that are brought out to the ship, also to spy on the Frenchman's activities as far as possible, and has had himself rowed out to the Edgar; *it seems that Macdonald is returning further eastward along the coast, and will know the situation there. Thurso did not ask his surgeon to accompany him, for which that same surgeon is grateful.*

Not long after he had gone a party of men under Haines set off to shore in the yawl with water casks and a variety of cutting tools. What these last are for I do not know. There is much that is not explained to me; I do not mean kept from me – I suppose my knowledge is assumed; and it would be easy to resign myself to this, cease enquiring about this world of the present, into which I have strayed by some accident and which appears more grievous to me every day, just as I have ceased to speculate, or much to care, about what is to become of me. Perhaps that is all that would be needed: by an act of will to relinquish curiosity and so have no need to skulk away from God when he walks in the cool of the evening . . .

But this, as he knew, was death in life. It was in a spirit of rebellion against his own self-abnegation that he abruptly closed his journal now and made his way up on deck. The weather was oppressively heavy and hot, with a darkening skein of cloud drawing over the sky from the distant headlands to the south. The wind had abated but the waves were high over the bar across the river mouth; he saw the glitter of the spray and heard the low thunder of the breakers. This distant violence of the surf, viewed across the calm expanse of blue unbroken water, appeared to Paris like the stealthy release of some vindicative mania long nursed. A sickening fetid smell came over the water from Macdonald's ship lying to windward of them with its full cargo of slaves.

Turning and looking down into the waist of the ship, he saw the negroes clustered under their canopy, their bodies patterned by shadows. The slight, continuous riffling of the awning made gleaming fluxions of light on the men's chains. The women had been given a piece of calico to tie round their waists so as to cover the pudenda, and these squares of white held an intense purity in the thick light filtering down through the canvas. Johnson and Libby were standing guard, armed with pistols and whips.

Forward of him, astride on the boom, he saw Hughes working on the tackle for the stay ropes, head and shoulders outlined against the sky. On the deck below Cavana was sitting cross-legged, with various bits and pieces laid out before him.

Paris made his way forward and stood near the starboard rail. Cavana had glanced up at his approach but his eyes were back on his work now, and he showed no sign of being aware of the surgeon's proximity. They had not spoken much together since he had treated Cavana for an inflamed condition of the eyes.

'What work is that you are doing?' the surgeon enquired after an interval of some moments.

'I am putting in new pins for these blocks,' Cavana's voice was surprisingly soft and musical. After an appreciable pause he added, 'They have wore loose. They were not well fitted to begin with.'

This was the longest speech that Cavana had made for some considerable time; but he felt relaxed this morning, in the sultry weather, under the slowly thickening sky, with customary aggravation absent for the moment, Thurso away on his visit, Haines ashore with the boat party, Barton below somewhere busy with stores. Besides, though he would not have gone so far as to admit to a liking, he had formed a favourable judgement of Paris over the weeks, and this though the surgeon had started out with the black mark against him of being related to the owner. In this Cavana shared the general opinion of the fore-castle. It was seen that Paris spoke fairly to people and that he was no crimp for Thurso – it was remembered how he had stood out against the captain over treating Wilson's torn back. Other things there were too. A ship is a public place and the *Liverpool Merchant* was little more than a hundred feet long from stem to stern. Paris would have been surprised to learn the extent to which his words and actions had been noted.

Cavana maintained silence for some moments more to see if the surgeon had more questions. He discovered in himself a reluctance to let this conversation come to an end. He said, 'They don't use hard enough wood for it, these days. They should use greenheart or ironwood for the pins.'

235

'I see, yes.' Paris thought he could detect the accents of Wales in the other's voice, much muted. He looked up briefly to see Hughes still straddling the boom, his bare feet against the smooth projections of the saddle on the bowsprit. Beyond him the sky was darker now and there was a hush over everything, presaging rain.

'There is quite some wear on the pins then?' he said.

Cavana looked for some moments at the face of the surgeon. He saw nothing there but a serious and kindly attentiveness. 'Well, the pins now,' he said at last. Unaccustomed feelings of friendliness rose in him. He was suddenly glad to have this work to do and to explain; and he felt something like gratitude towards this vague-seeming man for providing the occasion. 'The pins,' he said, almost eagerly, 'they have got to be as hard as you can get and they have got to fit snug because the wheel that is inside the shell of the block turns on them, d'you see; the hole is bored through the middle and the block-maker must take care to make it a one-tenth part less than the measure round of the pin.'

Paris, to whom this had not been entirely comprehensible, nodded gravely. 'Well,' he said, 'I can see that the choice of wood is of first importance.'

'I know about all manner of blocks,' Cavana said. He paused a moment, then added – and Paris did not know what a mark of favour was being shown him – 'I was apprentice to a block-maker for the navy. I worked three years in the dockyards at Plymouth.'

'Did you so? But you left it for the sea?'

'I took to the sea, yes.' Cavana looked down again to his work. He had spoken on a brusquer note which Paris at first thought due to the nature of his question, pressing too closely on the man's past; but then he saw that Barton had appeared and was sniffing at the air on the starboard side of the mainmast. Facing that way, Cavana had seen him sooner. Paris knew he would not speak again now and felt sorry for an occasion lost.

He turned away and moved to where Barton was standing. The mate gave him good-day and directed sharp looks towards Hughes and Cavana, whose head was now down over his work.

'Rain before long,' he said. 'The men ashore will get a good wettin'.'

'What are they gone for? I saw that there were casks for water, but they had cutting tools in the boat also.'

'Aye, they are gone to cut stanchions to make a barricado.' Seeing that Paris had not understood this, Barton gave his peering, strangely benevolent-seeming smile. There was nothing he liked better than the chance to deliver some felicitous phrasing. 'The barricado,' he said, 'is a fence we makes with wood stakes clear across the foremost part of the quarterdeck. Now you may ask what is the use of that. But you have to bear in mind, Mr Paris, that when we have our full copplement of slaves aboard, it might amount to two hundred and more. They will be kept below at night but in fair weather, in the daytime, they will be allowed up for air and exercise – they has to be let up if you want 'em alive an' kickin'. Captain Thurso usually makes 'em dance for a half hour or so in the mornin' an' that gener'ly answers the purpose pretty well. Now you think of all them black heads gettin' together an' talkin' soft in their own lingo – we don't know what they are sayin' an' we can't stop 'em whisperin' together. You may not think it to look at 'em, now that they are mallancholy and cast down, but they are treacly sly devils. If you could open up one of their skulls you'd find a plan of the ship printed in there. They knows all sorts of little things you wouldn't suppose. They knows where keys is kept, they knows where the gun chest is, they knows where they can get hold of spikes to break their fetters. While we are in sight of land is the dangerous time.' Barton made a theatrical gesture towards the shore. 'There it is,' he said. 'Before their very eyes. They waits for the right moment, then they rushes the quarterdeck, an' they are desprit by then so they ain't easy to stop. So we build a fence across an' we stick two of the swivel cannon through it. Think of the effect, Mr Paris. There they are, plottin' mischief agin us, like the varments they are. Then they see this fence.' The mate paused again to make a spreading gesture with his palms to show the breadth and impenetrable nature of the barricade. He rolled his ferret's eyes to indicate the consternation of the negroes, faced with this obstacle to their

237

plans. 'They see the mouths of the guns pokin' through,' he said. 'Think of the effect on 'em. It's all in the mind, sir.' Barton tapped his head and winked at Paris, to whom it came now that the mate was a considerable artist. The rain, which had been threatening so long, now began to fall, the first slow and heavy drops making distinct and separate sounds of impact on the deck and the stretched canvas of the slave awning.

The rain came down on the shore party as they worked among the mangrove thickets in the tidal swampland bordering the estuary, chopping at the bases of the stems, knee-deep sometimes in the salt mud, stumbling and cursing among the arching roots of the mangroves. The rain obliterated all sight except of what was immediately before them and all sound but that of itself. It fell with a loud continuous drumming on the patient leaves, so thick and fleshy that they barely dipped under the onslaught. Within a minute the men were wet to the skin, their clothes clinging to them. Under the eyes of Haines they worked on without a pause, figures so completely beset by water as to seem almost submerged, the deluge from above indistinguishable from the sprays they shook on themselves as they wrenched at the branches.

The downpour ended abruptly, as at some signal. The surge of the sea came back to them with a curious kind of tentativeness, like a vessel filling slowly. From somewhere nearby there came the low, bubbling celebration of pigeons, then a series of fugitive chatterings from further in among the dripping trees. It grew hotter. The sun was concealed but all-pervasive, spreading below the leaden skin of the sky with the energy of poison, until the whole was suffused and livid with it. Each of the men there, sweat replacing rain as they toiled on in the sickly heat, felt in some fashion that the sky was infected.

Steam rose from the ground, from the foliage of the trees and their soaked clothing. Their sweat prickled them and the sting-ing creatures of the swampland, taking to the air again, guzzled the sweat as a sauce to the blood. There was a sweet heavy smell of flowers and odours of decay rose from the spongy ground and from the brackish slime of the fallen mangrove leaves.

'Holy Mary, Mother of God,' Sullivan groaned, slithering in mud, bedevilled by mosquitoes, grasping at the wet stems to force them down enough for a blow of his axe.

'I thowt you had finished wi' that gibrish, long ago,' Billy Blair said, slapping at his neck, his small, blunt-nosed, belligerent face moist and furious beneath the red kerchief round his brows. 'You said as much, anyway. But it is dawnin' on me that you canna be trusted, Sullivan.' Billy felt an equal fury at the wretched discomfort of the work and at Sullivan's inconsistency in the matter of religion for adding to the baffling nature of the universe.

'I was born for better things,' Sullivan said, pausing to wipe away sweat and mucus from around his mouth, and leaving a smear of blood from the numerous small cuts on the back of his hand.

'Yeh,' sneered Billy, 'playin' the fiddle in a crimp-house.'

'You can keep your snot-box out of me fiddlin',' Sullivan said, on a note of anger rare with him.

These two might have fallen out further if McGann had not chosen this moment to voice some thoughts. His life was given over to small stratagems; his motive for philosophizing now was to obtain a breathing-space. 'Well, takin' it a' in a',' he said, 'we are still men, aren't we?' Sun and rain and a salty diet had set up a flaking process on McGann's face; strips of dead skin hung from brows and cheeks. Amidst this patchy ruin his pale-lashed blue eyes surveyed the world with an expression of spurious calculation. 'There is aye someone worse off than yoursel',' he said. 'We are free men, we can gang an' come as we please, not like them blackies we hae took on board.'

'You try it, shipmate,' Wilson said, face narrow-eyed and sardonic below the stained white cotton headband, the heavy bones of his shoulder-blades standing out under his soaked shirt.

'Ye dinna see what I am gettin' at,' McGann, said. 'I am talkin' aboot freedom. I am talkin' aboot –'

'Get on, you Scotch runt,' hissed Haines from close behind him, having approached silently on purpose to startle and affright. 'You make talkin' an excuse for not workin', and I'll make you sing while you work. You know what song, don't you?'

The pile of trimmed stakes grew steadily on the clearing of shingle above the moored yawl. By mid-afternoon they had enough. While they were loading the stakes a bushpig came through the mangroves and briefly into the open. Haines fired his pistol at it but the creature fled, with no squeal to register a wound. However, the shot brought a prize of another sort: within twenty minutes of it a number of wary black men arrived by canoe from further upriver. They were armed with short, thick-shafted spears decorated with white feathers below the blade. And they were carrying palm wine in calabashes, which they offered with gestures and guttural sounds to sell.

Some close bargaining followed, at which the seamen were at a disadvantage, it proving impossible for them to keep eagerness for the liquor out of their eyes. Billy's kerchief and a copper ring belonging to Deakin were all that the negroes seemed interested in, once they had clearly understood that the gold band in Haines's ear and the hand-axes were not negotiable. Neither Wilson nor Calley nor Sullivan had anything at all to offer. The bargain was finally clinched by Haines, who dug in his waistcoat pocket and produced a brass button. 'Here you are, I'll throw this in,' he said, and perhaps there was something in his voice and manner, and in the quality of stillness now investing all the white men, that caused the negroes to close on the offer.

'Let me see that button,' Sullivan said, but he was too late – it was in the black man's hand now; attempts to retrieve it might have led to dangerous misunderstandings. 'That was my button,' he said to the boatswain. 'That button was off me coat.'

'What are you talkin' about?' Haines said carelessly. His eyes were on the wine. 'Get out of the way. Come on, lads, it is share and share alike, hoist the liquor up on the beach.'

Thus Haines, with assumed good-fellowship, sought to appear to the others as the provider of the feast, so as to keep a semblance of authority. A natural leader might have carried this off, but a natural leader would have been more loved than Haines, who in fact was not loved at all and knew it, but was led into unwisdom now by his wish to get drunk.

The negroes departed with dignity and without farewells,

making upstream again, their paddles dipping in perfect unison. The first of the gourds began to pass round the seated circle of men. The wine was clouded and sweetish, still fermenting slightly, very potent. The men had eaten nothing since morning. For perhaps half an hour all was harmony and accord among them. The drink passed round. It was cooler now and they were grateful for the leisure after their hours of toil, and for the ease that came to their limbs with the slow onset of drunkenness.

Sullivan, however, brooded. He was a convivial soul, especially in his drink, but he sat silent now. He was not vindictive like Wilson, who was at odds with the world and could not absorb his wrongs without violence. Life had dealt blows to Sullivan. Vagrancy and beggary, interspersed by spells at sea, had been his condition for almost as long as he could remember and he had seen the inside of prison more than once; but he had been blessed with a spirit of optimism, feckless perhaps, but saving him from that saddest of human destinies, which we call learning from one's mistakes. Sullivan had a short memory for mistakes as well as for wrongs. But to be robbed and then treated with contumely is hard to bear. To see Haines making play with what he was convinced was one of his buttons had caused him deep offence.

By the time the third calabash began circulating, drunkenness was general and advanced. The talk had turned to money and what it could buy. It was the opinion of Wilson that money could buy anything. 'If a man has enough on it,' he said, 'it'll buy him owt i' the world. Anythin' an' anybody.' His deep-set eyes had a glinting look and there was a quarrelsome note in his voice as he looked round the circle of faces. 'I know the world,' he said.

'Nobody's sayin' you don't,' Blair said, roused as always to combativeness by any hint of it in another. He leaned his small, pugnacious face forward, blinking to get the hulking Yorkshireman into focus. 'No use yappin' on, shipmate,' he said. 'Billy Blair knows the world better'n any man here, but that's no bleddy argument. What about them that has all the money they need an' live in palaces an' have servants to wait on 'em? What about the Prince o' Wales or the Archbishop o' Canterbury? Are you sayin' King George would be interested in yor money?'

Wilson's head sank down and he passed a tongue over his lips as he considered this. 'Kings an' bishops, is it?' he said with slow displeasure. 'Why is tha bringin' them in?'

'Nobody has everything they want,' Deakin said in his flat, expressionless voice, to which the drink had made no difference. 'There would always be something, if you could find it out. Might be only some little thing.'

'Some little thing,' Calley said in slurred echo of his friend. He smiled slackly, his eyes wide and unsteady. What could it be? he wondered. Something he might find himself, a piece of coloured stone, a bird's feather . . .

Wilson raised his head and fixed Billy with a sombre stare. 'What dost tha mean by talkin' o' King George?' he said. 'Tha's always tryin' to be clever.' Suspicion came to his face. 'I see thy game,' he said. 'Tha's tryin' to trap me into speakin' agin the king.'

'Stow that gab, lads,' Haines said. 'What you are talkin' about was all writ in the Bible long years ago.' He gazed at the disputants with heavy-lidded dignity. 'Him that has got something already must always try to get hold of more,' he said. 'An' the more he gets, the more will be given to him. That is in the Gospels.' He paused, passing a hand over his dark stubble and squinting at Wilson and Blair. 'What that means, my likely lads, is that it is everyone's bounden duty to try to get more than they have got already. If you have got two shillin' you try to make it into four shillin' an' you try to make that . . .' The boatswain paused here again, slightly losing the thread of his discourse. 'There is no end to it,' he said. 'An' the more you have to show for it, the more the bridegroom will be pleased with you when he comes in the night. I was brung up on the Bible,' he said, with a sudden, bitter twist of the mouth.

He would have done better to keep quiet. His discipline had never been more than brutality and there was no one to support him here.

'Who the pox is the bridegroom?' Billy said with sudden ferocity.

'We was talkin' between friends, wasn't we, Billy?' Wilson said. 'Why is he stickin' his oar in? This cuddy got me a floggin'.'

242

He looked at Haines as though seeing him for the first time. 'Dost tha want thy jaw broke?' he said.

But it was Sullivan who was first on his feet. 'Is that why you stole me buttons?' he demanded, swaying slightly from side to side. 'That's the divil's book you've been readin'. You done well. You done better than thim fellers in the parable, you made no buttons into six buttons just with a snip or two of the scissors. The bridegroom will be proud of you, Haines, bejabbers, he will take you to hell with pleasure.'

The boatswain sat still for a moment. Then he scrambled to his feet, staggered, recovered. 'You blasted Irish scudder,' he said, 'are you callin' William Haines a thief?'

Sullivan had raised his fists but Billy was up now and between the two men. He knew Haines was too strong for the Irishman and suspected that his own chances were not much better, though nothing of this doubt appeared in his bearing. 'Come on, then,' he said, half naked and profane and dark red in the face with alcohol and excitement. 'Last time my hands was held behind, do you remember, you scut-head bastid?'

However, in the event, it was Wilson who fought the boatswain. Billy, his vision still clouded, found himself pushed out of the way by the gaunt Yorkshireman, who seemed to come from nowhere, shouldering him aside and striking out at Haines in the same movement and without uttering a sound. The others scrambled to give the two men room enough.

That first blow had jolted Haines but not hurt him much. The drink had slowed him down but he had a natural agility and recovered balance quickly. He caught the advancing Wilson with a sweeping left-hand blow to the side of the head which sent him sprawling to the ground.

He was up on one knee immediately, shaking his head to clear it. He was a heavy man, without Haines's natural athleticism, but his ugly temper had furnished him over the years with much experience of brawling. Even through the fog of drink a sort of cunning still operated in him. He got to his feet slowly and stood with his hands low and his head hanging.

The savage urge to inflict damage on his opponent while he seemed thus defenceless made Haines unwary. He struck at

Wilson with left and right. The other rode back from the full force of these blows, though the second split his lip. Then, in the moment that the boatswain was still off-balance, Wilson made his recovery, jabbed with his left hand at his opponent's eyes and when the boatswain gave back, followed with a straight blow from the shoulder which landed square on the other man's jaw. Haines staggered, tripped on the shingle and fell heavily.

He struggled up again but the heart was out of the fight now. The blows they had taken and the heavy falls, combining with the quantities of drink both had consumed, had put lead into their limbs. They staggered and flailed about for some minutes more, faces marked with blood, occasionally landing blows, occasionally clinging to each other for balance in what resembled a clumsy and ill-coordinated dance. The boatswain, blind now on his left side, got in the way of a swinging blow that landed high on the cheekbone and sent him reeling. Wilson, trying to follow this up, swung at him again, missed, staggered and fell flat, winding himself. It took him a long time to get up and when he did so the two men did not close but stood some paces apart, breathing heavily and regarding each other with a sort of bafflement.

Thus by unspoken consent the fight was abandoned, though not the quarrel – neither man offered to shake hands. The spectators had by now lost interest in the proceedings. McGann was already asleep and within a short while the others slept too, lying sprawled and stertorous on the shingle.

It was not until they were awake again and grumbling in the chillier air that they discovered that Deakin and Calley had disappeared and did not answer to their shouts. With them had gone two axes and Haines's pistol.

Deakin and Calley heard the shouts distantly from where they crouched in the shrub some quarter of a mile upstream. Calley had been sick from the palm wine and still did not feel quite well. It seemed a lonely thing to stay hidden and make no answer to these voices. Sitting there, lips tightly compressed to show his friend Deakin how determined he was not to make the slightest noise, he had a confused and painful memory of shouts of children on the streets, shouting his name in mockery, keeping him out – the children flowed away from him, re-formed somewhere out of his sight, always out of his sight, leaving only the fleeting, mocking reiteration of his name . . . These shouts now were different, asking for him, wanting to include him. They died away finally and he felt the silence settle round them both. He glanced at Deakin and saw that the other's eyes were not looking at him or anything near at hand, but were fixed on some distant point beyond the river. Then Deakin became aware of his gaze and smiled and said in low tones, 'Don't you worry, Dan'l. I shall see you all right.'

TWENTY-SEVEN

Thurso had returned from his visit to the *Edgar* in late afternoon, in much improved mood, having learned from Captain Macdonald that trade was brisk further east along the coast and especially in the vicinity of the Kavalli River. Thurso was intending to do some business on his own account – business which no one but Barton knew anything about. The Company of Merchants Trading to Africa, to which his owner, William Kemp, belonged, had taken over the dilapidated old fort on the coast, previously the property of the Royal Africa Company, and refurbished it, installing new cannon, strengthening the garrison and extending the slave-dungeons. According to Macdonald they had established excellent relations with the traders on the river and with the chiefs in the interior. Macdonald had bought two hundred and twenty-three slaves in the space of two months, he assured Thurso; only sixteen had so far died, and three of those suicides. He was staying only to take on rice and yams before leaving for the West Indies.

Had it not been for this encouraging news, the boat party might have fared much worse at their return, and especially Haines, who presented himself some several hours later than might have been expected, haggard and bruised, his left eye blackened and half closed, his shirt blood-bedabbled, minus pistol and cartridge belt and two axes, and with two of his party missing. Haines knew he had been a fool. He expected a flogging and felt it was deserved – he had been flogged in his time for much lesser offences. In the event, he was roundly cursed by Thurso, struck in the face and confined in handcuffs and double leg irons for the night. The value of pistol and ammunition was deducted from his pay.

Much of this was done for the sake of effect. Thurso did not have high expectations of the boatswain, or any of his crew. He knew they would drink to the point of insensibility if they could get hold of liquor and that some would run if they saw an opportunity. He was angered by the loss of the two men, but the chances were that they would be recaptured. If not, he would save their wages. It was later, when the ship was fully slaved, that a full crew would be needed; and he felt fairly sure of being able to take on more men later, at Cape Mount.

Next morning, having provisioned the yawl for three days, he set off for shore, taking Paris and Simmonds with him and six members of the crew. The principal dealer along the Sherbro River was a mulatto named Tucker and he had sent word that he had slaves to sell. Four of his retainers had been dispatched to meet them and conduct them upriver to Tucker's house. They were waiting in a light canoe in the shade of the raffia palms along the banks just within the bar, where the water eddied and sidled, flecked with muddy white.

The river was wide here and the current flowed strongly. The seamen at the oars had hard work of it to keep their guides in sight. These made against the current with astonishing swiftness in their light canoe, one man standing at prow and one at stern, leaning forward in unison to throw their weight on the long-handled paddles.

The sound of the waves breaking over the bar at the river mouth pursued them, growing sullen with distance. They were enclosed on either side by thick walls of glossy-leaved mangrove trees. Paris sought to distract his mind from the close heat and the zealous attention of various stinging creatures by noting, for future inclusion in his journal, the naked and adventitious-seeming roots of these trees, how they arched from the parent stem while some feet from the ground to form strange stilts and buttresses.

'He is a big man in these parts, Tucker,' Thurso said. 'All the people you see here belong to him on both sides of the river.' He was as near as he could ever be to good humour this morning, with the prospect of doing business, seeing an old acquaintance, though he was sweating, Paris noticed, in his hot clothes – he was dressed in his best, with braided tricorn hat and blue and silver coat with lace at the cuffs. 'There is no trading anywhere up this river without Tucker,' he said. 'He is what I call a success in life, Mr Paris. He is over seventy now and has his hair and teeth still and as rich as Croesus. And he has built it all up from nothing – not like you who had the benefit of a professional training. Everything he has got he has had to work for. It was the same with me. I don't mind admitting it, to you or any man.' Thurso leaned forward and said in a low, hoarse mutter, 'I was never handed anything on a silver plate. My parents were out of this world before I was four years old.'

'Indeed, sir?' Paris looked at the immobile, brick-coloured face, the small blue eyes that seemed now once again, this avowal or confession having been made, to seek for refuge further back and find none. The surgeon felt touched, though knowing this confidence quite probably came only because the captain despised him. It was the first in any case that Thurso had ever made. 'You were brought up by relatives then, sir?' he ventured, rather diffidently; he had learned that the captain suspected the motives behind all questions.

'I was brought up by the parish.' Thurso's face had become more forbidding. 'The sea has been father and mother to me,' he said. 'Aye, and more.' He fell silent now and looked fixedly before him in one of the fits of dark abstraction that Paris had noticed in him before.

The river had narrowed. As they went closer in to the bank Paris saw the gauze and glint of honey bees high up among the small white flowers of the mangroves and caught the brackish smell from the ooze at their roots. Voices came from somewhere among the trees. They passed a landing stage made with moored rafts where women squatted, washing clothes at the waterside.

'Yes,' Thurso said, 'Tucker may be a mulatto, but he is a man to be reckoned with.' He spoke as if there had been no interval. Small beads of sweat had started on his brow and he wiped them away with a cambric handkerchief from his sleeve, in a gesture oddly delicate for a man of his bulk. 'There are times he might have as many as fifty prime slaves in his pens,' he said. 'Of course he has some customs we might object to, as

248

coming from more civilized society. For example he has more than one wife – seven or eight, I believe. Now we might think that little better than fornication, but it is their practice hereabouts. He knows my feelings, but I don't let it stand in the way of business. Besides, you see, there is a sound practical reason at the back of it, which you have to know these parts properly to appreciate. Just counting his own blood kin and relations by marriage, he can send upwards of a hundred men raiding upriver, and when you add to that his personal slaves and people that are in bond to him . . . He gives out credit to the people when they fall on bad times. They all owe him money. They know they can be sold for slaves to pay off the debt, so they take care to keep on the right side of him. There is nothing like fear, for keeping people in order. No, Tucker has got things very well in hand considering that he came to this coast with nothing.'

The river took a wide curve between banks of low shrub; the trees had been cleared here on both sides. Their guides waited above a balustraded wooden jetty where a boat was unloading plantains in wicker baskets. On the bankside beyond, lines of washing were hanging. Tucker himself was waiting at the top of the wooden steps that went up from the jetty. He was a tall, stout patriarch, light brown in colour, with a reverend poll of white hair. He greeted his visitors with dignified ease and led them through a square compound formed by low huts where women sat in the shade preparing food and small children disputed the dust with chickens.

The house was handsome and spacious, built of timber on two storeys, with gables and a broad, open verandah. Thurso glanced at Paris as they approached it, as if to remind him that this was the property of a man who had come up from nothing. Once inside he presented the mulatto with the gifts he had brought – a case of French brandy and a pair of silver-mounted pistols.

The crew members were assigned to Tucker's retainers and led away to be fed at the back of the house. Thurso, Paris and Simmonds were at once – though it was scarce eleven – invited to table. They had green salad from Tucker's own garden, and bushpig stewed with paw-paws, and rice with a sauce of palm

249

oil and pepper, all served on fine plate and accompanied by French wine. In response to compliments on the quality of this from an emboldened Simmonds, their host explained in his soft, idiosyncratic English that he had taken two dozen cases a fortnight before in part payment for slaves and ivory. Not from a French ship, but an American – a twenty-gun sloop. How a Nantucket privateer had come by fine quality French wines it was better not to ask, Tucker said, with his restrained smile. Other than this, not much news. A ruffian by the name of Yellow Henry Cook had been causing trouble and poaching on trade in the interior, but he believed that had been dealt with; Paris noted that Thurso forbore from enquiring how. Then there was the garden – he was growing marrows and trying out a type of European potato, and he had planted lemon trees. They must see it afterwards.

It was not till the end of the meal, over the brandy, that the talk turned to business. It appeared that Tucker had only six slaves in his pens at present, though all were male and guaranteed prime quality. He was expecting more within the next two or three days. He had sent a big party upriver in charge of his eldest son. If Captain Thurso would trust him for the goods, there would soon be slaves aplenty.

If Thurso was displeased at this he did not show it. Tucker was not a man to cross or ruffle in any way. He would stay the night, he said, if he could trade on his host's hospitality so far, and leave next day. Perhaps the slaving party would return in that time. It would in any case allow his surgeon and the second mate the time for a journey further upriver to see what the English factor, Owen, had to offer.

Paris had not known that this was intended; and it was still with a feeling of surprise, and something of resentment too, at not being informed, that he found himself some half hour later seated with Simmonds in one of his host's canoes under a low matting roof, with two oarsmen and two domestic servants of Tucker's for escort. A second canoe, intended for slaves, led the way.

A thin haze of mist hung over the water, rendering more distant objects indistinct – the canoe in front was half hidden in it. Paris could make out the man standing at the prow, the shine of his naked shoulders as he threw himself forward on the oar, the dip and flash of the long blade; but the form of the canoe itself was lost; it was as if the negro were suspended there, to perform his regular obeisance to some deity brooding above. The sky was featureless and hot, the colour of pale brass. They passed a heron at the water's edge, to all appearance the same grey heron, hunched and dishevelled, that he had seen in Norfolk, round the reedy borders of the Wash. But the dark yellow river swirled with less familiar things: he saw the cruising jaws of crocodiles caught in misty glitters of light.

As the channel veered away and the sea airs were lost, the forest stood still on either side and Paris felt the sweat start from his body. At the edges, beyond the ripples of their passage, the water was darker in colour and glassy: along these motionless borders lay the pale ellipses formed by the mangrove roots with their reflections, a series of perfect ovals. So motionless was the air now, in these reaches of the river, that image and reflection were seamless, undetectable; Paris found his eyes straining to distinguish the join, watching for occasional eddies to mar the surface, betray the half that was reflection into shivers.

These were like the tremors of fever. It seemed to Paris now that disease lay like a tangible presence there on the river, that they were proceeding through the very exhalations of plague. Fever shivered in the currents of the water, muttered among the mangrove flowers, rose and fell with the insects over the surface. His own sight seemed feverish and disordered to him, one moment listless, the next strangely intent.

He was relieved when a turn in the river brought them to a small landing stage, where the first canoe was tied up already and their escort stood waiting with Owen beside them, a thin figure in a straw hat and crumpled cotton suit, very white in the face, who began talking with a febrile eagerness to them almost before they had stepped out on to the planks.

'I'm glad to see you,' he said. 'My people here brought me word you were on your way. Damned hot and sweltery weather, ain't it? How is trade? What are you carrying? Usual stuff, is it?'

'We're a good ways from slaved yet,' Simmonds said. 'I don't

251

know if you remember me. Name of Jack Simmonds. I was on the crew of the *Arabella* four years ago; you had just settled in, sir. This is our doctor, Mr Matthew Paris.'

'How de do?' The factor's hand was dry and hot. 'Four years is a lifetime in this trade,' he said in rapid and perfunctory tones. Paris met the gaze of soft, lustreless brown eyes, saw the white face move in what seemed an uncertain attempt at a smile. 'I was set to make my fortune within three years or get out,' Owen said, 'and here I am still beside this stinking river.'

There was a reek of rum on his breath and his eyelids were reddish and inflamed – the more noticeably so for the pallor of his face. A refuse of palm fronds and coconut fibre littered the bank above the landing stage, with here and there the corpses of smallish, mud-coloured crabs emitting an odour of sadness and decay. The sky above had lost all colour now. For some moments the three men stood in an uncertain silence by the water, as if some other purpose had intervened, some purpose not their own, not yet fully apprehended.

'Captain Thurso sends his compliments,' Paris said at last. 'He is not able to come in person, he is staying with Mr Tucker.'

At this, Owen appeared to recollect himself. 'Tucker, there's a man,' he said. 'You had better leave someone in charge of the canoes if there is anything worth stealing in them. These people are thieves, every man of them; they have no notion of private property, none at all, not an iota. They will not rob you to your face but they will pilfer you to kingdom-come.

'Case in point,' he continued with the same febrile eagerness as they climbed up from the mooring stage, 'and it is why you find me a trifle in disarray at present. I have been surprised this very morning with finding the storehouse broke open and goods carried off to the value of fifty bars at least, that is near the value of a prime slave, in rum and tobacco and other goods, and small signs of discovering who are the thieves, except you bring in the Mandingo priest, which I have done, just to try it, not that a Christian can believe in their hocus-pocus tricks, but yet I have seen them perform strange things at different times while I have been a trader on the river here. On top of all that,

252

just today my people have brought in three dead men from the bush. They are Bulum and one of them a chief of sorts – badly mutilated. He was a well-known character in these parts and so I am obliged to keep them here till they are fetched away by the Bulum priests. They are noisome already, but I can do no other, these people are particular when it comes to such matters.'

The house stood on the rise before them, a low rectangle, whitewashed mud brick on a framework of poles, with a sloping thatched roof. A wooden fence made a compound round it. Within this, in the shade of the fence, two men lay asleep, their spears beside them. A few thin hens scraped in the dust.

'These are Susu tribesmen,' Owen said, nodding towards the sleepers. 'They came down from the interior, twenty days' march from a great river, twenty times the size of this one, according to what they say – these fellows embroider everything of course. They came with a small coffle of slaves – twelve altogether, but one was dying, she couldn't keep on her feet. You won't believe it but they still expected me to buy her. The reason they gave was that since they had brought her all that way she must be worth something. They have got no idea of commerce. Then they wanted dashes far above the usual to make up for it. They are always optimistic; they are like children.'

His eyes were soft as a cow's. A small nervous pulse beat in the thin hollow of his throat. Paris read in his gaze a plea to be understood, to be approved. 'I wonder why it is we think children are optimistic,' he said. 'I don't believe I was very optimistic when I was a child, rather the contrary. Most of the future was dread.' As it is now, he thought. He was back in the dread of childhood now, with Owen's blacks soon to examine.

'Eh?' Owen appeared involved for some moments in some painful effort of memory. 'Well, no,' he said, 'perhaps you are right. All the same, do I look a man to buy a dying negro? I wasn't born yesterday, I told them. It takes more than a naked savage to get the better of Timothy Owen. I purchased nine in the end, six men and three women. I have got them in the barracoon behind. Would you like to look them over now or should we go in and crack a bottle first?'

253

'We should see to the business first,' Paris said. 'Don't you think so, Simmonds?'

The mate was visibly divided. But after some seconds of pause he said, 'Yes, let us get it done.'

'The rum will still be there,' Owen said. 'I am glad to see you go armed, gentlemen. I never go near a captive negro without a pistol loaded and ready and someone to cover me. We'd better have these fellows along too, I think.' He went over and kicked lightly at the sleeping men, gesturing to them when they sat up that they should follow.

They skirted the fence and passed behind the house where an acre or so of forest had been cleared. A tethered goat raised its beard at them. A full-bodied woman in a blue cotton shift was hanging clothes on the line; she did not look towards them as they passed. The barracoon stood over against the broken edges of the forest. As they approached, a vulture which had been perched on the ridge-pole raised a wattled head to regard them, then flapped indignantly away. Through a lattice-work of rafters and rush matting Paris made out the forms of the negroes inside the barracoon.

'I made considerable efforts to have a vegetable garden here at one time,' Owen said, with the same rapidity of speech, at once eager and distracted. He indicated a level patch of ground, as bare as the rest but marked out with a stone border. 'I planted water melons, pompions, guinea peas. And sallet – you can have no idea how much I long for a bit of sallet, it is highly beneficial for the blood in this climate. But the damn crabs came up out of the river and devoured everything in a single night. When I looked at it in the morning it was as bare as you see it now. I never thought to make a fence against crabs, you see. There *was* a fence, but it was not proof against those devils, they got underneath. I never had the heart to try again. Nowadays, any time I encounter a crab, I put an end to its life.'

A smell of excrement and wood smoke came over to them from the barracoon. 'My mind was all on larger beasts,' Owen said. 'I never thought of anything getting underneath. Well, gentlemen, here they are, and a finer set of slaves you would have to travel far to see. Through here.'

It was intensely hot within the shrouded enclosure of the shed. The fires on which their food had been cooked were still smouldering; the smoke was acrid, Paris felt it stinging his eyes. He peered through the miasmic interior. All nine of the slaves, men and women alike, were shackled in a line to a long metal bar that ran down the centre of the barracoon. They were completely naked. One or two looked up but most remained staring before them. The smell of excrement was stronger now, combining with the sour smell of metal and the body-musk of the Africans to form a compound which Paris had begun to recognize as the odour of captivity. Nausea stirred in him. 'We'd better look at them out in the open,' he said.

One by one, under the guard of two men with spears, the negroes were unshackled and brought out, blinking in the stronger light. Paris went through the sequence of peering, prodding and palpating now become familiar, beginning always with the face, the teeth and gums, the red pools between lid and eye-ball, the pits of the nostrils. Custom had reduced his repugnance for the task but, perhaps paradoxically, had increased his sense of the humanity of the captives. He was beginning to know, with the same strange combination of sympathy and dispassion, the patterns of colour on an African body, zones of dark and less dark.

There was not the same pulse of fear in these negroes. They had been penned here a week now, and fear had passed into some more quiescent misery. Freed, they moved heavily as if still in chains, performing the kicks and jumps required of them with dazed docility. Three of the men were fine specimens, long-limbed and broad-shouldered, with powerful muscles in the arms and chest; but they were in a nightmare trance like the others and made no resistance. In the second of the women he examined he detected enlarged neck glands. In order to be quite sure of it he lingered for some time, pressing gently at the sides of the woman's neck.

'Something wrong?' Simmonds said. He had been following Paris's examination with his usual phlegmatic air, whistling between his teeth and occasionally kicking at the slaves, more from habit than anything else, it seemed, as they were quite unresisting.

255

'She has greatly enlarged lymph glands,' Paris said.

'Let's have a look. Lift your head up, darlin'.' Simmonds tapped the woman lightly, almost playfully, under the chin with the back of his hand. 'Yes,' he said after a moment. 'Oh, yes.' He looked at Owen. 'We can't take this one. She has got the negro lethargy, what they calls sleepy-sickness. I seen swellin's like them before. This here is a dead woman.'

'I didn't detect anything,' Owen said. 'I gave a good price for her.'

'That is as may be,' Simmonds said without emotion. 'But she is not worth a groat now, to you or anyone. They always dies when they get them balls in the neck.'

The woman remained impassive, staring before her with discoloured eyes. A small pulse beat at her temple. Her mouth hung very slightly open; the everted lips were dark lavender in colour and puffy-looking, as if swollen. If she felt curiosity as to why her captors were spending so long over her, she gave no sign of it. Her gaze showed nothing but an exhausted endurance.

'Let me see.' Owen stepped forward, felt the sides of the woman's neck for some moments, then turned to the others with his uncertain smile. 'That is nothing, take my word for it,' he said. 'It is some feverish inflammation that will soon pass.'

'I am sorry,' Paris said, 'but I fear Simmonds is right. They are glandular tumours, quite prominent. I cannot be mistaken, I felt them quite distinctly. The blood is already morbid in her. I know nothing of how this sickness comes but I believe it is generally fatal. It is here you feel the lumps, towards the vertebral region.'

He touched the woman's neck again to indicate the place, then felt round the whole area of the neck and shoulders. The skin was smooth and resilient. 'Here,' he insisted, 'in the hinder part of the neck. I am sorry, but we cannot take her.'

'It seems them fellers bubbled you after all, Mr Owen,' Simmonds said, and his normally rather bovine expression lightened perceptibly. 'Nekkid or not,' he added, winking broadly at Paris, to whom the mate's jocularity at such a moment seemed insensitive to the point of sublimity.

256

Owen looked from Paris's face to that of the woman. He had nodded his head at the medical details in what seemed an attempt at dignified dispassion. But at Simmonds's remark his eyes widened and he swallowed convulsively. 'God rot me,' he said. 'How can a man make a living here? These people . . .' He gestured at the impassive tribesmen, who stood waiting in positions of loose attention, their long spears resting on the ground. 'You can't trust anyone. Everything you try and do . . . You buy a slave in good faith, perhaps you overlook something, we can't always . . . It is true I had been drinking a little when they came in; I have had a bad bout of fever and I needed the rum to get me through. I am not through it yet, as a matter of fact. I am quite alone here, you know. There is no one . . .'

His mood, which had veered towards self-pity with these last words, and the sense of his solitude, grew suddenly inflamed again as he glanced at the diseased slave. His lower lip had begun to tremble. With a violent gesture, startling to those around, he took off his hat and cast it with all his force on the ground before him. He took a stride towards the woman, advancing his face furiously at her. 'God damn your eyes,' he shouted, 'I am not going to feed you, do you hear? Do you think I am running a charity?'

The woman was astounded. A strained and staring quality of alertness had appeared on her face. Some low and broken sounds came from her that might have been words of entreaty. She shrank from the inexplicable fury on the white face near her own, glanced quickly to either side of her as if seeking a path for flight, then wildly up at the blank and colourless sky above the barracoon.

'Do you hear me?' Owen seized her arm and tugged at her as if in an infuriated attempt to compel her straying attention. 'Not another mouthful,' he shouted. 'You can get out.' Enfeebled by illness and emotion, he could not drag her back and forth as he seemed to intend. With an effort he swung her round and pushed her violently forward so that she took some staggering steps towards the edge of the trees. Liberated thus, she stopped and stood still for some moments, as if incredulous. She raised her head to look again at the sky. There was blood round her ankles with the chafing of the fetters. It came to Paris, with a sensation of surprise, that she was beautiful. He saw her swallow at hope or fear. Then she moved forward again lightly and rapidly, without a glance behind, and disappeared into the darkness of the forest.

There was a short silence. Then Owen appeared to notice his hat. He retrieved it and restored it to his head with an attempt at a flourish. 'I think you will agree I handled that with proper firmness,' he said. His hands were trembling and after some moments he thrust them into the pockets of his jacket. 'You think it is funny when a man is cheated, Mr Simmonds?' he said. 'Well, I must spoil your joke – those Susu people would not have known her condition when they sold her to me.'

Whatever his private opinion, Simmonds had the grace to assent to this, and the examination was resumed, though Paris found his mind still on the diseased girl and the lightsome way she had stepped into the dark refuge of the forest. He found nothing amiss with the remaining slaves and left the bargaining to Simmonds. This passed reasonably quickly as it was a question merely of agreeing on the purchase price in bars – Owen would come out to the ship within a day or two to haggle with the redoubtable Thurso and make his choice of the goods.

When this was concluded and the slaves back in the barracoon, the three men returned to the house. They took their rum on the verandah. Owen pressed them eagerly to stay the night but Simmonds was for returning downriver. He made it a matter of duty that the slaves should be conveyed that night but in fact he was not properly easy in his present company and the place was lonely. His shipmates were at Tucker's, there would be drink in plenty there, and women.

Owen turned to Paris. Would he not stay? He could get off early in the morning, there would be time enough. 'The life is monotonous here,' the factor said. 'I do not see much company of my own sort.'

Paris was not sure that he cared to be included in this category, but the pathos of the understatement half won him and the mild and desperate eyes did the rest. And so it was decided: Simmonds would convey the slaves that evening under guard provided by Owen, Paris would remain until next morning.

The mate began preparing to leave at once, desire for more drink routed by the fear of being caught on the river in the dark with a boatload of slaves. Fettered by the legs in pairs, their arms bound tightly behind them, the negroes were thrust into the waist of Owen's longboat. With a heavily armed Simmonds at the stern and the two Susu spearmen forming a guard, they cast off. Owen and Paris watched the boat out of sight then mounted again to the house. The woman who had been hanging out washing was now in the lean-to beside the house, sitting on a low stool, thighs spread, winding cotton thread round a wooden spool. She looked intensely black in the shade there, so black that her skin glinted blue like coal, reminding Paris of the Kru people who had ferried his first slaves. She watched the approach of the two men without expression. Her face was broad and flat-boned, with a low forehead and a wide, sullen mouth.

'This one friend me, he sleep here one night,' Owen said. 'Two person chicken rice, you sabee?' He indicated Paris and himself with rapid gestures then made motions of eating. 'I don't trust the bitch,' he said moodily to Paris. 'Here, come in here.'

The house was built on a single storey with rooms leading off a narrow verandah. Owen led the way into what was evidently his living-room. Rush mats covered an earth floor. There was a European-style couch in worn red plush and some upright chairs round a bamboo table. 'Have a seat,' Owen said. 'She'll bring in the rum, she knows my habits by this time.'

He had barely finished speaking when the woman came in with glasses and bottle and set them down on the low table. She was tall and full-bodied. The cotton shift was strained across her hips and fell above the knees, showing thick, shapely legs with a faint down of black hair. Having set down bottle and glasses, she looked at Owen briefly and insolently, uttered some soft and high-pitched words and swayed out.

'She is getting above herself,' Owen said, with a wry smile that seemed to be intended as an apology. 'I shall get rid of her one of these days. She has brought her family in and I am expected to maintain 'em all, father, mother, maternal

259

grandmother, two sisters and a man she claims is her cousin. I have reason to think she plays the whore with the men who come here in the way of trade. And moreover I suspect it is her relatives that broke into the storehouse and made away with goods. But I intend calling in the Mandingo priest to get to the bottom of that business. These are difficult times, Mr Paris. On every hand there is news coming in of things miscarrying one way or another. There is Captain Potter's being cut off by slaves at Mano and the ship driven ashore and the captain, the second mate and the doctor all killed in the most barbarous manner – the slaves were all taken by the natives again and sold to other vessels, so they in no way mended their condition by their enterprise. And along the river here things are rendered difficult lately: it is dangerous to pass and repass because Captain Engelduc, upon his coming up the river, has refused the king his custom, or dashee as we call it, which has bred a great palaver between the king and all the whites trading along the river. Come, Mr Paris, you are not drinking, sir.'

'I am well enough,' Paris said. 'You need not wait on me – I will see to my own glass.' He watched the factor pour himself out a liberal measure. The light was fading now, shadows lengthened over the rough walls. In the silence Paris thought he heard a faint, continuous pattering sound like distant drums – or perhaps it was the sea, audible even here. This was Owen's evening then, the rum, the fading light, the smell of hot palm oil, the view across the baked clay of the compound to where the land dipped towards the river . . . 'This is my first voyage,' he said. 'I am new to the trade and I do not perfectly know how it is conducted. I saw that you agreed on a price in bars with Simmonds, and that is the same as they do with slaves that are brought to the ship.'

'I trade at the same prices as they do who take slaves to the ship. That is only fair, as I keep them penned here at my expense, convenient for the ships' boats. There are two rates of bars, one up country and one aboard ship. The ship's bar is worth twenty per cent more. At present prices a male slave in good condition can be purchased up country, by those that will bring them down – travelling traders like the Vai people and these Susu that are here now – for twenty country bars, which when brought down here we buy for thirty-five or forty. The same slave, sold on board ship or here from the barracoon, will fetch sixty-five ship's bars, which is equal to above eighty country bars. So I get eighty for laying out forty and the difference is made up in trade goods.'

The dark was gaining now and Owen rose to light the oil lamp on the table. His hands trembled no longer, Paris noted – the rum had steadied him. The lamp had been badly trimmed and it cast a wavering light over the walls of the room and the coarse matting on the floor. Owen's brows and eyes were left in shadow as he sat back in his chair.

'It is in determining the value of a bar that you find yourself exercised,' the factor said. 'A man has to keep himself abreast of things. The value of a bar can go up or down, Mr Paris, depending on the supply of slaves. A man can incur losses. I have seen men ruined on this coast, decent men, traders like myself, ruined, sir, for failing to remember that the price of a slave can fluctuate.'

Owen leaned forward and the lamplight fell on his face. His eyes were unsteady and Paris saw him frown slightly in what seemed an effort to focus them. 'For instance, a country bar,' he said in slow recital, 'may be worth fifty flints today and sixty-five two days from now. A piece of blue baft is worth ten bars as I speak to you now. Tomorrow, who knows? A man's intellects are exhausted keeping up with it.'

'All the same,' Paris said, 'if I understand you aright, you are making substantial profits.'

'Aye, sir, I would be, but for the exorbitant behaviour of the people here, that carry it all away. Your profits are brought down by the expenses of the kings and your own people, which are very unreasonable and great. For example in Sherbro there are three kings who divide the country among them, as well as others of less note. Every one of these expects custom from a white trader, which comes to twenty bars at your first visit, and after perhaps ten or twelve, if you bring a shallop or a longboat. I tell you, I am standing still. I have no more stock now than I did twelve month since.'

Owen paused to refill his glass. His movements were slower now and more deliberate. When he spoke again it was in a different tone, more consciously sociable. 'You are lately from England, I take it,' he said. 'I envy you. How you must look forward to returning there.'

'No, I do not. To be frank with you, I think I would be content not to set foot in England again as long as I live.'

His voice, deep and rather vibrant at any time, had betrayed an intensity of feeling surprising even to himself. The question, Owen's assumption, natural as it was, had caught him off guard.

But the factor was too rhetorical with rum by now, and too much occupied with his own deprivations, to notice much of this. 'You surprise me, sir,' he merely said. 'When I consider what it is to live in England, the happiness of conversation, the pleasures of a life free from all inconveniences which must certainly happen in this wilderness, where the inhabitants are scarcely above beasts, ignorant of all arts and sciences, without the comfort of religion, destitute of all wholesome laws . . .'

'Comfort of religion?' Despite himself, Paris's tone had quickened. He had drunk considerably less than the factor, but what he had drunk had inclined him to acerbity rather than indulgence, and the phrase Owen had used was hateful to him. 'Do you think we have wholesome laws in England?' he said. 'I have heard my fellow-Englishmen described in precisely the words you are using, and by those that were busy penning them up. Our good captain uses terms not much different to describe his crew.'

Owen seemed about to reply, but then his expression changed suddenly. 'Here she is,' he said. 'She has come at last with our supper. You have taken your time, haven't you?'

The woman had entered silently. Her moving form in the lamplight sent shadows flexing about the room. She set down the dishes on the table, straightened herself and stood still for some moments, though without looking directly at Owen.

'Do you think I don't know where you have been?' Owen said. 'She pretends not to understand anything,' he added to Paris. 'Me go call Mandingo priest-man,' he said loudly. 'He catchee thief. Tomorrow – do you hear that?'

The woman glanced indifferently at him then turned and walked slowly out of the room.

'She has been plotting with her relatives,' Owen said. 'But I have given her something to think about now. Serve yourself, sir. Let us not stand on ceremony.'

Paris took boiled fowl and rice and a sauce of palm oil and chopped peppers. Small black flies had entered the room; he felt the occasional sting through his shirt. Glancing up, he found Owen's eyes on him in a wide, unsteady stare.

'The Mandingos have a fashion of finding things out,' the factor said. 'I did not believe it when I came here at first, but I have seen things with my own eyes ... They follow the law of Mahomit according to the Alchorn, as they learn it from the Moors of Barbary and elsewhere, and so fetches it down here by these wandering pilgrims. You may say it is not reasonable for a Christian man to believe they are able to perform anything above the common run. But I have seen them with nothing but a few feathers and a handful of sand find out the secrets of futurity and things that people have spoke of to no one. It is my belief they have the power of some evil spirit or familiar sent to them by the great enemy, to draw these ignorant Bulums to himself.'

The rum he had drunk, the wavering light, his host's oddly disconnected speech, had combined to confuse Paris. It seemed to him for a moment that the factor was referring to some powerful and malignant slave trader further in the interior. 'Who is that?' he said. 'Further upriver, is he?'

'I am talking about Satan.' Owen looked gloomily before him. His mood was turning morose. He had eaten very little and now thrust his plate aside and reached again for the bottle. 'It is by Satan's help these ignorant wretches are so deceived,' he said.

'The Bulum compose the local population, don't they? Is the woman ... your housekeeper, is she a Bulum?'

'No, she belongs to the Kru people.'

'They are darker, aren't they? Yellow Henry and his band are Bulum, I suppose. Well, he is a mulatto of course, but –'

'You were acquainted with Henry Cook then?'

'It was he who came with our first slaves.'

'He'll never come with another.' Owen clapped white, slender hands at a fly, looking afterwards with a sort of hallucinated intensity for traces on his palms.

'Why? What do you mean?'

But the factor had reverted to his former gloomy staring and made no reply. He remained silent for some considerable time with his head sunk on his chest. Paris was beginning to think he had gone to sleep when he spoke again, in the blurred and dogged fashion of a man contending with his own obscured senses to reach to the heart of truth. 'No,' he said, 'for all religion these Bulums have only the Porra Man.'

'Who is he?'

'There is a secret mystery that these people have kept for many ages, or for all we know since their first foundation. It goes by the name of Porra or Porra Men. These men are marked in their infancy by the priests with three or four rows of small dents upon their backs and shoulders. Anyone that has not these marks they look on as of no account. There is one among the rest who personates the devil or Porra. He hides himself in some convenient place within call and upon his priests shouting he in the bush answers it with a terrible screech. Wherever the women or white men or any that is not Porra hear it, they fly immediately to their houses and shut all the windows and doors. Any caught outside will be torn to pieces.'

Owen raised his head and fixed the surgeon with a sombre regard. 'I have heard them,' he said. 'I have heard the screams. Sounds carry in this place. The Porra hasn't come this far yet, though.' He attempted a derisive expression, but there was no change in his eyes. 'It is all nonsense anyway, no one but a savage could believe in it. They come into town afterwards, this mock devil with his gang about him, and he speaks through a reed, and he tells on what account he comes and demands liquor and victuals. Then he goes away with singing and dancing and all is quiet again. 'Tis all faking – anyone with the curiosity to peer out of their houses would see it was only a man dressed up.'

'They surely cannot lack for curiosity to that extent,' Paris said. 'Either they are too terrified to look out or – and this I think more probable – they accept the mummery for the sake of order, just as we do. You say these people are charlatans. Well, just look at England, she is a paradise for Porra Men: the Church and the learned professions and parliament are full of them.'

He hesitated here, with some feeling of compunction. Owen's eyes were mournful and moist – he had wanted only to confide his solitude, his fears of the dark. But the surgeon was a little drunk and the memory of his shame was hot in his mind and his old vice of prideful assertiveness had him now in its grip. 'The system works better here,' he said. 'It has great consequence for the peace of the country. In Liverpool, not long before I left, a gang of seamen started to break up a brothel where one of them had been robbed. Others joined in. The watch was powerless to do anything. In the end they had to call in a regiment of militia and read the riot act. Two seamen and a passer-by were killed outright and one of the girls crippled for life before they could restore order.' Paris paused, smiling his bitter, lop-sided smile. He was arrogant with superior wisdom and intensely dislikeable at this moment. 'If it had happened here,' he said, 'just one screech from the bushes would have solved all.'

'Are you comparing things at home to this benighted place? I see you are one of those who always think they know better.' Owen raised his head to look steadily at Paris. Anger had stiffened him, given clarity to his speech. 'You do not know better, sir. You do not know worse, even. You know nothing at all of the nature of life here, along this pestilential river.'

There was silence between them for a short while. Paris sat with shoulders bowed, his big-knuckled hands thrust between his knees as if for safekeeping. Then he looked squarely into the other man's face. 'You are right,' he said, 'and I am sorry that I spoke as I did.' Rage to have the better of it, unwillingness to compromise, these were old failings in him, if failings they be. New, however – no older than Ruth's death – was the swift remorse that would come to him, a feeling like sorrow, at having delivered a wound for the mere sake of argument. The kind of truth that can be asserted by argument had lost all glamour, all lustre, for him, seeming no more now than another aspect of that ancient urge – much older than the desire for truth – to command attention, dominate one's fellows. The fuddled man before him was truth enough. He had belittled the nature of the factor's servitude. Owen needed to despise his surroundings in order to endure them. That a man engaged in this cruel trade still deserved not to be treated with cruelty seemed a mystery to Paris rather than a truth; but it was one which contained a strong imperative for him. 'Why don't you get out?' he said gently. 'Why don't you leave this place?'

'Get out?' Owen laughed on a rising note. 'Where to? All my capital is sunk here. I cannot return a pauper, they do not welcome prodigal sons. No, I am caught here, seven degrees above the line, three thousand miles from my native seat.' He laughed again briefly and licked slowly and carefully round his mouth. 'I am hoping for an upturn in trade,' he said in low tones. 'Before the Porra Man gets me, eh, Mr Paris?'

It was Paris's private view that fever and rum would find Owen first; but he was relieved to see the expression of weak jocularity that had come now to his host's face. 'I was something of a Porra Man myself, in England,' he said, not knowing quite what he meant, wanting to keep Owen in this lighter mood.

In this he succeeded. The factor had come round full circle and was disposed to sodden laughter now. The notion of this rather gangling, crease-faced guest of his lurking and screeching was one he found very risible. And it was on this note of mirth and restored amity that the two men parted for the night, Owen unsteadily to his bedroom, where the Kru woman had lain asleep some hours already, Paris to the small guest room at the end of the house, with its bunk bed and net canopy and its own door on to the verandah.

Here he lay for a long time sleepless, in spite of the drink, thinking of the diseased slave woman and the voracious, mud-coloured crabs creeping up from the river, and of the extraordinary ramifications of this trade in human creatures. Fumbling in his mind for some grasp of the complex chain of transactions between the capture of a negro and the purchase of a new cravat by Erasums Kemp, his cousin, or the giving of a supper

266

party by his uncle, he thought he heard again that distant pattering sound of surf or drums. There were occasional cries of night birds. Some time during the night he thought he heard the mutter of voices and afterwards groans that might have been caused by love or nightmare. Finally he fell into a troubled sleep, only to be brought awake again, not much after dawn, by the need to void his bladder.

He dressed and passed out on to the verandah and from there to the side of the house that was nearest to him. There was a chill in the air but no breath of wind. A thin mist lay over the compound and the shrub beyond it. There were sleeping forms under brightly coloured blankets in the lean-to where the woman had sat winding her thread.

Paris passed behind the house, avoided approaching too near the barracoon, which was silent and partly shrouded in mist, and urinated against the far side of a low shed near the edge of the clearing. In the immediate, mildly scalding pleasure of the discharge, he noticed nothing; but as he buttoned himself and prepared to return he became aware of a smell of animal decomposition, cold, dank, quite unmistakable. It did not come, as he thought at first, from within the forest, but from immediately before him, from inside the shed. He hesitated briefly then advanced his face to peer through the splintered plank. In rapid review, in the seconds before recoil, he saw three naked bodies, bloodstreaked and dreadfully staring, one bigger than the others, on its back, a big-featured face he knew, despite the blood-filled sockets where the eyes had been, a mounded belly the colour of dry clay, incongrously soft and smooth-looking, with a smear of red on it like a cattle brand. Flies had found them out, even thus early – he saw the gauzy glint of wings. One outflung hand had a thumb missing. He remembered the men who had held up their hands and grinned . . . As though reinforced by this recognition, the smell grew denser, sickening. Paris went back as though pursued across the clearing. He thought he heard a faint rattling from the barracoon. Glancing up he saw two vultures, heads settled on necks, asleep on the ridge-pole.

Later, at breakfast, he said nothing of his discovery to Owen, who was sick-looking and uncommunicative this morning, though he produced coffee for his guest from a carefully hoarded store, for which Paris was profoundly grateful. The Kru woman was nowhere to be seen.

'Well,' Paris said, as one of his oarsmen pushed barefoot against the mooring post and the canoe edged out towards midstream, 'I hope your Mandingo priest will get to the bottom of things.' It was the only hope he felt able to express for Owen. As the river began to curve away he turned to look back. The factor was still there, diminutive and lonely, standing on the bankside amidst the detritus of palm leaves and dead crabs, watching him out of sight. At the last moment Owen took off his hat and waved it once. Then the canoe took the bend and he was cancelled abruptly; the forested banks resumed their sway, concealing all traces. That scrape of human lodgement, focal point of wretchedness, the house, the compound, Owen with his longing for salad and polite manners, the shackled slaves in the stinking barracoon, no smallest hint of it remained.

The river was the only reality here. The river was the link of trade. Slaves came down from the upper reaches, perhaps hundreds of miles. The river bore them down to its bellowing mouth, the terrible ordeal of the surf, the open sky, the waiting ships. Wherever on this coast that there were rivers it would be the same. The rivers of Africa admitted the slavers to her vitals . . .

The long, light canoe was making good speed. The oarsmen set up a rhythmic cry as they thrust on the poles, perhaps in warning of their approach, as the channel was winding and the craft in midstream. But the men who were rowing him were so like those he had seen in the barracoon, in colour and in general cast of feature – he was beginning to notice such things now – that this wild cry of theirs seemed irresistibly to Paris like a cry of mourning for those in chains, who were too lost to mourn for themselves.

TWENTY-EIGHT

When Paris got down as far as Tucker's he found the yawl ready to leave, with only Thurso waited for. The slaves lay bound amidships, crowded promiscuously together. Sitting apart was a slightly built, smiling African in cotton singlet and drawers. This was the newly hired linguister, Simmonds told him – a protégé of Tucker's. Simmonds did not look well, he noticed: the mate's eyes were heavy-lidded and he held his head as if movement gave him pain there.

Thurso came down to the landing stage with the dignified and gravely smiling Tucker by his side. After they had exchanged civilities and assurances of further trade, the yawl was cast off. The wind was up and there was a heavy sea over the river mouth, obliging them to make a wide tack westward so as to get more easily over the bar.

Back on board they found the carpenter, with four men to assist him, busy constructing a barricade of stakes across the fore part of the quarterdeck, lashing the upright stanchions to long horizontals of inch-thick board that extended from side to side, with gates above the companion ladders. The starboard side was already complete; Johnson and Libby had run the swivel cannon out of its port so as to turn the muzzle through the fence, down on to the slave deck below.

The captain had scarcely set foot on deck when Haines came to him with a complaint against one of the negroes. Bullies need not be cowards and in fact Haines wasn't one; but hireling bullies need the countenance of their chiefs and the boatswain had been more than usually officious since his disgrace, in an attempt to recover lost ground.

'Morgan reported it to me, sir,' Paris heard him say. 'I checked it myself this morning and found it to be true.'

Thurso, with the boatswain at his side, took some steps away and Paris did not catch the rest of what was said. Haines had strange eyes, he thought. There was a constant glitter in them that seemed nothing to do with his mood or feelings ... The surgeon felt tired, after the broken sleep of the night before, and at the same time curiously heartsick, as if at some loss or shock whose nature he could not precisely determine.

'Fetch the man aft,' he heard Thurso say with a sudden, hoarse ferocity. 'And bring the linguister.'

Standing against the rail, Paris watched one of the slaves unshackled from his fellow by Cavana and Sullivan and led towards them. He was a tall man, loose-limbed and rather shambling in gait, though Paris thought this might be due to weakness. His face was broad and heavy-boned, the eyes deep-set below the ridges of the brows. He was emaciated; the lines of ribcage and breastbone were clearly visible below the skin. The inflamed K of his brandmark lay high on the left side of his chest, above the heart.

'It seems it has been going on for some days past, sir,' Haines said, 'but that fool Morgan did not see fit to say nothing, nor Wilson and Blair, that has had the job of serving them their beans and yams.'

'Has Morgan anything ready now?'

'He is cooking the slaves' rice, sir.'

'Tell him to fetch some.' Thurso turned to the negro, who stood with head downcast. 'Now, you dog,' he said. 'You have been setting a bad example, have you? I'll teach you tricks.' He glared round irately. 'Where the devil is the linguister?'

'Standing by, Captain, sir.' He had been at Thurso's side all the while, but he was so short in stature that the captain had overlooked him. 'Jimmy is here,' he said. His smile was amazing, occupying the whole of his face, all but closing his eyes, exposing a row of pale gums. 'This Wolof man,' he said. 'Bad temper people. I don' spik Wolof. Try him Bambara linga.'

'Tell him,' Thurso said, 'that he is going to be given some rice and if he doesn't eat it I'll set him down below in the dark with the screws on him.'

'Skeroos?' Jimmy's smile diminished at this difficulty.

'Thumbscrews, you fool.' Thurso's temper was deteriorating. He made a gesture of turning a key against his thumb.

'Unnerstan' perfect.'

Jimmy spoke for some moments in a language of soft, rising inflections. The slave continued to hang his head, making no reply nor showing any sign that he was aware of being addressed.

The rice was brought from the galley by a flustered Morgan, plump and aproned and sweating copiously as usual. It was thrust under the nose of the slave, who turned his head mutely from it. Thurso's precarious hold on his temper was not proof against this defiance. He struck the man heavily on the side of his lowered head, sending him to the deck, where he lay motionless but with his eyes open still.

Thurso stood for some moments looking down at him. Then, in his hoarse and grating voice, which showed small variety of tone whatever his feelings, he said, 'Take him below, Haines, put the screws on him – both thumbs. Leave him in the dark on his own. We will try him again later and see if he has come to better sense.'

Without waiting to see the man hauled to his feet, Paris turned away abruptly. He had taken some steps towards the ladder-way, when Thurso's voice recalled him. He turned and stood facing the captain at some paces' distance.

'Mr Paris,' Thurso said, 'it is customary for the members of a ship's company, including the officers, to take their cue from the captain. You do not withdraw yourself without a word. You will remain here until you get leave to go, sir.'

Paris felt the blood rush to his face at this public rebuke. He was aware of the people looking on, the negro still sprawled on the deck, the grouped slaves behind him in the waist. All seemed to be waiting, to be expecting something from him. He paused to control his breathing. When he spoke it was in a voice deeper than usual: 'Sir, I know I am subject to your orders, as are all on board. But I am a doctor, and I take my profession seriously. I suppose I am here for all on the ship. I cannot easily see that crushing his thumbs is the best way to make him eat. It might be possible to try persuasion.'

'Persuasion?' The word came, hoarse and lingering, charged with contempt. Barton, at some paces off, uttered a suppressed sniggering and grins spread among the crew.

Thurso's tactical sense was formidable and he exploited it now. 'Persuasion?' he said again, and made a stiff gesture of incredulity.

It was to occur later to Paris that by using this word he had saved himself from some more violent expression of the captain's antipathy. Thurso's temper was at a dangerous pitch and the law supported his authority. But there was no need now to assert this further. In the eyes of the men looking on, all conditioned to violence, the surgeon had shown weakness – not of character, but in his grasp of reality. Condescension served Thurso better now. He knew it, and the knowledge went some way to restoring his temper.

'We have thirty-six slaves already aboard, Mr Paris. When we leave this coast we shall have a cargo, God willing, of more than two hundred, and a crew possibly of twenty-five. And you talk of persuasion. I thought you had more sense.'

Paris found nothing to say in response to this. He did not mind losing ground with the crew, if indeed he had done so; he had no wish to be a spokesman for them or any kind of leader; never again to take up a voice for others had been one of the first vows he had made in the ruins of his life.

He remained there while the recalcitrant slave was taken below. Thurso repeated his orders for the thumbscrews, adding a caution of 'not too sharp' to the boatswain. This done, he surprised the surgeon with a request to accompany him to his cabin.

'Have a seat, sir,' he said. 'You will take a glass of port?'

'Thank you.' Paris watched the captain take out decanter and glasses from the locker above his table. A certain feeling of wariness came to him. Thurso was predictable only in his determination to secure good profits. Otherwise, in the motions of his spirit, he unsettled expectation in the way that persons did who could not be accounted wholly sane . . .

'Your health, sir.' Thurso looked with concealed dislike at the man before him, taking in – yet again – the details of the surgeon's appearance, the awkward frame, the ravaged look of the face, the pale eyes that did not retreat before his own. It seemed an inventory he had been condemned through eternity to go on making. He wondered how he had transgressed against his demon to be visited with this plaguey fellow on his last voyage, wondered why it should matter, with himself and Barton so soon to do their private trade. The gold dust they would get for the muskets and his share of the profits on the voyage, together with what he had already, would see him through comfortably. But he was accustomed to think of his career as a monument to fidelity and good profits and satisfaction to his owners – and this was his present owner's nephew, and also a half-baked fellow who might carry tales back, garble things, cast reflections on a man's reputation.

But a deeper reason underlay these, one that even now he was unwilling to acknowledge fully to himself. There was a quality in the surgeon he recognized as dangerous. Thurso understood the nature of power as he did that of the sea, by instinct and experience. He had felt the force of the surgeon's intervention just now. Paris had obliged him to play to the gallery, something he did rarely . . .

'I will overlook your words and manners just now,' he said, 'on the ground that you are ignorant of the usages of the sea. This ship and all aboard her are in my hands. No one quits the captain's presence without a form of asking permission, whether he be the doctor or the cabin boy. I will request you to remember that in future. And no one makes remarks in any way reflecting on the captain's judgement. I will request you to remember that too. Now as to this slave who refuses food, he does it out of a perverse desire to frustrate us and make himself awkward. There is a wicked, contrary spirit in these people, Mr Paris. I know 'em well. If they would make the best of their condition, a slaveship could be a happy ship. But our lot is made harder by their sly and sullen ways. And mark you this, such a thing will spread to the others, if they see it spoils our game to any degree. They are watching us all the time without seeming to. One man starts refusing food and before you know where you are they will all be doing it. Most of 'em find their appetites again soon

273

enough after a whipping, but there will be those that take longer and if they weaken themselves now they are more than likely to die on the passage to the West Indies. And remember – for every slave that dies on board ship we lose the price we might have raised at Kingston market which presently stands at fifty pounds cash for a prime male slave.'

Here in this narrow space the captain's voice had declined to a hoarse mutter, little more than a whisper. He sat back now to drink some of his port, then set the glass down carefully, looking closely at the surgeon from the square cage of his brows. 'Fifty pounds, Mr Paris. That is money. A man can live a year in England on fifty pounds and not go short of much. And it is a dead loss if they die of sickness or any natural cause. The insurers will not pay except they die in the course of an uprising or insurrection, and even then 'tis scarce half the value. No, sir, we must strive to preserve them. A man who can't see that is a fool, and there's an end of it.'

It had been a long speech for Thurso and his face had flushed darker with the vehemence of it; perhaps too, Paris thought, with resentment at being thus driven to explanations. Why he felt so driven was not clear to the surgeon at present, though he saw clearly enough that Thurso had reduced the world to a dominant principle and wrenched his moral frame to accommodate it. By some odd quirk of spirit he found himself fancying that Thurso's occasional stiff gestures were a physical sign of this wrenching process.

Meanwhile he was at some loss as to how to reply. Silence would be safer, more politic; he was aware that the captain had made a bid for his understanding, perhaps even for his sympathy. But Paris found himself unable to remain silent. In abjuring argument, he had forgotten how bitter it can be to leave an adversary in possession of the field. Even while he thus hesitated he saw the captain's eyes narrow and the hand on the table slowly clench.

'I can speak my mind to you, I suppose,' he said at last, with that air of earnest pertinacity that Thurso had found odious from their first acquaintance, 'since you have done so with me, and in any case there are none to hear us. I saw that man's face, sir. I particularly observed his looks. He is not refusing food in order to spite us or inconvenience us, but because he is set on dying.'

'Are you such a fool that you cannot see that it is the same thing?'

'The same thing? How the same thing?' He looked in astonishment at the captain's face, saw the square jaws clench with a fury almost convulsive. It seemed that his question was by way of being the last straw for Thurso, who now leaned forward and spoke with an unconcealed violence of antipathy.

'I see it now, you are one of those radical fellows they speak of, who will accept no authority. You will question everything, you will always think you know better. Hark to me now. The black will be tried with food again in the morning. If he refuses to eat, I will set Haines to flog him before them all until the skin hangs off him, and I will continue so until he consents to eat or dies. That has been my practice before and it shall be the same now.' Pausing, he found the surgeon's eyes on him, intent, without fear, hatefully perceptive. The other man's presence was strong, oppressive to him, exerting some constraint that poisoned his fury with a sense of impotence, obliging him to explain, to seek to convert, to look for comprehension. He felt the blood beating heavily at his temples. 'You preachy fool, you should have been a parson,' he said. 'He cannot be allowed to die as he chooses. They must not believe they have the disposal of themselves. If you don't understand that, you understand nothing. If he is going to die it must be at our hands and in pain, so that the others will not be corrupted.'

Paris rose to his feet. He felt himself quivering internally with the offence of Thurso's words and the reciprocal violence the other's antagonism aroused in him. He thrust his hands behind his back. 'I understand your words, sir,' he said huskily. 'With your permission, I shall now –'

At this moment, while the two were looking fixedly at each other, there came a cry from deck of a craft sighted. Thurso at once seized his hat and without a further word or glance stumped out of the cabin, the surgeon following. They stood on deck watching the approach of a narrow dugout with a framework amidships covered with palm thatch.

'That is a river boat, Mr Barton,' Thurso said in his usual tones.

'Aye, sir.'

The captain raised his telescope. 'They look like Susu people to me,' he said. 'They have got someone there under the awning. It is a white man,' he added after some moments. It was not until the dugout was considerably nearer and riding broadside on to them that they were able to see that the man in the shadow of the thatch was Calley, wearing only a pair of filthy cotton drawers, with his arms bound behind him.

'So,' Thurso said grimly, 'one of our birds has come home to roost. These are up-country people. We shall need the linguister.'

'Standing by, sir, Captain.'

'What the devil is funny?'

'Nothing funny, Captain. Some these men mebbe speak Malinke.'

'Tell them they are welcome aboard,' Thurso said. 'Tell them they can come up.'

Jimmy shouted down to the men in the boat below in a language of high, wavering pitch changes. He listened to the grave reply.

'They say they not coming up, sir.'

'Why in perdition not?'

'They say they don' like come up on the ship. They perlite people, don't like to say it, my 'pinion they scared of being panyared for slaves.'

'They can trust me. I am known up and down this coast. I wouldn't carry off free Africans. I give them dashee, one demi-john brandy. Tell them I am pleased they catch this runaway buckra man.' He looked balefully down at the unfortunate Calley, who sat in the shade of the palm thatch, head down, a picture of dejection. His upper arms were drawn together behind him with twisted raffia, so tightly that his neck tendons and the powerful muscles at his shoulders were tense with his efforts to withstand the traction.

Jimmy translated, rubbing his chest in a circular fashion and half extending his right arm towards the boatman to indicate Thurso's deep and abiding pleasure at the capture.

276

'They say they trust you and they believe you.'

'Good. They are sensible fellows.' Thurso looked down approvingly. 'Why aren't they moving?' he said impatiently after a moment.

'They not coming up, sir. They say they believe you now but you may change mind while they on the way up and you cannot gantee that you will not change mind as nobody can gantee future thinking of his mind.' In relief at having got through to the end of this difficult sentence, Jimmy forgot himself again and smiled broadly. 'So they not coming up,' he said. 'That the top and tail of it.'

'By God,' Thurso said savagely. 'That man shall suffer for this when I get my hands on him. If we had been homeward bound, with the slaves discharged, I would have let him rot ashore. Tell them the brandy will be lowered down to them. All they have to do is to loose his bonds in a way that will allow him to mount the accommodation ladder.'

Jimmy spoke again and the man in the prow of the dugout replied in a long and statesmanlike speech marked by grave, emphatic gesture.

'Beggin' your pardon, Captain,' Haines said, still seeking favour and reinstatement, 'why don't we shoot one of the beggars? That one gabblin' now. We could pick him off easy. That would bring 'em round.' He paused a moment, clearly taken with the beautiful simplicity of his idea. 'Why not shoot 'em all?' he said.

'You blockhead,' Thurso said, turning upon him sharply. 'Risk rousing the coast against us? Who would come trading to the ship after that?'

'They not satisfy with the offer,' Jimmy announced.

'Very well, I can give them tobacco if they prefer.'

'No, sir, pardon me.' In pure nervousness now Jimmy smiled again. 'They want brandy *and* tobacco,' he said. 'That is dashee for catch him. They say they want also ten bar slave price.'

'What?' Thurso's brows drew together. For some moments it looked as if he might burst into some violent expression of rage. But then a different look came to his face, something resigned, humorous almost. He glanced aside and nodded to himself as if in recognition. 'Aye,' he muttered, 'but they are traders, these people. They sit there under our guns and hold us to ransom. They separate the merit of the capture from the man's price and make us pay for both. Tell them I agree, but I won't haggle over the bars. They can have ten head blue beads for him, take or leave it. And tell them he is not a slave but an English seaman.'

The offer was signalled satisfactory by the men below, who were more interested – for the moment at least – in beads and brandy than in definitions. The goods were lowered down over the side, Calley was untied and hoisted on to the ladder to make his slow way upward with cramped arms. The dugout, cast free of the ship, made speed shoreward, the four men throwing themselves on the oars for dear life.

Calley was seized by Johnson and Haines before his feet had touched the deck. He made no resistance. Exhaustion, the sense of being a wrong-doer, the knowledge of punishment to come, combined to take the fight out of him. He was parched with thirst and bleeding from a host of scratches and cuts. He was given shirt and breeches from the ship's store; then he was placed in leg irons and set on the forward part of the main deck under the eye of the first mate, whose watch it was.

The end of the afternoon watch, with most of the ship's work done for the day and nearly everyone on deck, was the time favoured by Thurso for the carrying out of exemplary punishments. It was then that Wilson had been flogged and Thomas True and Evans; and it was then that the time came for Calley. He did not plead but he whimpered while he was being tied and began to cry out terribly with the first blows. When taken down he was conscious still and uttering sounds in his throat curiously as if trying to reassure himself. However, he was not able to get to his feet without help or stand unsupported. Paris, who had battled to establish his right to ministration in the earlier cases, felt he needed no further permission now. With Blair, distressed and blasphemous, to help him, he got Calley to the sick bay, got the heavy, helpless body facing down on the bunk and began to do what he could to clean the mess of blood from the back and staunch the lacerations.

Under the spread of water blood frilled like petals from the wounds the knots of the cat had made from nape to waist, and stirred the torn skin at the edges of the lashmarks. Calley, so abjectly clamorous throughout the public ordeal of his punishment, behaved with fortitude now, helped by a constitution of phenomenal recuperative power. He kept his face pressed into the blanket. After a while sounds came from him, faltering and half choked.

'He's tryin' to say somethin,' Blair said. The surgeon had asked him to remain and he stood there now with a basin for the blood-sodden swabs that Paris passed to him. 'He better keep mum, hadn't he?' he said anxiously.

Paris glanced at him a moment. Blair's face had paled, the freckles showed over the bridge of his nose and his eyes looked unnaturally prominent. He had looked thus at the branding of the first slaves, the surgeon recalled suddenly. Not a callous man at all, Blair, he thought. Bluster and bravado apart. Tender-hearted, even – whenever he couldn't find a cause for rage to save him from it. 'No reason why he shouldn't talk, if he wants,' he said mildly. 'Can you make out what he is saying? The man is strong as an ox.' Saying this he remembered the only other time Calley had spoken to him: 'You gets a saddle to put on,' and the look of shy mirth that had accompanied it. His friend and protector standing beside him.

'What you sayin', shipmate?' Blair said, leaning down and talking loudly as if to a deaf man. 'He an't very bright,' he said confidentially to Paris.

Calley kept his face pressed to the blanket. 'Deakin gone,' he mumbled, forming the sounds from the red mist his consciousness was reduced to. 'I didn' go wiv 'im.' All the events of these last days, already scrambled hopelessly in his mind, turned on this central desolation. Blundering lost through the endless savannah, panicking at silence, tormented by thirst, struck and baited by the tribesmen when they had finally succeeded in subduing him – vengeance this, for the several that had been hurt in the process; none of it was more than a nightmare embroidery surrounding his desertion of Deakin. The words continued to issue from him. 'I come back. There was noises . . . I was scared.

279

Deakin gone by hisself now. He shouted for Dan'l. Shouted for me . . .'

The two men listening had not understood everything of this because Calley's face was muffled and the pain of the flogging choked the sounds in his throat. But after some moments they understood that the nature of the sounds had changed, they had become broken and gasping.

'Dinna be snufflin', lad,' Blair said, and to him too there came a memory: waking in the darkness of the hulk to pain and the sound of rats and weeping . . . 'No use snufflin',' he said.

Hearing something in the other's voice, Paris glanced at him quickly and then away. Blair had tears in his eyes. The surgeon felt a sympathetic prickling behind his own.

Oblivious to the words and feelings of those above him and to the touch of water on his back, Calley wept into the blanket for the betrayal of his friend.

When Deakin became aware of the silence and turned and called Calley's name and received no reply, he knew at once that the other was not far away, that he was crouching somewhere among the bushes, hiding. The world became very quiet to Deakin at this moment, so quiet that he thought he would be able to hear the pulse of Calley's fear if he listened closely enough. But he did not want to find Calley now.

'Go back, Dan'l,' he called. 'Make back to the river and follow downstream.'

The sound disturbed birds somewhere high above him; he heard the volley of their wings. No other answer came. He waited some while longer then went on. For a time he listened, but he knew that Calley would not come after him now. The silence persisted, enveloping him, absorbing the sounds of his passage.

He tried at first to keep north, following the course of the river; but the ground was swampy and treacherous and he stumbled among the intricate mangrove roots. He found himself longing for the open. All his passion for flight was in open country; he needed the complicity of the sky.

In the evening he turned westward, into more thinly wooded

ground that rose slowly from the river, interspersed with belts of shrub. Here the going was easier and he made some miles before nightfall. He drank water from the tin container that, together with the pistol, he wore at his belt. It was more than half empty now. He ate some of the ship's bread and salt pork he had kept wrapped all day inside his shirt. The bread was damp with his sweat.

Late in the afternoon of the following day he drank the last of his water. He was now in a country of broken woodland and spreads of tall, tussocky grass. The sky was open above him. Faint shadows of hawks moved over the ground. The silence intensified and within it Deakin spoke to himself, sometimes aloud. He would come to a village, people would come out from their houses. He would establish a trading post. Palm wine, lime juice, coconut milk. Don't sleep, they will sell you. He could trade in gold dust, parrot's feathers, teak . . .

He did not believe it. He could not imagine the shape of the houses in the village or the look of the people; and with this failure there came the knowledge that all his plans of trading had been only pretexts to find himself here, on the move, in this empty country.

Food he forgot in the growing torment of thirst. His own voice spoke no longer, but his father questioned him, cane in hand. Where are you making for? You know what will happen when you reach Jamaica, don't you? What will they do to you when they get you on a navy ship again?

There was no way of answering so as to avoid error. No possible answer could avert his father's rage. Whatever he said, he would be beaten and locked up in the dark shed. Thurso gets the bounty, he said, trying to evade punishment by answering a different question altogether. Thurso gets five guineas for me. But this was wrong, his father's face grew dark and swollen. It filled the sky and burst and Deakin drank what rain he could catch in his mouth and his cupped hands.

That was on the fourth day of his freedom. After the rain the long, tawny grasses were swept by whispers, the sun came out again and the ground steamed. His pace was slow now and he staggered a little, but he was cooled by the rain and his mind

281

was clear. He had no sense of a destination. It came to him that he had never had one. All his destinations had been only breaking loose . . . But that was not it either. Patiently, like a celibate remembering some cherished episode of love, he began to assemble the details of that first escape, the feel of the metal bar in the dark, the fear and exultation of the splintering wood. No tropical light had ever been so blinding as that of the dim dawn he had stepped into then, no sky at sea so vast as that one. That light, that enlargement, had been destination enough. He had never found it again, he had run ever since between narrowing walls, under lowering skies.

He slept in his damp clothes and woke feverish. At first light he was on the move again, but his progress now was very slow. He was beginning to lose his sense of the rhythm of his walking, stepping too short, not raising his feet enough, so that he frequently stumbled and sometimes fell. With each fall the recovery took longer.

Soon after sunrise, crossing a wide savannah, with the grass-heads glinting reddish and the low, broad-leaved trees beaded with fire, Deakin saw figures moving like dark flames to encircle him. One pointed or gestured, with a strange, repeated jabbing motion, and the sun ran in glitters on something.

They were round him in a circle. That is how you capture a man or a beast, Deakin knew – one that you think might be dangerous. To be enclosed on all sides is the end of a runner. Frighten them off. Again the gleam of the raised spears caught his eyes. They would want his pistol and his water bottle and his leather belt. They would want to tie him . . . His sight was confused. He fumbled the pistol out of his belt and fired at a flash of sunlight. The sound was shattering. It was inconceivable that any sound could ever follow it and for Deakin none did. He saw another flash, different, speedy, but he heard nothing. The spear struck him below the breastbone and pierced him almost through. He fell to his knees and rested there a moment, holding the shaft like something precious, and the destination of light briefly flooded his eyes from a sky that blazed and closed.

TWENTY-NINE

No one on board ever knew what had become of Deakin. He joined the company of those who have no official death. For the Admiralty he remained a deserter in perpetuity. On Thurso's crew-list he was entered as 'Run', and this was all his epitaph. Paris, writing in his journal at intervals that grew longer, gave him space only for good wishes. By this time, for the surgeon, Deakin's disappearance had been overshadowed by a death that was official.

Jack Simmonds, our second mate, is no longer with us. He departed this life yesterday. I had noticed on our return from Tucker's that he bore every appearance of fever. The day following he was sent out again and on return of the yawl was unable to get aboard without assistance and complained much of headache and a weakness in his limbs. That evening, the fever mounting, I had him conveyed to the sickroom and attempted to allay the heat by bathing of his limbs and administering an infusion of powdered cinchona bark, of which I came provided with a good stock; but the fever grew worse in the night – I have seldom seen such violent throes; they came close to paroxysm. Early next morning he began to exude small quantities of blood from his nose and gums and the corners of his eyes; I detected marks of blood also on his forehead and in his armpits. Within two hours of this discharge, the heat subsided abruptly, a clammy moisture succeeded and the poor fellow's face took on the look of death. He asked me to make sure that his wife received the wages due to him and I promised to do so. I had not known he was married. At three in the afternoon he began to vomit quantities of blood darkened with bile and shortly after choked and so died, I standing by quite powerless to save him or even much alleviate his sufferings. His body was committed to the sea the same evening, with Thurso reading the service.

I am persuaded that this is a case of the 'black vomit', as the disease is called, which often afflicts our soldiers, as I have read, on their tours of foreign duty. It is possible – I think probable – that Simmonds caught the contagion that very evening we separated, I to remain with Owen, he to return to his shipmates at Tucker's. He would have drunk heavily there and perhaps lain with a native woman somewhere out in the open, and slept thus, amidst the impure effluvia of air proceeding from that marshy ground, acted upon all day by solar heat and at night releasing its poisons.

Paris paused for some moments, pen in hand. He was thinking of his actions from the moment he had noted the violence of Simmonds's fever. He had gone to his cabin and quite deliberately eaten a certain quantity of bread dipped in vinegar – one should never attend the sick when the stomach is empty, the body being then at its most absorbent. He had looked at his face in the small looking-glass fixed to the locker, the deeply marked forehead, the lines that ran from the nostrils to the corners of the mouth, the pale eyes under thick brows that slanted downward with a slightly dog-like effect, at once mournful and alert. A face not unhandsome, though roughly made and too bony – the face, he knew it then, of a man who did not want to die, who was bolting these sops of bread in fear of death. He clung to the world still, for all his shame and loss and grief.

He had stopped his nostrils, before returning to Simmonds, with lint dipped in the same vinegar; and after the man's death he had washed out his mouth with camphorated spirits. To be of service on the ship, yes; but he knew that was secondary. What he remembered now was the bread dissolving in his mouth, all hope of life in that sour taste ... Thinking of it here in the close, confessional privacy of his cabin he felt a traitor, but to whom or what he did not know.

The number of slaves continues steadily to augment. Tucker, in accordance with his promise, has furnished a batch of twenty-two males and eight females, all captured by his people in the wars he has been fomenting inland. One of his sons was killed in the raid, which had the effect of making Tucker very oppressive and implacable when it came to the bargaining: he asked seventy bars for the adult males and pushed the equivalent in trade goods to levels that brought Thurso close to apoplexy; though one might have thought this exorbitance would compel our captain's respect, it being after all the mark of a true trader to compensate himself for loss. 'Fortunate for us he lost only one of his sons,' Barton remarked to me with that peering, foxy look of his, 'or he would have cleared us out of printed cottons altogether.' The mulatto's prices had to be met in any case, as he controls much of the trade on the river and I believe the supply of slaves can be much curtailed by his disfavour. What can happen to those who get in his way I saw some evidence of in Owen's shed.

The slaves are still kept on deck, except in squally weather, but there are more than seventy now and they will have to be accommodated below when we are at sea. To this end Barber is installing platforms between the decks. There can be no doubt that a carpenter on a slaveship earns his wages: Barber has had to see to the trimming and raising of the hatches, the construction of the barricade and now these divisions in the hold, which has meant fitting platforms and partitions to divide the space below the deck into separate lodging rooms for the men, the boys and the women. As there is no more than five feet of vertical space in the hold to begin with, and these platforms will halve it, it is difficult to see how the negroes will have room even to sit upright.

Thurso, made anxious by symptoms of melancholy and lethargy among the captives, has instituted a joyless ceremony known as 'dancing the slaves', which Barton tells me is an old practice among slavers. After the morning meal, Sullivan is brought out to play reels on his fiddle while the women, who are not shackled, dance about the deck and the men jump in their irons as best they can, though it is a torture to men with swollen limbs. Thurso is too absolute in his habit of mind to grant any exemptions and so they are forced to continue till their ankles are raw and bleeding, the sailors keeping them to it with whips. There are those among the crew, the more brutish, who visibly enjoy this exercise. I have seen Libby and Tapley and Wilson grin to do it and laugh at the sad antics that they oblige the negroes to perform. They are made to sing also and sometimes they independently set up a wavering song among themselves. Jimmy, our linguister, tells me that these songs are full of sorrow, as one might expect. That their slow movements and this sad singing are at ludicrous odds with the brisk tempo of his fiddling seems not to trouble Sullivan at all. It is clear that he loves his fiddle and he plays it here with the same spirit as I have no doubt he would at a country wedding in Ireland.

I have spent some time in talking to Jimmy, who is very friendly and open, sensitive too, I believe – he conceals a good deal under that smile of his, which is due more to an inveterate habit of the nerves, I think, than to any real amusement. It is his ambition to be a teacher with a school for local children here on the coast, at Cape Palmas, under the protection of the English garrison there. He hopes to accompany us back to England and find an employment that would allow him to improve his knowledge of English.

If Jimmy feels that he is betraying his enslaved fellows by thus acting as intermediary with their captors, he gives no sign of it; perhaps he does not feel that they are his fellows at all. Because they have all black faces we suppose

285

them close in fellowship, but when have we been so towards people only because they are white-skinned like ourselves? I have not noticed much affection and loyalty among us towards the Dutch or the French. Jimmy does not know how old he is – I should say about thirty. He is of the Hausa people, he has told me, and was brought to the coast as a child when his parents were enslaved by the Ashanti.

The captives themselves are not united: I have seen a good deal of squabbling and bad feeling among them. Yesterday, not long after Simmonds's death, I saw one throw his rice in the face of another. They are of different races and tongues and reach the ship by diverse routes – this too I have learned from our linguister. Some are prisoners of war, others have been domestic slaves already and are sold now by their masters to pay off debts or provide wedding portions; yet others have been seized by local slavers such as the late Yellow Henry. But however varied the routes by which these unfortunates reach the deck of the Liverpool Merchant, *once here they are brought to a uniform condition with remarkable –*

He was interrupted by Charlie, who came knocking at his door to tell him that one of the negroes was thought to be dying. 'The one that won't take his grub, sir,' Charlie said, his starveling face full of wonder.

Up on deck, however, there was no opportunity to see the man alone. The captain had been informed and was standing in colloquy with Haines on the quarterdeck at the head of the companion ladder. As always, because of Thurso's stillness and the unchanging pitch of his voice, his feelings were not at first apparent; but as Paris drew closer, he saw the furious look of the captain's eyes and the rigid set of his jaws, and he felt a curious weakness, as if brought cold and reluctant to some passage of arms.

'I'll see he eats,' Thurso said. 'He will sup before he dies. Lay forward there for the wrench and the funnel, Haines.'

'Aye-aye, sir.'

'The wrench?' Paris did not know what was meant. He had seen, like a premonition, a certain kind of satisfaction pass over Haines's face.

'I want the man brought aft, below me here.' Thurso turned to the surgeon. 'Yes, sir,' he said, 'you shall see this malingering fellow eat his rice at last.'

286

The negro came supported between two men, his head hanging. Paris, looking down from the quarterdeck, saw the marks of the lash across his shoulders, saw the red mess of his thumbs, saw at the same moment what Haines was carrying, took it at first for a large pair of dividers, then recognized the notched prongs and the broad wing-screw. 'But that is the *speculum oris*,' he said, and saw the faintly sneering look of knowledge of him, or expectation of some pretext for derision, rise to the boatswain's face. 'Aye, is it, Doctor?' he said. 'We calls it a gob-wrench.'

'But you will spoil his mouth,' Paris said, and watched the sneer deepen on the boatswain's face. He had seen the instrument used to force open the mouths of patients suffering from lockjaw and he knew the damage it could inflict if clumsily applied – the broken teeth and torn gums. 'You will reduce his value,' he said, in an attempt to impress Thurso with a commercial argument, a ludicrously inept one, he knew – the man was near death in any case. 'Let me try him with food,' he said. 'With your permission, sir, I will make an attempt with him.'

'You are for persuasion still, I see.' Thurso paused for what seemed some private reflection. 'Very well,' he said at last, 'I will allow you a few minutes. I care not how he comes to it, so long as he does so and is seen to. But you are wasting your time.'

Paris descended from the gangway to the main deck. The two men supporting the negro, Tapley and McGann, finding him a dead weight, had set him down against the base of the gangway ladder. The surgeon crouched in an attempt to look into the man's face.

'What shall we try him with, sir?'

This was an offer Paris turned sharply towards, a voice that held something for him. Glancing up he saw that it belonged to Hughes, the misanthropic climber, who had not addressed a syllable to him ever before. Hughes was regarding him with a sombre intentness, not unfriendly.

'Boiled rice, I think, as before,' the surgeon said. 'Can some be fetched?'

'There is a bit of hasty pudding left over in the galley,' Cavana said. 'I do know that because I seen it.'

287

'I seen it too.' This came fervently from the boy Charlie, who was always hungry.

'They like dried pease boiled in a cloth,' Sullivan said. 'All the black races is infatuated on that dish.'

'God damn me,' Blair said, instantly furious, 'we might ha' known you'd put yor clappers in. Are you goin' to tell us —'

'It would take too long to get it ready,' Paris said. 'And the hasty pudding is made with oatmeal, which he will not be used to.' He looked at their faces, struck by a sense of the mystery of things. This man had been taken from his home and tortured and brought to the edge of death – too close to be brought back, he suspected. And now these other men, who had assisted in it, were eager to find some way of tempting his appetite. He was aware of Thurso, up on the quarterdeck, ostensibly withdrawn from the proceedings but able to hear every word that was uttered. Is it concern for the negro they are expressing or support for me? The question sprang to his mind and he surprised in himself a feeling of mingled exhilaration and reluctance. And I? Which do I care more for, this man's life or proving right? He had not thought this question could come at him again; he had thought it dealt with, disposed of for ever. He looked down at the negro, as if to find an answer there. The man's thumbs were covered with blood and he could not understand this, until he realized that the pressure of the thumbscrews had caused him to bleed through the nails ... 'No, we will try with rice,' he repeated in his deep, vibrant voice. 'Here it is now. Thank you, Charlie,' he said to the boy who had come at a run with a dish of rice and a wooden spoon. 'Where is the linguister?'

Jimmy came forward. 'I don' know if he unnerstan' me,' he said. 'Mebbe unnerstan' Malinka.'

Paris drew closer to the man and crouched down beside him as he half sat, half lay against the foot of the steps. 'Tell him I want him to eat this rice,' he said. He felt suddenly helpless and ridiculous. How could he persuade the man to eat? 'Tell him I want him to live,' he said to Jimmy urgently and impatiently.

Jimmy squatted and spoke close to the man's ear.

'Wha'll tak a wee bet?' McGann said. 'I'll gie ye ten to one. Five shillin' to saxpence the doctor will no' get a crumb doon his gullet.'

288

'A penny to a shillin' he gets sommat in,' Wilson said.

'Aye, in his mouth,' Libby said. 'That's easy, man, that's not what McGann is layin' odds on. His mouth is open already. Naw, he's got to swaller, to win the bet.'

The negro showed no sign of hearing. His eyes looked at nothing, his head hung down at an awkward angle. 'I think this man goin',' Jimmy said. 'This man finish. I try him pidgin.' He brought his mouth close to the man's ear again: 'Dis buckra man doctor say you nyam-nyam, say you nyam an' dringi kaba, everythin' fine-fine.'

Paris freighted the spoon with rice, then put it back down on the plate again: he saw now that the spoon was too big. He took some of the moist and sticky rice between his thumb and first two fingers and extended this towards the man. He was aware of the silence among the people looking on – some of the women slaves had joined the circle of seamen. There was a ring round him, cutting off the air. The stench of captivity came to him, from the man before him, the spectators white and black, the massed bodies of the slaves under the awning.

'Eat,' he said. 'I want you to eat.' He could read no expression on the broad, flat-boned face, unless the approach of death can be an expression. The eyes were fixed on the strip of plank between his long and narrow feet. The mouth hung open, a spongy ellipse, allowing the pale loll of the tongue to show within it. As Paris crouched there, holding out in his fingers the sticky ball of rice, he knew that he was alone with this man, that the two of them were quite alone. The pale sky had clutched at them, gathered them into privacy, into some area of seclusion. He did not know whose was the greater arrogance, his or this dying man's.

'Eat it,' he said harshly. He reached forward and put the rice between the man's lips, feeling the helpless softness of the mouth as he did so, pushing the food between the barrier of the teeth. He dipped his fingers again into the dish, moulding a new ball. The man's mouth made no movement, his lips still hung slackly open; but as Paris again reached forward the eyes for the first time looked at him, registered his presence there, directly, immediately. Paris saw in the eyes the desire for death and recognized it as his own familiar; but in these same eyes that longed for the burden of pain to be removed there was what the surgeon had seen in his own looking-glass while the bread dissolved in his mouth – inveterate, unquenchable, the hope of life, the appeal to be saved. And Paris knew in that same moment that he had done a wicked thing to sail with this ship out of mere despair.

'Eat it,' he said again. He saw a blaze in the man's eyes, saw the mouth work to gather its contents. The negro raised himself a little and his face strained forward with a curiously patient effort. With a deep gasp, almost a groan, the mouth opened and sprayed out its contents. Paris felt the warm shock of the rice and spit on his face and saw the negro's head fall back against the ladder and his eyes turn upward.

Haines took a step forward, half raising his whip. 'Let me give him a go with this,' he said. 'I'll teach him spittin'.'

Paris got to his feet. 'Stand clear of him,' he said. 'Stand back from him.' There was an eagerness on Haines's face. On an impulse he did not understand, Paris took a step towards the boatswain and thrust at him violently. The power in his arms was a revelation – perhaps most of all to the surgeon himself. Haines was a big man and well planted on his feet but he was sent staggering back.

Paris took out a handkerchief and wiped his face slowly. 'There was not much gained by flogging him, even when he was alive,' he said, loudly enough for the captain and mate on the quarterdeck to hear. He glanced across the deck at the shackled men under the awning. They avoided his eye as usual, except for one tall and strongly built man, whom he recognized now as the first slave he had examined. This man was looking at him steadily though without discernible expression; and he did not look away when their eyes met – an unusual thing.

THIRTY

The dead slave was thrown overboard at once. He was followed two days later by a woman who, though eating her portions without protest, had been in a state of deepening lethargy for some time and was found dead on deck in the early morning with no sign about her as to the cause. Then the ship's boy, Charlie, began to sicken with the same symptoms that Simmonds had shown. As his fever mounted, the hammering and clatter on the ship mounted with it: under the supervision of Johnson, the gunner, the men were sheathing the fore parts of the main-mast and a space of the deck forward of it with lead plate, so that the furnace could be placed amidship with more security, there being more mouths aboard now than the ship's iron pot could boil for. Charlie, whose surname nobody knew, who had experienced little but blows and hunger in his fourteen years, died shivering and vomiting, not knowing whether these heavy detonations of sound were within him or without.

Paris could fathom neither the one death nor the other. Charlie had not berthed in any proximity to the second mate; he had not gone on the expedition to Tucker's and so had not been exposed to any poisonous airs from the river. Paris knew there were sexual relations among some of the men. Simmonds, after contracting the disease, might have sodomized the boy and so communicated the contagion. From questions such as these – and from his own ignorance – he sought refuge where he could find it, in memories of the past, in attention to the daily trafficking for slaves that still continued.

That steady look of the negro exercised his mind in the days that followed, though it was not repeated. It was the first time he had actually been regarded by any of these people. He could not decide if it had been a look of enmity or a recognition of something. *It was as if,* he wrote in his journal, *the life of the eyes was transferred from the man who spat at me, who died, transferred from him to the other . . .*

Fanciful, no doubt, he thought, sitting late in his cramped cabin, unable to sleep, for all the cradling motion of the ship. He felt that he was changed. He had become prey to superstitious fancies, as he had to impulses of violence.

Close weather lately, with lightnings and variable winds. The slaves have had to be kept under hatches a good part of the time – Barber has fitted the platforms and bulkheads now. Tapley is in irons up against the windlass, and has been so since yesterday. It seems that he seduced one of the women to go with him below, and there lay with her brutelike in view of those of his companions not on deck. It was not a rape, all are agreed, so he may escape flogging. He is a sly, rat-like man, Tapley.

At daybreak there came several canoes alongside us with traders to offer their services. They were sent back ashore by Captain Thurso to purchase slaves and rice, he having provided them on trust with trade goods. One came back within two hours with a man and two girls, bringing our number to eighty-three. There is in the offing now, as well as the Frenchman and a Danish slaver newly arrived, a London ship, the Astrid, *Captain Cockburn. In mid-morning Thurso went over to her in the punt, having been told she had eight slaves aboard to change for ivory. He returned shortly with that clamp-jawed, staring look of his when he is in a rage; it seems he could not take the slaves on Cockburn's terms, which was sixty bars per head round. According to Barton, there were but three of the slaves sizeable and two of the remaining five under three foot six inches. 'Sixty bars for dwarfs now,' Barton said, and laughed – though not so Thurso would hear. Barton keeps me informed, though not out of friendship – I do not believe he has feelings for anyone. It may be that he thinks to ingratiate himself for the sake of my uncle; but I believe he enjoys using some tone of disrespect to compensate for his usual sycophancy.*

Trade is slowing down. The local dealers will very seldom bring a slave to the ship to sell, and the boat trade is dearer and more precarious. As a consequence, whenever any do bring a slave, Thurso is obliged to accept him, being in fear that if he refuses, he will not get the chance of another. Meanwhile, the French are rumoured to be paying eighty bars for an adult male. 'The crappos are trying to ruin us,' Barton said. I do not know whom he means by 'us'; the ruin has been total for some aboard this ship already. I suspect we shall be leaving here soon and proceeding further along the coast to eastward, now that trade is slackening. We have lost two slaves and several more look very listless and low and will scarce move except they are whipped, though I cannot determine any disease in them. It is as if they cannot emerge from the shock of their capture . . .

Sometimes in storm weather the shore had fluttered with disabled swallows. They crouched lower for his approach, without strength to escape. In his hands they pulsed with that same pulse. He had taken a bird and warmed it between his hands or inside his jacket, brought the life back until it was able to fly. Sometimes, released from his hands, they circled once around him before flying away; in gratitude, or so the child had believed – and the belief had survived all the man's science.

It was Wilson who had come upon the dead woman. He told the story at the time favoured for stories, in the first of the twilight, before the night watch was set, when it was still early enough for most men to be on deck.

The captain was making his usual walk on the weather side of the quarterdeck, twelve paces forward, twelve back; Barton stood alone on the lee side and Johnson was at the weather gangway, mending a tear in his jacket by the lamp there. Haines, having seen to the coiling of the ropes, was smoking a pipe with Morgan in the galley. Two of those on half-watch, Hughes and True, were amidships guarding the slaves. The others were lying on the forecastle, smoking, talking together. It was a relaxed time on the ship, a time for speculation and hyperbole.

'She were crawled right under the gangway,' Wilson said. 'Behind the gangway ladder, up agin the side. Hardly space for a cat in there. She were crawled under, among some bread butts.' He had been sent forward with Calley shortly after turning-to that morning to wash down the deck, and had found her there, in the first light of the day, lying on her side, knees drawn up, in the narrow space between the butts. 'Not a mark on her,' Wilson said. 'She must have been took sick and crawled in there.'

There were things about this discovery that Wilson did not speak of to the others. He had thought her asleep. Her back was to him and in the carelessness of her condition the waist-cloth had ridden up over her buttocks to show the brandmark high on the left one. Calley was over on the other side of the deck. There was no one else near. Moving the butts clear, he felt half suffocated with eagerness. By good luck – as he thought – she did not wake. It was his idea to take her from behind while she was still too sleepy to make effective resistance. He had lowered himself against her and had a hand over her mouth before he felt the chill of the body and realized that he was jammed up against a corpse. 'Shark meat,' he said now, with resentment; Wilson never forgot an injury and this death seemed one to him, cheating his lust. Light from the forecastle lamps glinted on his dark stubble as he turned his face slowly from side to side. 'That's all she were, shark meat.'

'I never seen her,' Calley said. 'I was on the other side. I seen her but I didn' find her. Wilson shouted to me come an' looka this.' He wished he could have been the one to find her and have something to tell.

'Yer couldn't find yer own cock in the dark,' Libby said. The dead jelly of his eye emitted a thin, satiric gleam. 'Yer lost yerself, didn' yer, and had to be brought back by the quashees?'

A rare moment of felicity came to Calley. 'Well, I got two eyes,' he said, 'so I got more chance o' findin' things than what you have.'

This unexpected riposte set Blair chuckling. 'That's reet, lad, you ha' twice the chance o' some,' he said; and this support and the fact that Blair had laughed at his joke, secured him Calley's affection for ever.

'They dies of melancholy,' Barber said, round the stem of his pipe. 'I have seen it over an' over. They sets their minds on dying. I have been on ships where it spread like a plague. You put 'em below just as usual, two by two, an' they looks just the same as ever, an' in the mornin' you find a dead an' a livin' man chained together an' that is the first you notice any difference between 'em.'

'When one dies, others will follow,' Sullivan said, glancing about him as if disturbed in a dream. 'It was Simmonds set it loose, God rest his soul. Death has sailed with every ship that ever put out of port. Once he gets loose, there is no confinin' him again.'

'He is the only free fuckster on this ship then,' Wilson said. ''cept for the captain.'

'It is true that a curse will sometimes fasten on a ship,' Davies said. 'There was the *Black Prince*, Captain Bibby, which I sailed with in forty-four. We were tradin' on the Gambia an' the captain was a tartar – this one is a saint to him. He would flog a man every day for one reason or another. I seen him drown a black woman in a swill tub with his own hands for tryin' to pass a marlin-spike to one of the men slaves. I tell you, he was a devil. He had given out arms and ammunition to the natives ashore so they could make a war-party to take slaves, an' in exchange he'd taken eight men aboard as pawns.'

'What is that?' Blair asked.

'They are relatives of the chief or people belonging to the chief that offers themselves for it, on the agreement that unless slaves are furnished within a certain time, or goods to the value of what has been loaned, the pawns will be carried off instead. Our agreement was for three days, but Bibby did not wait the due time, he took advantage of a favourable wind to up anchor and make off. The result was that another ship was attacked by the natives in revenge, the *Molly*, it was, for no other reason than she was a Liverpool ship. She wasn't a slaver even, she was tradin' for beeswax an' pepper. The captain an' the mate an' five crew were taken an' tied to trees an' had their throats cut. The English sent a sloop from Goree with a platoon of troops an' a cannon to punish the blacks for this outrage, an' they burned their village over their heads an' killed several of them an' one of the soldiers was killed in the fightin'. Now all this blood was on Captain Bibby's head, as he had broke the bond. But there was a curse on that ship from the moment of leavin'. Bibby lost two-thirds of his negroes by the bloody flux on the Middle Passage, includin' all but one of the pawns he had taken, an' so it was paid back to him.'

'Paid back to him?' Blair said. 'What became o' Bibby then?'

'He retired shortly after. He had put savin's by. He went to live in Kent, with his unmarried daughter. He was a Kentish man, d'you see, Captain Bibby.'

'I have seen blindness spread on a ship,' Wilson said. 'There is a skin grows ower the eyes. Tha wakes up in the mornin' an' tha cannot see owt. The negroes come aboard with it already about them, an' it gets among the crew. I were on a ship once when everyone were goin' blind with it, skipper an' all. We were out in the Gulf o' Guinea when it started, bound for Barbados, but we had to put back to San Tomé. I were talkin' to the bos'n, name of Billy Fox, talkin' away one minute, next he says, "Christ, give us a fin, mate, my eyes have gone."'

'Did he get better?' Calley, whose sleep would be troubled, had been following this story with round eyes.

'Get better? He didn't have no chance to get better. Billy couldn't keep off the women. He went to a crackhouse back in San Tomé an' fell down some steps an' broke his neck. There were a canary on board an' that went blind as well. Soon as it went blind it started singin' – it were dumb before.'

There was a pause at this. Wilson was an unpredictable man and no one felt inclined to risk provoking him by seeming not to believe it. After some moments Libby gave it out as his opinion that Africans were able to put an end to themselves by holding their breath, this being the only explanation for deaths among fed slaves with no injuries or marks of disease.

'A man canna kill himself just by holdin' his breath,' Blair said, with some beginnings of the confused anger he always showed at contradictory or illogical statements. 'If he holds his breath, he'll fall down in a faint, an' when he falls down in a faint, he'll start breathin' again. If you dinna believe me, try it for yourself.'

'No use askin' me to try it.' Libby laughed and spat over the rail. 'I'm a Englishman, ain't I?'

'A Englishman cannot do it,' Tapley said. 'Only these here blacks can do it. They are closer to animals than what we are.'

'If they are closer than what you are, Tapley, they must be amazin' creatures indeed,' Blair said. 'I agree with what Barber says. It is melancholy kills them.'

'I will be dyin' of malincholly meself aboard of this ship,' Sullivan said. 'I am playin' me fiddle for them blacks ivery mornin' an' the sound of the clankin' they make is drownin' out me notes. I am goin' to have a word with the captain about it.'

'The only word you'll ever have wi' the captain is "aye-aye, sir",' Blair said.

'You said the same thing about me buttons, but I spoke up to Haines.'

'Aye, an' wha's still got 'em? Speakin' up to Thurso is a different matter. You have only to look at him wrong, an' it's bread an' water in the bilboes.'

'A man with justice on his side will always be listened to,' Sullivan said.

'Ye're all gab, Sullivan,' McGann said. 'We might tak ye more serious if ye'd put money on it. Will ye tak a bet in even shillin's? My shillin' says ye'll never hae the brash to speak up to Thurso.'

'The Scotch were always doubters,' Sullivan said. 'My shillin' says I'll speak to him, man to man. Billy, you are me witness.'

THIRTY-ONE

With the slaves' numbers now so much increased, the enforced
periods below decks rendered their quarters noisome; it was
Paris's duty to see the platforms well washed down and the area
between decks smoked for some hours to purify the air. Relations
with the coast negroes had worsened. The Frenchmen's yawl
had driven ashore at Little Bassa and been smashed and plun-
dered, and her crew roughly handled, by the natives. The news
had perturbed Thurso, who was afraid that this success would
encourage other attempts.

'These villains will copy any bad example,' he observed to
Barton, 'but show them a good model of behaviour and they
will sheer away from it as if it were the devil. They are inclined
by nature to every kind of mischief and evil-doing.' The thought
of losing the ship's boat worried him a good deal; there was no
trade anywhere along the Windward Coast without a sloop of
some sort. 'You can trade with 'em for twenty years,' he said,
'then some other white man does 'em an injury and they pretend
to believe we are all tarred with the same brush.'

'They are wrong there, Captain,' Barton said. 'It is them
what have been tarred.'

Thurso regarded his first mate with a displeasure he took no
trouble to conceal. He was an enemy to jokes, feeling an energy
in them beyond his controlling. 'Barton, I do not like levity,' he
said. 'You know my feelings and still you go on with it. I advise
you to be careful.'

'Aye-aye, sir.'

'We will be going on round the coast very soon, down to the
company fort. We will do our private business for the gold dust

there, upriver, as we did before. This voyage will be our last together. What course you set afterwards is no concern of mine, but while you are mate on my ship you will keep to my mood. I was remarking on the fickleness of these dogs and their readiness to follow any bad example.'

Then the yawl returned from six days' trading upriver, with eight slaves, a tusk weighing nearly forty pounds and two quintals of camwood – and with Johnson in the waist half conscious and shivering with fever and True hardly able to stand to his oars.

It was this that decided Thurso. Two of the crew were dead already and one had run; any more, and he could not keep the yawl manned and the negroes guarded at the same time and so would not manage to bring off slaves anywhere on this side of the cape. Next morning he sent ashore for water and more rice; they had more than a thousand pounds of it aboard now. Later he sent Haines and four men with twenty fathoms of remnants to exchange for yams, plantains and palm oil, but these supplies could not be brought aboard till next day, as there was so great a sea across the bar that Haines did not dare to venture over. When they came they brought with them also a single slave, a well-grown boy of fourteen or so, bringing the total number to ninety-seven, of which thirty were women.

In the course of the day the ship's sails were loosed and aired and the spare sails brought up and overhauled. It was found that the rats had done some damage to these; the ship was by now overrun with them, as the three cats they had brought out from England were all dead, and they had been quite unable to find one ashore. Under Barton's supervision – Johnson being too ill – the small arms were discharged and reloaded. With nightfall, the slaves were herded to their quarters below and the hatches fastened down on them, Thurso knowing from old that to leave slaves on deck, men or women, when the ship was leaving their home shores, was to invite trouble of the most serious kind.

'I have seen it happen,' he said that evening to Barton and Paris, whom he had invited to sup with him on this eve of departure. 'They become desperate when they see the ship putting out to sea. They will sometimes throw themselves over the side, chained as they are. And in their shackles, d'ye see, they cannot long stay alive once they are in the water. They are gone under before you can lower a boat for 'em. I have known 'em shout and laugh with the joy of cheating us. It is a dead loss to the owners, since we are not underwritten for suicide.'

They were sitting over brandy after the meal. Thurso was in a more than usually expansive mood this evening, with his trading done here and half his cargo already purchased. Since hearing Paris's report he was less troubled at the thought of being left undermanned. Johnson was still weak and complained of racking pains in head and limbs; but True's fever had left him. Both men had been drinking heavily and sleeping in native huts on shore. It was the surgeon's opinion that they had exposed themselves to malignant ground vapours and thus contracted marsh fever, though it seemed of an ephemeral kind.

'If the men have to sleep away from the ship,' the surgeon said, 'they should be sure to have a fire lit in their close vicinity, just sufficient to raise a gentle smoke. This would render the night airs less noxious.'

'Aye, it is the same practice we use aboard ship,' Barton said, 'to clear the air between decks.'

Thurso looked from the mate to the surgeon. He could not suffer men to show any accord in his company without prior reference to himself. 'You may be right, Mr Paris,' he said. 'But you will never get any discipline or good governance from these men. They will take no notice of advice that might tend to their good. Hard labour aboard, debauchery ashore and an early grave – that is the way of it for nearly all of 'em.'

Thurso paused for a moment, looking closely at the surgeon, feeling the customary irritation of moral constraint the other put upon him, by his silences as much as his words. 'We are living in the real world, Mr Paris,' he said. 'We have to shape our course to the weather.'

'The measure I am suggesting is practical enough, sir,' Paris said mildly.

Thurso raised a blunt forefinger and tapped slowly at the side of his head. 'It is in the mind,' he said. 'You have got to bring 'em to the right frame of mind. And when you have animals to deal with, it is done by fear, sir, not persuasion.'

There had been a jibe contained in this and Thurso saw it register – the surgeon's face had lost the look of youth but there was no concealment in it; what he felt changed the expression of his eyes and moved the corners of his mouth.

'Persuasion gets you a gobful o' rice in the face,' Barton said with his lackey's instinct for pressing home the attacks of his master.

Paris smiled slightly but he had felt his heart quicken. 'So you think the rice in the face was a victory for the method of fear, Barton, do you? I must say I find that a strange interpretation of the event.'

'Take the negroes,' Thurso said, with unmoved face. He often behaved as if no one had spoken since his own last remark. 'This mortality by which we suffer such losses is entirely owing to their brooding so much on their situation. If you want to get 'em to market in good condition, you must change their way of thinking. I remember once, many years ago now, it was one of my first ships, we were trading in the Bight of Benin and had taken aboard a cargo of Ibo. I do not buy Ibo nowadays; they have a reputation for being unreliable and do not fetch prices anything comparable to the Windward Coast negroes, though I know of skippers that deal in nothing else as the trade is well ordered in the delta and slaves in good supply, so you can reduce waiting time on the coast, and the feeding of your negroes while you are waiting. On this occasion we had not been a week at sea when these Ibo began to fall into a fixed melancholy. They could not be brought to eat by flogging and began to die in numbers. I discovered from my linguister that they believed that by dying they would get back to their own country. So what do you think I did, sir?'

Thurso paused to drink some of his brandy. 'Do you think I tried persuasion on 'em?' he said. At this moment there was a light tapping on the cabin door, but at this climactic moment of his story, he paid no attention to it. 'I'll tell you what I did, sir. I had the slaves brought up on deck and in full view of all I cut off the heads of those who had died with a cleaver from the

301

galley. Who the devil is that knocking? Give him a shout to come in, Barton. Yes, sir, that is what I did, and do you know why?'

In answer to Barton's summons, the door had been pushed open and Sullivan stood wild-eyed and dishevelled on the threshold. He was in time to hear his captain's concluding remarks.

'I did it so they might clearly understand that if they were determined to return home they would have to do so without their heads. I had no more trouble with 'em from that day forward. What are you doing here?'

'Beggin' your pardon, sir.' After the first glances, Sullivan kept his eyes down. He had prepared his speech and delivered it without faltering though rather too fast: 'The captives bein' in chains, sir, they cannot move their limbs freely to the sound o' me fiddle an' the noise they make with the clankin' is swampin' me notes. There is more than thirty pairs, sir, fastened at wrist and ankle an' all of thim jumpin'. The sound of the chains is drownin' out me fiddlin' intirely.' He paused, looked up briefly, then down again – he had remembered another point. 'An' the numbers is increasin' all the time,' he said. 'I'll niver be able to hear me own notes an' I'll forget what it is I am supposed to be playin'.'

Thurso turned frowning to his first mate. 'What is this man talking about?' he said. 'Is he drunk?' It was an old menacing trick of his not to address an underling directly.

'What are you talkin' about?' Barton demanded. 'How dare you come here with this riggermarool talk o' fiddlin'? Don't you know you should have gone through one of the officers?'

As often happened with Sullivan, his initial fear – strong enough to have kept him hesitating long at the door – had diminished now in the warmth and justice of his own advocacy. 'Beggin' your pardon, sir, but I was askin' meself if the chains could be taken off.'

'Taken off?'

'Just for the period of me playin',' Sullivan said.

Thurso's brows had drawn together in a ferocious frown. For a few moments he said nothing. Then they saw his mouth move in a curious grimacing, stretching way, almost convulsive in appearance. He raised his face as if about to sneeze and a series of hoarse, choking sounds came from somewhere deep in his throat. After a moment or two, the others regarding him meanwhile in astonished silence – neither of them had any idea to begin with what ailed him, never having seen such symptoms in him before – he took out a capacious handkerchief and wiped his eyes.

'By God, that's rich,' he said. 'I haven't heard anything so rich for a long time. Did you hear him, Barton? This gut-scraper wants the chains taken off 'em because the noise is spoiling his music.'

'He must be out of his senses,' Barton said blankly.

Thurso turned to Paris, traces of tears still in his eyes. 'Here is another fellow of the same kidney as yourself,' he said. 'He doesn't know what is the real world either.'

Paris looked at the fiddler in silence for a moment. Then he said, without smiling, 'I don't disdain the connection, if he doesn't.'

Sullivan was too concerned with bearing himself properly to look the surgeon in the eye; but the grace of these words went to his heart and he never repeated them to anyone, not even Blair. Everything else he recounted later in the forecastle with considerable embellishment and dramatic licence. 'I put me arguments fair an' square,' he said. 'I gave me reasons. Not surprisin' they refused me – Thurso has no feelin' for music any more than a toad. "If that is the case," I says to them, "you might as well not have employed a fiddler at all." An' I turns on me heel . . .'

Under the chaffing attention of his shipmates his spirits rose. He was by nature mercurial; and he felt sure of McGann's shilling. But the words of kinship, unexpected, unsolicited, as he stood there with his head down and Thurso's fearsome laughter still in his ears, these were to shine in his memory for ever.

Soon after midnight the first of the land breeze began making along the river and Thurso ordered sail to be got up and all to be made ready for purchasing anchor. At two they weighed and got out to sea, the wind by this time giving a good offing. In the cover of darkness, as quietly as possible, the *Liverpool Merchant* began to steer a course south-eastward. But when the ship met the deep sea swell, the rhythm of her movement changed and the people in the cramped and fetid darkness of the hold, understanding that they had lost all hope of returning to their homes, set up a great cry of desolation and despair that carried over the water to the other ships in the road and the slaves in the holds of the ships heard it and answered with wild shouts and screams, so that for people lying awake in villages along the shore and for solitary fishermen up before dawn, there was a period when the night resounded with the echoes of lamentation.

PART SIX

THIRTY-TWO

It was an uneventful voyage, apart from the attempt of one negro to put an end to his life by severing the veins of his neck with his nails. While dressing the wounds Paris learned from Jimmy that the man had been falsely convicted of witchcraft and sold to pay his fine. 'Very good way for make money,' Jimmy said. 'Man got nothin'. So they sell 'em.'

They rounded the cape and came to anchor in eleven fathoms, abreast of the river and within sight of the fort. Their approach was saluted with three guns and Thurso returned the same number.

In the afternoon a Company pinnace with twelve oars came out for them, rowed by looser-built, lither men, Paris noticed, than the Kru boatmen of the Grain Coast they had just left. Thurso left the ship in charge of Barton, and he and the surgeon embarked in the pinnace for shore. The town at this distance was a low jumble of native huts set in a mesh of greenery. Lying to the left of it, on a rocky eminence above the river bank, rose the white fort, shimmering in the sunshine, dramatic and imposing, with its block towers and high, crenellated walls. Paris made out the Union Jack flying from the battlements, and another flag, blue and white – the colours of the Company, Thurso told him.

With astonishing judgement and skill, the oarsmen brought them to shore through the violent paroxysms of the surf. They mounted the slope of the foreshore, past narrow fishing boats curved high at the prow, with tufted fetish-bundles tied at their heads. It was hot here, out of the breeze, and the strength of the light troubled Paris's eyes. Screens of nets were drying on poles and the scraps of fish scales caught in them glinted and flashed.

Escorted by the Company negroes, they made their way past marshy flats where naked children ran, flies rose in swarms, geese and ducks pottered in the muddy water. There was a strench of dead crabs from the river bank and of decaying coconuts that had been half buried in the sand to rot the fibre free.

The walls of the fort rose above them with an intensity of white almost blinding. There was to Paris a terrible strangeness in this great monumental structure amidst the squalid and provisional evidences of life around them: the cluttered, evil-smelling shore, the ramshackle town, the signs everywhere of a collaboration with the forces of nature that was tentative and temporary. The battlemented walls denied all this; they asserted the principle of permanence. There would always be profits to make, interests to defend. In the fertile interior of Africa her children, her greatest resource, would multiply endlessly and come down in endless procession to be sold below these walls, beside the sea.

The way they were following rose more steeply in the last few hundred yards as they approached the rocky bluff on which the fort was built. Then they were in the sharp black shadows of the buttresses and Paris felt immediate relief from the assaults of heat and light. The heavy gates stood open. The soldiers on sentry duty, one at either side, straightened from their position of ease without coming fully to attention, their tunics dark red in the deep shadow.

They were conducted to the Governor's quarters, up flights of stone stairs with steps of alternate white and black, freshly painted. On the landing, defending the approach, two small brass cannon squatted. Crossed pikes stood on the wall behind. There was a passage and a narrow hallway, also hung with weapons; then finally the door to the Governor's chambers.

He was there to receive them, a handsome, pale-mouthed man with a high bridge to his nose and a languid, murmuring manner of speech. His shirt was elaborately ruffled with lace at the neck and cuffs and he wore a short silver wig with curled rolls above the ears.

'Captain Thurso, Mr Paris,' he said, with minimum effort of the lips. 'I am glad to make your acquaintance. We have not had dealings before, Captain, I believe?'

308

'No, sir.' Bewigged, cocked hat under his arm, in his ceremonial broadcloth, Thurso looked out of his element here, in
this wainscoted room, with its several low tables and armless
leather chairs. Paris was reminded of their first meeting, in
Liverpool, with his uncle present, when Thurso had worn that
same look of staring outrage, as if he had been derided. The
captain was a fish that could only swim in a certain water . . .

'I did trade with Mr Charles Gordon,' he said now, in his
hoarse and lingering fashion. The words seemed forced from the
depths by the pressure of some urgent secret, as if only a rage to
confide could have steered them up through his windpipe. His
confidences, when they came, were not distinguished by tact,
however. 'In these last years,' he said, 'I have seen three Governors come and go, two under the old charter of the Royal
Africa Company and one since the new Company took over.'

'You are a man of much experience,' the Governor said,
moving his almost bloodless lips in the semblance of a smile.
'Please be seated, gentlemen. Will you take a glass of port, Captain?'

'Thank you, sir, I will.'

'And you, Mr Paris?'

'I would be content with a little lemon water, something of
that kind.'

'You do not care for port then?'

'Not in this heat.' Paris's tone was abrupt. Whatever the
progress he had made towards humility, he was no better able
than before to bear with condescension.

'You are right, sir,' the Governor said. 'You are a man of
sense, I can see. The captain is well seasoned and I dare say it
does him no harm, but I never touch it myself in the middle
hours of the day. I have some barley water here. Will that suffice?'

'Thank you.'

'Your port, Captain. Gentlemen, good health! I will not join
you at present, pray forgive me. What I generally have at this
time of afternoon, or just a little later, is a syllabub of cream
and thin cider, sweetened with a modicum of honey. I find it
answers very well. What do you think of such a dish, sir?'

'Think of it?' Paris found himself being regarded closely. For all the nonchalance of the tone, the Governor's eyes were fixed on him with a distinct sharpness of interest. 'I would think it healthsome and nourishing,' he said.

'I am glad to hear you say that, sir. I prepare it myself, with my own hands. To teach my last imbecile of an orderly how to make it in the right proportions took me months, gentlemen, and I cannot tell you what stores of patience. And no sooner was he schooled to it than he succumbed to an ague of some sort that is going round among the troops. I find myself unable to face the prospect of beginning all over again with another, so I do it now myself.'

The Governor paused and appeared to muse some moments, looking down his nose. 'Yes,' he said softly. 'I find it answers pretty well.'

It seemed to Paris now that he could hear screams, though he could not tell from where they were coming – somewhere outside, it seemed.

'Charles Gordon, whom you did business with, Captain, was my predecessor here,' he heard the Governor say in his well-bred, languid tones. 'He died of a putrid fever. He died in the room next to this one. *His* predecessor died in this room where we are standing, of a burst blood vessel. But whether we say they died of this or that, they both died of the same thing, gentlemen.'

'Oh, aye, what was that?' Thurso said with interest.

'They died through not taking proper care of themselves. Diet is the key to it. Would you not agree, as a medical man, Mr Paris?'

'I do not know. There are other factors in a climate such as this one. Certainly, diet is important.' The screams were coming from somewhere below them. Paris glanced towards the windows. The drapes were drawn against the strong light. He thought of the flights of stairs they had mounted to come here. The rooms must lie along the ramparts of the fort, facing the afternoon sun . . .

'Yes, I am sorry,' the Governor said. He had noticed the surgeon's distraction. 'There is a private of marines being flogged; they have chosen just this time to do it and sounds rise to us here from the courtyards in spite of –'

'Well, you need not apologize to us, sir,' Paris said, rather too hastily. 'Our ears will recover from the discomfort more quickly than will his back.'

The Governor's eyebrows had risen slightly at this impetuous speech, but when he spoke his expression had resumed its usual frigid composure. 'It was I who ordered him the flogging,' he said. 'He stole a snuff-box from my study and sold it for drink – it was quite clearly proved upon him. I ordered him a hundred lashes. The snuff-box was one I set particular store by, it had a sentimental value for me. You will understand my feelings when I tell you that it was a present from a lady.'

Paris could not for the moment find a response to this, though it was clear one was expected – the Governor had addressed him, not Thurso, no doubt supposing the captain incapable of finer feelings. It was he, the captain, however, who saved the present silence from lengthening awkwardly. Not finding much of interest in this tale of a theft and a flogging, he had been glancing into the corners of the room for some time and now said, 'I believe these chambers have been refurbished since the last occasion I had the honour to be here? And I noticed as we came up that the timber and the ironwork on the gates are new.'

'Yes, you are right, Captain,' the Governor said. 'There have been extensive repairs. The work was begun in the days of my predecessor and has not been long completed. The Company, when it took over the fort from the Royal Africa Company, which as you know is now dissolved, finding it dilapidated and in some parts ruinous, thought fit to expend some considerable sums on its reconstruction. They were right to do so, in my view. This fort is the visible evidence of our presence here; it must be made imposing. We are judged by it, sir, not only the power and wealth of the Company but that of our whole nation. By their works shall ye know them, as the Scriptures say. Competition for trade is increasing all down the coast. We cannot rest on our laurels. The Company is very much alive to the importance of the image it presents.'

The Governor lay back in his chair, as if the energy required for this speech had exhausted him. He drew out a square of cambric from his sleeve and dabbed at his temples and the corners of his lips. A scent of lavender expanded in the still air of the room. The screaming had stopped now, but the regular sound of the lash continued.

'They were obliged to bring craftsmen out,' the Governor sighed after a moment. 'All the oak for the interior panelling had to be imported. Imagine the difficulty we were under, in getting these wretched people to transport the stone. With their distaste for work of any kind, our labour here was worse than that confronting the pharaohs of old. Well, gentlemen, it grows time for me to busy myself with my syllabub. With your permission, I shall give you over to the care of one of our factors, Mr Saunders, who will take you down to see the slaves. After that you might like to take your ease for a while. Saunders will show you your quarters. I look forward to seeing you both again at supper.'

He rang a small brass handbell that had been lying on the table before him. An African in white tunic and drawers appeared instantly and was told to fetch Mr Saunders, for whom they waited some minutes in a silence made rather uneasy by Thurso's audible breathing and the Governor's total immobility. There was no sound at all now from the courtyard below, but it seemed to Paris that he could hear a faint but steady sound of hammering from some more distant source. The Governor kept his nose and mouth buried in his handkerchief, though he freed them once to ask the surgeon his opinion of the efficacy of watered spirits in preventing disease. 'The Company doctor here recommended a glass of red wine with the juice of half a lemon and a little sugar as a good defence against contagion,' he said, 'but he died of fever a month ago, leaving me in some doubt of his remedy.'

The surgeon was seeking to reply to this when there was a knock at the door and Saunders entered. He was youngish, perhaps not more than thirty or so, but sunken-eyed and haggard. With him as their guide they returned to ground level and thence through stone-floored passages towards what Paris thought might be the rear of the fort, the side facing away from the sea. But the corridors twisted and turned and after a while he had lost all sense of direction.

As they proceeded he began to feel a sort of remote terror, the anxiety that comes sometimes in dreams of labyrinths, when each turning threatens to confront us with something intolerable and we struggle to wake before we reach it.

What he might meet he did not know. No one can keep account of damage done to himself. We imagine we have absorbed the shock, the harm, but we have merely caged it, and not in a strong cage either. It waits within the bars for a signal. And however long the wait may be, the leap is always unerring; a man can after twenty years be struck by a horror he thought he had forgotten and it will be green and fresh as ever. Often the pounce comes before the mind knows the signal, as it came to Paris now with the smell of the dank stone, the smell of degradation somewhere ahead of him, a horror almost incredulous that he was lost here, in this place, that he, who had prided himself on his vigilant clarity of mind and ruined himself for it, could have been his own self-deceiver, could have made his own despair a reason for compounding the misery of the world, and that he could have called this monstrous egotism self-abnegation and offered it to a dead woman as a proof of love. The dead could only be mourned. Love is for the living, he thought suddenly, and the thought dispelled his fear.

A final turn brought them to the slave-dungeons, set side by side like cells, with barred fronts and stone walls and high barred windows, through which the afternoon sun was falling now in straight rays; he had been right, they were at the rear of the fort, against the outside walls. Three of the dungeons were occupied now, two with men handcuffed together in pairs and one with unshackled girls and women. Sunlight for this hour was caged there with them. Motes of dust moved with gauzy flies through the bright air. The bodies of the slaves were flecked and stippled and the straw that covered the earth floors was luminous gold. The smells of excrement and trodden straw seemed like a release of this flooding warmth of sunshine. Through the barred embrasures in the walls, Paris heard the hammering again, much closer now, a double-stroke, impatient and swift, metal on wood. Then he saw that one of the women had come forward and was standing pressed against the bars in a shaft of sunlight. She was looking directly at him – he saw the gleam of her eyes. But her face was shadowed. Sunlight fell on her from the window behind, her face and head were edged with fire. She was naked but he took in little of her form beyond that she was slender and straight-shouldered. She was somehow protected from closer scrutiny by her stillness, which struck him suddenly as sacramental, and by the edging of fire around her. He looked at her steadily but she did not look away. He had a moment of slight dizziness, as if he had made some too precipitate movement.

'Thirty-six in all,' Saunders said. 'We are expecting a batch from up country.'

In this stronger light Paris saw that the factor was younger than he had at first supposed, perhaps not much more than twenty, though much wasted by some recent fever. 'What is that persistent hammering?' he asked.

'There has been an outbreak of jail fever among the garrison troops,' Saunders said. 'There are two more dead of it since yesterday. The carpenters are making coffins for the dead. It has not touched the slaves, I am glad to say.'

'Shall we get to business?' Thurso said. 'We have had enough talking round the matter.' Away from the oppression of the drawing-room and the governor's presence, he was himself again, in his proper element, with the penned creatures and the bargaining. 'Those are never Wika people, those men there,' he said, pointing towards a group of tall, very robust negroes. 'See those heads, Mr Paris? Look at the limbs of those men, see how they stare back at us. Those are Corymantee negroes, Mr Saunders. What are they doing so far west?'

'There is a story to that,' Saunders said, a little uneasily as it seemed.

'I warrant there is.'

'They were taken from a Dutch slaver returning from Elmina.'

'Taken? How do you mean? Are you saying the Dutchman was already slaved and they were taken off her?'

314

'She wasn't fully slaved, she was still trading. She had about twenty Gold Coast negroes aboard and some ivory and gold dust. She was boarded by natives from King George Town. I don't know the details. I believe there were not more than four or five able-bodied crew on the ship at the time – some were down with dysentery and some away trading upriver. The blacks came in boats at night and got aboard her. They overpowered the people on deck and carried off the slaves.'

'And brought 'em here,' Thurso said, with a peculiar intonation.

'Yes. That is, they found their way here. As I say, I am not familiar with the details.'

'I dare say not. Well, I am not concerned to enquire too closely. In this business it is he who possesses the merchandise that has best title to it. And they are fine fellows. Intractable though,' he added quickly. 'Devilish proud. There are those who will not bid for Corymantee negroes on any terms. Too much trouble, you know. Still, I will take 'em off your hands, subject to our doctor here casting an eye over 'em. Fifty-eight bars is the price I have been trading at, up on the Sherbro. I will make it sixty for those Gold Coast men, for the sake of avoiding argument.'

'The price here is seventy-five bars,' Saunders said. 'For all male slaves in prime condition, independent of where they hail from. And sixty-eight for women.'

Expressions of outrage Paris had seen before on the captain's face; but the present one surpassed them all. *'Seventy-five bars?'* The words came in a harsh, incredulous whisper. He turned his body stiffly round towards Paris, his only ally now, however uncongenial. 'Did you hear that, Mr Paris? That is near twenty-five guineas in coin of the realm. The prices cannot have jumped so high. When Mr Gordon was Company Agent here there was not this difference; he kept to prices prevailing on the coast.'

'You had best speak to the Governor about it, not to me.' Saunders looked suddenly very young, despite his emaciation, and distinctly unhappy. 'No one else has any say. The Company sent me out as factor but I have no more scope than a dog here

– and it is a dog's life altogether, sir. So you would do best to enquire of the Governor.'

'I will, be sure of it,' Thurso said grimly. 'Come, Mr Paris, there is nothing to be done here for the moment.'

However he had no opportunity at supper, where he found himself seated at some distance from the Governor, below the commander of the garrison, a Major Donlevy, and the Company Treasurer, whose name was Eager, with a young man named Delblanc, described as an artist, on his other side, and Paris opposite with two silent Swedes beside him, whose names the captain hadn't caught. There were no women at table.

Thurso had already tucked his napkin under his chin and dipped his spoon into his soup when a tall negro in a dark suit and a clerical neckband, who had been introduced as the Reverend Kalabanda, rose to his feet, closed his eyes in the hush and intoned in a voice of considerable resonance: 'O Most Merciful Father, we give thee humble thanks for this thy special bounty, beseeching thee to continue thy loving-kindness unto us, that our land may yield us her fruits of increase, to thy glory and our comfort, through Jesus Christ our Lord. Amen.'

He resumed his seat in the midst of murmured amens, and addressed himself gravely to his soup.

'Your English is extremely good, Mr Kalabanda,' Paris said, speaking across the table. 'I congratulate you on it.'

The vicar smiled at Paris's compliments and the small scars high on his cheeks, which Paris thought might be due to ceremonial cuts, stretched with his smile. He was stout and muscular, his arms and shoulders straining his clerical coat. His eyes were coal black and lustrous and the skin of his face shone with health. 'I have spent many years in England,' he said. 'Most of my life. I was at school and at theological college there.'

'This man is a credit to his family, Mr Paris,' the Governor said, in his expiring tones. 'He is a living demonstration of what the African is capable of, given sobriety and good governance.'

'Aye, dammit, that is the key to the business,' the major said loudly, and Paris saw now that he was drunk and must have been well on the way to it when he arrived among them. The surgeon caught Delblanc's eye across the table and smiled a little and saw the young man's face break into an answering smile of great warmth and humour, though there was a degree of satire in it too, which he seemed careless to conceal.

'Your people taught me language,' the chaplain said. 'A great gift indeed. And I have profited from it to bless the name of God and that country where of all others his laws are respected, which I never cease from doing day or night. Language, Captain, what a great gift. The word. The Logos. God said, "Let there be light." *Said*, sir.'

For some reason he had fastened on Thurso for audience. The captain's great square cage of a face gave little away, but his eyes had retreated as far as possible back into his head.

'I do not allow my wife's vile language to be spoken in my hearing, Captain,' the chaplain said. 'I do not permit my children to use it. They speak only English.'

In an attempt to shake off the Reverend Kalabanda's gaze, Thurso addressed himself to the major, whose face was lowered over his roast duck and sweet potatoes: 'There has been a fort here for a fair time now, one way or another, sir.'

The major raised his head in the abrupt way of the drunken. He gave the impression of being held in place in his chair only by the stiff brocade of his uniform. 'Centuries, sir,' he said. 'The Portuguese built this fort and held it for a hundred years. Then the Dutch took it off 'em. Then we took it off the Dutch. Then the Danes had a try for it, but naturally they could not prevail against us.' He reached for his wine with deliberate care. 'The French came into it somewhere, too,' he said. 'I cannot recall exactly where.' He looked with dazed eyes down the table. 'Confusion to the French,' he said, raising his glass.

From the head of the table the Governor was still singing the praises of his chaplain. 'He has come back here to preach the Gospel in his ancestral lands. His father is Chief Peachy Kalabanda, who is a highly respected figure in these parts.'

'Yes,' the vicar said, 'I have returned to my homeland. I used to run about here as a little child. My father brought me here when he came with slaves to sell. That was in the days of the old company. I used to look up at this great monument, this big white fort. My father used to tell me this was the home of the

317

Great White King.' Kalabanda smiled and shook his head at the memory. 'I little thought that one day I would find myself sitting at this table, an ordained priest of the Church of England.'

'And so it is his home,' the governor said. He raised a napkin to dab at his pale lips as if to remove pollutant traces. 'Wherever the flag is planted, there is his home.'

'I hope he ain't going about baptizing among the slaves,' Thurso muttered hoarsely in Paris's ear. 'It makes 'em uppish. You persuade a negro he has a soul to be saved and he will be a source of trouble for ever afterwards, to himself and to his owner.'

It is possible that the chaplain's ears were keen enough to hear something of this, for he smiled again and said, 'I minister among the troops here and among my free brethren. That there are those who are not free helps me in my ministry. The mind is constituted to accept the god of the more powerful. This we must accept as human nature – and our human nature is given to us by God, so God himself has endowed us with this respect for the powerful. If you have to choose between the god of the slave owner and the god of the enslaved, naturally you will chose the former. All history teaches us that lesson.'

'It does not teach me that lesson, sir, for one,' Delblanc said, rather carelessly but with no trace of a smile. 'Christ spoke to the wretched and powerless as one of them, did he not? I have always understood that the Christian religion was spread among slaves.'

The Reverend Kalabanda leaned forward and Paris saw his nostrils distend slightly. 'A few ragged-trouser fellows talking in cellars,' he said with contempt. 'It was the Roman rulers who spread the faith, governors of provinces like this our governor here, officers of garrisons like our good major, the treasurers and keepers of –'

'Excuse me, please.' One of the Scandinavians had come to sudden and unexpected life. He laid down knife and fork and looked with large vague eyes at the eloquent chaplain. 'A new word we have now, and a new mission. Our mission now is to learn from Africa.'

His colleague nodded. 'Your efforts, excuse me, they are going in a wrong direction; it is from Africa to Europe that the spirit is flowing and we must open ourselves to receive it. The Church of the West is corrupted, God has declared a last judgement on it. Now is the time of the Fourth Church. We are forerunners, we go in advance to found his Celestial City.'

'Open ourselves to receive it?' A broad smile had overspread Kalabanda's face. 'The Celestial City?' he said. 'Out there in the bush? Excuse me if I laugh. Haw-haw. Have I been ordained into the Anglican Rite and subscribed after much self-questioning to the Thirty-Nine Articles only to come back here and open myself to receive the spirit flowing from people living in mud huts and talking in obscure languages?'

With the mildness of the utterly convinced, the first of the two missionaries began again to speak of God's plans for Africa. God had promised that the New Jerusalem would be founded among the heathen, and the Africans of the interior had been chosen because they, among the heathen peoples, were the most spiritual . . .

Under cover of this, Delblanc leaned forward and said in low tones to Paris, 'I don't know which is the madder, do you? What are you doing in this Bedlam, may I ask?'

'I believe it was mentioned to you that I am the ship's surgeon?' Paris spoke rather coldly. It was clear to him that Delblanc was a man of birth and education; but his own provincial and rather narrow upbringing had accustomed him to more circumspect modes of address and the lack of ceremony jarred a little on him, his pride suspected there might be some disparagement in it. But the expression of the other's face was humorous and friendly and his brown eyes were alert with the interest of his question.

'Well, of course I know that,' Delblanc said, with a hint of impatience – he was quick and open in all expression of feeling, as Paris was to learn. 'That doesn't explain anything. You do not seem to me to be typical, that is why I asked.'

Something extremely youthful, innocent almost, in the confidence of this pronouncement amused Paris suddenly and took the stiffness out of him. Delblanc, who like many enthusiastic persons often amused without intending to, saw the long, patient face opposite him break into a smile of singular sweetness.

'I have not had time to become typical,' the surgeon said. 'I suppose it takes time, doesn't it? This is my first voyage.'

'Ah, that is it then.'

The note of disappointment in this, as at some promising line of enquiry frustrated, made Paris smile again. 'What are *you* doing here, for that matter?' he asked, borrowing the other's directness. 'I believe you are an artist?'

'I do not know if I would so dignify it,' Delblanc said. 'I can paint a good likeness. Or so I thought.' A shadow had come to his face. He appeared to reflect a moment or two, then said, half to himself, 'It occurs to me . . . I wonder if your captain would agree to take me as a passenger.'

Before Paris had time to answer this, the Governor had risen to his feet, a signal for everyone else at the table to do the same, and remain so until he had left the room, the major by this time relying heavily on the back of his chair for support, and the treasurer, who had said nothing during the meal, also visibly befuddled.

'Mr Paris,' Delblanc said quickly, 'I know we have not been long acquainted, but there is a matter I would dearly like your advice on. I suppose you are staying here tonight? I would be most grateful . . . I have some rather good brandy in my room.'

Paris hesitated briefly. He had been looking forward to the solitude of his own quarters. But there had been a quality of appeal in Delblanc's tone, as there was in the clear, ingenuous eyes that now regarded him. 'Very well,' he said, 'but I had better make sure first that Captain Thurso has no further need of me.'

Thurso, who had requested half an hour with the Governor after dinner, was ready enough to confirm this; he did so, in fact, with discourteous emphasis. Paris's presence was increasingly an irritant to him these days. Nevertheless, it was in a spirit of resentment rather than relief that he watched his surgeon's retreat, the broad-shouldered, awkward form, the tendency to step a little short as if about to alter pace or make some bounding advance which in fact was never made. The man had been no earthly use from the start, merely a source of trouble and vexation . . .

He was conducted into a small chamber on an upper floor, which the Governor used as an office. Here he was offered brandy, while the Governor himself, now in pale blue robe and round black skull-cap, sipped at a glass of pale fluid. 'Camomile tea, sir,' he said with customary languidness. 'An excellent specific for the digestion. I take a glass of it lukewarm every evening, before retiring for the night. Lukewarm, not too hot – in case you ever feel tempted to try it.'

A small fire was burning in the grate, though the evening was not cold. He had one lit, he explained, in all the apartments he used. 'To combat the infernal damp that is constantly emanating from the stone,' he said. 'Well, sir, how may I be of service to you? I understand from Saunders that you saw the slaves but expressed some reservations.'

'Reservations.' The word came gravelled with effort, as if only outrage could have forced it from the reluctant larynx. 'Sir, I cannot buy the slaves at the prices you are asking. There is no profit for my owner at those prices.'

'Come now, Captain.' The Governor spoke with the same nonchalance, but his gaze had sharpened. 'You know well that there is still profit in it for you. If we were dealing privately together, no doubt I could offer you a lower price. But you must remember the heavy expenses the Company is under in the maintenance of this fort. There is a small army here of clerks, factors, artificers, who all have to have their wages. There is a chaplain. There are the permanent officers of the Company. There is a garrison of a hundred troops, at the Company's charge for victuals. Allow me also to remind you that you enjoy all the advantages of warehousing here, without a penny of cost. The Company acts as a depot for the goods, they are collected here and wait for you, saving you the trouble and danger of foraging in the unhealthy swamps behind. Moreover, the Company takes care of relations with local chiefs and all intermediaries in the trade, and lays out money to keep them well disposed. But I don't really need to remind you of this, do I, Captain? You are an old hand.'

'Yes, sir, I am. Of course I know the Company has expenses. But so they did in the days of your predecessor, and he kept the surcharge to five bars a head. I know these up-country prices – I would be surprised if you were paying more than twenty bars. Your predecessor –'

'My predecessor died here.' The Governor's face was still set in its usual expression of cold composure, but his voice had risen. 'He lies out there in the graveyard on the hill, with his name cut rough in the stone by a drunken mason. He lasted eighteen months before drink and the climate finished him. It is not my way to explain myself, Captain Thurso, but tonight is perhaps something of an occasion – it is a year to the day since I came out here.' The Governor paused for some moments, with head raised. 'That knocking still,' he said. 'They are working through the night.'

'They will have light enough for it,' Thurso said stolidly. 'It is a full moon tonight.'

The Governor compressed his lips. There was so little colour in them that only the moulding at the corners indicated the contours of the mouth. Again, in what was clearly a habitual gesture, he dabbed at his face with his handkerchief. 'A year to the day,' he said. 'And apart from some loss of colour and occasional qualms and fluxes, I am as well as ever I was. Sir, I spent everything I had to purchase this post as a Director of the Company. The competition for such positions nowadays is fierce, as I dare say you know. I spent many months soliciting interest on my behalf in London. I had to go to the Jews for the balance of the money, and agree to pay the interest they asked. I have to recover what I have laid out and make my profit while there is time, sir. This climate eats Europeans. War with France could come any day now, with French privateers lying off these coasts, disrupting our trade. You take my meaning? It is a question of time, Captain.'

'Well, sir,' Thurso said, 'it is a question of time for all of us, one way or another. If I am obliged to wait for more favourable prices, some of the slaves already purchased will die on my hands.' He had no hope now of getting any reduction in the prices; he knew obduracy when he met it, and he had met it now in this slack-wristed, invalidish fellow. But long experience had taught Thurso that an argument is rarely lost completely, if it is persisted in; and certain concessions he was still hoping for. 'What is to stop us trading independently?' he said.

The Governor smiled at this, not very pleasantly. 'There is no independent trade here, my friend,' he said. 'Not as far as our writ runs – and it runs far. You have heard no doubt what happened to the *Indian Maid?* Very sad business. They were attempting to trade privately upriver and were cut off by the natives and two killed and their longboat a total loss. We could do nothing to help them.'

'I have heard what happened to the Dutchman with the Corymantee negroes aboard.' Thurso fixed his eyes on the other but could detect no slightest change in the expression of his face.

'The natives are very loyal here,' the Governor said, with a return to his more nonchalant manner. 'They see the Company as their father.'

If Thurso had doubts on this score, he gave no indication of it. After a long moment he said, 'Well, it seems that I shall have to trade on your terms, sir, if I want to trade at all.'

'I am glad you take that view, Captain. You will have your pick of the slaves, sir, I can promise you that.'

And it was on this note of harmonious accord between them that Thurso obtained the spoils of the vanquished, which he had all this while, in his dogged and cunning fashion, been pursuing: on the understanding he would take the slaves presently in the dungeons, subject to their being passed as fit, the Governor agreed to let him have eight armed men and two canoes for a week's absence on private business, the expenses of this to be charged to the Company.

Meanwhile Delblanc had not yet made clear to the surgeon the nature of the advice he was seeking, though both men had made some inroads into the brandy by this time and had grown fairly confidential with each other. The painter occupied a single, square-built chamber, which seemed to have been intended originally as a guard-room. It was high on the ramparts, at the same level as the governor's quarters, but facing east, away from the sea.

The night was warm and Delblanc's windows were open; he had stretched squares of fine bobbin-net across them to keep out insects. 'I carry those nets around with me wherever I go,' the young man said. 'I had rather do without a bed than without those.'

Moonlight shone through these precious screens, silvering the mesh, as if to confirm Delblanc's high estimate. Though earlier wreathed about in cloud, the moon had ridden clear now and hung in the sky, serene and radiant. Blanched pools lay below the casement windows and Delblanc's shadow fell momentarily across them as he walked to and fro, holding his glass. An array of paints and brushes and jars lay on a low trestle table against one wall. In the centre of the room, masked by a square of pale cloth touched down one edge by moonlight, a canvas stood on an easel.

'This moonlight is amazing strong,' Paris said. 'Strong enough to read by, against the windows. I can hear the sea still, but it does not lie before us, does it?'

'No, the room looks east, along the coast. I am on the leeward side here – it grows confounded hot during the day. The best quarters are those that get the sea breeze, like those of our esteemed Governor.' As he spoke Delblanc glanced with a harassed expression at the veiled canvas. 'As you'd expect,' he added, running a hand through his thick, already somewhat disordered light brown hair.

'That is he, isn't it, under the sheet?' Paris nodded at the easel.

'Yes, that is he,' Delblanc said. However, he made no move to uncover the painting. 'Have some more brandy,' he said.

'I will.' Waiting for his glass, Paris was struck suddenly by the wonder of existence. He said, 'It is quiet, but for the waves. I could not tell for a while what the difference was, but it is that – they have stopped their hammering.'

'What? Ah, no, they will begin again. They need a store of coffins in reserve. You cannot keep corpses long in this climate. For most of the last week they have been at it, practically all the time I have been –' He broke off, as if struck by some notion. 'I wonder if that is the reason,' he said.

324

'What do you mean?'

'You will understand when you see the portrait, I think. But I shall need another glass before bringing it to view. Anyway, it is an ill wind that blows no one good. The Reverend Kalabanda has been kept busy with funerals, for which he gets an emolument from the Company.' Delblanc's expression of harassment gave way suddenly to a smile. 'There's a character for you. That unctuous way he talked about preaching to his free brethren. His free brethren have to listen to his sermons whether they want to or not. They are all in debt to the Company, which makes it a policy to give them drams and goods on credit. The Company could sell them tomorrow to recover the debts and they know it.'

'Like Tucker,' Paris said.

'Who is he?'

'Oh, he is a mulatto trader on the Sherbro River, where we have just been. He has a big trade connection there and is the principal man of the region. By advancing credit he puts people in fear of him and so gets everyone in his power.'

'Well, it is common practice,' Delblanc said, 'and not only in Africa. Though one sees it in a pure form here, not so much shrouded with hypocrisy. One sees the sacredness of money.' He passed a hand through his hair again. His eyes were light hazel in colour, very large in the iris and set rather shallow; with the clear, high forehead they gave to the whole face a sincerity almost disturbing in its nakedness and absence of concealment – and greatly at odds with the gentlemanly offhandedness of his manner. He was smiling slightly now but his expression was unhappy and rather bitter. 'Money is sacred, as everyone knows,' he said. 'So then must be the hunger for it and the means we use to obtain it. Once a man is in debt he becomes a flesh and blood form of money, a walking investment. You can do what you like with him, you can work him to death or you can sell him. This cannot be called cruelty or greed because we are seeking only to recover our investment and that is a sacred duty. Still, the negroes are not much worse off than the whites, from what Saunders tells me. He is one of the factors here.'

'Yes, we met this afternoon. He took us to see the slaves. He did not look in good health to me.'

325

'He will die if he does not get away from here. He would leave if he could, while he still has some chance of recovering his health, but he cannot – the Company has got him as fast as if he were in chains. Seventy-five pounds a year sounds well enough in Leadenhall Street. But when he got out here he found that it was paid in crackra.'

'What is that?'

'It is a kind of false currency that can only be used in the Company stores – at Company prices. It is all Saunders can do to buy cankey, palm oil and a little fish to keep himself alive. For other necessaries he has to go into debt. And the others are all in the same case. I tell you, they are all a company of white negroes here and it is the same in the other trading forts I have been in. The only ones who do well out of it are the high officials of the Company.'

He glanced again, involuntarily it seemed, at the veiled portrait on the easel. 'If they live long enough, that is. Death is good for my business as well as Kalabanda's. Or the threat of it, at least. There is nothing like the shadow of mortality for inclining a man to have his portrait painted. But what the sitter pays for, Mr Paris, is the promise of life. Just take a look at this, sir.'

Delblanc finished what was left in his glass and moved towards the easel. After a final moment of hesitation he threw back the cover.

'Good heavens!' Paris exclaimed. Whatever he had expected it had not been this. 'What have you done to him?'

The likeness was remarkable: the artist had perfectly caught the high-bridged, disdainful nose, the languid eyelids; but the eyes were fixed, the bloodless mouth frozen in avarice and the whole face stark with ultimate composure. It was a mask of death that looked at him.

'Now do you see what I mean?' Delblanc spoke as if making a point in an argument. 'A man who lives in perpetual fear of dissolution, who is for ever dosing himself and taking his own pulse, and I have depicted him as a death's head. It only happened in these last two days. The portrait was finished, or so I thought, he had done his sittings. I was intending only some finishing touches, heighten the flesh tones, ennoble the expression

326

and so on, the usual embellishments, you know. Then, I don't know how it happened, a touch here, a touch there, the line of the mouth, the set of the eyes, and this face emerged under my brush. And I can't bring myself to change it – it is the truth of the man, and something more than that. But of course he won't like it.'

'No,' conceded Paris, 'he won't like it.' He felt a little light-headed, after the wine at dinner and the brandy now, and the lapping light and shadow in the room, and this staring, moon-touched portrait of a stricken miser. 'He won't like it at all,' he said.

'And if he doesn't like it,' Delblanc pursued, with a sort of gloomy logic, 'he won't take it, and if he doesn't take it, he won't pay. But it's not really that – I'm not short of money for the moment. No, but you see, he could make things devilish unpleasant for me, if he wanted, and he would want, I feel sure.' Delblanc gestured at the portrait. 'You only need look at his face to see that. I could find myself in the dungeons on some trumped-up charge. We are a long way from home and justice is a relative concept at the best of times. Three degrees of latitude reverses the whole of jurisprudence . . . It was Pascal said that, wasn't it? I don't feel like taking the risk. It is for that reason I thought of taking passage with you.'

'As to that,' Paris said, 'I think it would be best if you deal direct with Thurso himself. My recommendation would not dispose him in your favour, quite the contrary.'

Delblanc nodded. 'He did not appear very fond of you. My purse, such as it is, will best recommend me to the captain. He will take me, I have no doubt of it. It is not only to save my skin I want to get away.'

He paused to replenish the surgeon's glass and his own. 'To be quite frank,' he said – and it was difficult to imagine his ever being much else – 'I am fair sick of what I am doing and assisting in here. I have had to paint a good number of faces in order to get to this one. For eighteen months now I have been painting likenesses of company officials and agents and resident merchants up and down from James Fort to Elmina, not only English, but Dutch and French too. And now I have come upon their collective face. It is no accident that it has sprung out under my brush. Since I came to this coast I have seen things and heard of things, Paris, that I will take to the grave with me. The ships come and trade on the edges. You may think only the edges are fouled with this trade but it is not so. The flood of cheap manufactures, for which the people have no need, destroys their industries. They become dependent on this trade and the demand for goods can only be met by enslaving their fellows. To do this they need muskets in ever increasing quantities – which we supply. And so we spread death everywhere. But that sacred hunger we spoke of justifies all. The trade is lawful, they say, and that is enough. Well, it is not enough for me. That face on the easel is the face of plunder and death, sir, it is the face of Europe in Africa. It is an unacceptable face to me, sir, and I cannot go on any longer painting it. I have come to the end of portraits, on this coast at least. A man can hold off the truth of things for purposes of making a living – that is legitimate, I suppose, though ignoble. But when the face is there, before your eyes ... It cannot simply be expunged, d'you see, as if it had never existed, not when heart and mind have worked together to produce it.'

'Heart and mind,' Paris repeated, struck by this simple and unaffected yoking of the two. Once again he was aware of some essential ingenuousness in the painter, a quality of innocence that had survived the wandering and makeshift life. He encountered the transfixed and horrendous stare of the face in the portrait. Moonlight lay along the pallid temples, revived a gleam of avarice in the dead left eye.

'Yes,' the painter said, with the same eagerness. 'To make a good likeness you must have heart and mind working together. But the heart comes first.'

'The heart is a vital organ,' Paris said, in his serious and slightly pedantic way. 'But it is a faulty guide to conduct. It is the mind makes judgements and comparisons, furnishes evidence on which ideas of truth can be founded.'

'I take an opposite view,' Delblanc said excitedly. 'No man will ever find virtue by the mind alone – to think so was the folly of the Greeks. This trade we are helping in our different ways – do you think it comes about through the dictates of the heart?'

'Nor truly of the mind either, but greed can take that colouring, as can other vices.'

'Yes, sir, and so our natural instincts are perverted. Do you think for a moment that men would enslave one another if they lived in a state of nature?'

'Well, it is a large question,' Paris said doubtfully. 'And one that cannot be easily answered.'

'You are right. Let us have some more brandy now, so that we can the better discuss it.'

Whether it was Delblanc's precipitation of speech or his readiness to forget his troubles at the prospect of debate, Paris did not quite know, but there was something about this eagerness that moved him now with a mingled sense of comedy and pain. Quite suddenly, with that lonely urgency that comes at times to reticent natures, he wanted to entrust something to this man, so frank and unaffected, so unforced in his transitions from thought and sensation to speech. 'We can discuss it if you like,' he said, 'but there is something I wanted to say before and didn't. You spoke about the need to make a living and how it inclines us to evade the truth of things, but I have not even that excuse.'

'But it is your livelihood, as I understand the matter. I suppose you do not offer your services free?'

'I did not need to take my uncle's offer,' Paris said. 'My uncle is the owner of the ship I am serving on. I could have gone to another part of England or to one of the colonies. I could have gone to America, where there is need for doctors.'

'You needed to get away then?'

The gentle matter-of-factness of this brought a tightness to Paris's throat that he had not anticipated. Those confiding their pain cannot know at the outset how much they will be required to relive it; but he knew that he was set on a course here, in this room from which the moonlight was receding, leaving it darker, before a man he hardly knew and a face of death. 'Yes,' he said harshly, 'I needed to get away, but I did not need to take a post on a slaveship, I did not need to use my profession, of which I was proud once, to certify people as fit for branding and chaining.'

'I suppose you thought it didn't much matter,' Delblanc said, in the same tone of gentle simplicity. 'What you did with yourself, I mean.'

At this the surgeon rose in his turn and began pacing to and fro across the room. 'It never mattered what I did, as far as only myself was concerned,' he said. 'It doesn't matter now. I don't care what becomes of me. But I had no right . . . I should not have argued in favour of the mind just now, that was only for argument's sake – I still have that vice. It was my insistence on opinion, concealed under the appearance of a desire for truth, that ruined me and killed my wife. Yes, sir, killed her.' Paris nodded fiercely, as if he thought the other might attempt to contradict him. 'By my arrogant folly I killed her and the child she was carrying.' He paused to drink what was left in his glass, though hardly aware of the action.

'We lived in Norfolk,' he said, 'where I practised as a surgeon-apothecary. I became interested in fossil remains and what they can tell us about the age of the earth, and also in the evidence of rises and falls of the earth's surface through long ages of time. I began to form a collection of marine fossils, some of them found high above the level of the sea. The existence of these cannot be reconciled with the account of creation given to us in the Bible. So far, if it had been a mere question of my private studies, all would have been well. There are men of science all over Europe quietly forming their opinions on such matters. But I, sir, I had to air my discoveries and opinions. I acquired a printing press and issued pamphlets in which I championed the views of Maupertuis. Perhaps you are acquainted with his work?'

'Not even with his name, I am afraid,' Delblanc said. 'I have not taken much interest in such matters.'

'He is a man of genius.' Despite his distress, Paris's tone had quickened with admiration for this hero of his youth. 'His name has been obscured by misapprehension and envy, but one day his worth will be known. By his investigations into heredity he has shown how, from two individuals only, the multiplication of the most dissimilar species could grow, owing their origin to some accidental formation, an error you could say, each error creating a new species . . .'

330

'But that would mean that we ourselves are the result of error also, that we need not have been as we are.'

'Yes, some different accidents might have occurred. Or so Maupertuis would say. Something impossible to imagine ... I was greatly struck by these ideas when first I read them; they seemed to offer an explanation of the diversity of creatures, something which had always puzzled me. And they confirmed my own conclusions about the age of the earth, because such changes would have needed great periods of time to accomplish.'

Paris paused, swallowing at some impediment. 'Great periods of time,' he repeated, in a voice that trembled slightly – they were dear to his memory, these early studies and speculations, his desk in the lamplight, Ruth busy somewhere not far. 'I published these theories,' he went on after a moment. 'They run counter to orthodox opinion and especially to the teachings of the Church. I was warned, not only by those who were hostile, but by friends and colleagues. Yes, I was well warned. But I paid no heed.' Paris stopped his pacing and stood still in the centre of the room, looking fixedly at Delblanc, who sat out of the candle-light, his face in shadow. 'I was clad in the armour of truth,' the surgeon said. 'Or so I thought. Or so I pretended to think.' He tried to smile but failed. 'In fact, I was merely obstinate and overweening, vices which I have still. I was arrested on a complaint of the Bishop of Norwich. The judge was in the Church Interest. He found me guilty of issuing a seditious publication, imposed a fine beyond my means and consigned me to prison until it was paid. My uncle redeemed the debt when he learned of it, but while I lay in prison a mob set on by the Church Party broke into my house with a view to smashing the press and in the course of this they terrified my wife so that she miscarried. She was not a strong woman and she did not recover. I did not see her die . . .'

These unguarded negatives broke the control which he had struggled to maintain by an appearance of reporting on facts. 'She died without me,' he said, and his voice broke on it. He saw the artist make a sudden movement, as if to rise and come towards him. He said quickly, 'You would serve me best by

331

staying as you are. I do not know why, for the life of me, but I am set on speaking to you as I have spoke to no one else, and I need a distance between us if I am to get through to the end.'

For some moments, however, he was obliged to remain silent, checking the tears that had threatened him at Delblanc's impulse to kindness. The hardest part still lay before him. Below the acknowledgement of blame, below the self-reproach, at the deepest level of confession, lay the words that would express the shame of what had been done to him. It was characteristic of Paris that he should seek a way to it through argument. 'You quoted Pascal just now,' he said. '"Three degrees of latitude reverses the whole of jurisprudence." Delblanc, no latitude makes any difference to what men will do to other men, whether for gain or in the name of justice. Publishing seditious material is a felony in our law. Before I began my prison sentence, they set me twelve hours in the pillory. In our enlightened land, for publishing the view that the earth is older than six thousand years, and thus contradicting Revelation, I was chained by the legs to a post, my head and hands were stuck through a board and clamped there and I was left to the mercies of the crowd for a night on the market square of Norwich. Pilloried alongside with me there was a man who had been convicted of sodomy. Fortunate for me, because he diverted the wrath of the mob and so I was saved from injury at their hands. He was stoned by the whores of the town. In the morning, when they came for us, he was insensible – I do not know to this day whether he lived or died.'

Paris's voice was unhesitating now; the droning fluency of nightmare had descended on him. As he spoke he had the sense of a steady seepage of filth and blood, a stain that spread with his words in this quiet room, with no check to him in Delblanc's motionless figure or the hideous silence of the governor, and only the distant booming of the sea for admonition. The festering restraint of months fell away from him and the agony of his humiliation returned, licensed, almost welcomed, that crouching, ludicrous, beast-like posture, the terrible exposure of the naked face and head, detached from the rest of the body, offered like a pumpkin at a fair for the crowd to shy at, the hanging

332

head and meek hands of the sodomist, his face and hair all pulped and bloody, like a burst pumpkin, lolling there, still unable to retract his head from his tormentors, his pleading mercy made indistinct by the blood that had filled his mouth . . .

He checked himself at last and a deep gasp like a sob broke from him. 'Legitimate means of livelihood? The face of truth that cannot be denied? I wanted to look them in the face, when they came to release me in the morning. I had prepared myself. But I could not stand upright, I was led away crouching still, with back bent like some submissive animal. And yet I came here. I knew what it is to be shackled and derided and still I came. How can that be forgiven?'

Another groan came from him. Humiliation almost worse than that grey morning's, the knowledge of his folly, to think that despair can exonerate, that the desire of death can remove the burden of conscience . . . 'And it is not even true,' he said turning half blindly and moving to the window as if for some refuge in the night outside. 'It was not true then and is not now.'

The moon was high and clear of cloud, astoundingly radiant, eclipsing the stars. Moonlight gleamed in a sheet of silver over the marshes and flats of mud they had crossed to come here, so cluttered and tawdry by day, all unified and resplendent now as if lying under some momentary blessing. And for a moment this transforming moonlight was confused in Paris's mind with the sunlight of earlier, the form of the woman edged with fire against the bars. 'It is not even true that I want to die,' he said, and with this ultimate confession he saw the moonlit levels run together and glimmer, as if washed in some thin solution of silver, and then blur to bright webs, as the tears, held long in check, came freely now to his eyes.

THIRTY-THREE

On the day following his return aboard, Paris resumed his journal, which he had neglected of late, with so many calls on his time and attention. He felt in any case disinclined for any more active occupation this afternoon: his limbs were heavy and he was experiencing a slight but persistent sense of oppression above the eyes. He would have liked to sleep, but to do so with the sense of a task unfulfilled went against the grain of his nature; self-denying generations spoke in his blood against it. Hunched at his small table, aware intermittently of the foul smell from the ship's bilges, he wrote on doggedly.

Delblanc was right when he said his purse would sufficiently recommend him. He came aboard this morning, with a small cabin trunk and a rather dressed-up, festive look. I suspect he is a man who likes changes and adventures, and perhaps especially those not much premeditated. Apparently he did not wait to see the effect of his portrait upon the governor. There is something reckless in Delblanc. I feel him to be a generous-hearted man, who might go astray in practice, though he would not behave ignobly. But he seems accountable to no one and free to follow the promptings of his nature. In this he is different from myself and perhaps it is why I feel drawn so towards him – the more now, in gratitude for his friendship and patience last evening. I am glad he is to be with us. We have had already some resumption of our discussion on the merits of heart and head; his arguments in defence of untrammelled liberty and the natural goodness of the heart are delivered with no less enthusiasm as he paces the deck of a slaveship. There is something touching in this fervour, something absurd too – like all good theorists he is not much troubled by incongruities of circumstance. Might it be true that men would live together in peace and harmony if only the coercion of authority were lifted from them? When I look into the faces of my fellows, I find it hard to credit.

With Delblanc there have come aboard two new crew members, recruited at the fort, Lees and Rimmer. The former seems a decent man enough, a cooper by trade, badly scarred with smallpox. He is a former seaman, though I understand he has been two years employed by the company here. The other man, Rimmer, has one of the most debauched and vicious faces I have seen, swollen with drink and rough living and with an ugly expression of the eyes, like a dog that would bite if it dared. He either ran from, or was abandoned by, another slaver that came earlier, and has since been living as he can here on the coast. Shortly after coming aboard he must have behaved with some insolence, or perhaps merely indifference, towards Barton, who struck him a blow with his open hand which could be heard all over the ship. I saw this incident myself. It was only a slapping blow, but Rimmer was knocked sideways. He knew better than to attempt a retaliation, but there was murder on his face. I did not see much change on Barton's. 'You do what I tell you,' I heard him say, 'and you do it prompt, or you'll never reach Jamaica.' Of course Barton knows that he must take such a man in hand from the outset. He is in command for these days; Thurso is gone ashore on some business of his own.

That look of the eyes is not so common among us. I saw it sometimes in prison. It belongs to men who will always be ready to do more hurt than they need. Tapley has something of it, but he is less bold than this new man; he needs the shelter and bidding of another, and his prefect, Libby, has not this wickedness in his face, but seems merely brutal and unfeeling.

It seems that I am become an expert on faces. Men like Hughes and Cavana have a savage eye, so intent in regard as to seem almost innocent, with that sort of fierce innocence which has known no chastening or softening. I saw that expression again on the faces of the Gold Coast negroes who stared at us through their bars. I do not know if the woman belonged with that group. Thurso had already looked them over and purchased them before I was stirring next morning, having apparently agreed on a price with the governor the night before. She is tall, like them, but lighter skinned, tawny rather than black, and her hair not so wiry. I am cursed with too much doubt, or compunction – I do not know what to call it. Perhaps it was only a figment of that mood of hope that came to me as I walked behind Saunders through those passages. But it was as if she waited there, in the sunlight . . .

Cavana came aboard mid-morning with a monkey on a rope, a bright-eyed little creature with tufted ears and a tail longer than itself, and very prettily coloured – a black crown on him and a small white face, and arms and feet pale orange colour. Cavana is very taken with it, though he does not like to appear so, at least not to me, I think out of some sort of shyness. Blair speaks to me freely since we treated Calley's back together and he told me they had gone ashore soon after sunrise with Haines to get firewood and shoot pigeons, *of which there are large flocks at present in the trees just a little back from the shore. While there they had met a party from the American grain ship in the road with us, who were on the same business. One of these had the monkey and seeing Cavana much taken with it had offered to sell it to him. Cavana had no money but he had a silver chain round his neck, his only possession. On the kind of impulse which seems common with these men when they want something that is before their eyes, he pulled this off and offered it in exchange. To my less impulsive nature this seemed extravagant, but I could tell that Blair would have done the same thing. The creature sat quite comfortably on Cavana's shoulder, turning its muzzle to look at our faces and raising the skin on its scalp in a very comical way, as if it were constantly being surprised by the tenor of our conversation.*

Thurso will not be back for some days yet. There is some mystery about his absence, as there is about our lingering here at all. Why trade for negroes through the fort, if prices are higher? Thurso is not a man to pay more than he needs, and it cannot be that he wishes to keep good relations for the future, as Barton once let fall to me that this is the captain's last voyage. I believe he has come down to this stretch of coast with some private purpose, and that Barton is privy to it . . .

Paris laid down his pen. He was feeling distinctly unwell. The heaviness in his limbs had intensified and his temples throbbed painfully with any slightest movement of his eyes. He made himself a strong infusion of powdered cinchona bark and took to his bed, where within an hour he was experiencing the first assaults of a violent fever.

There followed a period for Paris undistinguished by passage of hours, marked only by alternations of sweating and shivering. In the lulls he continued to dose himself within infusions of cinchona and battled to repair his copious sweats with lemon water.

Sullivan, who had taken over from Charlie the duty of seeing to the surgeon's wants – Thurso would not have given permission to a fore-the-mast man to do it – came that evening at the change of watch, found his charge muttering and tossing and conversing with shadows and ran to get rainwater from the butt so as to make cold compresses for the surgeon's face and chest. This had been done to Sullivan by a woman somewhere in his scattered past and it had been a memory of love to him. It was all he knew of treating fevers, but he was assiduous in it, and was a devoted attendant to Paris all through his illness, sponging his brow, running to the galley with dried yarrow leaves from Paris's stock so that Morgan could make him tea.

On the morning of the fourth day, Paris woke feeling weak but clear-headed. His restored senses brought sounds more typical of delirium, a hullabaloo above him of stamping feet, jangling chains, the jaunty persistence of the fiddle: the slaves were at their morning dance. He ate the breakfast provided by Sullivan: ship's biscuit, in which the occasional weevil was still to be found, and some rock-hard cheddar. He enjoyed both items hugely. He felt sure now that he had been suffering from the same type of fever which had earlier attacked Johnson and True, a kind of swamp fever, he believed, transmitted by the miasmic airs of the coast. If it were the same he could expect further bouts – Johnson had suffered some return of it already, though True so far not.

He dressed slowly and made his way up on deck, where the slaves were still exercising, Libby and Tapley moving among them with whips and curses while McGann and Evans stood to the cannon on the deck above. The whole mid-part of the ship forward of the mainmast moved with this noisy, disorderly seething of the black bodies. They had been hosed down that morning, and the decks washed, and the contents of the ordinary buckets discharged over the sides; but there still came to Paris, as he stood on the side gangway, the sickening fetid smell he had grown to recognize. The timbers were becoming engrained with it. No scrubbing could remove it entirely – they would carry it back with them to Liverpool . . .

The women and girls moved like sleepwalkers about the deck, sometimes raising their arms and swaying their bodies as if listening to some music more remote than that transmitted by Sullivan's quick elbow. The men jumped and lumbered in their shackles. Cries and groans and wavering phrases of song came from both men and women, mingling with the cracking of the whips and the heavy stamping of feet and rattling of chains, so that the notes of the fiddle were only intermittently audible. To Paris, with that deceiving clarity that comes after fever – a clarity in which there is still a sort of languid disorder – there

337

came the fancy that Sullivan was sawing at the negroes' chains. At this moment, with the same sense of heightened but unreliable perception, he saw that some of the younger boys, though moving to the music in apparent dance, were playing a game of ambush and kidnap in among the moving bodies of the adults. They were taking captives, he realized suddenly ... With a lurch of feeling he recognized among the dancers the woman who had looked at him in the dungeon of the fort. Her face was lowered now, expressionless. She must have been brought aboard while he lay ill. He looked among the men but could not for the moment make out the Corymantee negroes. The woman had been given the same cotton waistcloth as the others, covering the pudenda but leaving the sides of the thighs bare. The muscles of her haunches flexed smoothly as she turned in the motions of the dance.

He removed his eyes from her to see Cavana come up from the forecastle with the monkey crouched on his shoulder and disappear in the direction of the latrines at the heads. At the same moment Thurso emerged on the starboard side of the quarterdeck with a scowling look of bad temper, Barton immediately behind him. 'Glad to see you recovered,' the captain said, though nothing in his face showed pleasure. 'What the devil was that?' he said to Barton.

'A monkey, sir.'

'Tell the fiddler to stow his noise, will you? They have had enough of his infernal scraping and so have I.'

'Aye-aye, sir.'

Barton bawled across the intervening space of deck. Libby, who had been waiting for it, nudged the heedless fiddler. The music stopped and the dancing with it. The slaves were herded into their allotted space amidships by the men guarding them, who were eager now to finish and get below – it was close on eight bells.

'I won't have that confounded animal running loose on my ship,' Thurso said. 'Tell Cavana that.'

'It sticks pretty close to him from what I have seen,' Paris said, taking some steps towards the captain. 'You must have returned while I was ill, sir?' he said.

338

He encountered the small, beleaguered eyes, saw in them the usual fury at being questioned. It was clear that Thurso was in the grip of some feeling stronger than the irritation caused by the sight of the monkey. 'I returned to find that we have got a case of the bloody flux aboard,' he said. 'I returned to find that, sir.'

'I did not know of it.' Paris had sensed some accusation in the captain's words. 'I have been confined to my cabin these last few days.'

'He is only twelve or so,' Thurso said, 'so it is not as bad as it might be, but it is still a loss of forty bars. That is not the worst of it, however. We will be obliged now to leave the coast early. I could have taken a dozen more that now I cannot wait for. We must get out to sea and trust we can be blown clean of it.'

'He is dead then?'

'Dead? He is shitting blood. He may die or he may recover, it makes no difference, he must be got off the ship.'

'Got off the ship? You mean simply set down ashore?' Thurso's monstrous simplicity, as always, had taken him completely by surprise. 'But he could be treated,' he said hastily. For a moment, absurdly, he was under the impression that Thurso had overlooked this possibility. 'I can make up a panegoric,' he went on eagerly. 'Tincture of opium has often been found efficacious in cases of severe diarrhoea, with a preparation of fennel that I know of; fennel is an excellent –'

'Good God,' Thurso broke in with a sudden violence of fury that made Paris flinch. 'Must I waste my breath arguing with a damned landsman who knows nothing but country remedies? I am talking about bloody flux. If it gets a hold on us here, we can lose half our cargo. Do you know what that means in money? Am I to wait on the chance that you will cure him with your damned brews? And if you fail? No, sir, not another word.' Thurso paused, visibly struggling with his passion. All his detestation of the surgeon came out in this moment. He advanced his face, darkly congested with rage, and said in his hoarse monotone, 'I command on this ship. I will have you muzzled like a dog and sent to kennel below if you argue another syllable with me.'

339

Paris was silent, looking down before him at the deck. Brought to this pass, Thurso would do as he threatened. Owing perhaps to the weakness consequent upon his fever he could feel no saving fury now as he had on previous occasions, only an immense weariness and discouragement. It was not the other's brutality that was too strong for him, but his logic. There was no answering it. It was why they were all there. 'I do not argue further,' he said. 'May I have your permission to go ashore with the boy and take the linguister?'

'You need no linguister with you to leave the boy on the beach,' Thurso said. However, after a moment's pause, he gave his consent in an indifferent mutter. The punt was lowered, the shivering boy fetched up and soon Paris found himself making for shore with Jimmy beside him in the stern and four men to row them.

He had no plan of action; he did not believe there was any action to take. His request had been involuntary almost, an impulse to hurt himself, to share in what was being done to the boy. But it occurred to him now that they might find some help ashore for him or some shelter at least. 'Ask him where he comes from,' he said to the linguister. 'Perhaps he comes from this part of the coast.'

'He not belong here,' Jimmy said. 'Dis boy Vai people, I think so.'

He spoke a few words to the boy, who turned deep-set eyes on him, straining and imperfectly focused, as if he were staring through a screen of mist or flame. After a moment he replied in a soft mumble, raising a thin hand in a vague pointing motion.

'He say he comes from over dere.' Jimmy repeated the vague gesture. He smiled with pity and scorn. 'Dis boy don't know where he is,' he said. 'So he can't say where he come from. He points anywhere comes into mind. Point up at sky, all same-same ting.'

'I don't believe you understand a word of what he is saying,' Paris said. 'You are only pretending.'

'Pretendin' part of linguister's job,' Jimmy said with dignity. 'Dis boy speak one Vai language. Nobody unnerstan' what dis boy says 'cept mebbe few hunnert people round the Gallinas River. Dat ten-twelve days' sail from here, sir.'

340

The boy looked at their faces with his wide, strained stare, in which, however, there was something of appeal. He knew he was being discussed. He was quite naked. His teeth were chattering faintly and Paris could see the rise and fall of his thin chest. With an austere avoidance of Jimmy's gaze, he took off his shirt and placed it round the boy's shoulders.

Their departure had been witnessed by several people and it formed a subject of discussion among a group, clustered together forward, below the jib boom.

'Thurso never does owt without a reason,' Wilson said. 'An' there's nobbut one reason why he would put a slave ashore an' lose the price. The boy has got sommat wrong wi' him.'

'The flux or the smallpox, them is the two worst,' Cavana said. The monkey sat on his shoulder, turning its black muzzle to watch their faces, and repeatedly raising the loose skin on its scalp. Cavana was making a cage for it, constructed out of bamboo canes which he had cut ashore.

'Why is that animal always makin' faces,' Libby demanded, his solitary eye fixing the monkey with a look of dark disapproval. 'Monkeys spread the pox. I wouldn't be surprised if it isn't him that is spreadin' it now.'

Cavana split one of the canes down the middle with his knife. He was clever at making things, all the movements of his hands were neat and certain. 'He don't do it so much when he is just with me,' he said. 'Bein' in a crowd unsettles him.'

Blair winked at Sullivan. 'What it is,' he said, 'he does it when he gets to windward of bleddy great farts like those you've been lettin' go of, Libby. If I had a loose scalp, I would do the same.'

'He is clever,' Cavana said with pride. 'He knows what's goin' on. He knows me already. He won't go to no one else.'

The monkey, aware of being the centre of attention, retracted its head and tucked in its chin shyly. After a moment, with a languid and fastidious gesture of one reddish arm, strangely human and hairless on the inside, it reached out, fumbled gently in Cavana's matted hair, found something there, peered at it closely with wise, amber-coloured eyes and then swallowed it.

'Ha, ha!' Calley said. 'He found somethink. He found a nit.' His eyes were round. 'You are full o' nits, Cavana,' he said with delight. 'What is his name?'

'I'm callin' him Vasco,' Cavana said. There was a certain quality of defensiveness in his tone. 'That's a sea-goin' name I've heard tell of. He's a regglar sailor – the feller that sold him told me he will eat salt beef and biscuit.' He had begun binding the cross-pieces with strands of yarn and he lowered his head over the task to conceal his pride in the versatile and omniverous Vasco.

'A monkey can be the savin' of a ship,' Sullivan said, glancing round with his usual haunted expression. 'They have the gift of second sight. I knew of a monkey once, he was kept on a bit of rope like this one; the ship was standin' off the Bahama Bank. She was a two-masted ship with a square rig, like this one. Same type of monkey, same type of ship. That's a funny thing now . . . But she wasn't carryin' slaves.'

'I wish you'd keep to the bleddy point,' Blair said irritably. 'What the jig does it matter what type o' ship she was?'

'Thim channels are dangerous for any vessel,' Sullivan said, 'let alone a square-rig merchantman that can't keep close to the wind. Anyway, they are sailin' into the wind when the monkey slips his rope an' makes a dart for the riggin'. He climbs up to the crow's nest before anyone can stop him, looks out to sea, then starts gibberin' an' pointin'. No one can see anythin'. There is nothin' to see. The monkey is goin' frantic an' frothin' at the jaws. He runs down an' gets the captain's telescope from his cabin an' brings it to him, but the captain can't see anythin' wrong. Then the monkey starts swingin' from side to side, hangin' to the rat-lines by his tail, pointin' down at the water.'

Carried away by his narrative, Sullivan twisted his head to a grotesque angle and made stabbing gestures with a long fore-finger down at the deck. '"What the divil's upsettin' the cray-tur?" everybody's askin'. Nobody knows. The captain doesn't believe there is anythin' amiss but he decides to take a soundin'. He can hardly believe his eyes. They are in seven fathom water an' movin' in to the bank. Five minutes more an' they would have been grounded there, with a rising sea. They put about just in time an' it was all due to that monkey.'

'What was the point o' fetchin' the telescope?' Wilson said, after an appreciable pause. 'There were nowt to see.'

'Aye, I grant you it made a mistake there,' Sullivan said. 'There was limits to its sagacity, I'm not the man to deny that.'

'How did the monkey know?' Calley said.

'Ah, there is the question,' Sullivan said. 'There is things in nature very difficult to explain.'

There was a short silence. No one but Calley had completely believed this story. 'Weel,' McGann said, 'coming back to this blacky they hae shipped ashore, I'll lay even saxpences it is a case o' bloody flux. He didn't look to hae much fever. Libby, ye can find out from Haines. Wha'll tak the bet?'

'Will you listen to that now?' Sullivan said. 'You still owe me that shillin for standin' up to Thurso. Billy, you was me witness.'

'He cannot witness to what he never heard. How do we know what ye said to Thurso? Ye might hae gone in there an' said any trumped-up thing.'

'I told you the truth of it,' Sullivan said. 'Are you makin' to call me a liar, McGann?'

McGann looked at him with pity. He shook his head. 'Truth or lies doesna' come into it,' he said. 'This is a question o' money.'

Paris returned bare-chested and barefoot, having left his shirt with the sick boy and his shoes — for the sake of their silver buckles — with an old woman in a thatched hut on the shore above the beach, whom he thought must have mothered children in her time. Squatting on thin hams at the entrance, smoking a clay pipe, she had listened impassively while Jimmy said what Paris had told him to say. This child was sick in the stomach by *sovah monou*. He was under the special protection of the Great Fort. The Governor himself took a particular interest in this child, as he did in all the weak and helpless. The Governor and his redcoats would be watching from afar to make sure that this child was well treated. The Governor had a mighty telescope up in the sky, right at the top of the fort, and through his telescope he could see everything that happened.

The woman chewed briefly on bare gums then replied at some length in a high-pitched, querulous voice.

343

'What does she say? Does she undertake to care for the child?'

'She say she don' believe the Governor have any interes' in dis boy. He too busy sellin' healthy boy to bother 'bout one small boy with *sovah monou* belly. She say to redcoats kiss my arse, pardon me, sir. She talk big mouth,' Jimmy said in scornful aside. 'Nobody take ol' hag for slave. She say also, she don' believe in no telescope. But if you give the shirt an' also silver buckle off your shoe, she will look after dis boy.'

Paris, whose distress was mounting, hastily assented. He had taken his clasp-knife to cut off the buckles when the old woman spoke again. Having noted his alacrity, she was now asking for the shoes entire. He pulled them off and handed them over, together with a small quantity of powdered quassia in a paper packet that he had brought with him from the ship.

Jimmy transmitted instructions as to the preparation of this emetic. The woman took the packet into her hand but did not look at it. The boy watched everything with the same strained, hallucinated stare, his thin form lost in the folds of the shirt. Shame prevented Paris from meeting his eyes or saying any words to him. But he laid his hand on the boy's head for a moment before turning away. At the shoreline he looked back: the diminutive figure was still hunched there, but the shirt that had draped him was gone.

Next day Thurso took advantage of a Liverpool brig recently arrived in the offing, fully loaded with camwood and ivory and on the way home, to leave letters for Kemp announcing his intention to quit the coast immediately with a total of one hundred and ninety-six slaves.

Most of the following week was spent in preparations for departure. More yams and rice were taken on board and the water casks replenished. The crew were employed mending the sails, which had been much damaged by rats during this long stay on the coast. These were very numerous now and ravenous, so emboldened by hunger that they would bite at people they found sleeping and had even taken to gnawing the cables.

Things were not made easier during all this time by the strong winds from land and the continual high swells which caused the vessel to labour a good deal, especially at the change of the tide. In the worst of this the ship was made to ride so hard that on successive days she broke one of her main shrouds on the larboard side and a main topmast stay. The purchase of two women slaves was frustrated when the canoe bringing them off was smashed in the surf and they were lost by drowning, having their arms bound behind them. Then a woman slave who had wandered from the others was dragged below and raped by two men who hooded her with a square of sail-cloth. She could not say who the men were and if others of the crew knew it they did not come forward to say so.

These various irritations darkened Thurso's mood considerably and he scowled through the days. It was a time of grievance generally, compounded by impatience to be gone from the coast and its humid, sapping airs. The boatswain was out of temper at being saddled with the repairs to the rigging, and he drove the men hard. The crew grumbled at the work and at the constant labouring of the ship, which made the footing precarious. Even Vasco, the monkey, seemed affected by the prevailing mood. Cavana had killed a rat with a lucky throw of a mallet and, wishing to show off his pet's adaptability, gave it to him to eat; but Vasco threw the limp and scaly creature from him in unconcealed bad temper. 'He would have ate it if it had been cooked,' Cavana said. But he had found that what Vasco liked best was a mixed diet of flies and beetles and boiled plantains mashed with coconut, and he was continually badgering Morgan to make this last dish for him.

For Paris too it was a bad time. The fever had reduced him and depressed his spirits. He did not recover quickly from his abandonment of the diseased boy and kept to himself below as much as he could. He was surprised to find his face in the looking-glass unchanged, when he had so betrayed his profession. What worse was there that he could assent to now? In the cramped and heaving confines of his cabin he was haunted by the knowledge that he had not paid his score yet, there was worse to come.

Only Delblanc seemed unaffected by the prevailing mood. He was often to be seen on deck, dressed with careless elegance, conversing in his frank, unstudied fashion with anyone free to listen, not seeming at all inconvenienced by the heaving of the ship. Paris, emerging from his penitential cell, would find himself accosted with some theory of sentiment as the source of knowledge or the arbiter of action. On the very eve of departure Delblanc detained the captain some minutes with an ingenious metaphor derived from the workings of the ship. Feeling was the pilot, the passions alone could fill the sails and drive the ship forward, even if their excess might overwhelm it ... Thurso meanwhile, constrained to politeness by the other's status as passenger, looking as if excess passion might overwhelm him at any moment.

In the early hours of the day following, they weighed anchor and stood off from the south as the wind allowed, with all sails set. Stealthily, in the dark, the *Liverpool Merchant* began to make slow way against the head swell on the first leagues of its journey to the West Indies. But departure was not so stealthy and way not so slow that the slaves packed close in the hot darkness between decks did not feel the change and raise a cry of despair that echoed over the water and was the only farewell of the departing slaver.

On the second day after this Paris found three cases of fever among the negroes. Thomas True, who had seemed recovered, though much reduced by his illness, was taken again by a raging fever, this time accompanied by vomiting. The wind lessened, almost ceased, obliging them to tack for the advantage of what breeze there was. But the ship was now so foul that she did not feel a small breeze and by noon she had lost steerage way. The days that followed showed the same pattern of light airs and calms, the ship tacking when she could and loitering for long hours almost motionless. One of the sick slaves died and was thrown overboard into the sluggish, shark-ridden wake. And with this wind failed altogether.

The hysteria that lay deep within Thurso was roused by such enforced inactivity. He would rather have had storms to deal with. He had the spare sails aired, the yawl turned and coated with brimstone and pitch, the cables repaired from the ravages of the rats. Still the listless weather continued. After six days of

346

sailing, they still had Mount Daro to the north, with the Guinea Current running at two knots against them and not enough headway to get clear. Under the stress Thurso's temper deteriorated. He sat alone in his cabin, a bottle of brandy before him, brooding on his conspiracy of the elements, seeking to understand the reason. No counsel came to him, he sat in silence, abandoned by his helpers. A reason there must always be, he knew that, something done or left undone ... The brandy did not make him drunk but it rendered his mood violent and unpredictable.

Emerging in early evening on to the quarterdeck, his sight somewhat confused by brandy and by the splendour of the light – the sun was setting and had cast a wide swathe of flame across the surface to landward – he had a brief impression that there was a deformed, two-headed man at the helm. Then he saw that it was Cavana with the monkey at his shoulder. And at that moment his counsellor spoke to him at last: *It is the monkey.*

'Get that animal out of my sight,' he said.

'Aye-aye, sir.' Cavana's eyes started wildly. He sensed the danger to Vasco but could not leave the wheel. 'Out o' sight, sir? Where can I put him? Beg permission to be relieved at the helm, sir, there is no steerage to speak of, while I take him –'

The hesitation and bewilderment of the seaman was enough for Thurso. 'Do you dither there and debate with me, you dog?' he said. 'I'll get rid of him for you. Give me the rope.' The monkey, perhaps sensing the captain's rage, had begun raising and lowering his scalp in alarmed interrogation. Thurso stepped forward and slipped the loop from Cavana's wrist. Taking good hold of the end of it, he swung the animal clear over the side with a single sweep of his arm.

Cavana, standing rigidly at the helm, heard the splash the beast made but was spared the sight of its struggles. But Hughes, high up in the mainmast top setting the small sails, and Morgan, who was standing outside the galley to get some air, and Wilson and Sullivan smoking on the forecastle, and those of the slaves who happened to find themselves against the starboard rail, saw the monkey's brief trajectory, saw him land face down in the bright water and sink and rise again. Because of the bright

347

surface, it seemed to these spectators that Vasco fought for life in very shallow water, a few inches only, a zone shot through with light, agitated with his struggles – all the rest, the dark fathoms beneath him, seemed a different arena. They saw the monkey raise his thin neck, gulp for air. They saw him strike out with his arms as if set on swimming across that great track of light, saw his heavy tail lie briefly on the surface, slick as a snake. Then he thrashed and turned in the water, the black muzzle opened widely and Vasco yearned up at the sky. This brief struggle over, the monkey sank again, and they had a last glimpse of his orange-coloured arms and feet vividly refracted below the surface, dangling like roots. Then the ship had cleared him, he was lost to view.

Thurso said nothing more. He stood with feet planted on the deck. After a while he raised his head and sniffed for a wind. Cavana waited some minutes, looking straight before him, hands gripped tight to the wheel. Then, very slowly, he turned his head and studied the captain's face in profile as if trying to memorize the features.

Later that evening Thomas True died. A man of few words and unclean habits, he had had no friends aboard. Libby sewed him into his blanket and within half an hour of his last breath he was consigned to the sea, Thurso officiating in his usual hoarse mutter, barely audible except to those nearest him. As usual he omitted the lesson, confining himself to the short final office: 'We therefore commit his body to the deep, to be turned into corruption, looking for the resurrection of the body, when the sea shall give up her dead, and the life of the world to come . . .'

Thurso paused here before continuing. It was the briefest of pauses but every member of the crew knew the reason for it. Startling in the silence, unmistakable, there had come a long fluttering sigh through all the ship's canvas, first breath of a rising wind.

PART SEVEN

THIRTY-FOUR

The ship Thurso sent by made quick passage and the letters were in Kemp's hands within a month.

'He is leaving without his full complement of negroes,' Kemp said to his son as they sat together in their office overlooking the waterfront. 'He declares himself short by twelve.'

They sat at the mahogany table, on whose polished surface objects – jeweller's scales, a set of weights in silver, an ivory paper-knife, a japanned box – were reflected so deeply and with such lustre that they seemed afloat there. The February afternoon was cold and a banked fire of sea-coal burned in the grate behind them with flickering, rose-blue flames. The sky through the window was gravid with snow and the river ran slate-grey and sullen, half obscured by the warehouses and storage sheds along its nearside bank.

'Matthew says little beyond that he is well and in good spirits,' Kemp said, passing over his nephew's letter. 'I do not know how Thurso computes that twelve. The commonly accepted figure for capacity is two negroes for every unit of tonnage. The *Liverpool Merchant* is a hundred and two tons and so he is eight short, not twelve, by my reckoning.' He had aged in appearance of recent weeks; he had lost colour and the flesh of his cheeks had loosened and sagged. But he was as master of the facts as ever. 'That is allowing for headroom between the platforms of two foot six inches,' he added.

Erasmus looked down at the brief lines of his cousin's letter. He could see no reference to good spirits in it. Paris sent his best respects, was in good health, asked to be remembered to his aunt and cousin. The rather large, angular characters recalled the surgeon's physical being strongly and disagreeably to Erasmus. He remembered the subfusc suit, the awkward courtesy, the pale, lined face. That disgraced presence at the dinner table . . . Erasmus almost never revised opinion or reinterpreted experience. Enmity was like a sort of faith with him. After some moments he found that his teeth had clenched hard together with aversion.

'Of course,' his father said, 'Thurso is an experienced man, no doubt he has ways of disposing the negroes so as to make the most of the space. It seems there has been a case of virulent infection among them, very dangerous if it takes hold. A bloody flux. But he has hopes that by a prompt departure now and with God's grace a favourable passage, he will bring them without more loss to the West Indies.' Kemp paused a moment, looking up through the window at the charged clouds. Then he said, 'I hope I have not been mistaken in the reliance I have placed on Captain Thurso.'

Erasmus felt an obscure distress. It was like a betrayal, the breaking of a promise, hearing his confident father express doubts and misgivings. Such moments of discouragement had been frequent with him lately. 'Diseases among them are rather my cousin's business,' he said. 'It was to look to such things that he went with the ship.'

But Kemp seemed not to hear this. His eyes were still turned towards the window and the cold reflected light from the river lay along his brows. Erasmus saw an expression of bitterness and sorrow come to his father's face and heard him say in low tones, 'What devil was it counselled me to turn to cotton, I wonder? I should have stayed in sugar.'

These muttered words and the drawn mouth of his father made an impression on Erasmus never to be effaced; but for the moment it was their seeming irrelevance that startled him, the sense that his father was following some lonely track of his own. He experienced a sort of foreboding and an impulse of protective love. He sought for words but found none.

'Well,' Kemp said heavily after a moment, 'let us get out the maps.' It was a favourite occupation of his now to chart the course of the ship and this news of departure had provided fresh incentive.

They spread the map on the table before them, holding down the corners with the jeweller's weights. 'This is where they left from,' Kemp said. 'Here is situated the Company fort.' His nail touched the mouth of the Kavalli River, made a faint scraping sound across the flats of mud that Paris had seen transfigured by moonlight, stopped at the point where the two bound girl slaves, both roughly of an age with Sarah Wolpert, had choked and drowned in the surf.

In that quiet room, with its oak wainscoting and Turkey carpet, its shelves of ledgers and almanacks, it would have been difficult for these two to form any true picture of the ship's circumstances or the nature of trading on the Guinea Coast, even if they had been inclined to try. Difficult, and in any case superfluous. To function efficiently – to function at all – we must concentrate our effects. Picturing things is bad for business, it is undynamic. It can choke the mind with horror if persisted in. We have graphs and tables and balance sheets and statements of corporate philosophy to help us remain busily and safely in the realm of the abstract and comfort us with a sense of lawful endeavour and lawful profit. And we have maps.

'See, my boy,' Kemp said, 'Just about here they should be. They have been on the way a month now, near enough. They should be somewhere here, north of Caracas. They will be keeping on a latitude some fifteen degrees above the equator.' His finger traced the lines, caressed the contours of flying cherubs with puffed-out cheeks, and sportive dolphins, and the hulls of miniature ships with bellying sails that travelled this benign Atlantic. Meanwhile the real ship was beating to westward, packed to suffocation with negroes in irons, its hold swarming with rats, other merchantmen keeping well to windward of the stench. 'They will have caught the winter trades,' Kemp said with something of his old enthusiasm. 'I dare say as we sit here talking of it they are already in sight of the Sugar Islands.'

Erasmus assented to this. It was the best way to look at it. He was glad to see his father returning to a more sanguine mood. Afterwards, after the event, it was to come to him with bitter self-reproach that he had known all the time that more was worrying his father than the progress of the ship, though this became the focus of it. There had been signs – bills deferred, credit renewed on high terms, the abrupt suspending of their policy of buying land adjoining the roads into the city. He could not, of course, have known the extent of his father's losses. Even the indefatigible Partridge, whom Wolpert had set on to look into Kemp's affairs, had failed to discover the merchant's disastrous attempts to recoup himself on the Stock Exchange; none knew of these but Kemp and his broker. And throughout this time Erasmus too had been absorbed in his own insulating dream.

Sarah's eighteenth birthday was approaching, and with it the announcement of their betrothal; and it seemed to Erasmus that the changes in the seasons and all the sights and sounds around him were merely portents of this stupendous event. It was there in the usual din of the streets, in the smells of raw cotton and hemp that surrounded him in the warehouse, as it was in the silver skies of the March evenings, the bright drifts and linings burrowed out by the sun in the banks of cloud over the Mersey and the ruffling breezes over the water. There later in the new crop of dock and nettle in the waste ground and the songs of larks above the fields outside the city, the air full of climbing, singing birds, rending and repairing the sky with song. And the time from that freezing day when he had looked at the map with his father to this joyous stitching of the larks was for Erasmus all one indeterminate period of waiting.

Three days before the event, in the early afternoon, he rode over to the Wolpert house, having asked leave beforehand. Afterwards he could not remember any of the words he had exchanged with his father in parting – commonplace words in any case. But he remembered that his father had evaded his eyes.

It was around the time of year he had first ridden over to the house on the pretext of visiting Charles. He remembered his feelings of humiliation, his failure to understand the ancient footman – still in service there, more doddery than ever now – the clear, unearthly singing that had come to him through the trees and brought him stumbling into the open to be enrolled as Ferdinand . . .

Things were very different now. On the day of Sarah's birth-

354

day she would be his by title, by consent, by public acknowledgement. He would never again be required to go against the grain of his nature in order to please her. She would love and respect him too much ever to require it.

In the light of these triumphant feelings familiar sights seemed new this afternoon. The beeches bordering the avenue, in full leaf now, were a fresher green than he could remember, the singing of hidden warblers more deliberately sweet. In the parkland the chestnut trees were candled with blossom and the terraces below the house were vivid with geraniums.

He was early, which meant he could take his tea alone with Sarah and her mother, old Wolpert and Charles being out at business still and the younger brother, Andrew, in the schoolroom under the eye of his tutor. Afternoon sunshine filled the room, entering through the tall French windows. In this radiant light Erasmus looked round him and felt the same triumph, the same sense of newness in familiar things. The water-colours on the walls, the needlework over the chimneypiece embroidered by Sarah's maternal grandmother, now dead, Mrs Wolpert's beaded work-box on the low table beside her, the fine set of moulded beakers on their glass shelf, all possessed a special effulgence on this day. It was in this room, he remembered suddenly, that he and Sarah had once come face to face, during rehearsal of the play. He had been looking for his book ... He had failed in address that day, failed miserably, but she had known – he remembered the wave of colour that had come to her face. Afterwards she had seemed to disregard everything in her eagerness to play Miranda. How he had hated that transformation, all that posturing and make-believe. And the nonsense of an enchanted island where divisions could be healed and enemies reconciled ... He would never allow such a thing to happen again. He caught Sarah's eye and saw that she was happy.

Most of the time they spent discussing the arrangements. Flowers had been ordered – carnations, red and white. Invitations had been sent out long ago – there were more than a hundred on the list of guests. There was to be a ball, with an orchestra of five. If the weather stayed fine supper would be served out of doors on the terrace.

355

'We can dance out of doors, too,' Sarah said. 'We can dance on the lawns.' Her face wore its usual delicate composure, in which there was always something impervious, or perhaps obstinate; but her eyes were bright with excitement.

'Outside on the grass?' Erasmus laughed a little at the extravagance of it. 'That's an odd notion. Have you forgotten that there is a perfectly good ballroom inside the house?'

'Yes, but don't you see, it would be something different, it would be something to remember. People would remember my party for ever. Everyone dances in ballrooms.'

This, Erasmus felt, was precisely the point, but he merely smiled and shook his head, glancing indulgently at Mrs Wolpert. Better to say nothing, she would forget the idea soon – or so he hoped.

However, she was exalted now and took it into her head that he should see her new dress, the one she was to wear for the ball, and not merely see it, but see it on – a suggestion that her mother objected to immediately on grounds of propriety and some alarmed superstition. But Sarah insisted, demanded to be allowed, drawing herself up and raising her delicately moulded chin in the determined way she had when her mind was wholly set on something. In the end the mother gave in, as she generally did when the girl was wrought up in this way; she had learned to recognize the signs. And on this occasion she received no help from Erasmus, who remained silent, divided between his sense of correctness and the desire to view his love.

Sarah was away half an hour or more. When she returned, making an entry through the wide double-doors, Erasmus saw at once that she had done her hair differently, in a braid over the top of her head, and that she had added something to the natural glow of her cheeks. The dress was of silk, a soft apricot in colour, with narrow stripes in a darker shade and a vine pattern of flowers and leaves between, the skirt full, with a short train, and arranged over a hooped petticoat of cream-coloured quilted satin. High-heeled shoes with brocade straps completed the effect.

Sarah paraded before them for some time. She was flushed but serious, as befitted the occasion. For a while there was no sound in the room but the beguiling friction of silk. Having helped in the choice of material and seen the dress fitted at the dressmaker's, Mrs Wolpert had not many words to say now. She was still far from approving the exhibition and wished it over quickly. Erasmus was silent for so long that in the end Sarah stopped and looked at him in a way that was imperious, yet somehow supplicating too. 'You look beautiful,' he said then. 'It is a beautiful dress.' His own voice sounded husky and strange to him, so great was the sincerity with which he delivered this verdict. He could hardly believe, even now, that this radiant creature would so soon be promised to him. But even as he spoke something changed in his expression. Another, even so young, even in the joy of possession, might have felt something akin to compassion for what had been patient and somehow helpless in the girl's display, some quality of subjection in it, in the very vanity itself. But this was a reach of feeling quite beyond him. He had felt the joy – it had taken him by the throat. But below it an obscure feeling of offendedness had grown within him. Though she had looked at him and posed for him, he had begun to feel that this show was not for him only, he was sharing her with other spectators somewhere beyond the room. She was on stage again.

Displeasure at this did not last long, once he was able to assign it to weakness on Sarah's part – her weaknesses he was confident he could deal with. By the time he took his leave he had quite recovered equanimity. Sarah, restored to her house costume of light blue lutestring, accompanied him to the end of the drive. Walking beside her, leading his horse, he felt unmixed happiness. At the gate they kissed and he held her close. He felt her press against him and the blood rose to his head and obscured his sight for some moments.

She had heard the change in his breathing. 'My own love,' she said.

'Until Saturday then,' he said. He watched her walk away, keeping his eyes fixed on her until the curve of the drive took her from his sight.

It was nearly six o'clock when he reached home. His mother

heard him crossing the hall towards the staircase and called out to him. He found her alone in her small parlour, the tea things still before her.

'No one cares a fig for my convenience,' she began at once, before he was properly in the room. 'That is always the last thing to be studied; my poor father would turn in his grave if he knew, well, I believe he does. I have so long been used in this way, it would be strange if he didn't, but this goes beyond the bounds.'

From his mother's hasty, indrawn breaths and the bridling movements of her head, Erasmus saw that she was in one of her states. 'What is the matter, Mother?' he asked, and there had unconsciously come into his voice the tone his father habitually used with her, breezy, affectionate, patronizingly brisk.

'I have not even had the resolution to ring for the tea things to be removed,' she said on a calmer, more plaintive note.

'Well, I will do that.' He saw now that her hair was powdered and set in the rather elaborate coiffure known as French curls, and that she was dressed for going out in a brocade gown in pink and gold, with a lace stomacher. 'That is a handsome gown,' he said, in the same tone. 'You are altogether very elegant this evening, Mother.'

'Well, but your father is not come home, he will have forgot it.' Vexation had paled her, so that the rouge on her cheeks showed too prominently. 'I have had that fluttering,' she said, on a note of warning, laying a white hand over the brocaded bodice of her dress. 'Had it not been for the tincture of hellebore your cousin Matthew recommended, I don't know what would have happened, and now I can't be sure the apothecary is making it up in the exact same proportions, and Matthew is not here to advise me. I think it a great pity that my nephew must stay away so long and spend his talents on rough seamen and black people.'

'Well, I hope you do not blame father for that,' Erasmus said, smiling. 'You know he has much on his mind these days.'

'How should I know it? He does not talk to me of what is on his mind. He promised to be home today in time for tea. We were to have dined early and gone to the Mansion House

Gardens that are newly opened and a great draw to all the fashion of the town, to listen to the band.'

'He cannot be much longer now,' Erasmus said. He stayed with his mother and entertained her with the description of Sarah's dress – she entirely shared Mrs Wolpert's feelings about the propriety of the proceedings. They played some hands of whist together. Cards always calmed her nerves. She was a shrewd and accomplished player with a strong desire to win, which sometimes led her into cheating. Light in the room began to fail and the parlourmaid was summoned to light the lamps. Still the merchant failed to arrive. When the clock struck eight Erasmus got up. 'He must have overlooked it completely,' he said. 'If something had come up in the way of business to detain him, he would have sent word. I will go down to the office and see.'

It seemed too much trouble to have the mare brought out and saddled again. There were always chairmen waiting outside the Lion at the corner of Red Cross Street. Almost at once he found two men with a sedan that passed his inspection as not too impossibly verminous.

On the way he thought of little. The slight rocking motion of the chair and the whoops of the foremost man to clear the way made drowsy rhythm in his mind and he fell into a state between musing and dozing.

He paid off the men at the end of Water Street beside the Ram's Head and walked through the alley behind the inn on to the waterfront. There was a wind rising from across the estuary; he heard the rattle of a loose board somewhere and the creaking of the ropes that held the heavy inn-sign. A barge with a lantern at the stern lay some way out on the water.

There were no lights on the ground floor of the warehouse and the doors that gave on to the street were locked. He went round to the side of the building and ascended the short flight of metal stairs to the watchman's shed on the landing. He found the man sprawled on a ragged quilt, open-mouthed and oblivious in a thick fume of gin. After locking up below he had obviously deemed his watch over for the night and settled down to the bottle. Erasmus considered kicking him awake, but even that degree of contact was distasteful to him. It would be the brute's last sleep in the service of the firm, that much at least he promised himself.

From behind the shed a gallery ran the length of the building, giving access to a number of rooms that looked over the warehouse floor on one side and the waterfront on the other. His father's office and his own smaller, adjoining one were roughly halfway along; both father and son were accustomed to enter and leave the building by this route and each had his own set of keys.

He had taken the small, half-blackened oil lamp from the watchman's hut to light his way. The gallery itself was in darkness but he could make out a faint crack of light beneath the door of his father's office. He knocked, waited, tried the door – it was locked. He used his key to open it. There was no one in the room. The stub of a candle in a tall holder on the table burned with an unsteady flame, sending blurred ripples over the polished surface.

Erasmus stood still for some moments, aware of nothing but a sort of mild puzzlement. The room was quiet, at once familiar and strange at this late hour, with its odours of melted candle wax and old papers and the stealthy reek of river water that entered all these buildings in the cool of the night.

He saw now that the flame of the candle was not guttering as he had thought at first, but leaning over in some current of air. This it was that accounted for the tremulous waverings of light over the table and near the wall. Glancing beyond the table, he saw that the door of the small stock-room at the far end of the office was standing half open. Perhaps his father had gone that way for some reason – there was a passage beyond it which led back on to the gallery further along. Still holding the lamp he took some steps round the table and approached the door. 'Father,' he called, not very loudly. 'Are you there?'

He held the door open. Shadows were somehow too long in here. There was his own flickering shadow lying before him, but it extended further than the candle-light could have thrown it. There was another, cast by the lamp. He was holding the lamp too close to his face. He raised it and went forward a little, no more than a pace or two, but enough for him to see the dark bulk hanging above him and to take in, with the helpless particularity that accompanies shock, the exact look of the overturned stool on the floor and his father's shoeless feet which by some accident of balance dangled one distinctly lower than the other.

Some words broke from Erasmus but he could not afterwards remember what they had been, nor what had been the sequence of his actions after the first one: with the same instinct of secrecy that had possessed his father, he had run to lock the outer door. Everything else, everything surrounding this one deliberate act, was improvised, maladroit, violent, climbing on to a chair, sawing awkwardly at the rope above his father's head, clutching at the body in absurd scruple that it might be further damaged by a fall, falling with it, heavily, when he could not take the weight. Lying half-embraced there on the floor, he had fumbled to loosen the knot, not in the hope of restoring life – he knew there was no life left in the body – but as if in hope that the relief of it might close his father's eyes at last. But it did not, and he could not touch the face.

He left the way he had come, locking the door again carefully behind him. The watchman was snoring still in his hut. He took a sedan from the inn and gave directions to the porters in clear and collected tones. The necessity for concealment acted on him like resolution and kept him in a semblance of calm. Only when he was home again did this begin to break down. His mother, still in her brocade gown, sat in the parlour where he had left her, playing patience. She has been here all this time, he thought, here in this one place . . .

'Well, you have taken long enough,' she said pettishly. 'Is your father there? It is too late now in any case, I have given up all thoughts of it.'

When he failed to answer, she looked up at him sharply. Then her eyes widened and she started forward in her chair. 'What is it?' she said. 'Where is your father?'

'Something has happened,' he said and his voice broke on it, not in grief yet – the death was all horror still – but in distress at not knowing how to tell her, not knowing how to speak of it to his mother, who had always had to be shielded, humoured. For a while he was silent, thinking of words to say. 'Mother,' he said at last, 'you must prepare yourself –'

With a speed that took him by surprise she had flung down the cards and was out of her chair and standing close. Her head came lower than his chin but he felt no difference in height now, so fiercely did she look at him. 'What is it?' she said again. 'Why don't you speak?' Her voice rose. 'Has there been an accident?'

Still with an instinct of concealment or protection he said, 'I locked the office door. No one can get in.' It sounded like a boast. Then he felt the sharp clutch of her hands on his arms and he began to tell her but in his desire to be gradual he lost his way in the story; like a child, he grew enmeshed in the nightmare preliminaries, the clues that had led him to that hanging shape, the leaning flame, the half-opened door, the shadows that had seemed wrong, misshapen . . . 'He was there, in the dark,' he said, looking away from her in shame, his own, his father's.

'You say you locked the door? Did you bring away the keys?'

The sharpness of the question brought his eyes back to her. The patches of paint on her cheeks looked grotesque now, clownish, against the drained pallor of her face. But her eyes were regarding him closely and her mouth was compressed in a firm line.

'Why, yes,' he said, 'I have them with me.'

'His own will be there with him, if he had locked the door. And the watchman?'

'Watchman?'

'Yes,' she said with sudden angry impatience, 'the watchman, the watchman. Gather your wits. We must be quick if we are to keep this hid. The watchman, does he have keys?'

'Only to the storerooms below.'

'We must have your father brought home tonight, but it cannot be done by any of our own people, it must all be done through Dr Banks. We must see him tonight, at once.'

'But what use is that?' He was bewildered. 'I have told you he is dead,' he said. 'Would I have left him otherwise?'

362

'For the certificate,' she said, and he saw that her lips had begun trembling. 'The doctor must sign to a cause of death. Do as I say, Erasmus. Go and see to the coach. William will be there still, he has been waiting all this while to take your father and me to the Mansion House. He will not have stabled the horses without permission.' Her voice softened to a full tone of pity for him which he was never quite to forgive. 'You must come with me,' she said. 'My poor boy, nothing will be required of you, but I must have someone . . . I must have a man with me at this hour of night. Go now. I will change my clothes meanwhile.'

Mutely, as if in a dream, he obeyed her. It was gone eleven when they drew up outside the doctor's house, a large mansion in the newly opened and fashionable Bold Street. Henry Banks was now one of the leading physicians of the town but he had been doctor to the Kemps since the early days of his practice.

He received them almost at once in the small parlour he used as a consulting-room, apologizing for his evening attire of robe and skull-cap – he had been on the point of retiring for the night. He was a tall, high-shouldered man, deliberate and impressive in manner, with shrewd, equable eyes in a long face.

'You will take something?' he said, glancing from one to the other. He had recognized the hush of shock about them from the moment they entered the room. 'A glass of cordial, perhaps, something to warm you? The nights are cold still. You will not? Well, then, tell me how I can be of service to you.'

At this, Elizabeth Kemp began for the first time to weep. Between bouts of tears she spoke of an accident, a terrible misadventure, she did not know which way to turn, she was sorry it was so late, they were keeping him from bed and she knew he was a man with many calls upon him, but by the time they had got the coach out . . .

The doctor listened with sober patience, saying little, making no attempt to prompt her or check the weeping, evidently content to let her come to the business in her own time. But Erasmus could not contain himself. This foolish prevarication of his mother's, this flattering of the doctor, seemed shameful to him. His father was lying there, dead and disgraced and staring in the dark while she wheedled and dabbed at her eyes. Even the tears . . . He had to take the initiative, speak for both of them.

'My father has done a violence to himself,' he said harshly. 'By misadventure, of course, but it could be taken as design and it is that we want to avoid.' He paused, clearing some obstacle in his throat. 'We are come to ask if you will certify to natural causes.'

'Natural causes?' The doctor looked sharply and coldly at Erasmus. 'He is dead, then? And in circumstances of violence? No, I do not wish to know the manner of it. You must save that for the proper authorities. There are people appointed to examine into such things. Did you seriously think I would compound a felony, a man in my position? You would have done better to leave things to your mother.' He turned to the mother now and his expression softened. She had been coming to him with ailments largely imaginary for upwards of twenty years and he had grown fond of her. 'My dear,' he said, 'I am deeply sorry to hear of this accident, but really cannot see, under the circumstances –'

'My son is overwrought,' she said quickly. 'He does not know what he is saying. 'Twas he that discovered my poor husband. He is little more than a boy and has got the matter quite wrong. Please forgive him. We came only to seek your advice in this terrible pass we are brought to. I am a mere woman and have small knowledge of the world and my health is far from good, as none knows better then you . . .'

In fact she looked less sickly, more animated, at this moment than Erasmus could ever remember seeing her. The crisis of his intervention had driven away her tears, leaving her eyes brighter, and a glow had come to warm her cheeks. Sitting upright in her plain cambric dress and trimmed hood, her hands clasped together, she looked more than well, she looked handsome; and Erasmus sensed that Banks thought so too, for all the fellow's grave airs.

She paused a moment now as if in reflection and when she spoke again it was in a different, more considering tone: 'My husband, as you will recall, was a high-blooded man and rather short in the neck and suffered from dizzy fits sometimes and rushes to the head.'

Banks nodded slowly. 'That is so,' he said. 'He had a sanguine constitution of body. I remember letting him blood on occasion.'

'Well, it is my belief that he consulted another doctor for this condition at certain times, for example when you yourself were away from the town or otherwise not available to be visited.'

The doctor regarded her for a moment in silence. Then, still without speaking, he looked down thoughtfully at the signet ring on his right hand. Absently, he turned it this way and that for some little while. Erasmus glanced at his mother in surprise – he had not heard before of a second doctor and was about to say so when he was checked by her slight warning frown.

The doctor looked up. His face was quite without expression. 'Yes,' he said, 'I am sometimes away. To take a second opinion would have been quite a reasonable thing for Kemp to do under the circumstances.'

'Well, now, the difficulty is,' she said, 'I am so silly and not used to remembering and I cannot for the life of me bring to mind this doctor's name and I do not know how I can find it out on such short notice. I thought you might know it. You know so many things and have a wide acquaintance among the practitioners of the town . . .'

There was another silence. Dr Banks looked straight before him, tapping his long fingers softly together, his face composed in its habitual gravity of expression. 'I could support the condition of high blood pressure,' he said at last. 'That is, if asked, I could confirm that Kemp received treatment from me for that condition – if asked, let us say, by this other physician your husband had been seeing. That would not be to certify cause of death, you understand. But in the event of a certificate being signed by someone else, it might lend credence. Yes, I should say pretty certainly it would lend credence.' He got up on this and went to his desk, where he spent some time searching in a drawer and a further brief time writing. When he came back to them he held a slip of paper in his hand. 'The doctor your husband may have consulted in my absence is this one,' he said. 'The address is written here too. He is flexible in his hours, I believe, and can be visited at any time.'

365

She had risen to take the paper from him and for a moment she clasped his hand and lowered her head over it and the tears came again. Different now, impeding her thanks. The doctor too knew the difference in the tears and this time used words of comfort to her as he supported her towards the door. 'Kemp did not lack for friends,' he said. 'There will be those that you can turn to. And you have this fine son as your support. If there is anything more that I can do, I trust you will not hesitate to ask. You will understand that I cannot examine the poor fellow's body or have anything more to do directly with the business. If any should ask why I was not called in, you may say I was indisposed. But it is unlikely.' He smiled at them in farewell. 'The proceedings are quite regular, the man whose name I have given you is a qualified medical practitioner.'

It was only when, long past midnight, they had run the qualified medical man to earth in his ramshackle and evil-smelling quarters above a tavern, that things began to fall into place in Erasmus's mind. He had listened in silence while his mother bargained with the gaunt, unsteady fellow, whom they had roused, still reeking of spirits, from his sleep. Ten minutes' talk and twenty-five guineas secured for William Kemp an official death from heart failure, the due period of mourning, burial in hallowed ground. From the widow and the son was lifted the spectre of scandal and disgrace. Five guineas more obtained the services of two silent, out-at-elbow ruffians and a covered litter. The merchant was brought home in the dimness of the new day, wrapped in a length of good-quality blue cotton baft from his warehouse.

She had bargained with that scoundrel – Erasmus could scarcely believe it. 'Not for the sake of the guineas,' she told him, 'no price can be put on your father's reputation. But these people expect it.'

It was her own unexpected knowledge of what people expected that he held against her – that and her resourcefulness when he himself had been floundering. And she had deceived him, she had kept him in the dark. He writhed inwardly when he remembered how she had apologized for him to the condescending Banks.

'Why didn't you tell me, Mother?' he asked her once. 'Why didn't you say what was in your mind to do?'

'My poor Erasmus,' she said, 'I thought the less you knew the better. You had already lost your father that night.'

And with this – as he saw it – typical failure of logic on her part he had to be content. The worst of it was that despite his superior logic and the sense of rectitude to which he clung as if it were a mark of loyalty to his father, he knew in his heart that he had been given that night a lesson in the conduct of human affairs that he would never forget.

The feeling of having been somehow duped poisoned his grief in the days that followed. For of course his father too had deceived him. With sick incredulity he tried to imagine what his father had felt during the last hours of his life, tried to make the actions of that stranger somehow congruous and explicable. He remembered how his father had avoided his eyes when they had parted that afternoon, an unusual thing – both father and son were direct in their regard. He must have known then. He would have had the rope ready, he would have marked the iron hook in the beam. Perhaps he had known for much longer . . . But this was more than Erasmus could bear steadily to contemplate, the loneliness and treachery of it, sitting at meals, discussing business, with the intention of death constant behind the changing face.

Below his feeling of betrayal was a horror that never left him at the secrecy of the business, the deranged ceremony, locking the door, setting the candle on the table. Somewhere in the midst of this madness his father had removed his shoes so that the last steps of his life would be silent . . .

Erasmus was freed from this stricken state, though not yet enough to weep, by the sight of the face in its open coffin on the eve of the funeral. Once again it was by deception that Elizabeth Kemp revealed her love and fulfilled her duty. Alone she had bathed the body and shrouded it. She had waxed away the dark mottles below the skin, and shut the outraged eyes. She had closed Kemp's mouth over his swollen tongue and held it closed with a binding of linen.

Death itself is never false, she had merely falsified appearances

367

for the sake of the living. But to Erasmus, kneeling alone in the silent room, it seemed that he was seeing the truth of his father's face for the first time. The inessentials were gone, the changes of expression, the high colour and the hectic regard, erased by this draining of the accidental blood. Now it could be seen that his father bore the face of a zealot who had been proved right after all. It came to Erasmus, with inexpressible pain, that all he could remember of his father's life, all his gesture and assertion, all the peculiar vividness of expression that had belonged to him, had been no more than botched rehearsals for this final waxen immobility.

This pity for his father brought him close to tears. In the determined intensity of his efforts to hold them back – he had not so far wept – his gaze took on a preternatural fixity, blurring the face before him, giving it for the moment a look of merely momentary repose. The eyelids seemed to quiver and the nostrils to distend slightly, as if at the scent of something savoursome. Erasmus was carried back to the winter morning at Dickson's shipyard, more than a year ago now, when amid smells of cut wood and wet sawdust his father had crouched and advanced his connoisseur's nose to the fresh-cut timber of the ship's mast, and pronounced it first-rate. Another smell too there had been, coarser, the odour of decay. Not that day but somewhere near it, the time the ship was building. Eyes from which the light was fading, a startled movement in the half-dark, a mute plea for a death unwitnessed . . . Another man, adding the rank smell of his death to these milder ones of clean linen and essence of violets . . . Erasmus rose too hastily and felt a wave of dizziness. In the desolate clarity that came with its passing he understood that his father had been sniffing at his own death, his own decay, that day at the shipyard – it was the ship that had killed him.

THIRTY-FIVE

She was continuing to kill others; not on a grand scale, but steadily, day by day, as the dysentery gained ground in spite of all Paris's efforts.

This second attempt to quit Africa had been hardly more successful than the first. Perhaps the monkey was not deemed sacrifice enough and Thurso's tutelary spirit, in the arbitrary way of powerful beings, simply abandoned him; or perhaps, having lived longer than any man was supposed to in this trade, he had exhausted luck and credit alike. Whatever the reason, in the following weeks the *Liverpool Merchant* was subject to every perversity of weather possible in those waters at that time of year. The north-east trades fell shorter than usual for the season and she lay too far south to find them. Less than thirty leagues out she found herself again becalmed, prey to the currents flowing eastward into the Gulf of Guinea, edging her back towards the shoals. Day after day she dawdled in a latitude some points south of seven degrees, in that equatorial region of light currents and whispering convergence of breezes known as the Doldrums, where opposing winds meet and die in slow rises and wandering uplifts of air.

They had promises of change: light rufflings of the sea were perceived at a distance, like gentle strokes of a cat's paw over the surface, forerunners of a steadier breeze. From aloft Hughes saw these fugitive traces and following an old superstition he scratched with his nails at the backstays and whistled for a wind.

But no wind came. The canvas hung slack. The negroes were listless and sullen under their awning, whose fringes hardly stirred. The fear that had made them quick-eyed and febrile was quite gone from their faces. Their looks were fixed and heavy now, their limbs slow and reluctant, as if fear had been stilled by something worse.

Sea and sky joined seamlessly in a single tone of hot white, burnished and slightly smoky. The ship rested on the sea as if in some substance thicker and more inert than water. Yet this lifeless sea had its moments of energy. The clawing strokes across the surface deepened sometimes to a strange rippling or seething motion. Occasionally a line of foam would break in the vicinity of the ship, bearing an evil-smelling, gelatinous scum. A fierce argument, almost leading to blows, broke out in the forecastle between Blair and Lees as to the nature of this stinking freightage, one contending it was dead spawn, the other decayed fragments of jellyfish. Tempers were short among the men, with only dirty work to do and not enough to eat – their food was rationed now, on Thurso's orders. Cavana, whose hatred for the captain had not rested since the murder of his monkey, put it about that Thurso had pocketed the money that should have been laid out on provisions. This was consistent with what they knew of him and was believed for the sake of the grievance it afforded. A muttering grew up against Thurso, though not yet in his hearing.

To Paris, seeing the strange seething motions that sometimes disturbed this pale and fiery sea without bringing the faintest of breezes, there came the obscene suspicion that creatures were feasting just below the surface, growing fat on the polluted scum – a filth to which the ship herself added daily, tipping the bodies of the dead and the ordures of the living into the placid waste around, obliged from time to time to have her longboat hoisted out so that she could be towed forward, out of the zone she had fouled.

He was in those days prone to sick fancies, induced in part by the ravages of disease among the negroes, which he found himself powerless to prevent. In the later stages of the dysentery they grew too weak to use the necessary buckets, especially the men, who were still chained together in pairs, and their quarters below and parts of the deck amidships became noisome. Paris used all the means known to him of combating infection, working to keep the slaves washed down and the decks well scraped, and to purify the tainted air below. He had the slaves' rooms swabbed out with vinegar and he smoked the area between decks with tar and brimstone. Thurso too played his part, united with the surgeon in his urgent wish to keep as many of the negroes alive as possible. He gave orders for wetted gunpowder to be burned in iron pots in different parts of the vessel – a long-tried disinfectant which he swore by. But in spite of all efforts the deaths continued. And now, to add to his troubles, Paris began to find scorbutic symptoms among the crew.

McGann was the first. He had just assisted, with Sullivan, in throwing a dead woman slave over the side, and he came to Paris complaining of a disabling feebleness in his knees experienced while doing so. 'I could hardly hoist her over,' he said, 'an' she was nae mair than a bag o' bones hersel'. There's a weakness in a' me joints.'

He was a noted malingerer and exploiter of situations, so Paris did not at first take these complaints very seriously. However, his breath was very offensive and upon looking into his mouth Paris found the gums to be of an unusual livid redness and very soft and spongy – the small degree of pressure necessary in the course of the examination caused them to bleed freely.

'Then there is me legs,' McGann said dolefully, beginning to roll up his trousers, which hung even baggier on him now.

The skin of the legs was marked by several black and livid spots. They were equal to the surface of the skin, Paris saw, and resembled an extravagation under it, as if from bruising.

'The slightest thing an' I fall to pantin' an' catchin' for breath,' McGann said.

Paris nodded. 'You have got scurvy.'

'Oh, aye?'

Something in McGann's manner told Paris he had known this already. 'Your present diet is not sufficient,' he said.

McGann's voluminous cap, from which he would not be separated, fell forward over his brows. From below it his small, tight-featured face looked up with a kind of dogged tenacity at Paris. ''Tis true that I'm a'ways hungry,' he said. 'I cannot get enough to eat. If I could get a extry bit o' rice pudden, me strength would come back to me.'

'I understand that you are hungry,' Paris said, 'but if you ate twice the amount it would not make any difference to your condition. The cause lies not in the quantity but in the nature of the food, at least so I suppose.' He paused for a moment, then said rather helpessly, 'To be frank with you, McGann, I am not at all sure what it is that causes these symptoms. It is a deficiency of nutriment, as I believe. I have heard that lemon juice can do much for the condition, but we have nothing of that sort aboard. I will make you up a gargle and see how that answers.'

McGann showed himself sceptical of this remedy and generally disappointed and dissatisfied. Only the hope of getting extra rations had brought him, Paris now realized. Though not very confident, he made up a gargle of acidulated barley water and obliged McGann to take it.

Alerted now, he noticed during the following days a similar bloating of complexion and listlessness in other members of the crew. As far as he could ascertain, none of the negroes showed symptoms of scurvy and after some pondering he came to the conclusion that the reason for this must be the green peppers which had been served with their rice while supplies lasted. There had been no other significant difference in diet.

The prolonged calm and attendant sickness brought out different things in people, depending on temperament and circumstances. To the inward-looking Paris, with his abiding sense of guilt, the stagnation was also moral, and he was prey to depression and morbid imaginings. The people of the crew, less privileged in respect to space, grew more quarrelsome among themselves and more resentful of those set over them. Haines and Barton still drove the men but they went more warily and kept a loaded pistol at their belts.

Thurso too went armed, aware of the feeling against him. The captain was living in a purgatory of his own. He took his meals generally alone, in sombre silence. When on deck he spoke only through Barton. His small, raw-veined eyes darted suspicious glances from under their heavy brows as if seeking in the faces of those around him some clue as to the culprit, the killer of his merchandise, the agent of this blighting calm. He conveyed to Paris a definite impression of derangement.

Only Delblanc seemed largely unaffected – though this was a mistaken impression, as Paris came afterwards to realize. In fact, in this succession of unchanging days, Delblanc changed more profoundly than anyone, though this was not obvious at the time because he seemed merely to become more definitely himself. Scrupulously shaved, his hair dressed carefully, in cambric shirt and elegant, close-fitting breeches, he moved about the ship, talking in his frank and engaging style to any of the crew with leisure to listen.

What reflections he made in the silence of his cabin and how far he seriously attempted to foment revolt, or even hoped for it, was never made clear – he did not himself declare it. But there is no doubt that in this waste of sea, as the ship dragged her stench through the water and dead negroes continued to be cast over the side, Delblanc underwent a sort of conversion, of profound consequence for all of them, slaves and seamen alike. And the first sign of it was the way he sought to make converts.

A man may go through life and remain ignorant of himself; he may think himself as other than he truly is and he may die with this illusion still intact, because no circumstance of his life has obliged him to revise it. Perhaps this is true for most of us. Delblanc had regarded himself as an artist of a sort, a drifting person, rather a failure. He had espoused theories of liberty and equality, as many do who feel they have made no mark on the world; but these had been diluted in society at large and by his own diffidence. Now, in the present circumstances of the ship, he found a world reduced, concentrated, the perfect model of a tyranny. He was driven to question his life's purposes.

Quite frequently, on some corner of the deck or in Delblanc's more spacious cabin, he and the surgeon would continue the discussions that had begun with their first meeting. Paris's liking for the other persisted, grew stronger. There was a warmth, a personal attractiveness about him and a patent sincerity impossible to resist. Even without this Delblanc would always have held a special place in his affection and regard: it was to Delblanc that he had laid bare his soul that night at the fort, in the

373

moonlit room, with the death-mask of the governor seeming to follow his every word and movement . . .

However, they could never altogether agree. Delblanc's contention was that any people, any nation or group, could change their condition immediately and radically by changing their habits of mind. 'Let the most oppressed people under heaven once change their thinking and they are free,' he said, his brown eyes shining with that extraordinary openness and un-defendedness of expression, his hands – which were shapely and strong – gesturing sharply. He had recently developed a habit of gesture curiously at odds with the gentlemanly nonchalance of his bearing, abrupt, almost fierce, controlling and delimiting, cutting off possible dissent. 'Even these people on the ship,' he said, 'both black and white, for they are imprisoned both.'

And Paris, weary and oppressed, suffering these days from a sort of feverish insomnia, would marvel at this pristine shine of Delblanc's, the freshness of his face and clothes, his philosophical empressement, the increasing eagerness of his manner, in which, though this was not to occur to the surgeon until later, there were already the signs of that fanaticism which would so profoundly affect them all. 'We can change our situation by thinking, you say,' Paris would reply. 'But whence comes this faith of yours that thinking can be changed? You are like a man who wants to build the upstairs rooms before he is sure of the foundations. Do you believe that habits of mind can be so easily reversed? For myself, I do not believe so.'

'If ideas are not innate – and they are not – they cannot be so deeply lodged as to be beyond uprooting,' Delblanc would say, with one of his eager, delimiting gestures. 'It is only a question of supplanting one set of associations with another. I am convinced of it . . . I know it in my heart and mind, Paris. Man can live free and not seek to limit the freedom of others so long as no one seeks to limit his.'

So these discussions between them took usually an accustomed course. But Delblanc's sense of mission was growing and he did not limit himself to Paris. Anyone at all – the weasel-faced Tapley, swabbing down the decks, a disgruntled Billy Blair coming up from scraping the slaves' quarters, Morgan in his

374

galley trying to find some new disguise for the rotten beef –
might find himself addressed by Delblanc and asked whether he
did not agree that the state of society was artificial and the
power of one man over another merely derived from convention.
Delblanc's manner was the same with all, friendly and open. At
first, tactics lagging behind conviction, he made no concession
to any imperfections of understanding in his audience. 'By
nature we are equal,' he said on one occasion to a vacantly
smiling Calley. 'Does it not therefore follow that government
must always depend on the consent of the governed?' He was
bookish and he used the language he knew. He even spoke to
McGann, asking him whether he did not think it true that the
character of man originated in external circumstances and could
be changed as these were changed.

The men listened, or appeared to listen, out of deference,
because he was a gentleman, because he was paying for his
passage. Delblanc saw soon enough that he was using the wrong
language with them and was beginning to try out a different
one until warned by Thurso in terms not very civil that if he
persisted in thus distracting the crew, he would be confined to
his quarters for the rest of the voyage. 'I will silence his blab-
bing,' he swore to Barton. 'I will board him up in his cabin.'
This proved unnecessary. One look at the captain's face was
enough to convince Delblanc. It was in his reaction to this
threat that he showed the quick grasp of realities that later
came to distinguish him. A man can do no good locked up in
his cabin. He went more circumspectly thereafter.

In this he was wise. Thurso's punishments now were mere
savagery – there was no pretence of justice in them. Davies,
elected as spokesman, went aft to complain about the quality of
the beef, which was offensive to the smell and visibly putrid.
Though he spoke respectfully and kept his eyes down, he had
hardly got out a dozen words before Thurso, in an access of
fury, had him seized up to the gratings and flogged him with a
rope's end, groaning and panting himself with the force of the
blows, only desisting when obliged by exhaustion.

'Davies will niver forgive it,' Sullivan confided to Paris. 'Niver,
not if he lives to be a hundred. He feels it was not deserved.

Davies is a steady man, that is why he was chose, an' he spoke to the captain fair. It would have been the cat, but Thurso couldn't wait for it to be fetched, he was in such haste for blood-lettin'.'

'These are difficult days,' Paris said. He had made it a point of principle not to join in any direct criticism of the captain.

Sullivan hesitated briefly, then said, 'I know it is not me place to speak, but there is bad will buildin' up towards the captain an' the mate . . .' Again he checked, this time for longer. His next words came in a rush: 'I don't care a farthin' what befalls Thurso, he has treated us worse than the blacks. But you stand close to him, Mr Paris, because you are related to the owner, beggin' your pardon . . . I wanted to say you should keep a weather eye open.'

'Thank you, I will remember it,' Paris said.

Sullivan gave his gap-toothed smile, relieved that his words had not been resented. Ever since the surgeon had spoken kindly to him in the matter of dancing the slaves, he had felt a loyal affection for Paris. He had come partly to utter the warning, partly to ask for a favour: he wanted Paris to act as witness for him.

'McGann will not believe I did it,' he said. 'We had a shillin' on it, McGann bet me a shillin' that I would not dare to face Thurso. Well, he knows I went, but the miscreated Caledonian pretends not to believe I spoke as I did.' Sullivan shook his head at McGann's obduracy and his long, unkempt black hair swung round his face. 'He says he won't part with his shillin' till he gets proof it was me music I spoke of to Thurso, an' the fact that I could not hear meself playin' owin' to the clankin' of the chains.'

'Yes, I see.' Paris saw from the other's expression that this was a serious matter for him. Sullivan was naked to the waist and terribly thin now, the bones of his shoulders standing out clearly; but his eyes had their usual look of glancing after some vision of splendour glimpsed and lost only moments before. 'I don't believe McGann has a shilling,' the surgeon said after a moment. 'He hasn't had any wages, has he? You will remember that he came aboard in rags and every stitch was taken off him and burned.'

376

'I remember it well. They done the exact self-same thing with me, only I was turned out smarter than McGann by far, I had a good coat on me with a set of brass buttons. Thim buttons have niver, to this day, been give back.'

'I didn't know that. But I wanted to say that if McGann came aboard with nothing . . .'

'It is not for the sake of the money,' Sullivan said. 'If it was the money, he could give me a note of hand. I know somethin' of the law, bein' a travelled man, an' I know a note of hand is legal tender. But then again, what is the use of wavin' a note of hand about when there is niver a drop left in the bottle? No, he has got to admit that I won the bet, that is all I am askin'. McGann has the scurvy very bad, he could drop off tomorrow, I have seen men go sudden with that, jokin' one minute an' dead the next, an' McGann is beginnin' to have the look of it about him. The matter must be set straight before he goes, that is what we mean by justice, Mr Paris. An' I thought, since you were present and heard what passed, you might find it in you to tell McGann how I put me request to the captain with a firm voice an' meanwhile lookin' him straight in the eye.'

'Very well,' Paris said. 'It can do no harm to try. I will confine myself to your actual words, I think, and leave McGann to imagine how you bore yourself.'

But before he found an opportunity for this McGann had been put in irons for begging rice from the bowls of the negroes. These last would sometimes give food to the men who had so ill-used them, a charity mysterious and moving to Paris, but rousing the captain to particular rage as tending to weaken the slaves further and reduce their chances of survival.

The surgeon had to make his way forward in order to see McGann, past the slaves grouped together on the main deck, guarded at present by Wilson, Lees and Hughes armed with whips and weighted sticks – Thurso had ceased to issue small arms to the crew. The men slaves were still fettered in pairs, the women and boys and girls allowed free. Paris noted in passing that the woman from the fort was there among them, that she seemed well enough, though emaciated. He had learned from Jimmy that she was not from the Gold Coast at all but much further west. She was from a people of nomads called Foulani, who lived by herding cattle. She did not look at him now as he went by.

McGann sat in his heavy leg irons on the forecastle deck. He listened to Paris's testimony with head lowered, the ragged cap drawn down over his brows. The pale, yellowish hue that had marked his face at first had darkened now and he had visible difficulty in breathing. Paris took the opportunity to look again at the blotches on his legs and found that they had degenerated into ulcerous wounds.

'That is what passed,' the surgeon said. 'I was present at the time and I heard Sullivan say the words. He asked me to come and tell you, so that you would be satisfied he had won the wager fairly.'

McGann glanced up at this. There was a blankness now in his gaze but the lines of his face were set in their old expression of dogged and fruitless calculation. 'Ye're on Sullivan's side then,' he said. His breath wheezed. 'I am not done out of a shillin' sae easy. Put in a word with Thurso for me, get me out these irons, an' ye can hae the money.'

'I have already asked Captain Thurso to free you,' Paris said gently. 'I will ask him again in any case. It does not depend on what you decide to do about your bet with Sullivan.'

Whether McGann believed this or not Paris never knew. He made no reply at the time, merely lowered his head with a sort of bitter obstinacy. He remained in irons all night, despite the surgeon's pleas. He was still alive and able to talk when Haines went to strike off his fetters, but when they began to help him to his feet he groaned loudly once and fell dead to the deck. Within an hour he had been sewn in canvas and weighted and committed with the scantest of ceremonies to the sea.

Two days later there was a change for the better in the weather, raising the spirits of all, though it was to prove no more than a respite, the crueller for its promise. A fair wind sprang up from the east, variable at first, then settling. The *Liverpool Merchant* made good way, tacking to begin with so as to take best advantage of the breezes. The fair spell coincided with a lull in the progress of the dysentery. For nine days there were no deaths. However, the slaves were much weakened and when they were got up on deck for washing, a number of them could not stand without support, despite whipping. Losses had been considerable. According to Barton, whose task it was to keep the tally, seventy-six negroes had died aboard ship since they had taken on their first slaves at Sierra Leone.

In spite of this, Thurso seemed in better mood now that the weather had quickened. He invited Paris and Delblanc to sup with him, Barton making the fourth. There was still part of a side of fresher beef, taken on board ready-salted at Cape Palmas and reserved for captain and officers. This was minced with biscuit, onions and rice to make a stew. Over it – and a bottle from his stock of Bordeaux – Thurso became communicative, informing the others that the longitude of Kingston, Jamaica, by Dr Halley's Chart, was seventy-six degrees and thirty minutes from London, and that they were therefore, by his reckoning, one hundred and forty-two leagues from it, provided he was right in his computation of the longitude of Cape St Ann. And as he squared his shoulders and stuffed his pipe with the rank black tobacco and glared before him at a possibly relenting demon, everything about the captain's manner indicated his belief that the computation was indeed correct.

Paris, still worried at the presence of scurvy aboard, took advantage of this better mood to ask the captain for some of his claret to dilute and serve out to the crew.

'My claret?' Thurso looked at him with genuine astonishment. 'Your wits have gone astray altogether, Mr Paris. I am to give up my claret for that mutinous scum in the forecastle?'

'McGann died of scurvy,' Paris said. 'And there are three others who show signs of it. It is due to some lack of nutriment. I thought perhaps the wine might do something, it is the juice of the grape after all. I thought I might mull it with a little sugar and some dried sage that I have.'

'Did you so? I am obliged to you for thus disposing of my wine. McGann was a pox-ridden little beast and he died because there was no more marrow left in his bones. There is nothing wrong with salt beef. Our navy has fed on it for centuries. Why are all the crew not down with scurvy, if it is owing to the food? They have all eaten the same.'

'That I do not know exactly,' Paris said.

'Ah, so there is something you do not know? Take my word, those three you mention are dragging their feet. If I catch any man scanting his work he will get a good dozen. What he will not get, Mr Paris, is any of the captain's wine.'

This was final enough and left no grounds for appeal. Paris was driven to ponder again on the green peppers that had been served to the negroes. Without speaking of it to anyone, he took a bag of dried peas from the stores and kept them rinsed in his cabin until they produced shoots. These he persuaded Morgan to add to the men's lobscouse just before serving. But as things turned out, he was not allowed time enough to detect any improvement, nor indeed to continue very long with his cultivation.

Hughes the climber, high in the rigging, saw long-tailed tropic birds above him and shoals of brightly coloured sunfish below – signs that they were coming into more enclosed waters. He saw also, full in the wind's eye, a luminous halo on the edge of a distant cloud and knew it for the precursor of stormy weather. But the storm, when it came, struck with such suddenness that they had barely time to get the slaves battened down between decks. The ship staggered with the shock of a huge sea that seemed to rise on them from nowhere. The tornado that accompanied it came from eastward and attacked with awesome force and fury. Above the creaking and straining of the ship Haines bellowed for all hands. Thurso stood at the mainmast beside Barton, who bawled out the captain's orders. The men at the clew lines struggled to hoist the stubborn, thundering canvas to the yards. Up above, Hughes and Wilson and Cavana and Blair, swinging on the cross-pieces while the ship reeled below them, fought to subdue the topsails and get them furled. The men were debilitated but the habit of discipline and the long practice of endurance kept them to the work and with surprising speed the ship was hove to under reefed fore and main topsails.

Thereafter she was driven by heavy squalls that struck at her repeatedly, with scarcely a pause. For six days the slaves could not be brought on deck. Their meals were served below in lulls between the squalls. Because of the rough seas and heavy rain, the air ports set along the sides of the ship between decks had to be closed, and tarpaulins thrown over the gratings, thus effectively cutting off all the means by which air could be admitted.

The sufferings of the negroes, already weakened by their privations and many of them with dysentery, were of the most appalling kind. Their rooms soon became insufferably hot. The confined air grew stifling through lack of oxygen and noxious with the breathing and sweating and excreting of so many bodies so close together. There was little more than two feet of headroom and the boards they lay on were of unplaned plank so that as they rolled helplessly in the hot, suffocating darkness, the rough surface of the wood took the skin from their backs and sides. In lapses of the wind Paris heard calls for help come from them and wild, demented cries. Sometimes he saw steam rise through the gratings.

Several times, when conditions permitted, he went down among them, accompanied always by three men, one to hold a lamp, the others carrying loaded sticks to prevent the slaves from biting at their legs and ankles. To Paris the place seemed like some infernal slaughterhouse. The floor of the rooms was slippery with the blood and mucus that had resulted from the dysentery, making the footing hazardous.

He brought bread soaked in water to refresh the slaves and tried to discover any who had fainted so that they might be brought up and revived. He always pulled off his shirt before going down, but he could never stand the heat for very long. On the last occasion he was already feeling sick and feverish before descending. After no more than ten minutes he was so overcome with the heat and stench and foul air that his senses swam and he would have fallen had it not been for the assistance of the men with him.

This heralded a bout of the fever which had visited him earlier in the voyage. For a day and a night he lay in his cabin, sweating, shivering, sleeping in troubled snatches, while the squalls slowly grew less violent and the weather began to settle again.

It was while he lay thus that Thurso had his idea. It was a

simple idea, but Thurso was a simple man, being an incarnation, really, of the profit motive, than which there can be few things simpler. His idea was based on certain undeniable facts. Deaths among the negroes during the six days of bad weather had amounted to eighteen – ten men, five women and three boys. The ship had been blown considerably off course and a good number more were likely to die before Jamaica was reached. Those that survived would not look attractive to the planters that came to bid for them. Cargo dying aboard ship of so-called natural causes was quite worthless, whereas cargo cast overboard for good and sufficient reason could be classed as lawful jetsam and thirty per cent of the market value could then be claimed from the insurers ... There was also the fact that Paris, who might otherwise have given trouble, need not be consulted, as he was at present confined to his cabin with fever and with luck would continue so some time longer. With real luck, Thurso thought darkly, he would die of it.

These facts in synthesis were present to the captain's mind as he sat alone in his cabin over his brandy. His counsellor, it seemed, had not altogether deserted him, but returned and spoke to him now again – it was for the last time. The counsel was more than rational, it was virtuous. Thurso knew he had nothing much to gain – only Kemp would benefit from the insurance money. He knew he would be retiring at the end of this voyage. He had money saved, he had a three-quarter share in the gold dust purchased with Barton. The negroes could live or die, it would not much matter to him. But he had his reputation to think of. He had always, throughout his long career, done everything in his power to give satisfaction to his owners ... Mindful of the need for lawful proceeding, he called Barton, Haines, Davies and Barber to his cabin, these being the only men surviving with any status on the ship.

The results of this nocturnal conference were what Paris woke to in the early morning. He felt light-headed and insubstantial, but free of fever. He sensed that the ship was listing slightly and guessed there had been some displacement in her hold. As he lay there, not fully awake yet but grateful for the calmer weather and his restored clarity, he heard a series of sounds quite inexplicable: a heavy clatter of chains on the deck somewhere above him, then running steps of several men together, a single cry, sustained and strangely exultant, brief splashing to starboard. Before he could believe he was properly awake, it came again, the clattering of chains on the deck – it sounded like fetters falling. He had heard no voices other than that single cry. Possessed by nothing stronger than curiosity at first and a sort of disbelief, like a man following clues in a dream, he got to his feet, dressed as hastily as his weakness allowed and made his way up to the deck.

In all the years of his life remaining, Paris was to carry the impression of that emergence into light and space. It was to accompany his days, glimpsed again and again in the wake of experiences of a certain kind, increases of light, intimations of freedom, a sort of puzzlement too; he could not at first understand what was happening, he was bewildered by the placid sea and sky – a sky enormous and blank, sheltering and condoning everything.

His first impression was of a fight in progress. Haines and Libby were half facing each other with something of the wrestler's crouch in their posture. Thurso and Barton stood on either side like seconds in a duel. Perhaps a dozen men, armed with the same short, heavy sticks, made a semicircle around them, as if to make sure neither combatant broke free.

But it was no fight, he saw now, there were no combatants. Two naked male slaves stood together side by side, unchained, up against the ship's rail. He heard Thurso utter some words. Haines and Libby moved towards the negroes, joined now by Wilson. Three powerful men ... The slaves were about to be manhandled over the side. Others had gone before them – it was what he had heard. That sound – they had taken the chains off them. Chains had a value still ... All the people were absorbed in the business, no one had seen him yet. One of the negroes stood straight and impassive, but the other had given way to fear, he had brought his hands up to plead for him and thrust forward his head as if to make an obeisance before his oppressors. It was a posture beast-like, baited, derided, and Paris recognized it ...

All thought of consequences departed from him. 'No!' he shouted. 'No!' He began to move rapidly towards them across the deck. Obeying an obscure impulse he raised his right arm to the fullest extent, as if in witness. With all the strength of his lungs, aiming his voice at the sky, he shouted again: 'No!'

THIRTY-SIX

Erasmus expressed his belief that the ship was to blame some days later in the course of his final interview with the man who was to have been his father-in-law. In the passion of it he came near to betraying his father altogether. 'It preyed on his mind,' he said, white-faced, hot-eyed, dressed impeccably in his suit of mourning velvet and his white stock. As the full extent of the financial disaster was borne in upon him, he had grown more than ever fastidious in his dress and person, washing frequently and changing his linen twice a day. He had taken also to the fashion of powdering his hair. 'It was the failure of his hopes in the ship,' he said, 'that led him to . . . that led to the seizure.'

If Wolpert noticed anything in the altered form of words or the brief hesitation he gave no sign of it. He thought it odd for the young man to attribute his father's death to such a minor cause of worry, odd and excessive, but Erasmus's nature went to extremes; in that he was like his father, who had just proved it again, Wolpert thought wryly, by the magnitude of his debts. Twenty shiploads of slaves would not have saved Kemp, in the pass his affairs had come to. So much was common knowledge now. 'The ship is not late enough yet to be given up as lost,' he said. 'It is hardly more than a year since she sailed and the trading is slow at present on the Guinea Coast. Your father would have known that.'

He had spoken to defend the father's reason against this judgement of the son, moved by a kind of pity for both. But the stiff composure of the young man's face did not change. He seemed to brace his shoulders more, as if sensing – and rejecting – the intention of kindness in the older man's words. 'The ship

385

left Africa six months ago,' he said coldly. 'We had letters . . . We had a letter from the captain.'

'Your cousin is with the ship, I understand,' Wolpert said. Kemp had let this fall one day, when they had been talking together in the street. 'He will be hard hit by this. Kemp was his benefactor.' Erasmus himself had never mentioned his cousin. It seemed he would make no response now, save for a brief nod. But after a moment he said, 'I believe the ship is lost and my cousin with her.'

Wolpert sighed and put his heavy hands together on the desk before him. 'We must come to the point,' he said. 'None of this is your fault, but naturally it has changed things. When we talk of losses, it is seldom useful to consider where the fault lies.' He paused again, looking at the set, expressionless face before him. He had never really warmed to Erasmus Kemp, noting always something relentless and oppressive in him, even in his visible devotion to Sarah; but he had grown to respect the young man's energy and ambition and he felt more kindly disposed to him now, when he was left with nothing but these, than perhaps ever before. 'Your mother has some means of her own, I believe?' he said.

'She has a small income from capital left in trust by her father.'

'She will not remain long in the house there, I suppose?'

'No, sir. The house is to be sold and all in it. She proposes to go to her sister in Norfolk.'

'She has impressed us all by her fortitude in this tragic loss.' A certain delicacy prevented Wolpert from saying more than this. It was years since he had seen Elizabeth Kemp with such spring in her step and colour in her cheeks. 'I am heartily sorry to see you both brought to this,' he continued after a moment. 'In what I am about to say now there is no blame for you. You could not have suspected the extent of your father's losses, and particularly his unlucky investments of these last months.'

'There were signs, if I had but heeded them.' He would not suffer this stranger to distribute degrees of blame. 'I was taken up with my own affairs,' he said.

Wolpert shrugged a little. 'That is only natural,' he said. 'But it is about those same affairs I am afraid we must speak now. It will be obvious to you that there cannot in the present circumstances be any contract of marriage with my daughter. There can be no question of an engagement, either official or otherwise, or any sort of an agreement or understanding which would place you in a special relation to her. You will understand that clearly, I hope?'

'I had understood it already,' the young man said, and made to get up.

'One moment.' Wolpert raised a hand. 'I have not yet finished. These debts are not yours, they were incurred by the firm of Kemp, in which you had not yet become a partner. The creditors will recover what they can and that will be the end of the matter, as far as –'

'No, sir, excuse me, it shall not be the end.'

'Pray allow me to finish. I have been impressed by your abilities. I am prepared to offer you a place in the family firm at a salary to be agreed on. Thirty pounds a year was what I had in mind – I think you will agree that is not ungenerous. You would be an assistant to my son Charles, who conducts the transport side of the business. There is no need for you to answer at once, but I am sure that the briefest consideration will reveal the advantages of the offer.'

'To a pauper such an offer must have obvious advantages,' Erasmus said with a bitter twist of the lips. He remained silent for some moments, then rose to his feet. 'I have no need of time to consider,' he said, standing very straight. 'I thank you for your offer but I must refuse it. Your kindness requires I should explain why. I cannot agree with what you say about the debts my father has left. My father's debts are mine, whether I am legally responsible for them or not. I intend to clear his name and discharge the bankruptcy. All the creditors shall be repaid in full, with due interest. I cannot do this on the salary you offer, no, not if you tripled it.'

Wolpert sat still for some moments, taken by surprise. 'Well,' he said at last in a tone of some displeasure, getting up in his turn, 'you know your own business best, I suppose.' In fact, he did not at all suppose it at the moment. There was nothing at all quixotic in the merchant's outlook on life. Debts were the business of those who had contracted them. That Erasmus would persist in this he did not believe – nor even that the intention would outlast the rawness of his loss. It was the young man's high-handedness that had nettled him, as on occasion before. Below this lay a certain relief: he had done his duty – and Erasmus might have made a difficult subordinate. There was little left to say between them now – there never had been much. 'You have my good wishes, in any case,' Wolpert said as they shook hands. 'My daughter expressed the wish to see you. She is waiting for you in the small parlour across the hall.'

He found her standing against the tall window that looked over the terrace and the long slope of the grounds towards the lake. She made a movement towards him as he entered, but checked on seeing how straight and still he stood there, just inside the door.

'Your father said I should find you here,' he said. He had prepared himself for this interview, rehearsed it. The need to conduct himself properly took all feeling from his voice. Three days before, in the secrecy of his room, in the house that no longer belonged to them, he had wept for Sarah until he was feverish. There were no tears left in him now.

She waited a moment, then said, 'You have refused, I take it?'

'Refused?'

'My father's offer, you have refused it?'

She was standing against the light. He did not feel that he was seeing her clearly. His eyes felt strangely weak, perhaps with the constant effort of these last days to show the world a clear and defiant regard. He blinked to focus them. He saw Sarah turn her head to one side. There was some movement in the line of her shoulder as she stood in her summer dress against the light and he knew that she was crying.

'So, that was your idea, then?' he said. 'You set your father on to it.'

'Do you think he is a man to be set on?'

The tears were in her voice. Why was she crying? It seemed to him that all the loss was his. 'No,' he said, with an odd

388

attempt to judiciousness, 'I don't think that. But you asked him this favour. He doesn't refuse you anything, does he?' It sounded like a jibe, though he had spoken gravely. 'Weighing bales and measuring the width of cart wheels for Charles Wolpert,' he said after a moment.

'It would have been a way for us.' There was an attempt now, in spite of her distress, at the angry sarcasm she kept for quarrels. 'He would not take favours,' she said. 'Oh no, not Erasmus Kemp. This was not a favour, either – my father knows your worth. You did not think of me, not for one moment.'

'A way?' He could not understand what she meant. 'I would take favours,' he said, with a sudden passionate intensity. 'I would take any means to restore his good name. When I asked him, when I told him my feelings and asked his permission to marry, and he consented, he said that he and I were different, that we had different characters. He said he would stop to look at something but I would keep on with it until it had grown so that it couldn't be changed or touched. But it wasn't true, we are the same.' He raised one arm in a stiff gesture of emphasis. 'He let this grow until he couldn't touch it anywhere. It wasn't possible for him to disentangle one thing from another. So the ship came to stand for everything.'

'I have been mistaken,' he heard her say in low tones. 'I supposed you would fight to keep me – for the hope of not losing me. I thought it would be something to keep your heart up in this terrible time, if you knew that I didn't give you up, in spite of everything, that I would wait . . .' She paused, then said in a tone of wonder almost, 'You have not thought of me at all.'

'I am not the same as I was,' he said. 'We cannot marry now, it is over. I have lost everything.'

At this she came quickly towards him, placed her hands on his rigid shoulders, looked up into his face. 'Not everything,' she said. 'Not everything.' But she faltered at the set cast of his features, the bright, abstracted stare. He was not seeing her.

'I don't want to be thought different from him,' he said. 'There is something else I remember him saying.' He had made no move to take her in his arms or touch her in any way, and after a moment she turned aside from him.

Feeling the touch withdrawn, watching her move away, his loss was bitter to him. He had felt for that moment all the essence of promise in her, the warmth of her hands on him, the uncertain tenderness of her breath, the wide, undefended look of her eyes. Her words were brave but he knew she was wrong, she was deceiving herself, he had lost everything. He said, 'He told me he should never have gone into cotton. He began in sugar, you know.'

He was silent for some moments. He did not know what to talk about. There was nothing to say. She was part now of the debts and losses, part of the restitution he had to make – he was making a start with her. 'I intend to put that right,' he said. 'I intend to go into sugar.'

'You will do as you please,' she said. 'Nothing anyone else says will make a farthing of difference to you, I know that well, everyone knows it.' This calling of the world to witness was something she did often in argument; but her voice quivered now with the first real pain she had ever had to deal with alone. 'When you first began coming, when you looked at me so, I did not find you agreeable at all, I thought you overbearing and farouche, and everybody thought it too. Then you ruined the whole play and you knew that I so much wanted to be in it, and I thought that it meant you cared more for me than you cared about pleasing me, and this was different from the other young men that talked to me. I know now that I was a fool to think it – it was pleasing yourself that you were set on.'

He did not know how to answer her, nor why she was reviving past complaints when there was only this overwhelming present of his poverty. It was as if she was speaking in a language he was not fully familiar with. 'It is a simple matter enough,' he said. 'Your father has forbidden the match. I cannot go against him. I have been left without a penny. I have nothing to offer you.'

'No, Erasmus,' she said, and her voice was clear and unfaltering now. 'That is not the reason.' Once more, for the last time, he saw on her face the expression he had always found both fascinating and disturbing: the half-closed eyes, the luminous pause before the words came, that brief contortion of the mouth, like a prelude to ecstasy. But the words when they came were sad with final knowledge: 'It is not because you have nothing to offer me but because you have nothing now to add me to.'

He felt anger at this. She had belittled his sacrifice. With a brief phrase of farewell he turned away. She did not answer, but as he passed out of the room she called loudly after him in a voice that returning tears had made inarticulate – perhaps it was an attempt to call his name.

The declarations had been made already in the course of these interviews with father and daughter; but they needed to be uttered in the shrine of his room, where loneliness and custom could bind them into the sanctity of a vow.

As always, his possessions, things deeply familiar to him, acted on his sensibilities like objects of ritual. The fact that the house and most of its contents would soon be coming under the hammer gave force and fervour to his words, as a promise takes more poignant strength when uttered in the midst of danger and change. Kneeling at his bedside while sparrows chirped their loves in the eaves over the window, he spoke to God and his silver spurs and the pistols on the wall and his mother's framed embroidery extolling the virtues of the meek.

'Every penny.' It was less than a whisper. There were only the slight, plosive sounds of his dry and fervent lips, the click of tongue in the dry mouth. 'I will restore my father's good name. I will go into sugar.'

BOOK TWO
1765

PART EIGHT

THIRTY-SEVEN

Sir William Templeton, His Majesty's Principal Secretary to the West India Office, was at his dressing-table, still in turban and flowered banyan. His levee had scarcely begun. He had just dismissed with promises a half-pay naval officer, unemployed now that the wars with France were ended, who was seeking his influence with the Admiralty but lacked the guineas necessary to assure it.

His footman entered to announce the name of a gentleman on business waiting at present in the ante-room with the others, but not the sort to kick his heels long, the footman remarked – there was between servant and master a close understanding of mutual convenience.

'He would not be fobbed off,' the footman said. 'He has a short way with him, sir.'

'Aye, and a long purse, you rascal, I make no doubt,' his master said. 'He must have shown you the lining of it for you to bring his name with this dispatch.'

Briefly pleased with this piece of wit he twitched thin lips in the looking-glass. His face was narrow and long, very pale beneath the crimson silk of his turban, with a mouth that turned up at the corners in an accidental simper oddly at variance with the generally downward-sloping, lugubrious cast of his features. He knew who this visitor was, though he did not say so to the servant, whose eye was upon him keenly.

'Where the devil is my hot chocolate?' he said. 'Why am I kept waiting in this fashion? Now is the time I need sustenance, sir, as I address myself to the business of the day. Get within and see to it and send Bindman hither to me so I may discuss with him what I shall be wearing.'

'Yes, sir. And the gentleman?'

'When you have seen to all that,' Templeton said with assumed carelessness, 'you may admit this person.'

He spent the interval before his mirror. Entering, Erasmus Kemp saw the Secretary's long face, gaudy with rouge just applied but not smoothed in yet, looking fixedly at him in the glass, framed by the swimming or flying putti round the rim and beyond this by the pale blue and rose pink stucco cornucopias round the arches of the recessed bedchamber.

For some moments the two men regarded each other thus. Then Templeton rose and advanced with languid affability, taking short and mincing steps in his loose Turkish slippers. 'My dear sir, curse me, this is a pleasure,' he said, holding out his hand. 'Will you take a seat, sir? I trust you are well?'

'Tolerably well, I thank you.' Kemp regarded the Secretary with a sombreness the warmth of his welcome had done nothing to relax. The years had taken colour from his cheeks and compressed his lips with a certain grimness of endurance or denial – though it was not evident whether of claims from within or without. But the eyes were unchanged: narrow and very dark, with a piercing insistence of regard that verged always on the antagonistic. He was dressed faultlessly in a suit of dark brown velvet set off by foams of lace at the neck and cuffs. His black hair was longer now, in accordance with the fashion; he wore it free of powder, caught in a dark red ribbon behind.

'We need not make a long business of this,' he said. 'I shall not encroach on your time more than is needful. You have affairs of state to look to.'

'Cares of state, sir, I prefer to name 'em. There is a neat epigram to be got out of that rhyme, but these days, alas, I have no time for composition. Do you scribble yourself, sir? No? One needs peace for it. You will not mind if I continue with my toilette? I am bidden to my Lady Everney's in the forenoon.'

'Indeed? By all means, continue. I would not have you disappoint Lady Everney.'

Templeton shot him a sharp glance in the mirror, but made no reply. He had begun touching in the paint with a small brush.

398

'You know me and you know whom I represent,' Kemp was beginning, 'so there is no need for –'

A small negro page boy in a white turban and surcoat came in bearing a sugar bowl, a steaming cup of chocolate and a plate of wafers on a japanned tray.

'About time, my pretty fellow,' Templeton said. 'Set it down here beside me. You must learn to be sharper.'

The little boy smiled and his eyes flashed eagerly. He had teeth of amazing perfection.

'He doesn't know much English as yet,' Templeton said. 'I haven't had him above two weeks. I got him at auction at George's Coffee House in the Strand. I gave the last one to my Lord Granville, who had taken a fancy for him. This one is even better-looking. One should buy them pockmarked of course, 'tis more secure, but I like a smooth skin. Will you take some chocolate?'

'Thank you, no,' Kemp said. 'I have breakfasted but lately.' This was not strictly true as it was now mid-morning, but a certain kind of disgusted impatience was growing in him and he had no wish to share more than was necessary with the man before him – the knowledge there was between them had to be shared, and the space of the room and the stale air in it.

'So then,' Templeton said to the negro boy, waving an irritable hand. 'Why are you waiting there? Shoo, shoo, shoo. Go.'

'I am come on the same grounds as last time,' Kemp said in level tones. 'Nothing of substance has been achieved on your part since then, in spite of the monies made over to you for your use as you thought fit.'

'Ah, base metal, curse me, I knew we should soon come to money,' Templeton said in a tone of disdain.

'Yes, sir, money,' Kemp said with a slight smile. 'You find it a wearisome topic, I dare say, but those who dispense it incline to take an interest in how it is used.'

His disgust persisted. It was more for himself now. I should have sent someone else, he thought. But he trusted no one. He knew that Templeton was frightened and that his every gesture and inflection was assumed to disguise the fact. He knew more: he knew the man's circumstances, his connections, those who

399

were in his interest, those who were in his pocket, his gambling debts, his taste for boys, his wife of the days before his preferment alone and drunken in their country house, consoling herself with footmen. He was sick to the soul with his knowledge of Templeton.

'No doubt it is perverse of them to press enquiry so far,' he said drily, 'but there it is.'

'You are sarcastic, sir. It is not true to say that nothing has been achieved. I have risked displeasure at court by resisting demands for increased sugar duties to swell the revenues. There has been no increase since they were raised to help finance the war with the French, and that is close on four years now.'

He had spoken with indignation, real or assumed. But there was nothing assumed about the unsteadiness of his hands when he set down his cup. 'Not to have agreed then would have cost me my place, it would have branded me as unpatriotic,' he said.

'If you will forgive me,' Kemp said, in the same level tones, 'the duties would have been kept down in any case, even without your support. As you are aware, we have fifty-three members of the House of Commons voting in our interest directly, as well as some others, whom we both know, whose pockets are affected one way or another. We are strong enough to turn the balance in parliament on any West India business. It is not for the conduct of bills in the House that we need your interest. You know that well, I think, Sir William. We need your voice behind the scenes, in the Council, your urgent –'

At this moment the valet entered with garments draped over one arm, holding a long stick with a half a dozen wigs on it before him like a lance.

'Ah, Bindman,' Templeton said, grateful for the diversion. 'Let us see, now.'

'I thought the claret-coloured suit, sir, with the silver stitching,' the valet said, after a brief bow to Kemp, 'and a silver wig to go with it; a dull-toned wig will not do well with silver threaded on wine-colour, especially seeing that the suit is satin and has a high shine to it.'

He had spoken as he was obviously accustomed to speak, in high-pitched, intimate tones, as if there were no one else present.

He took some gliding steps into the bedchamber and laid the clothes on the bed. 'This one?' he said returning, lifting one of the wigs delicately from the stick. He had produced from his pocket a little powder-bellows.

'Wait, you rogue,' Templeton said. 'Why do you always hurry me so?'

'I would have this interview in private,' Kemp said coldly. 'I cannot speak to you while this fellow capers about with wigs.'

Dignity required some delay in response to this. Templeton had commenced already to unfasten the high turban. He continued to do so, glancing at Kemp through the glass. Typical of the low-born fellow to be rendered uneasy by the presence of servants. Son of a provincial bankrupt. The times were bad that could throw up such creatures into positions of power. Templeton had his own sources of information and there was a file on Kemp in his office at the Ministry.

He took in the careless, lounging posture of his visitor, a carelessness at odds with the tight lips, the insolent intensity of the eyes. A man who had come from nothing and nowhere. It was a career meteoric even in these times of opportunity for the clever and unscrupulous. He had begun as an employee of the firm of Thomas Fletcher, which carried on an extensive trade with Jamaica, dealing on the London Exchange in sugar grown on its own plantations and imported in its own ships. He had made himself useful to his employers in a number of ways, some of them on the edge of legality and some beyond. Templeton knew something of these last, though not enough to be useful. Kemp had been twice to Jamaica to increase the firm's holdings by bribing or intimidating local officials to sign foreclosure orders on small tenants who had fallen into arrears. These services and others more nebulous had brought him to a full partnership in five years. He had married sugar too, in the person of the daughter of Sir Hugo Jarrold, whose merchant bank had been founded on his connections in the West India trade. Elizabeth Jarrold had neither looks nor elegance but had made up for both by the fortune she had brought, said to be eighty thousand pounds. Kemp's present wealth could only be guessed at; but the most important fact about him from

Templeton's point of view was that he had lately become Vice-President of the West India Association and could thus speak for the entire faction . . .

The turban was removed now and Templeton's long, nearly naked head stood revealed. 'Bindman is discretion itself,' he said at last. 'He has been with me these five years.'

'He has been with me no more than five minutes but I find it enough,' Kemp said. 'I should esteem it a favour.'

'Very well.' Templeton assumed an air of fatigue. 'Bindman, you can go. I will dress myself this morning.'

'Dress yourself, sir?' The valet's attentive bearing was ruffled by solicitude and surprise.

'Yes, yes, yes. Dress myself. 'Sblood, man, do you think me a puppet with no independent powers of locomotion? Go, sir. And tell Biggs to send away all those who are waiting. I will have no time for anyone this morning.'

Kemp waited till the servant had withdrawn before resuming. He was telling Templeton what for the most part the latter knew already. The local assembly in Kingston, elected by popular vote in the colony and controlling the purse-strings, was bringing pressure to bear on the Governor, whose salary they also controlled, to authorize policies hostile to the interests of the absentee landlords whom Kemp represented. They were seeking to confiscate tracts of land and to redistribute them among small farmers on the island. These measures, of course, were opposed by His Majesty's Government . . .

'Or they should be, sir,' Kemp said. 'If they are not, we are abandoning one of the most sacred duties of government, which is the preservation of property. The great end of men's entering into society in the first place is the enjoyment of their properties in peace and safety.'

'That is most certainly true, sir. And this present administration of my Lord Rockingham, in which I have the honour to serve, has ever been dedicated to ensuring it.'

Kemp's air of nonchalance fell away and he sat forward abruptly. 'Then why is this policy allowed to continue unchecked?' he demanded. 'The legislation is there. Why is it not enforced? Why, above all, are you not more active on our

402

behalf, in view of the sums, the very considerable sums, that you have received? Why am I thus obliged to come in person here and wait on your pleasure and consume my time away? Do you think I find it agreeable, sir? Do you think I find it congenial? Do you?'

'Good God!' Templeton was shocked at the blaze of antagonism that had come to the other's eyes. 'How can I answer you?' he said. He had an impulse to get up and put the dressing-table between them. It was almost as if the fellow were gathering for a spring, as he said later that day to a crony at White's: 'I tell you, I feared for my person,' he said, 'and there was nothing there but the stick with my wigs on, which that wretch Bindman had left behind.'

It had seemed inexplicable, this spasm of fury, quite out of keeping with their conversation, which had been progressing on accustomed lines. Templeton was astute enough, but we never fully succeed in understanding what we cannot feel and so he did not suspect the sense of outrage that had come to Kemp to find himself using the same language, exchanging similar phrases with a man he so despised, as if they were both of the same kidney, as if he had waded through the years only to make an embrace of minds with this depraved fop. If he had suspected anything of this, Templeton would have found it grotesque, in a man who was so strenuously engaged in protecting his own interest. That he did not suspect it was a mark of virtue in a nature not otherwise richly endowed with this commodity. He was venal and corrupt but he did not dignify his motives to himself – only to others.

'It is not so simple,' he said now, in a tone he strove to make conciliatory. 'Let me play the adversary for a while and point out to you the arguments on the other side. The plantations you speak of are owned by landlords who do not set foot on the island once in ten years. Their estates are mismanaged by overseers regrettably subject to the corruption of the climate, in other words liquor and whores, sir, and milked by dishonest attorneys, with consequent loss of duty to the Crown at a time when the demand for sugar is rising. Then there is the disproportion in population, with dangers of a slave revolt. There must be found some way of encouraging more Englishmen to settle in the colony – there were barely twenty-five thousand in the last count, against more than a hundred thousand blacks. The Deficiency Laws have failed to restrain the practice of absenteeism, hence the clamour for redistribution of land in the local assembly. There are those in parliament sympathetic to these demands, especially among the followers of Chatham. Need I name 'em to you?'

Kemp looked down for a while in silence. His anger had gone, leaving a certain familiar sense of desolation. 'No, you need not,' he said. 'I know well enough who they are. For us, you see, the issue is simple, in spite of what you say. We are ready to guarantee an income for the Governor, whomever he be, that will make him independent of the assembly. But the real change must come in the workings by which the decisions of the Council are put into effect. The Council has the power, the statutory power, to disallow local legislation even when backed by the Governor. If there is delay, it must be because some person or persons are obstructing the procedure. This is not a question of legislation, it is a question of influence. That is why you were approached in the first place, so that you could use your voice behind the scenes.'

But how strong was this voice? he wondered, looking at the rouged and sorrowful face before him, with its thick eyebrows and slight, incongruous simper. And how often, and how earnestly, was it being raised? It had been his private belief for some time now that Templeton was taking bribes from the opposite party too. Men like this, grown old in the practice of chicanery, were difficult to frighten for long; they could not easily believe that the streams which had nourished them so long could dry up. In the purlieus of Westminster bribes were paid like pensions, long after it had been forgotten whose interest was secured by them . . .

'We want results,' he said quietly. 'We are tired of waiting. It is possible that you imagine we would rather pay you for nothing than risk your disfavour by ceasing. If so, you had better disabuse yourself. That may have been the case in the time of my predecessor, but I assure you it is not the case now. I take the view that when a man's friendship has not helped us we have nothing to fear from his enmity.'

He got up, looking squarely at the man before him. 'You, on the other hand, have much to fear from ours,' he said. 'Put on wisdom with your wig today, Sir William, and ponder my words well. I trust I make my meaning clear to you?'

'Abundantly crystalline, sir, curse me, translucent,' Templeton said, meeting the other's gaze with tolerable firmness.

On this less than cordial note the two men parted. Kemp found his chairmen waiting in the courtyard with the sedan, as instructed; but he paid them and sent them away, feeling the need for air and movement.

He left the Albert Gate on his left and began to walk towards Hyde Park Corner, crossing the Westbourne by the little wooden footbridge. After a while he became aware of a stinging sensation in his right hand and saw that the palm bore shallow lacerations which were bleeding slightly. He could not at first understand this, then he realized that it must have happened during his interview with Templeton: he had clenched his fist so tightly that he had cut himself with his nails. Only the right one, he thought vaguely – he had been holding his cane with the other. Increasingly these days he found himself becoming aware of overwrought feeling through some discomfort felt later, rather as one is woken by some pain in the night.

He had the wall of the park now on his left. Across from him, on the opposite side, there was a row of small houses, then the White Horse Inn with St George's Hospital beyond it, fronting on to Knightsbridge. He crossed the road and turned off along-side the hospital garden, which ran into Grosvenor Place. This had no buildings at its lower end, giving directly on to the open heathland known as Five Fields. Kemp stood for a while here looking out over the ponds and brick kilns.

It was a quiet corner. The rumble of carts and coaches on the cobbles of Piccadilly and the cries of hawkers came to him, but distantly. A ragged, crippled man was playing a barrel-organ at the Knightsbridge end of the square, dragging one leg and glancing up at the windows for pennies. The music carried to Kemp, softened and distorted, unrecognizable. He could see the gleam of the ponds and gulls wheeling above them and the figures of fishermen. It was early October and the weather had been wet and windy, though today there was some faint sunshine. He could smell the damp leaf mould from the garden behind him.

He recalled with distaste the conversation just past, the posturing and evasions of Templeton. He had nailed the fellow, though, in the end. What steps could have led him to such a man? He could almost believe he had come upon him by some unrepeatable chance, as one might come upon a creature in a labyrinth. But of course it was not by chance . . . He experienced a slight feeling of nausea at the openness of the sky, the flashes of the gulls' wings over the pale water, the spaces beyond. London ended here, his London at least. It lay all to the back of him, the precincts of government, the banks and counting-houses; and with it lay all he had achieved in these twelve years: his partnership in Fletcher & Company, his holdings in his father-in-law's bank, his house in St James's, the power and position that had come with his money. He had laboured and denied himself and stopped at nothing, however unworthy. His promise, his father's memory, had purged everything of wrong. In restoring his father's name and credit, he had established and consolidated his own. Kemp was a name to be reckoned with again. And he was still some months away from his thirty-fifth birthday.

It was a triumph . . . He looked again at the solitary fishermen, dark in the distance. There would be pike in those deep ponds. Beyond them, he knew, there was the toll-gate and beyond that the road through the market gardens of Marylebone and the fields where the cowkeepers had their shacks . . . Something, some nostalgia or desire for completeness, came to him with the strength of a physical impulse, though without aim or direction. The music of the barrel-organ was nearer now. Kemp moved away across the square but after a moment returned to give the man a florin. For a moment he met the dark eyes, saw marks of hardship on the face, had a fleeting sense of the streets the man would drag through, grinding out the same tunes.

He went down the steps and cut across the park past the

keeper's lodge and came out on Piccadilly, turning off again when he drew opposite the reservoir. His house was on one corner of St James's Square, overlooking the railed gardens.

He found his wife at home as he had expected, still in her bedroom. It was past midday now but she had just risen. He knew her movements well: she would spend two hours at least on her toilette, take her tea and leave the house in late afternoon on a round of visits. They would not meet again that day – perhaps not until this time tomorrow. He wanted to speak to her about her father, Sir Hugo, with whom he was now on rather bad terms because of recent business disagreements and because it was to her father that Margaret complained of him.

The elderly French maid was in the room, clearing away the remains of breakfast. He noted that as soon as he appeared she began to delay. Fritz, his wife's poodle, yapped when he entered – there was an old enmity between them, unyielding on both sides. Margaret Kemp chided her dog and greeted her husband in more or less the same tones. Across the top of her head there lay a large round cushion covered with black crêpe, over which the hair was combed back and fastened with curlers. She was a martyr to fashion and the fashion now was for a high, piled-up style. Her face was completely covered with white cream.

'Will you ask her to take away the things and leave us alone for a while?' Kemp said, receiving in response a snap of black eyes from the maid – Marie shared the poodle's feelings precisely.

'Why? You know she does not gossip.'

Kemp sighed. It was the second time that morning. 'I know nothing of the sort,' he said. 'Can you not exist for ten minutes without her presence in the room?'

'I am glad I have not a suspicious nature,' his wife said. 'Go, Marie, I will ring when I need you.'

Kemp waited until the maid had gone, then began to speak to her about her father's latest passion, which was for speculating in negroes. The old man had somehow become convinced – and how and by whom were among the things Kemp most wanted to know – that the trade in slaves was shortly to be made illegal by Act of Parliament. He had instructed his agents in Barbados and Virginia to buy up as many blacks as possible in order to get compensation from the government when the bill was passed into law.

'He is going mad,' Kemp said. 'That is the only possible conclusion. There is no such a bill in prospect. There are not above three members of parliament who take the abolitionist line. I am told reliably that your father is buying up negroes of no quality whatever, with no value on the market. Old, diseased, crippled, it makes no difference. He has got fixed in his mind this absurd notion of compensation. The blacks will all have to be fed and kept alive somehow, at great expense. Half of them will die on his hands in spite of everything.'

The mask of cream which covered his wife's face allowed no expression, except what showed in her eyes. These were brown and glistening and full of ill-humour. They were not looking at him.

'Could you not find an occasion to speak to him and dissuade him from this folly?' he said.

'Lord, sir,' she said, 'you speak with rare feeling. 'Twas in those very tones you wooed me. I would not have credited you with such tender solicitude for my father's welfare.'

Kemp said nothing for a while. Pride made him wish to seem indifferent to the sarcasm, with the same indifference he showed towards the irregularities of her conduct, her absences from home, her suspected infidelities. At heart he felt it to be no more than justice. He saw it as he might have seen a balance sheet. The money she had brought had provided substantial investment funds much earlier than he had hoped, at a time of expanding opportunity in the London property market. She had saved him the many years of scheming it would still have taken to pay off his father's debts. He had protested love in order to get her and since he had not repaid her in that currency, she was free to choose other means of repayment. He kept to his side of things by not reproaching her. And it was this that gave her the greatest offence of all.

He looked at her obscured face, the grotesquely high setting of her hair. Seven years of marriage and he could not remember a time when there had been trust between them. 'Well,' he said at last, 'if you have any regard for him you will disabuse his mind.' A thought struck him suddenly. 'Try to discover who is communicating these ideas to him,' he said.

She had begun to remove the cream from her face with moist pieces of cotton, dropping the used swabs into a little silver dish on the bed beside her. The clear complexion she had possessed when he married her, and which had been her best feature, was gone now; unhappiness had made her sallow and frequent use of cosmetics was clouding the skin.

'You are asking me, in other words, to spy on my own father,' she said after a moment.

'It is for his good and ours, the good of the bank. I am asking from you no more than the duty of a wife.' Kemp had no sense of irony in saying this and was surprised to see a smile come to his wife's face. The interests of the bank were paramount in his mind. He took a few steps across the room. 'I would be interested to know who is spreading these rumours of abolition,' he said. His movements had brought him too close to the cushion on which the poodle was reclining and it set up a furious yapping, baring its teeth, and shaking the beribboned tufts of its mane at him.

'Be quiet, you little brute,' he said.

'Pray do not disturb poor Fritz.'

'Poor Fritz, is it?' Kemp eyed the beast. 'I have never been able to see what a dog like that is good for.'

A silence fell between them. Now that he had said what he had come to say, he did not know what else to talk about. His wife's activities and interests were remote to him, her circle of acquaintance quite different.

'I shall not be home this evening,' he said at last. 'I am dining out. I shall not need the coach, however.'

'Well, that is a blessing. You are at your club?'

'No, it is a celebration banquet of the Association. I have spoke to you of it, I think?'

But he saw that she remembered nothing of the matter, and he himself could not be sure whether he had mentioned it to her or not. He certainly would have said nothing about the plans of the younger element to go on afterwards to a Covent Garden tavern for a meeting of the Trionfi Club, of which he had now, as Vice-President of the West India Association, become the leading figure. The activities of the Trionfi were under oath of secrecy. But he thought it possible he had mentioned the banquet, as it was such a great occasion. The Assembly in Jamaica, in order to raise revenue, had sought to impose a duty on every negro imported into the colony. The Sugar Interest, supported by the Company of Merchants Trading to Africa, had naturally resisted this iniquitous tax on their profits. There had been a protracted legal battle, but the Association's lawyers had pleaded the matter successfully and the Board of Trade had finally condemned the law as unjustifiable, improper and prejudicial to British commerce.

Something of this he tried to tell her now, but quite soon she interrupted him to ask if Marie could be recalled. 'I must have her back,' she said. 'I did not think you would stay so long. She must positively come and unpin this cushion, she is the only creature in the world that knows how to do it.'

On this he took his leave. He spent the afternoon closeted in his study with his secretary, dealing with correspondence of various sorts. His position in the Association, which he took very seriously, had involved him in much extra work. The President, Sir James Wigmore, over eighty now and increasingly infirm, did little these days but put in an appearance on ceremonial occasions – he was due to make a speech at the banquet that evening. This was to be held at the premises of the African Merchants off Chancery Lane. The members of the Association were guests of the Company for the evening.

The streets were miry after the recent rain and he wore a long riding-cloak to protect his royal-blue satin suit. He stabled his horse in the courtyard, consigned cloak and boots to the stable-boy, changed into the elegant wedge-heeled shoes he had brought with him and mounted to the ante-rooms, where he was announced in stentorian tones. There were a number of people already assembled here, several of them known to him. Sir James arrived and passed directly into the dining-hall. Distributing smiles, his head in its full-bottomed wig trembling incessantly, he was deftly supported to his place at the head of the table by a liveried footman of Herculean proportions. His installation was the signal for the call to dinner. The orchestra in the gallery struck up with 'Conquering Heroes' and some seventy persons trooped to their places at the long table amidst the splendour of coffered ceilings, double rows of Doric pillars and gleaming stucco mouldings in blue and gold recently completed by the Italian plasterer, Pietro Francini, at very considerable expense.

The first toast came, as usual, after the soup. It was delivered by the Chairman of the Company, who welcomed the guests and drank perdition to any who would lay import duties on British goods. Sir James was then helped to his feet by the footman who stood behind his chair. He gave thanks to their hosts on behalf of the West India Association and raised his glass to the principles so triumphantly vindicated by the recent decision of the Tribunal. He added his congratulations to those who had pleaded the case and particularly the advocate who had led them, Mr Joshua Moore, who was a guest of honour that evening. Through their victory the value to the nation of the Triangular Trade had been clearly recognized. The East India trade was pernicious, in his opinion, draining England of bullion and committing her to buy unnecessary wares. The Africa trade, by contrast, was a sane and healthy trade, carried on by means of English manufactured goods and rendering the nation independent of foreigners for her supply of tropical products ... Sir James drew himself up and looked with palsied benignity round the table. 'And to what tropical product do I refer in particular, gentlemen? May I hear your answer?'

The reply came in jovial shouts: 'Sugar, sir! Sugar!'

'So here is to sugar,' the old man said, and drank a second glass amid cheers.

Kemp, sitting a little lower down the table, glanced at the lawyer, who had been placed opposite him. Moore had a sharp-boned, watchful face, flushed a little now with what he had drunk. He had listened with good-humoured impassivity to Sir James's congratulations. Meeting Kemp's eye, he nodded and raised his glass. 'Your health, sir,' he said.

'And yours.' Kemp rarely drank enough to disturb his

judgement, but he was drinking more than usual tonight. He felt some tension about the meeting of the Trionfi planned for later; it was his inauguration as the new president of the club and his conduct would come under scrutiny . . . 'Some of us may differ from Sir James as regards the East India trade,' he said to Moore, 'but we are unanimous in our admiration for the way you conducted our case.' The fellow would have been just as eloquent on the other side, if his fee had come from that quarter, he thought with some disgust. Lawyers were mercenary creatures. This one was Irish, too – a nation of talkers.

'I am glad of your good opinion,' Moore said with a slight smile. 'I take it you approve of the East India trade?'

Kemp hesitated a moment from habitual caution. But this was public knowledge. 'My firm supports the Company of Elliot and Son,' he said. 'They are one of the main importers of China tea. Did you know that duty was paid on more than six million pounds of tea coming into this country last year? And the volume will increase. All reports indicate that our new Colony of India is capable of large-scale production. The East India Company is doing us a service. The more tea, the more sugar – it takes no prodigious wit to see that.'

'I see you are far-sighted, sir,' the other said. There was something slightly ironical in the tone of this. Kemp found himself being regarded by a pair of humorous blue eyes. 'Tell me now,' the lawyer said softly, 'with all this tea coming in, do you not think the price will fall so that the common people can afford it?'

'Why, yes, in time.'

'In quite a short time, do you not think? And if they take to drinking tea, will they not require sugar in vast quantities?'

'Of course.' Kemp refilled his glass. He was nettled by the other's manner – it was as if he were being rather teasingly cross-examined. He was aware that others nearby were listening. 'And that will help our business,' he said curtly. 'Any fool can see that.'

'Here is one who can't,' the lawyer said with unruffled good humour. 'You are digging your own pit, sir, if you will pardon me. We are talking about a time when tea will be cheaper than beer. Once the true magnitude of the sugar market is grasped, do you think that control of the prices will be left in the hands of a few West Indian planters? People will look elsewhere for their sugar, sir – wherever it is cheapest. There is no divine right in commerce.'

Kemp was indignant. He could not imagine any government, of whatever complexion, exposing the nation to foreign competition. One country could only grow rich at the expense of another – it was an axiom and an article of faith with him. But he had no time to retort upon the lawyer. The remains of the beef were being cleared, they would be bringing in the sorbet, it was time for him, as Vice-President, to propose the health of their hosts, the Africa Merchants. He got to his feet and rapped with his spoon for silence. This took some time to obtain, as the guests were loud and heated now with food and drink. He spoke easily and well, timing his pauses, inserting the humorous remarks prepared beforehand. Though still as scornful as ever of actors, he had learned much about the art of pleasing over the years.

When he came to the heart of his speech he grew serious, pointing out the value and importance of the slave trade, on which every man in the room in some way depended. It was a sign of this value and importance that through all variation in the administration of public affairs, through all variation of government and party, this trade had always been approved, its encouragement voted, its benefit to the nation recognized on all sides . . .

These were the things above all that this company of men enjoyed hearing and he resumed his seat to general applause. He did not speak again to the lawyer or look at him but devoted his attention to the man on his right, who was already well known to him, as to most people in the room, and always to be found at these gatherings. Dr Ebeneezer Slingsby, familiarly known among his associates as Dr Sugar, was a man who had done more for the trade, in his own way, than almost anyone, having been for more than thirty years a tireless publicist for the medicinal virtues of sugar in every form, and having published not much previously a learned treatise entitled 'A Vindication of Sugar', in which he proved beyond doubt that sugar was

beneficial to everyone, of whatever degree or age or sex. Throughout all this time his researches had been helped forward by
generous subsidies from the West India Association.

Slingsby was corpulent and somewhat short of breath and his
teeth were ruinous; but his full, round face had a good high
shine on it and his eyes glistened as he described to Kemp his
new remedy for all ailments of the eye: two drams of fine sugar-
candy, one grain of leaf gold, one quarter-dram pearl. 'Made
into a very fine and impalpable powder, sir,' the doctor said.
'When dry, blow a convenient quantity into the eye. Relief will
be felt within two minutes.'

'The pearl and gold leaf will make it an expensive remedy, I
fancy,' Kemp said. 'Beyond the means of most.'

'That is true, sir, it is designed for people of fashion. But I am
presently seeking patents for a hand-lotion made from sugar
paste which will be a sovereign cure for all manner of external
lesions and well within the means of the common general. And I
am working also on a dentifrice made with powdered sugar,
which should come out cheap enough. Alas, too late to save my
own teeth.' The smile he gave at this point attested in a graphic
fashion to the terminal condition of these. 'But we do not work
for ourselves alone,' he said. 'It is the younger generation who
will thank us. There is a Slingsby Sugar Snuff now on the
market which I believe will replace tobacco entirely, to the
better health of the whole population.'

The doctor paused to drink some of his wine. His nails, Kemp
noticed, were a strangely uniform whitish colour without any
evident presence of blood behind them. 'Well, that is good
news,' he said. 'I had not thought sugar could be put to so
many uses.'

Dr Sugar set down his glass. 'Sir,' he said, 'sugar has a thousand uses, it is the most versatile of all commodities in the
world. It is first of all a food, of course, and an excellent one. A
man can live on the products of sugar alone for many weeks
together without the smallest detriment, as I have proved upon
my own person. But sugar is also a preservative, a solvent, a
stabilizer. It is equally valuable as excipient or diluent. It gives
consistency of body, it masks bitter-tasting drugs. It can be used

in syrups and elixirs, as a demulcent or as a binding agent for tablets. It is a base for confections, oil sugars, aromatic sugars, candy cough lozenges. It improves the eyesight, preserves the hair and sweetens the blood. Sir, there is no end to the virtues of sugar.'

By the time Kemp had followed the doctor through this catalogue he was beginning to feel the onset of drunkenness. However, when the guests rose he was still steady enough in his movements and clear in speech.

The place used by the Trionfi for their meetings was the Bell in Covent Garden, which boasted a good-sized dining-room. In the cloakroom, where he had gone to divest himself of cloak and boots, Kemp found four men, all members of the club, sitting at cards with brandy on the table before them.

'Here is our worthy President,' one of them said. 'Stab me, why do you look so glum, man? Here, have some brandy, get your flipper to the bottle.'

Kemp saw that the man, whose name was Fowler, was drunk already. His waistcoat hung open and the lace front of his shirt had a wet stain on it. Kemp drank from the bottle and sighed loudly and smiled round at the men, widening his eyes in a way that was peculiar to him, slightly devilish. 'This will wash out the taste of all those confounded speeches,' he said, and drank again. The men at the table had been looking at him expectantly. They all laughed now, as if in some kind of relief. Kemp had found something of his father's friendly manners in the course of paying off his debts. To the advantages of good looks and a well-knit figure he had added the useful gift of bonhomie. But there was nothing of the father's simple and unaffected good-fellowship in the way the son noted now, for future reference, that these men had not thought fit to attend the banquet, preferring to sit here over their cards. He knew them all for profligate and idle. They were the sons of plantation owners, men who had never known the want of money . . .

'They have got the ladies in already,' one said.

Kemp could hear a considerable noise of voices from the dining-room adjoining, and the sound of the fiddlers playing a reel. 'I must go in,' he said. 'I hope that fool of a landlord has not let the women into the dining-room yet – they are to come in later.'

'No,' Fowler said, with a loose smile. 'They are upstairs getting dressed for it, powdering their fannies.' He tilted back his chair and patted his crotch with an imaginary powder-puff.

'You will need something more than powder on it, Fowler, to stiffen you tonight,' Kemp said. 'Are you gentlemen not going in?'

They began to get up, but he did not wait, passing alone into the long, low-raftered room, where a fire of logs burned at one end. He greeted the dozen men there and took his place at the head of the table. Immediately on his right, as tradition required, was their guest for the evening, a man named Armstrong, the only one there not connected with sugar – he was a lieutenant in the Guards, a relative of one of the members.

While all remained standing the retiring President, lisping in speech but impressively serious in manner, welcomed Kemp to his new office, and handed him the ceremonial white baton, known as the 'Cane'. No member could command the attention of the others, nor speak to them collectively, without having this in his possession. Kemp tapped three times on the table with it and formally declared the proceedings open. The serving man came forward with the port.

Voices were raised, now that the gravity of protocol had been laid aside. The drinking was reckless. Most of the men there had been tipsy when they sat down, but they drank off bumpers of wine as if it were water. There were toasts to King George and the Royal Princes and Squinting Kate, the Queen of Camden. Kemp got up while he still had his senses about him and expressed the hope that he would give satisfaction as the new President, a sentiment which was greeted by loud and sustained hammering on the table. Some wine was spilled in the course of this and one or two glasses broken.

An undercurrent of excitement ran below the high spirits. It was hot in the room. Kemp felt perspiration break out on him. Several of the men had discarded coats and waistcoats. The air was heavy with tobacco smoke and vinous breath. A low chant began from lower down the table: '*Trionfi – trionfi – trionfi.*'

416

Kemp made a signal to the two fiddlers, who broke into a rendering of 'Lads and Lassies'.

This was the cue for the club's Italian sugar chef, Signor Gasperini, to advance into the room in his tall hat and spotless white apron. Behind him, greeted by a rousing chorus of yells and whoops, came three attendants bearing a litter on which stood a three-foot high model of a negress fashioned in chocolate. Except for bracelets, anklets and pearl collar, which were all made of sugar-crystal droplets, and the red sugar-paste rose in her hair, she was naked. To the continuing strains of the fiddle, they made the round of the table with her. At her base was a plaque of chocolate with letters picked out in spun sugar: THE SABLE VENUS.

Kemp rapped with his baton for silence. 'In accordance with custom, Signor Gasperini will now explain to the company the mysteries of this delectable lady's composition.'

The chef had a lively eye and a smile so extensive that the corners of his lips and eyes seemed almost to join in a circle. The negretta was made of *pasta di cioccolato e cacao*, sweetened with fanid, flavoured with vanilla, moulded by his own hands – he threw them up with the gesture of a conjuror. 'The hairs is made from caramella,' he said jubilantly. 'her leeps is pink pasta of sugar, the eyes *zucchero fino*, she have sugar cherries for neeples, *dolcissimi, no? Ecco Signori, a voi!!!*' He swept off his tall hat and gestured proudly towards his creation, who regarded the company with gleaming, affrighted eyes. 'Only the best sugar go to make this *fanciulla*,' Signor Gasperini said.

'What the devil is fanid?' muttered the young lieutenant in Kemp's ear. It seemed he had experienced a moment of intellectual enquiry. His eyes were round with drink and wonderment.

'It is the juice of the sugar cane after it has been boiled down and skimmed,' Kemp said. 'It makes a sweet black dough, like thick syrup.' He stood up rather unsteadily and inclined his head to the chef. 'Gasperini,' he said, 'you have excelled yourself. My congratulations. The guest may now be served.'

Armstrong, after some fuddled hesitation, and to the accompaniment of much profane advice, chose the left breast with

its cherry nipple. He was served with dexterity by the attendants, who could not, however, avoid some of the shoulder coming
away with it. Thereafter the others were served, beginning with
Kemp, who took her nose and eyes, proceeding down the table,
the least senior members having to pick among the fragments.
Sauternes was served and a sweet, heavy Malaga wine.

Kemp saw one of the junior members get up suddenly and
make for the door, his face overspread with a chalky pallor.
Fowler had slumped forward in his chair; his head rested on the
table among the remains of his chocolate. So much for the
powder-puff, Erasmus thought. He was distinctly drunk himself
now, but his stomach felt firm enough. The chanting began
again, this time accompanied by a flat-handed striking at the
table: '*Trionfi – trionfi – trionfi.*' The volume rose, drowning out the
fiddles. On the crest of it, laughing among themselves, the
women came in, sent by the prudent landlord before things
started to get broken.

There were eight of them, scantily dressed and painted and
high-stepping – they had been given drink while waiting. They
sat in the laps of the men who were quickest to catch them,
except for one, who came unbidden to Erasmus, a wild-haired,
gypsy-looking young woman with a bold mouth. She wore
nothing above the waist but a muslin bodice. Her breasts moved
unconfined below it, the nipples showing through with a dark
glow. She drank from his glass and smiled at him, her eyes
shining below the thick fringe of hair.

Erasmus, whose senses were swimming now and whose only
care was to see that no one took away his precious baton of
office, fumbled with the buttons of her bodice, at the same time
trying to explain to Armstrong, with a vestigial sense of his duty
as host, that the *trionfi* were due to appear now: it was these that
gave the club its name, little figures made from cast sugar. 'Cast
on marble,' he said, enunciating with immense care. His tongue
felt too thick for his mouth. 'The marble first lubricated with oil
of almonds . . .' Armstrong did not appear to be listening closely.
The girl on his lap had slid a hand inside his breeches.

Gasperini's men brought them, in boxes tied with red ribbon,
one for each person in the room. They were unwrapped and

418

held up and turned this way and that in the lamplight, glistening white replicas of horse-shoes, pigs, rosettes, shells, keys ... A long-drawn aaah went round the table: Erasmus's girl had extracted from her box – as all had known she would, since it was marked for her – a sugar penis, gleaming with crystals, heroically tumid, with a red tassel attached. Smiling, she held it up for all to see. And as she did so, the chanting began again, a single barking syllable now: '*Up-up-up.*'

She laid the dildo before Erasmus and leapt up in a single movement on to the table. Dishes, glasses, remnants of food were swept aside. She tossed her head and snapped her fingers at the hollow-eyed fiddlers, who went into the rhythm of a gavotte. She commenced a swaying dance in the centre of the table, removing her garments piece by piece and throwing them down among the spectators, petticoats, bustle, bodice, stockings. Naked, she was beautiful in the lamplight, her skin like warm pearl. She swooped for her gift, danced into a half-squatting position. Still to the stately rhythm of the music, she inserted it between her legs, pressing it slowly into herself with both hands, raising her face with an expression of simulated ecstasy, while the voices round her rose again, overlapping, indistinguishable, like the baying of dogs.

The woman rose and raised her arms to show the hands were empty and danced a few gyrating steps, keeping her knees close, working her thighs, rounding her mouth to make oohs of bliss. The crimson tassel hung down between her legs like some trailing tissue of blood. She kept to the centre of the table, stepping short, turning to avoid the hands that snatched, though more in jest than earnest, at the swinging cord.

She came to rest where she had begun, before Erasmus, and smiled down at him and swayed her hips, while the whole table loudly exhorted their new President to take it out-out-out, and he reached up and took the strip of velvet and drew on it and a roar went up at the expected sight of how wilted and eroded that proud prick was now, how it dangled grotesquely misshapen on its thread – in accordance with hallowed custom it had been made of powder sugar, designed for quick melting in the hot spice of the vagina.

419

Erasmus knew what was expected of him. He rose and swung the naked woman off the table and set a staggering course with her towards the door. Then he remembered the Cane, symbol of his office, and came back for it. On inspired impulse, he turned his lapse into triumph, raising the baton and making a sign of the cross with it in a gesture of blessing and farewell, adding that night – though without design – to the proud traditions of the Trionfi Club.

The girl led him down the candle-lit passage into a small room with a narrow bed. On this, with some laughter but no words, she lay down and waited for him. The melted sugar had leaked from her, he saw the shine of it on her thighs. Without words or touch of the mouth, they copulated briefly and violently. She clutched at him and made an angry cry and he felt the slight knifing of her nails. He was released in a series of groaning shudders and fell down beside her like a stone and slept at once.

He woke to a throbbing head and a feeling of utter desolation. There was a grey light in the room. The woman was gone. The tavern and the streets outside were silent and he judged it to be not long after dawn. There was a jug of water and a basin on the small table against the window. He washed his face and hands, drying himself with his handkerchief. The room looked out over the courtyard and the stables, half obscured in mist. Erasmus shivered a little in the chill air. A certain impulse of escape came to him. He would rouse the lad in the loft over the stables, have his horse saddled, his cloak and boots fetched. The streets would be quiet. At this hour even crime was sleeping . . . But he made no move yet to leave. His white baton was still there by the bed where he had let it fall. He went to pick it up. The movement sent shoots of pain through his head. Holding the baton he stood for some minutes longer in the dim room, going over things in his mind, recapitulating his assets. He had passed his initiation triumphantly – he knew it. Everything lay in his hands. He was acknowledged leader of the younger set, and his position in the Association would enable him to influence events and steer business the way of Fletcher and Kemp. Fletcher was old and he had no sons; day by day he was relinquishing control. Now that the debts were paid, more money would be free for investment. He would go into banking on his own account. The future lay with those who dealt in money, not commodities ... It lay with people like himself, people who could *see*. Why then did he feel this desolation, which was not sickness of body, which would not be dismissed as the aftermath of debauch, coming as it did at other times and often quite unexpectedly, a feeling of being thrust without shelter under remorseless skies? The successful cannot be unhappy – it was a contradiction in terms. But as he stood there, in this time of licensed introspection, with night over and duties of day not yet resumed, he fell again to rehearsing in his mind the actions he was about to take, as if seeking to give them, and with them his life as a whole, some fuller reality. Crossing the greasy cobbles, shouting for the stable-lad ... Perhaps he would climb to the loft to shake him awake. His horse would be led out, snorting in the cold air. And he would turn her head south towards the river and ride through the empty streets ... Suddenly he felt like a man who has played by the rules and been cheated by an opponent more cunning – so cunning that it was not possible to see how the trick had been done.

THIRTY-EIGHT

At home he found his man, Hudson, already up and dressed and waiting with his usual discreet blend of deference and reproof. Hudson had been with him for almost eight years now and was licensed in various ways, but Erasmus cut him short this morning, sending him off in a hurry to make tea and get water heated for a bath.

He stayed a long time in the scented tub, Hudson labouring back and forth with buckets of warm water to pour over him. When he rose from this long immersion, he was feeling slightly languid but triumphant again. He dressed as usual with the greatest care, in a plain shirt and a suit of dark broadcloth. He was intending to spend the rest of the day at the offices of the bank, on Cheapside, where he was due to meet the owners of a shipping company in need of short-term credits.

However, he had scarcely finished dressing when Hudson came to announce a visitor, a Captain John Philips, who had called without appointment.

'A sea-captain?'

'Yes, sir. A merchant captain, by the look of him.'

'There is none of that name on our books. Does he say what he wants?'

'No, sir. When I asked him to state his business, he spoke short to me, as if he thought I should be hauling on the ropes. All he will say is that he has something of interest to impart to you.'

Erasmus sighed. 'I don't doubt it,' he said. 'But whose interest, his or mine? That is the question, Hudson.'

'Yes, sir.'

'Well, you had better show him into the study.'

Making his way there some minutes later, Erasmus found himself facing a thickset, weathered-looking man of middle years, in nankeen trousers and a buff-coloured top coat.

'I am Erasmus Kemp,' he said, advancing to shake his visitor's hand. 'You have some business with me, I believe. I am rather pressed this morning . . .'

'Not business, sir, not exactly business,' the captain said. He hesitated for some moments, as if not sure how to proceed, though his gaze remained firmly on Erasmus. 'I knew your father,' he said. 'By repute, I mean, not personal. I am a Liverpool man, sir.'

'Indeed?' Erasmus had stiffened involuntarily at this reference to his father. But the captain's blue eyes under their thick, fair brows wore a frank and friendly expression.

'Aye, sir, and I knew Captain Thurso. On rather closer terms – too close for comfort. I sailed under Thurso once, before I got my own ship. Once was enough – more than enough.'

'Sir, excuse me, my time is short this morning. May I ask where this is leading?'

'The *Liverpool Merchant*, that was her name, his last ship. There was a deal of talk at the time. There is always talk about a ship that goes down. And this was a new-built ship. I remembered it, being your father's ship and skippered by Thurso.'

'Well, you are right enough, that was her name.'

'She had a figurehead on her of a big-breasted woman with flowing hair. That is right, is it not, just to be sure?'

'Why, yes.' Into his mind there came the memory of that distant afternoon in Oates's workshop by the Mersey, the staring figures, the smells of pitch and varnish, the irascible carver limping among his creations, his father's enthusiasm for the huge, garish duchess looming above them with her yellow hair and blue dress, her look of a captive giant. He had shared that day, in that sorcerer's den, something of the feeling for the ship that had possessed his father. He had his love for Sarah then, to open his heart to wonder . . . 'What do you mean,' he said on a note of anger, 'to come here and talk to me of a ship that was lost twelve years ago with all aboard her?'

423

'She was not lost.'

Erasmus raised a hand quickly to his temple, a habit since childhood when he was distracted or confused. 'Not lost?' It came to him now that his visitor might be dangerous. There was a heavy glass paperweight on the desk before him, the only thing that could serve as a weapon in this room. He moved his right arm a little nearer to it.

But there was nothing of madness in the tanned, bluff-featured face of the man opposite him. If the captain had noticed the movement he gave no sign of it. 'I saw her less than six months since,' he said. 'What is left of her. I am here fitting out a ship and took occasion to find you out and tell you of it. She is beached up on the south-east coast of Florida.'

Erasmus stared at him. 'Beached? You mean wrecked on the shore?'

'No, I mean hauled up deliberate. She was a good way from the shore.' Some of the diffidence or uncertainty had returned to the captain's voice: it was as if he too had been visited by disbelief. 'Further than a man would ever expect to see a ship,' he said, in a lower tone.

'*Florida?*' Erasmus raised a hand to his face again. 'What should the ship be doing there, so far to westward? She never reached Jamaica. What rigmarole is this?'

'I am speaking of what I have seen with these eyes.' There was an angry brusqueness in the captain's voice now. 'I thought it my duty to come,' he said. 'I will not take any more of your time, sir.'

'No, no.' Erasmus raised his hand. 'Pardon me,' he said. 'I intended no offence. I must hear the rest of what you have to say. Your words came as a shock to me ... My father died in that same year the ship failed to return, and the circumstances of my life were altogether changed.'

'I know it.' Philips was gruff still, but mollified. 'I was sorry to hear of it.'

Erasmus smiled at him. 'Will you not sit?' he said. 'I have some good Madeira here in my cabinet. Or if that is not to your taste, my man can fetch you something else.'

'What you keep close at hand is good enough for me,' the captain said, returning the smile.

Pouring out the wine, Erasmus found his hands slightly unsteady. 'Now, sir,' he said. 'You have my full attention.'

Thus encouraged, and more at ease now, coat unbuttoned and glass in hand, the captain began his story. He had been in the Africa trade, it seemed, but not for slaves, except incidentally. His main trade now was in timber and hides between the North American colonists and the Spanish islands of the Caribbean. He had been following his usual route northward through the Florida Straits, bound for Norfolk, Virginia. They had anchored at a latitude of some twenty-seven degrees, south of a point on the coast known as the Boca Nueva, where there were fresh springs. He had sent a party ashore for water and firewood, and to shoot whatever game they came upon.

'No man is perfect, sir,' the captain said, shaking his head, 'and seamen less so perhaps than others, being confined together for long periods. They contrived to draw off some rum from the ship's stores and carry it to shore with them. It was not enough to take their legs away, but it was enough to make them wild and heedless. They sighted a party of Indians and gave chase, hoping to catch the women among them. At least, that is how I understood the matter – they tried to pretend otherwise later, to lighten their punishment. There are Indian bands along that coast, sir, so much is true. They are hostile to white men and their arrows can give a death-wound if they strike in the right place. What these men did was folly, to rate it no worse. They were led on further than they intended, especially the two foremost, and found themselves in a swampy wooded ground where the only way forward was by following the course of a dry creek bed. This took them round in a blind curve and so they came upon her quite sudden, they said, tilted over in the bed of the creek, one side of her jammed against the bank, with creepers trailing over her and her decks half rotted away and both her masts down. That is how they told it to the mate and that is how the mate told it to me.' The captain shook his head again. 'Out of sight of the shore, she was,' he said, 'in the middle of swamps and trees, sir, where no ship has any business to be. She was an uncanny sight even for me, who was prepared for it by their account. Her name was there, on the scroll below the quarter figure. Faded, but you could still make it out.'

He had gone himself, led by the men who had found her. He had clambered over the sloping, gaping planks of her deck and found his way below, to the captain's cabin. 'Nothing much there but rubbish,' he said. 'She had been well picked over. By those who left her there, I suppose, and by the rats that were aboard with them and maybe the Indians after. But I found this behind a rotted bulkhead.' He put a hand into the pocket of his coat and drew out a square-shaped book bound in black buckram, shredded and ragged now. ''Twas in a wood box,' he said. 'The damp has done for most of it, but some pages can still be read. It is the ship's log.'

Erasmus reached out his hand for it with the sense of slow, protracted motion sometimes felt in dreams. His thoughts too had slowed; there was nothing in his mind but the strangeness of what the captain had told him. 'But is it sure?' he said, with some instinct of gaining time. 'Can you be sure it is the same ship?'

'She is a snow, sir, a two-master, Liverpool made. And there is the name on her, and the figurehead.'

'But how could she have got up so far, away from the water?' He felt again the need to compose himself, the need for time. He was aware of the captain's eyes resting steadily on him. 'Perhaps you will tell me she crawled,' he said.

'The land keeps low on that piece of coast, it does not rise more than a few feet, and it is soft, sir, sand and shingle and mud. The Atlantic tides come in very strong. But perhaps you know those parts?'

'No, not at all.'

'The sea makes roads into the land and they run deep sometimes, I have known of four- and five-fathom depth. Behind the shore it is a maze of mud flats and streams and lagoons and they are changing all the time, silting up into swamp, changing their courses, running into creeks that go for miles. That coast never looks the same from one year to the next, and I know it better than most. Your father's ship lies in a channel that is narrowed now and half choked up, but it could have held deep water twelve years ago, deep enough to tow a ship, taking her at full tide and hauling from the banks.'

'But the men who did that, who laboured to do it, must have been desperate to hide her from sight of the sea.'

'Aye, that is what it looks like. And they succeeded in it – she would not have been found now, but for the accident of the men getting drunk. A hundred ships could water there without knowing anything of her. Men go to shoot pig in the scrub or fowl at the edges of the lagoons, but no one goes into the swamps behind. Why should they?'

'And the captain?' Erasmus spoke with a strange constraint. It was as if he wanted the other to supply him with judgement. 'Surely he could not . . .'

'Thurso was not a man to abandon his own ship, not willingly. But this is speculation – I was concerned only to tell you what I could vouch for.' He set down his glass and rose to his feet. 'I saw the vessel with my own eyes,' he said. He moved towards the door, then stopped and looked back at Erasmus, who had also risen now. 'It is all I know for definite,' he said. 'But I sail in those waters regular, now that Florida has been given to us by the Spaniards, and I have heard stories. I did not pay much heed to them before . . .'

'What stories?'

'The Indians who trade with Cuba from the Florida Keys tell of a kind of settlement somewhere back behind the coast, where white and black live together and no one is chief.'

'But twelve years,' Erasmus said. 'How could men remain hidden there?'

'It is feasible,' Philips said after a moment of reflection. 'The southern part of Florida is a wilderness. It is trackless and empty of human kind, save for some scattered Indians. The Spanish never went down so far, not that I know of. There was no reason why they should. For seven of these last twelve years they have been fighting a war to keep the colonies that really matter to them. A remote part of the Florida peninsula was of interest to no one. Yes, it is feasible.'

Erasmus was silent and the captain, perhaps taking the silence for disbelief – he was a prideful man and sensitive in his own way – held out his hand rather abruptly. 'I did not say I believed the stories,' he said. 'With Indians you do not know if

427

they are speaking of today or yesterday or a hundred years ago. Well, I have done what I came to do. Now I must take my leave of you.'

'One moment.' Erasmus appeared to rouse himself from some private musing. 'I am extremely obliged to you for this intelligence you have brought me. Be good enough to let me know where you are lodging, so I may send you a mark of my gratitude.'

'So much is not necessary.'

'I do not imply that it is necessary.' Erasmus practised his smile again. He had formed no conscious intention other than to send a sum of money. It was right that a man should be rewarded for his trouble, and there was not a sufficient sum in the house. But he knew even now that the money was merely a pretext: he had to know where Philips could be found. 'I would esteem it a favour,' he said.

Pressed thus, the captain complied. He was staying at the Bull in Southwark. He took his leave and Erasmus found himself alone again with the tattered black book on the desk before him. The interview had made him late: there was no time now for more than a cursory look. Philips had been right, the log was largely indecipherable. Mould had attacked the covers and outer pages, obliterating the names of captain and ship. Everywhere damp had spread the ink, running the lines together into blurred webs. The quality of the hand did not help: it was crabbed and uneven, the writing of a man not at ease with a pen. But occasionally, and particularly in the latter part, there were entries that could still be made out, dates, details of weather and navigation. His eye caught a name: Haines, set in irons for some offence not named . . .

He had no time now for more. When he left the house the log went with him, but it was not until late in the afternoon that he was able to look at it again. All through the day's business he had found himself recalling, half incredulously, fragments of his interview with the captain, dwelling on details of his visitor's words and manner as if to detect some falsity in them that would discredit his story, dispel this monstrous notion that men had deliberately abandoned his father's ship.

428

He was alone now in his office. In the larger room adjoining, the clerks still laboured at their long counter, heads studiously lowered – he could see the line of heads and backs if he chose to, through the spyhole set in his door. The offices were at the rear of the building, looking towards the quiet courts south of St Paul's. The din of the streets was muted here. The evening had darkened early and he had lit the lamp on his desk. Behind him a fire burned in the grate with a faint, persistent whispering.

He took the logbook from his drawer and began to look through it again. He saw an entry for November 1752, again with a name – it was names he paused at:

. . . bartered with a frenchman for 4 anchs of brandy. Bought 13 cwt rice of Tucker's people. They brought a man slave aboard, but it being late . . . promised to bring him off betimes in the morning . . .

A musty odour came to him from the softened, slightly swollen pages. Misfortune was apparent even through the bare entries that had survived: *No slant of wind any way,* he read. *Buried a woman of a fever which destroyed her in 5 days. There are now 67 lost and still in the . . .*

It was near the end of the log, on a page largely effaced, that he found what all this while he had been looking for:

. . . sea breeze came in but soon overpowered by a smart tornado obliging us to furl all and come to anchor in 25 fathoms . . . Following morning when hatches raised found 4 slaves dead in their irons. My cnsllr tells me jettison the sick. The men are muttering against me, they are given countenance by Paris who sets himself . . . sorry now I gave passage to . . .

The name that followed was illegible. Erasmus read through the entry again with utmost care. When he looked up it was with a feeling of gratitude he did not yet understand, though it was fierce enough to contort his face. His cousin had been there then, still alive at the end – for the log was finished now, only a page remained, and that quite illegible. Paris had played a part in what had happened to the ship . . .

The abbreviation puzzled him somewhat. He could not understand who might have given Thurso this advice – there was no doubt now that this was Thurso's log. Perhaps the first mate.

His mind went back to a day at the shipyard when he had seen them come round together, passing through the shadows of the ship's bows, out again into the sun, the heavy, deliberate captain and the sharp-faced mate. Barton, his name. He had lifted his head and sniffed at the breeze like a dog . . .

His thoughts reverted to his cousin, settled on him slowly and with curious care, as though aiming. The clumsy, laughing boy with the sleeves too short who had lifted him away from his failure on the beach, thereby becoming a mortal enemy; the studious youth of his mother's recommendations; the pale man with the lined face and the hedge-parson's hat and the shadow of misfortune and disgrace upon him . . . He was unable to imagine how his cousin might look now; but he knew him in that moment for a leader of mutiny, a man with blood on his hands.

It must be so, if Philips was to be believed: they must have murdered the captain. They had hauled the ship out of sight of the land, hacked down her masts. They could never have intended to return. Return to what? They had taken the negroes off her. That was theft – they had appropriated the ship's cargo and carried it to shore. So there was piracy to add to the other counts. *White men and black men living together with no chief.* Not only Thurso's blood. My father, waiting for his ship to come home, scanning the maps . . .

Afterwards it came to seem to him that the intention had been formed then, with the quiet sound of the fire behind him and the faint rattle of traffic coming through from Cheapside. But it was not until some days later that he knew beyond question that he had to go, had to see – and not just the wreck. He knew it by the desolation that swept through him at the thought that Philips might have left already, might be out of his reach.

Until this fear was allayed he could not rest. He had sent Hudson in the coach with twenty-five guineas and a note of thanks. And it was Hudson who accompanied him now and waited below while Erasmus spoke to the captain about the two men who had come upon the ship. Were either of these still with him? It seemed that one, the ringleader in the business, had been too much of a troublemaker and Philips had handed him over to the harsher discipline of a naval frigate at Savannah. But the other, a man named Harvey, had signed on again and could be found. An altogether steadier man, this, a good seaman, he had been led astray on this occasion by rum and the foolish hope of catching one of the women . . .

'They are simple men, sir,' the captain said. He was not best pleased to learn that Erasmus was proposing to take Harvey away from him, a reliable fore-the-mast man being not so easy to replace. But he was conscious that he had himself been treated with generosity; not to comply would have been ungrateful, even had he felt inclined to go counter to the other's will, which he did not. Kemp was a man who wielded influence, one whom it was unwise to cross. But it was more than that: there was a quality of suppressed passion in him which Philips – strong-willed enough himself, and used to intractable men – found daunting.

So Harvey was found and brought to the Kemp house. He was blond and ruddy with a usual expression of cheerful competence, though this was overlaid now at finding himself in such surroundings.

'Now,' Erasmus said to him, 'how old are you, Harvey?'

The seaman was of those whom nervousness makes more confiding. 'I am twenty-nine or I am thirty, sir, depending on how you looks at it. I never knowed my father, my mother gave me up to the parish when I was little, an' sometimes they told me one thing, sometimes they told me another.'

'So then, let us say you are thirty. You have your health and strength now, but few seafaring men get much beyond forty with those possessions still, certainly not on ships plying to the tropics. You know this yourself, you have not the look of a fool. Even if you last so long, what would there be for you on leaving the sea but rags and beggary? If you will agree to conduct me to this place where you came upon the remains of my father's ship . . . I suppose you would be able to find it again?'

'Yes, sir, I could find it.'

'If you will take me there and show me the place, I swear you will not be sorry. You need never return to the sea if you do not

431

wish to. I will take you into my service on good terms, or if you would rather, I will give you a sum that will set you up in some business ashore. I am a rich man and what I say I will do I will do – anyone who knows me will tell you that. I am asking you for a year of your life and offering to free you from want for the rest of it. Come, what do you say?'

'I say yes, sir, and trust I will give satisfaction and God bless you for an open-handed gentleman.'

Erasmus relaxed a little. He had offered more than he needed to, which was not a habit of his when bargaining; but he had been in fear that the man would refuse. 'It will take some two or three weeks for me to make arrangements,' he said. 'During that time you will live here and you will be dressed and fed. Then you will accompany me, as my servant, to the Florida coast. While in my house you will be expected to conduct yourself properly. Do you take my meaning?'

'Yes, sir.'

'No drunkenness, no rowdiness, no harassment of the maids.'

'No, sir.'

'You will find me worse than any Indian if you get up to those tricks.'

It was not often that Erasmus made witticisms of this or any other kind; perhaps only relief could have produced this one. He was surprised almost to see a smile come to the other's face. It was a smile of considerable charm, broken-toothed, guileless, totally unabashed by the reference to his offence. And in it Erasmus saw the beginning of a retribution twelve years delayed. 'And you will speak to no one of this business,' he said. 'No living soul.'

THIRTY-NINE

There was much to see to, but not so much as he had feared. It is when we make plans for an absence that we learn the extent to which we are needed at home. A good deal of business had to be left in the hands of the junior partner, Andrews; but Erasmus's secretary was entirely familiar with the workings of the firm and could be trusted to guide and advise. The old man, Fletcher, was still active and hard-headed enough; he grumbled at having more to do, but made no real objection. Someone was found to deputize at meetings of the Association. Many of the members had holdings in the West Indies, so prolonged absence from London was not uncommon.

There was the chartering of a ship to see to and letters of introduction had to be obtained for Colonel Campbell, the recently appointed governor of Florida. None of this presented much in the way of difficulty, but it took time. While waiting, he informed himself as far as he could about this new Colony, acquired by accident almost: Spain had handed her over some two and a half years previously to buy back her jewel of Cuba, taken by the English fleet. It seemed that what Philips had said of her was largely true. The Spanish had never much valued the possession, except as safeguarding their trade routes from Mexico and the Caribbean. They had done little to develop the territory or even to explore it. It offered nothing, after all, to anyone's notions of usefulness. The southern part was an uncharted, sub-tropical wilderness. There was no gold or silver to be found there and any Indians that were captured soon died when enslaved, a fact that greatly reduced their value. During the latter part of the recent colonial wars, the Spanish had scarcely ventured from their capital of St Augustine in the north, penned in by the warlike Creek Indians, who had been incited and supplied with arms by the English in Georgia. It was with the main task of pacifying these Creeks and assuring them of English gratitude that Campbell had been sent there. Or such, at least, was the declared policy. Privately Erasmus was given to understand that the expressions of gratitude would be accompanied by appropriations of traditional Creek hunting grounds to offer to English settlers.

Harvey, meanwhile, kept to his side of the bargain and behaved well. Metamorphosed into a superior servant, in a suit of good cloth and paste buckles to his shoes and his hair dressed in a pigtail, he entertained his fellow-domestics with stories of the sea and aroused the beginnings of tenderness in the cook. He could still hardly believe his luck. He had entered a world where anything could happen. His new master was rich, the rich had unaccountable fancies – and Harvey was glad of it.

Erasmus found a certain kind of happiness in this period of planning. His cause was just: a wrong had been done, and the perpetrators of it might be living still, while his own father had lain underground these twelve years. He said nothing of this, however, to anyone at all. To his associates, as to his wife and father-in-law, he explained the voyage as a business venture. This was plausible enough. Florida was a new Colony, it was His Majesty's declared policy to encourage settlement by assisted passages and grants of land. Many could be expected to take advantage of this, there was certain to be a demand for manufactured goods.

'I shall form useful connections up there in St Augustine,' Erasmus said to his father-in-law. 'This new Colony is a potential market of very great importance, I believe. Those who strike while the iron is hot will get the best share of it.'

'Do you seriously think that Florida colonists will buy their sugar from us and pay the tariffs when they have Havana just across the water?' Sir Hugo looked without friendliness at Erasmus from under white, dishevelled eyebrows. 'You must have taken leave of your senses,' he said.

Erasmus met the old man's gaze with unconcealed antagonism. He had always been impatient of opposition but of late years, with all his opinions confirmed by increasing wealth – that infallible testimony – any slightest criticism drove him to anger. 'I was not talking of sugar,' he said coldly. 'Do you think there is naught but sugar in this world? Do you think people wear sugar on their backs or turn the earth with it? And if it is madness we are talking of, what is this indiscriminate buying of negroes but madness? I am reliably informed that your factors in Kingston are buying men with no mouth left and women with dugs to their knees, and keeping them all in compounds with nothing to do.'

'The compensation we receive from the government will take no account of sick or whole, it will be paid on the number of heads and calculated on current prices.'

'Compensation?' Erasmus affected a look of frigid puzzlement. 'Whence comes this notion? Some incubus must have visited your sleep.'

'They are going to abolish the trade. It is coming, I tell you, there is a bill preparing now. I have it on authority.'

'A parcel of clerks and petty fellows that hang about the ministries and sell information by the shilling,' Erasmus said with contempt. It was hardly believable that Jarrold should give credence to such stories. He was a man whose shrewdness and ruthlessness were legendary, who had risen from lawyer's clerk to merchant banker and amassed a fortune on the way – he was worth half a million at least. In a lifetime of trading he had scarcely touched anything that did not turn to profit. And to be visited now with this quite unfounded but unshakeable fear of the abolitionists, which was like enough to ruin him. No, not fear, more like a need, something he was seeking. The intervention of God, perhaps . . . It was an unusual kind of thought for Erasmus and he was uneasy at it – uneasy and perplexed: his father-in-law's career had after all been highly meritorious in its single-minded pursuit of wealth. Even now, in the shadow of this Apocalypse of his own creating, the old man was trying to realize a profit . . .

'You will lose by it,' Erasmus said. 'A negro is valuable only in terms of the work that can be got out of him in the period

435

immediately after purchase. He is not a capital asset, the merchandise is too perishable. It is not like cattle, you cannot breed him for profit. This movement for abolition of the trade is a chimera, there will be no bill, there are no voices against it but some few members of the Quaker Faction and one or two meddling fools outside parliament. But it is useless to talk to you.'

The money being thus squandered might have ultimately come down to him through his wife. He had thought at one stage of trying to have the old man declared incompetent, but apart from this particular mania he seemed rational enough. The only thing to be hoped was that he might die soon and so limit the damage. Erasmus's own money at least was not in any danger. He had given instructions for his twelve per cent holding in the bank to be quietly sold in small lots while the stock was still high.

His farewells to his wife on the day of departure were scant in the extreme. He was embarking that evening, the coach was waiting below with Harvey and the baggage already inside. He had to wait while Marie announced him: his wife had lately decided, or been told by one of her friends, that too much ease of access between married persons was vulgar.

As he entered Fritz the poodle yapped at him as usual from its cushion and showed its pink gums. A travestied and unrecognizable woman in a peach-coloured gown, her features concealed behind a mask of greyish, pimpled skin, reclined on a sofa in the dressing-room adjacent to the bedchamber. 'Is it you, Margaret?' he said, advancing. 'What in God's name is that on your face?'

'It is a chicken skin,' she replied in a voice slightly obscured. 'I am advised by my friend Lady Danby that it is the non plus ultra for restoring one's complexion.' The ragged fringe of skin round her mouth moved with the movement of her lips. 'It has to be a freshly killed bird so as to be moist enough.'

'So your husband, who is to be away several months, is to make his farewells to a chicken skin.'

'I cannot see why you should need to look at my face just because you are going away, when you take such small interest in it while we are under the same roof. This must be kept in place for an hour at least, so Lady Danby says, if it is to do anything.'

'Lady Danby is little better than a whore and I am sorry to hear you call her friend,' Erasmus said. 'I cannot wait that long, we are sailing with the tide.' He took her listless hand and kissed it. 'I hope you will take care of your health,' he said. 'Your complexion, I see, is in no danger of neglect.'

In the coach, as they jolted past Tower Bridge, it occurred to Erasmus that his wife must have donned the chicken skin shortly before his visit, though she had known he was coming. She had wanted to conceal herself. Her complaint against him had some truth in it: on the occasions, rare enough now, when they slept together, he did not look much at her face; at all other times when they met she was masked or disguised in some way, with fard and rouge and patches or with some charlatan lotion. It came to him that he almost never saw Margaret's real face. He wondered if he would recognize her passing in the street, or in the midst of a crowd . . . There was one face he would know instantly, after twelve years or twenty, the green eyes, so pale as to seem like some solution of silver, the deeply marked brows, the patience and obstinacy of the expression . . . With a sudden rush of detestation Erasmus realized that he knew this face of Matthew Paris more intimately than that of any other person in the world.

It was a face that returned frequently to him during the voyage, accompanied always by further remembered details of his cousin's appearance and manner, this process resembling a story he repeated to himself, more elaborate with every repetition. But wherever the story began it ended always in the same place, with those stronger arms lifting him, swinging him away, violating his body and his will. He had uttered no sound, submitting in furious silence, making himself a dead weight in his cousin's arms . . .

He recalled Paris's appearance on that last visit, the gaunt and awkward frame, the thick wrists and clumsy-seeming hands that were yet so precise in their smallest movements, the deep voice with the odd vibration in it and the sardonic, lop-sided smile. There had been that disturbing suggestion of physical power, of imperfect control . . .

437

The possibility that this face, this bundle of attributes, should have continued in being all this while, surviving his father's ruin, his own loss of love and home and all the long struggle to pay off his father's debts, was something he found difficult at first to endure. That the survival had been achieved by such heinous crimes – murder, piracy, the theft not only of the negroes but of the ship itself and then only to abandon her – made it the more monstrous. The thought that his cousin might be alive still was literally monstrous to him, a shape of ugliness and deformity in the natural order of things, something to be extirpated. It subverted all the rules that men lived by. If such wrong-doing was allowed to succeed, what price duty, what price honour? What price his own faithful discharge of obligation to the family name?

But as the days at sea followed one another in monotonous succession, with the wash of waves against the ship's bows and the slow creaking of her timbers, he found himself in the strengthening grip of paradox. The less Paris seemed deserving of liberty and life, the more Erasmus found himself hoping that he was still in possession of these, so that he could be brought to justice and deprived of both together. For the other miscreants who had been aboard, whom Paris had doubtless persuaded to join him, Erasmus cared little. They were scum in any case. But his thoughts tended always to a passionate preservation of his cousin's life, until the fear that he was not there, that he might not be able to be found, even that the whole story might still prove to be a fabrication, set him burning with a fever of anxiety as he lay sleepless on his narrow bunk, rocked tirelessly by this barren mother who could give him no security, no relief. The chafing of the sheets brought him to sexual arousal sometimes, a mechanical tension that was like a transference of his tense will. At these times he brought himself to a cold release and lay empty, waiting for dawn.

As the leagues mounted between himself and what he had left, the years fell away, became unreal, and he returned to the elemental feelings of childhood. His life dwindled to one intense focus, of such simplicity and power that it reduced the rest to shadows. This falling away was like the slow dismantling of a

438

scaffolding that had never been necessary; but he could not discern the structure it had supported, or seemed to support – that too was an illusion. There was the intense and brilliant focus of his resolve. Outside of this little was visible to him. The blankness of sky and ocean seemed evidence only of more stripping away. But in lieu of possession and identity there was the notion of justice, which deepened and grew abstract and religious, renewed every day in the promise of the dawn, confirmed by the simple sunlight, solemnized by the approach of the dark.

Harvey he questioned from time to time and always closely, as if intent to find him out in some contradiction; but the seaman's story was too simple for that, and at the same time too vague. Harvey had no picture in his mind of the route that had led him to the creek. He had blundered on to it. 'I had taken drink, sir,' he said, always with the same expression, wry and philosophical, as befitted references to this common accident of the human condition. He could remember, so he said, the watering place and the general lie of the coast where they had anchored. And indeed he felt pretty sure of this, though apprehensive of failure; he knew his master well enough by now not to relish the thought of disappointing him.

However, he was not a man who worried overmuch and he was otherwise enjoying the voyage mightily: it was the first time in his life that he had been at sea without having to sweat at the ropes. He messed with the steward and other crew members exempted from watch and regaled them with extraordinary stories about the world of fashion into which he had been introduced. His own simple wonder disarmed his listeners and he was popular with everyone aboard.

The same wonder governed his relations with his employer. That a man with a fine house and servants and money – in short, everything he needed in life – should want to go halfway round the world merely to look at a stinking hulk in a creek bed was so far from reasonable, so opaque to normal understanding, that it placed Kemp on a different level of humanity altogether, lordly, superbly unaccountable, needing to be humoured like the mad.

This humouring Harvey took seriously, conceiving it his duty, part of the terms of his engagement. His story gained in fluency and dramatic colouring without acquiring much more in the way of substance. It was also refined in the direction of virtue: someone else had drawn off the rum from the ship's stores, someone else again had been for trying to catch the women. To the discovery itself he could add little. The elements after all were few: the drink, the headlong chase, the stumbling through the mangrove swamp, the curving bank of the channel and the tilted wreck lying there amid the debris of her masts, the vegetation trailing over her from the banks on either side. Sometimes he added details. 'She was a slaveship,' he said once. 'I been on slavers. There was the remains of the bulkheads markin' off the rooms.'

At the same time he tried to defend himself against possible mistake. 'That bit of coast,' he said, 'it never looks the same. Sometimes it an't even the coast you are seein'. You see what looks like land but it is only shapes of mist built up on the horizon and they disappears as you come closer in.'

As they passed through the Santaren Channel and out into the Florida Stream, these words came to seem prophetic. They struck a season of wandering and irregular mists, warm air above the current meeting with colder on the edges. Through these they loitered for some days with the low green shapes of the Keys, glimpsed intermittently on the port side, vivid and brief enough to seem like hallucinations.

Anxious to avoid the shoals to eastwards, the captain kept in mid-channel until they were north of the Great Bahama Bank, then approached the Florida coast at the rough latitude of the Boca Nueva – the only landmark Philips had supplied and so far invisible in the continuing mists. He did not dare go in too close. The only charts they had were Spanish, well drawn enough but not to be relied on, the configuration of the coast in this south-eastern part having undergone constant change as the sea nibbled at it. 'It is like a flobby old prick hangin' down, gettin' wore away all the time,' Harvey remarked in a moment of gloom to the steward, after studying the map of the peninsula. 'With poxy Spanish names on it, which no Christian can read.' He could not read in any language, but this did not lessen his sense of aggrievement.

However, next morning they woke to clear weather and a succession of fine days followed. They drew closer to the coast, and made gradual way northwards with the current, scanning the shore as they went. Towards noon on the second day of this they sighted the green mouth of the *entrada*, with its long, curving sand bar on the north side, where the sea broke white in the shape of a sickle, just as Philips had described. They anchored in ten fathoms and the shore party put out in the punt with provisions for two days, Erasmus, Harvey and six of the crew armed with musket and cutlass.

It was a day of clear sunshine, almost windless. The shore and the scrub beyond were completely deserted. Low waves broke on the sand with scarcely any sound at all. Erasmus was never to forget the sense of terrible incongruity that descended on him as he stepped out of the boat on to the white sand and felt the peace of the place settle round him.

Before him the beach sloped gently upwards to a fringe of motionless palms. A flock of birds with black wings and white faces and crimson, blade-like bills rose and flew out to sea, keeping low over the water, making no sound. Here, he thought, or somewhere not far, perhaps on a day like this one, the fugitives had made landfall. It was hardly possible to believe it. There was no print of man anywhere to be seen.

He began to walk up the beach. Feeling firm ground under his feet, he staggered slightly, after the weeks at sea. But the unsteadiness seemed to him due more to the shock of this hush that lay over everything. He came to a stop, glancing in something like bewilderment along the empty shore, with nothing in his mind but his own loneliness and the incongruous violence of his intentions.

Such faltering was unusual and it did not last long. If anything, his resolution was strengthened by the difficulties that followed. It emerged that Harvey could not immediately locate the place where they had watered. He would know it when he saw it, he said, in an attempt to deflect his employer's wrath. But he could see nothing directly before him, here on the shoreline, to indicate which direction it lay in.

Since all he knew for sure was that the place lay south of the inlet, Erasmus judged it best to take the point of their landing as central and seek north and south from it along the coast. Creeks there were in plenty, running into the wetlands behind the shore; but they were not the streams of Harvey's memory. It took two days of casting thus, with their escort now openly surly at being made to row long hours in the sun, before they came upon the stretch of slightly higher, rockier shore scattered with pines that Philips had described and Harvey now recognized.

The springs were here right enough – there was fresh water below the ground over a wide area, emerging in pools among the rocky scrub. As if to compensate for his failure before, Harvey led now without hesitation, skirting the pools, plunging into the mangrove thickets that grew beyond them. Sweating profusely, stumbling among the intricate roots of the trees, sometimes floundering knee-deep in swamp, they kept a rough course between the shore and a chain of small brackish lagoons that ran parallel to it.

The mouth of the creek, when they came to it, was dark as a cavern, roofed over with branches. There was no more than a foot or two of water in it, almost black and quite still, half choked in places with spreads of heavily scented, hyacinth-like flowers. Keeping as close as possible to the bank, they followed the channel as it wound inland. A crocodile, which had been sunning itself in a break among the trees, slithered without apparent haste down the bankside, broke the dark water into brief glitters and disappeared among a tangle of bushes. The creek began a wide curve away from the sea. Quite unexpectedly, following this round, they came upon the ship.

She lay where the retreating water had left her, keel embedded in the mud bottom. In settling she had leaned heavily to port and the refuse of her decks had piled against the gunwales on that side. Creepers had found their way over her bows and clothed the ruined trellis of the forecastle railing. Drapes of pale green moss like horses' tails had lowered on to her from the trees that arched overhead. Thick-stemmed vines had lassoed the stumps of her masts. Only the upper slope of her quarterdeck was left bare. She was tied down here, bound by the lacing of creepers, a rotting captive in this forgotten channel.

442

From somewhere on the opposite bank Erasmus heard the sudden chattering cry of a bird. The smell of salt, mud and vegetable decomposition came to him, and the smell of the softened, worm-riddled timbers of the ship. He walked forward until he came level with her bows. There was the Duchess of Devonshire, eyeless and cracked and faded now, and her bosom crumbling, but still yearning forward in her pinions. She was turned away towards the farther bank: some distant ebb had tugged the ship athwart the stream. Boarding would be easier by the stern, he decided, where she was closer up. 'I want no one with me,' he said. 'You men will wait here. Space out along the bank and keep a watch.'

These words came as a disappointment to Harvey, who had hoped to accompany his master aboard. He had convinced himself that there was something of immense value on the ship, which only Kemp knew about, this being the only thing he could think of that could explain what they were doing there. All he got in the event, however, was mud on his back from Erasmus's boots. The ship's side was rather far for a leap, especially as she was tilted so awkwardly. Too impatient to wait for a bridge to be made, Erasmus swung over to the stern post by means of a rope, using Harvey's back as a launching pad. Taking advantage of the footholds afforded by the carving of the quarterheads, he climbed up over the side, encountering as he did so the raddled, reproachful stare of the Merchant, still in periwig and cocked hat, still with hectic traces of red in his cheeks. Above this, affording an excellent toe-hold, was the scroll of the City of Liverpool in blistered gilt.

A final effort brought him on to the deck. Here he stood clear in the sunshine. He heard faint scuttling sounds from among the warm boards. A delicately fronded, fern-like plant grew thickly amidst the burst planking of the deck where the rotted wood had mixed with leaf mould and drifted dust to make a soil. With a small shock of surprise he heard the humming of bees from somewhere and moments later two tiny, buff-coloured birds flew up out of this undergrowth and disappeared among the foliage on the opposite bank.

He began to make his way forward, moving crabwise along

443

the slope of the deck. A debris of broken staves and a section of mast lay over the after-hatch, too heavy for him to lift aside. He went on towards the main hatchway. He saw a snake, dandified as only the very venomous can be, in bands of red and black and yellow, go slithering across some feet of open deck and disappear below a pile of broken casks and scraps of cordage.

He drew the cutlass at his side and went forward. The intensity of his purpose was near to choking him now. He would have braved any danger to get below and find his cousin's cabin, though what he expected to see there he did not know.

The hatchway was open, though partly grown over with bindweed. The stairs were in place, leading down. At the foot he began to make his way aft again, leaning awkwardly against the portside bulkhead to keep his balance against the tilt. Shafts of light came through from the gaps in the planking overhead. Some yards along he found a skull and a scattering of bones, part of the ribcage still in its hoop. Had Philips mentioned human remains on the ship? He could not remember. An adult this, but whether black or white it was not possible to determine. Hardly big enough to belong to Paris . . . There were two more skeletons, one of them a child's, lying a little further, at an angle to the bulkhead.

The discovery, his aloneness in these unaccustomed surroundings, took all guard from his thoughts. As he stood in this dim, cluttered place, he could not defend himself against the knowledge that there had been terrible suffering here, in the heart of the ship; it was as though the timbers gave off the odour of it. It had survived this ruin, would survive the dust the ship was destined to . . .

This was no more than an aberration, a brief deflection of purpose. Next moment he was shuffling on again, through the broken sunlight. He had been over the vessel often enough with his father to remember where the surgeon's quarters lay, but the dimensions of the cabin were not so easy to make out now; the light inner bulkhead had fallen in, as if from some splintering blow. There was a litter of old yarn and bits of tackle that had jolted down here with the tilt of the ship. But the frame of the bunk was still there, loose at the foot where it had swung free from the splintered partition.

Erasmus kicked at the rubbish, dislodged a rusted band of iron and some pieces of curved wood, saw beneath these a curled shape, a snake he thought at first, then saw it was part of a belt. He picked it up. The leather had rotted and the buckle was missing, perhaps cut off. It was narrow – not a seaman's belt. He began to look about him with more purpose. Below where the planking had buckled and split he found a glass stopper with a round lid, of the type apothecaries use for small bottles and phials. This mark of his cousin's presence was as precious to him as a token of love and he pocketed it with care. However, apart from a small china inkwell, he found nothing more of any interest. It was clear that the cabins had been diligently picked over, and probably more than once.

On the point of leaving, obscurely disappointed, he pushed with a sort of vindictive violence against the frame of the bunk. He felt the head of it swing heavily round, then check against the splintered bulkhead. There was some obstruction there, something reinforcing the partition. Forcing the frame as far as possible from the wall, he saw a small cavity there, which had perhaps been fronted with panelling or some light veneer. He could see nothing inside, there was not light enough, and he was unwilling to put his hand where his eye could not follow it. He found a piece of wood and poked with it in the cavity. His stick encountered some object there that took up nearly all the space. When he reached in, his fingers touched the side of a wooden box.

It seemed to him afterwards that he had known from the first touch what this box would be, so that when he drew it out there was no surprise, only a sense of confirmation. The lacquer was roughened and pitted, but the resinous varnish had held off the damp and the gold and blue design of peacocks on the lid was as clear now in this narrow space where he stood as it had been the afternoon thirteen years ago when amid the tea-cups and the talk of her ailments his mother had made a present of it to Matthew Paris. He remembered with absolute clarity the quality of the light, the gown his mother had worn, his cousin's courteous gravity, in which there seemed always something sardonic, and his large hands taking the box . . .

445

Holding it carefully he went some paces forward to where the sunlight shafted through from gaps in the deck above. There was no lock but the wood had warped; he had to use some force to open the lid. Inside was a loose sheaf of papers and a stoutly bound book edged with red leather. A glance at this told him that it was a journal of some kind; the pages were covered with the angular writing he recognized as his cousin's. The loose sheets too bore his cousin's hand. There were words and phrases crossed out here and there. He took a sheet at random, raised it to the light and looked at the first few lines:

Thus it is that while the heart remains unharmed, life can chance to be restored to all parts, and health recovered. But if the heart be either chilled or affected with some grievous ill, it must needs be that the whole animal will suffer and fall into corruption . . .

Erasmus looked up towards the source of light. There was a spider's web directly above him, the strands dusty-looking in the sunlight, the fawn-coloured host motionless in the centre. Vaguely at first, then with a sudden tightening of the throat, he remembered how his father had enjoyed singing Paris's praises, how delighted he had been to be sending such a well-qualified surgeon with the ship. Among these accomplishments of his nephew had been the fact that he was translating a medical work from Latin, a treatise on the heart.

Erasmus could hear the voices of the men stationed on the bank. The angle of the sun had changed in this brief space of time: the light fell now directly on his face, the web was in shadow, scarcely visible. Within these rotting bowels of the ship he sensed a life that had cautiously resumed, faint scurrying sounds, minute displacements. This crumbling structure, coffin of his father's hopes . . . But it was Paris who had deserted him, left him to die in ignorance. This box, which had been a parting gift, these papers, he had not forgotten them, not overlooked them: he had left them here because they belonged to a life that was over, one to which he had not intended to return; either that or he had been no longer among the living when the ship was drawn up here.

Erasmus replaced the papers, closed the lid. One or the other it must be – it was the doubt that had brought him so far. If his cousin was dead, the ledger could be closed. If he were alive he had to be found and hanged. Somewhere in this wilderness they might be still, those who had survived. The stories of the Indians came to his mind. Stories or legends, Philips had not seemed sure . . . They would never have stayed here among the swamps. They would have made for higher, drier ground. Unlikely they had gone so very far, hampered and burdened as they must have been, and in such difficult terrain. His mind moved among possibilities with an insistent logic. They might not have stayed together, they might have scattered, gone their different ways. But there was safety in numbers. They might have made north-wards in a body for Georgia or Louisiana. But that would have meant hundreds of miles through Spanish territory, with hostile Indians all along the northern borders. Could the remnants of the crew have abandoned the negroes and escaped by sea, perhaps to Cuba or Hispaniola?

But he did not believe it. He was convinced, in a way that went beyond logic, that this ingrate jail-bird cousin of his had compounded his crimes and made his disgrace complete by siding not only with the mutinous scum of the crew but with the runaway blacks as well.

The conviction transcended his hatred for Paris. That high sense of justice that he had experienced during the voyage returned to him now. 'It is not finished,' he said in a low, impulsive mutter. Once more he lifted his face to the broken sunlight. 'The debts are not paid yet. If he is alive, I will find him.' As always, he gathered his surroundings to him, took them to witness. He promised the silence and dilapidation around him, the whole rotting hulk of the ship, that he would find his renegade cousin wherever he was skulking – find him and see him hanged.

FORTY

As soon as Erasmus Kemp had rejoined the ship she weighed and set a course northwards for St Augustine. In the south-westerly land breeze she made good time. Erasmus stood at the rail scanning the coast through a telescope, but he saw no sign of human habitation, only the pale stretches of the shore and the low line of scrub beyond it, broken occasionally by dark, dome-shaped belts of forest like sudden islands. When they were still south of Cape Canaveral the wind veered eastward, obliging them to stand further out for fear of the shoals, and he lost all sight of the coast.

Late in the afternoon, after some hesitation, he settled down to look at the journal. Some reluctance he did not fully under-stand, some fear of being mastered, held him back, though he was conscious of no curiosity in regard to his cousin's thoughts and feelings, only of the desire to find evidence of his crimes.

He began at the later pages – evidence would be here, if anywhere. The ink had faded badly in places and mould had attacked the edges of the leaves here and there, but a good deal was legible still. He turned the leaves, his eyes moving im-patiently over the obliterated passages. The journal gave off the faint, sweetish perfume of neglect.

. . . perhaps seeing some advantage to be gained from me as the owner's nephew, a matter he refers to frequently and with significant inflections. He is sniffing for a source of power, or preparing to shift allegiance. Certainly Thurso may not now be such a star to follow. Feeling among the people against him is strong, it can be sensed in the men's looks and mutterings among themselves. Cavana has scarce said a word since the casting overboard of his monkey . . . a

favourable wind, but the terrible deity who may have sustained Thurso all these years of his trading for slaves shows himself whimsical at last, as we see in these calms that have descended on us and keep us still among the shoals with seldom enough wind to give the ship steerage way, for she is now so foul she will not feel a small breeze.

April 20

Woke this morning to strains of 'Nancy Dawson', played by Sullivan for the negroes to dance to. It is in his face that he does not much relish this use to which his music is put, but Thurso . . . considerations of humanity, but for the sake of his 'prime', that is the four per cent promised him by my uncle on every slave reaching Jamaica and sold there. I care not if we never reach Jamaica nor any . . . Dancing will not keep them alive while the bloody flux moves among them; this demon was with us when we set sail from the coast and grows apace in spite of all my efforts to air and fumigate their rooms below deck. Almost every morning now we bring up dead shackled to the living. Yesterday one of the women was delivered of a dead baby, which Libby threw over the side.

April 26

I continue, in spite of these terrible conditions, to hold long conversations with Delblanc, and they are a solace to me, though I think him not enough of a realist. He maintains there could be a world, a society, without victims and without injustice, where the weakness of one was not an invitation to the strength of another, except to succour or protect. I go so far with him as to believe it true that the moral character of man is formed by what happens to him in the world and that our nature originates in external circumstances. Why then do we languish under wars and tyrannies? Delblanc would say it is due to the harmful effect of government upon us, government being powerful for evil only and powerless for . . . conditions on this ship one would be bound to agree. We are a sick and disaffected body of men, with a human cargo constantly dwindling, presided over by a man who grows every day more mad in appearance, hoarse and staring, with congested-looking features, and accompanied always . . . flogged a man today only for going to complain about the condition of the salt beef, which is black and glazed over and clearly putrid, as I have myself verified . . . Barton sends those he does not favour to scrape and swab out the slaves' quarters, a task much hated by reason of the poor creatures sometimes being so enfeebled by the flux as not to have strength to reach the necessary-buckets. There are four of these in each of the apartments. It often happens that those who are placed at a distance from the buckets, in endeavouring to get to them, tumble over their companions in consequence of their being shackled. These accidents, though unavoidable, are productive of

449

continual quarrels, in which some of them are always bruised. In this situation, unable to proceed and prevented from going to the tubs, they desist from the attempt; and as the necessities of nature are not to be resisted, they ease themselves as they lie.

There followed now several pages which some particular wear or friction, or perhaps the poorer quality of the ink, had rendered illegible. Erasmus felt hot and half stifled in the close confines of the cabin. The sweetish smell that rose from the pages came like some repugnant claim on him. He had retrieved this record from its journey to dust, and the rescue seemed to make him for the moment his cousin's accomplice. Perhaps in the final pages Paris might have written something to incriminate himself. The writing here was more hasty and ragged, though still for the most part clear enough.

This morning we consigned to the sea Evans, who had been declining these two weeks past with a low fever and died on deck. Also two slaves, a man of the bloody flux and a boy of the gravel and stoppage of the urine, thus bringing . . . McGann in irons for the second time, for begging rice from the negroes' bowls. Now that supplies are running low, the slaves get more than the crew, which is reasonable from Thurso's point of view since he has no hope of selling the latter and may save their wages if they die. Water too is growing scarce – the men are rationed to one pint a day. McGann is sick with scurvy, but his appetite seems not to be affected. On being detected he was beaten by Barton with a rope's end, then set in irons on the deck. He sits there in his shackles with his face screwed up tight and the red bonnet, which he has worn all the voyage, still hanging over his brow . . . not far from death, in my judgement, but still has not relented in the matter of his wager with Sullivan.

He is not the only one of our people to beg thus. I have been surprised to see the negroes give sometimes from their own portions, notwithstanding the grievous condition they are themselves in. It cannot be pity, how could they pity the men who have brought them to this pass? Crew and slaves are in the embrace of a wretchedness so profound that it precludes all animosity, all personal . . . my cabin here, I can hardly breathe in the mid-parts of the day and seek what breezes I can get on the weather side. The stench of the ship is truly terrible, there is not only the reek that rises from the bilges, but the smell of the slave quarters grows daily less supportable, for all our applications of vinegar and sulphur. My fancies grow sick, I feel the breeding of disease in the pores of her timbers and . . . We are a foul breath on the ocean that bears us.

450

Not only fancies are bred in these days but memories dredged up as it were from the sea. I have been thinking much of you lately and of our child that we never saw. It haunts my thoughts that you cried out for me and I was not there. Worse than this, against all reason and yet beyond my power to suppress, there is the fear that you were there in the crowd, that you saw me, head and hands thrust forward in that grotesque position, my face bleeding and fouled, and it was this memory of my face that you carried to the grave, while yours in my memory is flawless and . . . these ugly thoughts, my dearest.

I know that if I had not persisted in publishing my opinions – which I did out of arrogance . . . into prison and ruin. Because of this I took Kemp's offer, not from any necessity of a material nature, but from the necessity of my shame . . . regard myself as valueless, as disposable for any purpose, however unworthy . . . throw my life away but I have been brought with despair to see that this was the same self-regard as before. I have assisted in the suffering inflicted on these innocent people and in so doing joined the ranks of those that degrade the unoffending . . . This has been my crime and I am more guilty in it than the common seamen, who can plead the dire necessity of –

Erasmus closed the book with sudden violence. He understood better now the initial reluctance he had felt. Reading had brought his cousin too close. In some such cramped and narrow space as this, where he himself was now, Paris must have written the words. His image came through them, undimmed by the years: the awkward, heavy-shouldered form in its clerical black, the lined face with its look of obstinate patience. He had suffered . . . Erasmus felt the touch of an intolerable compassion. At the same time he could hardly believe what he had been reading. It struck him as verging on madness. This wild confession, this owning to a crime so outlandish, so totally different from the true ones of mutiny and theft of the negroes, outraged him with its insolence and perversity. In the conflict of these feelings Erasmus was swept by doubt and loneliness. His whole being seemed under threat of dissolution. What became of law, of legitimacy, of established order, if a man could assume such attitudes of private morality, decide for himself where his fault lay? It turned everything upside down. He could think of nothing more damnable. And yet . . . He remembered suddenly the second, rarer smile his cousin had, the one that came slowly, transforming his face. Briefly, unwillingly, Erasmus glimpsed the possibility of freedom.

His face and hands felt hot, feverish almost. He went to the water jug on his narrow table and washed, cupping the cold water in his hands and throwing it repeatedly up into his face. After this, feeling the need for air, he mounted to the deck and found a sky still smouldering in the aftermath of sunset. Embers of cloud glowed in the east and there were long rifts of fire low over the sea. He stood at the rail, breathing deeply, watching the flame die slowly to colours of cinders and ash, allowing his knowledge of his cousin's wickedness to return and comfort him.

FORTY-ONE

On the second day following, helped by the constant flow of the stream and a fair wind from the south-east, they drew level with Anastasia Island and by the middle of the afternoon, crossing the bar at high tide, they had anchored in the harbour of St Augustine.

Turned out as elegantly as conditions at sea permitted, in a cocked hat and dove-grey suit, and accompanied by Harvey in sober black and a powdered pigtail, Erasmus stepped on to the quayside to find himself being saluted by a young lieutenant of Dragoons, resplendent in full dress uniform, waiting for him beside an ancient, creaking four-wheeler. Word of the ship's approach had come post from Anastasia Island, the lieutenant explained, flicking with his gloves at the cracked leather seats of the coach. The Governor was detained in the port at present over some business with stores. He apologized for the state of the conveyance, but there was nothing better to be found, the Spanish having allowed things to run down to a degree quite shocking. With the Colony now in British hands, things would very soon be improved . . .

At a pace consistent with the powers of their skinny horses and ragged, consumptive-looking driver, they proceeded over the bridge and causeway spanning the estuary of the St Sebastian River, with the decayed fortress of St Mark, built by the Spanish, looming up across the flat, marshy landscape. The city was built along a narrow ridge of land between marsh and river mouth and lay a good two miles from the ocean, though within sight of the bar and lighthouse.

The lieutenant, who was very young, had been instructed to

make himself agreeable to the distinguished visitor from England and he strove to fulfil his instructions, pointing out features of the landscape, apologizing yet again for the Governor's absence. Colonel Campbell had left word he would be back within the hour. Would Mr Kemp care to wait at the Residence? The lieutenant ventured to think they could make him tolerably comfortable . . .

Erasmus considered. He had never taken easily to waiting; and there would be some advantage, slight but ponderable, in having himself properly announced and received, rather than appearing to wait on the governor's pleasure. They had entered now the precincts of the city. A pleasant, well-shaded avenue led between gardens and orange groves. 'If you will be good enough to set me down in the principal square,' he said, 'I will walk for an hour and view the town.'

The offer of an escort was declined with polite firmness. In a short while Erasmus was sauntering through the lanes that ran north and south, parallel to the sea wall, Harvey a pace behind, laden with his sword and his gloves and the small box containing his letters of introduction and soon – since the afternoon sun was still hot – his coat and hat.

He was struck by the silence and abandonment of the place. There were no surfaced roads. There were no pavements or sidewalks. The houses were built in the Spanish style, with projecting balconies and latticed verandahs. Time and weather had softened their colours and crumbled the walls surrounding their neglected gardens. For the most part they were shuttered and silent. The whole city lay under the hush of desertion. The stores in the square were boarded. A few listless Indians sat on the steps of the Spanish Mission Church. He encountered small groups of red-coated soldiers from the garrison, but no European civilians at all. The British, it seemed, had taken over an empty city.

It was early evening when he presented himself at the Residence, a white, Spanish-style mansion of good proportions, facing to the sea. He was conducted to the drawing-room, where he found Campbell, together with another man, an officer in uniform, awaiting him. He delivered his letters and expressed himself delighted to make the Governor's acquaintance.

'And I yours, sir,' the Governor said. 'I bid you heartily welcome here in our new Colony of Florida.' He was a lean, wiry man, with an energetic manner and the accents of his native Banffshire. His eyes were small and watchful and they held a twinkling light. 'I have the honour to present Major Redwood, the commander of our garrison here,' he said.

'Your servant, sir.' The major brought his heels together with a jingle of spears. He was big and fair-browed, with a good-humoured, careless face. 'We have a damned good brandy here,' he said, 'if you want to celebrate being on terra firma again. I hate ships myself. The Spanish left a cellarful of it. Just about all they did leave, apart from rusty cannon and dying Indians.'

'Come, Redwood, we must not give our visitor the wrong impression.'

This had been said with a smile, but Erasmus heard the note of reproof and understood it perfectly. He was swift and acute where his interest was involved. There were two different types of men before him here and the difference might be useful. 'We should drink to them for leaving it,' he said with a smile of good-fellowship for Redwood. 'Then another bumper in gratitude to them for taking themselves off and allowing us to drink in peace.'

This was a sentiment that appealed to the major, who broke into a loud laugh. Erasmus turned back to the Governor. 'They could not take this happy climate away with them,' he said, 'nor the fertility of the soil.'

Campbell showed some cautious pleasure at this. 'You are right, sir,' he said. 'I perceive you to be a man of sense and observation. Why, you can get three crops of vegetables a year out of this soil and figs and oranges in abundance. This could be a paradise, if settled with subjects of King George and properly cultivated.'

'Let us drink to that and be damned to the Dons,' Erasmus said, raising his glass.

'You are proposing to remain some time with us, I believe?' Campbell said, after they had drunk. His small, twinkling eyes rested steadily on Erasmus for some seconds. 'Such at least is my hope,' he added.

'You are very good, sir. Yes, some little time. There is much of interest here, and I shall need to inform myself before I can make a full report to my partners in London as to the prospects for development in the Colony.'

Campbell nodded with the vigour characteristic of all his movements. When he spoke, however, his voice was softer and the Scottish accent more clearly audible. 'Yes, sir, we shall hope you carry away with you a favourable impression. But perhaps there is something more particular that you will be requiring from us?'

Erasmus sipped his brandy. There had been more than politeness in this query. It was almost as if the other were reaching for an accommodation between them already. Campbell was a shrewd fellow, by no means the simple soldier he might have wanted to be thought. 'There are things we might profitably discuss, sir, bye and bye,' he said. 'Time and your other engagements permitting.'

'In the meantime, what do you say to some more brandy?' Redwood said, turning towards the sideboard. He moved lightly for a man of his bulk. ''Twill evaporate completely if left too long.'

'You will stay with us here, of course, for the length of your visit?' the Governor said. 'I dare say we can make you rather more comfortable than you will have been aboard ship.'

Erasmus made some demur, but not much; he had been expecting the offer. He was engaged to dinner and shown his quarters, while Harvey, who had just discovered a source of grog below stairs and had begun to harbour designs on a serving girl with Spanish brows and Indian colouring, was dispatched back to the ship for some further necessities of his master's.

There were only the three of them at dinner. An orderly in uniform served them with quail pie and roast venison and an assortment of fresh vegetables, accompanied by a good Burgundy. Erasmus commented on the excellence of the meal.

'We owe it to Redwood,' Campbell said, glancing at the commandant with his usual careful, close-mouthed geniality. The major, it was now explained, had been in charge of the British occupation force when the Colony was handed over by

456

the Spanish, and had served as administrator until the Governor's arrival eighteen months later. A good deal of his time had been spent on food, one way and another – organizing field kitchens for the garrison, recruiting and training kitchen staff for the Residence, ensuring a supply of fresh meat and vegetables from the surrounding countryside.

'Well, my congratulations, sir,' Erasmus said. 'The results do you credit.' Much of what Campbell had just been telling him he knew already, though he was careful to give no indication of this. In his usual methodical way, he had made enquiries before leaving England and he knew more about both men than either would have suspected. As they sat after dinner on the terrace with their brandy and cigars, he reviewed this knowledge in his mind. Redwood had been a professional soldier from the age of eighteen when he had joined as an ensign in a regiment of infantry. Since then he had seen service in a dozen campaigns. He was brave, competent, perhaps not greatly ambitious, though he would doubtless be hoping for promotion now, after his services in this interim period. He struck Erasmus as a man who would do much for the sake of friendship or even from a careless kind of generosity. Not so Campbell . . .

He thought again about the Governor's record. A cavalryman by training, he had fought with Cumberland against his fellow Scots and held a command under Ligonier in the expeditionary force to Flanders. He had come to North America in 1757 and fought the French and their Indian allies in Pennsylvania and South Carolina. In 1761 he had helped in the defeat and decimation of the Cherokee nation, distinguishing himself as much by his adroit manipulation of rivalries among the tribes as by skill in the field. His present post was a recognition of these services to the Crown. He would need all his diplomacy now, since the main task facing the new administration was to persuade the fierce and numerous Creek Indians to the north and west of them to surrender large tracts of their territory. Campbell had risen on a certain kind of shrewd and dogged merit, without great influence or flavour. He would not want to make enemies at home now.

The knowledge of all this was present to Erasmus as he sat

457

there at his ease in the warm evening, with the land breeze bringing a scent of autumn roses, and the sound of the sea in his ears. Speculation, if not knowledge, there must have been on Campbell's part too, as he now broke a short period of silence by saying in that softer voice he used for more deliberate speech, 'You suggested earlier, if I am not mistaken, that we might be of some service to you. But perhaps you would prefer some later occasion to talk of it?'

'No, no,' Erasmus said. 'I have no objection to discussing the matter now, none at all.'

He began to speak about the *Liverpool Merchant*, the delayed return, the assumed loss, the lapse of twelve years, the visit of Captain Philips, the ship as he had last seen her, grounded and abandoned. He spoke of his belief that the mutineers and the remnants of the negroes had survived and the possibility they had continued living together in the wilds of south Florida. 'Life would be possible there for a small number and they had women with them,' he said. He had not mentioned his cousin. 'It is my intention to pursue these men and bring them to account. I know I can count upon your help as the newly invested Governor. These men have formed a colony of criminals within His Majesty's Colony of Florida and they must be rooted out and punished with the law.'

A short silence succeeded this. Then Campbell said, 'You are speaking of a company of renegade whites and runaway negroes beached up in south Florida twelve years ago. Sir, the times have been violent. They are most likely to be dead or scattered long ago.'

'It is the violence of the times that affords me reason. It is obvious that they did not plan to escape by sea. And the overland route northwards would have been difficult, extremely so, with the Spanish here and the tribes hostile. Their safety would have been in keeping together. They had blood on their hands, if I am right. Where were they to make for?' He had spoken with confidence but as the silence continued he felt a touch of panic. These were men of experience. He had not realized until now how much he wanted his reasoning to prevail with them. 'Then there are the stories that the Indians tell,' he said, into

458

the silence. 'They talk of a community of black and white living in the south part of the peninsula.'

'I have heard of no such community,' Campbell said. 'The evidence for it seems slight to me, sir.'

This brought a welcome anger. Scepticism from such a quarter was only to be expected – it afforded the best excuse for denying help. 'I have judged the evidence sufficient,' he said coldly. 'I have given you full and adequate reason. I am the one who is injured in this. I have the same right to redress here as I would anywhere else within His Majesty's dominions. Those negroes who were on the ship originally and any offspring they may have had subsequent to their escape are mine by right of purchase.'

'Speaking of those same negroes . . .' Redwood had leaned forward and was regarding him with a look of good-humoured curiosity. 'Tell me,' he said, 'did it never occur to you that the negroes might have risen against the crew and killed them? Such rebellions have been frequent enough on slaveships – more frequent than mutinies. In that case, none of the seamen would have survived and the blacks might have made south for the Keys. I don't say this is what happened but I am surprised that you do not think of it as the first possibility.'

The question took Erasmus completely by surprise. He returned the major's gaze for some moments without being able to think of an answer. He did not like the expression of curiosity on Redwood's face; it was the look a man might have on seeing something odd, but not dangerously so. The silence on the terrace lengthened from moment to moment. It came to Erasmus in his disarray that his cousin's guilt was not a matter of logical deduction but a terrible necessity . . . 'Why, but of course,' he said, 'it could not have been the negroes. It would have needed able seamen to bring her in so close, find the mouth of the inlet and then take soundings so she could be towed.' He felt as if he had passed some crucial test.

Redwood nodded. 'Certainly men unused to the sea could not have done it,' he said. 'When you say help, I take it you mean troops. You can hardly go down there on your own, waving a warrant.'

459

'I have estimated that I shall need a force of fifty men under an officer and two sergeants, and two light cannon,' Erasmus said.

The Governor uttered a short exclamation, somewhere between a laugh and a snort. Thereafter there was silence, which neither wanted to be the first to break. It was Campbell who yielded. In a voice that this shock had softened almost to the caressive, he said, 'I beg you will listen to me, my good sir. I intend to be quite frank with you. I am a plain military man, so you will forgive my bluntness. In the days before us there is no slightest prospect of your obtaining five troops, let alone fifty. I should be compelled to say the same whoever asked me and whatever bad report I might suffer for it back home among people who do not understand the exigencies of the situation. You could not have come at a more awkward time with such a request. Perhaps you know something of how things stand with us here?'

'I know you are on the eve of talks with the Creek Indians.'

'Sir, the tribes are camped in the woods on the west side of the St John River. They will not cross the water yet. They give the care of their horses as excuse. They are cunning and they have had things their own way in East Florida for a long time.'

'It is a monster of our own making,' Redwood said. 'The Lower Creeks were allied with us in these late wars. We supplied them with muskets and rum in equal measure. They helped us to victory here by keeping the Dons cooped up in their forts.' He was in the light that fell on to the terrace from the dining-room behind them and Erasmus saw that he was smiling, it seemed rather bitterly. 'Now they think we owe them something, the poor benighted heathen,' he said.

'Aye, man, we know all that, those are the necessities of war,' Campbell said impatiently. 'What I am talking about are the problems of peace. The tribes are assembling at the river, not thirty miles off. We have a force of fewer than two hundred men, cavalry included. That is all they have thought fit to give me, sir. There is no prospect of raising a militia, the province is empty, the resident population have followed the Spanish to Havana. In three days we ride out to Picolata to receive the chiefs. The Indian agent is due to arrive from Georgia some time tomorrow to take part in the talks.'

'And the talks will be directed . . .?'

'To the establishment of mutually agreeable frontiers between the lands of the red people and those of the white.' This came with a certain suavity, as if Campbell were rehearsing his lines for the conference. He had a way of turning his irritation into an occasion for rhetoric.

'In short,' Redwood said, 'our red brothers have to be persuaded to surrender large areas of their traditional hunting grounds. What makes it just a trifle delicate is that they outnumber us at present by roughly twenty to one.'

Campbell made an irritated bridling movement of the head. It was clear that he found the major's sarcasm irksome. The sarcasm itself seemed to Erasmus in some way factitious or assumed and he was once again aware of stresses between these two men.

'No question of using force,' Campbell said. 'The future of the colony depends on settlement. A fair and proper settlement which will lay the basis for lasting peace. We must secure land in quantity enough to bring settlers from England and we must be able to guarantee the frontiers.'

'I quite understand the situation,' Erasmus said. 'I will be content to wait until these discussions have been completed.' He knew this form of words would not be greatly agreeable to Campbell, suggesting as they did that a promise had been made. 'I can employ my time very profitably in the interval,' he added quickly, 'by making a survey of the surrounding countryside. I suppose I may have the use of a horse?' This laying of a small question over a larger one was a device he had found useful in the past.

'Why, as to that, certainly,' Campbell said. 'And a groom, if you like. But I cannot be so definite –'

'You will have read by now the letters I brought with me?'

'I have read them, yes.'

'You will know, then, something of the interests I represent. I don't go into it at present, it is something we can discuss in the days ahead, but they are very considerable, especially in the

461

matter of capital at disposal for investment –' He broke off and drew out the watch from his waistcoat pocket. 'Is it really so late? Time passes quickly when spent in company so congenial. I will not keep you from your rest any longer, gentlemen.'

With this he got to his feet. Redwood walked with him as far as the courtyard which gave access to the guest-rooms. The stables were on that side, the major explained; he had a ride of a mile or so to the house where he was quartered; the officers and a good number of the men had been accommodated in private houses, which had caused trouble in the early days.

'The Spanish generally quit the houses when someone was quartered on them,' Redwood said. 'Then they made a claim on us for compensation, a hundred and eighty dollars a week in the case of Cochrane and me. You have met Cochrane, I think – he came to meet you. I told them that British subjects all over America had troops quartered on them when there were no barracks to contain them, without any expense to the Crown, and how could I put the Crown to expense in their favour when it was not allowed to British subjects?'

He paused, smiling. The moon was up and a pale wash of light lay over the courtyard, silvering the silent stone fountain in the centre and the sharp leaves of the orange trees lining the sides. 'We took a stand on principle,' the major said. 'Always a very convenient thing to do. In fact we had no money to pay. But Campbell will tell you about that – shortage of money is one of his favourite subjects.'

He was silent for a moment, then said in a different tone, 'There is something I was intending to tell you . . . I thought it better not to speak of it before the colonel. It is an old maxim in the army not to seem to know more about anything than your superior officer, but he has only been here a few months, you know. The fact is, there is some evidence for the existence of this settlement you spoke about just now. What I said about the negroes rising was only my curiosity.' Something of the same slightly quizzical expression was on his face as he looked at Erasmus now. 'It struck me as odd, you know, that you hadn't thought of it. Anyway, in the first weeks I was here, early in 1763, I talked to a half-breed trapper who had brought in some skins to sell and he told me he had seen black men and white fishing together in a creek back behind the shore. He had heard them shouting to drive the fish into the traps and had gone to look. I remember he said they had bamboo harpoons and there were some children watching from the bank. He said he spoke to them. They talked a lingua franca among themselves, a kind of pidgin. It was summer and they were naked save for loincloths and they had oiled themselves with something fishy-smelling. One of them asked him if he could get horsehair, offered him racoon tails for horsehair, a good trade, the trapper thought, but of course he hadn't got any . . .'

'Horsehair,' Erasmus repeated wonderingly. 'What would a man in that wilderness want with horsehair?'

'It was a garbled story. A fiddle came into it somewhere. I don't recall the details, perhaps I never knew them. The trapper's English wasn't exactly –'

'You need horsehair to make a fiddle-bow . . .' Erasmus looked for a moment across the moonlit courtyard. 'There was a fiddler,' he said with sudden and rather startling loudness. 'He was mentioned . . . They had a fiddler aboard to dance the slaves.'

'Did they so? That may be it then. I didn't think too much of it at the time. In the months after the Peace Treaty people came with all sorts of stories, just to gain our goodwill.'

'Did he say where it was?'

'He did not say exactly. It was in the country north of Cape Florida and the Miami River. That is a region of pinewood ridge and jungle hummock, completely trackless – it has never been mapped.'

'Could the man be found again?'

'I shouldn't think so. Not in time to be of any use to you. These fellows go off for months into the wilds. But I can make enquiries among the Mission Indians who have stayed on here. Most of them speak some Spanish, it is not difficult to find an interpreter. Someone may be found who knows something of the matter. There may be trade links. It is not really so improbable that a small settlement could have survived down there. They are marshlands mainly, I believe, but game must be plentiful, fish too, and it is healthier than the west side because of the sea breezes. During the years of the war there were no troop movements or landings in the far south of Florida. What would have been the point? Miles from anywhere, no use to anyone. There are reports of mixed bands of negroes and Indians from Mississippi raiding in West Florida, but nothing south of the St John River. I'll see what I can find out.'

'I would be extremely grateful.' Despite his efforts at containment, Erasmus's voice quivered slightly. He had felt his soul expand with delight at this confirmation of his hopes.

'It means a lot to you, doesn't it?'

Erasmus straightened up at this and glanced away. Only feelings of gratitude to Redwood prevented him from resenting this intimate question more. He felt the eyes of the other man fixed on him still. 'I have come from England expressly to see justice done,' he said.

'Ah, yes, I forgot – justice.' Redwood raised his head and smiled and his strong teeth gleamed in the moonlight. It was a careless smile, though with something bitter in it, not the smile of a stupid man. 'Justice is a mighty fine thing,' he said.

FORTY-TWO

Mr George Watson, Superintendent of Indian Affairs for the Southern District, arrived from Savannah on the following afternoon. He was a tall man, rather cadaverous, with a thin, high-bridged nose through which the breath seemed to come with some difficulty or reluctance. There were few men who knew more about the ways of Indians than Watson. He said as much himself to Erasmus not long after his arrival. In the name of the Great White King he had made deals of one sort or another with them throughout Georgia and the Carolinas, from Pantico Sound to Brunswick. The Tuscarora, the Yamassee, the Choctaw, the Chickasee and the confederate tribes of the Creeks – Watson knew them all. Perhaps because of this long experience his manner had become like theirs: slow and dignified and impassive.

He spent much of the time before the conference closeted with Campbell, deciding on policy, studying maps of the north-east tidewater area, which was where they hoped to obtain the major concessions. Occasionally they emerged to pace together on the terrace or in the gardens behind the house, affording as they did so a remarkable study in contrasts, the wiry, tenacious Governor with his soft voice and emphatic gestures and the dignified, sonorous Agent in his long-skirted coat and old-fashioned, full-bottomed wig.

For the most part, however, Erasmus saw little of either, a circumstance he did not mind, as it left him free to explore the district surrounding St Augustine and compile his report; he had been perfectly sincere, while at the same time knowing it would be a powerful inducement to Campbell, in what he had said about the possibilities of investments in the colony.

465

It did not take him very long to see that these were considerable indeed. As he rode about the countryside, he was able to mature his intentions with regard to his renegade cousin while at the same time calculating the profits that could be made here, in advance of the influx of population which must inevitably come, once the Indians had been pacified. These considerations of justice and pecuniary advantage, though one belonged in the moral and the other in the material realm, seemed of the same order to Erasmus, and gave him a similar kind of satisfaction, sanctified equally by law and the dictates of feeling.

There was no doubt that the territory offered much to the colonist. The cold in winter was only sufficient to mark the difference of season, without preventing the growth of vegetables – green peas could be had at Christmas without the aid of fire or glass. The same field could give two crops of Indian corn in a year and Erasmus was reliably informed that indigo, which he knew to be a highly profitable export crop in South Carolina, could here be cut four times a year and need not be planted more often than once in three years. The rivers that ran through the country made the cost of transport negligible. The St John River admitted vessels of nine-foot draught for a considerable way – how far he was not able precisely to determine; and there was an excellent harbour at the mouth of the Mosketto. His mind was busy with schemes. Settling accounts with his cousin might keep him in Florida some time yet, but he could send his instructions to London. This was Crown property now and the Crown always needed money. The land could be purchased through an agent. Then concerted advertising to attract settlement . . .

He did not speak of these plans to anyone, but he threw off various possibilities when he was alone with the Governor, partly in order to keep him well disposed, but also because he had recognized from the start that Campbell, though highly cautious, had an instinct for commerce which might be turned to good account. It would be necessary to form a company, with an office in St Augustine, so as to increase profits by levying a local tax on the resale of the land. Someone of local standing would be needed for this, someone with strong backing, in case of disputes.

However, Campbell was not able to give these matters much of his mind at present. As the day appointed for the conference approached, he grew brusquer and more irascible, though his eyes still held their twinkling light. Things were not going well. The Indians had remained camped on the west bank of the river. It was reported that their supplies of food were running low. A schooner and a pilot-boat were on the way from Georgia, loaded with rum, tobacco, parched corn and a variety of gifts – beads, kettles, mirrors, knives – but unfavourable winds had slowed their passage and they had not yet arrived. Meanwhile, the braves were becoming disgruntled.

'Curse this weather,' Campbell said, not for the first time. 'Not having the baubles to distribute sets us off to a bad start. The devils will start raising mischief before much longer. The chiefs can't control the young men indefinitely. They have got no liquor, heaven be praised.'

'They will not relish being kept long there, at the start of their hunting season,' Watson conceded with his usual gravity.

They were sitting at dinner on the eve of the conference. At the Agent's suggestion Erasmus had been invited to attend this as an observer. He could be presented as a special envoy from England, a proof that the Great White Father took an interest in his red children. Such things impressed them, Watson said. Erasmus had accepted eagerly enough, curious to see how the business would be managed. 'These Creeks were our allies in the late wars,' he said now. 'Surely that will provide a good foundation for these talks we are entering upon tomorrow?'

'Allies?' Watson's brows rose without otherwise disturbing the solemn composure of his face. 'My dear sir, these fellows have no concept of loyalty, none at all, except in their own clans. They are fickle and they are treacherous, sir, they are wilder than their own ponies. I know them, by God, I have been dealing with redskins for thirty years. They have to be treated as we treat children, with gifts and material inducements. They will not act from a spirit of service, they will do nothing except they see a profit in it for themselves. They fought for us, as you

467

rightly say, but that was more because they wanted the run of
the hunting grounds on this side of the river than out of friendship.'

'We were not entirely governed by motives of friendship
either, if I remember rightly,' Redwood said, smiling down the
table at Watson. 'And it might even be thought by some that
we had territorial ambitions of our own.'

Campbell had developed a habit, in these anxious days, of
glancing aside with a sharp compression of the lips, as at some
sudden pain. He did it now. 'This habit of sarcasm is growing
upon you, Redwood,' he said testily. 'You cannot compare the
policy of national states with the petty intrigues of these
savages.'

'Ah, no, of course not.' Redwood poured himself more wine.
He drank a good deal, though without looking much the worse
for it.

'Now England is the occupying power, not Spain,' Campbell
said, 'and it needs little for them to transfer their hostility to us.
Aye, by God, very little – a few more days kicking their heels in
the woods there might be enough to do it.'

'But you will have told them the ships are on the way,'
Erasmus said.

'Sir, they are not like us. If I say to you that there are ships
on the way, loaded with the things you want, but they are
delayed by weather, and if I give you my hand on it, you will
take my word, because we are men of honour. But these people
never trust assurances completely. There is some confounded
division in their skulls, sir, I know not how to describe it, they
are capable of believing a thing and not believing it both at the
same time.'

Erasmus nodded, tightening his lips. There could hardly have
been anything he found more reprehensible. He could understand consecutive beliefs that might be contradictory, each filling
the mind in its season; but not this appalling confusion. Every
promise, every glance, would be tainted by it. It was like believing a man innocent and guilty of the same offence. Madness . . .
The memory of an entry in his cousin's journal came suddenly
to him. A dying negro. Death in his eyes and the invincible

468

desire to live. Paris had presided over life and death. Looking up he found the Governor's twinkling gaze upon him. 'That is the savage mind, I suppose,' he said.

'Aye,' Campbell said, 'and even when the vessels come in, I cannot be assured that they will be sufficiently stocked to feed the Indians and satisfy their appetite for trade goods until the Treaty of Limits is signed. Nine hundred pounds, sir, that is all the Government has seen fit to grant me for the conduct of this business, which is vital for the future prospects of the Colony. It almost defies belief. I can only think that His Majesty has not been properly informed of what may happen if we fail here. I have made an outlay of seven hundred and six pounds and two shillings on provisioning the ships. It needs not much calculation to see that our margins are perilously slight. I tell you this, sir, in the hope that you may be able to bring some influence to bear on your return to England.'

'I will do what I can,' Erasmus said. Campbell still thought in terms of a public official, which did not differ much from those of a shopkeeper. It was natural enough – he had to account for every penny. But it was a pitiful waste of labour to solicit a few hundred pounds more from a miserly Exchequer when there were vast profits waiting to be picked up here in the Colony. However, this was not the time to say so. At present, he knew, it was the value to Campbell of his influence in England that held out the best prospect of obtaining the troops and cannon he wanted. 'If the matter were represented as a legitimate concern of the Sugar Interest, we might do much,' he said. 'And it could be so represented – there is no reason that I can see why sugar should not be grown in Florida. In the meantime, however, while the vessels are delayed, the Indians must be brought to trust our intentions.'

'They do not trust one another's intentions, let alone ours,' Campbell said.

'That is to our advantage.' Watson's head turned slowly as he glanced up and down the table. The wine had brought a flush to the parchment of his cheeks, but his features were as grave and composed as ever. 'They will find it easier to trust us than to trust one another,' he said. 'I have seen it happen again and

469

again. We may be few but we speak with one voice, whereas among them it is as Terence said, *Quot homines tot sententiae*, as many opinions as there are men. As for the ships, we differ there, Campbell, the main thing is that they should arrive and be seen to have arrived. Lying there at anchor with their holds full of rum and tobacco and trinkets they will work very powerfully in our favour. I would be opposed to making gifts of any kind until the treaty is safely signed and in our pocket.'

He got to his feet, still nodding solemnly. He was a tall man and he made an imposing figure as he stood there in his dark suit and full wig, with his deep-set eyes and long, cadaverous face. 'I don't speak of the corn,' he said. 'The red men are hungry, their stocks are low, it is fitting we should give them food. We must on no account appear to them ungenerous. It is a quality they despise above all others.'

'I bow to your judgement in the matter of the presents,' Campbell said. 'They are better given out after than before.'

Watson smiled slightly. 'This giving and withholding is a difficult balance to achieve,' he said. 'It calls for judgement. Well, I shall bid you goodnight, gentlemen. It is growing late and there is much to do tomorrow.'

FORTY-THREE

Fort Picolata, the site chosen for the conference, was some twenty miles distant, on the east bank of the St John River. It was a stone tower within wooden palisades, built by the Spanish during the war as an outpost against the Indians.

Watson and Campbell, accompanied by Erasmus and escorted by a detachment of troops, rode over in the morning. The headmen of the Creeks left their horses on the west bank and crossed the water by canoe with a hundred warriors. An open pine-log pavilion had been put up inside the palisade and the white men awaited their Indian visitors sitting within this. Branches of pine had been laid over the roof and sides to give protection from the sun and there was a long table in the centre to act as a speaker's podium. Vari-coloured beads on long strings of leather lay coiled on the table like snakes. On either side poles wrapped round with blankets were laid for the chiefs to sit on.

They did not immediately take up position here, however. The whole company of Indians assembled before the pavilion at a distance of some hundred and fifty yards and formed silent ranks behind their chiefs. To Erasmus, sitting unobtrusively to one side in the shade of the pavilion, this forming of rank was strangely like a movement – and a stillness – of the sea; the white plumes of the headdresses swayed and came to rest like foam on the eddy of a dark red tide. Within the enclave of the pavilion colour was deepened. The colonel's high-necked tunic was ruby-coloured, Watson's wig stood out silver against the dark cloth of his suit and the cheap trade beads on the table glowed like gems of price.

At some signal not perceived by Erasmus the Indians began to move forward at an easy pace. He saw now that the chiefs leading the two centre files, distinguished by headdresses that fell below the shoulder and beaded armbands, were carrying feathered objects which he took at this distance for dead birds. They came on for some twenty paces, then rattles sounded among them and a wild, ragged singing, and the whole company broke into a shuffling, lunging dance, raising and lowering their heads and turning their bodies inwards towards the two chiefs carrying the feathered bundles.

In this manner, singing and dancing, they advanced until they were within twenty yards of the pavilion, when they halted and stood silent, their only movement the deep rise and fall of their chests. For perhaps a minute they stood thus, then the two chiefs came forward with a fast dancing step and Erasmus saw now that the objects in their hands were long-stemmed pipes tied with feathers.

Without hesitation, still dancing, they entered the pavilion and advanced to the white men. Erasmus watched while they stroked the faces and hands of the Governor and Superintendent, neither of whom moved a muscle, with the feathers of the pipes. Then one came to him. He felt the soft brush of the feathers and smelled the ignited tobacco in the bowl of the pipe. He met for a moment the gleaming, strangely impersonal eyes of the Indian below the beaded headband. Two braves came forward from the ranks, loaded with dressed buckskins, some of which they laid on the floor and some on the table. The remaining headmen advanced and sat in their places. A pipe was held out by the bowl and the white men smoked solemnly in turn, followed by the seated chiefs. There was a further interval of deep silence, then the Superintendent rose to his feet and began to speak in slow, deliberate tones, pausing frequently to allow his interpreter time to translate.

He declared himself happy that the chiefs and warriors had accepted the invitation for this meeting and kept their word for the hour. He believed they would be well pleased with what they were going to hear from the Governor and from himself. He introduced Erasmus as an emissary from the King of England.

He requested his Indian brothers earnestly to listen and pay attention to the words that would be said to them.

At the conclusion of these remarks he took one of the strings of beads from the table and dropped it with deliberate movements on the earth floor, where it fell with a muffled crash. This ceremony, and the words which had preceded it, were greeted by the Indians with complete silence and impassivity.

The Governor now came forward to the table. Glancing keenly at the expressionless faces of the chiefs on either side of him, he began speaking in his usual brisk, direct and somehow confiding fashion: 'Friends and brothers, the Great King, my master and your father, after driving the French and Spanish from this land, was graciously pleased to appoint me to govern the white people in this part of his newly conquered dominions.

'I know and love the red people. I have lived long with them and I am acquainted with their customs and manners. The Great King knows that I will do everything in my power to keep up peace and harmony between his white subjects and his red children.

'You are apprehensive and have been told that the white people are desirous of getting possession of your hunting grounds. Your fears are ill-founded for my sentiments with regards to the hunting ground of an Indian nation are well known. Such of you as have been in the Cherokee nation must know and all of you must have heard that in the Treaty signed at Charleston after their defeat I spoke against taking their ancestral lands and I prevented it. If I did that for a people with whom I had been at war, who had been prevailed upon by the French to strike their English brothers, you may be sure I will do nothing to the harm of your people who have always been our friends . . .'

Erasmus listened to this with feelings of distinct approval. He had heard a lot of speeches in his time, and this was a good one, though it was difficult to read anything in the set faces of the Indians. Campbell spoke with a kind of gritty dignity that was native to him and made his appeal to matters that lay within the knowledge of his audience. And the accent of sincerity in his words was unmistakable; his voice had grated with feeling when he spoke of his defence of the beaten and demoralized Cherokee. Once again it came to Erasmus that Campbell would be an excellent man to head his Florida Land Company.

The Indians who sat beyond the pavilion were motionless, their eyes fixed on the speaker. The sun was high now; these preliminary ceremonies had taken up the morning. Sunlight lay on the white feathers and the beaded ornaments and the smoothly muscled bodies. Campbell paused to take up a string of beads and drop it from shoulder height to the floor.

'Your profession is hunting,' he said. 'You therefore must have a large tract of country, but it is your interest to have your English brothers near you. They only can supply you in exchange for your skins with clothes to cover you and your wives and children, with guns, powder and ball for your hunting and with a number of other things which you cannot make for yourselves though you cannot exist without them. To induce the white people to live in your neighbourhood you will no doubt think it reasonable to assign them a certain district of country to feed cattle and raise provisions, for without lands they cannot maintain themselves, much less supply you.'

He ended on this with another ceremonial dropping of beads. The Superintendent spoke again briefly, emphasizing that a boundary had to be ascertained, leaving them to determine the limits but recommending them to behave in such a manner as would show their gratitude to the Great King, by whose permission they enjoyed the advantages of trade.

A profound silence followed these words. None of the headmen seated in the pavilion said anything at all. But for the fiery expression of the eyes, their faces might have been cast in stone. After perhaps ten minutes – though it seemed much longer to Erasmus – a young man in the front rank of those outside the pavilion stood up and advanced to the table. In vehement, broken-sounding sentences, strangely at odds with the hesitant English of the interpreter, he began to complain of the high prices the dealers were asking for trade goods. The Superintendent, he said, had promised to lower the rates at a meeting with his people at Pensacola six months before. He was Sempoiaffe, he was a leading man of his nation, but he was not the mouth of

474

his nation and was not seeking to answer the Governor's talk, he left that to the chiefs, but he wanted to say that this thing had been promised and had not been done. Also, it was his opinion that if all the country was going to be settled by white people his people would find nothing but rats and rabbits to kill. Would the white people give them trade goods in exchange for rats and rabbits?

Throughout this the chiefs had remained silent but short grunts of approval had come from the men seated in the open. The speaker dropped a string of beads to the floor and looked full at the white men before returning to his place. His eyes flashed and Erasmus saw the deep intake of his breath and realized that he was moved, though whether by anger or some other emotion he could not tell.

In reply, Watson said that he had not promised to lower the trade as it was not in his power to do so and that he had said the same thing at Pensacola. He appealed to Tallechea and Captain Aleck and the other chiefs who had been present at that meeting whether they had not heard him say so, and Erasmus saw that some of the seated inside the pavilion nodded in agreement.

No other speaker now presented himself and after a further period of unbroken silence and immobility on the part of the Indians, the Superintendent declared the meeting adjourned till the following day.

Not much was said by either Watson or Campbell as they returned to St Augustine. The three men did not meet again till dinner and only then did it become fully apparent to Erasmus just how badly this opening session of the conference had gone.

'But it seemed to me that you were listened to with respectful attention,' he said. 'None of them spoke in rejection of a boundary line.'

'Sir,' Watson said, 'they are devious, they set their meanings out by a system of signals. None of the principal men spoke at all, which is a bad sign to begin with. He who spoke is a leading warrior among the Kasihta Creeks, but not of headman rank. What he said about trade prices was a mere piece of bravado and fabrication. Everybody knows I made no such promise.'

'He knew it too then?'

'He knew it perfectly well,' Campbell said. 'He wanted to put us on the defensive. I have seen it before often enough – they argue from emotion more then you might suppose. What he said about rats and rabbits was just as much beside the point. That fellow's town is on the east side of the Chattahoochee River, up in Georgia. He was talking about Georgia, not Florida.'

'It is all one land to them,' Watson said. 'They have not yet learned to think in terms of state boundaries.'

'What is likely to happen tomorrow then?'

'We shall see,' Watson said, with deepened gravity. 'Tomorrow the chiefs will speak and then we shall see. But I am afraid it will not be easy. The signs are bad. We must hope that with God's help they will be brought to see reason.'

After dinner Redwood asked Erasmus for the favour of some words in private. The major had come from his quarters on foot; it was a fine evening and Erasmus offered to walk some way back with him.

At this hour the streets were almost deserted. Sand and dust had drifted thickly, muffling their steps. The houses were shuttered and silent for the most part. The concrete of sand and ground shell with which they were built had crumbled with time, giving their outlines a softened, abraded appearance in the faint moonlight.

'I have been making enquiries among the Indians here, as I promised you,' Redwood said as they walked along together. 'I am afraid I have not been able to find anyone with knowledge of a settlement in the south of the peninsula. In a way, the times are against you. Some might have known of it who left with the Spanish. As you know, the region is depopulated at present. There are practically no Europeans and the Indians that remain are a sedentary sort of people, who scrape a living here, God knows how.'

'Well, it cannot be helped.' Erasmus had not allowed himself to hope for much from the major's enquiries, but he was none the less disappointed. 'I am grateful for your efforts on my behalf,' he said.

476

'There is no point even in trying to engage a guide from among them,' Redwood said. 'However, I have not failed altogether.'

They were passing a tall, deep-balconied house, which showed some light behind the shutters. As they went by a sound of voices and laughter came from somewhere on the upper floor.

'These are about the only places which show any sign of life,' Redwood said. 'The whores didn't all follow the Spanish to Cuba.' He stopped on this, as if suddenly struck by an idea. 'We are about halfway now to my quarters,' he said. 'It might be rather long for you to walk back the whole way. What do you say to breaking a bottle inside here? I don't suggest we try the girls. I could head you in the direction of something much better if you were ever interested in that line. These have been worked pretty hard by the Spanish and some of our men use them, though there is a brothel nearer the barracks. No, but the Mother Superior here, Mama Rosalita, knows me. I have been here on occasion to deal with affrays and pay for damage. She will give us a room out of the way and serve us a bottle and we can talk in peace. What do you say?'

'I say yes.' He had no particular desire for more to drink but Redwood had not told him everything yet, he had paused at a crucial point, perhaps by design. It came to Erasmus that there was some loneliness about the major for all his conviviality.

They passed through the overgrown garden, knocked, were admitted by the massive Señora Rosalita. It was at once clear from her manner that Redwood was a highly regarded visitor. They were shown without delay to a room at the back of the house and served by the señora herself with a sweetish, dark red wine.

'That's better.' Redwood unbuttoned his tunic and stretched his long legs before him. 'I don't know how it is,' he said, following some train of thought of his own, 'but that preachy fellow Watson sets my teeth on edge, for all I might drink at dinner. Anyway, as I was saying, I did not find anyone in St Augustine, but I have been given the name of an Indian who lives at Matanzas, about fifteen miles away. He is a Lower Creek, the same breed as those you saw today, but he lives solitary. His name is Nipke, though he seems also to be known as the Young Soldier. I am told he knows the southern regions well, having taken part in raids against the Timucua Indians during the war. We paid them a bounty for the scalps of any Indians friendly to the Spanish, you know.'

'I didn't know.'

'Any that were not with us were regarded as being against us. It was part of the policy of terror adopted by our forces to unsettle the region. You couldn't always tell who the scalps had belonged to, but the bounty was paid all the same. The point is that this Nipke has worked for the English before and so he knows the clink of guineas, which makes him easier to talk to. He may not know of your fugitives, but he knows the terrain and will be skilled at following tracks and moving quietly.'

'He sounds just the man.'

'If you are interested, we might ride over to Matanzas tomorrow and see if we can find him. I could spare an hour or two in the morning. Things are at an awkward pass here but there is no danger while the treaty is under discussion. It is the only way, if you want to come to terms with this Nipke. If we send for him, he may come next week or next month or he may not come at all.'

Erasmus hesitated. 'I should like it of all things,' he said. 'I am anxious to get the matter settled. But I am due to attend the conference tomorrow.'

'As to that, I fancy Watson and the Governor will not mind your absence, quite the reverse in fact, they will be able to put it to good account.'

'How do you mean?'

'Things have not gone well today, I gather, and they seem likely to go even worse tomorrow. It will be found necessary to sow dismay among the Indians, for that is the surest way of disuniting them – that and the jealousies among them and their fears of being left out when it comes to the presents. The ships have been sighted, by the way, did you know?'

'No.'

'They are expected to cross the bar some time tomorrow morning. That will strengthen our hand considerably. Watson will simply tell the Creeks that the envoy of their Great White Father has not seen fit to be present.'

'Yes, I see.' Erasmus was silent for some moments. 'It is like dealing with opponents in business,' he said. 'You seek to unsettle them and divide their counsels. Quite lawful, of course.'

'Oh, quite.' Redwood drank some wine. His eyes were partially concealed under lowered lashes – long lashes for a man, Erasmus noticed now, and giving a certain delicacy to the fair-skinned, careless, rather sensual face. 'That was the idea behind our paying bounties for the scalps,' the major said. 'It unsettled the Timucua and divided their counsels very considerably.'

'I cannot say that I see much similarity.' Erasmus spoke rather coldly. He had not liked this joking repetition of his own words. There was a sort of arbitrary quality about Redwood's style of speech which he was beginning to find irksome. He felt that he understood now that grimace of irritation, resembling pain, that would sometimes come to Campbell's face. All the same, Redwood was doing him a favour, and it was obvious now that he was the worse for drink. His colour was high and his voice had thickened slightly. 'However it may be,' Erasmus said in more friendly tones, 'I thank you for your offer of tomorrow and I would be glad of your company.'

'Good, that is settled then. Tell me, what did you think of the business today?'

'Much of the time was taken up with ceremony. It was interesting for me, of course, who have not seen these Indian customs before. They were all decked out in their best beads and feathers.' He laughed a little saying this.

'So were you I suppose?'

'What do you mean?' Erasmus said, staring.

'Campbell in his dress uniform, Watson in his best broadcloth and his silver wig and you, as always, irreproachably turned out. Just a question of fashion, really. Theirs suits the climate better.'

Obscurely displeased at this comparison, Erasmus made no immediate reply. Redwood waited a moment, then said, 'You were talking of the Calumet ceremony, the peace pipes. I have seen it often. They have come singing and dancing to their ruin with those pipes in their hands all over America.'

479

'It is hardly ruin, Redwood – you are exaggerating. They will be left in possession of large tracts of land, as I understand the matter from Colonel Campbell.'

'For how long? We daren't do otherwise at present, or they will rise against us and sweep us into the sea. Campbell is a reasonable man in his way. He knows the Creeks and has a feeling for them. But he is set on getting a favourable treaty – his career hangs on it, and that makes him wonderfully single-minded. That Indian who spoke today, who complained of trade prices, he wasn't so wide of the mark.'

'Not wide of the mark? He accused Watson of breaking promises he had never made. He wasn't even talking of Florida, but of Georgia.'

'That is the point. He has seen thousands of land-hungry white settlers pouring into the Georgia back-country from Virginia and the Carolinas. Many of them have crossed the treaty line and fenced the land on the other side. Nothing has been done to stop it and nothing will be done. And why? You know the answer as well as I do, Kemp. I suggest you know it much better. You have been having a look round, haven't you? This is prime land, there are fortunes to be made out of it – but it is worth a lot more with no Indians on it.'

Redwood sat back, smiling with the slightly bitter carelessness characteristic of him. There were brief sounds from above them, voices, steps on the stairs; then silence. 'And it is hardly necessary for us to use force of arms,' he continued. 'They are prevailed upon to cede their lands by treaty. Trade is the thing that has undone them, this great blessing of trade. Watson tells them they should be grateful for the advantages of trade. Campbell tells them they should give up land to their English brothers for the sake of the trade goods they will get by it. They have hunted over these lands for centuries without ever knowing that what they needed for happiness were muskets and looking-glasses and beads and bits of printed cotton. Now they are persuaded that they cannot live without these things. Strange, is it not?'

Erasmus smiled, but without much warmth. He found himself caring less and less for the other's company. What he had taken for a good-natured, rather thoughtless expansiveness, seemed

480

quite other to him now: Redwood obtruded his views more than a man should, without first making sure they were welcome. And what he was saying was perverse, subversive even. Trade brought benefits to both sides – so much was common knowledge. Erasmus had always disliked people who took a view contrary to what was broadly agreed by men of sense. 'If the Indians want blankets and guns, that is their business,' he said. 'They should try to get them on the best terms. Our business is to supply their wants on terms as favourable to ourselves as we can secure. This is bound to be mutually beneficial in the long run. It is only common sense. You take a very negative view of things, if I may say so, Redwood.'

There had been a curtness of reproof in this which Redwood obviously noticed, as his smile faded and his brows drew together slightly. 'In the long run, you say? But we have only got the short run, Kemp – you and me and the Creeks. If you had fought alongside Indians as I have, and seen what they will do for friendship's sake, you might take a more complicated view. Campbell knows it too, none better, but he is a wonderfully single-minded fellow, that's the difference. You are a single-minded fellow too, aren't you? Let's see now. Months taken from your business, a chartered schooner awaiting your pleasure in the harbour, fifty troops to maintain, a hazardous journey before you into wild country. And all for an old loss that is unlikely to be recovered now. Yes, I would call that single-minded. I do my duty, at least I hope so, and I put my King and country first, but I have always found it plaguey difficult to be single-minded.' He paused for a moment then in a very passable imitation of the Governor's soft voice and brisk manner he said, 'They have a confounded division in their skulls, sir, I know not what to call it.'

He did not look at Erasmus to see the effect of his mimicry; some quality of warmth had passed from their relation, never to be recovered. And it was as well he did not, or he would have seen on the other's face a degree of displeasure he might have felt bound to answer – he was not a man to overlook such things. 'I know not what to call it either,' he said, as if to himself. 'But it is the reason I shall end my days as a half-pay major.'

481

Only his sense of obligation and his knowledge that the major was slightly drunk held Erasmus back from angry words. Redwood's presumption had come too close to the doubts that would sometimes attack him in the midst of all his plans, as he was riding round the countryside or sitting with the others at meals or walking alone in the garden of the Residence, a sense of wonder edged with panic at the strangeness of his presence here, at the time and money he was spending. What could be gained from it now? Then he would remember his high purpose, his mission of justice ... Of course, Redwood was after all an ignorant fellow, with a very partial view; his remarks about trade had shown that. All men of sense knew the benefit of trade. The major was simple-minded, that was it – not single, simple. The conceit pleased Erasmus and restored his calm. 'Just enough left for a toast,' he said, smiling full at the other man though with narrowed eyes. 'Here is to the benefits of trade – and to single-mindedness!'

The major raised his glass. 'What was the other thing?' he said. 'Ah yes, justice. Here's to justice – long-term, of course, I mean!'

FORTY-FOUR

As Redwood had predicted, Erasmus's absence from the conference was accepted with a certain polite alacrity. He confided his reasons to Campbell in the hope that the Governor, seeing the seriousness of his intentions, would give him some more explicit assurance of the troops and cannon. But Campbell was preoccupied and did no more than nod and mutter.

Nipke, the Young Soldier, turned out to be older than expected, stocky and taciturn, with a heavily lined face the colour of wet, reddish clay. He had a pine-log cabin beside a creek and a cowpen and a field of maize and two wives. Redwood had brought an interpreter with them, but there was scarcely need for one: Nipke knew enough English to understand what was wanted. He listened intently to their questions, though his face remained immobile. He had seen no black men on his forays to the south. There was said to be black men on Key Biscayne, but he had never seen any and did not believe it. There were escaped slaves living among the Upper Creeks, he had seen this himself, they had taken wives among the Indian women, but these men had come from the English colonies in the north.

He remained silent for a considerable time when asked if he would go ahead of the expedition as a scout. Erasmus was afraid he would refuse: he was settled here, with fish in the creek and game in the woods and his wives to grow the corn and feed the chickens. But he was quite willing to go — the hesitation had been merely a ploy to obtain better wages. They agreed finally on five shillings a day for him as leader and three for the others he would recruit to make up the scouting

483

party – four more men would be needed. The money would be payable from that day onwards but not in advance; Redwood had warned him against this, as Nipke would almost certainly buy rum with the money and get into trouble of some kind or be found drunk and insensible just when he was needed. In sign of good intention, however, Erasmus gave the Indian a leather cartridge belt which he had brought with him.

The ride there and back and the protracted silences and solemn talk and the consumption of milk and maize cakes had taken up most of the day and it was mid-afternoon when they got back to St Augustine. Redwood had duties in the garrison and Erasmus made his way back to the Residence alone. He found an air of gloom there: the conference had broken up early, he was told, owing to the intransigence of the Indians.

'They were not prepared to yield a single inch, sir, not one iota,' Watson said, with solemn indignation. 'The chiefs came to the rostrum one after the other, all of them in turn, Tallechea, Captain Aleck, Wioffke, Latchige, Chayhage, and all gave voice to the same sentiments.'

'And what were they?'

'They want to keep us to the tidewaters,' Campbell said tersely. He was still in uniform, booted and spurred, with his cavalry sword at his side.

'I am not clear what that means,' Erasmus said.

'Well, they are talking about the salt tide, of course. The saltwaters flow as far as Picolata and they are seeking to restrict English settlement to a line north of that as far as the mouth of the St John River.'

'A meagre acreage indeed,' Watson said, 'and by no means offering scope for settlement on the scale we have in mind. By no means. It is quite unacceptable. And the tone of their speeches was threatening. Veiled threats, of course, but that is their way. They would be sorry, but they could not answer for the consequences if any cattle or white people strayed over the line. Yes, that was the sort of insolence they offered us, sir, the representatives of His Majesty in this new Colony of the Crown. It was all I could do to keep my countenance.'

'I had no difficulty keeping mine, sir, by God,' Campbell said

484

with considerable asperity. Certain strains had begun to show between soldier and civilian. 'A wrong word now and you are like to lose more than your countenance, Watson, you are like to lose your scalp, sir. Our intelligence gives their numbers at not less than five thousand. They know the ground, they have had years of fighting the Spanish over it; we oppose them with a few hundred men fresh from Europe, whose only training is to form a square in open ground and fire volleys.'

'What grant of land are we demanding from them?' Erasmus asked.

'We must have the sweet waters too. We are asking for all the land east of the river from mouth to source. Also some portions on the west bank.'

'That is a difference indeed. I cannot see why they should agree to such a thing.'

'Well, we are now purposing to take a different tack with them.' Campbell gave Erasmus a tight, cautious smile. 'Have you ever sat at dinner with Indian chieftains?' he said.

'No, I can't say I have.'

'You will be doing so this evening, sir.'

'What, you have invited them to dinner here?'

Watson chuckled suddenly, a rather startling and incongruous sound, seeming to rise from cavernous depths. 'Not all of them,' he said. 'Nothing would be gained by that. We have asked two – Tallechea and Captain Aleck. They are the two most powerful men. These savages are so constituted, sir, the honour of an invitation to the governor's house means a great deal, a very great deal, sir, both for those that are included and those that are left out. They will see that their threats of today have not had the effects intended, quite the reverse, in fact, quite the reverse, and it will puzzle them. I also have a little inducement of my own devising . . .' He refused to say more than this, however, contenting himself with further chuckling sounds. 'God willing,' he said, restored to gravity, 'we shall succeed by these means in creating discord and dissension among them.'

They parted on this, Erasmus to rest and refresh himself after his ride. When he descended again it was to find the two chiefs already at table, seated opposite the Governor and

Superintendent, with the half-breed interpreter, whose name was Forrest, a little further down. Redwood entered at the same time as himself and they were introduced together. Erasmus found himself looking into two faces that seemed closely similar in their foreignness, mahogany-coloured, with a regard at once fiery and sombre under prominent brows. His hand, when he extended it, was gripped firmly, not shaken, and his forearm too was grasped for a moment. The Indians smelled of woodsmoke and some kind of sweet oil they had rubbed into the skin – their faces glistened slightly with it. They were not now in ceremonial headdresses but plain headbands and they wore waistcoats over cotton shifts and breeches of fringed buckskin.

Campbell had been to great trouble with the food, making sure the Indians were served with things they were used to and liked: roast wild turkey, maize cakes, pumpkin, sour oranges filled with honey. No rum or brandy was put out, as Creeks generally had a fatal weakness for spirits, but there was wine and root-beer.

Tallechea and Captain Aleck ate in silence, cutting their meat with the small knives they carried at their belts, using their fingers to carry it to their mouths, eating round the bones very delicately and neatly. Erasmus was surprised at their self-containment and the ease and grace of their movements; the unaccustomed surroundings and the alien manners of their hosts seemed to occasion them no physical constraint. Even their silence struck Erasmus as due more to their custom than to any shyness or lack of ease. Only the eyes were savage; these held a constant gleaming light, not changed by what they rested on.

When they had finished eating, both remarked through the hatchet-faced Mr Forrest on the excellence of the meal, nodding heavily for emphasis and uttering deep exclamations. Captain Aleck complimented the Governor on the size and splendour of his house and said that a man who lived in such a stronghold need have no fear of enemies. Following upon this, Tallechea made a brief speech. They knew him as Tama, Flame of Tongue. He hoped there would always be straight paths between their nations. The English had kindled their fire on the sea coast, and it was the will of the Giver of Breath that they and the red men

486

should live in amity, so that their children might grow up to be men.

In reply, the Governor welcomed them to his table and expressed the hope that there would be further occasions of a similar kind, as Tallechea and Captain Aleck were his red brothers and particularly dear to him, but that the paths could not run straight so long as the red people would not behave generously towards their white brothers in the matter of the land. What was being asked was something they could easily spare. As they knew, the ships from Georgia had arrived and now lay at anchor. They contained blankets and ammunition and rum and many things his red brothers desired. But if they gave no land they could expect no presents. The Great King would ask him what he had got for his presents. And how would he answer? He hoped that Tallechea and Captain Aleck, as dear friends and intended Large-Medal Chiefs, would speak to their people and prevent them from taking the same unconstructive attitudes as they had today.

The two Indians listened impassively. But it seemed to Erasmus that the quality of their stillness had deepened with the mention of the ships. After a long, reflective pause, Captain Aleck asked for the Governor's words about medal chiefs to be more fully explained to them, as they had not heard of this matter before. Nor had Erasmus, but he realized at once that this must be what the Superintendent had been so archly mysterious about earlier.

Watson began to speak now with the utmost solemnity. The Great White King had provided special medals to be bestowed upon those of his red children that showed friendship for their English brothers. These medals showed the Great King's face and they were of bronze. Some were as big as a man's palm and they were intended for the most important men, who would be known as Large-Medal Chiefs. Some were smaller, about the size of a dollar. These medals, both large and small, were to be hung round the necks of those who had shown their love for the Great King. This would be done in a special ceremony before all the headmen of the nation.

The Creeks listened to this intently but without further

487

comment. After further assurances of friendship they took a dignified leave. Before Mr Forrest left he was instructed by the Governor, on whom he knew his trade in liquor would in future depend, to move among the Creeks and whenever he heard differences of policy among them to point out the value of English friendship and the line they should take next day at the conference.

'We must leave no stone unturned,' Campbell said, on parting that night. 'An interpreter moves in both worlds. He has an aura about him, he inspires trust.' He looked at Erasmus with his small, canny smile, the twinkle in his eyes as relentless as ever. 'These are cunning fellows we are dealing with, Mr Kemp, and we must try to match them, however much it goes against the grain.'

FORTY-FIVE

It was deemed inadvisable, in Watson's view, for Erasmus to attend the next day's meeting. In the present delicate stage of negotiations his presence there might have seemed like an attempt at conciliation and as such taken as a mark of weakness. So he had to wait until the evening before learning the result of the Governor and Superintendent's combined diplomacy.

He saw at once that things had gone well. Both men showed their satisfaction in ways peculiarly characteristic, Campbell with an air of preternatural shrewdness, Watson more orotund of phrase than ever and with a tendency to rub his long-fingered hands together. There had been a dramatic reversal of attitude on the part of their two dinner guests, both of whom had spoken in favour of granting all the land east of the river and even some on the west side; and this, coming from such respected and influential figures, had found general support among the chiefs.

'They must have talked half the night, sir, after leaving us,' Watson said. 'Character will show, in the end. They have no firmness of purpose, none at all. I have seen it before, they try to impose upon us, they see it is of no avail and that we are people that cannot be intimidated. Then comes the fear of losing what they had thought wé would be coerced to give. We seize the moment to make some special offer. Result?' He made fluttering gestures with his hands. 'Capitulation, sir,' he said, 'absolute and total.' His large, yellowish teeth were exposed in a smile – the first Erasmus could remember seeing on his face. 'I have transported those medals all over the southern states of America,' he said. 'And they weigh, sir, they are deuced heavy.'

'We will present the Treaty tomorrow and there is reason now

489

to think they will sign it,' Campbell said. 'And a good piece of business it will be for England, and King George, God bless him, and I hope our services will be recognized.'

On the following day, at Fort Picolata, thirty of the principal men of the Lower Creek nation put their marks against their names, and the whole of the land from the coast to the river and southward to its source was made available for settlement. Large medals were then bestowed upon Tallechea, Captain Aleck and another chief named Estime, who had supported the English cause; while Wioffke, Latchige and Chayhage were all made Small-Medal Chiefs. This was done in a solemn ceremony, the Superintendent presenting the chiefs to the Governor, who hung the medals about their necks, while the guns of the fort sounded out, repeated by those on board the East Florida Schooner.

That evening, at the Residence, there was a celebratory dinner to which all the chiefs were invited. The Governor, resplendent in scarlet and gold, made a speech in which he declared that Florida would be held by the Crown in perpetuity and that he looked forward to a long and fruitful cooperation between the red men and their white brothers.

Tallechea, his large medal shining on his chest, replied for the assembled chiefs. He was Tama, Flame of Tongue, and he was glad to hear the words of the Governor. He hoped that blankets would soon be given to the people as it was getting cold and one blanket was not enough. These remarks were greeted by the assembled chiefs with deep, guttural exclamations of agreement.

The Superintendent then congratulated the Medal Chiefs, both large and small, and said that all the people of the Creeks, whether or not they had been honoured with medals, had acquired that day a friend and father in the Great White King.

In point of fact the Great White King was just then embarking on policies destined to lose him the whole of North America within two decades and bring about the total destruction of the Creek nation. He had begun already to talk rather rapidly and incoherently at times and his urine had started to show a dark red colour mystifying to his physicians.

At around midnight the chiefs left in a body, many by this time unsteady on their feet and some needing to be helped on to their horses by the young braves who had been waiting in the compound of the Residence. Watson, who had a weak stomach and not much liking for festivities in any case, had retired at an early stage and the garrison officers now returned to their quarters, Redwood flushed and staring with what he had drunk but still sufficiently in command of himself. In leaving he expressed to Campbell his belief that the Medal Chiefs would find their trophies useful some day in stopping the bullets of their English brothers, a remark the Governor found in questionable taste.

His departure left Erasmus and Campbell alone together. Neither of them was yet inclined to retire for the night. Neither had drunk more than moderately, sharing a certain kind of abstemiousness and a dislike for any loss of control. Both men, in their different ways, were in happy mood, though Erasmus was aware that matters had still to be settled with regard to his expedition.

'This is a great occasion, Kemp,' Campbell said. 'Let us have a drop more brandy. We can go into my study, it is more comfortable there.'

This was the room where the conduct of the negotiations had been plotted with Watson, and the pages of Campbell's uncompleted report still covered the desk. 'A historic occasion,' the Governor said, when they were settled in armchairs. 'We have gained all we asked and more. His Majesty's Province of East Florida now includes all the sea coast as far as the tide flows and all the country eastward of the river from its source to its entrance to the sea. I must say that Watson managed that matter of the medals consummately well. He and I have had our differences but I have to admit that his sense of timing was impeccable.'

'He knows his business, so much is certain,' Erasmus said.

'He has had the happy thought, which he explained to me tonight before retiring, of holding back some of the goods promised to the Indians, keeping them in storage for a few months.'

'Where would be the virtue in that?'

'At present they know what we give them is in the nature of a reward. If, a little later, they see us give presents and ask for nothing in return, it will bind them closer to us.'

'If Watson ever needs a post in the City of London he can have one. He would be just the man to deal with our shareholders.'

The Governor sipped at his brandy. 'The best of it is that we have been able to keep within the limits set by the Board of Trade,' he said. He glanced quickly at Erasmus and a look of simple happiness appeared on his small, cautious face, as if he had reverted suddenly to some triumph of boyhood. He said, 'There were four hundred pounds allotted for the expenses of the conference, excluding the cost of provisions, and we have kept it to three hundred and eighty pounds, sixteen shillings and eight pence. I shall be making out the invoices first thing tomorrow. I trust their Lordships at the Board of Trade will take note of it.'

Watching Campbell's face, listening to his self-congratulatory tones, Erasmus knew that the time had come to extract a definite promise. The fire of his purpose had been burning all this while, but low; the Governor's simple pleasure at having cash in hand was fresh kindling, highly combustible – Erasmus felt the flames curl around it and leap. In throwing off hints about land deals he had been misjudging Campbell: the governor was not a man of vision like himself, he was too cautious, too parsimonious. He would be interested more in the immediate prospect . . .

'I am delighted at your success,' he said, 'and this infant Colony has all my good wishes. With you at the helm, Colonel Campbell, she is set fair. Now that things are satisfactorily concluded here, I shall be able to leave shortly for the south of the peninsula. In fact I shall be ready to go as soon as the troops and guns are made available to me.'

He saw an immediate shadow fall over Campbell's face. The Governor set down his glass carefully and Erasmus noticed for the first time that the backs of his small, strong hands were covered with wiry-looking reddish hairs. 'That needs some studying,' Campbell said. 'There are the redskins still to be reckoned with.'

'They will go their separate ways, surely, when the presents have been given out. Think, sir, of the contribution you will be making to the coffers of the new Colony, and just at this time when money is so sorely needed.'

492

'You have lost me now.' A look of alertness had come to Campbell's face. 'What contribution do you speak of?'

'Sir, what would happen if I could not rely on you for the soldiers? I would have to recruit and arm irregulars from Georgia, half the profits would go to a parcel of mercenary rogues who have no ounce or scruple of patriotism among them.'

'Profits? I am slow tonight,' Campbell said. 'Perhaps it is the brandy.'

'No, sir. As a military man and a servant of the Crown you naturally do not take a view of private advantage. You have not fully considered the implications of this business. If my calculation is right – and my enquiries here have yielded some confirmation – there might be upwards of a hundred down there, in this upstart colony within your own, including women and children. They will have been breeding. The great majority will be black or mulatto. At Charles Town an adult slave in good condition, it makes no difference whether black or mulatto, will fetch fifty pounds for a man and thirty-eight for a woman at current prices. Children over the age of ten fetch good prices in proportion. The cost of transporting the cargo to South Carolina will not be great. It takes no great head for figures to see that there is a lot of money for the man who gets them to market. Now if the capture were made by troops acting on your orders, you could make claim to it – for the royal coffers, of course.'

'Of course.'

'And if any of the men are lost in the action, it will be viewed as acceptable in such a cause.' Erasmus was silent for a short while, then he said, in a thoughtful, reflective tone, 'I should say there is something like two and a half thousand guineas in it, clear profit.' He met now the full regard of the Governor's small, keen eyes, with their misleading twinkle still in evidence.

'Do I understand you to say that you do not want the money?' Campbell said, in the softer voice he used for moments of emotion.

'I did not say that. The negroes were purchased by my father and I will recover some of his investment. I shall expect to reimburse myself for the expense I have been put to. And I shall

493

expect a half share in the proceeds of the sale. I am aware that these are liberal terms, but my interest is not entirely financial. The people of that ship are murderers and thieves, the black men and women and all their offspring are stolen property. I want the former brought to justice and the latter recovered and sold. I have personal reasons – their nature I won't discuss, but they are compelling. The years have changed nothing, how could they?'

His tone had quickened in speaking. He experienced now a faint shuddering in his lower jaw and realized that he had set his teeth too close in the stress of his feeling. 'I have money enough,' he continued more calmly. 'I would be content to sign over to you one half of my rights in the cargo, subject to a deduction for expenses, say three hundred and fifty pounds, in exchange for your official countenance and your help in the matter of the men and guns. We can see to the papers, it is a simple enough matter.'

Campbell, nodded and glanced aside, compressing his mouth to a thin line. He reflected for some moments then said, 'I respect your motives, sir, they show you to be a man of both sense and feeling. But you must realize my position here. There may be loss of life among the troops, if these people make resistance. There may even be damage to the cannon, a serious matter, for which I would be held accountable. Under the circumstances, will you not reconsider? I would think it more reasonable if you were to deduct expenses after the sale, from your half-share, rather than before.'

'Sir,' Erasmus said, 'any loss or damage would be favourably viewed, since it would have occurred in the course of smoking out a nest of vipers in the heart of His Majesty's Province. That is the kind of energetic action that brings a man to the notice of his superiors. They will think better of you for it than for saving them a few pounds and shillings on the conference expenses. However, I don't wish to appear unreasonable. As I say, my interest is not only financial. I will lower my figure for expenses by a hundred pounds, but it must still be deductible before the sale of the negroes. Come now, that is the best offer I can make you.'

Campbell's face still showed some reserve. With a sense of timing rivalling that of the masterly Watson, Erasmus chose this moment to say, with studied nonchalance, 'It would be a private matter between us, of course, I would not ask for any accounting. I would take my half in cash if possible, or in bills of credit, and the other half would be made over to you, together with all receipts and records of the sale. I am content to leave the matter in your hands for the better governance of this new Colony of Florida.'

'Sir,' Campbell said, 'here is my hand on it. Give me three days. The Creeks will be drunk for that time on the rum we shall give them and our full force will be needed in case of disturbance. After that they will disperse. Three days, and the men and the guns will be placed at your disposal. You have my word.'

They drank to this, and shook hands again, before parting for the night. Alone in his room, Erasmus lay hot and sleepless, excited by thoughts of lawful profit and just retribution. His plans had knitted together most wonderfully. Somewhere to the south of him Matthew Paris was lying at this moment, asleep or awake, with no knowledge of the nemesis that was drawing near. He had no doubt now that his cousin was there, was alive, was waiting, he too, though unconsciously, for this last act to be played out between them. The nightmare fears that Paris might be dead or somehow beyond his reach had gone now: Paris was necessary to the completeness of things, to the workings of justice, and so he must be there. It was a faith almost childlike, and all the faces that came now to visit him in the darkness confirmed it in one way or another, his father's faces living and dead, the actor in the shipyard sniffing at the fatal timbers, the flushed and handsome dominator of conversation, the staring creature in the candle-light. Sarah's face came too, stately as Miranda, calm with love, then with tears on the cheeks and some ultimate accusation in the eyes. His wife's grotesque masks floated before him and his mother's face of recovered health, which he had never been able to forgive. Last, eclipsing the others, the laughing face of the youth who had lifted him away . . .

Yes, the days were numbered now for cousin Matthew. *You*

will hang by the neck, as my father did, he promised that laughing face. Lying there in the dark he could feel the noose tightening round his cousin's throat, feel it so surely that it was like a constriction of his own breathing.

PART NINE

FORTY-SIX

The passage of Erasmus's ship up the coast towards St Augustine had been observed by Hughes the climber, who also noticed the unusual length of time she dallied at anchor. He was high in the branches of a gum-resin tree in a jungle cluster surrounding a freshwater pool where white-tail deer came to drink – he had been waiting for the deer since early morning.

He saw the ship in the distance and noted by old habit the set of her sails: two square topsails, fore and aft rig – she was a schooner. He had grown accustomed over the years to the fleeting sight of sails on the horizon, high-bowed Spanish merchantmen bound for Cuba, an occasional frigate patrolling off the coast, the long, lateen-rigged fishing canoes of the Indians. They showed their shapes to his indifferent gaze, drew away and dissolved like a doubtful memory.

Hughes was fifty-four now and had long ceased wanting to be anywhere else. The purposes of his fellows did not much occupy his speculation. He had noticed that this ship stayed longer than she needed for taking water on. But he soon stopped thinking about her altogether and fell to watching a woodpecker with bright yellow wing-feathers feeding in the branches of a tree some twenty yards away. He watched with close interest the movements of its feet and beak as it swung to get at the clusters of small red berries. Any life before his eyes that was not human could absorb his attention for hours. Inviolate here, high in the branches, his rope ladder drawn up and coiled on the lashed driftwood of the platform, he felt the solitude like an accustomed drug in his veins.

Community life had come too late for Hughes – too late to

499

soften much the savage misanthropy of his nature; but he could escape now, into these empty places, and the impulse of violence had quietened in him. He ranged far and wide, from the pinewood ridges near the shore to the swamps and jungle islands behind them and the great sea of saw grass that stretched far inland from the settlement. He cultivated no ground, living on what he could kill or gather, bringing in skins sometimes to trade for food, going to Lamba, his woman, at irregular intervals.

This last habit had caused trouble in early days, made worse by his demand for Lamba's immediate and total attention whenever he arrived. It violated established rules of sexual behaviour, which were founded on the woman's consent, and reflected on the dignity of the man he shared Lamba with, a negro known as Mando Tammy. The three had come to fighting over it, Tammy receiving a knife-gash in his arm which had to be stitched by Matthew Paris, and Hughes lucky to escape permanent damage to an eye from Lamba's nails. But habit is a skin that can grow over any shape and they had reached a kind of understanding over the years. Hughes could not be brought to any concept of the mutal rights involved in sharing; but he was granted some latitude as a special case. It was never forgotten that he had once, by his vigilance, saved the settlement.

He watched the woodpecker until it disappeared among the lower foliage and then, with the same attention, a honey-coloured bee at the flowers of a smooth-barked tree which grew almost as tall as his own, ending some feet below his platform. He followed the movements of the bee as it clambered among the drooping white spikes of blossom, observing how the insect vibrated its body each time it entered one of the flowers. His mind moved slowly over possible explanation. Could the bee do this to help the flower spread its pollen? From time to time he glanced across the short space of clearing towards the black water below him. In this dry season, when the levels sank below the roots of the saw-grass, the deer came more often to these pools in the jungle islands. He knew they came to this one: he had see their traces in the soft earth at the edge and the nibbled-off tops of the spider-lilies.

500

The dark water mirrored with absolute fidelity the bushy cabbage palms standing nearby and the spikes of air plants that grew on them and the pale drapes of moss that hung over the surface. No faintest tremor marred these reflections for the moment, all was glassy calm, but Hughes knew that there was always danger in the vicinity of these jungle pools. Not only deer came to drink here: he had seen snake tracks and the pad marks of a panther at the edges.

It was a good place to wait. At forty feet above ground he was not much troubled by mosquitoes. There was small need for camouflage, deer almost never looked upward; and at that height his smell would be undetectable to them. His bow and cane arrows lay on the platform beside him. The bow was as tall as he was. He had cut and seasoned the wood himself and strung it with deer-gut. He had to use his full strength to draw it. Most men in the settlement had adopted the Indian habit of pointing their arrows with sharpened fish-bone, but Hughes preferred flint arrowheads, lengthening the shaft to balance the extra weight. He had become expert with the weapon. At this range, if he caught the deer drinking, he could break its neck with a single shot. An instant kill was better, there was more respect in it; and the meat was sweeter when the beast had died without fear.

Sooner or later, perhaps in the early evening, they would come stepping through the trees. Meanwhile he was content to wait. More than content: there was in this exercise of patience the nearest thing to happiness that Hughes had ever known. The feeling lay far below his capacity for words, but it was as if the casual elements of his surroundings, the foliage and the dark water and the bright air and the life of small creatures around him, were freed by his waiting to be truly themselves.

In early afternoon it rained a little. There had been a succession of similar days. The mornings began warm and clear, then towards midday clouds gathered in the east and drew rapidly across the sky. Out to sea the shafts of rain squalls were visible, shaped like inverted fans and imbued with a smoky radiance. These spread to the land and there were showers of rain, sometimes heavy. By mid-afternoon the skies were clear again, without visible stain, and the sun shone as warmly as ever. At this season clouds formed and dissolved casually. The rain was like a brief smudge of breath on a clear window, bringing no consequence, leaving no trace.

Hughes leaned back against the trunk, drew up his legs and sat still under the rain. Afterwards a faint steam rose from the wet leaves. Before they were properly dry he saw a hunting spider lower itself on an invisible thread and come to rest directly before his face. This type of spider he had seen before: they made no web, but hunted their prey through the foliage and among the litter in the clefts of the branches. He leaned slowly and carefully forward and looked at the creature closely. Its eyes were saucer-shaped, unmoving. When he looked into them, he saw there a pulsing, flashing light. It was as if a shutter were being drawn rapidly back and forth over some brightness at the back of the eye . . .

Another person who saw the ship pass was Temka Tongman. He was paddling out to his fishnets in the reedy verges of an inlet a mile or so down the coast from the settlement. He paid little attention to the passing vessel. His mind was on the Palaver, due to be held in some days' time, at which he had agreed to be the speaker for Bulum Iboti, who was accused of practising witchcraft. Tongman's abilities as a speaker were widely recognized – he owed his name to them. He was thinking now of the fact that Iboti, a notoriously unlucky man, had agreed to pay him in labour, instead of the acorn flour he had offered at first. Tongman had no need for acorn flour, but he wanted ground cleared for planting pumpkins and sweet potatoes, both of which grew well in the rich soil at the edges of the freshwater lagoons. Iboti had agreed to clear fifty paces by ten of roots and vines if he won the case. Naturally, there would be no fee if he lost. Two witnesses had seen them strike hands together . . .

'Dat ten day work, Iboti,' he said aloud. 'Where you from?' Tongman liked the sound of his own voice and in these lonely places he often talked to himself. After twelve years pidgin came more naturally to him than the Temne he had spoken as a child. He had been surprised when his client agreed to complete the work, rather than simply promising a fixed number of days. Iboti could have got away with half of the time. He was not merely unlucky, he was foolish too. Perhaps it was the same thing.

Tongman was a dealer by instinct, a settled, sedentary man, wily of speech. As he paddled out through the narrow channels in the mangroves into the ruffled, gleaming expanse of open water, he wove a golden future for himself. He would exchange the surplus of his vegetables for the salt and flint that more adventurous spirits like Cavana and Tiamoko, working in partnership, brought down from the north. Salt and flint were goods that could be kept indefinitely, until the time came when shortage would increase demand.

His net broke the water. A large, green-mottled lizard fish threshed in the depths of it, its long jaws snapping to show the rows of teeth.

'Dis fish palava too much,' Tongman said. 'Look at me bad yai. I got de answer for you, my fren'.' He took up a short club from the floor of the canoe and gave the lizard fish a blow on the head with it, stilling its movements instantly. 'Where dat bad yai now?'

He was pleased to find the silver-blue fish with the big fleshy lump on its forehead, which he knew from the rivers of home. 'You come a long way. Got a big head, live a long time, finish now. Only one time fish ken die, same as man.'

He felt confident he could win the case. He had made his own enquiries and had a surprise witness, whom he had sworn to secrecy. All the same, there were aspects of the business that worried him, the main one being the identity of Iboti's accuser. Shantee Hambo was a fellow tribesman of Danka, one of the men with whom Tongman traded, and more importantly of Kireku, whom it was better to have for a friend than an enemy. These three were all the Shantee that had survived, but they formed a powerful group. And they had begun to claim their male children, which was contrary both to rule and custom . . .

The net was in now. Apart from the big parrot-fish, it had not been a good catch. But there were two bait fish, which he knew from the strong, brassy lustre of their colouring. They were not good to eat, but they were full of oil and could be chopped and scattered to attract the the big, black and silver food-fish that lay in the deep water of the creek mouths. This he remembered doing in another life, on a wider, swifter river.

Tongman had been a boy of fourteen when he was caught by a slaving party and sold aboard ship. His memories of childhood lay beyond the misery and terror of the voyage. They were thus in a charmed place, not altogether believed in but vivid and piercing when they came, and curiously arbitrary too. He had remembered scattering bait on the bright, flecked surface of the Roketa River, rocking in a dugout canoe not much different from this one, his father in the stern with a long spear. The memory was changeless: there was always the bright, eddying water, the crash of waves over the bar at the river mouth, the conical roofs of huts along the banks. And there were big white birds with forked tails that flew endlessly over the water. He could remember their quick shadows over the surface but he could not remember hearing any sounds from these birds, nor ever seeing them settle. In his memory they dipped and wheeled for ever in total silence . . .

Past and present were also interfused in an argument taking place on the outskirts of the settlement at more or less the same time, between Billy Blair and the negro named Inchebe.

'Oh, Billee, Billee, I so sorry for you, I ready for cry,' Inchebe said, shaking his head from side to side and blinking sorrowfully. 'You don' know de shit of de fire from de burnin' of de fire, dat you great trouble, man.' He was small and coal black, with a mobile, slightly twisted face, very quick and delicate in all his movements.

Blair's frayed and battered palm-leaf hat dipped over his brows and the lower part of his face was hidden by a fair, curly beard. But his blue eyes were wrathful as ever, wide now with the furious protest with which he greeted all the manifold contradictions and failures of logic in the world. 'You talkin' bigbig rabbish, Cheeby my son,' he said. 'You altagedder tellin' me you got stone make rain? You want me b'lieve you knock bleddy stone tagedder make rain? Dat all my arse an' Betty Martin.'

One of Inchebe's great strengths in argument – and it was one peculiarly infuriating to Billy – was that he never sought to persuade. He radiated always a placid, unassertive confidence of being in the right. 'What you b'lieve you business,' he said. 'I tellin' trut.'

Both men were somewhat out of temper. They had spent most of the day trying to shoot turkey in the swamps without any success, stumbling and slipping in pursuit of that most wily and sagacious of birds, making gobbling noises in the vain hope of drawing one to them. All they had got were two small squirrels, hardly enough for a stew. In such situations they each tended to lay the blame on the other. They were in any case on terms of exasperated familiarity owing to the fact that they shared the same woman. Sallian Kivee had grown very fat and had never been a beauty, but she was a good-tempered woman, very faithful by nature and an excellent cook. She had been content for ten years now with these two.

'I hear you talkin' bigmowf Dinka Meri,' Billy said, 'say her you got rainstone, make yourself out big rainman.'

Inchebe returned no answer to this, merely gazing around him with his small, bright eyes. Billy too was silent for a while, as if baffled. Of late years a habit of suspended consciousness had grown in him. At any time, when he was alone or with others or even, as now, in the midst of argument, there would come a certain kind of hush over things, everything before him would seem fixed somehow, arrested. Accompanying this was a kind of perplexity at the strangeness, the ultimate illogicality, of his being where he was. He felt this now as he looked away towards the first huts of the settlement. Only the sloping thatches of the roofs were visible from here; the rest was concealed behind the stockade of palm logs that encircled the whole area. He and Inchebe were standing outside this, lower down, on a track that led through thin forest. Some children were playing together up against the stockade and two women stood talking nearby. Beyond them, in the distance, he saw the hulking form of Libby go past, carrying what looked like fencing for a fish trap. Probably on some errand for Kireku, he thought with faint contempt. 'Dinka never go b'lieve you,' he said. 'She not born yestaday, she sabee you jus' tryin' git you leg over.'

505

Inchebe was unmoved. 'I not born yestaday, neever. I sabee you tryin' git *you* leg over.'

Dinka was young, twenty-two or three, it was computed, tall and graceful, scornful of smile but melting of eye. She was visited by a man of the Bulum, middle-aged and taciturn, known to everyone by the single name of Amos. But her regular man had failed to return from a fishing trip and was now presumed drowned.

'You jaloos, Billee,' Inchebe said. 'Dat what it is.'

Billy feigned laughter. The floppy brim of his hat nodded up and down. 'Me jaloos? Dat a good 'un. Ho, ho, look de big 'portant rainman of Africa.'

'Prentiss man.'

'What you say?'

'I prentiss rainman.'

'Aha!' Billy's eyes shone with triumph. 'Dat a different song,' he said. 'Dat not what you tell Dinka.'

At this moment Sullivan came up the track and joined them. He was carrying a palm-fibre basket three-quarters full of fresh-water mussels. 'Well, me brave lads,' he said. 'Will you look at this now?' He took up a handful of mussels and let them slide off his palm into the basket, watching the clattering blue shells with eyes that were hallucinated-looking in the deep tan of his face. Sullivan was a great man for mussels and clams and knew all the best places. Gathering them he was sometimes taken back to his childhood in Galway, foraging for shellfish in the salt recesses of this same ocean.

He was naked except for his deerskin moccasins and a breech-clout of braided palm leaves and he smelled of the fish oil he had rubbed on himself against mosquitoes. His black hair fell almost to his shoulders and was held off his face by a band of fibre tied across the forehead. 'You make swap?' he said, reverting to pidgin at the prospect of trade. 'You make me good swap five pint measure mussel? What you got?'

Neither Billy nor Inchebe said anything. Sullivan regarded the two small, limp squirrels hanging head downwards from Billy's rope belt. 'Dat all?'

Billy looked away from the mussels with assumed indifference.

'De time come for *trut*,' he said doggedly to Inchebe. 'You tell Dinka you got rainstone, you show me dem rainstone. Where dey?'

Inchebe turned to Sullivan, twisting his mouth and widening his small expressive eyes. 'You hear dis man? He tink rainman carry cargo rainstone aboard all de time.' He turned a pitying glance back to Billy. 'Dey kept secret place, close water,' he said. 'No tell where. Anyone know anyting bout rainstone know dat. Why you care soso much what 'pinion Dinka have? Dat no secret, I tell you why, you want get in Dinka bed, get *you* leg over.'

'For the love of God,' Sullivan said. His face had assumed an expression of astonishment. His green eyes glanced after a lost vision of human reason and decency. 'You feller sniffin' after dat no-good Dinka when you got a soso jool at home? Yeh, yeh, dat right, I talkin' bout you Sallian. She cook good too much, she fuck much you want, she never naggy. What man do when he got woman like dat? I tell you what, he *treasure* dat woman, he put de grapple on dat woman, he climb aboard an' stay aboard.'

At this point he found himself being regarded closely by Inchebe, who was more devious than Billy and so more prone to suspicion. 'We glad too much get you idea on dis subjec',' he said. It was known to everyone that Sullivan, by one of those shifts of fortune sometimes occurring in the settlement, where relations between the sexes were a complex blend of the casual and the binding, now found himself having to share his woman with two others. 'You say Dinka no good,' Inchebe said. 'Mebbe you tink Dinka not bootiful girl, not have bootiful butties an' so on an' so fort, what you say?'

This was a very cunning question and Sullivan, aware that he had possibly overdone Sallian's praises, was thrown out by it. 'Thim things you mention is steadily deterioratin',' he said. 'Any man with a knowledge of commerce, like meself, will tell you it is no arthly use investin' your money in a deterioratin' asset.'

Some of Inchebe's calm fell away from him. 'What shit lingo dat?' he said. 'You want say me someting, you talk people lingo.'

507

'Bootiful butties, what dat madder?' Sullivan said earnestly. 'You feller lucky have soso ugly woman. Bootiful go way soon soon, niver come back. Ugly go on gettin' more 'n more.' He cast about for a way of changing the subject. 'What you talk about?' he said. 'Sallian look after you so good you like twin, you like bun same oven, one bake bit longer.'

This was a true observation. Both men were short and quick of movement; and both were dressed identically in clothes that had been made for them by Sallian. A tactful and loving woman, she made no distinction of any kind between them. They had exactly the same palm-leaf hats, deerskin drawers decorated with plaited fibre tassels dyed red, and sleeveless smocks of faded blue, made from a remnant of cotton from the trade goods that had been brought off the ship.

'Subjec' not Dinka, subjec' not Sallian,' Billy said austerely. 'Subjec' not bleddy twins. We talkin' 'bout rainstone. Easy too much no tell where. Ho, yes. Last rain come late. Why you no knock stone tagedder fall rain before?'

'De time no right.'

'What you mean, time no right? Dat de time people need.'

'Rain no come for people need, no care bugger people need.'

'Aha! I got you in de corner now, Cheeby.' Billy's expression was again triumphant. 'I got you pin down. You wait you see rain come den you knock stone.'

Inchebe nodded placidly. 'Sartinly,' he said. 'Dat de right time knock stone.' He raised a thin forefinger. 'But only rainman ken see dat.'

'He right.' Sullivan had begun to take an interest in the argument. 'Why the pox man knock stone if rain no come?'

'Jesus, you bad as he is.' Billy felt himself sweating. There was a contradiction of appalling proportions at the heart of Inchebe's argument, but he could not see it clearly enough to be able to expose and refute it. He raised his heated face to an uncomprehending sky. 'Give me strength,' he said.

Sullivan was shaking his head slowly. 'Aye, bejabbers, wasted effort,' he said. 'Where de point in dat?'

Suddenly Billy saw a way. 'Tell me dis, den. How you know dey de right stones?'

'What you mean?'

'How you fin' dem? You no born with stone, eh? Only stone you born with is you ball. Or mebbe you rainman bebby, you knock you ball tagedder make rain?'

Inchebe greeted this with dignified silence.

'Well, den,' Billy went on, 'you got to look here, look dere, fin' de good stone. Right or wrong?'

'Right.'

'Got you now.' Billy paused, savouring his triumph. 'One bleddy stone like anadder. How you know you stone de right one?'

Inchebe looked at him with genuine astonishment. 'What kind question dat? Dey de wrong stone, rain no come down.'

FORTY-SEVEN

On his return, happening to pass Matthew Paris, Hughes mentioned the ship and the fact that she had anchored overnight. Most things came to Paris's ears sooner or later. The people of the crew reported to him out of habit and a kind of deference that had survived the familiarity of the years; and both black and white confided in him sometimes when he was treating them for sickness or injury or discontent in the long, palm-thatch lean-to on the edge of the compound that he used for a sickroom.

He thought for a while about what Hughes had told him as he sat there at the corner of his hut on a low stool he had made out of driftwood, with his hat tilted forward against the low sun and his naked, long-shanked legs stretched out before him. He did not see anything very remarkable in a ship lingering a day or two longer than usual – there could be a score of reasons. That it was Hughes who had delivered the information was the only remarkable thing. In remote communities legends form as imperceptibly as clouds change shape and colouring; and Hughes, while still alive amongst them, had become a legendary climber and watcher. This lonely man had saved them once, or so it was generally held, in the violent early days of the settlement when the threads that held them all together had been stretched taut, close to snapping.

In the first rainy season it had happened, when the vast prairies of saw-grass lay under water. Hughes never spoke of it, taciturn in this as in all else; but the words with which he had come to tell the others had always been remembered – and repeated. Delblanc in particular had seen from the first the importance of telling things over; he had been clear-sighted in those times of danger, always seeking to encourage a sense of unity among the fugitives, ready to seize on anything that could be celebrated by the whole people together. Delblanc lay under the ground now, but this had been his legacy.

Jimmy, the linguister, had aided this work, especially with the children. He had found his vocation as a teacher, though his school was very irregularly attended and subject to changes in the weather. He taught the children to form letters and he taught them simple arithmetic; but his lessons were mainly story-telling and play-acting. He was helped sometimes by Paris, who had no idea of teaching, but would read extracts from his small stock of books. The children dozed or fidgeted to the sound of Pope and Hume.

The years had stiffened Jimmy's back and thinned his wiry poll so that the scalp showed through. His habit of smiling was unchanged, but in class, for the sake of drama, he would compel his face to seriousness, and this was effective, even sometimes fearsome, because of the contrast. He always began the Hughes story in the same way, speaking in his high, musical, rather plaintive voice, raising his hands and assuming a fixed stare, so as to engage the children's attention: 'One time Oose climb dis big tree. Oose ken climb anyting. Dis tree go high in de sky too much. S-o-o-o big dis tree . . .' Jimmy raised his arms and spread his fingers, looking up in a daze of wonderment at branches and foliage lost in the sky. 'Now why he do dat?'

A number of hands were raised immediately.

'Ya, Sammy?'

'Oose want git up top.'

The simplicity of this answer occasioned some mirth. Sammy glanced round him smiling, then slowly allowed his head to sink forward on to his hands.

'Very good, my pikin, very good,' Jimmy said. 'Never mind dem sniggin' ones. Easy to laff. Dey laff diffrent baimbai. You answer hunnerd per cent right. You only four but you a thinker. But dere anadder reason come behind dat one. Ya, Tekka?'

Tekka was a strong, sardonic boy of nine, deep black in colour, with prominent cheekbones and bright, intrepid eyes.

There was always a high shine on his face, as if it were kept polished. 'Mebbe black bear chase Oose up de tree,' he said. 'Mebbe black bear come after him an' Oose fraid lose him arse.'

There was some laughter at this, spiced with the sense of sacrilege. It was the ambition of all the children to add in some way to the body of the story, and Jimmy sometimes admitted new material. But this attempt of Tekka's failed altogether.

'No black bear.' Jimmy shook his head more in sorrow than in anger. 'No arse or any portion Oose 'natomy.' To assert authority, or deal with subversion, he found it effective some-times to use words outside the range of the children's pidgin. Besides, he enjoyed the sound of them in his mouth. 'Dat not in de story,' he said. 'Ya, Lamina?'

Lamina, who was a little older than Sammy, had a mouth whose upper and lower lips were full and exactly symmetrical, forming the perfect shape of a flower. She always hesitated long over her answer, however eagerly she had thrust up her hand. 'Oose want git up dere for lookout,' she said at last.

'Dat right, my pikin. An' when he git up dere, what he see?'

And so it would go on, from question to answer, both ques-tions and answers known by heart, until Jimmy settled into the story in real earnest and then it was just his voice rising and falling, a sound that belonged there, like the hiss and crackle of evening fires or the dry rustle of wind in the cabbage palms, while the children sat silently listening, all shades from ebony to dark sand, in the shade of the long fronds.

'Oose he see like snippy bit colour, mebbe dey was colour, mebbe dey was shine a white man face . . .'

The climber hero, from his eminence there in the close-growing hummock, had found himself able to look down over a narrow valley, or canyon rather, a long strip where the rock rose near the surface, giving lodgement only to low growths, palmetto and bush willow. Beyond this, mangroves marked the course of a creek which wound through swampland, taking its rise from the flooded saw-grass plain. In the distance Hughes could see the winking rim of this vast lake.

Through the lower leaves of the mangroves, in the long shaft of sunlight that lay along the defile before him, he glimpsed a flash of red, saw light reflected from broken water. He trained the ship's telescope, which had belonged once to Thurso and was now common property, over the belt of barer ground to where the creek water glinted behind the screen of mangroves. He waited. Then, for a space of perhaps fifteen seconds, before it was again hidden by denser foliage, he saw a long canoe pass downstream, a white man paddling at the prow in a ragged straw hat, with a musket slung across his back. Behind him, huddled together on the centre thwarts, were three Indians with faces painted or tattooed – he could not determine which, in this brief space of time. They sat with heads hanging, roped together, their arms bound behind them. Three more men, two of them negroes, all armed with muskets, sat in the stern. One of the negroes had a red kerchief tied round his head – it was this that Hughes had glimpsed through the screen of trees.

This was the tale he had come back with. The long canoe, the armed men, the bound Indians. They were going towards the sea. But this creek would not take them far, Hughes knew that – and reported it. It was a summer stream only, swollen by the rains, running out into the marshy edges of the lagoons.

Perhaps they did not know this, someone suggested. Or perhaps they were not making for the sea at all, but looking for some great river they knew of, which would take them north, where they could sell their captives. That it was their intention to sell the Indians everyone was agreed – there could be no other reason for taking men and binding them.

Nothing much else was clear. At this time the people of the settlement knew only their immediate surroundings. They knew the shore and the sheltering pineland and the swamps behind. They had not ventured far into the interior for fear of the Indians, who had already killed and mutilated Haines. Thus they could form no idea of where the men had come from. But some of the crew remembered stories of whites and runaway negroes banded together down among the Florida Keys, who lived by wrecking craft on the reefs and selling any Indians they caught to the Spanish.

'Dis de story Oose come back with,' Jimmy said. 'Den de

513

people talk tagedder bout dis. Some dem say, let canoe alone, dem feller no danger to us, come for take Indian, not us. But Parry an' Delba, dey say no. Mebbe some you member Delba, he get sick, die after. An' Foulah woman Tabakali say no an' Nadri say no, s'pose dem feller come back agin. What den? But dere anadder reason back behind dis why dey say no. Why dem Indian in de canoe fust place? Ya, Kenka?'

Kenka was a slender, tawny-skinned mulatto boy, who often did not put up his hand even when he knew the answer, but Jimmy had learned to recognize the look on his face when he wanted to be asked and the tense position of his body. Jimmy knew too that Tabakali, the heroine of this debate, was Kenka's mother.

'Dey take Indian for slave,' the boy said proudly.

'Dat right. Take dem for slave. Dat very 'portant reason for help dem. All people got a right to be free. Nadri say dat an' Delba say dat. You let dem take slave? You stand one side, let dem take slave? You was slave youself. You forget so quick?'

Jimmy paused and smiled round at the children. 'I was dere,' he said. 'Dem time people no talk pidgin like now, people talk lingo belong dem. I big linguister dem time.'

It was not the first debate he had assisted in: that had been held on board the ship, blood still on the deck, Thurso's body still warm. The children knew this story too. Jimmy always went through all the stages of these famous debates, but he was a moralist as teachers often are, he wanted to instil a sense of community in the children so there were certain aspects that he omitted to mention or even falsified, his version of events was not necessarily that which lived in the memory of others who had taken part. People read into things their own truths and meanings. But everyone who had been present – and that was all of the fugitives, men and women, black and white, who had survived the voyage and the landing and the hardships of the first weeks – knew that the actions stemming from this debate had saved the settlement.

One thing Jimmy always omitted was the naming of those unheroic ones who would have let the slaver-takers go unmolested. Only Wilson was named – he took the burden of all.

514

The others still walked the earth, their offspring were among Jimmy's pupils; but Wilson had died in public view, disgraced and without issue, and so everything discreditable could be laid at his door. In the course of time a legendary wickedness had gathered round Wilson's name. It had been his fate to become first scapegoat then ogre. Now mothers sometimes hushed their children with the threat that Wilson would hear them and come.

But in fact there had been others to take his side in this debate. Libby had done so, and a big, morose man from the Ivory Coast named Tiamoko. None of these had been able to see any point in intervening to save the Indians.

'Them Indians aren't nothin' but savviges,' Libby said, his solitary eye staring furious and bloodshot. 'Yer seen what they done to Haines. They took the scalp off him while he was still alive. Them white fellers done me no harm. Why should I raise my hand agin my own kind?'

It was then, when these remarks had been explained to her, that Tabakali, the Foulani woman, joined in the discussion. She spoke no pidgin at that time, but she was a bold, independent woman from a nomad people and had ranged far west along the Guinea Coast, and she could speak some Malinke, which Jimmy was able to translate. He had not been able to do full justice to the contempt that rang in the words of this tall and magnificent woman, but enough of it came through, even in the bare pidgin of his rendering: 'She say, what you mean raise you hand agin you kind? You kind slave-taker, dat what you mean? She say, in dat case you no belong here, you ken git out. Den she say, Haines killed stealin' gold dust from de ship. Who weepin' for Haines? Barton sabee dat good. Sabee different, he ken speak now, we waitin'.'

Barton had remained silent. Everyone knew he had joined with Haines in the ill-fated attempt to escape with the gold.

'She say, Libby make sick she belly. She say, Libby missin' one eye an' both him ball. If Libby her man, but she tank great god he not, she put him out de door. She say Wilson an' Tiamoko same same Libby.'

'Hooray!' Billy Blair said, delighted at this discomfiting of his old enemy.

But Wilson was not amenable to the rules of debate, had moreover an ugly temper; not many weeks later it was to be his death. He took two steps towards the woman. 'You black bitch,' he said, 'is tha callin' me names?'

'Stand back.' Without conscious thought Paris had interposed himself. Wilson's darkly bearded face was on a level with his own, the eyes in their cavernous sockets curiously vacant and unseeing. 'Stand back,' he said again, though not loudly or threateningly. 'This is a time for words, not blows. Or do you not know the difference?' he added with a sort of involuntary contempt.

Wilson continued to look sullenly at him. He showed no sign of being cowed, but after a moment, perhaps sensing opinion was against him, he fell back.

Paris turned and looked at the woman standing there. She had not given ground. She was wearing still the coarse cotton shift they had given her on the slaveship. The passion of her words had deepened her breathing. Her eyes flashed and her head was thrown back on the splendid column of her neck. Paris, who still had no woman at that time, was swept by a tide of admiration and desire more urgent than anything he had known, flooding his whole being, like a sudden brimming of the vessel in which lay all the thoughts he had had of her from the very first, when he had seen her behind the bars in the sunlit slave dungeon of the fort. He could not keep the feeling out of his eyes and Tabakali saw it.

But it was above all for Delblanc that this debate – the first one of the whole people together – was a turning point and a revelation. And the nature of this revelation did not feature in Jimmy's account either, because it was mainly concerned with Delblanc's knowledge of himself. He had seen at once that the Indians should be rescued. Such an act would assert the principles of freedom and natural justice on which he hoped to found this infant republic of his dreams. And it might well improve relations with the Indians, fear of whom, after the terrible death of Haines, had kept them penned in this narrow space of woodland between the exposed shore and the flooded savannah behind. But he had seen further than this. With a perception colder than he had believed possible in himself – and herein lay the element of revelation – he had seen at once that what became of the Indians was in a way a secondary issue: the slave-takers had to be killed *in any case.*

It was their death that he argued for, with all the force at his command, speaking directly to Paris and the people of the crew, leaving Jimmy to make the best of it he could, knowing that the whites, though in a minority, were more cohesive, had a certain ascendancy still, which would not last long but might be exploited now; knowing too that the intention to kill the men must be formed and stated here, not left to the chances of the pursuit.

'We have no choice,' he said. 'It makes no difference what is decided about the Indians and what are the rights and wrongs of rescuing them. Personally, I think they should be rescued. But above all the men who have taken them must be killed. Some of you have already said it. Suppose they come back? Suppose they have seen some of us? We cannot afford not to suppose it. They might return in more strength. Even if not, can we take the risk of stories about us being carried up and down the coast? You know we cannot. We must go after them now, before they escape us.'

Delblanc was a man transformed. He was still wearing the waistcoat and breeches with which he had left the ship, torn and muddied now; but nothing else about him seemed the same. The years of vague theory, half-ironic rhetoric, generous, egalitarian sympathy, came together now in this focus of fierce clarity. More than he had wanted anything in his life, he wanted this desperate experiment to succeed. All the people before him, black and white, whether they knew it or not, had been enslaved. He intended now that they should live in peace and freedom, without coercion, in this untouched corner where they found themselves. Four lives seemed little against such a dream.

To Paris, his friend's face had become unrecognizable almost, cold, preoccupied and yet elated too. 'You are talking about killing four men in cold blood,' he said.

'Yes, I am, of course I am,' Delblanc said, with a vehemence barely held in check. 'Don't be a fool, Matthew. Are you

517

suggesting it should be left to the bungling of hot blood, a thing like this, affecting the lives of all of us?'

For a moment then it had seemed to Paris that here, in the close heat of this rocky clearing where they stood, with the cicadas loud around them and the sun harsh on the blades of the palmetto, they were once more engaged in the old argument as to the relative merits of reason and nature that had occupied so much of their time aboard the *Liverpool Merchant*. But now the positions were reversed: it was Delblanc now who was the enemy of impulse . . .

For a moment Paris continued to look into his friend's face, uncertain how to answer. Then quite suddenly he knew that this man, whose openness had so drawn him, was leaving his deeper reasons unspoken. It was typical of Paris that to understand this by intuition was to feel partly convicted of it himself. He was going to speak but Delblanc, as if sensing himself discovered, drew closer and muttered, too low for anyone else's ears: 'We must kill them. Don't you see? It is providential – they are mixed white and black, just as we are. By killing them we cancel the distinction. It is the only way . . . It is the only thing that will keep us together.'

That had been the knowledge shared by these two, never afterwards referred to by either. But it was Tiamoko who settled things. He came from a society where the respect of women was important, and the scorn of the Foulani woman had affected him more than his impassive demeanour had indicated. With an abrupt swing of mood he now stepped forward and declared himself willing to kill these slave-takers alone and unaided if need be.

Others followed suit. In the end all the men took part in the pursuit, divided into two groups, one keeping close to the line of the shore, the other, guided by Hughes, striking further inland. But for the sake of silence and surprise only six made the final approach, three white and three black, and they were drawn by lot once it was known where the slave-takers had camped.

'Who dem six?' All the children knew the names: Paree, Kavna, Barba, Kireku, Kadu, Zobi. It was a roll of heroes.

'Dey foller dem slave-taker. Now it git dark, night come

down.' Jimmy opened his eyes as wide as they would go. 'What dey go do? Dem slave-taker 'fraid in de night-time, dey 'fraid crocdile, for sample. What else dey 'fraid of?'

'Dey 'fraid snake.'

'Dey 'fraid leppid.'

The children always took part eagerly at this stage, sharing these fears in large measure. 'Dey 'fraid black bear,' Tekka said.

'You right, boy. You great man for black bear, an't you? Dem slave-taker 'fraid dey own shadder. Why dat? Dat 'cause dey bad wickit man, dey sabee take sell slave bad ting too much, dey feel bad inside demself. But us people go after dem no 'fraid. Why dat?'

'Dey more of us.'

'No, Sammy, dat not de answer. Us not 'fraid 'cause us *in de right*. When you in de right, you heart strong, you no 'fraid nottin'. So dey camp on de bank, make fire, set one man watch. Den dey go sleep. Indian still tied tagedder. Now dese slave-taker bad man too much but us people no go for kill dem, very bad kill anadder man, we all man got to live tagedder in dis world, but dis time got to kill for free dem slave . . .'

Sitting outside the small hut adjoining his sickroom that he used when not with Tabakali, Paris thought about those distant killings again now. He could never see Hughes without some memory of them. There were men and women like this in the settlement, so charged with a particular event that they carried an evocative aura about them.

It had been about this time when they set off in pursuit, evening, the sky draining slowly to an opalescent, milky blue. With the approach of darkness they heard the cry of frogs, some solitary voices at first, then the great glimmering expanse of flooded saw-grass had resounded with them, a loud, unbroken, pulsing chorus, strangely like sustained lamentation to Paris's ears.

The men they were following had bivouacked on a sandbank among sea-grape trees and palmetto, as high as they could get above the water. They had lit a fire and one had settled to watch, a white man, musket across his knees. The Indians they had roped to a tree. Paris remembered the firelight on the pale

519

trunks of the sea-grape trees, and the shadows of their long, deformed-looking branches.

That ceaseless litany of the frogs had concealed all sound of their approach. The Shantee, Kireku, had gone first, tall and lithe and soft-footed, with a visible appetite for murder. Or is it only now, Paris wondered, in the distrust and division of these later times, that I attribute this to him?

Kireku had slashed the guard's throat from behind before he could stir or utter a cry. But the man had choked and bubbled in his death and one of the others had started up, seen the moving forms and shouted once before Barber reached him, chopped at him with the short axe he had brought among his carpenter's tools from the ship, pursued him still chopping as he tried to crawl away. The others were roused now. All Paris could remember, after this bloodied, crawling form in the fire-light, was a confused and violent struggle in which Zobi had been struck down by the stock of a musket and he himself had shot with his pistol the man wielding the musket, a powerful negro, shot him through the body, seen him blunder away through the trees and followed, not knowing how badly hurt he might be, and found him coughing out his life in the dimness beyond the light of the fire. Expiring in blood, the negro had begged to be spared. Paris remembered the eyes fixed on him, the soft mumble of the voice. And he remembered the hush that had fallen all around himself and this dying stranger. He had not been able to understand it at first, then he realized that his shot had silenced the frogs.

On this blood and that of Wilson, whose death was still to come, their small republic had been founded. This was the Battle of Red Creek, as Jimmy told the children – he knew the importance of names. The colour came from the red stain in the water made by the fallen mangrove leaves.

The Indians they had taken back with them, still bound. By yet another stratagem deriving from the inspired Delblanc they had only been released later, ceremonially, before the whole people. They were copper-coloured, slender but robust, small-boned, with long straight black hair and depthless, glittering eyes. They had remained mute in the hands of their new captors and they made no sound when released from their bonds, refusing the food that was offered them, seeming slow to understand that they were free but then slipping quickly away and vanishing into the darkness.

Gratitude, however, there had been, or acknowledgement at least. Two days later, a party of twenty men, their bodies shining with oil, their hair dressed with ornaments of shell and bone, came in deputation under the leadership of one with a headband of feathers and heavy earrings of shell-lining. They sat for an hour in complete silence and left gifts of shell ornament and carved arrowheads, sour oranges brought from abandoned Spanish settlements further north, above all cakes made from koonti flour: it was to these Indians that the people of the settlement owed the knowledge of the koonti plant that had given them their staple food. From the Indians too, in the course of time, they had obtained the foundations of their husbandry, pumpkin seeds, tubers of sweet potato. They had made gifts in their turn, in the early days, using goods brought off the ship, clasp-knives and kettles which it had been Thurso's intention to sell off in Jamaica. Some, like Cavana and Tongman and the Shantee people, had joined by degrees in the trade in skins with the settlements on the banks of the St John River to the north.

These neighbouring Indians, whose faces were tattooed in a pattern of concentric circles coloured red and blue, though hunting and fishing over the same grounds and though skirmishing incessantly with tribes to the west of them, offered the settlement no further hostility. For them too the past merged easily into legend. The story of this rescue was repeated among them, the alliance became a kind of custom and went unquestioned.

There could be no doubt of it – Delblanc had been right: in saving the three Indians they had preserved themselves and made possible the survival of their colony. Not long afterwards the execution of Wilson had brought acceptance of the need for the men to share the women, a problem on which they had nearly foundered, though it had been a matter of simple arithmetic from the start with only fourteen females surviving.

Twelve years, Paris thought. Twelve floodings of the saw-grass plain, with the great freshwater sea slowly flowing

521

southwards, following the gradual tilt of the land. Twelve dry seasons with the mud cracking and the eroded shapes of the rock exposed, and the alligator, which Paris had long ago observed to be the true benefactor of these marshes, burrowing in the mud and maintaining small colonies of life in the water-holes thus made. One of the most ancient of beasts, an aboriginal reptile. He had watched them whenever he could, marvelling at the perfect adaptation to the circumstances of their lives. In this case, for reasons obscure to him, there seemed to have been no diversifying of the species. The alligator had neither died nor changed. The churchmen who had pilloried and imprisoned him and given him before ever he stepped on to the deck of a slaveship the horror of degradation that had led him by devious courses to this place, they might have pointed to the alligator as a proof of original creation, one of those who had voyaged with Noah. Climates might have cooled and warmed again, mountains risen, continents formed, but in the watery recesses of the world this same beast lived on. And it was because he was perfect . . .

On such a scale of time the twelve years of the colony was too short for detection, let alone measurement, it was less than a breath. Yet it was a whole life to him in the beating of his heart. He had been happier than he could have believed possible in this forgotten corner. But increasingly nowadays it seemed to him that this short history was assuming, had assumed, a definite shape, determined by the violence of its beginnings. A shape implies an end . . . With a sudden deep uneasiness he thought again now of Kireku and of those who moved in his orbit, Barton, Libby, men by nature subservient, quick to see a rising power. Kireku was growing rich – he had trade links not only to the north but even, it was said, with the sea-going Indians who crossed the straits in their dugouts, carrying dried fish and heron plumes and freshwater pearls to the Spanish islands. The man who had accused Iboti of witchcraft was a fellow-tribesman of Kireku . . .

Made restless by these thoughts, Paris got up, crossed the corner of the compound and passed through the gate in the stockade. He walked some way through the forested ground

522

that lay on the seaward side of the settlement until he found the little rocky eminence among the tall slash-pines where he often sat in early evening, his favourite time here as it had been at home in England. Trailings of cloud had formed earlier but these cleared as he sat there and the sky took on a look of readiness for the dark, that depthless clarity which is no colour and the womb of all colours.

He was looking eastward to where the sea lay, invisible but always present, revealed by something wild in the quality of the light above it. They had built their huts out of sight of the sea on the slightly higher ground between the barrier hummocks near the shore and the lagoons and grasslands behind, a site affording some defence against marauders and some protection from the storms that swept the coast in late summer, while still open to the prevailing sea breezes that combed through the pineland ridges and freshened the exhalations of the swamps.

It seemed to Paris as he sat there that he had somehow earned the right not merely to live in this place but to love it – a stronger claim of possession, one enforced by the things of deepest familiarity that surrounded him, the invisible sea that cast its light, the dark snake-birds already flying up to roost in the high branches, the breeze moving in the palmettos, stirring the leaves against the palm trunks with a sound like the faint clashing of cymbals, the slender blades of the leaves themselves, curving in perfect gradation like the first whorl of a green shell. Fear of loss gave a sharper intensity to his perception. This was the place that suffering and crime had made their own, where he had been able to save some lives and ease some pain, where he had found a refuge and a physical passion undreamt of in the arms of a woman still in most ways a stranger to him.

A vagrant beam of sunlight fell across the clearing and lay briefly on the papery bark of a gum-resin tree, lighting the peeling strips to a red glow, as if the tree were burning. The upper branches were hung with drapes of green moss, dark in the centre, fluffed with sunlight at the edges. Paris looked up beyond this, to where branch and foliage and festooning moss melted and fused into a single veil-like substance. Slowly his anxieties receded.

As he began to return he was met by a voice calling for him through the trees and knew it by something sorrowing in the tone for that of Kenka, who was Tabakali's son and – though this had never been declared between him and the boy – his too.

'Here,' he called and after a moment saw the boy come out into the small clearing and approach silently. Kenka followed him sometimes for no seeming reason but to be in his company and this gave great pleasure to Paris, who had from Kenka's earliest infancy watched him and sometimes stalked him as it were about the place, to find occasion to speak to him. Children lived with their mothers and they had all the men for their fathers, such at least was the general principle. But it happened sometimes that men took a particular interest in those they knew for their own. Paris had seen his own lineaments in the child's face, in the shape of his eyes and the set of his mouth; and he had known that this was his and Tabakali's child and the child that Ruth had not lived to give him.

'How you sabee I here dis place?' Paris said.

'I see you talk Oose, see you go,' the boy said. He had eyes that seemed to look inward until startled by speech, and in this he was like his mother. Tabakali's too the straight shoulders, the sturdy column of the neck, the quick, restless turns of the head. But the look of patient enquiry his face would assume, this was all his father's. He wore the look now. 'What Oose say?' he asked.

Paris said gravely, 'Oose climb tree see ship stay two-three day. He tink hum-hum, pass by, tell me.'

Kenka reflected for a moment but it was clear from his next words that he was not interested in this news of the ship. 'Oose ken climb anyting,' he said. 'Ken you?'

'Some man good dis, some man good dat. Everybody climb tree, who go catch fish? You want walk dis way?'

The boy had a small, particular smile for proposals that pleased him. 'You good more ting dan Oose,' he said. He had a way of prefacing certain of his words with a light frictive sound, not quite a consonant; a habit derived from the Foulani speech habits of his mother, with whom he talked more quickly and easily than with Paris, using with her some African words.

As they walked along together, Paris felt his hand taken in a small, tenacious paw. 'One time in de class,' Kenka said, 'Tekka say Oose climb dat tree he see slave-taker cos black bear after him arse. Dat de trut?'

'What Jimmy say?' Paris asked cautiously. There were aspects of Jimmy's teaching he was not sure he approved of.

'Jimmy say dat not in de story.'

They had come now to the edge of the jungle hummock that lay just below the pine ridges. The path they were following opened on to the bank of a shallow, brackish lagoon. They heard the plop of a turtle as they approached the water and two grey doves flew up from the undergrowth at the edge. 'How ken Jimmy sabee everyting in de story?' the boy persisted. 'Not Jimmy climb de tree. Mebbe Oose no tell 'bout black bear an' fraid him arse.'

Paris thought about this for some moments. The turtle had stopped swimming and lay some dozen yards out, with the blunt nob of its head and the glistening curve of its shell just above the surface. 'Dis what I tink,' he said at last. 'Nobody sabee de whole story. Mebbe Oose forgit, mebbe change some ting. Oose got arse same like you, me, Tekka, he want save him arse same like everybody. An' you sabee why dat, don' you?'

The pure pleasure of knowing the answer had spread over Kenka's face. 'Man lose him arse no ken climb tree, no ken do anyting.'

'Dat right. You member dat, Kenka. Now I go tell you different story 'bout tree. You see where we standin' now, we standin' side of tree big too much grow close tagedder we call jungle ammack. You sabee dat name?'

The boy nodded.

'Dey got big big tree grow in dere, in de heart of it. Man look up, no see de top. Animal in dere, deer an' leppid an' rabbit. You ever walk all de way roun' dis ammack? You big boy now, we do it one day baimbai. Take axe an' knife, ask you mamma make nyam for us eat on de way. Grass land grow all roun', all covered water in de rainy time. Dis ammack an island in de grass.'

'What mean aylan?'

'Same like land in de sea. You sabee? Grass land like de sea. So de question is, how dis aylan come here dis place? One time all same same grass. Mebbe dis place jus' little bit high. Mebbe dis much.' He made a gap of some inches between finger and thumb. 'High nuff catch seed come on de wind.'

'Come from where?' Kenka was absorbed. The area of his face seemed to have contracted and his eyes opened wide and startled-looking as though the next thing coming might be too much for him.

'Come over de sea from de aylan in de sea where de big tree grow. Mebbe seed resin tree or palm. Mebbe seed mastick tree I use for make medsin, you sabee? Mebbe so small seed no ken see. Den build up slow too much, root keep ground tagedder, water stick on leaf, den anadder seed catch. So it go on mebbe two-three hunnerd year.' But he saw this meant little to the boy. 'Long time ago, before I born,' he said. 'Now we got dis big ammack, tree start fightin'. You come dis way I show you someting.'

The turtle, which had been watching them all this time, nose-dived as they began to walk along the bank. Shoals of tiny black fish darted here and there in the warm shallow water at the edges. A butterfly with zebra stripes of cream and black wavered past them. Paris led the boy some way in among the trees. In the gloom here, bordering black water, amidst a tangle of palmetto and the strange, leaning, festooned trees of the swamp, he found a strangler fig enfolding an oak in its murderous embrace, its network of creepers embedded in the trunk of its dying host.

'See dis tree?' he said. 'Dis killer tree. Dis tree find anadder tree den grappul him, climb all over de trunk till fust tree life choke out.'

Kenka did not know this word and Paris placed hands round his own neck in illustration. He tried to explain the operation of this strange, deadly plant, which had seeded in some crevice on the oak and from these tiny beginnings and over many years had clambered relentlessly up to the light, murdering its host by infinitesimal degrees on the way. It had tentacles as thick as a man's body now; one of them had leapt a dozen feet and put a smooth loop round the branch of a nearby mangrove.

526

'In de finish, kill dat too,' Paris said. He was aware that this had become a different story from the one he had set out to tell. Some darkness from himself had intruded. He felt suddenly guilty, as if he had committed some sin of the spirit, perhaps irreparable, seeing the boy's rapt face in this dimness among the trees. 'I want tell you,' he said. 'You listen good an' member it. Dis a tree, we talkin' 'bout, not a man. Man ken climb an' live in de sunshine tagedder.'

This had come perhaps too belatedly. Kenka's face had a considering look but his mind had taken a different turn. 'One tree chok anadder,' he said. 'Den anadder chok dat one. In de finish all dem fall down.' He made a sharp gesture with one thin arm. 'We come back grass agin, no aylan.'

'What den?' Paris asked, amused and somehow touched at this rigorous conclusion.

Kenka answered his father's smile with the look of serious pleasure he always had when he knew the answer. 'Anadder seed come on de wind,' he said.

FORTY-EIGHT

Father and son walked back together in the failing light. The lagoon water was steel-coloured, glimmering faintly, quite motionless. They kept well above it. In this deceptive light it was better not to go too near the water. Alligators sometimes entered the lagoons hunting for turtles. They could lie at the shadowed verges almost without breaking the surface. A moving adult was not likely to be attacked, but in the early years of the settlement a small son of Iboti had been seized and dragged under and no one had forgotten it.

High in the branches of a tree on the far side of the water a black snake-bird stretched its fantastic neck and uttered a single screaming cry. And as if this were a signal, while Paris and Kenka began the gradual ascent towards the first huts of the settlement, there began the evening clamour of the marsh birds rising to their roosting places, shrieking at the touch of the dark with a sound harsh and sorrowful like a fanfare of defeat. This lasted some minutes only, then the birds fell silent.

The compound was smoky with cooking fires and loud with the drum-beat sound of mortar and pestle. Tabakali's hut was near the centre, facing the stockade gate but further back than most of the others, nearer to the dense foliage of the hummock that lay immediately below the pine ridge. The clashing rustle of palmetto fans was audible here in the slightest breeze and in the mornings the tallest of the palms cast thin shadows over the thatch.

The hut was the same as the others, built on a rectangle with more frontage than depth, with a palm-thatch roof sloping down on either side from a central ridge-pole. Woven mats hung from the split-log rafters to divide the space inside. In the hot season the huts were open-sided, but now in November mats had been hung all round to make an enclosure.

Tabakali was crouched at a low fire cooking silverfish on a cane grid. She smiled as they approached, but said nothing – she never spoke in greeting. Kenka, seeing that the food was not ready yet, disappeared round the back of the hut, where he found his sister playing knuckle-bones with some other children and joined in.

Paris stood for some minutes near the fire. The new moon was rising now, rimmed with the old one. The sky still held a lingering radiance, the few clouds very dark and soft-looking, as if charred. In the clearing of the compound there was light enough still, though figures at any distance were shadowy and indistinct in the smoky haze. Tabakali's face was lit by the glow of the fire. She was unaware of him, lost in thoughts of her own. She was dressed in a piece of the new cotton, dark red in colour, that Nadri, her other man, had bought for her. Nadri, an ingenious maker of traps, had given three fox-skins for three yards of it, an exorbitant price but she had desired the material greatly. With a tenacity that had surprised Paris she had always contrived to dress here as she had done in Africa, with a length of dyed cotton flung over one shoulder, covering the breasts and gathered at the waist to make a short skirt. Earlier she had hoarded remnants of the trade cottons they had taken from the ship; but of late bolts of cloth, dyed in vivid colours, had began to appear among the people of the settlement, brought from an undisclosed source by the trade partnership of Cavana, Tongman and Tiamoko. Several of the women wore this new fabric now, in their different ways, though there was a tendency among the younger ones to imitate Tabakali and cover the breasts. She herself wore nothing beneath the garment and her narrow feet and long legs were bare.

He looked steadily at her, enjoying the licence of watching her when she was heedless. She had less now of the elegant sharpness of bone that had drawn him at first. In these years she had borne four children, one of whom had died. Her breasts were heavier and the years had put flesh on her shoulders and hips and softened the sheer planes of her face. Her mouth was set in a fuller pout, resembling now a dark pink, crumpled rose. But the long-browed, slanting look of the eyes was the same, somehow both insolent and docile, and her arms and legs were slender still; he could see the supple play of muscle in her thighs as she shifted on her heels. Suddenly he was swept by a longing for the refuge she could give him, a need for darkness and the simplicity of her embrace – need made fierce by the desire that waited upon it, loosening his loins with heat as he stood there in the smoky, echoing compound.

She glanced up at him now, with her habitual, rather startled-seeming abruptness of movement, as if to appeal for his support in some argument she was conducting within herself. But her expression changed at the sight of his face and she raised her head and straightened her shoulders. 'You got big yai,' she said. 'Dat me or de fish you lookin' at?'

'Dat you.'

'Good, I happy for dat too much, never mind den, we forgit 'bout fish, buzzad bird ken have dem.'

'No, no,' Paris said, smiling. He knew that it amused her to catch him in contradiction of any kind. 'You plenty sabee man keep more dan one ting inside him head same-same time.'

She rose in one lithe movement and turned towards him. 'Keep ting in your head same-same time, head go sick,' she said in the tone of finality she used when it was a question of Paris's well-being – an area in which she felt sole and undisputed authority. 'You docta, you no sabee dat? Better one ting one time. Fish ready now.'

The fish had been brought that afternoon by Blair in thanks for the curing of Sallian's latest-born – whom Paris had delivered three months before – of a colic. This had not been a difficult matter; the baby's cramps had been alarming in their violence but had been eased within a short time by a mild infusion of wild mint and quassia root. But Sallian's gratitude was as large as everything else about her and she had dispatched Billy with the silverfish.

They ate in a circle at the fireside, sitting on rush mats that Tabakali had made with a skill learned in childhood and stained

530

blue with the leaves of a dye plant that grew wild further north in abandoned plantations; Kireku and the Shantee brought it down sometimes, together with the small, bitter oranges that grew there.

With the fish they had swamp cabbage, eaten raw, and koonti cakes – excellent these last, as Paris several times exclaimed. The koonti plant, knowledge of which they owed to the Indians, grew plentifully in the shore hummocks and in the pine ridges above them, and it was the exclusive concern of the women to gather the roots and make the flour. But Tabakali's koonti cakes had a particular excellence known to everyone in the settlement, rivalled only by those of Sallian, and this despite the fact that Tabakali came from a nomadic people who did not cultivate the ground and so – unlike almost all the other women – she had no experience of similar root crops like cassava. But she was meticulous almost to a fault and addressed herself thoroughly to everything from gathering and cooking to cleaning her teeth and oiling her body. She had developed her own methods of pulping the roots and washing the starch free, fermenting the sediment not just once or twice but four times, so that the flour was purer and her cakes lighter in texture, pale yellow in colour instead of the usual orange. With wild honey, when this could be found, there were few things in Paris's experience more delicious.

After supper the younger children were put to bed and Kenka went off to see his friend Tekka – his friend for the moment, at least: these two were of an age and by turns friends and enemies. Just now they were united in a common excitement as they were both to be allowed to accompany Paris and Nadri and Shantee Danka on a hunt for deer due to take place before the moon reached the full.

Inside the hut they lit a thin, foot-long pine quill resting longways in an upright stand fashioned by Barber from a cask-hoop. The resinous wood gave off little smoke and the light from it was reddish, slightly wavering.

Tabakali sat near the light on a low trestle. She was sifting through some wild cane seeds she had gathered to make porridge, taking them handful by handful from a skin bag on to a

531

board across her knees. Paris sat with his back against a corner
post, saying little, enjoying the peace that came to him always
within this warmly lit enclave at nightfall, compounded of the
silence, the gentle light, the deft movements of the woman. No
call would be made on him here; Tabakali rarely enjoined any
task on him or Nadri when they came to her. She had a strong
sense of territory, and that included the division of labour;
Nadri's work was trapping, at which he was a notable success,
applying skills learned from his father in childhood, snaring
quail in the wide grasslands; Paris's work was his sickroom and
his garden.

Kenka did not return, but this caused no concern to either of
them. The boy knew better than to go alone outside the compound after dark. It was a lesson drummed in from an early
age: night was the time of the bear and the panther and the
crocodile. He would be sleeping elsewhere, as he frequently did
– perhaps at Tekka's. The night was silent now except for the
occasional cry of nightbirds. Paris rose to light another splinter
of wood. Tabakali looked up at the movement and her long
fingers rested among the seeds. 'You worrit, an't you?' she said.
'Why you keep mum? What good dat serve?' She never missed
any change in his demeanour, though it was sometimes long
before she spoke of it. Lately she had seen some unhappiness
drag at the lines of his mouth, though the expression was fleeting,
soon lost in the patience and obstinacy that his face wore in
repose. 'Keep mum, end up poison belly,' she said.

'It's nothing,' Paris said. 'No wort' palaver.' He moved
towards her and put out his hand to touch the warm soft skin at
her nape. He had always loved the strong column of her neck,
thick but shapely and unblemished. The musky scent of her
body came to him and the sweet smell of the acorn oil she used
on her hair.

'We see if wort' palaver,' she said. 'You tell me, den we see.'
She smiled suddenly and he realized, without being able to
share it, that her amusement came from something she saw as
contradictory in what she was saying. 'I wait dis palaver,' she
said.

Paris hesitated still. Tabakali was a fighting woman, prompt

532

to action or decision when confronted with the need; but he did not know how to discuss feelings of anxiety or foreboding with her as this involved some appeal to shared expectation and she lived far more closely from hour to hour and day to day than he did, making her – at least in his view of things – a natural victim of those who saw further. In this, as in a number of other ways, she had remained alien to him. He knew little of her past before enslavement, and she had no concept of his. And the lingua franca that had developed among them, derived from the trade pidgin of the Guinea Coast, though it had provided the only possibility of a common language, offered small register for feeling.

The tendencies that worried him most – the growth of trading partnerships and the increasing rivalry and secrecy of their operations – he could not find words for. He began to speak to her of something more tangible and immediate, the forthcoming Palaver at which Tongman was to defend Iboti against the charge of witchcraft brought jointly by his woman Arifa and Shantee Hambo, who was Arifa's other man. A number of things about this case troubled him, not least among them the fact that Hambo was a fellow-tribesman of the powerful Kireku. Accusations of witchcraft were rare these days; most disputes concerned property or trade. Even in the early days there had been nothing like this. Some disputes concerning the evil eye there had been, born of jealousy and soon settled. Since then the nature of life in the settlement, the variety of language and race among the negroes, above all the violence done to traditional morality by the need to share women, had wrenched the people away from their accustomed styles of thinking, ideas of the supernatural had been driven below the surface.

There was, moreover, a disturbing aura of domestic intrigue about this case. Iboti was very slow in understanding and already one of the poorest people in the settlement, depending on Arifa for some of his necessities. If he lost the case Arifa would be entitled to deny him admittance to her hut and he would have to pay compensation to Hambo. If he won with Tongman's help, he would avoid disgrace but he would have to pay Tongman's fee. Either way he would be impoverished. This was not the first time that Tongman had spoken on someone else's behalf at a Council . . .

'Tongman big man for Palaver,' he said. 'He talk clever. Tongman is a good advocate.'

'Avokka, what dat?'

'Avokka talk in de Palaver, talk any way, say any ting, dis way, dat way, never mind de trut.'

'Avokka,' she repeated. 'Man talk clever pas' other man, dat his work. Docta sabee medsin pas' other man, trappa make trap pas' other man, dat dem work. Dat same-same ting everywhere.'

'Docta an' trappa, dey don' change you head,' Paris said with a smile. He was amused and strangely reassured by the invariably non-moralistic quality of her judgements. She admired all outstanding achievement of whatever kind.

'Tongman no ken change you head cos you *sabee* he a talkin' man,' she said now, answering his smile with a triumphant one of her own. 'You say hum-hum, dat jus' Tongman agin. When he don' talk, dat danger time. Okpolu by de water, you no 'fraid. Okpolu climb fence, den you watch out.'

'What is okpolu?'

'Okpolu is frog.'

Paris nodded gravely. 'Okpolu,' he said, as if in serious intention to remember it, and this made her laugh and look down and raise a hand to her mouth in the strange gesture, half modest, half superstitious, with which she always covered her laughter.

He laughed a little in response, moved by tenderness and renewed desire at this familiar and strangely helpless movement of hers. She sat carelessly, exposing her inner thighs below the short skirt – modesty and indifference were blended in her in a way he had never understood. With the sensitivity that she showed in all physical matters, a swiftness far surpassing his, she kept her eyes down for some moments. When she looked at him it was with a certain quality of steadiness that he also recognized, proud, calm, quite unselfconscious.

He heard a movement and a brief muttering from one of the sleeping children on the other side of the partition. Then silence again. 'You finish dat now,' he said, pointing towards the cane seed beside her on the trestle. At once she began to sweep the grain into a clay bowl, tilting the board and using the edge of her hand. Paris watched, remembering the first time he had come to her, the desolation of his desire, standing outside in the dark, a cool wind from the sea, his feet kicking in the debris of fallen palmetto leaves, the loneliness of need possessing him and Ruth's image lost among the rustling fronds at his feet. The same soft light, the same sense of warmth and safety . . . He had shared her with several men since those days but nothing had changed the feeling she gave him of having reached a safe haven. Just so had she looked at him then, as he stood dumb before her, with the same steadiness, without subterfuge and yet with a pride and decorum that had survived all the brutalities of the slaveship.

'Make dead de fire,' she said softly. She slept naked but for reasons that seemed cogent to her she would not undress before him nor ever make love except in the dark.

They lay together on the bed of rush matting and deerskins. Faint light came through where the woven mats joined the eaves. He could make out the line of her cheek, and her eyes in their shadowed hollows. Her smell came to him and he nuzzled his face against her neck and kissed the pulse in her throat and then the full mouth, which softened to his kisses; having early discovered his eccentric taste for kissing on the mouth she had practised the way of it that pleased him most. She pressed against him, but softly; her first movements of love were always gentle and slow. She moved her hands over his chest and abdomen and traced the bones of the pelvis. Preliminaries between them never lasted long. For him her touch and nearness in the dark were enough and when he turned to her he found her always ready. Tonight as he rode to his peace he muttered that he loved her, loved her, but the only reply that came was in the quickened breath of her excitement.

Afterwards she was asleep almost at once, almost before his weight was off her. Sleep, however, did not come to Paris despite the torpor of his body – indeed his mind seemed the clearer for this. He lay awake for a long time, his thoughts moving outward

535

in concentric ripples from the solitary phenomenon of himself to the human creatures sleeping around him, then to the spaces of the night that wrapped them all.

Once again the wonder of their existence on this remote strand came to him. In terms of odds defeated and probabilities defied it verged on the miraculous. Even the first condition of survival, the unity preserved among them after Thurso's death, in the aftermath of the mutiny, when staying made them all accomplices in murder, even this had been due to accidental factors, the presence of the gold dust on board, the extraordinary fervour of Delblanc.

No one had known of the gold dust at that time but Barton and Haines – and Haines only because Barton needed his help. The knowledge had been enough to make these two throw their weight behind the mutiny. Fear too, of course – both men were hated; but had they not planned to return to the ship they might have opposed the idea of grounding her. Once she was grounded there had been no turning back.

The presence of the gold, then, had been an accidental blessing. But the man who had done most to keep them together had not been a member of the crew at all. He saw Delblanc's face before him now, with the starkness on it of a truth belatedly, overwhelmingly, perceived. Delblanc had seen more clearly than anyone that only concerted action could save them, not only from surrounding dangers but from one another. Perhaps there was already present to his mind the marvellous opportunity the mutiny presented to test his theories, vindicate man's natural goodness in this dream of a community living without constraint of government or corruption of money. A ship blown off course, a scuffle of sick and desperate men, the blood of a madman clumsily and almost casually spilt, he had seen in these a truth of politics, a revolution, the founding of a new order. But it was I, after all, who began it, Paris thought, I who stepped forward under that witnessing sky. For the sake of others or myself? The old question, as far as ever from being answered. Was it to halt a crime or merely to straighten my back at last, face at last those who had set me in the pillory, made a hobbling beast of me? Impossible, now and for ever, to be sure . . .

In the landfall itself, where others saw merely a refuge, Delblanc must have seen also a violent birth. Paris thought of that dawn, the unreal calm after the long buffetings of the wind, the listing ship with her decks washed clean by the night's rain, the sight of the long, sickle-shaped sand bar fretted with waves, and the curving sweep of the inlet. It was afternoon before they could bring the ship into the channel, but the sun was high enough still to cast a band of light across its mouth, making it seem like a glorious threshold.

In the event, however, more suffering had lain beyond. Those early days had been the worst. Weakened by hunger and privation, huddled together on the rim of the limestone pineland, they had lived as they could on beach plum and palm berries and a species of blackberry growing along the shore. These fruits, insufficient as they were, had probably prevented deaths among the crew, several of whom were suffering from scurvy; but more negroes died in those first days and some ran off and were not seen again.

More would have run and almost certainly died, if the fate of Haines had not come as a fearful warning. He and Barton had disappeared on the first night, Barton to return two days later, half raving, bearing still the ripped jute sack that had held the gold dust, as if this evidence of his loss could somehow, as well as proving his words, exonerate him, plead in his favour. The story he came back with, garbled afterwards in pidgin and a variety of African languages, had lived in the minds of them all.

The two had returned to the ship with what speed they could. In spite of their enfeebled state they had brought the sacks off her. Their first plan, of making off in the longboat, was frustrated because she was fouled and they were too weak to free her, and too much in haste – they were possessed by fear of being surprised at their work. Ever the actor, even in his state of shock, Barton had sought to convey this fearful haste to his listeners. He wanted them to understand, to see that his conduct had been rational, laudable even. 'We had to get clear of the vessel,' he said again and again, rapidly and tonelessly. 'You can see that, shipmates.' And then, with his inveterate fondness for the polysyllabic flourish, 'It was iniquitous dark, lads, we didn't dare to show no light . . .'

Paris found himself smiling involuntarily as he lay there. Barton's impudence surpassed everything. The thin face blood-less with exhaustion, staring with a fear still not overcome, the ripped sack – his gauge of truth – still in his hand. And the incorrigible flourish of the phrase.

They had blundered with the sacks for some distance and settled down to wait for daylight. This, when it came, brought further problems. Their idea was now to bury the gold, but the ground was too marshy. They had stumbled through thickets of mangrove and swamp willow, carrying the sacks, looking for a place. Eventually they had come to the edge of a shore hum-mock, where a stream ran like a tunnel into thick vegetation. Here, above the stream, there was a deep mould of leaf and soil. But now a difficulty arose, strangely unforeseen in the midst of all their labours: they could not agree on a hiding place because neither man could trust the other not to return to it alone and take all the gold for himself.

Strange and absurd situation, Paris thought, lying wide-eyed in the darkness, the two exhausted men quarrelling there by the stream as the sun climbed above them, coming to blows at one point, if Barton was to be believed, over two sacks of dust. 'It came to me that Haines was not a man to be trusted,' Barton said, glancing at the faces round him, restored to the community of honest men.

The solution they had hit upon was for each man to bury his sack in a place of his own choosing. And it was then, in the interval between reaching this decision and summoning the energy to carry it out, that an amazing stroke of good fortune occurred to save Barton's life. 'Luckiest shit I ever had in my life, lads,' he said, looking haggardly from face to face, inviting them to share his luck, repeating the fact in that rapid, toneless voice of his nightmare: 'Luckiest shit of my whole life . . .' Luckyshit Barton, Blair had begun to call him after that, and so he was known to everyone now, even the toddlers who did not yet know why.

The diet of beach plums and palm berries had left Barton with violent diarrhoea and he had felt the gripes of it just at that moment. Leaving Haines there by the streamside, he had removed himself into a thicket of bushes. He had taken his musket with him, but he had left the gold with Haines. Because of this he had not gone too far away; and he had chosen a place from which any movement Haines made along the stream would be visible to him.

As he crouched there in the first easement of his pangs, he had heard a slight sound. He had looked up and seen with heart-stopping shock a party of naked savages, fearsomely tattooed in whorls of red and white on their faces and chests, come drifting down through the trees, moving with a lightness that seemed to have no need of stealth. They had not seen him, but it was immediately clear to him that they had seen Haines.

They had passed quite close, it seemed – within thirty yards. He had his musket there beside him. Haines would have heard him if he had called, would have had at least some warning, some chance to defend himself. What sort of hope or calculation had passed through Barton's mind in those moments could only be conjectured. It was possible of course that he was simply petrified with fear. In any case, he had done nothing. 'There was no use,' he said. 'They was too many. I couldn't be sure a shot would drive them off and I wouldn't have had no chance for a second.' In the fever of his veracity he did not attempt to cover his cowardice. His chief thought, he told them, in the babbling of his honesty, was that the Indians might smell his shit and find him. He had tried to cover it, when they had passed below him, with the edge of his shoe.

But before many seconds the smell of butchery had been in their nostrils. Barton had not seen, from his crouched position there, what was done to Haines. He had heard a sound of surprise, like a cough or a loud grunt, then a wailing cry. Some other broken sounds there had been, more like effort than pain, but these had been made indistinct by some chattering syllables of the Indians and then by their laughter, rather high-pitched.

He had remained there, not daring to move, crouched over his own excrement, tormented by flies. He did not see or hear the Indians again and supposed they had taken a path below the stream. Long after silence had settled he waited still. When he went finally, moving his cramped limbs with utmost caution, he had found Haines lying there and the sacks ripped and empty. Haines had been scalped. He lay on his back across the slight track above the stream, presenting to the trees and to the sky beyond them a face unrecognizable, obscured by blood from crown to chin.

'He was always proud of his hair, Haines was,' Barton said. It was the boatswain's only epitaph.

There was not much more to the story. The horror showed in the mate's eyes, and everyone understood it. The quiet, sunlit path, the glint of flies about the terrible red face of the corpse. He had crawled some way, it seemed – the Indians had left him alive. 'Mebbe that was what they was laughin' at,' Barton said. 'I heard the varmints laughin'.'

He had begun to make his way back, halting at nightfall and shivering through till first light – he had not dared to make a fire. Next day he had gone on, staggering with exhaustion, involved in endless detours among the mangroves. He had been at the limits of his strength when he had found them again; but he was still clinging to the vital evidence of the ripped and gutted sack.

'Look what they done, shipmates,' he said, holding it out in witness to an insane universe. 'Them iggerant beggars . . . They cut the sacks open an' shook the gold out, down into the creek.' On the point of collapse, Barton looked round with a drained, exhausted triumph at this ultimate proof of human folly. 'How can you unnerstand people like that?' he demanded.

Sullivan was the only one to find anything to say to this, Paris remembered, with a feeling of amused affection. Sullivan always liked to have an answer to everything. He had fastened on the tottering Barton the fleeting speculation of his gaze. 'Clear as daylight to a thinkin' man,' he said. 'They was hopin' to find somethin' valuable, and they got disappointed like, when they didn't.'

It was an old story now, but not forgotten. Haines's face of blood was part of the collective memory of the settlement, though only Barton had seen it. The body was never recovered. The rains came and the grasslands were flooded. By the time the people were able to venture so far there was no trace. But the place where he met his end was called Goldwater by Jimmy in his classroom stories and it became as legendary in its way as Oose Tree or Red Creek, enshrined like them in the imagination of the children. It was said that at certain times, when the water ran clear in the stream bed, glints of gold were still to be seen there.

It had been Luckyshit Barton's last attempt at private enterprise. He was Kireku's lackey now and generally despised, a man without friends and without a regular woman. To Haines something was held to be owing, simply for the manner of his death, and this was also true of Wilson. It was strange that these two, bad men both and sworn enemies, should have been the martyrs and founding fathers of the community.

Delblanc had known how to use these deaths, as he had known how to use everything. Not least of the mysteries that touched Paris's mind as he finally drifted towards sleep was how his dead friend, an itinerant portrait painter of good birth and easy manners, had been able to forge men of such metal into instruments of a higher purpose. But of course it was not a higher purpose at all, he thought, despite the rhetoric of the time. It was *our* purpose, Delblanc's and mine; his based on doctrines of liberty, mine on some inveterate hope. Men living free and equal in a state of nature . . . What gave us the confidence to suppose that a state of nature could only mean what it meant to us, a notion of Eden, a nostalgia of educated, privileged men?

FORTY-NINE

Calley woke at dawn, released from a dream in which he had been lost in a desolate place and bitterly weeping. He whimpered on waking and lay for some time without moving, not knowing where he was, still involved in the grief of his dream. Then he knew the feel of the sand on which he was lying and saw the branches overhead of the rough shelter he had made for himself.

He crawled out, away from his sorrow, into the misty light of morning. He shook himself and urinated and shivered, looking up at the sky above the sea, where trailing clouds were touched with faint pink. Crouched again in his shelter, he ate the koonti bread and scraps of dried fish left from the day before. Then he started back through the jungle of the hummock to make a scratch-hole for water on the landward side. It was several hours' walk to the settlement, but Calley had been combing the beaches and ranging through the pine ridges for years now and he knew there was water here, just below ground, as he knew there were acorn trees and pig nuts and the tunnels of the big red land crabs.

Now he did things exactly in the way Nadri had taught him years before – Nadri had always been kind to him and protected him and to some extent had taken Deakin's place in his life. With the long-bladed knife that was his only weapon and practically his only possession, he dug down into the soft, sandy mould until he came upon the water. It was muddy at first, but Calley knew that it would clear if he waited some minutes, because the water below the ground was always flowing, very slowly, towards the ocean. Nadri, who knew a great many things, had told him this and he had always remembered it. When the water was clear he lowered his head towards his moonface reflection: alone among the crew people, Calley grew no hair on his face, only a soft, whitish down. He drank, careful not to disturb the bed of the pool.

This done, he put on his harness, which he had carried with him from the shelter. It consisted of a broad back-pad, rather like a saddle, made of matted palm fibres, worn high on the shoulders and secured with rope straps. Calley quite often found logs of pitchwood in the forest and he had learned that this black, heavy wood was in great demand as fuel and could secure him food and shelter and sexual favours sometimes – he had no hut of his own and no settled way of life. He was extremely strong and he would arrive at the settlement with his squat and heavily muscled figure bowed under a great pyramid of logs.

He began to walk, following a faint track in the direction of the sea. The air was bright and he knew the sun had risen clear, though it was too low in the sky to be seen. Sharp folds of limestone rose here and there above the ground, but Calley's soles were thickly calloused and he felt little through the deer-hide bags he wore tied to his feet.

The vegetation thinned as he drew nearer the sea until there was only the saw palmettos and torchwood trees and the smooth writhing forms of the sea-grape. Finally there was nothing but the fringe of tall, dishevelled palms growing above the shore. He emerged into the open to see the sun riding clear of the water and a sky that seemed surprised by the brilliance that had come to it, just as he was himself surprised. Calley found echoes for all his feelings in the look of things around him.

He began to walk southwards, in the direction of the settlement. A breeze from the sea stirred the palms, and the pliant, yellow-green spines of the fronds were touched to gold by this early sunshine. Calley felt the beauty of the swaying leaves and the radiant sky and the surprised clouds. His soft mouth hung a little open as he settled into the rhythm of his walking and lowered his eyes to the scattering of pebble and shell fragment that marked the tide-line. Things could be found here, things of

543

value. Calley had learned and memorized them: sea beans, polished and smooth after their long washing in the sea, odds and ends from wrecked ships, tiny white cone shells to make necklaces and the bigger, cunt-shaped ones that some of the women valued for good luck in childbirth.

He made little whistling sounds to himself as he walked along, happy to be out here in the open where there was no danger. As the sun rose the sky took on a deeper blue but the marbling of cloud remained and there were bursts of light and falls of shadow across the surface of the water. The low waves broke and milled briefly in splinters of light and the suds frilled out and fizzed and shrank back, leaving gleaming levels of sand that confused Calley's eyes when he looked along the shore. A company of pelicans, disturbed by his approach, flapped up awkwardly and headed out to sea, one behind the other, gliding on stiff wings. He walked steadily at first, keeping his gaze on the tide-line. But before long the jellyfish began to distract him. Dead and dying jellyfish lay here and there along the shore, stranded by the tide, their iridescent, bladder-like forms sometimes alone on the wet sand, sometimes entangled in seaweed. These lilac-tinted bubbles could deliver a lash-like sting, as Calley knew from painful experience: he had once tried to pick one up and ever since had harboured vindictive feelings towards them. Whenever he came to one now he stopped and pricked it with the point of his knife. As the gas was released the puffed-out sac collapsed with a comical squeak like a fart of farewell. Each time it happened Calley chuckled to himself and mocked the deflated jellyfish with squeaking sounds of his own.

He looked up gleefully from this sport to see a fretting and worrying of waves round a dark shape at the water-line some distance ahead of him. He thought at first it might be a section of the trimmed hardwood timber sometimes washed up from cargo ships; but it was too short for that and too light – the water was lifting and moving it this way and that. Then he saw that it was the body of a negro, not fully grown. The sex he could not determine yet. As he drew nearer the movements of the body seemed like a sort of languid play. He saw now that it was a boy. Calley stopped and stood looking. It came to his mind that the sea was bringing this body to life. Calley knew there were spirits, he saw and heard them everywhere about him, they informed his dreams. In a shaft of awe below any power of words it seemed to him that this negro boy would presently crawl up out of the sea. Then he saw the staring eyes and the slight, helpless gestures of the hands and he knew the boy was dead.

He went forward and drew the body out of the water and laid it higher up on the beach. The boy was perhaps ten or eleven years old and his body was whole – he had escaped sharks in the deep water and crabs in the shallows and the vultures that would have found him soon. He was emaciated; his cage of ribs was clearly visible beneath the skin, the collarbone like a halter on him. There was a brandmark on his chest, on the right side, above the nipple. The scar was red, still new.

Calley fell now into a painful state of anxiety and indecision. He stood looking from the dead boy to the empty shore and sea and sky. He was absolutely alone with the responsibility of this discovery, nothing to guide or help him. He could leave the body where it was and walk on as if nothing had happened. He would never speak about it, no one would know. Would Deakin have done that? Deakin would not just walk away from the dead child. Deakin would take the body and show people . . .

He stopped and picked up the boy in his arms. The body was ice-cold and Calley shivered slightly at the contact of this cold flesh against his own. He hoisted the slight form across his shoulders and resumed his way. Soon he became accustomed to his burden. He walked on steadily, his mind vacant, aware only of the washing sound of the waves, the growing warmth of the sun.

Also abroad early was a young man called Sefadu, whom love had made restless. He had risen with the first light and paddled for two hours through the channels on the edge of the flooded saw-grass plain towards the dark line of a jungle island on the horizon. The water levels had begun to sink but he often hunted here for duck and quail and he knew the floodlands well. He had been born in the Bolilands of Sierra Leone, a region not much different, flooded in the rainy season and dry in winter. In the narrow, flat-bottomed canoe, which he had hollowed out himself from a single trunk, he could pass at a level of a few inches.

The tall grass grew close and the minute teeth on the blades cut his arms and shoulders sometimes. But his purpose was fixed and the fire in his mind steady, so that he hardly noticed these wounds, or the indignant herons and spoonbill birds that flapped up with heavy wingbeats at his approach.

He tied up the canoe at the edge of the hummock among pads of water-shield plants still cupping their catch of dew, and stepped into the green twilight of the trees. He had been here before and knew there was a wide sink-hole on this side, not far into the trees, a deep hollow in the rockbed which was the hummock's foundation. Thrusting through the close-growing vegetation, beating before him with a stick to warn snakes, he came upon it. It was deep still, brimming with clear, dark water. A lacework of duckweed floated at the edges, but the centre held nothing save the glinting reflections of the foliage above it.

Here among the trees there was no sound. Sefadu stood at the edge of the pool, looking across to the sharp outcrop that thrust like wrinkled knuckles through the peat mould on the other side. These creases of rock were what had brought him. He had remembered the dark interior of this hummock, the cracked limestone and the complicated roots of the trees edging the pool. It was a perfect place for ground pearls, the most coveted of all ornaments among the women. He wanted to make a necklace for Dinka, so she would know his love.

He was three years younger than she, the youngest adult of the settlement, having been not yet ten years old when brought here – he had been a well-grown child and Thurso had thought him older. He was Temne-speaking like Tongman, but that was all they had in common, since Sefadu was not interested in dealing but in making things, and especially decorative things, though he made cutting tools and arrowheads also. He was tall and long-legged, rather narrow in build, with heavy-lidded eyes that gave his face a totally misleading expression of indolence.

546

The pause had been for something in the nature of a strong wish addressed to the spirit of his maternal grandmother, who had been a great gleaner and finder. Now he moved carefully round to the far side of the pool and began his search. After he had been there some time a brief but heavy shower descended. He stood patiently where he was, waiting to resume, watching the bark of the trees darken with wet. The rain stopped abruptly and he immediately began searching again, with the drenched leaves dripping down on him and the slow ack-ack of the grateful tree frogs resounding through the hummock.

It was an hour or so before he found the first pearls, caught among the exposed roots of a pond apple, four small opaque lumps, roseate and waxy, glistening softly among the dark root-hairs. There were two more in the soil below.

He put them in the skin bag he wore round his neck and searched on without pausing. He felt neither hunger nor fatigue. By mid-afternoon his bag contained thirty-eight pearls, all roughly the same size. Enough to make a necklace.

He set off back immediately, wanting to make the most of the light. Once again in the compound, he started work without pausing to eat or rest. His hut was also his workship and he had everything here that he needed: sailmaker's needles, steel pins, chisels, all begged at various times from the people of the crew, some when he was still a child – he had always been clever at making things. Now he worked with application to pierce the pearls, the movements of his hands assured and delicate, his face set in a slight frown of concentration, joy and anxiety contending within him.

Somewhere not far away he could hear the voices of children. They were acting out the story of Wilson – he recognized the dialogue of the quarrel. Sefadu knew this story well; he had witnessed the execution of Wilson as a child and he had never forgotten it, the big man and his white, unbelieving face, the ragged volley of the muskets, fired by black men and white men together, all the men of the settlement. The voices of the unseen children carried to him, rapid, high-pitched, the actors scarcely distinguishable one from another, using words they knew by heart:

547

'*We here is two man one woman. You ken do matta mattick, yes or no? We got to share dis woman.*'

'*I no share wit you, I wan' fuck dis woman for wife.*'

'*We go ask woman den. Woman, you take us share two husban'?*'

'*Yes, sartin, I take you . . .*'

No excuse had been found for Wilson's crime. He had waited in hiding and stabbed a man to death, a negro, over a quarrel about sharing a woman.

Sefadu had not understood matters fully at the time. Those early days were clouded and confused with the terrors of the voyage and the hardships they had suffered on first landing. As a child, aboard the slaveship, he had seen death come in fearsome ways; he had heard people shrieking around him in the stinking darkness and he had joined in, screaming, not knowing whether it was fear of death or desire for release. But this public death that Wilson had suffered was not like any other he had seen. The white man had been brought out and tied up and slaughtered like an animal. He had not struggled, he had not believed it, he had walked among the people as if in a dream. Wilson had been killed by *everybody*. It was this that made his death special, the children had been told. It was justice, it was all the people showing how much they hated this crime. Killing was justice when everybody joined in.

At ten, Sefadu had not been able to understand this because his idea of justice was more personal. It puzzled him still, twelve years later. Killing Wilson had been good for the settlement, it had shown the black people that their lives were valuable to the white people, but he could not see how that could be called justice. Delblanc, dead now himself, had been the great talker for Wilson's death, just as he was talking for it again now, in piping tones, outside the hut:

'*Turn you arse about, I talkin' to you. What you name?*'

'*My name Wilsoon.*'

'*Wilsoon, you kill one man. How ken people live tagedder if dey do dat? How ken dey learn share woman if dey do dat? The worl' fall in pieces if dey do dat. So now we all go kill you, Wilsoon . . .*'

They had tied Wilson to a tree and discharged their muskets at close range into his body. Sefadu remembered how at that sudden explosion of sound great flocks of birds had risen from the marshes. For some moments their wings had filled the sky. Wilson had hung in his ropes all that day and the next for everyone to see . . .

Sefadu paused to blow dust from the mouth of the tiny hole he was making. The little pile of pearls on his low bench was diminishing slowly. He sat cross-legged on the floor to work, in the light of the entrance. The image of Dinka came into his mind as he had seen her last, the shapely arms, the proud carriage of the head, the long, narrow eyes both languorous and mocking. On her lower lip, close to the join, there was a tender flush of blood, dark pink, as if at some previous time this lip had been turned a little more inward, into the protective softness of the mouth . . .

Sullivan too was busy that afternoon. He was replacing a broken string in his fiddle. He would win Dinka by the power of music, and he desired the instrument of persuasion to be in best possible condition. Sullivan's life from earliest childhood had been too hard for him to maintain much consistency of principle or opinion – that is for more sheltered folk – but he had retained a belief in music as an aid to love.

He had been alerted to the need for swift action by his talk with Billy and Inchebe and his realization that both of them had a fancy for Dinka, in spite of being settled men with a good wife. He was by no means convinced that his praise for Sallian had done much to make them see the error of their ways. Indeed, he was rather afraid that his words had misfired and roused their suspicions, Inchebe's particularly. Inchebe was a subtle and a guileful fellow; there was a good deal to fear from this quarter, Sullivan felt.

Fortune had favoured him in the shape of a fresh-killed deer brought in by Hughes the day before. He had selected a length of gut from the carcass and had squeezed and nipped the blood and excrement out of it with utmost care, pulling it repeatedly between finger and thumb until it was as clean and sweet as he could make it. All night it had been soaking in a strong lye of wood ash. Now he had begun to peel away the softened film of

549

skin lining the outside, a task requiring patience and devotion and lightness of touch, all of which qualities Sullivan brought to it and desired also to bring to Dinka. Meanwhile, as he worked his hopes rose, he whistled between his teeth a tune of his boyhood, 'Katy Brannigan'.

His plan was formed and he felt that it was a good one. He would tune his fiddle to the maximum tenderness it was capable of. He would wait for nightfall. After the evening meal, when things had settled down, he would make his way to Dinka's hut, which fortunately was one of those on the edge of the settlement. Once there, he would sit outside her door and give her a tune or two. He would serenade her. He had chosen the tunes already: 'Oh Hear Me' and 'Rose of Ireland'. She would be moved by the beauty of it, she would take him in, he would be home and dry. Perhaps she would offer him, in the way of preliminary courtesy, a drop of grain beer. Dinka made an excellent grain beer . . .

Of course, there would be something public in it, people round would be certain to hear him, they would come crowding out to see this prodigy of song. But Sullivan had never been averse to an audience. And Dinka would not mind her neighbours knowing she was desired by one of the main music-makers of the place. She would be pleased. It was, he sought for the word in his mind, *homage*. Sullivan knew women. Women liked homage the world over.

He made a narrow loop at one end of the gut and passed a short toggle through it. The other end he tied to a corner post of his hut. He began to twist the gut, pausing often to run the twists higher with his fingers, increasing the tension. She was a beauty, taut and supple as any man could wish.

As soon as he left the shore and began to strike inland, Calley stopped from time to time to gather pieces of pitchwood. These he laid on top of the dead child and then roped the body and the logs together so that the stack rose high above his shoulders. He was almost doubled under this weight when he reached the first huts of the settlement.

The logs were deposited for safe-keeping outside Tabakali's

hut. He knew she would not cheat him and he knew she was charitable with food. On her advice he carried the body to Paris's sickroom; he was mightily relieved to be told there, by Paris himself, that he had done the right thing.

The body lay there for the rest of the afternoon under a blanket to keep off the flies. It was quite unmarked and Paris could discover no certain cause of death. The boy had not died by drowning, there was no water in the lungs; he had been dead when thrown over the side. It seemed likely that a flux or fever had carried him off. Or the shock of captivity, Paris thought, remembering some of the deaths on board the *Liverpool Merchant*. *Fixed melancholy*, that had been Thurso's phrase for it. But no children had died from this cause, none that he could remember, only adults. Children did not die of unhappiness, they were still too close to the dawn of life ... The brandmark on the boy's chest was an S and an L joined in the shape of a loop with one side curving and one straight. It could be the mark of any of a thousand merchants from a dozen nations. The only one that could be definitely excluded was his uncle. *K for Kemp*. A long way from Liverpool to this wrecked life. There came into his mind an old adage of the Guinea traders which Barton had let fall to him once – Barton could seldom resist a quote: *Heaven is high and Europe far away* ...

For some time he stood there, in the long, open-fronted hut where he kept his jars of herbs and his instruments and his few belongings, looking at the face of the dead boy. The faces of the dead resemble no living face, but Paris judged this boy to be about the age of his own son. Quite unexpectedly he felt the pricking of tears. Only by fortunate accident had Kenka been born to freedom and kind treatment ...

Several people had seen Calley with his burden and the news of the dead boy passed around. Almost everyone in the compound or the immediate surroundings came at some time during the afternoon to see the body. They stood for a while and discussed with one another where the boy might have come from and what people he belonged to. Most saw some resemblance to their own people. Kireku's woman, Amansa, came with a funeral mat of palmetto leaf. The children stood in a ring and

551

stared at the face whenever it was uncovered. Paris gave Kenka a task of special responsibility, much envied by the others: he was armed with a fly-whisk in the form of a stick with palm fibres fastened to it, and told to sit at the boy's head and guard his face from flies. This he did with utmost diligence and gravity, resisting all attempts of other children to relieve him. It was to remain a day of high event in Kenka's mind through all the years to come, coloured by the pride and importance of this task enjoined on him by his father.

So the dead boy lay there while his grave was being dug by Calley and Bulum Iboti. Patterns of light and shade moved over him as the sun shifted lower, until finally it sank below the trees and he lay in shadow. They had decided to bury him in the common burial place, which was on a bluff at the edge of the pine ridge, overlooking a sizeable creek. Here were the mounded remains of an ancient settlement of the Indians, long abandoned. The ground had been raised to a dozen feet or more by an accumulation of earth and a heavy dust of shards and shell fragments, making it possible to dig graves deep enough to cheat the animals. Customs vary, and some of the dead were elsewhere. Some lay under the huts they had lived in; two had been exhumed and their bones placed in palm-leaf baskets. But most who had died in the years of the settlement were buried here and their graves marked by posts with an initial or abbreviated name burnt on. Stitched in their palmetto shrouds, Delblanc and Wilson had been laid to rest here, and the man Wilson had killed, and the child that Tabakali had lost. There was a post here too for Deakin; occasionally the wandering Calley came and sat beside it and remembered his friend.

The boy was stitched into his tough shroud and slung to a pole borne by Billy Blair and Shantee Danka. On the mound of the cemetery there was some sunlight still, broken by the long, straight shadows of the graveposts. Nadri was in the last of the sunlight as he stood beside the grave. As a man generally respected, he had been chosen to say a few words.

'Nobody sabee where dis boy come from,' he said. 'To Vai people he look like he come from Vai people, to Susu people he look like he Susu an' so it go like dat. Everybody say he look

552

like dey own people. Dis boy got no tribe cut, he got no cockskin cut. Slavemark on him, look like done only two-three day, mebee dis boy nearly die already when dey put burnmark, mebbe not. Who put dis slavemark on him, Frenchman, Inglisman, Danaman? Only ting we ken say buckra man slaver done it. If he got no mark tell us who he belong, we oblige say dis dead pikin belong nobody. But wait one minnit, what dat mean? My pinion dat mean he belong everybody. He belong all of us here.'

Nadri's voice had deepened on this and his listeners saw that he was moved. 'Dis pikin belong everybody,' he repeated. 'So we go bury dis one here, longside us people, an' we go put dat burnmark on him gravepost. Dat burnmark him name.'

With that, the body was lowered into the grave. Iboti, who had helped to dig the grave, stayed behind to fill it in. He was too poor a man to work for nothing and had been promised a rabbit and a bag of chestnut meal – quite valuable this, as the nearest chestnut trees lay far to the north. This was a bad time for Iboti, perhaps the worst since the terrible days of his capture and enslavement. His woman did not want him and treated him with scorn. He was due to be charged with witchcraft next day and he was deeply frightened and unhappy at this. Also he was afraid of being caught here among the dead at nightfall. For this reason he worked rapidly, protesting his innocence and uttering propitiatory phrases in a continuous mutter as he worked. He was a fearful man and not blessed with great intelligence. Only fear of devils and hope in Tongman's advocacy kept him from running off into the night.

Sullivan adhered to his plan in every detail. He ate no supper. The tension of his feelings took away appetite. There was not much to eat in any case: he had neglected to provide for himself and he felt in no frame of mind for the communal supper at his woman's hut, along with one and quite possibly both of her other men, Libby and Zobi, and her four children, the latest only a year old.

He waited in his own hut until the cooking fires were low and the meal-time gossip over. The shouts of children continued afterwards but they too were hushed after a while. The moon was high when he emerged and a faint light from it lay across the compound. There was a chill in the air and a smell of wood smoke and mist. Sullivan shivered a little. He had taken pains with his appearance, tying back his long hair with a leather thong, trimming his beard, chewing mastic to clean his teeth and sweeten his breath.

There were people still moving about here and there, but no one took much notice of Sullivan as he made his way to the corner of the compound where Dinka lived. No light showed from her hut, but he was not particularly surprised at this; people in the settlement generally slept early and rose with the sun. Dinka would be roused from her first sleep by his music and what better way for a woman to wake?

He chose a place some yards from the entrance and seated himself on the ground. After waiting a while to steady his breathing he settled the fiddle to his shoulder and began to play the air of 'Oh, Hear Me!' He had a husky tenor voice, not very strong, but pleasing – he had used it in dusty lanes and cobbled streets of the past, in another life, singing for coppers, dragging a leg for more pathetic effect. Now he put all the feeling he knew into it:

> Oh, hear me, my charmer!
> Wouldst kill me with scorn?
> See, the east lightens,
> Soon cometh the dawn.

He was aware of movements, voices, people stirring in the huts around, but he kept his eyes on the entrance to Dinka's. There had been no response from this quarter so far. He repeated the first two lines of the melody on his fiddle, drawing out the notes as tremulously as possible. Still no sign of anything. He began the second verse:

> Hear me, oh, hear me,
> Give ease to my pain . . .

Abruptly he fell silent. A figure had at last appeared at the threshold, naked, but not the one hoped for and not the right

554

sex even – a fact grossly apparent to the staring Sullivan considerably before he knew the face for Sefadu's. The voice, when it came, was not unkind: 'She no ken hear you now, fiddleman, she busy too much. Come back in de mornin'.'

The strains of the fiddle had come to Kenka as he lay between waking and sleeping. He had heard fiddle-music before and knew that it must be Sullivan. At the same time, perhaps because he was not fully awake or because the music was distant and sad, it seemed like a voice of the night, not coming from any particular place or person. There was something magical about it and for this reason Kenka never asked any questions concerning the music, nor indeed mentioned it to anyone until many years later in a different place, when he was an old man and nearly blind.

As he lay looking through the darkness he heard the silence left by the ceasing of the music fill again with small accustomed sounds, faint rustles in the thatch above him, the deep, regular breathing of his brother and sister lying nearby, the distant sibilance of the sea – not exactly a sound, this, but a very faint escape of silence.

He began to think about the night-time deer-hunt which he had been promised – his first. It was due to take place very shortly now, before the full moon. Shantee Danka was back, after an absence of several days. He had returned for the Palaver. It was Danka who had seen the deer-tracks and the cropped shoots in a hummock no more than an hour away, beyond the freshwater lagoon. Danka would be leading them. He was a notable hunter and very strong – Kenka had once measured Danka's bow against the thickness of his own wrist and found no difference. About him, as about almost all the older men of the settlement, there was a legendary glamour. Danka had been one of those who brought the ship up from the sea . . .

Kenka had never been to the hummock where the tracks had been found, but he felt he knew it because he had questioned both Paris and Nadri at different times and both had described it to him in detail, just as they had described the method of the hunt. There was a bayhead over a narrow stream. The stream

555

flowed out of a tunnel of moonvines and there were small red fish in it and it opened into a pool that was completely roofed over by the branches of trees like a room with a floor of water.

He began to rehearse the hunt in his mind, as he had done often before. Every phase of it had taken on the colour of ritual, and everything had to be done in a precise, unvarying order. They would leave while it was still light. He would see the silver stream flowing out of the vines and the red fish flashing in the clear water. He would wade upstream with the others, through the low opening in the tangle. They would wait at the edge of the clearing, making sure they were on the right side of the wind so that their scent would not be carried to the thickets where the deer came. The deer liked dark and secret places, Kenka knew, they were timid and swift to take alarm. But in spite of this, they always wanted to know the meaning of things and it was this that was their undoing. *Dat de ting capsai dem,* Nadri had said. *Same-same ting every time.*

When it was growing dark he and Tekka would be allowed to light the fires of splinterwood in the shallow pans that the men carried on their backs in a rope harness. These made a light just strong enough – too much light would frighten the deer away. *Deer don' stan' for blazelight* . . . Kenka lay completely still, on his back, his hands held down by his sides. The dark shapes of the deer would approach silently through the trees, drawn by the light. They would be dazzled but still they would come nearer, not seeing the forms of the hunters or the tightened bows with the heavy arrows. The light of the fire would shine in their eyes – their eyes would be wide open and blind. Perhaps at the last moment some fear would turn them away, but then it would be too late. There would come the twang and swish and the deer would fall and kick for a little while and then be still.

With the death of the deer the night would be empty . . . Kenka was obscurely troubled as he lay there. The deer was killed because it wanted to know the meaning of everything and he understood this because he was the same himself. He had heard his father say it to Tabakali. *Dis Kenka cur'us boy, allus want de answer, what dis mean, what dat mean* . . .

His father had seemed pleased . . . The glowing, sightless eyes of the deer faded in the darkness among the trees and Kenka drifted towards sleep.

FIFTY

Palavers were held at irregular intervals, whenever disputes occurred which could not be settled privately. They took place in the compound, in the open space between the stockade and the first huts. Though serious enough to the disputants, they were regarded as a form of entertainment by those not involved and were always well attended. In the hot season evening was the preferred time but now, in the cooler weather, mid-morning was judged suitable, particularly as that evening would be taken up with the naming of Neema's latest child, under the joint fathership of Cavana and Tiamoko – friends and partners, these two, sharing wife and trade interests. Neema had decided to have the naming on the same day as the Palaver so as to ensure a good attendance – desirable alike for prestige and the volume of gifts and good wishes.

It was early still, not long after sunrise, and Paris was in his sickroom administering an infusion of quassia and dried orange peels to Libby, who had a jaundiced look to his solitary eye this morning and had come with complaints of a night disturbed by vomiting. This morbid condition, accompanied in the first hours by a low fever, was one that Libby had suffered from at intervals for a good number of years now.

He was not alone in this. Others of the crew people, though none of the Africans, were troubled by a recurrent fever, mystifying in its cause to Paris, as there seemed to be no evidence of reinfection. In some cases it took the form of a single mild bout lasting a day or two, in others there was a more dangerous period of closely spaced peaks. Libby's fever was accompanied by an evident obstruction of the bile, but this was not so with

558

any of the others. It was difficult to see a pattern anywhere. However, the men seemed well enough between times and there had been no deaths from fever since Rimmer's, five summers ago. Paris himself had experienced no recurrence of the illness that had stricken him aboard ship, except for a tendency to ache and shiver when he caught the mildest chill.

He had long since exhausted his store of cinchona; now, to allay the fever and clear the blood, he relied on the powdered bark of the bitter ash, of which he had discovered isolated specimens growing on the shorewards side of some jungle hummocks, or on a concoction of sassafras.

Libby was grateful enough, in his surly way, and Paris took the opportunity to ask his opinion of the charge against Iboti, due to be heard later that morning. As he had expected from a hanger-on of Kireku – and it was really the purpose of his question – it was the Shantee view that he got.

'It is clear as daylight,' Libby said. 'Iboti is guilty. He tried to kill Hambo just as much as if he had stuck a knife into him. He was seen gatherin' dust from Hambo's footprint to make the fetish. Why should Hambo's woman say she seen him if she never did?'

'She is Iboti's woman too. Why she says this or that is what we hope to find out at the Palaver.'

Libby made a gesture of contempt. 'Palaver's a shaggin' waste o' time,' he said. 'The death fetish was found on Hambo's roof.'

Paris looked curiously at the other man's face, which was pallid and swollen with the bad night he had passed. Libby borrowed opinions from those he served. Why not beliefs too? 'I did not know you set so much store by fetishes, Libby,' he said.

'Me? A few sticks an' feathers an' a bit o' spit?' As he got up to go Libby uttered a short laugh, not altogether convincing. 'When I am sick,' he said, 'don't I come for medicine? I don't go to Amansa, beggin' for a charm.'

After he had gone, Paris stood quietly, without moving. There was an ugliness of spirit about Libby, which showed even when he was trying to be amiable – perhaps more then. A period of silence seemed necessary before the place could be healed of his visit. Paris knew this was a superstitious feeling, but superstition of one sort or another, like nostalgia, moved among them all; and this sickroom, though open to everyone, was a very private place for him, it was where he came to commune with himself and with the past.

Everything he possessed was here. His mahogany medicine chest stood on trestles of split palm log, with his small set of instruments, cleaned and polished, laid out in their slots of frayed plush and his glass-stopped bottles set in a row. Barber had made him a cabinet out of mangrove wood and he kept his collection of roots and oils and dried leaves on the shelves and his few books in the drawer.

In a certain way the past was gathered here, as it was in the cemetery. Paris had kept the splints he had used to set a broken leg, the charred cane with which he had vainly tried to cauterize a snake-bite and save a life. In a jar on the shelf of his cabinet he kept the eel-skin – carefully cured – from which in desperate haste he had fashioned a catheter to pass down the throat and into the stomach of a baby of six months that had swallowed some flakings of koonti root – poisonous before pulping and draining. The child had been at the point of death, pulse and respiration had almost ceased. The improvised tube had enabled Paris to use his syringe to inject an emetic – it was a common pewter syringe, still there among his instruments. The effect had been miraculous: within minutes the pulse had become perceptible again at the wrist, the convulsed action of the mouth had ceased and the child had taken a quivering breath. Verging on the miraculous too that fortunate chance of the fresh eels caught from the creek and the tiny quantity of ipecacuanha still remaining at that time among his medicines. The little girl was six years old now . . .

Memories are grafted together in ways beyond our choosing. He could not think of the child saved without some memory of his lost Ruth, though his thoughts of her in these days most often went back before the time of their misfortunes to the early days of courtship and marriage. Now there came to his mind a day in spring when they had walked together along the shore near her parents' home, in Norfolk. They had walked a long way, hand in hand, far beyond the harbour, to a deserted stretch of shore. The tide was out, he remembered. Levels of rippled sand, the pale blue of the tide-pools and the real sea beyond, darker, uniform to the horizon. Sunlight: the shingle was bright along the beach and the bunches of wet kelp were gleaming. Terns were screaming overhead – he had brought his telescope to watch them plunging for fish. Ruth had felt cold in the ruffling breeze from the sea and he had used his tinder-box to make a fire of driftwood up among the dunes. Bright flame against the pale dune grass. They held out their hands to the flame and laughed at nothing but the joy of being there together. Her pale hands reddened by the chill and then the fire. She had gone a little way alone to gather the blue flowers that grew there, that kept their colour when dried – he could not re-member the name. He had followed with his eyes the slight, lonely figure against the sweep of the dunes. On an impulse he had taken up the telescope and trained it on her. She was brought suddenly close before him and he was amazed and deeply moved to see the cherishing and tentative way she put out her hand to the flowers. All the gentleness of her nature was in it. He had realized then that this was the way she touched everything, and he had been swept by such love for her that his sight for the moment seemed darkened and her figure lost . . .

He was still standing in the same place half an hour later when Nadri approached, carrying a fish trap he had made, which he was intending to leave here while he attended the Palaver. In fact he could have left it anywhere with perfect security. Theft was rare in the settlement, the nature of life was too public. But in any case no one would have dreamed of carrying off his trap because it was instantly recognizable for Nadri's: no one else made traps the equal of his, either for cunning or beauty. This one, which he set down at a corner of the sickroom, was quite large, a yard or so in diameter, cylindrical in shape, with one end open and a funnel-shaped passageway leading to the interior. Warp splints made of willow sticks curved inward, admitting entry of the fish into the maze-like filling of the trap, and the closed end had a wicker lid.

'That's a fish-trap?' Paris said. 'I don't believe it.'

Nadri smiled. His perfectionism in the matter of traps was a long-standing joke between them. 'Why, what you think it is?'

Sharing the same woman had thrown them together and over the years Nadri had picked up a good deal of English from Paris, helped in this by a good ear and a quick intelligence and also, Paris had learned, by a grasp of language derived from his education – he was a Moslem and had been taught as a child to read and write and figure in Arabic. Other things too Paris had learned by degrees. Nadri came from a region of high grasslands and wooded valleys behind the Ivory Coast and had been clerk to a merchant, subsequently marrying his employer's daughter. It was while journeying on business for his father-in-law that he had been taken by a slaving party. He had a daughter who would be fourteen now if she was still alive.

'Mebbe looks good, I dunno,' he said now. 'But this trap is going to catch plenty of fish, I know that. One thing I find out, Matthew, while I have been here in this place.'

'What is that?'

'A trap looks good gives good result, whether you after bird or fish or fox.' He smiled again. It was an attractive smile, lighting up the normally rather stern expression of his face with the prominent bones at the cheeks and temples. 'Twelve summers here I learn one thing,' he said. 'That is not so bad, I think.'

Paris was silent for a moment, looking at this man to whom he was close but who would never fully be his friend. Nadri was tall – the eyes that looked back at him were on a level with his own. They were the eyes that had looked into his in pain and bewilderment on the slaveship as Nadri was whipped forward to be examined and branded. He was naked now above the waist and the brandmark of Kemp showed livid on his chest. He had been the first that Paris had violated with his touch, as Tabakali had been the first of the women he had looked at and wanted. Now they shared her together. The woman had forgiven him, or so it seemed – perhaps because he had needed her so much; but for the man there could be no forgetting that first encounter, for all the affection that had grown between them.

'It is a great pity that what you say of traps is not true also of people,' Paris said. 'At least then we would not be deceived.'

Nadri spread his hands, revealing the paler, vulnerable-

562

seeming skin of the palms. 'Trap is a very simple thing,' he said. 'Only has one purpose. When we say the name of it we say what it is. People are not like that. I dunno why it is, Matthew, you are all the time wanting to make some kind of *laws* for people. Why you never content to look at one person then another person?'

There was a note of reproof in this, stronger, as it seemed to Paris, than his own rather mild words had warranted. Some of the warmth left his face. He took no more kindly now than he ever had to being told how to shape his thoughts, and Nadri's constitutional unwillingness to generalize about human behaviour had caused arguments between them before. 'If we cannot proceed from particular truths to general ones our thoughts will get nowhere,' he said.

'Better for us you get nowhere,' Nadri said. 'Partikklar to gen'ral is story of the slave trade, I think.'

'That is not fair, Nadri. If you bring everything down to that, we cannot discuss things at all.' However, he had seen quite suddenly that Nadri's resentment came from wanting to be separate and free, not wanting to be herded as it were into a law of human nature. 'It is only an attempt at understanding,' he said more gently. 'We are all here by accident.'

'No, excuse me, *you* are here by accident, I am here because you bringed me. For accident there must be choosing somewhere. That is one big difference between us, Matthew. The crew people here because they kill the captain. You say an attempt understanding but it is only an attempt proving your ideas the right ones. First you bringed us, say we are free, then you want to make us serve some idea in your head. But the people cannot serve your idea, you cannot make them do that.'

Paris did not reply at once. He was not so much dashed by the argument – he could not see how he could be held guilty of coercion simply by virtue of his own mental processes – as hurt in some obscure way by Nadri's remark about the difference between them. It was true he bore a responsibility that none of the black people could be expected to share. Even the people of the crew he felt to be less accountable than himself. They had shared the physical misery of the negroes in a way he had not, they had been flogged in the negroes' view, they had begged from the negroes' bowls. No doubt it was for this reason they had been able to settle here together on equal terms. Paris had found happiness here, he knew himself to be useful and respected. But he knew also that in certain essential respects he was quite alone.

'Only way to live here is day by day, same as anywhere,' Nadri said in a different tone. 'A wise man know his limits. Like the trokki, you know?'

'What is trokki?'

Nadri was fond of Paris and had seen that he was hurt. He allowed his face to assume the expression, sly and slightly ironic, which it always wore on his excursions into folk wisdom. 'Trokki is tortos',' he said. 'Mebbe tortos' wan' fight but he sabee him arm short.'

'You arm long nuff,' Paris said, smiling in sudden relief. 'You arm long pas' anyone dis place.' A surge of affection for Nadri came with the words. The use of pidgin often released feeling between them in this way. Between those men who shared a woman, which was still the case with most, feelings were rarely neutral. There sometimes grew enmity and sometimes a close bond. But Paris knew that the grace of the friendship came from Nadri and the sense of this, a feeling close to gratitude, pained his throat still when he thought of it. Now, true to the restraints of his upringing, he sought for a way to continue that would not betray his feeling. 'Tabakali,' he said, 'dat one woman look good an' good insai.'

'Dat de perfec' trut,' Nadri said gravely. 'She one fine woman.'

The two nodded together on this and the silence of total accord fell upon them, broken after some time by Nadri. 'Time for Palaver,' he said. 'They are coming together.'

They left the sickroom and made their way across to the wide clearing before the stockade gates, where people were already assembled, men, women and children, seated on mats brought for the purpose, in two files facing inwards, separated by the space of a dozen feet or so. Paris noticed Hughes among them and Amos and Cavana – men often away from the settlement.

Cavana, of course, would have returned for the naming. Tabakali and the youngest child were there already and Paris and Nadri joined them.

The beck-man, or holder of the stick, elected for this occasion, was Billy Blair, a man without discernible interest to serve save that of justice, having no cultivation in common or trade connection with either of the disputing parties. He sat between the files, at one end, holding the elegant, silver-headed cane that had once belonged to Delblanc; he it was who, a year or so before his death, had introduced this regulating device into the chaos of their earlier debates. No one could address the assembly unless he was on his feet between the files and holding the cane; and it was the task of the beck-man to make sure this rule was observed.

As was customary, the accuser spoke first. Hambo walked to and fro between the lines, gesturing fiercely with the cane. Iboti, he said, had tried to kill him by making a powerful fetish and attaching it to the roof of his hut. He had returned to his hut to find the fetish-bundle in the thatch. Danka had seen him find it. The bundle contained dried leaves, two sticks, one of them sharpened, and two cane whistles, one of them filled with dust. He knew Iboti had put it there because Iboti had threatened to kill him. He had threatened this in the hearing of Arifa, the woman they shared. 'He say he kill me,' Hambo said, with a prolonged flourish of the stick. 'He say make me eye blind, gut rot, spit blood. Arifa hear him say it.'

'Dat lie,' Iboti shouted suddenly from his place beside Tong-man. 'Hambo, you say lie.' He swallowed and the whites of his eyes showed prominently as he glanced from side to side of him.

'You call me lie?' Hambo stopped near Iboti and glowered down at him. 'You pig Bulum, you call me lie I break you troat,' he said.

'Iboti,' Billy said, 'you turn come baimbai. Hambo got de stick now. Hambo, you talk badmowf, I take back stick, you altagedder finish.'

Sullenly Hambo gave back a little and after a moment resumed his pacing. He was shorter than the other Shantee, stocky in build and deep-chested. The column of his neck was not much narrower than the back of his head, which gave him the look of having been hewn from a single block. In contrast to his fierce gestures, he spoke rather slowly, pausing sometimes to marshal his thoughts. In these pauses, he made loud spitting sounds in token of the truth of his words. Arifa, he said, had not only heard the threats but had seen Iboti gathering dust from a footprint, as she would shortly be telling them. 'Now I show fetish, you sabee I speak trut',' he said. He went to his place, took up the bundle and held it above his head for all to see. 'Leaf look like dey *bombiri* leaf,' he said. 'Mebbe Iboti find *bombiri* tree.'

Tongman rose. It was the right of the accused person, or the one speaking for him, to address questions to the beck-man. 'What dis sarve?' he said. 'I ask what puppose all dis sarvin'. Whedder dey *bombiri* leaf or no, who care bout dat?'

'What de puppose?' Billy asked Hambo.

'*Bombiri* leaf fall quick when him stick cut from tree. Dat mean bad fetish, make house fall down me. Tongman, you head go soft, you sabee dat before.'

Billy thought for some time, his small, pugnacious face tight with the seriousness of his office. There was tension in the air of the meeting and he was feeling it along with everybody else. Apart from the occasional voices of the smaller children, complete silence reigned among the people gathered there. 'Hambo got de right,' Billy said. 'He tryin' show us dis fetish strong too much, capsai him house.'

Encouraged thus, and aware of the intense interest of his audience, Hambo went on to draw attention to the two sticks, one blunt and one sharpened, the sharp one being *unkumba*, the second spear of witchcraft. Finally he held up the dust-stopped whistle. 'Dust under him foot,' he said. 'Arifa see him take it. Dust in whissul make Hambo die, foul him win'pipe.'

He strode back and forth some time longer, still waving the cane, but it was clear that he had stated his case and was now merely repeating it, a favoured rhetorical device of the Shantee.

After some minutes of this Billy asked for the return of the stick, which passed next to Arifa. She was a big woman, built on voluptuous lines, with heavy features and a stolid expression,

566

somewhat redeemed by the coquetry of luxuriant eyelashes. She had taken particular care with her appearance for this public occasion: white cowrie shells, exactly matched, adorned the large lobes of her ears and a gold coin, found on the beach by Calley and obtained from him by means everyone knew of, hung shining between her breasts. These were not very much concealed by the cotton wrap thrown with studied negligence over her shoulders, and they swayed and swung magnificently with the motions of her narrative. Yes, she had heard Iboti utter the death threats. He had threatened, among other things, to open up Hambo from *puga* to chin and to cut off his testicles and compel him to eat them. Some laughter came from the audience at this, whether from the sense that a man with his belly cut open would not be in a fit state to eat his own testicles or at the very evident contrast in physique between the two men. But the silence of total absorption returned when Arifa began to tell of seeing Iboti gather up the dust.

She had seen him stoop and take up the dust in the palm of his hand and move away with it in the direction of his hut. It had been just after sunrise, she was outside her hut putting pulped koonti roots into a basket so as to take them and wash them in the creek. 'He hol' dat dust like it water in him hand,' she said, in her strong contralto voice. 'Like cargo gol' dust. Never take me like dat – Iboti ball go sleep long time ago.'

Iboti lowered his head in humiliation at this. Paris heard Tabakali beside him utter a harsh exhalation of anger and contempt. She had never liked Arifa. 'Dat one bumbot woman,' she said loudly. 'She put man out when Hambo say, den she say fault him ball. Dat one fat bumbot hussy.'

'Tabakali, stow you gab, you 'pinion Arifa not de bleddy question,' Billy said.

'You no 'fraid, Iboti,' Tabakali called. 'You find anadder woman good pas' dis one.'

'Matthew, Nadri, you woman no keep mum, we still here tomorrow. Stick pass to Hambo agin, ask for Iboti punish.'

Hambo's plea for the punishment of his alleged evil-wisher was brief. 'Dis man try kill me,' he said. 'What he go give me now? He poor like *kabo*, like rat. He give me bag koonti root?

567

Hah! Hambo life wort' more dan bag koonti. My country, man try kill me, I kill him. We kill Wilson long time ago for kill one man. But Hambo good heart, no ask Iboti kill, ask him sarve me three year gremetto, carry cargo for Shantee. I finish now, give back de stick.'

Silence at this was complete. Paris saw Kireku and Danka sitting side by side nodding in grave assent and behind them the face of Barton, raised and peering in that old expression of his, that relish at the scent of weakness. Libby was there too, and Hambo's woman had returned to her place among them. It was a phalanx of power.

The shock of the announcement brought a sense of cleared vision to Paris, like a slap that first blurs the eyes then sharpens them. He understood now that Hambo had never meant to ask for goods in compensation, that he must have intended all along to demand this term of labour. Others must be realizing it too ... He glanced at some of the faces nearest him: they were deeply absorbed, but he saw no sign of any strong dissent. Nadri was frowning slightly, it seemed in concentration, and Sullivan's face showed a sort of startlement, as if he had just awoken. Beyond them Jimmy sat cross-legged. The smile for once was absent, but Paris knew in that moment, with a sort of prophetic chill, that Iboti's bondage to the Shantee, if it became a fact, would be incorporated by the teacher into the history of the settlement, it would become a story with a moral like the mutiny, Wilson's execution, the freeing of the Indians. In the course of time the people would come to believe that a term of servitude was fitting punishment. The slave who had tried to kill himself with his own nails on board the ship, there had been a fetish somewhere in that too – he had been wrongly accused. It was Jimmy who had explained it ...

The silence continued as the stick was returned. Billy was beginning to look harassed. There was no precedent for Hambo's demand. Labour had sometimes been imposed, but only for specific tasks and when there was clear evidence of some previous contract or undertaking – to repair a roof, for example, or cut a certain quantity of wood. 'We listen both sai, den see,' Billy said at last.

Paris scrambled to his feet. 'I ask Hambo change him word,' he said to Billy, in a voice vibrant with feeling. 'I ask him tink what we do here. He forgit how we come here, where we come from? We come dis place make man free or make him slave?'

'Dat not question, dat you 'pinion.' Billy shook his head from side to side as if to clear it. The familiar nightmare of logical incoherence was descending on him. '*Sound* like question, but it not. You no ken say 'pinion without de stick, no ken get stick till finish both side Palaver.'

'But if he is found guilty,' Paris said, abandoning pidgin in the stress of his feelings, 'if the vote goes against him, it will be a vote also on this demand for servitude, not only on the crime itself. It will be too late to modify the punishment, except in degree – not in its nature. And not only that, it will establish –'

'What lingo dis?' Kireku was on his feet now, a tall, imposing figure. 'Why you talk dis rabbish lingo?' He surveyed Paris steadily for some moments with an expression of frowning severity. 'My fren', you talk people lingo or you get down stow gab altagedder,' he said. He extended his arm in a sudden fierce gesture, notably at odds with the dignified calm of his speech. 'You, beck-man,' he said, turning towards Billy, 'you no sabee keep palaver, you get down, give place better man.'

'Dat man not you,' Inchebe shouted, in immediate defence of his friend. 'Shantee beck-man say everything for Shantee.'

Billy's face had gone red as fire and he had taken a hard grip on Delblanc's cane. His first words, perhaps fortunately, were impeded by rage and not properly audible to Kireku. It was at this point that Tongman, with a superb sense of timing, rose to his feet. 'Why dis palaver bout punish?' he demanded. 'Iboti not punish, done notting wrong. I speak for Iboti now. I ask for de stick.'

Once armed with this, he moved between the files, portly and unruffled. His forensic style was completely different from Hambo's. He did not gesture and declaim, but appealed directly to his audience with an air of taking them into his confidence. There were some strange features in this case, he said, and one of the strangest was the ease with which Hambo had come upon the fetish. In his, Tongman's experience – and he had no doubt

569

this corresponded to the experience of his audience – when a man went to the trouble of making up a fetish-bundle and placing it on another man's roof, he generally concealed it well, intending that it should remain there for as long as possible, so as to have its full effect. Indeed, it was usually only when a roof was repaired that a fetish was found in the thatch.

Sounds of assent came from here and there among his listeners and Tongman nodded and smiled. Then the smile faded and he compressed his lips in an expression of perplexity. Was it not surprising, then, that Hambo had so easily come upon this particular fetish? By his own account he had returned to his hut and found it on the roof. Danka, his friend and fellow-tribesman, had seen him find it.

Tongman's strolling between the lines had brought him, it seemed accidentally, opposite to Danka now. He stopped and looked mildly down. 'You see Hambo find de fetish, dat right?'

'Dat right,' Danka said.

'You see him klem up roof, look roun', find de fetish?'

'Dat right, I see him. He say, "Danka, look dis, someone try kill me."'

'I no ask you what he say. I sartin he say many ting. You see him look de roof adder time?'

'Adder time?'

'You see him look de roof adder time or jus' dat one time?'

Danka was a loyal friend, but his wits were nowhere near equal to Tongman's and he had been taken by surprise. He hesitated a moment, then uttered a short grunt of contempt for the question. 'I no see him look adder time. Why he look adder time?'

'Why he look adder time? Dat a very good question.' Tongman resumed his perambulation between the lines. 'Danka no see Hambo look adder time. Nobody see Hambo look adder time. I go tell you why.' However, for a moment he hesitated, his confident expression wavered a little and he passed his tongue quickly over his lips. Then, with a dramatic increase of volume, he said, 'Hambo no look adder time *cause he sabee well fetish no on de roof adder time.*'

Hambo shouted a denial and rose to his feet, taking some

steps between the files towards Tongman. The latter, his brief attack of nerves now quite overcome, demonstrated his sense of theatre by turning his back on his furious opponent, drawing himself up to his full height and raising Delblanc's cane high in the air. 'Who got the stick?' he demanded loudly. Neema's baby, disturbed by all the noise, set up a lusty bawling.

'I tell you one time, Hambo,' Billy shouted over the hubbub. 'Now I tell you agin. Tongman got the stick. Shove you oar in one more time, Palaver finish, Iboti go free.'

Hambo's face expressed violent displeasure, but he was obliged to return to his place. After courteous thanks to the beck-man for his timely intervention, Tongman resumed his case. He had the audience now in the palm of his hand. They might think, he said, that if a man knows exactly when and where to look for a thing, he either has some special information about it or he has put it there himself. But Hambo had made no claim to special information, except only the knowledge of the death threats and the business of the dust – both derived from Arifa. Perhaps Arifa could now throw some light on these extremely puzzling questions . . .

Arifa had been pondering all this while and had hit upon what she thought a good way of neutralizing the damning point that Tongman had just made. In her eagerness she did not wait for questions, a serious error as it turned out. 'Hambo no look de roof adder time, ha-ha, dat easy say why. He no sabee Iboti badmowf, I no tell him Iboti badmowf, I no tell him Iboti pick up dust. I tell him after. When I tell him, den he look.'

'You no tell him?' Tongman raised his eyebrows. 'We go see now. Day you see Iboti, dat de day you take koonti root wash in creek, seven-eight adder woman same-same ting altagedder? Dat de day, yes? An' you no tell Hambo dat day?'

'No, I no tell him.'

'Man try kill you bootiful Hambo, you no tell? Why dat?'

Arifa settled the wrap over her ample shoulders and lowered her lashes. 'I 'fraid Iboti too much,' she said.

There was laughter at this, especially from the women. Arifa was bigger than Iboti and noted for her termagant temper. 'Poor little *kuku*, poor *mwona*,' Tabakali called, 'I so sorry for you.'

Under this provocation, Arifa forgot her role of fearful woman. Her eyes flashed and she clenched her fists. 'Foulani baggage, crow pick you eye,' she said.

'Never mind dem,' Tongman said, giving her a look of sympathetic understanding. 'I sabee why you no tell Hambo. You not sartin, dat why. Early mornin' light no very good. You see Iboti pick up someting, but mebbe piece string, mebbe piece flint. Mebbe not Iboti. Dat right?'

Flustered by the laughter and misled by Tongman's sympathetic tone, Arifa was brought to agree that in fact Iboti had been some considerable distance away and that a man picking up dust would not easily be distinguished from a man picking up any small object. But she still swore it was Iboti and said she knew it was dust because of the careful way he had carried it.

Tongman turned away from her to address the assembly at large. The evidence against Iboti was completely discredited already, as he felt sure they would agree; however, he proposed to call one witness who would demolish any shreds of credibility still remaining. There was something of a sensation at this, for Tongman had told noboby about this witness, for fear she might be intimidated. It was Koudi, who had been sitting silent among them all this while. She was a quiet, long-limbed, rather shy and self-effacing woman with a kind expression of the eyes.

Gently, amidst complete silence, Tongman drew out her story. She had seen Iboti on that particular morning – she knew it was the same day that Arifa had been referring to, because it was the day for the washing of the pulped koonti roots. She herself had gone down to the creek, though a little later. There had been several women already there, Arifa among them.

This evidence as to the day carried complete conviction. Everyone knew that the washing of the pulp was planned in advance and that it was collective work, involving repeated saturation and straining, the women helping one another with the heavy baskets.

'So now de day fix, you tell us where you see Iboti,' Tongman said.

'See him nearby de graveyar'.'

'What time day?'

'Mornin'. Sun jus' come up.'

'What he carry?'

'Carry chop knife an' baskit.'

'An' you comin' from graveyar', dat right? Come from Wilson an' Tibo grave?'

'Dat right.'

This too, no one would have dreamed of doubting. It was common knowledge that Koudi visited the graveyard frequently in the early hours of the day so as to sprinkle water on the graves of Wilson and Tibo and conciliate their spirits. These two men had died because of her in the early days of the settlement, one murdered for her sake and the other put to death for the crime. An aura of evil fortune had hung over Koudi ever since. Nobody held her directly responsible, but a woman who brings death to two men can never be quite as others are. Koudi was regarded as an unlucky woman and so, to some extent, guilty. However, on this occasion, for Iboti, she was lucky enough.

Tongman had allowed an appreciable pause for the significance of her statements to come fully home to the people. Now he put his last, crucial, question to her: 'What course Iboti lay? He lay for hut, he lay adder way, for bush?'

'Adder way,' Koudi said, without hesitation. 'Iboti lay for bush.'

'Iboti lay for bush,' Tongman repeated loudly. 'I tank you. Dat all. Now, Iboti, stan' up, hoist up you head. You no 'fraid. Only one ting you say dese good people. Where you go with you baskit an' knife?'

It was Iboti's moment. He raised his head and straightened his shoulders. 'I go cut cabbage in de ammack,' he said, in his drawling, thick-tongued voice.

'Iboti, you good man,' Tongman said. 'I sorry you have dis trouble.' He was standing still now between the rows. It was time for the plea for acquittal and he was conscious of the need to tread carefully. The case was won, he knew it from the faces round him. His fee was sure, his reputation enhanced. But a wise man thinks of the future. The Shantee were strong and likely to get stronger; they were warriors as well as traders,

573

whereas he was a trader only. It was highly inadvisable to make enemies of them. He had caused offence already, but this had been unavoidable. Now he would do what he could to mend matters.

He cleared his throat and began, addressing himself to Billy. There were still elements of mystery in the business, they must all feel that, but one thing was abundantly clear: whoever had put the fetish on Hambo's roof, it had not been Iboti. There was no case against Iboti at all. Arifa had seen a man pick something up, but that man had not been Iboti because he was on his way to cut cabbage at the time and he was only a mortal man and could not be in two places at once. However, Arifa's mistake was natural. It was early morning and the distance considerable. The identity of the man she had seen would perhaps never be known. Possibly, if he resembled Iboti, it was the ghost of one of Iboti's relatives come to pick up something he needed.

The fact that Hambo had known exactly when and where to look for the fetish could be explained by some message that had come to him in a dream or vision, which had now disappeared from his recollection – such things were known to occur. He, Tongman, was very far from wishing to make accusations against anyone. It was enough for him that Iboti should be cleared.

On this, Tongman rested his case and returned the stick. The matter was put to the vote by Billy, as custom required, though now it was the merest formality: the show of hands in favour of acquittal was so overwhelming that a count of those against was not deemed necessary. The Shantee contingent stalked off in stony silence, not waiting for the formal verdict. Billy pronounced Iboti not guilty of witchcraft and within a very few minutes the clearing, scene of so much excitement, was once again quite empty of people.

FIFTY-ONE

Relief at Iboti's acquittal overlaid at first all other feelings in Paris. Before long, however, uneasiness came seeping back, something of that cold and half-incredulous dismay with which he had greeted Hambo's plea.

Certainly the verdict had been a victory for truth. Tongman's advocacy, the fortunate fact of Koudi's presence at the graveyard, the good sense of the people, these had combined to triumph. But tyranny could take many such blows and still prevail; and it was this terrible resilience and recuperative power that was most in Paris's mind in the hours that followed. For all Tongman's attempts to gloss things over in his summing-up, it was evident that there had been a conspiracy, that Hambo, with the connivance of Arifa and the probable complicity of Danka and Kireku, had practised to incriminate an innocent man and make a slave of him.

The more Paris considered the matter, the more convinced he became that Kireku was the key to it. He was cleverer and more able than the other two Shantee, and more far-seeing – a natural leader. He had been careful not to seem directly involved in the case and had taken no direct part in the pleading, but Paris felt sure he must have known of the enterprise and given it his blessing in some measure. However, the extent to which he might have encouraged Hambo remained in doubt and it was suddenly clear to Paris that this element of doubt could provide a basis for talk between them. It would be better to go immediately, if he were to go at all, while he was likely to find Kireku still at home.

All the same, the sun was well down in the sky before he

575

finally made up his mind. Kireku's hut was on the southern edge of the settlement, the side furthest from the lagoon. Like Tongman, he had built a second hut, alongside the first, for storing his trade goods. Libby emerged from this as Paris approached and called out, though whether in greeting or to notify his master was not clear. Amansa, Kireku's woman, whom he shared with no one, sat outside the hut, shelling acorns and milling them between two blocks of wood, smooth and polished from much use. She glanced up but made no other acknowledgement of Paris's presence.

Kireku appeared at the entrance, looked gravely at Paris for some moments without speaking, then motioned him to enter. He was naked to the waist and his chest and shoulders gleamed with the acorn oil which it seemed he had just been putting on himself. The palm matting on the side of the hut facing west had been raised and sunlight reached into the interior, where the corner poles cast long shadows. Paris found Barton inside, sitting on a mat in one corner with his back against a post. He lifted his narrow face and nodded as Paris entered, but said nothing.

Kireku gestured towards the mats on the floor, waited for Paris to sit, then sat himself. His long, narrow eyes were bright and fathomless in the sunlight and those parts of his body in the shade shone with blue-black glints at every smallest movement. 'You welcome,' he said. 'You drink someting? You drink beer?'

'Thank you.'

'Barton, go git de beer.'

'Aye-aye,' Barton said, and Paris, as if in some uneasy dream where one struggles against recognition, heard in these syllables the same irony — too faint for insolence — the same servile alacrity as in the days when Barton had been mate on the slaveship. The response, too, was the same: Kireku directed a look of intimate disdain and irritation at his minister. 'Look live, den,' he said. 'Stir you stumps.'

The beer was good — cool, unclouded and not too sour to the taste. They had to draw close to drink, following the sociable custom of the settlement, by which the beer, like the gruel

576

sometimes made from the same grain, was taken with long-handled shell scoops from the same wooden bowl.

Paris smacked his lips politely at the excellence of the beer and commented on the beauty of the scoops – they had been made, he was told, by Sefadu. He answered Kireku's queries as to his health and well-being and waited through the long, hospitable silences.

Whatever displeasure Kireku might have felt at the way the Palaver had gone, he showed nothing of it now. The face that regarded Paris was equable and handsome, with its broad nostrils and wide, full mouth. Thin diagonal scars of tribal incisions showed faintly on his cheeks. The marks of thought were on Kireku's face, there were fine wrinkles at the corners of his eyes and slight vertical folds between the brows. But its general expression was confident and resolute. It was the face of a man in command of his passions and of the circumstances of his life. Now, either from indifference or contempt, he gave Paris the opening he needed. 'Well, so it look like Iboti not de man,' he said.

'Not less he got wing,' Paris said.

Kireku chuckled at this and tapped his temple with a long forefinger. 'Iboti got brain of de bird, no got de wing,' he said.

'He not clever, dat is sartin,' Paris agreed. 'But dat not a reason make him Hambo porter.'

Grasping the opportunity thus afforded, he began to speak of his fears for the future of the settlement if it became accepted among them that a man's weakness or stupidity or simply his poverty was reason enough for that man to be made the possession of another and forced to do that other's bidding. Some men had short memories, but Kireku's was longer and he would remember his own sufferings as a slave. If Kireku, as a leading member of the community, would speak to his fellow-tribesman Hambo and explain these things to him, it might be possible to stop this tendency now, before it took hold among them and became customary practice. Kireku was a man of sense and experience and he would know that once a thing became customary it soon came to be regarded as lawful and was then extremely difficult to root out . . .

Concerned above all to find words that would express his

577

meaning clearly and show at the same time his confidence in Kireku as an ally, Paris had not looked very closely at the other in the course of speaking. When he did so now, he saw at once that his words had failed of their effect. Kireku's position had not changed; he sat cross-legged, his strong, well-shaped hands resting lightly on his knees; but his face had assumed the same expression of frowning severity it had worn during the Palaver when he had intervened to protest at Paris's lapse from pidgin.

'What man you tink me, Paree, what man you tink yourself?' he said, after an angry silence. 'You come here my house for ask favour. Man born me I favour dat man, no madder what, but you no born me, you buckra white man come off slaveship.'

Paris took care to keep his eyes steadily on the other: any shift of gaze would be taken as weakness. 'White man, black man, all free man, all bradder, live tagedder dis place, all same boat,' he said.

'Same boat?' For a moment Kireku seemed to waver between anger and amusement. Then his face settled into a fierce smile of derision. 'Dat de slaveboat you talkin' bout?' He glanced round at his minion, who was seated to one side and slightly behind him. Barton, responsive as always to the need for background effects, sniggered loudly.

'Hear him laff, heh, heh?' Kireku said. 'Barton, he sabee when to laff.' With a sudden gesture he brought his right hand across his body and pointed to the livid scar on his chest. 'Barton do dis,' he said. 'Barton put hot iron, burn me. How ken he do dat? I tell you. It cause Barton strong pas' me dat time. Now Barton my man, fetch dis, carry dat. He no do it I kick him arse. Dat de same boat? You bigman doctor, look me eye, mouth, ball, make me dance, people laff, heh, heh. Now you come sweetmowf, ask favour me, say we fren', sai by sai, no more slave. Dat de same boat?'

'He got you by the bollocks.' Barton was grinning. He seemed no whit abashed or put out by the slighting references to himself. 'He got a headpiece on him like I never —'

'Barton, stow you gab,' Kireku said.

'All dat finish now,' Paris said, after a brief pause to gather himself. 'Dat in de past. Twelve year live tagedder dis place.

578

We no tink come here. Come here by wind an' sea. Come here by God hand, you like say so. We jus' *happen* here, Kireku, but give us de chance put ting altagedder right agin.' He paused again, casting about for words that might somehow clinch the matter, failing to find them. Kireku's face had returned to seriousness, the look of derision quite gone. The sun was close to setting, shadows inside the hut had lost form, seemed merely now a vanguard of darkness. Paris saw Amansa pass outside with an armful of kindling. There was a smell of wood smoke and he could hear the voices of children, happy-angry, in the distance. It was a world, and precious to him. 'Give us secon' time here,' he said heavily, 'give us secon' chance.'

'Mebbe give you secon' chance, not me,' Kireku said, and his deep-throated voice now held a quality of conscious forbearance, sarcastic or sympathetic, Paris could not tell which. 'I no panyar people from house put slavemark on dem, take for sell. You de one do dat. You tink one mind belong all us here, dat mind same-same you mind. Why you tink I belong you idea right-wrong? I tell you why, Paree. It cause you tink you clever pas' me, you think you idea right-wrong strong pas' my idea.'

His voice had quickened and stumbled as he spoke and his hands had clenched. He made a brief pause, staring before him. When he spoke again it was more deliberately.

'Dat you big trouble, you never change. You allus try make adder people belong you idea. Like you play game wit dem, move here, move dere, like *amati* game, you sabee? You try make people here dis place do like you want, so you feel good, make man free. Den Paree feel good, oh-hoh! No feel bad no more, make man free, win de game. But Kireku not piece *amati* game pick up, put down. I no stay in place you want. I strong pas' you. You a fool. You tink dis speshul place but it altageddar same adder place. Iboti, Callee, Libbee, dese men slave, you no change dat never. Go look for Iboti now, where you find him? Find him Tongman field, workin' for Tongman. I build hut need man guard dat hut, build boat need boatman, do trade need porter for cargo. Need dem *all de time*, not jus' when dey wan'. Dat de way ting go dis worl', Paree, where you been? Dis de real worl', you no sabee dat?'

579

'Thurso was another who talked about the real world,' Paris said after a moment and as if to himself. He looked at Kireku and attempted a smile. 'Funny ting,' he said. 'Dey talk bout real worl', dey never mean real worl' where man help adder man or spend him life do good for people, dey allus mean real worl' like rat in de cellar or dung-heap cock try git on top.'

Kireku said nothing to this and it was clear from his face that he thought it not worth answering.

Paris too sat silent for some time. It was not so much the force and penetration of the other's argument that daunted him, considerable as these were, but the certainty and finality of the tone. He sought for a memory of Kireku aboard the slaveship, as if some clue to their present impasse could be found there. But no such memory was available to his mind. That shuffling, clanking dance to the sound of Sullivan's fiddle, the mass of listless limbs and faces in the shadow of the awning amidships, the terrible cries from the fetid darkness of the hold, the stench of defecation, the corpses one so like another . . . Somewhere among those herded, brutalized people, featureless, indistinguishable in misery from the rest, this drive to power still dormant, undeclared. Perhaps it could only have declared itself here, he thought, with a painful sense of paradox. His mind staggered suddenly at the thought of what manifold talents, what capacities for good and ill, had been thrown from the deck of the *Liverpool Merchant* to feed the sharks. The moral argument, he now saw, had been a mistake, they were both trapped in the same bog. Perhaps all that was left was the argument of expediency. He thought of Delblanc and his doctrine of necessity. Even freedom and equality might be seen as necessities of survival . . .

'My life in dis place, jus' like you life,' he said, in low tones. 'Some man weak, some man not clever, I same mind wit you 'bout dat. But suppose I use weak man make me strong pas' adder people an' you do same-same ting, den we go fight, dis place altagedder finish.' But he knew as he spoke that he had failed, that the discussion was over.

'You wrong.' Kireku smiled, a genial smile of complete equanimity. He now wore the same air as when Paris had first

580

arrived: unruffled, sure of himself and his world. 'Barton,' he said, 'I cold, go git my jackit.'

'Aye-aye.'

Kireku nodded humorously at Paris. 'Barton no slave,' he said. 'Barton too close me, he too bad man for slave. Poor Paree, you no sabee nottin', no sabee de shit of de fire from de burnin' of de fire. I no ask come here. Now I here I fight for place. Strong man get rich, him slave get rich. Strong man make everybody rich. Everybody dis place happy an' rich come from trade. Some man not free, nevermind, buggerit, trade free. Dis palaver finish now. Barton, take Paree show him way along.'

It was a dismissal. Kireku looked austerely away while Paris rose and barely acknowledged his departure. As instructed, Barton walked some way with him.

The former mate seemed disposed to say something on his own account and they stood together for a few minutes some way beyond Amansa's cooking fire. The last of the sunshine lay over the settlement and there was no breath of wind. Smoke from the fires rose in slow plumes and the cabbage palms outside the stockade stood motionless and stiff, the dead, withered lower fronds bright rust-colour where the sun caught them.

Barton's face still bore some traces of the amusement which the recent conversation seemed to have afforded him. 'Kireku is in the right of it,' he said. 'He hasn't had the benefits of a lib'ral eddication, but he got the better of you. Stands to reason, you will not stop men of talent from risin' up, any more than you can stop cuddies like Iboti from sinkin'. You will never stop ooman bein's tryin' to improve themselves, that is the way we go forrad.'

'Improve themselves?' Paris was tired and discouraged and disinclined for further talk, but a kind of curiosity kept his attention directed to the other man now. The years had leeched colour from Barton's eyes and dishevelled his brows and put grey into his wiry, ragged beard; but the peering, relishing expression was the same as ever, the shape of felicitous syllables forming on the thin mouth – these things would be the same until the day he breathed his last. 'You think it an improvement when we prosper at the expense of others and reduce them and take away their dignity?' Paris had a sense, half resigned, half despairing, that the terms he was using were in the wrong language. 'It is a very selective notion of improvement.'

'You're a regglar sticker, you are.' Barton spat delicately aside to express his disgust. 'You got no sense of the future. If it was left to you, the march of ooman betterment would be slowed down to a crawl, we would be in the doldrums without breeze enough to give steerage way.' There had risen to his face the old look of pleasure at the rich resources of language. 'We have got to reach out for somethin',' he said virtuously. 'Take a bebby now, what is the first thing you will see a bebby do? He sees somethin' before his eyes, he reaches for it. He don't know what it is, might be a lump of shit, might be a di'mond. He has got to learn for hisself. When we stops reachin' out, we are done for.'

'Last time you reached out you came near to losing your scalp,' Paris said, with a degree of unkindness unusual in him. 'You only saved it, I seem to remember, by keeping pretty low to the ground.'

Barton spat again. 'Times a man has to keep his head down,' he said. 'Any fool knows that.' There was a truculence in his manner which seemed new to Paris; it indicated – better perhaps than anything else could have done – the divisions that were growing among the people now. 'Times change,' he went on after a moment. 'This place is changin'. There is pickin's now such as never before. The land between us and the St John is almost empty – these local Indians are poxed-out an' dyin'. We know there is peace now with the French and Spanish. The seas will be safer – we can trade skins to Cuba. The English have took Florida for King George, there is an English Gov'nor in place now in St Augustine; we shall have justidge an' fair play, no more of these blaggard dons linin' their pockets an' grindin' down the people. I will tell you somethin' now, I am a man that sees ahead. There will be a place up there for a man like me, I am a serviceable fellow. Do you think I am goin' to rot down here the rest of my nat'ral life? Why do you think I answer to that black devil now?'

His face had grown envenomed as he spoke and his voice had risen. It was clear that Kireku's contemptuous treatment was resented more than Barton dared openly show – resented enough to take the guard off his tongue now. Or perhaps, Paris thought, it was this he had wanted to say all along, the rhetoric about human aspiration merely a preamble. Barton was devious enough and probably by this time more than a little mad. Asserting a readiness to betray Kireku might seem to him like proof of integrity.

'I do not know why,' Paris said.

'I use him to serve my turn,' Barton said, in a rapid and confidential tone. 'I wasn't Thurso's fool and I ain't Kireku's neither. I am waitin' my time.' He raised a finger and laid it along his thin nose. 'I keep my nose to the wind,' he said. 'I am a man that sees ahead, I tell you.'

Paris was silent for a short while. He was aware, as always with Barton, of a mystery. You could not call such a man wicked even; he seemed to have his being below distinctions of good and evil, in some sunless Eden of his own. 'You see ahead, Barton, God help us,' he said. 'But what a man sees must still depend on what he looks for. While I have got eyes of my own, I shall not need to borrow yours.'

With this he turned away and left the other standing there. He made his way back to his own hut and remained there for some time in total silence and immobility. Then he thought of the clearing in the pine hummock where he had sometimes gone when his spirit was heavy. He would go there and sit for a while and let the accustomed descent of evening bring its peace.

He took the track that led in the direction of the lagoon. On reaching the edge of the pine ridge he glanced back. From where he was standing most of the settlement was invisible, cut off from sight by the trees. He could see the pale gleam of sunshine on the thatched roofs of the nearer huts. The stockade gates were open. Just beyond them, on the level ground before the first of the trees, children were playing together.

They were full in the sunlight. He could see the rapid play of their shadows as they moved. No voices came to him at first and he could not determine the nature of the game. There was a line of small children, somehow linked together, perhaps tied. Two larger boys, armed with sticks, appeared to be guarding them. A group of older children stood in a cluster some yards off. Kenka was among these: there was a quality of eagerness in his son's slight figure recognizable to Paris even at this distance. A moment later he picked out the form of Tekka, tallest of the group. There was one standing slightly apart – it was the mulatto boy, Fonga, whom he knew well, having treated him regularly for an inveterate condition of congested sinuses. Fonga was a delicate, rather gangling boy, a year younger than Kenka, not well coordinated in his movements, something of a butt for the others. One of the guards, Paris now realized, was not a boy at all, though as tall as most of the boys there – it looked like Lamina, whose life he had saved when she was a baby.

As he stood there the wish rose in him to know the nature of the game they were playing. It came as a reprieve from his unhappiness; and then there was something potently suggestive in the way they had grouped themselves, something of ceremony or accustomed ritual about it, in this last, lingering sunlight of the day.

He saw Fonga point at the line of small children. The guards raised their sticks and made whipping motions at the captives. It was a game of slavery ... Then Kenka stepped forward, a lonely figure between the group he had left and the linked line of slaves. Paris saw the raised hand, the uplifted face. The echo of the shout came to him – it was the first sound he was conscious of hearing. He understood now what the game was and he was swept by the poignancy of his son's loneliness there, immobile, his arm stiffly raised, between opposed factions. Paris knew that the loneliness was his too and had never changed, the same now as at the moment of his intervention on the deck of the slave-ship.

It was Fonga who played Thurso and this too was only to be expected, he thought. Power had its ironies of reversal; the weaker had been coerced or cajoled into performing the detested role of the strong. Entirely appropriate too that it should be Kenka, with his eagerness to shine and to excel, who had secured the empty role of glory, over in seconds, leaving him with nothing more to do.

With close attention he watched the game to its conclusion, saw Thurso draw his pistol, saw Cavana make the gesture of throwing the heavy spike which had destroyed the captain's right eye and sent him staggering back against the bulkhead. Then came the wild shot that brought down Tapley with a shattered leg – performed now with much impressive writhing by a boy he did not recognize. Tapley's wound had turned gangrenous and he had died five days later. Tekka the cynic it was who struck the decisive blow. As Rimmer, he stepped forward while the cursing Thurso fumbled to reload, and stabbed the captain to the heart.

A great advantage of the stage that actions of irrevocable violence could be endlessly repeated, modified, Paris thought, as he resumed his way. Some profounder sense of the difference lay in his mind, though he could not immediately express it to himself. The sunlit arena, the quick shadows of the children . . . It was the orderliness of the performance, mysterious in its effect, that marked it off from the confused reality. This, to the touch of his memory, was glutinous with blood, thick with discordant sound, grotesque, Tapley's groans mingling with the imprecations of Thurso, as their blood was to mingle on the deck, Cavana shouting at the wounded captain about a drowned monkey, the late appearance on the scene of Delblanc, still in his nightshirt.

Of course, Jimmy must have related the events in precise order. Jimmy was a good teacher. He was one of those who had stumbled on a vocation here. He was gifted alike at pointing a moral or adorning a tale. And this was history now: heroic protest, concerted rebellion, execution of the tyrant, a new social order. It ran like a clear stream – useless to require it to resemble the viscous substance of truth.

FIFTY-TWO

With nightfall people began to congregate outside Neema's hut. Mats had been spread and there was a good fire. Neema sat at the entrance, the baby in her lap, greeting the visitors as they arrived with their gifts and good wishes. She had been busy with preparations since the closing of the Palaver that morning, sweeping out the hut and the space all around, cooking, tending the fire, pausing only to give milk to the baby. At the approach of the dark she had stopped and gone to dress herself in her best, then taken up her position here. The results of all this labour lay spread on a litter of sea-grape leaves. Calley's eyes glistened at the sight and the lean Sullivan invoked the saints. There were pieces of boiled fish, kebabs of venison on cane spits, a sweet dough made from acorn meal and dried coco plum. Various people had made contributions. Tabakali, a friend and near neighbour, had made koonti cakes for the occasion; the day before, Danka, most accomplished of hunters, who had a friendship for Tiamoko in spite of conflicting trade interests, had brought a big turkey which he had stalked and shot on the edges of the cypress swamp; the unpredictable and taciturn Hughes surprised everyone by presenting a wild honeycomb and then leaving almost immediately. Children of various ages moved among the guests, round-eyed with excitement at so many voices, the leaping of the fire, the display of food. Tiamoko and Cavana, both a little drunk by this time, gave out the beer. It was Neema's first boy and they had used up their entire stock of wild grain to brew enough beer for the party.

By the time Paris arrived things were in full swing. Fortified with beer, Sullivan had already given the company a couple of reels on his fiddle. He had now been joined by Sefadu with a cane flute limited in range but piercing in sound and by Danka with a finger drum made of deerskin stretched over a hollowed-out section of black gum tree. These three had performed at similar gatherings before and varied in their effects from a loud and cheerful dissonance to occasional wild harmony.

Paris went up to Neema and laid his gift on the ground before her, beside the others. He had not much skill in making things, but during the summer he had discovered a variety of sapodilla tree and had collected a number of the seeds with a view to planting them in the spring. They were like flattened beans in appearance and glossy black. He had strung some of them on plaited palm fibre to make an unusual, and distinctly handsome, neckband. 'Dis for de boy when he liddle old pas' now,' he said. 'I wish he live long time for you.'

He looked down at the baby, which returned his gaze with singular intensity. Its eyelids were polished and shiny, as if by some gently frictive agency of the air; they were tiny – the narrowest of rims for eyes so amazingly lustrous that they seemed to take up all the face. The hands were the only other visible part. Paris had seen a good many babies in his time, but the perfection of the hands moved him always. In the light of the fire he could see the paler webs at the base of the fingers and the tiny pink cracks of the knuckles as the baby gripped the edge of its blanket with the oddly fussy, faintly spasmodic clutch that marks the very young.

'What name you give him?' Only now could this be asked: it was never divulged until the evening of the naming, for fear of the ill-fortune that could so easily come from premature and presumptuous mention of a name.

'Him name Kavamoko.' Neema smiled. She was happy. She knew she made a good appearance in her shell necklace and blue cotton wrap; the baby had been much admired and the party was going well. She nodded in the direction of her two men. 'Dey two give him half piece one name half piece adder,' she said indulgently.

Her eyes were as bright as the baby's and Paris saw the reflection of the firelight move in them. Some touch of awe came to his mind. The seated woman, prepared and composed, the simple thatch behind her, the gifts before her on the swept earth, the regard of the baby that seemed full of some precocious knowledge . . . 'I wish he live long an' happy for you,' he said.

'Dis de fust man pikin,' she said. 'Dey two give de name.'

'It a very good name,' Paris said.

As he spoke the music ceased and Cavana stepped forward holding his battered pewter tankard, once the possession of the dead gunner, Johnson. Tiamoko meanwhile was making sure that everyone had enough beer to drink the impending toast. In his troubled preoccupation of earlier, Paris had forgotten a cardinal point of etiquette, which was to bring one's own drinking vessel on occasions of this kind; now there was found for him one of the pumpkin calabashes held in reserve for the forgetful and for people like Calley, whose personal possessions did not extend even thus far.

'De boy name Kavamoko,' Cavana said, when silence among the guests had been achieved. 'Dat de name we give him, dat de name he keep.'

This had been said very seriously: it was the official naming. Now Cavana paused, as if in search of some flourish of rhetoric. His face for the moment was sombre, dark red in the firelight. Suddenly he broke into a broad smile and raised his tankard. 'We drink him health an' happy an' good long life,' he said.

All the people present echoed this and drank. The orchestra struck up again with renewed vigour. Paris glanced round. As always, he looked first for Tabakali in order to know that she was there, and well. She was standing with Sallian and Dinka, tall and very beautiful to Paris with her smile and the proud movements of her head. He saw some of the parties to that morning's dispute mingling together without apparent animosity. Hambo and Iboti and Billy were standing together in the same group. Kireku had at least deigned to make an appearance, though he kept apart, Barton as usual at his elbow.

Paris drank and felt the sourish beer spread a warmth within him. His mood lightened. He found hope in this enclave of firelight and mingling voices and din of music – a hope that was inveterate, perhaps ultimately beyond defeat, tenacious enough in any case to acknowledge that only the surrounding darkness conferred unity upon them. An accident then, perhaps; but they had met here together to celebrate the appearance of a new life; and that, surely, was also to affirm a future in which new life could grow without stunting . . .

Heated with his efforts, Sullivan laid down his fiddle and went to replenish his can. This brought him up close to Billy Blair, who was about the same business. Billy was in the best of moods, but he had drunk enough to make him slightly abrasive and Sullivan, to whom he was very attached, always roused his spirit of satire.

'What fettle?' he said. ''Tis a funny thing, but you havna' changed one iota, Michael. Still scrapin' away, just as you was doin' in that whorehouse in Liverpool, the neet you an' me come alongside all them years ago.'

Sullivan detected at once the note of disrespect for his music, but he was not much put out by it; he was in a particularly exuberant frame of mind this evening, due in part to the beer, but mainly to the encouraging glances he had been getting from Koudi, whom he had always thought a fine woman, despite the aura of misfortune that hung about her. She was young too, not so many years older than Dinka. He had been playing with particular feeling tonight for her sake and he felt that she had understood this and would not be averse to a man like himself appearing on the doorstep.

'Aye, bejabbers,' he said, 'you are right, Billy, an' to think of it, I would niver have come here at all, if it hadn't been for you walkin' in that night, full of boastin' an' vainglory. You haven't changed neether, Billy, all these years in the wilderness, an' still full of yourself.'

'Lucky for you, bonny lad, that I come in that neet,' Billy said. 'You was on a downhill path. I saved you from yourself.'

'Oh aye, very lucky,' Sullivan said with deep sarcasm. 'I might have been livin' in a grand house by now, with silver buckles to me shoes an' lace to me cuffs an' drinkin' brandy from a crystal glass stead of beer from a ship's cannikin.'

'You would ha' been dead o' drink or clap or both by this

time,' Billy said. 'You didna' look set on a prosperous career when I sighted you hove short in that poxy tavern.'

'The trouble with you, Billy,' Sullivan said, 'an' it is the same trouble as affected you in them days, I remember makin' a mental note of it at the time, you are not a truly travelled man, in the best sense of that word, you are not acquainted with the usages of society. If you was, you would know without needin' to be told that all doors are open to the artist.' He caught Koudi's eye and smiled at her and raised his cannikin. 'Never mind, shipmate, you cannot help it,' he said, 'I drink your health in spite of shortcomin's.'

Billy returned the health and drank, but the blood had come with a rush to his head at this condescension. Like practically everyone else he had heard by now of Sullivan's failed attempt on Dinka. He had thought to say nothing of it, as taking advantage of a man who was down; but the other's unabashed and unrepentant air destroyed his resolution in a moment. 'All doors open to the artist, are they?' he said. 'They wasn't open to you last night, was they, doors nor legs?'

'You have lost me, Billy. What legs is that?' They had turned back now towards the fire and Sullivan was making to where he had left his fiddle.

'Dinka's door wasn't open to you, by what I hear. While you was exercisin' yor elber outside, Sefadu was exercisin' sommat else indoors.'

Sullivan opened his eyes wide. 'What?' he said. 'You'll niver believe I was tryin' to intrude meself? Is that what they are sayin'? Holy Mary! I was givin' the young couple a love-song.' Suddenly he noticed the majestic bulk of Sallian close by and realized she could hear them. 'You got de story all foul up,' he said, raising his voice a little. 'I give de couple love-song, give dem music make de fust night sweet for dem. I music man dis place. You no tink man ken give something, ask nottin' back? I real sorry for you, Billy. Look what Sallian do for you, she ask nottin' back. Dat one good woman. All dese year she cook for you an' Inchebe, she niver shut you out.'

Billy too had now realized the proximity of Sallian. 'Dat trut',' he said hastily. 'She good woman pas' anyone. Inchebe an' me, we sabee dat good.'

590

'You sabee dat good?' Sallian broke in, her broad, good-humoured face as severe as it could ever possibly be. 'You sabee dat so good, mebbe you sabee dat dere no nyam in de house for eat tomorrow cept dry corn an' koonti, no meat, no fish. You drink plenty beer, talk plenty fine. Inchebe altagedder same-same. You tink I feed two man six pikin koonti mush an' squirrel-tail?'

This public complaint stung Billy's pride. 'Why you say dis now, middle de bleddy neet? Dat jus' like a woman, she wait de time man happy drink some beer den she say hum-hum, go find nyam in de dark.'

'Fish in de creek, dey no die when dark come,' Tabakali said, joining in on Sallian's behalf. The slighting reference to women had not pleased her.

Faced with this formidable combination, Billy glanced round for Inchebe, but he was too far away to be of any help. He drew himself up. 'Right den,' he said. 'Me an' Inchebe, we go out catch fish soon de party finish.'

'Head full of beer, you no catch nottin',' Sallian said scornfully. 'Catch fall on you face.' She smiled in spite of herself and her body shook a little. Billy often made her laugh, though he rarely knew precisely why; it was one of the things that had kept her tenderly disposed towards him over the years. 'Catch *paka* bite you ball,' she said, still laughing. She did not believe that he would go.

But Billy was on his dignity now. 'You go see,' he said. 'Billy Blair, him word him bond. Say do one ting, he do dat ting. Inchebe altagedder same-same.' He moved away in good order, turning short on Sullivan when he was out of range. 'See what you done? Now I got to go out fishin' in the middle o' the bleddy neet.'

Sullivan appeared unmoved. 'Ah, what we do for the ladies,' he said. 'But then, where would we be without 'em, Billy, tell me that. There is one here tonight that sees me worth.'

'She needs glasses then,' said the exasperated Billy. 'Michael, I make you out to be round forty-four years old. You've got precious little to offer, a rabbit now and then, a few rows o' pompions and pumpkins, a basket o' clams. You'll never get a young 'un now, not with all these lads comin' up.'

Sullivan smiled and shook his head. 'You are forgettin' one thing, Billy.'

'An' what may that be?'

'You are forgettin' the power of music.'

The sound of the music carried far through the night. Occasional strains came to the ears of Erasmus Kemp as he advanced cautiously in the faint moonlight, with Nipke and the Creek scouts leading the way and the labouring troops strung out behind. Guessing that some sort of celebration was in progress – and thankful for it as reducing the vigilance of those he was seeking – he asked Cochrane to order a halt. It was his idea to encircle the settlement while everyone was sleeping and attack in the early morning before they had time to make any resistance. Surprise was the essence of this plan; they must be taken before they could scatter and run – once in the bush they would be impossible to capture; he had no resources for pursuit, and the troops would be vulnerable in the extreme to ambush and harassment. Everything, then, depended on this dawn attack. If successful, there need be little bloodshed, the whole population could be disarmed and bound and brought to where the boats had been left. With luck they could all be at sea again by the evening of next day, on the way to St Augustine.

So Erasmus reviewed his plans, while the troops crouched waiting, straggled over a low outcrop of limestone which was the driest land they could find. They were newly arrived from England, mainly country boys from Wiltshire, weary and dispirited now after long hours of struggling through this unfamiliar and difficult terrain, alternately scrambling and wading, burdened with musket and pack, dragging the high-wheeled cannon behind them. It had not occurred to their superiors that the hot, close-fitting, conspicuous tunics might be in any way unsuitable for an expedition of this kind. They had had to be disembarked the night before under cover of darkness and had spent the whole of the following day lying concealed, waiting for nightfall. Two men were already disabled, one bitten by a cotton-mouth snake, the other with a broken collar-bone from falling down a pothole in the limestone ridge.

None of this affected the issue and so it was not of much concern to Erasmus. He was close to his quarry now. It was not weariness he found himself having to contend with, but a tearing impatience. For a good hour after the music had ceased he governed himself to remain there, on this rocky strand, with the misty exhalations of the marsh rising all round, weirdly shot with moonlight, vicious with mosquitoes, echoing occasionally with loud percussive sounds, like metal striking stone, produced, so Nipke had told him, by the jaws of infant alligators snapping at frogs and crayfish in the shallow water. When he was sure that all was silent ahead of him, he informed Lieutenant Cochrane that he was ready to proceed.

By the time this order was given Billy and Inchebe had set off in an opposite direction on their fishing expedition. They were not on very good terms to begin with. Inchebe felt, not without reason, that his consent had been taken too much for granted and Billy's appeals to their joint honour were received coldly. But Inchebe was not a man to bear a grudge and he had grown fond of Billy, despite the fact that they argued frequently together – indeed, with Billy's constantly baffled sense of logic, argument was impossible to avoid. Quite apart from this, when two men are engaged in a task requiring such a degree of cooperation as does spearing fish at night, they had better put aside any difference between them.

Once afloat in their shallow canoe between the low banks of the creek, the two forgot everything but the business of catching fish. They had made a hearth in the middle of the craft, raised nearly to the level of the gunwales, and on this they built a fire of lighter-wood, the dried-out, resinous heartwood of the pine. This, split into small slivers, would blaze up and burn from end to end, like a candle. It fell to Billy, as the less accomplished harpoonist, to tend to the fire and keep it flaming, also to help control the motions of the canoe as required. For this a very fine, almost instinctive judgement was needed and Billy was expert at it, even when slightly clouded by drink.

Inchebe stood at the stern with his cane spear. He had fashioned this himself, pointing it with fish-bone, carving the barbs and hardening them with fire. He used the butt end to guide the canoe, very gently, so as to steal upon the fish without any noise or disturbance of the water. For a man as dexterous as Inchebe, who had been given his first throwing spear at the age of ten by his father as a circumcision present, fishing at night had distinct advantages. The dazzled fish would lie still for long periods gazing at the flame; and the river bottom was revealed more closely to the fisherman than was possible in daylight.

None the less, it was generally a slow business and slower tonight than usual perhaps, since Inchebe too felt the effects of the beer. A shadow, a wrong movement, the faintest marring of the surface, and the fish would vanish in flickers of silver. Often enough the thrust would fail and then they were obliged to wait, drifting on the slow current, till all was calm and the fish drew near again.

It was a long time before the first successful strike, but then two more came quickly, snapper fish, like the first – they had found a shoal. Lanced through, the red fish twitched briefly on the skewer, yielding in this death-display the marvellous iridescence of its colours, pink and deep gold, burnished in the light of the flames.

Billy, while not ceasing to concentrate on the fire and the stealthy management of his short paddle, fell slowly into a state of contemplation, induced by the silence around them and the gentle progress of the canoe. The flames before his face shut out the tree-lined verges of the river. Beyond their fire the night was limitless, without boundaries. Within its range all was a play of light and shadow. The surface of the water on either side was clearly illuminated and he could see the fish lying tranced with light – a condition not much different from his own. Except that I am safe, I am the hunter, Billy thought. He was a man impulsive to the point of rashness and ignorant in many ways; but he had felt the need lately to understand the meaning of his life. He was convinced there was a meaning if only he could find the key; and because of this he was always open to wonder, which is where, if anywhere, any such understanding must begin. It was wonder he felt now as he leaned forward to feed the fire with splinters and looked up at Inchebe standing poised beyond the flames, the reddish light cast upward on the wet shaft of his spear and the upper part of his chest with its livid scar. Somewhere amidst all this the meaning lay, if only he could find words to state it . . .

He had a sense that the sky was beginning to lighten. They would be returning soon. They would have fish to take back, perhaps half a dozen good-sized snappers. In the self-congratulation of this thought the sense of being on the brink of some momentous discovery faded. But Billy knew at that moment that he was happy and that he would not change places with an earl or a duke.

However, in returning Inchebe suffered an accident which, though slight enough, set the two men arguing. While drawing the canoe up the bankside in the first light of day, he slipped and fell against the hull, grazing his knuckles rather badly. He swore at this in a language unknown to Billy. Then he declared, with bad-tempered glances at the bush all around, that his accident, without a shadow of doubt, had been due to *kudala*, witchcraft.

Billy stopped short on the path. 'You on dat tack agin? I real sorry for you, Cheeby. Everything *kudala*, eh? We no fin' fish, you say *kudala*, we fin' fish, you cut you han', you say *kudala*. You no sabee such a ting *acciden'* dis world? Man cut him han', dat acciden'. Jus' happen, nobody wan' it.' He saw the usual dignified, slightly somnolent expression of dissent come to Inchebe's face. 'You allus puttin' on airs,' he said, with the beginnings of exasperation. 'Dat you big fault. Puff youself up, make youself big man, fust rainstone, now somebody put badyai on you. You soso 'portant, you tink somebody care you fall on you arse?'

Inchebe made no reply to this, keeping his eyes turned away. 'Who wish it on you?' Billy demanded. 'Nobody care dat much.' He swung his basket of fish to indicate the world around them indifferently waking to daylight, taking form from moment to moment in the misty air, the thick-leaved mangroves that seemed to guard the last of the darkness, the marshes beyond lying shrouded in mist, the blanched moon above them. 'Nobody wish it, nobody care dat much,' he said.

595

Inchebe resumed his way along the path. 'Tell you before,' he said, 'tell you agin now, no such ting acciden' dis world. Plant yam bad get bad crop. Nobody say *kudala*, say fool man. Plant yam good, get bad crop – dat is *kudala*. Inchebe allus riggin' trim sharp, look where he steppin'. So dis is *kudala*. Any *dabo* ken see dat.'

'Jesus save us! Dat not *kudala*, dat de law of bleddy evridge,' Billy said. 'Man pull a boat up hunnerd time, one time he fall down de bank. Jus' happen like dat.'

'Jus' happen like dat,' Inchebe repeated scornfully. Annoyance at his fall and badly grazed knuckles, and conviction of malpractice against him, had combined to sour his temper. 'Dat all you ken say?' He glanced at Billy with his small bright eyes. 'Tell me one ting, you soso clever. Why it happen dis partikkler mornin'?'

At this, Billy's previously clear view of the matter began to mist over from the edges. It was a strange fact that although they had argued about *kudala* intermittently over the years, this question of particularity always caught him unprepared. 'Why dis partikkler mornin'?' he repeated now, with an instinct of prevarication. 'What kin' question dat? Dere no answer dat question.'

'Dat anadder ting bout you, Billy, same-same all buckra white man, you say dere no answer mean you no have answer. I pull up de boat hunnerd time, do same ting every time, dis one time fall down. Why dis time? Why not anadder time? Boat same, bank same, Inchebe same. *Why dis time?*'

'Bank wet,' Billy said. 'You put you foot wrong.'

Inchebe smiled sadly. He had Billy on the run and knew it. 'My fren',' he said, 'you sabee good dat not de right answer. Bank wet many time before. Inchebe foot same-same adder time. I ask you why dis time, you say foot wrong. I ask you why dis time foot wrong you say jus' happen dis time. You go roun' in circle, Billy. I tell you bout one uncle now.'

'Curse me,' Billy said, stopping short again to glare at his companion. 'What de fuck you uncle got to do with it?' This unexpected intrusion of a relative had fogged his mind further.

'Middle of de day uncle sit under roof of de grain store – sit in

596

de shade, you sabee, people do same ting every day. Dat day roof fall down, uncle kill. Why dat happen?'

'What kind question dat? Mebbe pole rot in de groun', mebbe tarmeet 'stroy dem. Mebbe timber worm 'stroy de beam.'

'You tink I fool man? Tarmeet an' timber worm, dat not de question. Question is, why it happen when my uncle sittin' under de roof?'

'Well, I go tell you dis,' Billy said, after a long pause. 'I sorry to hear bout you uncle, but dis story prove nottin'.'

Nevertheless, he was agitated at his failure to find a convincing reply, at finding himself once more in these thickets of doubt and contradiction. He glanced up at the sky, which shone now with a faint light. Mist lay over the low ground in shifting swathes. The fan-shaped fronds of the palmettos rose here and there clear of it, hanging heavy and gleaming with wet, quite motionless – there was no breath of wind. The swamp willow alongside the path was coming into flower: he noticed the tight green pimples of the buds on their dangling stalks. It was a particularity of vision unusual with Billy, due perhaps to the indistinctness of everything farther off, in this ubiquituous shrouding of mist.

The *kudala* notion had its points, he suddenly saw: it saved a man from chance, for one thing. And it took the blame from the Almighty, thus solving a problem that had often bothered Billy. 'Dey fin' de one make *kudala* agin you uncle?' he said, but the other did not hear him. The track had narrowed, obliging them to walk in file, and Inchebe had paused to crush some cress leaves over his injured knuckles and so fallen behind.

They were nearing the settlement now. The track skirted the lagoon, went some way along the edge of the hardwood hummock, then turned away from the water to pass through a tangle of sea-grape and cabbage palm and wild coffee before emerging on to the open ground where the first huts of the settlement began.

Among the trees it was dark still; emerging from them was at first confusing to the eyes. As they came out into the scrub, Billy saw a form move suddenly in the mist, no more than a dark shape at first, but then as he advanced he saw that it was surmounted with a face and a tall hat. While he still gaped at this, he saw the figure raise its elbows as if to work a pair of bellows. He caught a gleam of metal, then the dark red of the tunic. He turned and took some running steps back towards Inchebe, who was still in the cover of the trees. 'Redcoats!' he shouted loudly. 'Get round through the –' The crack of the shot came from behind him, drowning out whatever more he said, or tried to say. With this sharp report all arguments were finally resolved for Billy, the frenzy of logic left him for ever. The ball took him in the back, on the left side, and pierced his heart. He ran some further steps but he was dead before he fell.

Inchebe saw Billy turn and run towards him, heard the shot, saw the issue of blood from Billy's mouth and the heavy pitch of his fall. He hesitated no more than a moment. Billy was beyond help. The people had to be warned. He threw down the string of fish he had been carrying and plunged aside from the track in the nearest direction to the settlement, finding what way he could through the close-growing vegetation. He sobbed lightly as he ran, with fear and shock. The broad-leaved trees of the hummock discharged their moisture on him, the saw palmetto slashed at his legs and arms. He stumbled through stretches of swampland, knee-deep in the sloughs, his feet catching in the stilted roots of the mangroves. Behind him, not very far way, he could hear sounds of pursuit. From moment to moment he expected a shot, but none came and he could not understand this, having forgotten that alive he was worth money. The cane harpoon impeded him, catching in thickets, but he did not abandon it.

Nipke it was who gave pursuit. He had been standing near the panicky fool who disobeyed orders by firing and had seen the sergeant strike the man down with his fist. He knew that the people of the settlement, whether black or white, had to be taken alive if at all possible, this being the English lord's express command. He knew too that time was needed for the troops to complete their encirclement of the huts. Above all he was eager to earn praise, because with praise came a bonus of dollars and Nipke looked forward to returning a rich man – rich enough to be drunk for a week and buy another cow and possibly a blanket. So he began running almost before the echoes of the shot had died away, cleared Billy's body as it lay across the path and was in time to crouch and listen and hear the faint crashing sounds of the black man's flight.

Though past his first youth he was a fine runner, as the Creek people commonly were, and he knew the ground, having ranged here for Tequesta scalps to sell to the English during the wars with Spain. Thoughts of reward sharpened senses already acute; he was alert to every change of direction ahead of him. Following was not difficult – his quarry had no time to rest or hide or lie in wait. He knew by the sounds that he was gaining. There were sounds behind him too: other of the Creeks, similarly inspired, had joined in the chase. But he would be first . . .

He ran through a stand of sea-grape trees, ducking and weaving to avoid the low branches. This was the edge of the hummock. Beyond was an area of marsh grass and willow scrub. He could catch glimpses now of the man before him, hear at times the splash of his steps in the watery ground. He was gaining ground with every stride, the negro was flagging. No more than twenty paces separated them. As he came closer he drew the hand-axe from his belt, intending to stun the man with the flat side. But he was gaining too fast, it came to him now, with a sudden, belated sense of danger. He saw that the man was carrying a pointed cane and checked momentarily, then came on with a rush: the negro had left it too late, there was no time now for him to turn and set himself for a throw. This was a serious misjudgement on Nipke's part and it cost him his life. He had seen many deeds of blood in his time and he had fought with various weapons at long range and close; but he did not know what a man from the headwaters of the Niger could do with a spear.

As they came into the open Inchebe had slackened speed. He knew that with such a light missile, designed for fish not men, the throat was the only target. And he knew that he only had one chance. When the panting and the steps were close enough behind, he whirled, and without pausing to set himself or even shift his grip on the shaft flung the spear upward from waist height, aiming instinctively, the turn and the throw one single movement. The distance was no more than a dozen feet. The barbed head of the spear with its needle-sharp fish-bone point caught the advancing Indian in the base of the throat and penetrated deeply, half severing an artery. Nipke dropped the axe and sank to his knees, raising his hands as if in some attempt to arrest the copious flow of blood. Inchebe waited only long enough to be sure that this enemy was disabled. When the others came up they found Nipke bleeding out his life in the marsh, no sign of the negro. They resumed the pursuit, but more cautiously.

This killing of Nipke, and the greater circumspection it imposed on the other Creek scouts, gave Inchebe a period of respite long enough for a circuitous approach to the settlement from the shoreward side. He made his way under cover of the stockade to the low gate in the rear and crawled under, into the compound. The shot had been heard, people were moving here and there, the main gate was barred. Inchebe began to shout the news of Billy's death and his last mysterious words and the presence of flat-head Indians not painted or tattooed. His eyes started wildly and he gulped for breath. Distress and exhaustion combined to render his pidgin barely intelligible.

'What Billy shout?' Nadri asked, taking a firm grip of Inchebe by the shoulders. He had been with Tabakali and they had come out together at the sound of the shot, she naked to the waist with a piece of cotton cloth wrapped round her middle.

'Say bout red cot,' Inchebe panted. He had no idea what these words meant. 'Say bout red cot den dey shoot.'

'Holy Mary!' Sullivan said. 'Dat sojers he talkin' bout. *Redcoats*. They have sent sojers after us.' His eyes were wet still with the quick tears that had come with the news of Billy's death. 'It is redcoats have killed Billy,' he said.

To Paris, standing among the others in his breechclout and a shirt strangely patched and shortened, these words of Sullivan's carried immediate conviction. He was shocked, but not surprised. Ever since learning that the fighting was over and the British established in the north, he had been expecting some sort of expedition against them sooner or later. News followed trade; there would have been rumours of merchandise down here more valuable than salt or flint or anything the traders carried ... 'We can still get out,' he said. 'We can't fight men armed with guns, not from inside here. We can break out before they have time to form round us.'

'Dat right.' Kireku's eyes flashed fiercely. He had his bow slung over one shoulder and heavy arrows in a bark quiver at his belt. 'Nobody see Inchebe come,' he said. 'Nobody try stop him. Dey not in place yet. We ken git out same way he come in. In de bush nobody fin' us. Redcot try fin' me, stick him like pig, make him cot red pas' now.'

It was to be long remembered of Kireku that even at this desperate moment he had made a joke. He was already moving away when a booming voice reached them from somewhere beyond the stockade: 'You are surrounded on every side. You cannot escape. Lay down your arms and open the gates. We are armed with cannon and can destroy you all at will . . .'

The voice was frightening, unearthly, distorted by an amplifying instrument of some kind which made it impossible to determine the direction. But the flat accents of northern England were clearly recognizable in it.

'There may be time yet,' Paris said. 'They may not know of the gate in the rear.' He hesitated, looking at Tabakali and the children standing close beside her, Kenka between the two smaller ones. 'We wait here, catch in a trap,' he said. 'Dey go make you slave again.' He had spoken rapidly and was not sure if she had understood, but she looked at him steadily and after a moment nodded.

'It wort' tryin',' Nadri said.'We git clear, adder come behin'.'

They went at a run through the lines of the huts. Beyond the narrow gate the space of open ground was deserted. The mist had lifted now and a pallid radiance showed in the sky above the listless fronds of the palms. Looking upward, Paris saw gulls in lazy flight, the hidden sun eliciting flashes of brilliance from them as they turned. The first trees were less than half a minute away to a running man but the distance seemed vast to Paris. He saw Kenka regarding him with an intent and painful seriousness and he reached out and briefly touched the boy's cheek. 'We go two-three fust time, see what happen,' he said.

'Nottin' happen, rest all go tagedder. You wait we in de bush, den you start runnin'.'

Nadri opened the gate and crouched a moment longer in the shelter of the stockade. His eyes met those of Paris and he smiled. Then he was up and running, with Paris and Kireku close behind.

Younger than the others by a good ten years and a natural runner, Kireku at once drew ahead. He moved with long strides, head up, the quiver swinging against his thigh. A shout came from somewhere slightly ahead of them, to the right. Kireku was almost in the shadow of the trees now. Then shots rang out in ragged unison and Paris saw Kireku pitch forward on his face. A moment later he felt a violent blow to his left leg. He staggered aside and fell heavily and lay on his back looking up to the sky, feeling nothing at first but the shock of the blow and the fall. Then pain gathered in his leg and with it a sense of the damage done to him: he knew now that the bone was broken. Raising his head a little he saw that Kireku was still lying where he had fallen, quite motionless. The trees were no more than twenty yards away. He heard shouts and scattered shots from somewhere on the other side of the compound. Edging round on to his right shoulder he made an effort to drag himself forward, but it was too soon, neither his body nor his will was braced enough for the pain and almost immediately he lost consciousness.

When he opened his eyes again, he found himself gazing up at the face of Erasmus Kemp, close above him. He was not conscious of any interval of doubt or any struggle for recognition. He regarded the face silently, noting with a strange sort of dispassion that it was clean-shaven and very pale and that the dark eyes held a singular brightness and intensity. He felt a certain wonder at the sight, but not really surprise: in a way it seemed natural, and even inevitable, that his cousin should be here to preside over the last hours of the settlement. The older Kemp had given, though inadvertently; now the younger had come to take away. 'Of course,' he said, 'you have come to claim your father's cargo.'

To Erasmus this reference to his father seemed the height of unrepentant insolence. Looking down, he saw the lop-sided smile he detested appear on his cousin's face. 'I have come to hang you,' he said, striving to keep all passion out of his voice. He took in the details of Paris's appearance, the beard, the sunburn, the long hair tied behind. 'I would not have known you but for that rascally Barton pointing you out,' he said with disgust. His cousin's shirt – and this seemed to Erasmus almost more heinous than anything – reached scarcely to his navel, having been cut off all round, apparently to make patches. The garment he wore below it was little more than a loincloth. His naked, long-shanked legs were outstretched on the ground, the left one a mess of blood below the knee. Erasmus had felt a leap of alarm at first sight of this damage; but the wound after all was not serious – the leg could be dressed in St Augustine. 'Have no fear, you will walk to the gallows,' he said.

Paris looked beyond his cousin to the sky, which in this short while seemed to have become much brighter. The gulls still wheeled there, breasts flashing with light as they turned.

'All in one swoop, pretty nearly,' Erasmus said, in a tone of satisfaction. He felt the need to drive his triumph home. 'None of the troops got a scratch.'

Paris wanted to ask about Kireku and whether any others of the settlement had been hurt. But he saw Erasmus turn at this moment and speak to someone approaching. 'Ah, so you have it ready,' Erasmus said. 'It has taken you time enough.'

Two men came into Paris's field of vision, carrying a blanket slung on poles to make a stretcher. Erasmus looked down again and his eyes had a light of fever. 'Your turn now to be lifted, cousin Matthew,' he said, words not immediately comprehensible to Paris, though for a moment he felt that he was trembling on the verge of understanding. Then the soldiers began to lift him on to the stretcher, his senses swam and the bright gulls dissolved in the sky above him.

FIFTY-THREE

Privileged by his wound, Paris was conveyed as directly as possible to the shore and rowed out to the ship in the late afternoon. Before midnight both troops and captives had been embarked and the ship set a course northward for St Augustine.

It was Erasmus's hope that he might avoid the delays of a long sea journey home to England, and the risk of his cousin cheating justice even now by some obscure and private death, by having the people of the crew tried and condemned either at St Augustine by Campbell or, if the latter felt this exceeded his competence, by the Governor of South Carolina, where the negroes were to be taken and sold. To this end it was important that at least one of the wrong-doers should be persuaded to inform upon his comrades in exchange for a pardon. Erasmus felt that he knew human nature passably well and did not anticipate any problem here. It would come better from a common seaman, one who had taken an active part; an officer of the ship might be able to claim that he had acted under duress. However, Barton had already proved willing to cooperate and Erasmus decided to interview him first so as to establish the facts.

The intention once formed, he could not wait for the morning. He had slept little for two nights now and the emotions of that day had exhausted him but he could not rest. The ship was barely under way when he had Barton shaken awake where he lay on the open deck and brought below.

There was rum and salt beef and ship's biscuit laid out on the table. Also, close to Erasmus's right hand, a loaded pistol. A soldier with bayonet fixed stood outside the door. Barton sat opposite at the table and a candle-lamp lay between them. The former mate wore nothing but a round cap made of rope yarn, the tattered remains of a red silk scarf and a pair of deerskin drawers, and he shivered like a dog in the warmer air of the cabin. Erasmus poured him a glass of rum and he swallowed half of it, hissing on an indrawn breath as the warmth spread through him. He took off his cap and laid it on the table beside him. His lank, gingerish hair fell forward round his face.

'I know who you are,' Erasmus said. 'You were mate on my father's ship. You have already answered to your name today and so it would serve no purpose to deny it now. I intend to ask you some questions. If you know what is good for you, you will answer me frankly and fully.'

Barton raised his head to drink again, draining his glass. The sharp edge of his Adam's apple pricked like a thorn against the loose skin of his throat.

'If you are honest with me now,' Erasmus said, 'I will speak on your behalf when the time comes.'

Whatever calculations Barton engaged in were of short duration. 'I knowed this would happen sooner or later,' he said. 'I am a child o' misfortun' an' no mistake. A man o' sorrows, I am, and on noddin' terms with grief. That is in the good book, sir. I was brought up for better things than what you see now. I can read an' write, if you will believe me, my sainted mother taught me at her knee, but misfortun' has been my lot in this life.'

'You will deepen your acquaintance with grief very considerably, my friend,' Erasmus said, 'if you thus persist in going round and round about things. What befell the ship?'

'What befell her?' Barton eyed the rum. Cornered as he was, his sense of theatre did not desert him. And he was not altogether destitute, he now perceived: he possessed knowledge the other needed – how strong the need could be seen from the quality of attention he was receiving, the starkness of interest on the handsome face opposite him. 'There is a story in that,' he said, reaching to take some of the meat.

But he had paused too long. Erasmus struck the table with a blow that made the glasses rattle. 'God damn your eyes,' he said, 'you impudent rogue, you, stop your cursed play-acting or I will shoot you where you sit.'

'She didn't go down,' Barton said in sudden haste. 'She never went down, sir. We was blown off our course by a storm that comes in them parts in late summer, what they call hurricanoes, sir, but we never sank. That was a stout ship, she was a gallant ship in every line of her, I was proud to sail on her.'

'I will crop your ears yet,' Erasmus said between his teeth. 'What the devil do I care for your pride? Tell me what happened.'

'By that time there wasn't enough healthy men aboard to man her an' we was in fear the blacks would rise on us. We was blown westward here, on to the coast of south Florida. The captain was dead by then . . . We was unlucky from the start. The trades fell short of us more than usual for the time o' year an' we had the bloody flux among the negroes before we cleared the Gulf o' Guinea. 'Tis a sea o' thunder there, sir, an' a breeding ground o' plague, with rain an' fire comin' down by turns. Six weeks an' we was still south-west o' the Cape Verde Islands and they was dyin' on us every day. 'Tis a terrible trade, them not in it will never know the hardships, to see your profits dribblin' into the sea an' nothin' you can do. I felt for your father an' you, sir, my heart bled, Barton has always been faithful to his owners.'

Erasmus poured out more rum. In these close quarters he could smell the sharp reek of sweat, mingled with some fishy odour, that came from the other's body, and he tensed his nostrils against it with involuntary repugnance. There was a glaze of the gutter about Barton that no outdoor living had been able to affect; it was there in the abjectness of the manner, which had something insolent in it too, and in the ragged, jaunty finery of the silk scarf. The voice was husky and dry, for all the rum, making its claims of constancy and fidelity, seeking to find the right note, enlist favour, strike a course that would bring him in safe from wind and wave. Erasmus set no store by the protestations, but he did not interrupt. Barton appeared to be in the grip of his own story now, staring and eager with it.

'We had to keep 'em under hatches a lot o' the time, increasing the mortality considerable. I tell you, it would have broke your heart to see it. The doctor worked like a slave himself to keep the beggars in the world . . .'

Erasmus looked up sharply at this and found the mate's eyes fixed on him in a sort of stealthy appraisal, disturbing in one whom he had thought so lost in his narrative. 'What are you looking at?' he said. 'Do you mean Paris?'

'Aye, him. Feed 'em with his own hand, he would. That would be your cousin, I believe, sir, on the materlineal side?'

'What is that to you?' Erasmus said violently. He was silent for some moments. Then, more calmly, he said, 'He did no more than his duty, I suppose.'

'No, sir. Well, on the materlineal side, so they say, it is not so strong.' No change had occurred in the mate's voice but there was a certain cautious relaxation in the peering expression of his face and the spread of his elbows on the table. He had found a direction. 'He only done what he was paid to do,' he said after a moment. 'We all done that, every man of us. This is a excellent quality o' rum, sir.'

'I don't want to know your opinion of the rum. Here, damn you, have some more. How did Thurso die?'

'There was various wounds, but the cause o' death was stab-bin'.'

'Who struck the blow?'

Barton narrowed his eyes as if in a sustained effort of memory. 'Things was confused,' he said. 'It is long years ago now, sir, an' my remembrance is not clear.'

'You had better endeavour to clear it,' Erasmus said. 'I shall want to know these things from you.'

'I dare say it will all come floodin' back to me in the course o' time. Anyhow, it was the ship's people that killed Thurso. They rose on him. I spoke out agin it. With Barton, duty always comes first. They would have killed me but they was stopped from it by Mr Delblanc, he was a passenger aboard, an' by the doctor.'

'What part did he play? Mr Paris, I mean. He was the leader, then? He led the others into this mutiny?'

Barton paused. There was no doubt expressed on his face,

607

only a kind of intensified alertness. 'Yes, sir,' he said, 'he was the leader, without the shadder of a doubt.'

'Was he the first to raise his hand against the captain?'

'In a manner o' speakin', he was. You see, sir, we had decided to jettison a good part o' the cargo. That is, the captain had decided it an' he put it to me an' Haines an' the carpenter, Barber, the night before. Haines was the bos'n. The second mate was dead by then of a putrid fever and so we was the only officers left, if you don't count the –'

'Jettison them? You mean throw them overboard?' Erasmus passed a hand over his brow. 'What, alive as they stood, and fettered?'

'Only them that was sickly, sir. We knowed we could never make Kingston market with 'em. An' if we did, we could not have sold 'em, they was too far gone. The worst o' the weather was over but we was blown far westward, Jamaica was a good ten days off by the captain's reck'nin', even in fair conditions. The water was givin' out, we was already on half a pint a day. We was wastin' water on the negroes, d'you see, sir, because they was dyin' anyway. That is not a efficient use o' resources. Not only that, but a negro dyin' o' nat'ral causes was a total loss to the owners, that is to your father, sir, beggin' your pardon, an' to you as his son an' hair. If they was jetsoned we could claim the insurance, an' that stood at thirty per cent o' the value in them days. But you had to show good an' sufficient cause.'

Erasmus was silent for some considerable time, holding a hand over his eyes as if to shield them from the light. 'Shortage of water would constitute sufficient cause,' he said at last. 'It could be seen as a question of survival. But wait, did you not say that there had been storms of rain? The casks should have been full.'

'My,' Barton exclaimed admiringly, 'you have got a head on your shoulders, sir, an' no mistake. The main cask was holed, the water leaked away unbeknown to us.'

'Yes, I see,' Erasmus said slowly. 'The cask had suffered damage in the rough weather.' A court was likely enough to accept that, he thought, with Barton spruced up to say so and one more to support him. 'I find that Captain Thurso acted lawfully and within his rights,' he said.

'That is how we seen the matter when the captain explained things to us. Haines would tell you the same, but unfortunately he has passed over, he was murdered by savvidges.'

'And my cousin intervened, you say? He set himself up against the lawful authority of the captain?'

'Yes, sir. It was early mornin' an' Mr Paris was below with a fever. He must have heard some commotion – we had already sent some o' them over the side. He come up an' seen what was happenin' an' he shouted an' raised his hand agin it. The captain drew a pistol on him an' that was what started things off.'

'Thurso went armed then?'

'He had taken to it, sir. The men was mutterin' agin him.'

'As pretty a piece of arrogant meddling as ever I heard of,' Erasmus said, as if to himself. 'The more I think about the business,' he said more loudly, 'the more it seems to me that the captain's decision was a sound one, not only in practical terms, but also more humane, as shortening the sufferings of these wretches.'

'Them is the sentiments I remember experiencin' at the time.' Barton raised his thin face as if sniffing at the air, and for the merest glimmer of a second lamplight was confused with sunlight in Erasmus's mind and he remembered again the day of the accident at the dockside, Thurso and the mate emerging side by side from the shadow of the ship's hull. Barton had spoken to him about the building of the hull, he recollected. He wore the same relishing look now and Erasmus had the same sense that the mate was trying to form some alliance, some intimacy of understanding, between them. 'I am not interested in your sentiments,' he said. 'Keep them to yourself. Thurso could hardly have done more for those negroes, short of killing them out of hand.'

'He couldn't do that, sir.' Barton spoke softly, seeming in no way put out by the snub. 'That would be unlawful. The underwriters would never have consented to pay money on negroes killed aboard ship, not unless it was in the course of a uprisin', an' these was in no case to rise on us.'

Erasmus nodded. 'As I understand it, the mutineers, led by Mr Paris, later appropriated what remained of the negroes and carried them ashore. That is correct, isn't it?'

'Yes, sir.'

'First mutiny, then murder, then piracy,' Erasmus said. 'Any one of them a capital offence.' As he spoke the ship's bell sounded on the deck above them – it was two o'clock in the morning. The night was calm and the vessel sat evenly upon the water with no sound but the slow, irregular creaking of her timbers.

'They needed the negroes,' Barton said. 'They couldn't have got the ship in behind the shore without the blacks to help with the towin'. She had to be towed from the banks, sir. Every man, woman and child that could stand on their feet had to bear a hand with the ropes.'

'Yes, yes, I know that part of it. In your opinion, was there any intention to return?'

'The vessel was grounded, sir. They hacked through her masts.'

'Did they declare they would not return? Did you hear Mr Paris say that?'

'Yes, sir, I did. Him an' Mr Delblanc. They talked about settin' up a kind o' colony in the wilderness, where men could live in a state o' nature.'

'In a state of nature? What the plague does that mean?'

'Curse me if I know.' With instant responsiveness Barton's tone had changed to match the amused contempt he saw come to Erasmus's face. 'They talked a lot about freedom an' justidge,' he said. 'They was goin' to found a colony where everybody would be equal an' have no use for money.'

'That den of thieves.' Erasmus, suddenly, was smiling. There is a broad division between those who laugh at the perception of incongruities in the world and within themselves, and those in whom laughter is released as a celebration of their own successes, a perception, not of incongruity but of total, triumphant correspondence. Erasmus was of this latter sort. Everything had fallen into his hands. He had Paris alive; the guilt was confirmed, the evidence overwhelming; in Barton he had found an instrument of justice infinitely pliable. And now to hear of these ridiculous aspirations . . . It was like crystal sugar on the cake. 'By God, that's rich,' he said.

And Barton, seeing his new protector's smile deepen, felt something of the delight of one who has found the key to a puzzle he had feared might be too intricate. 'They thought they could start afresh,' he said, with contemptuous indulgence.

FIFTY-FOUR

Through the hours of darkness Paris lay on the borderlines of fever, where thought and dream and sleeping and waking are confused together. Towards morning the throbbing of his wound eased for a while and he entered a phase of clearer recollection. He was back again in the public room of Norwich Jail, with its dark, greasy walls and echoing pavement and the usual lords of the place, violent criminals all, occupying the coveted area round the fireplace. One of these he remembered in particular, and even his name, Buxton, a man convicted for robbery on the highway, on appeal for his life, a broken-toothed, staring fellow of unpredictable mood. It was Buxton, wearing a towel on his head tied up in knots in imitation of a judge's wig, who had presided at the 'trial' of the young debtor. The mock-serious expression of this unbalanced ruffian was present to Paris's mind as vividly now as if there had been no interval, as was the lost and frightened look of the young man. The two faces had remained in his memory side by side, Buxton and Deever, natural complements one to the other. Two hours in the pillory had been the sentence of this court. With his head through the legs of a chair and his hands tied up to the sides, Deever had stood stock-still in full view, head thrust forward tortoise-like below its absurd carapace, too afraid to do more than absorb his shame . . .

I did not intervene, Paris thought. Perhaps I lacked courage, perhaps I was afraid I might make things worse for him. It was impossible now to be sure. Memory, which still retained clearly enough the impressions of sight – Buxton with his grotesque trappings of justice, the flushed and humiliated face of the young man – did not permit any exact recollection of feeling. Certain it was that he had done nothing; the victim had been released finally on the promise of five shillings.

But what chiefly occupied him now, as the first light strained through the port of his cabin, was not his failure to protest or intervene, but his failure to learn the lesson so conveniently offered. For the men who did this cruel thing had suffered themselves in real courts and had been condemned.

I should have known it then, he thought. Nothing a man suffers will prevent him from inflicting suffering on others. Indeed, it will teach him the way . . . Was it always wrong then to believe that the experience of suffering would soften the heart? Those who were fond of declaring that they understood human nature would no doubt conclude so. But as the light strengthened slowly, enabling him to make out the bare furnishings of his cabin, it came to Paris that he did not want to be numbered among these knowing ones, that such understanding was worse than error, worse than hope endlessly defeated. If that is what it means to be wise, I choose folly, he told himself, and slept again and woke to daylight and a sweat of pain and the sight of Sullivan's face above him. 'What are you doing here, Michael?' he said.

The beautiful, vague eyes of the fiddler sharpened with a sort of triumphant satisfaction. 'I told him I was the one looked after you before,' he said. 'I went up to him an' I introduced meself an' enquired if he had seen anythin' of me fiddle an' he said he had not seen hide nor hair of it an' he was very much afraid I would have to consent to be hanged without it. So I looked him in the eye an' I told him hangin' was a matter for the judge an' if I got off I would want to know what had become of me fiddle. While he was thinkin' over this I told him I looked after you before when you was sick an' he damned my eyes an' give me permission to do the same now.'

'That was well done,' Paris said, smiling. 'My cousin wants me looked after so that he can the better hang me, though why he has pursued me so I cannot tell. There is not much you can do for me in any case. I applied a tourniquet as soon as I was able, to stop the bleeding, and the sergeant – who knows the business better than a number of surgeons I have met – helped me to set the leg in splints before I was carried aboard. So long as I keep still, I shall be tolerably comfortable.'

'I thought you might like to have the comfort of washin'.' Sullivan said. 'I have brought a bowl of warm water. An' I can fetch you vittles from the galley as required – he has give his permission to that.'

It was Sullivan's standard medical procedure, which Paris remembered now from the time of his fever. 'It is very good of you, Michael,' he said. More in order not to disappoint than for any other reason – he felt weak and disinclined to move – he submitted to the bathing of his face and arms and chest. Sullivan was gentle and deft and kept up a stream of talk. There had been two deaths among the people of the settlement in addition to those of Billy and Kireku. Cavana had been fatally wounded when he tried to break out with Danka and Tiamoko on the other side of the compound; Neema, seeing him fall, had lost her head and rushed out after the men and been killed before she had gone a dozen steps. Her baby, which they had named only the night before, was being suckled by Sallian. Nadri had succeeded in reaching the trees but he had been tracked down and taken by the Creeks.

'And Tabakali?'

'She is there with the rest of them,' Sullivan said. 'Kenka is with her, an' the other two children. They are all together on deck under guard of the sojers. The crew people are kept separate.'

'Yes,' Paris said, 'we have a separate future now. They cannot sell us, you see, so they will try to hang us as the next best thing.'

'Koudi is there, among the others,' Sullivan said. 'She looked at me kindly while I was playin'. I should have gone to her straight, but I did not. We are not allowed near them now. After we get to St Augustine I'll never see her again in this life.' He paused a moment and his face brightened a little. 'Mebbe I will, after all,' he said. 'I have had a good omen.'

'What was that?'

'There is a bit of a story to it. When I was first brought

614

aboard the *Liverpool Merchant* in company with poor Billy, God rest his soul, I was wearin' a fine coat with brass buttons down the front. Now this coat was took from me without so much as a by-your-leave, along with ivery stitch I had on, an' I was given slop clothes from the ship's store. That was bad enough for a start, but the worst of it was, they niver give me back the buttons. Thim buttons was niver mentioned again. Now you know the world, Matthew, like meself, an' so you will know there is always somethin' that will rouse a man, howsoever patient an' long-sufferin' that man may be.'

Thus appealed to, Paris nodded. 'Yes,' he said, 'sooner or later there will always be something that we cannot overlook or pretend indifference to, something that sticks in the throat.'

'You have hit me meanin' exactly. Thim buttons stuck in me throat more than anythin' else I can call to mind. They were worth money, but it was more than that – a man has his self-respect to think of. I always suspected Haines of stealin' them an' I got proof of it one day when we were ashore cuttin' stakes. I offered to fight Haines for them, but Wilson took the quarrel on himself an' so me chance was lost.'

Sullivan paused in his task of drying Paris's shoulders and neck, and gave a smile of considerable sweetness. 'He would have beat me anyway,' he said. 'The long an' short of it is that I niver got me buttons back. Then Haines was killed an' as time went by they went out of me mind. Then yesterday, as they were drivin' us through the bush to where the boats were waitin', I tripped over me own feet an' fell down the side of a stream, nearly in the water. There I was, lyin' on me face in the mud with all the wind gone out of me sails and the corporal cursin' at me from the bank. An' it was then I seen it, not six inches from me eyes. It was crusted over with clay, but I knew it.'

He bent down quickly and fumbled a moment at the string of his moccasin. When he straightened up his face wore its usual serious, slightly melancholy expression. On his right palm, held out to view, a smooth round metal button the size of a shilling gleamed yellow in the flat, shadowless light of the cabin. 'I give it a bit of a polishin',' he said. 'I couldn't understand how it had come about at first, not for the life of me, then I bethought meself – that must have been the very spot where Haines met his end at the hands of the Indians. It must have dropped from him somehow an' the Blessed Virgin tripped up me feet at the very place.'

He was still standing there, with the miraculous find shining softly on his palm, when they heard sounds beyond the door. Sullivan brought his hands quickly to his sides. A moment later the door opened and Erasmus stepped over the threshold. 'You can suspend your ministrations for a while,' he said curtly to Sullivan. 'I want a few words with Mr Paris.'

'Yes, sir.' Sullivan, however, did not leave quite at once, but turned first to Paris and said, 'Will there be anythin' more I can do for you?'

'No, thank you, nothing.'

'In that case,' Sullivan said, 'I'll take meself off.'

Erasmus watched him leave. 'There is a brazen fellow,' he said. 'He had the impudence to ask me the whereabouts of his fiddle. That is a gallows-bird, if ever I saw one.'

'If you think that, you cannot ever have seen one.' Paris was propped up in his bunk now and able to get a steady view of his cousin's face, which was white and strained-looking. 'To what do I owe this visit?' he asked. 'I must tell you, cousin, it is not welcome to me.'

'I do not care if it is welcome or not,' Erasmus said. 'You have forfeited your rights in such matters.' On this, however, he paused. He was conscious his cousin's question was one that could not be answered altogether frankly. After dismissing Barton in the early hours of the morning he had slept deeply – his first good sleep for days. But he had woken once again to desolation. There are forms of triumph or fulfilment, and these not always virtuous, that require no witness, they are sufficient in themselves and can be enjoyed in the quietness of the soul; but the sense of being an instrument of justice was not, it seemed, of this order, not for Erasmus at least; he had felt the need to see it registered on a human face, and there was only one that would do: in all the world there was only Paris that could make the triumph of justice real to him. 'I have been learning something of this settlement of yours,' he said at last. 'I am told that it was founded on the best philosophical principles.'

616

Paris saw the mockery of this move the tense lines of his cousin's mouth and realized that Erasmus had come to bait him. Despite his weakness and the pain of his leg, the old combative urge rose in him, the refusal of intellect – or pride – to allow another to interpret the world for him, least of all a man who held him captive. 'It sounds as if your informant was Barton,' he said. 'He is not much acquainted with principles of any kind.'

'No, but it is rich, don't you think so,' Erasmus said, 'considering that your little colony took its rise from murder and theft?' He had wished to maintain a tone of levity, but with Paris's first words a rigidness had settled over his features and his lips tightened as he spoke.

'Murder and theft?' Paris looked at his cousin with something like wonder. 'You have just stolen these people from their homes and murdered three of them in the course of it. Their blood is on your head, no matter who fired the shots. Two of them had nothing whatever to do with Thurso's death – in fact they were some of the stolen goods that you came all this way to recover.'

The folly of this took some of the tension from Erasmus's face. 'Your stay in this wilderness has unsettled your brain,' he said. 'You must be mad to make such comparisons. Thurso was set in authority over you. He was engaged in a lawful trade. These people are fugitives on the one hand and chattels on the other. I have proceeded at every step with total legality. I have a warrant from the Governor of Florida.'

'Useful thing, a warrant. Murder and theft change their names if you have one. I suppose the Governor himself was armed with one when he took Florida for the Crown?'

'That is a treasonable speech,' Erasmus said. 'I have noted it.'

'I can only be hanged once,' Paris said. 'I do not think we will get far along these lines, Erasmus. But I assure you I had no principles worthy the name. It was Delblanc who was our theorist.' His head felt heavy and there was a pain gathering behind his eyes. What had Delblanc believed? It was an effort now to think about it. *Men are moral beings in their untrammelled nature. If constraint and coercion can once be removed they will be happy and if they are happy they will also be good . . .*

617

'I did not really share these views,' he said, under the momentary impression that he had explained to Erasmus what they were. 'But I knew people are held together by having the sense of a common destiny. And of course I had certain hopes.'

'What hopes were those?' The tone was sneering, yet there was an ardour in the question that Erasmus could not conceal. He had been outraged by his cousin's manner. Flushed out from his bolt-hole, wounded and helpless, with his crimes brought home to him, Paris showed no trace of contrition; he spoke as if engaged in some vague and desultory debate. It was monstrous. And yet Erasmus was held, and in some way fascinated, by what the other was saying; he was conscious of effort, of needing continually to make a wider embrace of hatred and contempt to encompass these movements of his cousin's mind, to let nothing escape.

And Paris too felt driven, perhaps to disarm or somehow outflank this enmity which he felt as a pressure almost physical and which he could not altogether understand. 'I knew we had done them harm beyond reckoning,' he said. 'It was impossible to pretend otherwise. It was impossible not to see that we had taken everything from them and only for the sake of profit – that sacred hunger, as Delblanc once called it, which justifies everything, sanctifies all purposes. You see, I began my career as ship's surgeon in ignorance and carelessness. Because my life was in ruins I thought it was unimportant what I did, what I assisted in – I thought it could only degrade myself. This was an offence to reason as well as feeling. We have a duty to be vigilant . . .'

He fell silent again. The burden of explanation seemed too heavy. Had it not been for pain of body and weariness of spirit he might have seen that it was useless in any case. He had sufficient store of irony and under other circumstances might have realized that he was not the ideal man to offer illumination of any kind. His genius was for error. He had blundered once through confusion between obstinate pride and the disinterested promulgation of truth; and then again – though perhaps it was not much different – through the illusion that his own despair was of cosmic import. Throughout the days of the settlement he

618

had mistaken his desire to make amends for a belief in the capacities of the human spirit. And now, ragged and feverish captive, he was blundering again, prating of wisdom and virtue to a man determined to believe him wicked, a man to whom virtue meant well-cut clothes, a proud bearing, money in the bank.

What, more than anything, he seemed to Erasmus – who had no resources of irony whatever – was an object lesson in how not to conduct one's life. It was only by a persistent operation of the will that Erasmus could maintain belief in his cousin as a scapegoat worthy enough. He glanced at Paris now, saw the deathly pallor below the tan, the small beads of perspiration that had appeared on the brow. How could a vessel so sickly bear so much blame? There was a terrible discrepancy here and Erasmus flinched from it as from a mortal threat.

'It is a lesson strangely hard to learn,' he heard Paris say in low tones.

'I don't know what you mean,' he said coldly. 'What lesson? A man with anything about him knows what he wants and tries to get it.' This was so obvious that it made him impatient. 'That is the way the world goes forward,' he said, 'whether in your settlement back there or my larger one on the banks of the Thames. Nothing would ever get done otherwise.'

'Well, that might not be such a bad thing,' Paris said, rather faintly.

'You have not yet told me of your precious hopes.'

In spite of the weariness that was gaining on him now, Paris heard the malice in this question, and something more, something strangely like appeal. His cousin was desperate for him to admit failure, disappointment, defeated hope. 'You want to take everything from me,' he said. 'I cannot understand why you hate me so. Why should I explain further to you, who only want to hear a bad report? I owe you nothing. If I wronged anyone, it is your father. He showed me kindness and might think I have made a poor return. I hope I may be allowed to speak to him and given some chance to explain.'

He had closed his eyes on these last words. He heard a single harsh note of laughter and opened them again to see something wild and disbelieving on his cousin's face. He saw Erasmus raise a hand briefly to his brow. 'What is the matter?' he said.

'You do not know it,' Erasmus said. 'How could you? I had forgot . . .'

With this, it came from him in a stream there was no stopping, his father's death – and he did not conceal the nature of this now from Paris – the ruin it had brought, the loss of his bride, all the years of paying back the debts. That these years had brought him also wealth and power he did not mention. The fact was evident enough in any case; and he could think only of his wrongs, only of his cousin's monstrous guilt. And because of this all caution departed him, all the lessons he had learned in a hard school: that you must keep your object firmly in mind and rigorously exclude all that might be prejudicial to it, that you must always hold something back, keep something in reserve, because that is the way to retain control. All this, in the treacherous fluency that swept him, was forgotten. He found himself talking to this hated cousin, whom he had pursued and crippled and intended more firmly than ever to see hanged, as he could have talked to no one else, with a fervent intimacy that in some part of his mind astonished him still as he spoke, with revelations of feeling long buried within him, the deceit of his father's silence and its wounding lack of trust, the bitterness of his mother's superior wit in their dealings with the doctor, old Wolpert's patronizing treatment of him and Sarah's inability to see the true meaning of his renunciation. 'She accused me of wanting to add her to my store of possessions,' he said. He had never forgotten the words. 'I was forced to go into sugar when I wanted to build canals. I married against my inclination for the sake of the alliance . . .' Sarah was long since married, he knew it from his Liverpool acquaintance; she had married a local squire and there were children now.

All this he sought to lay at his cousin's door. But to Paris, listening with face averted, it seemed that Erasmus was not accusing, but confessing: he was begging to be released. 'Nothing that becomes of me can mend these things,' he said. 'You will still be where you were.' He saw that Erasmus had drawn himself up into a position of rigid attention in the course of speaking, as if braced for some ordeal. The pathos of his cousin's singleness of vision came to him, the terrible emptiness of conquest. 'Can you not see that?' he said gently.

Erasmus heard the change of tone, detected amidst the lines of weariness and pain on his cousin's face traces of an insolent compassion. All his life he had hated to see knowledge of him on any face. After a moment more he turned and walked out of the cabin. Outside the door, at the foot of the ladder, he stood for a short while as if uncertain of his direction. Tears had risen to his eyes, a rare thing with him. Of all the injuries that Paris had done him it seemed to him for a moment that this kindness of tone was the worst.

FIFTY-FIVE

Early in the morning of the following day Paris awoke to pains in the lower region of the chest, on the left side. They lessened after a while but were followed shortly by a feeling of constriction in the lungs, forcing him to take shallow breaths, as any deeper inhalation brought renewed pain. As he lay thus it seemed to him that he could hear an occasional rattle of chains from the deck above; but he was feverish and there was a singing in his ears and so he thought it might have been an illusion. Sullivan, arriving with the morning gruel, heard the quick breaths as he entered and saw that Paris's face was terribly changed. He could not eat and would not submit to be washed.

'Will you listen to that now?' Sullivan said in a voice disguised by scolding. 'What can I do for you then?'

'You can stay beside me here.' Paris saw the other man turn his head aside sharply. 'It is all right,' he said. 'It is only that I don't want to be moved.'

'No one will move you,' Sullivan said.

Paris lay without speaking for a while, then said, 'I thought I heard the sound of fetters up on deck. I must have been mistaken, there are soldiers enough for a guard.'

'No, it was no mistake. During the night, two of the sojers took a hold of Dinka an' started dragging her off, an' Sefadu tried to prevent them an' one felled him with the barrel of his musket. Then Hambo, who was standin' alongside, struck this one with his fist, puttin' thoughts of ravishment out of the feller's mind for a good time to come. Then Calley got excited, you know how he is sometimes, an' he caught hold of a lad standin' near him, an' set off to strangle him with the strap of his own hat. But that they are forbid to shoot without the order, Hambo and Calley would be dead. As it is, them and Sefadu are in irons for the rest of the voyage, Sefadu with a split head an' all.'

'So,' Paris said, 'the wheel has come round in a full circle. They will all be in irons once the troops have been disembarked.' The pain came again, somewhere just below the breastbone, and he closed his eyes, waiting for it to subside. 'We are back where we began,' he said.

'No, we are not,' Sullivan said. 'That is not a thought to be havin' in your mind now. You can niver come back to where you start. You are a travelled man, Matthew, like meself, an' as a travelled man you must know things niver join up again once you have gone to any distance. How can they, seein' as there is a gap of time between? There is twelve years between this craft we are on now an' the *Liverpool Merchant*. Even if them years were not everythin' you wanted them to be, you can't say they niver happened. Billy is dead but he still had them years of hoppin' about an' arguin' the toss, which is what he liked doin' most of all. I keep thinkin' of Koudi an' that last night when we named the baby. She looked at me, she was impressed with me playin', an' I am not surprised, I played like a demon that night, there was power in me. Now I know I missed me chance, I should have gone to her straight. But you cannot say I am back where I started. I have the spirit of me playin' to think about an' the hope of Koudi's smile. Do you hear me, Matthew?'

'Yes,' Paris said, 'I hear you.' The pain in his chest was better for the moment but he could not breathe deeply enough to get the air he needed. 'I have taken a turn for the worse, I am afraid,' he said. He saw Sullivan bend down and straighten up again quickly. 'What are you doing?' he said.

'I want you to take care of this for me,' Sullivan said. 'I want you to keep it for luck. They would only take it from me, sooner or later.'

Paris felt the smooth metal of the button pressed into his hand and his fingers closed over it. 'I have nothing to give you, Michael,' he said.

623

'You give me somethin' beyond any price when you spoke to me that time aboard ship,' Sullivan said. 'Do you remember? I came to ask them to take the chains off the negroes because the noise of the rattlin' was spoilin' me music.'

'I remember, yes.'

'You spoke to me as if I was a man, an' I have niver forgot it.'

Paris saw now that Sullivan's eyes had filled with tears. 'Don't be concerned about me,' he said. 'If you get a chance tell Tabakali that I think about her. Tell Kenka to look after his mother. I'll rest for a while now, I think.'

His sight seemed in some way obscured. He could not see clearly across the narrow space of the cabin. He heard the door close softly behind Sullivan. He fell into a doze, though without relaxing his hold on the button. After an interval that might have been hours or minutes he opened his eyes to see his cousin looking down at him. 'I wanted to explain,' he said, as if there had been no lapse of time. 'When I raised my hand against Thurso it was not with the idea of leading a revolt against him.'

The words came between short breaths, noisy and irregular. He fell silent again now and closed his eyes. Why had he done it? He had a sudden memory of the rain-washed deck, the calm of that morning, the vast, indifferent sky. 'It was against my profession,' he said. But he knew that wasn't the reason.

'We shall arrive at St Augustine this evening,' Erasmus said. 'There is a doctor there, belonging to the garrison. We shall have you put to rights.'

'I fear there may be nothing a doctor can do. I have seen this before, after an amputation or some violent accident . . . There is only one path from the leg to the lungs. I am afraid I have suffered some occlusion of the blood.'

'You cannot die,' Erasmus said violently. 'Not in this hole-and-corner fashion, not after I have come halfway round the world to smoke you out. It makes nonsense of everything.'

'You wanted something more spectacular, I know,' Paris said with an effort. He was silent after this for a long time, then he asked for a candle to be lit, as he could not see well. The flame moved but the light from it did not spread. Someone was bathing his face again. In a sudden wash of colder, clearer light, he saw the picture on the easel, the Governor's face fixed in its rigid sneer. 'That fort was full of hammering,' he said. 'There was no order in it.' The metal of the bars and the flesh of her limbs all one substance in the sunshine. His labouring breath came to his ears as from a distance beyond him. Nor on the ship, he thought. How else but in a state of chaos could such things be done? That was it, he had wanted to find order again, he had shouted up to the sky for order . . .

And now you will tell me that your hope was realized?

These words were strangely disembodied, like his breathing; it was difficult to be sure who had said them; but he knew it was for him to answer. In his eagerness to do so he started forward from the bolster that supported him against the bulkhead. He extended his right hand and something fell from it on to the blanket. 'Yes,' he said, glaring across the room. 'As much as any hope can be.' He did not know, as he fell back, whether this was the truth of the matter or whether he was blundering yet again and it was merely the voice of his old intransigence, his incorrigible need to have the last word. But doubt is the ally of hope, not its enemy, and together they made all the blessing he had.

Erasmus, not having heard any question, had failed to understand his cousin's words. Half mechanically he had clasped the hand extended to him and he was still holding it some minutes later when Paris caught his breath and struggled forward again and died. After a little while he released the hand and crossed it with the other one over the chest and closed the eyelids over the pale eyes. He stood looking down at the dead man's face. All marks of pain had gone from it. Paris wore a look of patient obstinacy as if, eyes closed, he were memorizing his arguments. On the blanket before him, where he had dropped it, lay a smallish brass button. After hesitating a moment Erasmus leaned forward and picked this up. Then he left the cabin and made his way above.

He stood for a while at the forward rail of the quarterdeck. It was a clear morning, rather cold, but sunny. The bayonets of the soldiers on guard glinted in the sunshine. He looked down at the slaves huddled amidships. One or two glanced at him but most kept their eyes sullenly or listlessly turned away. From somewhere in their midst a baby was crying fitfully. He noted the differences in skin colouring among them and thought with some disgust of the promiscuous relations that must have prevailed in the settlement. They had lived like animals there . . . Negro and mulatto, men, women, children – they had little more distinction in his mind than cattle might have done. They were in prime condition, however, and would fetch best prices at Charles Town. A good number of infants among them – they would have to be sold with the mothers. This was not usual and he was not sure how far it would affect the price. Like so much else, it depended on the temperament of the buyer. Some would regard it as an investment, others grudge the outlay on feeding . . . It occurred to him now that there might be bastards of his cousin's among these children. With this thought the image of the dead man's face came back into his mind. What had Paris said at the end? It had not made much sense – he had been talking to himself. Something about hope.

Erasmus glanced to either side of him at the unruffled expanses of the sea. The sky was cloudless. To eastward there still lingered the faint stains of sunrise. He knew land could not be far distant on the port side, but there was no sign of it; sea and sky met in a clear line. On a beach as vast as this sea to the memory of childhood, Paris had lifted him, swung him clear of the ground. It had not been to cheat him of victory – he knew that now, perhaps he had always known it – but to save him from defeat. It had been an act of kindness, perhaps even love. Only superior strength had enabled his cousin to do it. No one since then had been strong enough. And now there was no one at all. Paris was dead and could save him from defeat no longer. Ever since the morning that Captain Philips had come with his story of the beached ship, the thought that Paris might still be in the world had given his life meaning and purpose. Sarah had done that once. What was there now? He had thought his defeat lay in not delivering Paris to the hangman; but he knew now that the more terrible thing was not to have kept his cousin alive . . .

In the stress of this knowledge he clenched his fists, as his habit was. As he did so he felt the edge of the button press painfully against his fingers – he had been holding it all this while. He opened his hand and looked at it closely. An odd thing for a dying man to hold on to. Erasmus might have thrown it into the sea, but it occurred to him that it was a kind of gift, though accidental. After a moment he put it carefully away in the pocket of his coat.

EPILOGUE

This evening no different from others. He knows where he is by the quality of the light, the shape of the pale sheet of mirror behind the bar. Waterside bar, early evening sunlight falling through the open door – there are no windows. The light is broken, disturbed by movements of bodies. The interior of the bar is dark, he can see nothing there – he always sits facing the light. Between himself and the door shapes loom and melt. He knows that he is a licensed clown for the sailors, dockers, whores, who use this place. He knows that he is alone.

The drink he pays for himself, as long as he can, from the day's yield of dimes, hoarding the coins together on the counter. When he runs out of money he might start to sing, snatch of some old slave song, in a high, cracked voice. Frail eyelids over ruined eyes, head trembling a little, yearning towards the light. The Paradise Nigger is dying, but he never looks any different; no more damage can show on his face.

He talks to anyone that he senses to be close; or to no one. Sometimes one of the customers will set him off, winking round at the others: 'Come on, old Sawdust, what's the news from paradise?'

'Cause you ain't seen it you don't believe. Doubtin' Thomas had to see the Lord wounds. But this nigger seen it. An' they makes bellerin' sounds an' blow up water an' got birds live inside they mouth, eat the pickin's of they teeth, that's 'nough food fo' them birds, don' need nuthin more. No sir! Dragon flies you heerd tell of. Please inform this nigger if you ain't never heerd tell of dragon flies. Well, these dragon *birds*.'

He pauses for a moment, then says with sudden scorn, 'I hear you laughin'. Yeah, you pissin' youselves.'

'You keep civil or I got to show you the door,' the barkeeper says.

The mulatto lowers his head, an old reflex of submission. 'Heart's delight,' he says, somewhere between a groan and a sigh. Some accidental gleam falls on the whitish sheaths of his eyes. He talks on, but to himself now, about the birds in the dragon's mouth, and with rum they grow increasingly marvellous. Other birds too, white herons rising on slow wings, black snake-birds, and a sea of grass brimming and winking with flood-water. 'Red-colour fish in them pool,' he says, 'an' leather-shell turtle. I kin see it now. It never snowed nor frosted neether. I kin see the clouds, kinda like mist but then blue back of it. We come off a ship. That place nobody boss man. All the people live together friendly, say good-mornin', good-evenin', white or black don' make no diff'rence . . .'

Someone puts a drink in his hand and he drinks and goes on talking, muttering, after they have stopped listening, when no one could have heard anyway because of the noise in the place, voices or music of a fiddle, he chokes himself up with a sudden crazy spasm of laughter, soft choking laughter that seizes his throat. 'My poppa tell me dat, one time. He show me in a book. Long time ago now.' Sparse tears run from his eyes. His mind fills with hyperbole, visions fed with hunger and rum, glowing moons, gilded palmettos, clouds pierced with splinters of sun-shine. And faces, black and white, belonging to the time of the dragons. 'I allus thought I goin' to git back but I never did. You ain't never goin' now, nigger. Ah, Jesus.'

Sometimes, with the rum, he would get dogged about something, quarrelsome even. Or he would get tearful and wild. One way or another he would be thrown out sooner or later. This evening it is stray words of a woman heard earlier that get inflamed in his mind.

'Why you say that? I warn't born on no plantation. I ain't a Guinea nigger neether. 'Cause I yaller, don' mean my fadder a slave-driver neether. My father a *doctor*. I born in a paradise place. You hear me? You hear me there?'

He is put out into the alley; not very roughly, but he falls, allows himself to fall, to break the hold on his arm. So he sprawls there in the dark, the harmonica dangling round his neck, while his rage fades and his mind grows blank as his eyes. Some time later, on this particular evening, he limps and fumbles his way to the kitchen of the *Cupola*, where Big Suzanne presides.

Indigo evening of summer, he sees stars floating and dilating in it. Big red pansies bloom and die on Suzanne's vast hips as she moves below the lamp. Standing unsteady in the doorway, he confides in her massive and contemptuous kindness.

'I give them a piece of my mind.'

'Sure,' she says. 'Same as every night. You been rollin' around again, ain't you? They's some meat gravy if you wants it.'

'We come on a ship,' he says. 'Not *here*.'

'Don't I know it? Here, take some of this here biscuit, mop it up with.'

'Heart's delight,' he sighs, standing in the doorway with his plate.

Her sweating face smiles over at him. 'That a fine name for a ship.'